Sometimes the things meant to destroy you lead you exactly where you were meant to be.

Whiskey & Secrets
Book One:
The Whiskey Tango Foxtrot Series
By Ali Wren
The Wren's Hollow

Table of Contents

Dedication

To my family, your love and support mean the world to me.
To my husband, thank you for always believing in me and standing by
my side as I chase my hopes and dreams. Your unwavering
encouragement makes everything possible.
To my children, who inspire me every single day. And especially to my
son, whose passion and imagination sparked the idea that brought this
story to life. Thank you for sharing your sense of adventure with me.
And finally, to the scientists, researchers, explorers, and endlessly
curious minds who see wonder in the unknown—this story is for you
too. For everyone who has ever fallen in love with discovery, history,
and the mysteries still waiting to be uncovered.

This book is for you.

Author's Note

This book contains themes that may be distressing to some readers, including abduction, violence, shootings, sexual assault, sex trafficking, and obsessive behavior. These elements are integral to the story, but I understand they may be triggering for some readers. Please read with care.

Your well-being is important. If you need to step away from this book at any point, please do so. Thank you for reading.

The Yanomami featured in this book are a real Indigenous people living within the Amazon Rainforest, though the specific village, events, and locations portrayed in this story are fictionalized. One of my goals in writing this book was to highlight the existence of modern hunter-gatherer societies and the importance of studying and preserving human history.

Anthropologists like Sarah study contemporary Indigenous cultures to better understand humanity's past, helping bridge the gap between the archaeological record and the living traditions that still exist today.

However, many Indigenous groups throughout the Amazon continue to face growing threats, including deforestation, illegal mining, disease exposure, and displacement. Conservation efforts remain critical in protecting both the rainforest and the people who have called it home for thousands of years.

Amazon Rainforest

Prologue

Five Years Ago
Sarah

The Amazon rainforest, sprawling, untamed, a labyrinth of emerald green, has haunted my dreams since childhood. Its ceaseless hum. The way sunlight filters through the dense canopy in fractured gold. The chorus of unseen creatures just beyond sight.

It's lingered in my memory like a half-forgotten melody. It started with a family trip to Brazil. I was eleven, far too young to understand how much that journey would shape my life, but old enough to feel the pull of something bigger than me.

I remember standing at a vendor's stall, fingers brushing over woven necklaces and bracelets, the scent of earth and rain thick in the air. My uncle bought me a small, intricately braided piece, one I still have.

A quiet beginning to something that would grow into obsession. After a week in São Paulo, we traveled north. The world changed. Concrete gave way to green. The air thickened. The sounds shifted from traffic and voices to something older. The landscape was wild and alive. It was there, in a remote village, that I met Paya.

She sat cross-legged in the shade, weaving patterns into a basket with steady, practiced hands. She was about my age, but there was nothing uncertain about her. While the adults around her remained guarded, distant, she watched me. Her dark brown, almost black eyes we curious and assessing.

Indigo markings traced along her arms, geometric lines that meant something I couldn't yet understand. When she finally spoke, it was in Portuguese but hesitant, like it wasn't the language she preferred. I don't know why she stayed with me. Why her face lingered when everything else faded. Maybe it was the way she tilted her head, deciding if I was worth her attention. Maybe it was the faint smirk when she realized I was trying to understand her world.

Whatever it was, that moment planted something in me. Something that led me here. Now, at twenty-two, I'm just starting my graduate degree, finally getting my first real chance to study the people who shaped the way I think.

The jungle wrapped around me like a humid, heavy and breathing living thing. It pressed in from all sides, thick with the endless hum of insects and distant animal calls that never fully stopped, just shifted, like something always watching, always moving. The air clung to my skin, damp and suffocating, each breath tasting faintly of earth and decay.

I crouched behind a massive kapok tree, its roots twisting up from the ground like ribs breaking through skin. My fingers dug into the wet soil, nails packing with mud as I leaned forward, straining to see through the dense wall of green.

Sweat slid down my temple, stinging my eyes. I didn't dare wipe it away. A flicker of indigo vanished into the undergrowth. She moved like she belonged to the forest, bare feet silent against the jungle floor, her body weaving through the trees with a fluidity I couldn't even begin to mimic. The faint markings along her skin caught the light for only a second before she disappeared again, swallowed whole by the foliage. My pulse kicked harder.

The Yanomami were notoriously reclusive. Outsiders weren't just unwelcome, they were avoided, ghosted, erased from sight before they even realized they'd been seen. Yet, here she was. And here I was. Years of study. Papers. Lectures. Obsession, if I was being honest. Everything had led to this moment, standing deep in the Amazon rainforest, on the edge of something most people would never even glimpse. Learning about their way of life.

I should have felt exhilarated.

Instead, something uneasy curled low in my stomach. The jungle felt wrong today. Too loud. Too alive. A sharp snap cracked behind me. I spun, heart slamming against my ribs, my hand flying to the pepper spray clipped to my backpack. My breath caught in my throat as I searched the shadows, a figure stepped through the foliage.

Dr. Anderson. Relief hit first. Then vanished just as quickly. Something was off. She didn't move like herself, her posture stiff, her usual effortless confidence replaced with something controlled. Forced. Her face looked pale beneath the humidity, lips pressed tight like she was holding something back.

"Sarah," she said, her voice low, too tight. "There you are."

Every nerve in my body went on edge.

"We need to get back to camp."

My stomach dropped. "What's wrong?"

She hesitated. That was what did it my pulse kicked into high gear. That had nothing to do with me running around with Paya. Dr. Anderson didn't hesitate, anytime she needs to correct me on something or adjust my way of thinking or studying, she did it easily with kindness. Her eyes flicked past me, scanning the trees, the canopy above us, like she was checking or listening for something I couldn't hear.

"It's Carly."

The jungle noise seemed to dull, like someone had pressed a hand over my ears.

"What?" My voice barely made it out.

Her gaze snapped back to mine, and whatever she'd been trying to hold together... cracked. "She's missing."

The word didn't fit. It didn't belong to Carly. Carly was careful. Deliberate. She triple-checked everything. She *made* me double-check everything. We didn't go anywhere alone. Not here. Not ever. We stayed together, stayed close to the guides, followed the rules because the rules were the only thing keeping this place from swallowing us whole.

"No." I shook my head, the word coming out too fast, too thin. "She wouldn't—she wouldn't just—"

"She was last seen heading down a path near the shabono." Dr. Anderson exhaled slowly, but there was no calm in it. Only restraint.

Only fear.

The jungle didn't feel like something we were studying, anymore. It felt like something we'd stepped into...and couldn't get out of. That was two days ago. A chill slid down my spine, even in the suffocating heat. We had to find her.

For three days, we searched.

Not wandering. Not blindly calling out into the trees.

We moved in lines, ten feet apart, just like we'd been trained. Sweeping the jungle in slow, methodical passes. Eyes scanning the ground, the brush, the canopy. Looking for disturbances. Broken branches. Shifted soil. Anything that didn't belong. Looking for her flash of light blonde hair or her green eyes, but there was nothing.

The Yanomami moved with us, though "with" didn't feel like the right word. They were ahead. Around us. Sometimes gone entirely, only to reappear without a sound. They read the jungle in ways we couldn't, every bent leaf, every scuff in the dirt, every subtle absence of noise.

The rest of us, we called her name.

"Carly!"

Over and over again, until the word stopped sounding like her and became something hollow. Our voices cracked, swallowed by the dense canopy, absorbed by a forest that refused to give anything back.

We should've found something. A footprint. A torn piece of fabric. A dropped pack. Anything.

Instead, we found nothing. Not even a sign she'd ever been there.

By the second night, fear had settled in.

By the third, it had roots.

I walked in line with Dr. Anderson, ten feet to my left, her movements precise, mechanical. To my right was Benjamin, his usual easygoing demeanor stripped away, replaced with something tight and unreadable. He was the last one to see her, they were walking together to the shabono, to meet with one of the elders. Our field school is done, this week is reviewing most of our notes and getting any last details we might need.

Tomorrow, we start the journey back out of the jungle and then going home. We didn't talk anymore as we continued our search. There was nothing left to say.

I forced myself to focus, scanning the underbrush the way I'd been trained, grid patterns, overlapping lines, slow and deliberate. Paleoanthropology had taught me how to read landscapes, how to find meaning in fragments, in what was left behind.

But there was nothing here.

No story. No trace. Just jungle. Endless, suffocating jungle. I told myself we would find her. That she'd stumble out from the trees, covered in mud, dehydrated and maybe eventually we would laugh at how turned around she'd gotten. Carly always had a way of making things feel lighter, even when they weren't. But as the sun dipped lower, staining the sky a bruised purple through the canopy, that hope began to rot.

She wasn't lost. She was gone. Even with the Yanomami guiding us. Even with every protocol followed. The Amazon had swallowed her whole. By the time we made our way back to the village, defeat clung to us like the humidity, it was inescapable.

I stopped at the base of the towering kapok tree, pressing my palm against its massive trunk. The bark was rough, solid. Real. In this moment I needed it to ground me. This tree had been ours all season, Carly's and mine. Our tent sat just beneath its sprawling roots, tucked into the only space that had ever felt even remotely familiar in this place. I stayed there for a moment, breathing. Trying to make sense of everything that didn't.

I was here for ethno-archaeology, studying how present-day remote tribes could offer insight into how our ancestors lived thousands of years ago. Patterns of survival. Social structures. Adaptation. Carly had been here for cultural anthropology. In a lot of ways, our work overlapped.

In a lot of ways…so did we.

Dr. Anderson wasn't just our professor, she was my mentor. She'd been guiding me through the beginning stages of my dissertation, pushing me, believing in me long before I fully believed in myself and now she looked like she was holding everything together by force. We weren't alone out here, either.

Dr. Willis had joined the expedition, new to the university, already making a name for himself in geological research. He and his grad student, Benjamin, were here to map ancient formations. Tracing how the last ice age may have shaped parts of the Amazon.

Benjamin. I glanced toward him. He stood a few yards away, staring into the trees, his jaw tight. He was Carly's boyfriend. The first day, he'd been frantic, shouting her name louder than anyone, pushing ahead and refusing to slow down. But after that, something shifted. Now, he barely called out at all. I could see the exhaustion written in his face, the look of shock that I am sure is etched in my own face. I haven't slept since we got the news, I just want to find her.

Dr. Anderson came up beside me, her voice barely above a whisper.

"Sarah... we have to call off the search."

"No." The word left me before I could stop it.

Her hand tightened on my shoulder. "I'm sorry. It's been three days. If she were out there... we would've found something by now."

My throat closed, a pressure building so thick I couldn't pull in a full breath. Carly was gone. And the jungle wasn't giving her back.

Even the Yanomami, who could read the forest in ways we never could, had grown quiet. Reserved. They had promised to send word if they found anything. But none of them looked hopeful.

The flight home felt unreal. Like I'd stepped out of my own life and was watching it from somewhere just outside my body. I hated leaving. Hated that the world kept moving like this was something we could just walk away from. Like she wasn't still out there. Like she wasn't still waiting.

My chest tightened as the plane climbed higher, the jungle shrinking beneath us until it blurred into nothing. And I couldn't stop thinking... I made it out. She didn't.

When we landed, I still had Carly's backpack clutched in my hands. I hadn't let it go. Not on the flight. Not in the car. Not even when my fingers started to ache from holding it too tightly. It still smelled like her.

Her parents were waiting. I'd seen them so many times before. Shared dinners, holidays and weekends at their house in Wisconsin when I couldn't afford to go home to Missouri. Carly, Fallon and I had shared everything. A dorm room. Then an apartment. Our lives had intertwined so completely that somewhere along the way, her family had become mine too.

Dr. Anderson stood beside me. Fallon hovered just behind, close enough that I could feel her presence, even if I couldn't look at her. I tried to hold it together. I told myself I had to be strong for them. That I owed them that much. But the second her mom, Linda, stepped forward and wrapped her arms around me—I broke. A sob tore out of my chest, raw and uncontrollable, as I clung to her, the backpack crushed between us like it could somehow fill the space Carly had left behind.

"I'm so sorry," I choked. "I'm so, so sorry..." Her arms tightened around me, and I felt her shaking too.

Behind her, Carly's dad stood frozen, his face pale, his eyes searching mine like I might still have something to give him. An answer. Hope. Anything. But I had nothing.

After they left, Fallon took me back to our shared apartment and I didn't leave for weeks. Not until school started again in the fall.

Chapter One

Present Day
Sarah

Now, as a doctoral candidate preparing for my final field study, I find myself returning to where it all began.

I push open the heavy glass doors to the anthropology department, the familiar resistance of the handle grounding me before I even step inside. The hum of fluorescent lights greets me first, followed by the low murmur of voices echoing down the hall.

The space feels like a museum of unfinished questions.

Glass display cases line the walls. Fragments of pottery, replicas of ancient tools, bone casts carefully labeled in neat, academic handwriting. Bulletin boards are cluttered with overlapping flyers: field study applications, guest lectures, grant opportunities, faded notices curling at the corners from months of neglect. Maps stretch across entire walls filled with migration patterns, excavation sites and territories outlined in ink that tries to make sense of something far more complicated.

It smells like dust and aged paper, layered with the faint bitterness of stale coffee that's seeped into the walls over decades.

Students weave through the halls, some animatedly discussing summer plans, others hunched over laptops, faces drawn tight with end-of-semester panic. A few glance up as I pass, recognition flickering before they return to their own worlds.

For a second, I feel suspended between two versions of my life. Here, which is full of structure and predictability. In two days, I will be back in the Amazon. Six weeks deep in the jungle. Heat, isolation, unpredictability. The culmination of everything I've worked toward, years of research, proposals, rejections and grant applications that felt like they would never come through.

I should feel proud. Excited, even. Instead, something uneasy settles beneath it all. I shift my bag higher on my shoulder and move down the hall, my mind already turning over the meeting ahead, final logistics and expectations, the last chance to prove that I belong here.

That this is worth it.

I pass a cluster of students gathered near the lounge, their voices overlapping with the faint sound of a video playing from someone's phone.

"…American researcher missing in the Amazon near the Venezuelan border—"

My steps falter. The words hit like a shockwave, cutting clean through everything else. I feel my pulse skitter over my skin. The hallway noise dulls, like someone's turned the volume down on the world. A cold prickle runs down my spine.

No.

Not again.

My stomach tightens, a familiar, unwelcome pressure building in my chest. Carly. Five years. Five years, and it still feels like this, this sharp and immediate, soul crushing grief. It's impossible to outrun. The rainforest had once been a place of wonder. Discovery. Now it carries something else entirely. Something darker

The last time I saw Carly, she was laughing, her eyes the same color as the trunk of the kapok tree, bright with excitement as she talked about the next step in her research.

"This is just the beginning, Sarah," she'd said, brushing damp strands of hair from her face, the humidity curling them at the edges. "Imagine what we'll discover out here."

And now, five years later, I was going back to the place that had swallowed her whole. A chill slid down my spine. I force myself to move. I can't let this rattle me. Not now.

When I reach Dr. Anderson's office, I slow just enough to steady myself and the door opens. Benjamin steps out. For a split second, something flashes across his face. Irritation. Sharp and unguarded. Then he sees me and it's instantly gone. Replaced with something smoother, it's entirely fake, practiced.

"Sarah," he says, his tone warming instantly. "I was hoping I'd run into you."

Of course you were. I keep my expression neutral as I take him in. Even if the urge to roll my eyes are strong.

Benjamin has always been put together. Handsome in a way that feels intentional—like every detail has been chosen for effect. Light brown hair styled just messy enough to look effortless. Piercing blue eyes that hold your gaze a beat too long. The kind of smile that's meant to disarm.

There's something underneath it. Something I've never quite been able to name. Something that makes me keep my distance. We stayed…friendly after Carly disappeared. Or at least, we tried to. We'd meet for lunch at a small diner near campus, picking at food neither of us really wanted, talking around the one subject we couldn't seem to face head-on.

For a while, it felt normal. Then, about six months in, it started to shift. The conversations lingered longer. His tone changed. Compliments slipped in where they hadn't before. Casual touches that didn't feel accidental. I shut it down. I never saw him that way, I never really even liked him and Benjamin didn't seem like the kind of person who heard "no" the first time.

It wasn't just me, either. He flirted with everyone. Undergrads. Grad students. Anyone who gave him even a second of attention. It was easy for him, like it was just natural. Like a habit he'd perfected over time. He was like that before he even started dating Carly.

He'd transferred into the program around the same time, coming from another university somewhere in Minnesota. Rumor was his uncle, Dean Wagner opened doors for him. Dean Wagner, Associate Dean of Research and Field Programs.

Benjamin was studying earth processes, especially the last ice age and how it transformed the earth as it melted. The geology and anthropology departments overlapped enough that he was always around. Always just close enough to show up where I was. Close enough to keep trying again.

"Benjamin," I reply, polite but curt. I don't want to invite any further conversation, I just want him to go away.

He shifts, leaning casually against the doorframe like he has nowhere else to be, like this moment is exactly what he planned. Confidence rolls off him, easily.

"It's been a while," he says. "Excited for the trip?"

"Of course." I adjust the strap on my bag. "Are you?"

His smile tightens, barely noticeable, but there.

"Yeah," he says. "I was just talking to Dr. Anderson about the final roster."

There's something in the way he says it. A subtle edge that makes my stomach twist.

"Any updates?" I ask, glancing toward the office.

"She hasn't finalized the undergrads yet," he says, rolling his eyes like it's an inconvenience. "Said she'll release names soon." A pause. "Guess we'll find out who the lucky ones are. At least you and I will be there."

Lucky. I nod, already shifting my weight, ready to move past him, but his hand closes lightly around my arm. But enough that a sharp, instinctive shudder runs through me before I can stop it. I pull back immediately, forcing a polite smile like I didn't just react. Like I didn't feel it. The thought of reporting him flashes through my mind. I just don't know if I have enough to warrant anyone taking a real look at him. Mostly he flirts. Pushes boundaries in ways easy to dismiss. But now he's touching me and I really don't like it.

His expression doesn't change. But something flickers in his eyes. Gone just as quickly as it appeared.

"See you in a couple days," he says, that same easy smirk settling back into place. Then, after a beat, "I'm looking forward to six weeks in the jungle with you."

The words are casual. But they don't feel like it. It felt more like a threat. I don't respond. Instead, I turn and knock on the door before he can say anything else, already pushing it open at the faint sound of Dr. Anderson's voice saying, "Come in."

I step inside quickly, shutting the door behind me putting a barrier between me and Benjamin. Inside Dr. Anderson's office, the tension in my shoulders finally begins to ease. It always does.

Her space feels different from the rest of the department, less sterile, less hurried. Lived in, with ayers of research and years of experience tucked into every corner. Books spill from overfilled shelves, stacked in uneven piles beside artifacts and field notes that look like they've been handled a hundred times over. A worn map of South America stretches across one wall, marked with faded ink and handwritten notes.

Dr. Hazel Anderson sits behind her cluttered desk, a pen tapping absently against her notepad as she reviews something in front of her. Sunlight filters through the window behind her, catching in the silver strands woven through her dark hair and softening the lines of her face. She looks exactly like she always has.

For a moment, the sight of her pulls me backward, to this same office, carrying the scent of old paper and lavender tea, weeks earlier when everything still felt uncertain. *"You don't have to go back,"* she'd said then, her voice calm but firm. *"No one would blame you."*

But I wanted to go, needed to. Not only did I need to finish my dissertation, I needed closure too. This might be my last chance to ever return. Future research could take me somewhere entirely different. This was my moment to say goodbye. Maybe it was stupid, but part of me hoped that when I got there, Carly would be waiting for me. I knew that was impossible. Still, I hoped anyway. Only... the opportunity never came. There were too many reasons we couldn't return. Concerns over her disappearance. Budget cuts. And now the growing instability in Venezuela. Until now.

The memory fades as Dr. Anderson glances up from the papers in front of her. Her reading glasses rest low on her nose, and her expression softens the second she sees me standing there.

"Sarah," she says, a small smile tugging at her lips. "Glad you could make it."

"Of course." I step fully into the room, letting the door fall shut behind me before lowering myself into the chair across from her desk. "You wanted to check in before the trip?"

She nods, studying me intently over the rim of her glasses. Like she's reading more than just my words. "I just wanted to see where your head is at," she says. "This is a big step for you. This is a lot."

Excitement and apprehension stirs in my chest, taking a deep breath, "I'm ready," I say. "I've been packing, double-checking all my research equipment—" My gear was packed. Mostly. Field notebooks. Waterproof cases. Enough insect repellent to kill something twice my size. But there's still that lingering feeling. Like I'm forgetting something. Not just physically. This isn't just another field study. This is going back. Back to where everything went wrong.

Dr. Anderson's lips curve slightly, like she can see straight through me. "That's not what I meant. I know you're ready for the trip physically, just it might hurt going back and with the growing tensions near the Venezuelan border." Her expression softens, the warmth there but threaded with something heavier.

I shift in my seat, forcing myself to stay steady. "I've been following the reports," I say. "It seems contained. We'll be far enough away."

She nods but there's hesitation in it. Calculation. "If things escalate, we cancel," she says plainly. "No exceptions. If it gets worse, you will need to be pulled out and brought back home." That's Dr. Anderson. Kind but never careless. "In light of everything," she continues, folding her hands on the desk, "we're taking additional precautions. The U.S. and Brazilian governments advised against the trip, but we've been approved, on one condition."

A flicker of unease moves through me. "What kind of condition?"

Her gaze holds mine. "Security."

My brow furrows. "Security?"

She leans back slightly, completely composed. "The U.S. military is assigning a Special Forces operative to accompany your team."

I blink. "I'm sorry—what?"

She chuckles at my expression. "I know it's unusual, but with everything happening, it's necessary. They said the operative is close to retirement."

A laugh slips out before I can stop it. "So… what? An old, cranky soldier is going to babysit us in the jungle?"

"Something like that." But Hazel's smile fades quickly, her expression turning more serious as she studies me. "Sarah," she says gently, "are you sure you're okay with this?"

The question settles heavier than I expect. For a moment, I can't answer. Five years ago, I lost Carly to that rainforest. Now I'm going back. Not just as a student this time. Not as someone trailing behind and trying to keep up. As the lead investigator. I should be scared and I am, but underneath that fear is something sharper. Something that has followed me for five years, quiet and relentless.

I owe Carly. I owe myself. I draw in a slow breath, forcing steadiness into my voice. "Yeah," I say. "I'm sure."

Hazel holds my gaze for a long moment, like she's making sure I mean it. Then she nods. "You've earned this," she says softly. "And I have no doubt you're going to do great things."

Emotion catches unexpectedly in my chest, but I swallow it down and manage a small smile. I hope she's right. Because in two days, I'll be heading back into the jungle. And this time, I know better than to believe I'll come back unchanged.

"One last thing," Dr. Anderson says, her tone shifting slightly. "We've run into budget concerns again." My heart drops, I really hope they're not canceling. "As you know, the geology team will still be returning. Dr. Willis and Benjamin will continue their research, and they'll be selecting one undergraduate to join them."

I nod slowly, waiting.

She exhales, then meets my eyes. "I won't be going this time."

The words hit harder than I expect. "What?" I sit up straighter. "Are you sure?"

A small, reassuring smile touches her lips. "Before you protest, this was my decision, too." She folds her hands together on the desk. "I trust you, Sarah. You're ready for this. And if I'm being honest..." she lets out a quiet breath, "six weeks sleeping on the ground in that heat doesn't hold quite the same appeal it used to."

Despite everything, a faint smile pulls at my lips. I don't think that really appeals to anyone honestly.

"However," she continues, "you'll still have support. They've approved you to bring one undergraduate, if you'd like. Or you can go on your own and focus entirely on your research. The choice is yours."

The choice is mine, it settles heavily in my chest.

An undergrad would be helpful, extra hands, another set of eyes. And it would look good. Leadership experience. Mentorship. But it would also mean responsibility, teaching and translating. Watching someone else in an environment that doesn't forgive mistakes. And without Dr. Anderson there, the thought alone feels overwhelming.

I glance down at my hands, turning it over. "I think..." I hesitate, then look back up at her. "I think I'd rather not bring anyone this time."

The words feel strange leaving my mouth, but once they're out, I know they're right.

"I know it's a great opportunity," I add, "but it just feels like a lot for this trip."

She nods immediately, like she expected that answer. "I think that's the right call," she says gently. "You need to focus on yourself out there." Relief flows through me, knowing I made the right decision.

"When you go..." Her voice softens. "Just be careful, alright? Make sure you come back home."

Something in her expression shifts, and her eyes are glassy. My throat tightens instantly, emotion rising faster than I can stop it.

"I will," I manage, though it comes out quieter than I intended.

She stands, stepping around the desk before I can say anything else, and pulls me into a hug. I don't hesitate. I wrap my arms around her, holding on a little tighter than I mean to.

I let myself into my apartment, the door creaking softly as I step inside. Music drifts through the space, something upbeat and I don't even have to look to know Fallon is home. She's in the living room, dancing as she folds laundry on the couch. Actually dancing.

Spinning barefoot across the worn carpet, a pile of clothes half-folded at her side, completely unbothered by the chaos she's creating.

She's impossible to miss, all long lines and effortless confidence. Her fiery red hair falls in thick, wild waves down her back, catching the light as she moves. Even in something as simple as shorts and a tank top, she somehow looks put together in a way I'll never quite understand. Her energy fills the room. It always does.

Our apartment isn't much, just one open space pretending to be a kitchen, dining room, and living room all at once. The kitchen is barely tucked into the corner, and our bedrooms sit on opposite sides like an afterthought. It's small. A little worn down but it's cheap, because it's close to campus, close to everything.

"Hey!" Fallon calls, spotting me mid-spin, not missing a beat as she tosses a shirt onto the growing pile. "You're back. How was your meeting with Dr. Anderson?"

"It was good," I say, dropping my bag by the door. "There's been some updates to the field school…"

She pauses, her bra dangling from her hands. "Oh no," she says immediately. "Tell me they're not canceling it."

"No, not canceling." I shake my head. "Apparently because of the risks, they're sending… security. Like, a retired Special Forces operative."

She blinks once and then a loud snort flies out of her.

"Oh, great. So you're going to have some old, jaded guy stalking you around the jungle?"

"I don't know about stalking," I mutter. "But yeah. Something like that."

She shakes her head, already amused. "Anything else?"

I hesitate. "Yeah. Budget cuts. Dr. Anderson's not going this time."

That gets her full attention. "What?" Her brows pull together. "So who's going?"

"Me. Dr. Willis. Benjamin. And one undergrad, they haven't picked yet or announced yet."

Her face scrunches immediately. "Oh, gross." She actually shudders. "Six weeks with that douche?"

"Yeah," I sigh. "Unfortunately."

"Please tell me you won't be stuck with him the whole time."

"I'm hoping they'll mostly be doing their own research," I say. "Maybe I'll only have to deal with him at dinner."

"Still too much," she mutters.

Then, just as quickly, her mood shifts. "Hey, I'm almost done here. Want to grab dinner?"

"Yeah," I admit. "That actually sounds good. Then I should finish packing."

Fallon stops mid-fold, slowly turning to look at me. "We're not doing that," she says, already shaking her head.

"What?"

"We are not spending your last night here packing."

"I just want to make sure I have everything—"

"You will," she cuts in. "You always do." She points at me like that settles it. "In two days, you're leaving me for six weeks. I deserve a proper send-off."

I narrow my eyes slightly. "That sounds like more than just dinner."

Her grin turns wicked. "You should know me by now." She scoops up the stack of clothes and heads toward her room. "Maybe we'll even find a couple of cute guys to bring home for the night."

She throws me a wink before disappearing. I shake my head, heading into our narrow kitchen to grab a bottle of water and something small to eat. Some things never change. A few minutes later, Fallon reappears and of course, she's already transformed. She's wearing a low-cut black dress that somehow looks both effortless and intentional, hugging her curves just enough without trying too hard. Her hair is still wild, still free, but now it looks like it belongs exactly that way.

Like she planned it. I don't even have to ask. We're going out. It's not something I do often. The drinking, bars, random conversations with strangers, it's never really been my thing. Neither are random guys.

In fact. I've never been with one. The thought hits, as it always does, quiet, sharp and a little embarrassing. I'm almost twenty-seven. It's not that I'm not interested. I am. I just never felt ready, never met a guy I wanted to try with. At first, I was scared. Then I was busy. Then Carly happened. And somehow, time just kept moving. Now it feels like I missed something I was supposed to figure out years ago. I want it to mean something. I want it to feel safe.

"Go get dressed," Fallon says, snapping me out of it. "And I mean something cute, Sarah." I glance up at her. "We're going to celebrate," she adds, softer this time but still smiling. "Properly."

I reluctantly go change. I pull on my favorite pair of skinny jeans, the ankle boots Fallon insisted I buy a few years ago, and a soft blue tank top that makes my eyes stand out just enough to feel intentional. Not overdone.

I tuck my ID and some cash into my pocket before heading back out. Fallon is already waiting, leaning against the doorframe like she's been ready for twenty minutes. Her eyes light up the second she sees me.

"Okay, yes," she says, pushing off the wall. "That top? We're working with that." I roll my eyes, but I can't help the small smile that slips through.

After dinner, we walk to the bar a few blocks from our apartment. It's the kind of place every college town has, cheap drinks, loud music and just enough charm to keep people coming back. The bass hits before we even reach the door, vibrating faintly through the pavement.

Inside, it's dim and already packed. A DJ is set up near the back, music pulsing through the room as people crowd the dance floor. We squeeze through bodies shoulder to shoulder, Fallon leading the way like she owns the place. Which, honestly, she kind of does. We finally make it to the bar, elbows planted just enough to claim space.

The bartender walks over, he looks familiar, I know I've seen him around campus before.

"What can I get you?"

"Two shots of tequila," Fallon says immediately. "She'll have a Sex on the Beach, and I'll take a beer."

He nods and disappears. I turn to her slowly. "A shot of tequila and a Sex on the Beach? I don't think I've ever even had one of those."

She grins, completely unapologetic. "Exactly. We're fixing that."

"That feels aggressive."

"It's called balance."

I snort. "What is that even supposed to mean?"

"It means," she says, leaning in slightly, lowering her voice like she's sharing something important, "I'm putting good energy into the universe for you."

"Oh no."

"Yes," she nods, fully committed. "You're going to meet some ridiculously attractive man and have a life-changing experience on the beach."

I stare at her. "I'm going into the middle of the Amazon rainforest. The only 'ridiculously attractive man' within a hundred miles is Benjamin."

Her face immediately twists in disgust. "Absolutely not," she says. "I rebuke that."

I laugh despite myself.

"Plus," she adds, pointing at me, "aren't you staying in São Paulo with your aunt and uncle after?"

"Yes. Still no beach."

She rolls her eyes like I've personally offended her. "Please. They're absolutely taking you to the beach and you know it."

"You're making a lot of assumptions."

"I have faith," she says, completely serious. "In you. In your future. In hot men."

"Of course you do."

"Here you go." The bartender sets our drinks down, and Fallon immediately grabs the shot glasses, sliding one toward me.

"Cheers," she says, lifting hers. "To a safe, successful research trip…" She pauses, her grin turning just a little mischievous. "…and to you finally having some fun."

I narrow my eyes but lift my glass anyway. "Cheers."

We clink them together and knock them back. The tequila burns all the way down, sharp and immediate, and I cough slightly as Fallon laughs beside me.

"See?" she says. "You're already thriving."

I take another sip of my drink, glancing over at Fallon as she leans against the bar, laughing easily with the bartender like they've known each other for years. It wasn't always like this.

When she first moved here, back when it was just me, Carly, and Fallon crammed into that tiny dorm room, she was different. Quieter. Smaller, somehow. She used to wear clothes that swallowed her whole, like she was trying to disappear into them. Always looking over her shoulder. Flinching at loud noises. Waking up in the middle of the night with screams she tried to smother before they could wake anyone.

After she finally told us what happened to her, we both cried with her. It was horrific, we never pushed her for details. Never asked for more than she was willing to give. We just stayed. Listened when she needed it. Sat with her when she couldn't sleep. Held her when the nightmares followed her into the daylight.

Slowly, things started to change. About six years ago, she signed up for a self-defense class. Then another. Then another. She dragged me along once, I lasted exactly one session before deciding it definitely wasn't for me. Fallon, on the other hand. She stayed and somewhere along the way, something in her shifted.

She started standing taller. Speaking louder. Laughing more. Trading oversized hoodies for clothes that actually fit, clothes she chose. Now she moves through the world like she owns her space. Like no one gets to take that from her again. She never pressured me to follow her lead, never made me feel like I was behind for not keeping up.

She just lived. And I've always admired that. Even if I don't always understand it. I shake my head, reaching for my drink, but I'm smiling now. Really smiling.

For the first time since the meeting—since the news, since everything—I feel it. A small, fleeting moment of normal.

Chapter Two

Wade

"Yo, Wraith! Heard you're gearing up for one last mission. Babysitting scientists, huh?" Nate's voice cuts through the noise, edged with humor as he jogs up beside me, a wide grin already in place. "Sounds like a real adrenaline rush."

At six feet, Nate's not small but I still have a few inches on him. I straighten just slightly, tipping my chin down like I'm looking at him. He notices and his eyes narrow. I smirk. It's a long-standing joke between us at this point.

"Yeah," I say, easy. "One last hurrah. No insurgents this time." I glance past him briefly. "Just scientists."

Nate huffs a quiet laugh. "Trading bullets for bugs. That's a downgrade, man."

"Depends who you ask."

He studies me for a second, grin easing just a fraction. "You're thinking too much already."

"Always am."

A beat passes before he taps his temple lightly. "You know, the hardest fights aren't the ones out there," he says. "They're the ones up here."

I glance at him. "Did you get that from your quote of the day calendar?"

His grin snaps back instantly. "You're just jealous you don't have depth."

"You're just old," I deadpan. "Don't confuse that with wisdom."

He flips me off without hesitation. I laugh. Some things don't change.

"Well," I say, shifting my weight slightly, "we head out tonight. Six weeks in the Amazon."

"That's a long time to play tour guide."

"Yeah," I mutter. "Especially with everything going on near the border."

Nate's expression tightens, subtle, but there. He knows exactly what I mean.

"Should be quiet," he says.

"Should be," I echo.

But I don't believe it. Not with terrain like that. Not with instability creeping in from the edges. And definitely not with a group of civilians walking straight into it. I roll my shoulders once, pushing the tension down.

"After this, I'm done," I add. "That's it."

Nate studies me again, longer this time. "You ever think you won't know what to do with yourself?"

I huff a quiet breath. "Not my problem yet."

We've been operating out of Comalapa International Airport the last few years. Not home, but close enough. South of San Salvador, where the heat sticks to your skin and everything smells like jet fuel, salt, and rain. Missions send us all over Central and South America, but this is where we come back to reload, regroup, and wait for the next fire.

I joined the Army at eighteen. Didn't take long to figure out where I belonged. Special Forces wasn't just a career path, it was structure. Control. Something solid. Something I didn't have growing up. My parents were there, technically. But that's about it. Always chasing something, parties, distractions—anything that kept them from paying attention to what was right in front of them.

I learned early not to expect much. If I needed something, I figured it out myself. If something went wrong, I handled it. No one was coming to fix it. So I stopped waiting.

The Army gave me something different. They gave me clear rules and clear purpose. No more guesswork, I learned to rely on myself and then eventually learn to trust the men on my team. I earned my place as team lead in the Special Forces and we've had ten years of perfecting our missions. Becoming a well oiled machine that moved in sync. There's a level of trust between us, most of the time we know what's expected and where to be without having to voice it. There's been plenty of times we had to move without uttering a word.

Nate ended up here around the same time. Different branch, he's a Navy SEAL, but close enough that our paths crossed more than once. His team runs out of the same region, usually offshore, but they rotate through base when they're in between deployments.

We met in a bar just outside the military compound. Neither of us spoke enough Spanish to avoid trouble. Almost got into a fight with the wrong group of locals. He had my back and that was enough. We've been tight ever since. His team, the Full Metal Jackets, runs operations parallel to ours sometimes. When missions overlap, we link up. It works.

The temporary barracks come into view ahead, cutting hard lines against the surrounding jungle. Made of concrete and steel, straight edges. A sharp contrast to everything around it. Nothing close to what people would consider comfortable or luxury.

The air is thick, heavy with the scent of rain and damp earth, storm clouds gathering low on the horizon. It feels like a warning. Out here, things don't stay calm for long. It's not the jungle that gets you, it's everything you don't see coming.

"So," Nate says, glancing up at the sky before looking back at me, "six weeks in another jungle. What are these scientists even chasing?"

I huff a quiet breath. "Command said something about land formations. Earth processes. Didn't sound like anything worth dying over."

Nate arches a brow. "Sounds thrilling."

"Yeah," I mutter. "We babysit, keep them breathing, and get out."

Simple. On paper.

"And then you're done?" he asks.

"Yeah." The word comes out flat. Final. "Discharged when we're back stateside."

He studies me for a second. "Starting that 'life' you keep talking about?"

I let out a quiet scoff, shaking my head slightly. "Guess so." The words don't land the way they should. Starting my life. Like this hasn't already been it. Like I haven't spent years building something out of nothing. Now I'm supposed to just what, walk away? Do what? Go where? I push the thought aside. Not today, that's a worry for another day.

"Still thinking Montana?" he asks.

I nod once. "Maybe. Not going back to Missouri."

That much is certain. "Rest of it, I'll figure out when I get there."

He exhales, nodding like he gets it. "I'm getting out too," he says. "Decided not to reenlist."

I glance over at him. "Yeah?"

"Yeah," he shrugs. "Figured I'd try one of those things you call a life."

I huff a quiet laugh. "Let me know how that works out for you."

"Same to you," he shoots back.

"Well," Nate says, clapping me lightly on the shoulder, "when it goes sideways. And it will, let me know. I'll come rescue your ass."

I glance at him. "We handle our own."

He grins. "Yeah, yeah. Keep telling yourself that."

We've both been on the wrong end of that argument before. Neither of us says it. We slow as we reach the barracks, the building looming ahead.

"Have fun with your 'mission,'" he adds, throwing up air quotes.

I snort. "Yeah. That."

He starts backing away, already turning. "Don't die, Wraith."

"No promises."

He grins. "Wouldn't expect any." I give him a short wave and head inside. I grab my duffel, running through the familiar routine. Clothes. MREs. Comms. Map. Everything laid out with purpose. Everything exactly where it needs to be. My hand pauses over my dog tags, the metal cool against my palm.

Something about this mission feels off. I don't have a reason for it, just instinct. I shake it off. Like the storm building outside. Four hours. That's all I've got before wheels up. I zip the bag and leave it there. No point overthinking it now.

The bar is already buzzing when I walk in. Low light. Music humming under the weight of voices and clinking glass. The air smells like beer, sweat, and something fried that's been sitting too long. Normal.

Except it's not. I spot my team in the back corner. Sitting at the same table we always claim when we're here. Every one in the same seats, just habit at this point. The energy is different today, always is before our next deployment. Quieter than normal, like something's coiled just beneath the surface.

Reaper's the first thing that stands out. He's never been the loudest, but this is different, more contemplative. He turns his glass slowly between his fingers, eyes fixed somewhere past the window, like he's already gone. Already thinking about what comes next.

Magellan sits beside him, elbows on the table, casually checking his sidearm. Slow. Methodical. Not because it needs checking. Because it gives him something to do. Keeps his mind from wandering too far. There's a joke sitting just behind his eyes—I can see it—just hasn't let it loose yet.

Stitches leans back in his chair, trying to carry the mood like he always does. "Never a dull moment, huh?" he says, flashing that easy grin as I walk up to the table. It's a little tighter than usual. But he's trying. He always does, he's always the calm one that holds things together when shit goes south.

Glitch is slouched back, boots hooked under his chair, jaw tight. "Babysitting," he mutters. Barely loud enough. But we all hear it.

Ghost doesn't even look up. He's already working. Tablet in hand, fingers moving fast, pulling data, cross-checking, building the picture before the rest of us even ask for it. No jokes. No commentary. Just work.

Sparta leans back, chair tipped slightly, watching all of it unfold like it's a show he's seen before. Which he has. A hundred times. He catches my eye and gives a small smirk. There it is. I pull out a chair and drop into it, forearms resting on the table.

"With everything heating up near Venezuela…" I start. I don't finish it. I don't need to, they already know the dangers and the risks. It's not even the first time we've been in this jungle dealing with guerrilla groups.

For a second, the bar fades and I'm back there.

Heat pressing down like a weight. Humidity thick enough to choke on. The jungle so dense you can't see more than ten feet in front of you. We were moving slow. Then gunfire erupts around us. Sharp cracks cutting through the trees. Pieces of bark are splintering around me, far too close for my liking. Magellan dropped first, dragging Stitches down with him behind a fallen log.

Reaper was already returning fire before the rest of us even hit the ground. Ghost calling movement in our ears, calm and precise, like he wasn't standing in the middle of chaos.

"Left flank—three moving!" There are clicks of acknowledgment. They weren't trained like us. But they didn't need to be. They knew the terrain. That made them dangerous.

Rounds tore through leaves overhead, splitting bark and small branches, kicking up dirt inches from where we were pinned. The jungle swallowed the sound and threw it back at us from every direction. No clean lines. No clear targets.

Just moving shadows and working on instinct. Sparta circles wide, disappearing into the brush without a word. Glitch kept comms steady, voice tight but controlled, keeping us connected when everything else was noise.

We pushed them back hard and fast. Ending it before it could be dragged out, before any casualties. The silence that follows is always the worst, the unknown while we breathe. Make sure no one was it, not on our side anyway.

No bodies. No trace. Just silence creeping back in like it had never happened. The jungle doesn't hold onto things. It erases them.

The bar comes back into focus. The weight of it settles in my chest.

Reaper exhales slowly. "More movement?"

Ghost nods once, still focused on his screen. "Yeah. Not military. Armed groups. Cartels. Some guerrilla spillover."

Magellan shifts in his seat. "Trafficking routes?"

"Among other things," Ghost says. "Drugs, mining, weapons. They move through the jungle because no one can track them out there."

Sparta taps the table lightly. "And if they start pushing further south…"

"They don't stop to check borders," I finish.

Ghost finally looks up. "They use the rivers. Old trails. Some of those routes run closer to where this team's operating than command wants to admit."

That settles over the table. Heavier now, we all remember what we went through. No one is excited to be back in the jungle.

Stitches leans back slightly. "So what? Wrong place, wrong time?"

"Best case," I say.

Reaper tilts his head. "Worst?"

I glance down at the map again. "Territory overlap. Or someone deciding they don't want witnesses. Unfortunately, people living in the remote spots are in danger, too."

Silence. Reaper finally looks over. "What intel do we actually have?"

I shake my head once. "Not much. Study on a local tribe. Northern Brazil."

"That's it?" Magellan asks.

"That's it."

He exhales through his nose. "Yeah... that checks out."

"Civilians," Reaper mutters.

"They think it's controlled," I add.

"Until it's not," he finishes.

Ghost starts explaining more, always down to business with him. "Yanomami region," he says, eyes still on the screen. "Remote. Dense canopy. Visibility's garbage." He taps the tablet once, rotating it slightly so we can all see. "Closest militia movement is outside their projected zone. Not far enough to ignore." That lands, you can feel it settle over the table.

"I sent everything to your devices," Ghost adds. "Routes, terrain, team layout. Flight, bus, and foot movement."

"Foot movement? Is that what we're calling walking now?" Magellan mutters.

Ghost finally glances up. "Three kilometers in."

Magellan groans quietly. "Yeah, I love that for us."

Sparta smirks. "You'll survive."

"Barely," Magellan shoots back. "And I'm going to complain the whole way."

That gets a quiet laugh out of Stitches. Even Reaper's mouth twitches. Glitch doesn't laugh. I lean back slightly, looking around the table at my team. Six weeks in the jungle, covering clueless civilians near an unstable border. Yeah. This isn't going to be as simple as it sounds.

"How far from the border?" Sparta asks, already leaning over the map, one hand braced on the table.

Ghost zooms in, the glow from the screen casting sharp lines across his face. "Close enough," he says. "If they push south, we won't get much warning."

Silence settles again, just that familiar feeling, like we're missing something.

"What about the civilians?" Stitches asks, quieter now.

Ghost shrugs slightly, still scanning. "Small team. Academic. Same group had an incident out there five years ago." That gets everyone's attention. "One of them didn't make it back."

The table goes still. No movement. No jokes. Even Magellan stops fidgeting with his gear.

I lean back in my chair, exhaling slowly. "Yeah," I mutter. "That tracks." My gaze drifts over the map. "People go in unprepared, jungle does the rest." I tap the edge of the table once. "Any indication the tribe was involved?"

Ghost shakes his head. "No. Reports say she disappeared. No signs of foul play. Just an accident," he adds, though his tone doesn't fully commit to it.

"And they want to go back," I say. It's not a question.

Reaper lifts his glass, watching the liquid inside for a second before answering. "Means they don't understand what they're walking into. Or they think they do," he adds.

"Same thing," I reply.

Sparta taps the map again, more deliberate this time. "Terrain's the bigger problem. Movement's slow. Dense coverage."

He glances up. "Extraction's worse."

"And they'll wander," Magellan says, leaning back with a quiet huff. "They always do."

I nod once. "Yeah. They always do."

Glitch shifts in his chair, restless, jaw tight. "Babysitting," he mutters again. No one argues.

I drop my gaze back to the map, tracing the route without really seeing it. Just a dense jungle, clueless civilians, a prior disappearance and a dangerous guerrilla group moving in. Yeah. This has all the makings of something going sideways.

The flight is quiet. Not peaceful. Just focused. We're on a commercial aircraft with standard seating, narrow aisles and the low hum of engines vibrating through the frame. Civilians scattered throughout, headphones on, screens glowing, unaware of anything beyond their own destination. Nothing special and not our preferred way to travel, we're all too big to sit comfortably in these seats.

We blend in. That's the point. I've got the window seat with Reaper sitting beside me. Tablet open. Maps pulled up as we plan our op.

The jungle spreads beneath us in fractured pieces, green layered over green, broken only by winding rivers that cut through it like veins. From up here, it looks manageable. It's not.

I zoom in, adjusting overlays, terrain, elevation and waterways. The details start to matter. Ridges that slow movement. Lowlands that flood. Dense canopy that kills visibility and comms. I mark potential exit points. Clearings. River access. Anything that could buy us time if things go sideways. Because they will. They always do.

Across the aisle, Ghost is already working ahead of me. Head down. Tablet glowing faintly in the dim cabin. Pulling intel. Cross-checking.

Filling in the gaps command didn't bother to.

Magellan's a few rows up, half turned in his seat, talking quietly with Stitches. I catch a low chuckle, he's keeping it light. He always does.

Reaper sits still, when we're done talking, His arms folded and eyes closed. Just conserving his energy. Glitch hasn't said a word in over an hour. That's not like him. Sparta shifts in his seat behind me, leaning forward just enough to see my screen.

"You're already planning exits," he mutters.

"Always am." He doesn't argue. He just nods. I switch screens, pulling up the files Ghost sent over. The civilians.

One professor. Two grad students. One undergrad. Three have been there before. That should mean something. Make them more prepared, but it doesn't. Not if they are willing to go back into the unknown, into dangerous territories.

I scroll further and find the incident. Five years ago. There is a minimal report, she disappeared days before they were set to leave the jungle to go back home. They searched for days and never found anything. No body. No trace. I stare at that line longer than I should. No trace. Yeah, I don't like that.

By the time we start descending into Belém, I've already started placing my team. Not officially. Just in my head. Magellan stays with the village. He's fluent in Spanish, it's not the same as Portuguese but he will be able to catch most of it. Language matters. But it's more than that, he's steady. More relaxed and approachable than the rest of us. People trust him without realizing it. We'll need that. remote tribes notoriously don't trust outsiders. The rest of us will rotate. Jungle coverage, movement control and overnight patrols. Eyes on everything that doesn't belong.

The plane hits the runway hard, tires screeching briefly before settling into a steady roll. The cabin shifts, people waking up, stretching and grabbing bags. Normal again. We're anything but.

The moment the cabin door opens, the heat hits. Humid air that clings instantly to your skin and settles in your lungs. Northern Brazil is the hottest, like Central America it's closest to the equator, making the heat even more oppressive.

"Alright," I say, low enough only my team hears. "Stay tight until we're clear." A few nods. No questions. We move with the crowd quickly, but not like them. It's a small airport with an open layout, large windows letting in natural light. Fans overhead doing nothing to cut the heat. The scent of earth, fuel, and something faintly sweet lingers in the air.

We grab our gear first. Duffels. Hard cases. Everything accounted for. Magellan does a quick count without being obvious. I don't even have to ask. Ghost checks his tablet again. Signal's weak, but usable. We don't linger. We refill our water, use the restrooms and get a quick reset before we head toward the bus terminal. We will have to meet the team, then two bus rides that will take us deep into the jungle.

I didn't even see her coming, I started turning from the water station and she walked straight into me. I hadn't been expecting it. But I noticed her immediately.

Her phone slipped from her hand, but I caught her before she could fall back, my grip firm at her arms. Her breath caught, a soft and startled sound, for a second, everything else faded. Just her. Flushed cheeks, wide eyes and something I couldn't immediately place.

"Ope—sorry! Desculpe!" she blurted. Fast. Flustered. Color rushed into her cheeks, and hell. That hit harder than it should have. I let go, slower than necessary.

"No problem," I said, my voice steadier than I felt. "Hope your phone's okay." She crouched to grab it, and my gaze dropped without permission, then stopped. Lingering on her perfectly rounded ass. Just enough to register the shape of her, the way she moved. She was natural and unguarded. Real. I forced my attention back up. She threw me off balance and I don't know if I like that. I'm not used to anything distracting me, still, I didn't step away. Not right away.

When she walked away, my eyes stayed on her longer than they should have. Until she turned the corner and disappeared. From the intel brief, I already knew she was part of the team. One of the scientists. That alone should've been enough to keep me away from her. But it wasn't. This mission had already shifted.

Chapter Three

Sarah

Two days later, my plane lands at Belém International Airport, in the northeast of Brazil. The second my feet hit the ground, the air feels different. Definitely warmer and way more humid than the spring air of Minnesota.

We're starting the field school the second week of June, six weeks in total. Maybe a little less, depending on travel. It's nearly a full day just to get here, and another six hours by bus before we even reach the edge of the rainforest. I step into the terminal, adjusting the strap of my backpack as I pull out my phone, connecting to the airport Wi-Fi.

First, Hazel. *Made it to Brazil safely.*

Then my parents. My sister. Fallon. Before finally calling my uncle.

He picks up almost immediately. "Olá! Tudo bem?" His voice is warm, familiar. "Did you land?"

"Of course," I say, smiling despite myself as I weave through the terminal. "Just trying to make my way to the bus station now. Long trip ahead."

My uncle Tony has lived in Brazil for years now, retired here with his wife, who grew up not far from where I'm headed. He's always been more than just family. The kind of uncle who shows up with stories, spoils you without asking, and somehow makes anywhere feel a little more familiar.

Around me, the airport hums with movement. Families cluster near baggage claim, children half-asleep against their parents' shoulders. The steady clatter of the conveyor belts blends with overlapping conversations, all of them in Portuguese. They're speaking so fast, fluid, just slightly beyond my comfort level.

Belém's airport isn't massive, but it's open, airy. Sunlight pours through tall windows, reflecting off polished floors. Large potted palms line the walkways, a quiet reminder of what waits beyond the city. The jungle.

"Olá?" my uncle says. "Did I lose you, Sarah?"

"Não, desculpa," I reply, shifting my bag higher on my shoulder. "Just trying not to get lost on my way out."

"Of course you are," he laughs softly.

I round a corner and walk straight into something solid. My phone slips from my hand, clattering against the floor.

"Sorry—" I start automatically, already crouching down to grab it, heat rushing to my face. I really need to start paying attention. A dull ache pulses in my arm where I made contact, and I rub it absently as I straighten and realize I didn't hit a pillar.

I hit a person. A very large person. I blink, my gaze lifting slowly and then stopping. He's tall. Easily over six feet, easily at least a whole foot taller than me. Broad shoulders that are solid and unmoving, like he barely felt the impact at all. Dark hair, slightly longer on top, like it hasn't been cut in a while but still somehow intentional. His features are sharp, defined, but it's his presence that hits first.

The kind of stillness that doesn't feel passive, it feels deliberate. For a second, I forget what I was about to say. Then I catch something warm and earthy. Something like sun-soaked wood and salty air, layered with a subtle spice I can't quite place. It lingers, pulling at something in my memory, something distant and unfamiliar all at once. It clung to the air around him, intoxicating and undeniably masculine. Reminding me of Brazil's beautiful beaches.

"Ope—sorry! Desculpe!" I blurt, the words tumbling out too fast as I realize I've just been standing there, staring.

Smooth. I crouch quickly, grabbing my phone, using the movement as an excuse to collect myself. When I straighten, I let my gaze lift again, more carefully this time, attempting to be subtle.

He's tall. Not just tall—*imposing*. At least a foot taller than me, maybe more. Solid build, the kind of presence that takes up space around him without trying. His features are sharp, almost too perfect, strong jaw and clean lines but it's the faint curve of his mouth that throws me off. Not quite a smile. Something quieter. Something... knowing.

Then I notice what he's wearing. Dark, fitted shirt stretched across his shoulders, sleeves hugging muscle without trying to show it off. Durable pants, cargo, maybe tactical and worn in just enough to look used, not new. Boots that look like they've seen a lot of rough places.. Everything about him is practical. Intentional. Like he's dressed for whatever comes next.

His eyes a golden-brown. There's depth there, flecks of gold catching the light, shifting when he looks at me. Focused in a way that makes it feel like he's actually seeing me. Really seeing me.

I forget, for a second, how to breathe. Behind him, five other men stand in formation or close enough to it. Same posture. Same build. Same quiet awareness, all dressed similarly. Military. The realization clicks into place just as he speaks.

"No problem," he says, that faint smile deepening slightly. "Hope your phone's okay." His voice—It's low. Controlled. A deep, steady rumble that settles somewhere in my chest before I can stop it. I swallow, my grip tightening slightly around my phone.

"It's fine," I manage. "I—uh—wasn't paying attention." Understatement.

His gaze lingers a second longer than it should. Or maybe I'm imagining it. My heart stutters, suddenly out of rhythm and before I can stop myself, my eyes flick down, to his mouth. Heat rushes to my face instantly. What am I doing?

I snap my gaze back up, mortified, but there's the slightest shift in his expression, like he noticed. I've never reacted like this before. Not to anyone. Not like this. My pulse pounds, my thoughts scrambling for something—anything—to blame.

The long flight. The heat. Anything but the strange, magnetic pull drawing me toward a man I don't even know. A quiet snicker breaks the moment. I blink, the spell snapping as I become aware of the others behind him, low voices, amused, just watching.

Watching *me*. My face burns hotter. Right. I'm still standing here like an idiot.

"Olá! Sarah, você está aí? Are you there?"

His voice crackles through my phone, louder now, pulling me out of whatever just happened. I take a small step back, heat creeping up my neck as reality settles back in.

"Sim, sorry," I say quickly, bringing the phone back to my ear. "I dropped it. I'm okay."

I risk a glance up. He's already stepping back, slinging a duffel bag over his shoulder like it weighs nothing. Even with the distance, I still have to tilt my head to meet his eyes.

Then he winks. Not exaggerated. Not playful. Just enough to feel intentional and confident, before he turns to leave. My eyes betray me instantly, tracing the movement of his shoulders beneath the fitted fabric of his uniform, the way he moves like everything he does is controlled and deliberate. Damn it, Sarah. Focus.

I'm still standing there, half dazed, when a voice calls out behind him, "Yo, Wraith! Careful, man, don't bulldoze pretty girls!"

My face burns. Oh my God. I stare down at my phone like it might save me from existing, but I can still hear the low voices, a round of laughter, something he says in response that I can't quite catch as they keep walking. I shouldn't look. I know I shouldn't. Just a quick glance over my shoulder and he's still watching me. A small thrill sparks in my chest before I can stop it.

Maybe I wasn't imagining it, still, it's not like it matters. Plus, I'm sure I look like a disaster after an overnight flights, leggings, oversized sweatshirt, hair pulled back in a way that stopped being intentional hours ago. Definitely not Fallon-level "approachable." She'd have turned that into a full conversation already. Probably gotten his name, his number, and a plan for later tonight. I barely managed to say sorry.

"You worried me there," Tony says through the phone. "Are you still headed to the bus?"

Right. Real life.

"Yes," I say, shifting my bag and starting toward baggage claim. "I'm almost there. I just need to grab my luggage, go through customs, and meet the team."

We only had forty-five minutes from landing to departure. And I've already wasted too much time.

"Okay," he says. "Send me updates when you can. And Sarah, stay safe. Call me if you need anything."

"I will," I promise. "Love you."

"Love you too. Tchau, tchau." The line clicks off, I quickly shoot off another text to Fallon, telling her I just ran into a giant and I slip my phone back into my pocket, picking up my pace as I head toward baggage claim.

By the time I grab my bags and make my way outside, the heat has already settled into my skin, thick and unrelenting. I spot the group near the bus almost immediately. This is it. The start of everything.

Dr. Willis and Benjamin are already there, deep in conversation. Dr. Willis looks exactly like I expected, lean, slightly stooped, dressed head-to-toe in practical field gear. A khaki button-down, sleeves rolled despite the heat, matching pants tucked neatly into worn hiking boots. Very *Indiana Jones*—minus the hat. Though honestly, I wouldn't be surprised if he owns one.

His wire-rimmed glasses that frame pale blue eyes, sit low on his nose as he gestures while speaking, his expression calm and thoughtful. There's a steadiness to him, the kind that comes from years in the field. Experience etched into the lines of his face, softened by an easy, approachable demeanor. The kind of person who makes you feel like you're in capable hands.

Benjamin stands beside him, nodding along but his attention flicks up the moment he notices me. Of course it does. I shift my focus past him. The undergrad, Jenna, approaches from the side, her attention fixed on her phone until the last second. She's petite, almost delicate in build, with blonde hair pulled into a loose, effortless bun. Hazel eyes, quick and observant when she finally looks up.

There's something sharp behind them. Not nervous. Not overwhelmed. Curious, like she's already trying to figure everything out. She's dressed like I am, in comfy leggings, long sleeves, practical enough for travel.

"Hey, guys," I say as I approach, forcing a smile while my eyes sweep the area. "What did you think of the flight?" And definitely not scanning for a certain six-foot-something distraction.

"It was fine," Dr. Willis says. "I was hoping to sleep more." A few nods of agreement follow.

"Yeah," I say. "Those long flights can be rough if you're not used to them." I shift my bag on my shoulder, glancing around again. "So, we're just waiting for the military escort? Dr. Anderson said he was close to retiring, so I'm guessing we're looking for someone a little older?"

"The 'military escort' is here." The voice hits first. Low and newly familiar. "And for the record, Mouse," he adds, amusement threading through the words, "I'm not old."

Heat floods my face instantly. I turn slowly and there he is. The same man I bumped into. Of course it's him. My mouth actually falls open before I can stop it, and his gaze drops briefly—just for a second —before lifting back to mine.

Oh my God. I just called him old. I snap my mouth shut, trying to recover, but my brain is nowhere near caught up. I'm just staring at him. Again. He's still just as distracting up close. Still, controlled in a way that feels deliberate, like every movement is measured. And those eyes—still locked on mine.

My heart kicks hard in my chest. Get it together. He takes a step closer, closing the space between us without hesitation, and for a second it feels like the rest of the world fades out again. Like it's just— someone clears their throat behind him.

Right. Reality. I blink, forcing myself to take a small step back, suddenly very aware of how close he'd been. The heat of him lingers even as the moment breaks, and I hate how easily my focus slips back to him. Like I'm being pulled in.

"Dr. Frank Willis," Dr. Willis says, stepping forward and extending his hand. "I wasn't aware it would be a full unit. We were told a Green Beret would be accompanying us."

"Sergeant Wade Blakely," he replies, his tone shifting—controlled, professional. "Team Lead. We were asked to bring additional support," he continues, his tone calm, professional. "Given the location."

Green Beret.

Special Forces. Hazel *did* say that. I just didn't fully process what that meant. I glance past him briefly, taking in the others behind him, equally built, equally composed and watching everything with quiet awareness. It looks like they are a well oiled machine, they keep watch as the Sergeant makes introductions.

This isn't just security. This is something else. Out of the corner of my eye, I catch Benjamin watching me. His gaze lingers a second too long before he looks away, exchanging a quick glance with Jenna and then Dr. Willis. Something about it sits wrong. But before I can figure out why, my attention drifts back. Right back to Sergeant Wade Blakely.

He gestures behind him, introducing them one by one. "Miller— Reaper. Second-in-command." Reaper gives a short nod, his expression sharp, assessing.

"Lewis—Ghost. Communications and intel." Ghost barely moves, his gaze already scanning the area like he's cataloging everything.

"Davies—Stitches. Medical." Stitches offers a calm, almost reassuring half-smile.

"Ramirez—Magellan. Weapons specialist." Magellan lifts a hand in a quick greeting, relaxed but alert.

"Jackson—Sparta. Operations and planning." Sparta stands solid, grounded, exactly what Wade implied. The kind of presence that keeps everything running smoothly.

"Thompson," he adds. "Assault and comms support." Jake doesn't say anything, but there's an edge to him, like he's coiled energy instead of controlled stillness.

Wade's attention shifts back to us. "We're here to keep you safe," he says. "We'll coordinate coverage based on your schedules and work zones."

A quiet stillness settles over the group. Not uncomfortable, just aware. Like everyone is adjusting to the reality of what he is. What they are. His gaze moves across each of us, measured. Assessing. Then it pauses, on me, just long enough to make my pulse stumble.

"Is it just the four of you?" The question hangs there for a second. Not uncertain. Like he already knows the answer. Before anyone else can respond, Benjamin steps forward. Closing the space between us like he's inserting himself into the moment. He looks up at Wade, he's not short, but Wade still has at least half a foot on him.

"Hi, I'm Benjamin," he says, flashing that practiced, confident smile. "PhD student working with Dr. Willis. I'll be assisting with geological research around the Amazon basin."

He gestures toward Jenna. "This is Jenna, our undergrad." There's subtle shift in his tone, like he's trying to prove something. Wade doesn't react. Just a single, measured nod. Unimpressed.

Benjamin shifts slightly, like he feels it too. Good. Jenna, on the other hand, is staring. I don't blame her. I glance at Wade, watching as his attention flicks briefly toward her. Acknowledgment. Nothing more. Then he turns back to me.

One corner of his mouth lifts. There it is again. That small, knowing smirk. He definitely caught me staring. Again. Great.

"And you?" he asks, that low, steady voice cutting through everything else. "What's your name?"

I straighten instinctively, clearing my throat as I meet his gaze. "Sarah," I say. "PhD candidate. I'll be conducting ethno-archaeological research with the Yanomami."

My voice stays steady. Somehow. Even as heat creeps up my neck. Out of the corner of my eye, I catch Jenna smirking. Of course she is. Wade's gaze doesn't shift. Not even a little.

"Sarah," he repeats. The way he says my name—too deliberate. Familiar. A small shiver runs down my spine before I can stop it.

"I'd like to hear more about your work," he says. "I'm familiar with environmental and terrain-based research... but not your field." There's a pause. Like he's choosing his next words. "But I'm interested." Something about the way he says it makes my stomach flip. Because it doesn't feel like he's talking about just the research.

"Do we have a departure time for the bus?" The question is directed at the group but his eyes never leave mine. Not once. Like he already knows the answer.

"About ten minutes," Dr. Willis says. "Then we can start loading up."

The words snap me back. Right, there's other people. The moment, whatever that was, dissolves as the world rushes back in. Voices. Movement. Heat. I take a small step back, creating space, I hadn't even realized how close we had gotten. Without looking at him again, I turn and follow the group toward the bus stop. My duffel bags feel heavier now, digging into my hands as I lag slightly behind the others. Before I can adjust my grip, one of them is lifted away. I glance up. Sergeant Wade or Wraith, I don't know what to call him.

"You don't have to carry that," I say quickly. "We're almost there."

"It's fine," he replies easily. Like it's not even a question. He looks down at me, that faint smile pulling at his lips again. Dangerous. My stomach flips over. I don't understand why I react like this around him. No one has ever made me feel so off balance. Like I'm not entirely in control of myself. I don't like it. I definitely don't trust it.

An hour later, we're on the highway, heading north. The bus is bigger than I expected. It has a wide row, two seats on each side that are pretty large and comfortable. The kind of seats that are almost comfortable enough to fall asleep in.

When we boarded, the unit hung back, letting us get on first. Even though I know it's childish, I dropped my bag into the seat next to me. Just in case. No Benjamin. No Special Forces soldier. No distractions.

Surprisingly, there's Wi-Fi, so I pull out my phone and message Fallon as the city slowly fades behind us.

Me: OMG. He's one of the Special Forces guys coming with us.

Fallon: Is he hot?

I huff out a quiet laugh.

Me: So hot. And he keeps looking at me. It's freaking me out.

Fallon: That's because he wants you 😾

Me: Absolutely not. He is *way* out of my league. You should've seen Benjamin trying to intimidate him lol

Fallon: Benjamin is a loser. Ignore him and enjoy the hot bodyguard for six weeks.

Me: You're insane. That is not happening.

Fallon: I'm telling you, this is the universe working. That Sex on the Beach was a sign 😉

I shake my head, smiling despite myself.

Me: You're not helping.

Fallon: I always help. You'll see.

I tuck my phone away, leaning back in my seat as the road stretches ahead of us. No. I'm not doing this. I'm here for a reason. I'll stay professional. Keep my distance. Focus on the work. That's it. No distractions. Especially not one with golden-brown eyes and a voice that lingers a little too long in my head. Besides, I won't even be deep in the jungle most of the time. I'll be near the village. Separate from the others. Separate from him.

But even as I try to convince myself, my thoughts drift back, to the way his voice wrapped around my name, the way his gaze felt almost tangible, like a touch I couldn't quite shake. What was it about him that made me feel so... seen? I shift in my seat, exhaling quietly. Maybe I'm overthinking it. Maybe he just thinks I'm funny. He did laugh earlier. His team too. My stomach tightens.

Was I that obvious? God, I hope they're not laughing at me. I press my lips together, forcing the thought away. I just need to stay professional. Keep my head down. Focus on the work. That's it.

I pull my phone back out, messaging Sam this time, anything to keep my mind off him. Off everything. But before I can type more than a sentence, I feel movement beside me. I glance up and there he is. Standing right next to my seat. My heart stumbles. I quickly flip my phone over, screen down. Smooth. Not obvious at all.

His gaze flicks to the phone, then back to me, that same knowing smirk settling in like he caught exactly what I was doing. Which he probably did.

"Mind if I join you?" he asks.

But he's already moving. My bag is lifted from the seat and set carefully on the floor before I can answer. Okay. That's a little rude and also completely unexpected. I shift slightly, giving him space as he sits, his presence immediately noticeable.

"So," he says, settling back, his voice low and even. "What exactly is ethno-archaeology?"

I keep my gaze forward, focusing on the seat in front of me. Of course he's asking because it's his job. That's all this is. It has to be.

"It's the study of living cultures to help interpret the past," I say. "We observe daily behaviors—how people build, use tools, organize space and use that to understand what similar patterns might look like in the archaeological record." My words come a little faster than I intend. Filling space. Filling silence. Because I don't want him to lose interest. The second that thought forms—I scold myself, why does that matter?

He's here to protect us. That's it. Nothing more. But when I finally get the nerve to glance over, his eyes are still on me. They're focused and attentive on me. Like he actually *is* interested. Despite everything I just told myself, I want him to be.

"I want to get to know the people who live there," I say, glancing down at my hands before forcing myself to look back at him. "Observe how they hunt, how they interact with each other, their daily routines. The small things that don't always get documented."

I shift slightly in my seat, settling into it as I continue. "Their tools, their food, their social structures, how they live alongside nature instead of against it. It's not identical to prehistoric life, obviously," I add, a small smile slipping through. "They use metal tools, and there's some contact with nearby villages. But their subsistence patterns and the way they sustain themselves, that's where the real insight is." I pause briefly, realizing I'm rambling. "This is the final piece I need for my dissertation," I finish, a little quieter. "I graduate in the fall."

Heat creeps up my neck as I glance at him again. When I do, he's closer, leaning in just slightly, one arm resting along the back of the seat. His presence closing the space between us without fully crossing it.

That scent hits me again. Warm. Earthy. Sun-soaked wood and addicting. I inhale without thinking and instantly regret it. His mouth curves. Of course he noticed.

"Hmm," Wade says, his voice lower now, thoughtful. "That's interesting." I can he's not just being polite or dismissing my interests.

He's actually interested.

"I've always liked history," he continues. "But I never really thought about learning from people who are still living it." His gaze stays on mine. "Makes you wonder how much we've lost."

There's a brief pause before he adds, "Dr. Willis mentioned you speak Portuguese. You'll be translating for us?" He shifts slightly as he speaks, angling toward me just enough that the world beyond him fades again. The aisle, the noise, the movement, all of it feels distant. Like it's just us.

"Yeah, Sergeant Blakely," I say, steadying my voice. "I'll handle most of the translation. The Yanomami don't speak much Portuguese, and mine isn't perfect, but it's enough." I hesitate for a second. "You'll probably be in the forest most of the time with the others anyway," I add. "I'll mostly help in the evenings, when everyone's back together."

That's the plan. At least, that's what I'm hoping. Focus on my work during the day. Stay out of the way. Keep things simple. I glance past him for just a second and catch Benjamin watching us. His jaw tight. Eyes narrowed. Something sharp flickering there, it sends a quiet chill up my arms. I look away quickly. Whatever his problem is, it's not going to matter. Not with someone like the Sergeant here.

"Call me Wade," he says, that small, easy smile softening the edges of him. "Or Wraith. No need for formalities." His gaze lingers, "I'm just here to keep you safe."

"Okay...Wade it is," I say. Then, before I can stop myself, before my brain even has time to process or filter my thoughts. "Does that make us friends?"

The second the words leave my mouth, I freeze. Oh my God. Where did that come from? I'm not like this. I don't *say* things like that.

A quiet chuckle rumbles from him, low and warm. "That's a good place to start." There's something in the way he says it, easy, but not dismissive. I wonder if maybe, he's not laughing at me.

I open my mouth to respond and come up with nothing. So I don't say anything at all. The bus hums quietly around us, the steady rhythm of the road pulling at my focus. He lets the conversation dip, I don't know where they came from but I am exhausted after that flight.

The bus slows. The change in motion pulls me back slowly, the world coming into focus in pieces. Warmth surrounds me. Too warm for a bus seat. Too solid.

My stomach drops. I blink awake and realize my head is resting on Wade's shoulder. There's a faint damp spot on his sleeve. Oh no. Oh no.

Heat rushes to my face as I jerk upright, mortified. Did I seriously just—I swipe quickly at my mouth, hoping and praying, it wasn't as obvious as it feels. I risk a glance up. He's already looking at me. Smiling. Of course he is. His arm is still around me, resting easily, like it had been there for a while. My hands are loosely curled around his forearm, I drop them instantly.

I don't even know how that happened. I don't want to know.

"I'm so sorry," I blurt, looking anywhere but at him as I reach for my bag.

"Don't be," he says easily. I glance up and meet his eyes. "You were comfortable," he adds, that same quiet amusement in his voice.

My face burns hotter. "You talk in your sleep. What were you dreaming about?"

My eyes widen. "What? What did I say?" I ask, my voice coming out quieter than I intend.

His mouth curves, just slightly. "Nothing I'm ready to share yet."

Oh.

My.

God.

I look away immediately, staring out the window like it might save me. There is absolutely no way I'm admitting I was dreaming about him. None.

"I don't remember," I say quickly.

"Oh, I think you do," he replies, the corner of his mouth lifting into that same maddening smirk. "But don't worry, I've got my ways of finding out." He gives a subtle wink.

I narrow my eyes. "Oh, so you're a jungle interrogation expert?"

A low chuckle escapes him, and I hate the way it sends a small thrill through me.

"Comes with the job," he says easily. Then, after a beat, his voice drops just slightly, "But I can be persuasive when I need to be." Of course he can.

I roll my eyes, turning away before he can see the reaction on my face and start gathering my things, shoving them into my bag a little faster than necessary. We still have another leg of the trip ahead, another bus, then a three-kilometer walk before we even reach the village. Focus. As I zip up my bag, the others begin filing off the bus. One of his teammates pauses at the front.

"I've got your gear, Sarge."

"Thanks," Wade calls back. The bus empties. It's just us. I sling my bag over my shoulder, then pause. He hasn't moved. I glance over. He's still seated, one hand pressing into his right knee, his jaw tightening for just a second before he releases the tension. It's subtle—quick—but I catch it. The pain he's trying to hide.

"Are we getting up?" I ask, softer now.

He exhales lightly, like he's pushing past it. "Yeah," he says. "Sorry. My leg acts up if I sit too long."

He stands, slower this time, more controlled but once he's upright, that steady presence settles right back into place. Like the moment never happened. But I saw it and I don't think I was supposed to. He steps back, reaching for my bag before I can stop him. I follow, falling into step behind him and that's when I notice the slight hitch in his stride. The way he favors his right leg, just enough to be noticeable, before it smooths out the longer he walks. Like he's used to pushing through it. I file it away without meaning to.

I rejoin the group, slipping into conversation with Jenna as we move toward the next bus. Anything to keep things normal. Anything to drown out the tension still lingering in my chest. I can feel it, though. Wade's presence and going back into the jungle.

I don't look back. I focus on Jenna, nodding along, letting the conversation carry me. I'm here to work. That's it. I didn't come here to get distracted. I definitely didn't come here to get involved with anyone. I came here for my work and for Carly.

"Why did it take you so long to get off the bus?" Benjamin's voice cuts through everything. His tone is sharp and accusing.

I turn, meeting his scowl head-on. "Well, it's none of your business," I say evenly, adjusting my backpack on my shoulder. "But since you asked so nicely, his leg was bothering him." I roll my eyes at him.

His eyes flick toward Wade, then back to me, something tightening in his expression.

"Anything else?" I add.

He doesn't answer. Good. I turn away before he can, stepping toward the bus as the bags are loaded. No more explanations. No more attention. I don't look at Wade. I don't look at his team. And I definitely don't look at Benjamin. This field study was supposed to be straightforward. But already, between Benjamin's simmering attitude and Wade's quiet persistence, I can feel it shifting. Something tells me, the next six weeks are going to be anything but simple.

Chapter Four

Sarah

I turn toward the next bus, heading for it without looking back. Mostly, I just need a second. Away from Benjamin. Away from Wade and the way I can *feel* his attention lingering at my back. It's ridiculous. But it's there. Like a slow warmth spreading under my skin.

I drop my bags into the compartment beneath the bus and step up inside. The metal stairs creak under my weight, and I already know, this ride is going to be worse. The engine rumbles low and rough, the whole frame vibrating beneath my feet. The air inside is thick and stale, it smells like diesel and dust. The air inside is heavy despite the weak attempt at air conditioning.

If anything, it's just pushing the heat around. We'll be heading deeper now. Through jungle. Through mountains. Further away from anything familiar. I move quickly to a window seat and sit, placing my bag beside me without hesitation.

Trying to create a barrier, again. I pull out my phone, even though there's no signal. Just something to focus on. Something to make it look like I'm occupied. I should be grabbing my book and powering my phone down. It's going to be useless to me now.

A second later, he's there. I don't turn, I pretend I don't even see him. I don't need to look to know, it's that same warm, earthy scent, sun-soaked wood with something faintly spiced. It drifts toward me as he steps closer, carried by the slow rotation of the fan overhead.

My skin prickles. Goosebumps rise despite the heat pressing in from all sides. I stare out the window. Okay, just breathe. Pretend I don't notice him, maybe he will go away. No such luck. He stops beside me, reaches down, and lifts my bag without hesitation, setting it between our feet before taking the seat. Like it was never a question.

My grip tightens around my phone. I don't react. Well, I *try* not to react. Why does he keep choosing me? I keep my gaze fixed outside, watching blurred green pass by, willing my pulse to slow. He makes me nervous. Not in a bad way, but in a way that is too aware.

This bus is smaller. Older. No Wi-Fi. No distractions. The seats are tighter, forcing us just close enough that I can feel the heat from his body beside me, steady and constant. It shouldn't matter. But it does. One by one, the others file in, spreading out across the rows.

No one sits near us. Good, I need the space. Even if Wade clearly doesn't. Benjamin climbs on last. His gaze finds us immediately. That same cutting look. I meet it for a second, trying to read what's behind it. I can't, the only thing I can see was jealousy and maybe anger, for what I don't know. He looks away first, jaw tightening as he drops into a seat near the front.

That makes everything feel even more complicated. Wade leans back slightly, lowering his voice.

"Mouse," he says, glancing toward me. "What's with that guy? Benjamin?"

My eyes widen just a fraction. Of course he noticed. I glance toward Benjamin before answering, weighing how much to say. I don't want to say too much or anything too personal. When I look back, Wade's watching me, steady and focused. Reading me. Like he's trying to piece something together.

"Mouse?" I ask quietly instead, deflecting. "You've called me that twice now." Something flickers in his expression. Surprise. Maybe a little amusement.

He leans in just slightly, not crowding, just enough to keep his voice between us. "Yeah," he says, the corner of his mouth lifting. "You're quiet."

My cheeks warm instantly.

"Observant," he adds. That doesn't help. "Quick. A little on edge. Not a bad thing."

My breath slips out before I can stop it, soft and unsteady. I don't know what to do with that. With him. It's obvious he's flirting, I think and I have no idea how to respond. At least he doesn't think I look like a rodent. My gaze lingers on his for a second too long. There's something in his eyes. He's not teasing me or mocking me, it's real. Real interest. I look away first.

"I don't—" I start, then stop myself, shaking my head slightly. Focus. Safer ground. "Well… this is our second field school together," I say quietly. "We're… friendly. I guess." Even I can hear it. That word doesn't fit. Friendly is definitely a stretch. My voice dips, and I glance around the bus again, making sure no one's listening. I don't want this conversation overheard. I don't want to explain more than I have to.

"He just—" I hesitate, choosing my words carefully. "He doesn't really understand boundaries."

That's putting it lightly. My fingers tighten around my phone. Memories flicker, things he's said, the way he looks at me and the way it never seems to mean anything to him. I swallow it all back down. Not here. Not now. Wade doesn't interrupt, he just listens.

"You ever been with him?" he asks, nodding slightly toward the front. "Or interested?" The reaction is immediate.

"God—no," I whisper, wrinkling my nose. "Absolutely not." Heat rises in my chest, sharper than I expect. "He's a player," I add under my breath. "Only cares about one thing."

I don't know what Wade thinks about me. Not really. But I want that part clear. Benjamin isn't an option. He never has been. Out of the corner of my eye, I see Wade shift slightly. Some of the tension in his shoulders eases. It's subtle, but I notice.

"Do you know why he keeps watching you?" he asks.

I do. I just don't want to get into it. Not like this.

"He's been flirting with me for a few years," I say instead, keeping my voice low. "I made it clear I'm not interested." A small pause. "He's persistent."

Again, that's putting it mildly. That's all he's getting.

"Do you think he's going to be a problem?" Wade asks.

I contain the snort that threatening to bubble out of me. Yes, I do think he will be a problem, but I think it will mostly be my problem. I hesitate. Because I don't actually know.

"I don't think so," I say finally, giving a small shrug. "He's forward, but harmless." The word feels uncertain even as I say it. There's a beat, before Wade shifts the conversation.

"How'd you get into studying remote tribes?" Relief settles in my chest, quiet but immediate. Something easier. A safer topic of conversation.

"The Yanomami" I begin, my voice steadier now. "They're very reclusive. They don't seek out contact with outsiders, and they're cautious about who they let into their community." I pause, choosing my words more carefully. "But once you're accepted it's different." I glance at him briefly before continuing. "They take hospitality seriously. Guests are treated with respect, protected, even. It's part of their culture. They're good people."

My fingers trace the edge of my phone absently. "They have their own language, but a few speak broken Portuguese, so we manage. It's not perfect, but it works. They're friendly," I add. "But cautious." The word lingers.

"I actually met them when I was younger," I continue, a small smile forming before I can stop it. "There was a girl—Paya. About my age. We met on the beach during a family trip." I let out a soft breath. "We didn't speak the same language, but we still played together."

"And that's what started all this?" he asks.

I nod. "At first, I thought I'd go into cultural anthropology. But once I started school," I pause, searching for the right words. "I fell in love with the history side of it. Human origins. How we lived." I glance at him briefly. "So now it's both. Bridging the gap between cultural anthropology and archaeology."

"That actually sounds…" he pauses, considering. "Interesting." There's a small smile on his lips. He's not teasing me or being dismissive. And for some reason, that matters more than it should. Not everyone understands anthropology or calls it a waste of time to study.

"I get the basics," he adds. "Mostly from *Indiana Jones*."

I hesitate. Because that's not even close. A small breath leaves me as I nod anyway, biting back the instinct to correct him. It's not worth it. He doesn't actually want to hear about preservation methods or ethical excavation practices. No one ever does.

But Wade watches me. Really watches me. His head tilts slightly. Like he caught something. "That was a bad answer," he says.

I blink, caught off guard. "What?"

"I can do better than that." He leans back slightly, arm resting along the seat behind me, relaxed but deliberate. "Try again."

I frown, confused. "Try… what again?"

"That look you just gave me," he says, the corner of his mouth lifting. "The one where you were about to tell me I'm completely wrong."

Heat rushes to my face. "I didn't—"

"You did," he says quietly, amused. "And then you decided not to."

I glance away, embarrassed. Okay. Maybe I did. "Well…" I mumble, "it's just—not really accurate."

"Good," he says.

I look back at him. "Good?"

"Yeah," he says, his tone shifting just enough to make me pause. "I'd rather hear the real version."

There's something in the way he says it. Like a gentle command. He wants to know about my life. "Tell me what I should actually know," he adds, his voice lower now. My fingers tighten slightly around my phone. I hesitate before I give in. Just a little.

"Archaeology isn't about taking things," I say slowly. "It's about understanding them. Preserving them." My voice steadies as I go on. "It's context. Culture. Why something exists, not just what it is."

He doesn't interrupt. Doesn't look away. And that's new, most people feign interest but don't actually care.

"It's about people," I finish quietly.

"That's better," he says, softer now. "You don't have to hide anything from me, I want to hear all your thoughts and concerns." My stomach flips. And I hate that I like hearing that.

As the bus rumbles to a stop, I press my forehead lightly against the window. The rainforest stretches endlessly beyond the glass, a sea of green so dense, so alive, it almost doesn't feel real.

Layers of canopy rise and fall like waves, sunlight slipping through in scattered gold, catching on leaves slick with humidity. The air—even from inside the bus—feels thick. Heavy. Like it's waiting for the rain that hangs low in the clouds above us.

For a moment, I forget everything else. Just… take it in. Then my thoughts drift back to him. A small smile pulls at my lips before I can stop it. Wade. The way he'd listened. The way he'd looked at me, like what I was saying actually mattered. Like I mattered. I tuck a strand of hair behind my ear, trying to hide the smile, even though no one's really paying attention.

Why me? The question comes just as quickly as the warmth. He's confident. Experienced. The kind of man who looks like he belongs anywhere he stands. And me? I'm just…me.

The bus doors creak open, letting in a wave of heat and damp air that clings instantly to my skin. Reality settles back in. One by one, everyone starts filing off. We're the last again. I glance over at him as he stands. He shifts his weight, and I catch the slight hitch in his movement. The way his hand brushes his thigh, just for a second too long. It's subtle. But it's there.

"How's your leg?" I ask quietly. He looks down at me, offering that easy smile.

"It's fine," he says. "Just stiff from the ride." But there's a tightness in his eyes that doesn't match the words. "Walking'll fix it," he adds. "Don't worry about me, Mouse." That nickname again. My heart does a strange little flip, before butterflies take off in my stomach. We step off the bus together, the ground uneven beneath my boots.

The heat wraps around me instantly, thick and damp, carrying the scent of earth, greenery, and something faintly sweet I can't quite place. Our bags are already being pulled together in a pile nearby. I reach down to adjust my backpack, still trying to ground myself, in the moment. In the research. In anything other than the way my thoughts keep circling back to him.

Wade steps closer, guiding me toward the group. His hand settles lightly at my lower back. It's a small touch. Barely there. But I feel it everywhere. Warmth spreads through me, quick and unexpected, and I have to focus on putting one foot in front of the other so I don't trip and fall. I glance up at him. His expression is calm. Controlled. Almost unreadable. Nothing like the man who was leaning in close on the bus, voice low, eyes focused only on me. And I can't help but wonder, if that version of him was just for me.

To my right, near the narrow path that leads deeper into the village, I spot them. Dori stands slightly ahead, exactly where I would expect him to be. Waiting. Watching. His presence is steady, grounded, like the forest itself bends around him. The woven textile at his waist is simple, practical, and the black feathered armbands rest high on his arms, unmoving. A single white tooth hangs from a cord at his neck, catching the light as he shifts just slightly. His gaze is fixed on us. He's assessing all of us and even from this distance, I can feel the weight of it.

Beside him stands Paya. Her long skirt, woven from bright natural fibers, moves softly with the breeze, colors shifting in the filtered sunlight—reds, golds, deep blues. Layers of handcrafted necklaces rest along her collarbone, beads catching the light with every small movement, while bracelets line her wrists and forearms, each piece intricate, intentional.

She looks the same and completely different. Stronger. More sure of herself. Her dark eyes are sharp, observant, until they land on me. Both of them stand still, their expressions serious, almost intimidating to anyone who doesn't know them. But I do.

A laugh bubbles up before I can stop it, bright and uncontrollable and I break into a run toward her.

"Paya—!" The moment I reach her, she's already smiling. A wide and radiant smile and then we're wrapping our arms around each other, holding tight.

"I missed you!" she says in Portuguese, her voice warm, breathless with excitement.

"I missed you too," I laugh, pulling back just enough to see her face again. It feels like no time has passed. We fall into slow Portuguese, both of us careful, deliberate, searching for the right words as we go. Neither of us fluent. But understanding enough.

"It's been so long," she says, her hands still lightly on my arms, like she's making sure I'm really here.

I nod, smiling. "Too long. How are you?"

I glance briefly toward Dori, still standing nearby. There's something grounding about his presence—even now.

"I've been good. Things around here are the same. How about you?" Paya asks, her smile easy and familiar.

"Good. Busy with school but it'll be worth it when it's over," I say.

A soft throat clears beside us. I look up to find Dori watching us, a faint smile pulling at his mouth. Without thinking, I step forward and wrap my arms around him. He returns it, firm but brief, and we pat each other's backs before pulling away. A proper greeting. When I first met them, it was handshakes. It was distant but respectful. This means something more.

Dori stands before me, steady and composed, his presence as grounded as the earth beneath our feet. He doesn't need to raise his voice to command attention. It's simply there. He is more than an elder. He is a mediator, a keeper of balance, someone who carries the weight of his people's traditions in everything he does.

"How are you?" he asks, his voice deep, rough with age and authority. His gaze shifts past me, scanning the group behind us. "You have brought many people." There's no accusation in his tone. But there is concern.

"I'm doing well," I say, lowering my voice slightly. "I'm glad to be back." A small pause, trying to find the right words. "We were assigned security. Because of what's happening near the border... and after last time."

Understanding shifts in his expression. He remembers. Of course he does. "Yes," he says quietly. "I understand." His eyes linger on me for a moment longer before moving back to the group. "Do they have a leader?" he asks. "I would speak with him."

I nod, offering a small smile. Then I turn. Wade is already watching. Focused on me. I feel it the moment our eyes meet, that same warmth, steady and unsettling all at once. I lift my hand, motioning him forward. He approaches at an unhurried pace, controlled, measured. When he reaches my side, he pauses just long enough that I'm aware of him—of his presence—before his hand briefly brushes the small of my back. I feel the zing of his touch shoot through my spine and yet it grounds me. His hand is gone just as quickly. The contact is fleeting. But the zing lingers, little tingles like every nerve is firing.

He steps into place beside me, his posture relaxed but alert, feet planted, attention shifting seamlessly from me to Dori. He's protective and not completely taking over this situation. Letting me lead. I can feel the difference.

Dori notices too. His gaze sharpens slightly, something thoughtful passing behind his eyes. Assessment again, he misses nothing. Heat rises to my cheeks before I can stop it. I clear my throat, forcing myself to focus.

"Dori, this is Wade," I begin, steadying my voice. "He's leading the security team assigned to us."

"How long have you known this man?" Dori asks. His tone is calm, but there's weight behind it, quiet authority. His steady gaze shifts to Wade, not unkind, but not unguarded either.

I hesitate. "Since this morning," I say softly. Heat creeps up my neck.

Under Dori's watchful eyes, every small movement suddenly feels magnified, like he's reading more into it than there actually is. Or maybe exactly what I'm trying not to show. Instinctively, I shift a half step to the side, putting just a little space between Wade and me.

When I glance at him, there's a slight frown pulling at his brow. Not annoyed, just trying to understand.

"What's going on?" he asks quietly, his voice low enough that it stays between us.

"Nothing," I say quickly, a little too quickly. "He was just asking how I've been. It's been a while." Even as the words leave my mouth, I know he doesn't buy it. He studies me for a second.

Then, softer he says, "That didn't look like nothing."

I exhale, tension tightening in my chest. This is a lot. Too many people. Too many eyes.

"He asked how long I've known you," I admit under my breath. "And I just... I don't want anyone getting the wrong idea." I glance around briefly, lowering my voice even more.

"There's a lot of people watching. And you—" I hesitate, then force the words out. "You being close, it just makes me nervous."

There that was honest. Enough. Understanding shifts in his expression. "Alright," Wade says quietly. "I didn't realize. I'll give you space." Some of the tension in my shoulders eases before I can stop it. Even if part of me feels bad.

"Thank you," I murmur. I take a breath, grounding myself and turn back to Dori.

"This is Wade," Switching back to Portuguese and gesturing between them. "He's leading the security team assigned to us." I add more gently, "He's here to help keep everyone safe." Dori studies Wade for a long moment.

Then nods once. "Tell him we understand there are concerns, we understand all to well what people do in the jungle" he says. "But weapons will make my people uneasy." His gaze sharpens slightly. "I do not want my people to be afraid."

I relay Dori's concerns to Wade as best as I can. The translation isn't perfect, but he seems to understand the weight behind it.

"We'll be discreet with our weapons," Wade says, his tone steady. "Unless there's a threat, they stay out of sight. We're not here to interfere, just to keep everyone safe."

I translate for Dori. He listens without interrupting, then gives a single nod. Satisfied.

"He seems close to you," Dori says quietly. Heat floods my face.

"He's just doing his job," I mumble, my gaze drifting toward the trees, anywhere but them.

Dori studies me for a moment, then gestures subtly toward Wade. "Tell him I will be watching him," he says. There's no hostility in it. Just certainty. And I feel the heat crawling all over me.

I hesitate. This is awkward. Still, I turn back to Wade and translate,

"He just said... it's a long walk," I tell him, keeping my voice even. "He hopes we can keep up."

His mouth twitches slightly, like he's holding back a reaction. He knows I'm lying but he doesn't call me out on it. Behind me, there's a quiet bark of laughter, one of his men but I don't dare turn to look. I don't want to know who heard that.

I move on quickly, making the rest of the introductions. Dr. Willis and Benjamin are already known to them, though I don't miss the brief, unreadable look Dori gives Benjamin. It's subtle, but it lingers longer than it should. Then, with Wade stepping in to help, I introduce the rest of his team. I use their given names. Trying to translate their call signs or titles would be impossible and meaningless here anyway.

As I speak, I catch one of them with bright green eyes, watching me. He looks irritated. I don't dwell on it.

"Shall we get going?" I ask Dori. He nods once and turns without another word, already leading the way down the narrow path.

The group shifts into motion, people adjusting packs, gathering gear. The jungle waits just beyond the tree line. Wade steps closer again but not as close as before. Not touching, he's respecting my wish to keep some distance.

"What did he say?" he asks quietly. "The part that had you blushing."

I hesitate. "I already told you." I say quietly looking away just as Dr. Willis, Benjamin, and Jenna move ahead, falling in behind Dori. Benjamin glances back once, his expression tight, something sour flickering across his face before he turns away.

Wade's team begins hauling their gear with ease, lifting heavy cases like they weigh nothing. I shift my own bag on my shoulder. Already feeling the heaviness that's going to weigh me down. This is going to be a long walk.

All that's left behind are Wade, two of his men and me.

"Magellan," Wade calls, shifting his pack higher on his shoulder. "You catch what he said?"

Magellan is a tall, broad-shouldered man, with dark hair and an easy, almost lazy confidence. He glances back at us, a grin already forming like he's been waiting for this.

"Oh, I caught it," he says, clearly entertained. "Something along the lines of... he'll be watching you."

Wade pauses. "Me?"

Magellan's grin widens. "Yeah. You." A beat. "Probably didn't help how close you were standing."

Wade huffs quietly, more amused than bothered. "Hmm." That's all he says before his gaze drops to me, that small, knowing smile tugging at his mouth again.

"Alright," he says. "Let's go." He reaches for one of my bags before I can stop him.

"You really don't have to do that," I protest, tightening my grip on the strap. "I can carry my own stuff. You've got enough."

"I want to help," he says simply, already lifting it. "I'll just take one." A slight tilt of his head. "Besides... I'm trying to earn points."

I glance ahead. Dori is watching, everyone else has already past him and of course, he's smiling. Heat rushes to my face, so I quickly look away.

"Fine," I mutter. "You've got the tent anyway, and I hate carrying that thing." I glance at his leg, just briefly. "Just don't push it."

A quiet laugh slips from him as we start walking. Ahead of us, his team adjusts their pace, a few of them glancing back with amused, knowing looks. I ignore it. Mostly. I already feel like I'm under a microscope. Translator. Outsider. Now, whatever this is.

We walk in silence for a few minutes, the jungle beginning to close in around us, thick and alive.

"So," Wade says, stepping just a little closer, not touching, just there. "Think we should take advantage of the local customs while we're here?"

I glance at him, confused. "What? Marry me off to the tribe?" I ask sarcastically rolling my eyes.

His grin deepens. "Something like that."

My steps falter. Oh my god, I was only kidding. "Wade—"

"I'm kidding," he says, holding up a hand, still smiling. "Mostly." A beat. "We'll save that for when we get back."

He winks and I choke on my water. Behind us, laughter breaks out, louder this time. Magellan and another one of his crew pass us easily, their strides effortless despite the weight they're carrying.

"Sarge," Magellan calls over his shoulder, "you're bringing up the rear. Try not to flirt the whole way."

"Yeah," the other one adds, smirking. "Some of us are trying to survive this hike."

My cheeks burn. Wade flips them off without missing a step.

"Don't listen to them," he says, his voice lower again as he looks back at me. "They just like giving me a hard time."

I nod, keeping my eyes forward. Watching the path. The backs of the men ahead of us. Dark shirts, damp with sweat, sleeves rolled, muscles shifting beneath the fabric as they move through the jungle like they belong here. Anything but him. Because I don't know what this is and I don't know if I should trust it.

Chapter Five

Sarah

The trek through the jungle was both grueling and awe-inspiring. Thick vines draped from towering trees, their broad leaves weaving together into a dense canopy overhead. Sunlight filtered through in scattered beams, turning the air gold in places, shadowed and heavy in others. The humidity pressed in from all sides, thick and suffocating, every breath carrying the scent of damp earth, decaying leaves, and something faintly sweet beneath it all.

Three kilometers shouldn't have felt this long. But the terrain was uneven, the ground soft in places, tangled with roots in others and with the weight of our packs, we had to stop more than once. Well, we as in the four researchers did. Dori, Paya, and the soldiers moved like it was nothing. They were completely steady and unaffected, barely out of breath. I focused on putting one foot in front of the other.

On the ground. On the path. On anything but the man walking just behind me. Eventually, the trees began to thin. The dense wall of green opened into a wide clearing, sunlight spilling fully across the space for the first time since we'd entered the jungle. Just beyond a sparse line of trees is the village. Relief loosened something tight in my chest, the walk is awful. It's going to be even worse after 6 weeks of little sleep.

We had stayed here before. It was familiar. The clearing stretched wide, packed earth beneath our feet, with signs of use, paths worn into the ground, fire pits, scattered tools. This was where smaller gatherings happened. Ceremonies sometimes, but not the main ones. Those were held in the shabono, their large, circular structure set slightly deeper within the village. Some of the tribe lived there, sharing the structure. The rest of the village spread outward in smaller, rectangular homes made of wood and straw, simple but purposeful. Family spaces. Private, in their own way. Further out, smaller structures stood apart from the others. For newlyweds. Or meetings. Or things not meant for everyone.

The group began to separate naturally as we reached the edge of the clearing. Like last time, Dr. Willis and Benjamin headed toward the tree line, already picking out spots for their tents near the path leading deeper into the village. Close to the shabono. Jenna followed them, adjusting her pack as she went. Benjamin said something to her, offering to have her set up nearby and I rolled my eyes before I could stop myself. Of course he did.

To the left, Wade's team moved together, choosing ground further from the rest of us. Their movements were efficient, practiced as they started dropping packs. At the same time they are scanning the area, already settling into position. Close enough to respond. Far enough to stay separate.

Wade and I brought up the rear. He still carried one of my bags. Even after I told him not to. My pace had slowed without me realizing it. The jungle had gone quieter around us now. Or maybe I was just too tired to notice anything else. No one talked much during the last stretch. Just the sound of footsteps. Heavy breathing and the weight of everything waiting ahead.

My steps slow. Then stop. Of course it's still here. The same tree. The same place. It's just me that's changed. My chest tightens before I can stop it. This is where we stayed. Where *she* stayed. The massive kapok tree rises into view, it towers above everything else, its thick trunk pale against the darker greens, its roots sprawling outward like something alive. The twisting roots, rising and weaving across the forest floor. A sentinel. Unmoving. Unchanged.

The air feels heavier here, thicker, like it's pressing the memory into me whether I want it to or not. I stare at the roots, at the space between them where our tent once sat.

And suddenly, I'm not here anymore. I'm back. To five years ago.

Carly's laughter cuts through the humid air, bright and unrestrained.

She's sprawled across her sleeping bag, hair sticking to her face from the heat, grinning like none of this, none of it, could ever touch her.

"This is insane," she says, pushing herself up onto her elbows. "We're actually here."

I laugh, shaking my head. "You've said that like ten times already."

"Yeah and I'm going to say it ten more," she shoots back, nudging me with her foot. "Because it is. This is what we worked for, Sarah." Her eyes are alive. Excited. Certain.

"Just wait," she adds, her voice softer now. "This is only the beginning."

The memory flickers and shatters. My throat tightens. Because it wasn't the beginning. It was the end. If I had known that, I would have grabbed her hand and drug her right back home. I blink hard, dragging myself back to the present. Back to the tree. Back to the space where she should be standing beside me. But she's not anymore. The roots stretch outward, just like before, leaving pockets of space between them. Enough for a tent. Enough for shade. Enough for, everything we had.

My vision blurs. I swallow hard, but it doesn't help. The lump in my throat only grows heavier. I knew this would be difficult. I told myself I was ready. I wasn't. Not for this. Not for how real it still feels. Like it happened only yesterday. The urge to start screaming her name is right there, ready to flow out of me. I force myself to move, my feet carrying me toward the tree without fully deciding to go.

Toward the place that still feels like it belongs to us. Carly and I. The rest of the group fades behind me. Not far. But far enough. I just need a minute, before everything breaks open. I start toward the tree, forcing one foot in front of the other.

I can feel it before I see it, someone watching me. I glance to my side and see Benjamin. His eyes on me. Of course. I just look away and continue forward. Behind me, I hear Wade's footsteps, still steady and unhurried. Like the extra weight doesn't bother him. He hasn't said anything yet. He's waiting.

"Where are you going?" he asks.

"Just… over there," I say, lifting a hand slightly toward the trees. "I don't really want to be around everyone right now." My voice is quieter than I intend. Tighter. "You can leave the tent here," I add quickly. "I'll get it set up." I keep my gaze forward. Not looking at him. Not risking it. Because I know if I do, he'll see it. The tears pressing behind my eyes. The way my throat won't quite cooperate. I just need a minute.

"I'll be near my guys," he says after a beat. "But I'm not letting you wander too far. Not here." There's an edge to it. I glance at him then. His eyes soften.

"I'll be fine," I say, trying to steady my voice. "You don't need to stay close to me. I know you've got a job to do." I shift my bag higher on my shoulder. "I won't be in my tent much anyway. I'll be working in the village most of the day. Translating. Observing. By the time everyone settles in, I'll probably just crash."

He studies me for a moment. "I'd still feel better if you were close," he says. "I'll set up on the other side of you. Closer to my team." A small pause. "Is there a reason you don't want to be near the rest of your group?"

I swallow, forcing the tightness in my throat down. "No," I say, a little too quickly. Then softer, "Not really." I glance toward the clearing. "It's just by the end of the day, I'm talking constantly. Translating, explaining, answering questions. Sometimes I just want a little space where I don't have to do that."

It's not a lie. Just not the whole truth. His gaze lingers on me. And even though I am trying to hide it, I know he sees it anyway. The shine in my eyes. The way I'm holding myself a little too tightly together. For a second, I think he might say something. Call me out. Push. He doesn't, instead, there's the faintest hint of a smile as he nods once.

"Alright," he says quietly. Just like that, he lets it go. "I get that," Wade says. "After a long day, sometimes I don't want to sit around with my guys either."

We continue toward the spot I chose, the roots of the kapok tree stretching wide enough to give me space without feeling exposed. I drop my bag and start clearing the ground with my foot, brushing away small rocks and sticks before kneeling down to unpack. The tent is near the bottom. I pull it out carefully, smoothing my hand over the worn fabric.

It's old. Faded from years of sun. But it's familiar. My sister and I used to share this one on family camping trips, crammed side by side, and whispering long after we were supposed to be asleep.

I brought it here last time, too. The same one Carly and I shared. Somehow, it felt right to bring it again. Even if it's seen better days.

The seams at the top are starting to wear, threads pulling just enough to make me notice. I pause, running my thumb along one of them. It'll hold. It has to, I hope.

"I want you to stay close to us," Wade says, his voice quieter now, but firm. I glance up. His posture has shifted completely. No teasing. No ease. Just focus. His gaze moves across the tree line, scanning, alert in a way that makes something tighten in my chest. It's not just for show. He means it, this is his military experience speaking. My eyes scan the trees, too but I don't see anything. I look back down, pushing the thought aside as I start setting up the poles.

Wade lets out a low breath behind me. "This your tent?" he asks. There's something in his tone that makes me pause.

I glance over my shoulder. "Yeah," I say, a small smile tugging at my lips. "Isn't it cute?" I shrug lightly. "My sister and I always shared it growing up. My parents got a new one, so they let me take this."

His expression doesn't change. In fact, he looks more concerned.

"Sarah…" he says slowly, crouching slightly to get a better look at it. "This thing's worn."

I straighten a little, defensive without meaning to be. "It's fine," I say. "I've used it for years. I had it here last time."

He runs a hand along one of the seams, his jaw tightening just a fraction. "It's a rainforest," he says. "We're going to get hit with rain, probably storms. You trust this to hold up?"

I hesitate. Just for a second. Then I nod. "I staked it properly," I say. "It'll be fine." Even if I'm not entirely sure. He studies me for a moment longer. Like he knows that. Then he exhales, shaking his head slightly.

"Alright," he says. "Then I guess it's a good thing I'll be close."

My head snaps up. "Close?" I repeat.

He nods toward the space just beyond my tent. "I'll set up there. That way if anything *does* happen, I'm right here."

I blink. I hadn't realized he meant *that* close. Of course he is. By the time I get my tent halfway up, Wade's already finished his. It unfolds in seconds, one of those compact, pop-up tents that snaps into place like it's been trained to do it. Camouflage fabric blends into the greens and browns of the jungle, sleek and efficient. I glance around. His entire team has the same setup.

Tents already up. Gear organized. A couple of them working together to secure a larger canopy nearby, movements quick and practiced. It's impressive. Wade crouches at the entrance of his tent, unzipping his pack and pulling out supplies like he's done this a hundred times before. His tent is longer than mine, low to the ground, narrow and a dark olive canvas stretched tight over a compact frame. More like a sleeping compartment than anything meant to sit in.

I stare a second too long. "Trying to figure out how you'd fit in there with me?"

My head snaps up, my eyes meeting his again. Heat rushes to my face instantly. "I—what? No!" I stammer, turning away too fast. "I've just never seen a tent like that before." Smooth, Sarah.

"Relax," he says, clearly amused. "It's not as cramped as it looks." Then, just a hint of that teasing edge, "But you'd probably make it feel cozy." I freeze for half a second. Then immediately focus on my tent again, fumbling with a pole I've suddenly forgotten how to assemble.

"Not happening," I mutter under my breath.

His quiet chuckle follows me, low and satisfied. "Sarah!" I turn at the sound of my name, only pronounced differently. They say both the A's like ah. Paya and Dori are approaching. Right. Dinner, back to work, I go. I straighten quickly, brushing my hands off on my pants, already preparing myself to switch gears. Translate. Observe. Focus.

Dori's gaze shifts past me, toward my tent. And something in his expression tightens. He says something to Paya in their language, gesturing toward it. My stomach drops. Did I set up somewhere I shouldn't have? Paya looks back at me, a little hesitant, like she's weighing the words in her head.

"He wants to know if that is your tent," she says gently. "It doesn't look... very strong." I blink.

Then exhale sharply. Seriously? "Yes," I say, a little more firmly than I mean to. "It is." I gesture toward it, frustration creeping into my voice. "It's stable. No holes. It's staked down properly." I cross my arms slightly, trying to rein myself back in. "I've used it before. It's fine."

Even if now—with *both* of them questioning it—I'm starting to second guess that. A chuckle sounds behind me. I turn and glare at Wade. Which only makes him laugh harder.

"He doesn't think your tent's going to hold up, does he?" Wade says, amusement clear in his voice.

I groan, dragging a hand over my face before turning back to Paya and Dori. Of course this is happening in front of everyone. Out of the corner of my eye, I see his entire team watching now. Great.

"What is he saying?" Paya asks, curiosity lighting her expression.

"He already made a comment about the tent earlier," I reply in Portuguese. "So, he thinks this is funny." Paya grins. Even Dori's expression softens just slightly. Of course.

"Do you need to stay with us?" Dori asks.

I shake my head quickly. "No. I'll be fine." Hopefully. Dori's gaze shifts upward, scanning the sky. The clouds are darker now. Heavier. When he looks back at me, there's hesitation there.

"The clouds carry a warning," he says quietly. "This storm will test you." A chill runs down my spine despite the heat.

"I'll be fine," I insist, forcing a small smile. "If something happens, I'll come find you." Please let that be enough. Paya nods, stepping back.

"Dinner will be ready soon. If you can gather your group, we will begin introductions." I nod, grateful for the shift in topic. They turn and disappear down the path. The moment they're gone, I exhale. That was embarrassing. I glance up at the sky again. The clouds are thickening, their edges dark and heavy, pressing low over the canopy. Storms here aren't just rain. They're something else entirely.

"What did they say?" Wade's voice pulls me back.

I look over at him, his expression more serious now, the earlier amusement gone. "They said the clouds are a warning," I answer quietly. "And dinner's ready. I need to gather everyone so we can start introductions."

He studies me for a second. Then nods. "Alright." Simple. Steady. Something about that settles me more than it should. I turn back to my tent, reaching inside for my camera. If I'm here, I'm working. I sling the strap around my neck, the familiar weight grounding me as it settles against my chest.

Document everything. That's the job. I straighten, taking a steadying breath before looking back up at Wade.

"Hey, Sarah!" My head snaps toward the voice. Magellan is leaning against one of the packs, that same easy grin already in place. "I hear you might need a new tent," he says. "Plenty of room in mine."

Heat explodes across my face.

"Magellan," Wade growls.

Magellan just lifts his hands in mock surrender, completely unbothered. I turn away quickly, wishing I could disappear into the ground.

"I'm going to go find Dr. Willis, Jenna, and Benjamin," I say, backing up a step. "Let them know it's time." I gesture toward the path. "You can gather your guys. Just follow that, it'll lead you to the shabono. There are benches set up."

I don't wait for a response. I just go. Because if I stay any longer, I might actually combust. I quickly tell Willis, then continue on towards the shabono. The path is narrower than I remember. More overgrown. Branches brushing against my arms as I push through, the jungle already reclaiming the space. I can hear footsteps behind me. Most of them must have followed.

When the trees begin to thin, the shabono comes into view. It looks refreshed. Fresh palm leaves layered across the roof, the structure fuller, stronger than the last time I saw it. Alive.

I step off to the side, lifting my camera.

Work.

Focus.

The lens frames the structure first, the curve of the roof, the open center, the filtered light spilling inside. Then the surrounding greenery. The path. I take a few more shots as Dr. Willis and Jenna walk into frame.

Click.

Just as I adjust for another, Benjamin turns. His gaze locks onto mine instantly. Too direct. Too intentional. Not an accident. My stomach tightens at his expression. I lower the camera slightly, angling away like I hadn't been looking at him at all. But the feeling lingers. Like he meant something by it.

I force myself to keep moving, snapping a few more pictures to shake it off. Then Wade passes through my frame. His broad shoulders and controlled movement. Solid and steady against the shifting chaos of everything else. My finger presses the shutter without thinking.

Click.

He turns at the sound. That smirk. It barely shows on his face, but his eyes brighten. Like he *knows*. I take another picture anyway. And this one, I already know, I'm not sharing.

Chapter Six

Sarah

The villagers begin to emerge from the shadows of the shabono, one by one. At first, it's just movement. Shapes shifting in the dim interior. Then faces start to appear. Dark eyes, sharp and observant, sweeping over our group with quiet intensity.

They don't rush. They don't speak. They simply watch. There's a stillness to them, that's measured. Their movements are fluid, deliberate—each step placed with a kind of natural precision that feels instinctive, practiced over a lifetime.

Some wear painted markings across their faces and bodies, deep reds and blacks, patterns that feel intentional, meaningful, though not immediately understood. A young girl catches my eye. Her face is painted in soft, uneven strokes, her dark hair falling around her shoulders. She studies me for a moment, then give me a quick smile. Like a secret shared just between us. And just as quickly, it's gone.

God, I missed this.

The shabono itself stretches wide behind them, its circular structure towering above us. Thick wooden supports hold up a roof woven from palm and thatch, layered densely enough to shield against rain while still allowing light to filter through in scattered beams.

The center remains open to the sky. This is their communal space. A place for gathering, for ceremony, for life to unfold in full view of the community. Around the perimeter, individual family spaces form a continuous ring, hammocks, small fires, tools and personal belongings all arranged in a way that feels both shared and distinctly individual.

Nothing here is accidental. Everything has purpose. This is how they've lived continuously for generations. I recognize a few familiar faces. And others I don't. There are new families and new children. Life continued to move forward, even when I wasn't here to see it.

My gaze finds Paya. She stands near the edge of the group, her posture relaxed but aware. Beside her is a man I don't recognize. He's very tall, quiet, his eyes are watching, assessing our group. He's not hovering over her but he does stay close. His hand brushes lightly against her back as people move around them. Paya glances up at him, something soft flickering across her expression.

A familiar, comfortable smile. This is all new to them, still growing. However, until I ask her question I won't assume. I've learned not to. But I do recognize what it might mean. In their culture, relationships aren't always built the way we expect them to be. Connection comes differently here. And sometimes, it comes later.

Her eyes find mine and she smiles. Unlike, some of the other villagers hers lingers. Some of them recognize me, but they are still apprehensive of outsiders. I smile back.

"Hey, Sarah" Jenna's voice pulls me back. "This is all so strange and exciting," she whispers, eyes wide as she takes everything in.

I huff a quiet laugh. "I know," I say. "My first time felt exactly like this." I glance around the shabono again, letting it settle over me. "You get used to it. The rhythm. The food. The way everything feels different at first."

"I just wish I could understand what they're saying," she adds.

"Yeah," I nod. "It's hard. Even when they speak Portuguese, it's different. Their dialect isn't the same as what you'd hear in São Paulo." I shrug slightly. "I can get by, but it's not perfect. You'd have to live here for a while to really understand it."

Jenna nods slowly. "I guess that makes sense. Even back home, people talk differently depending on where you are."

"Exactly."

Before I can say anything else, Benjamin drops onto the bench between us. Intentionally too close, I start leaning away, working on getting just a little distance. He turns toward me, smiling. But it doesn't reach his eyes. The warmth of the village feels just a little less steady, now.

"So," Benjamin says, glancing at me as he takes a bite of his food. "How'd setting up your tent go? You looked pretty worked up."

I glance at him briefly, then back to my food. "They just don't think it's safe," I say. "But it's fine."

He makes a face, chewing slowly like he's not entirely sold on whatever he's eating or what I just said. "Well," he adds, leaning back slightly, "I've got plenty of space in mine if you need it." He winks.

My stomach turns. I force a neutral expression, focusing on my plate. The food is growing cold now and I think I just lost my appetite. When Wade made the joke my stomach did a flip in anticipation. When Magellan made the joke, I was embarrassed but I knew it was harmless flirting. With Benjamin? I feel sick.

"Yeah," I say flatly. "If anything happens, I'll just stay with Dori and Paya." That shuts it down. At least, I hope it does. Movement catches my attention. Wade and his team are approaching, plates in hand. His expression is tight at first, something unreadable there, until his eyes land on me and it shifts ever so slightly to a softer look. Then he notices Benjamin and the tension snaps right back into place. I frown faintly, watching the change. What is that about?

Before I can think too much about it, everyone settles into place, and the quiet begins to shift. Dori steps forward. He speaks in Yanomami, his voice low and steady, carrying easily through the space. The entire village stills. Even the children. Paya moves to my side, translating softly into Portuguese as he speaks.

It's a welcome. A traditional prayer, acknowledging the land, the people, and the presence of outsiders. His prayer is full of respect and balance. I wait until he finishes before speaking quietly to our group.

"He's welcoming us," I explain. "To the village and to the land." The weight of it settles over us. Then Dori continues. He speaks of our group, why we're here, what we're doing. And then Wade's team. There's a shift in tone when he mentions them. It's ver subtle, I don't know if anyone on my team would even detect it.

Paya translates, her voice careful as she explains. "They know about the tensions to the north," I add quietly for the others. "That's why they're allowing security."

Not everyone looks reassured. When Dori finishes, all eyes turn toward us.

Right. Introductions, my least favorite part. I take a breath. One by one, I begin. I start with the researchers, giving their names, their roles and their purpose of being here.

Then Wade and his team. I need his help when I stumble over something or need clarification. There are a lot of them. Too many names at once. I'm definitely not remembering all of these tonight. Paya translates everything back into Yanomami, her voice steady beside mine. We fall into a rhythm quickly. Back and forth. Language crossing language. Meaning carried between us. It's slow but its working for us.

The tension eases just slightly as the introductions continue. Some of the children edge closer, curiosity outweighing caution now. Their attention shifts toward the soldiers. I suppress a small smile, of course they are curious for the big men that seem to be prepared for anything and completely at ease.

I do my best to translate their questions, though military terminology doesn't always carry cleanly across languages. I simplify where I can. Gesture when I can't. And in between it all, I lift my camera.

Click.

Moments captured between words. Between worlds. By the time the conversations begin to slow, I realize I haven't eaten. Not even a bite. My stomach twists in protest, but there's still so much happening, so many voices, stories and pieces I don't want to miss.

Two marriages since I'd last been here. New families. New connections. Paya explains to me one of the new ones are pregnant they both look so proud. I'm listening closely as one of the elders describes the ceremonies, trying to keep up with the rhythm of his words, when that familiar warm and steady presence settles beside me.

I don't even need to look. Still, I do. Wade. He's holding a plate. "You need to eat, Little Mouse." It's not a question. I blink, like the thought hadn't fully formed until he said it.

"I was going to," I murmur. My stomach betrays me instantly. A low, very obvious growl.

His mouth tips at the corner. "Yeah," he says, unconvinced.

He places the plate in my hands. No hesitation. No asking. Just handled like it was no big deal. I glance down. It's exactly what I would have grabbed. Fruit. Cassava. Fish. I don't remember telling him that. I don't remember him asking and yet, somehow he knew. I take a bite, and the relief is immediate, bringing me back into the moment. Wade lowers himself beside me, close enough that his knee brushes mine.

"Keep talking," he says, nodding toward the elder. "I like hearing you." Simple. He knows how to say the right things to get me to relax. I nod, swallowing before picking the conversation back up, translating between bites. The words come easier now. Steadier. I'm not as nervous now. And all the while, he stays.

I can feel it in the background of everything. The way his attention never fully leaves me. The way his gaze keeps shifting between the village, people, shadows and then back to me. It should feel overwhelming. But it doesn't, it feels safe. Not in a way I'm used to. Like even if I forget something, miss something or push myself too far, I know he won't. That makes it easier to breathe. I've never felt like I needed protection, never scared of something happening, just cautious. Until Carly disappeared. Being back here has made me more aware of how things could go wrong in an instant.

Paya guides me toward the man standing beside her. "Sarah," she says softly, "this is Kaori."

He inclines his head slightly. Up close, he's even more imposing, quiet, controlled and the kind of presence that doesn't need to prove itself.

"A warrior," Paya adds. "From a neighboring village to the northeast." I nod in greeting, offering a small smile.

There's something measured in the way he looks at me and then I realize, he's not looking at me. He's looking past me. I turn to find Wade standing directly behind me. He isn't touching me this time. But he's there. Close enough. His posture is relaxed but his attention isn't.

I glance back at Paya. "Is he concerned?" I ask quietly. She turns, speaking to Kaori. He answers without hesitation, his gaze shifting between me and Wade again.

Paya looks back to me. "He thinks the danger may be closer than you've been told."

My stomach tightens. It makes sense that they might know more than we do. The Yanomami and nearby tribes—have dealt with outsiders, violence, and territorial threats for generations. They don't ignore warning signs. I hadn't been letting myself think about it. But clearly they are. I turn toward Wade.

He's already watching me. The second our eyes meet, his expression shifts. Softens again, I wonder if he's only ever like this with me.

"What's wrong?" he asks, stepping closer, closing what little bit of distance there was.

"Kaori's been watching you," I say. "He thinks the threat from the north might be worse than we realize."

Wade's jaw tightens slightly. He doesn't look surprised in the least. Just confirming something he already suspected. He steps in closer, this time his arm settling lightly around my back. Protective. Like he's making a point but not saying it out loud. Sometimes gestures can speak louder than words. My breath catches. Clearly, he gave up on not trying to hide it. I don't know if that's good or bad. I really want to like it. I do like it. I just don't want to be deemed unprofessional.

"I won't lie to you," he says, voice low. "We don't know their intentions. We don't know if it's guns or drugs or if they making a play for territory. We're here as a precaution. To keep you scientists safe." His eyes stay on mine. "And you're part of that."

My chest tightens slightly at that. It doesn't feel like he's claiming me, just including me in their job. Which makes me more confused.

"It's serious enough that both governments wanted coverage in the field," he adds. I knew there were dangers, I just also thought it was far enough way it wouldn't matter. I mean they would have to cross thousands of miles of rough terrain to even get to this point.

I turn back to Paya, translating the gist of it for her. She relays it to Kaori. He listens. Then gives a small nod. He's not reassured but he accepts what Wade is saying. One warrior to another. That's enough for now.

The night settles back into motion after that. I move through the group, translating where I can, slipping between conversations, bridging gaps. Paya and I fall into rhythm again. Back and forth. It feels easier with her beside me. But I start to notice something else. The adults. Some of them linger at the edges, watching Wade and his team. Wide-eyed. Both curious and cautious, a little afraid of these outsiders. Large, armed outsiders moving through their home, it's not something they're used to. Even if they've accepted us. Even if they understand why we're here.

I glance toward Wade. Toward he guns holstered at their sides. Toward the way his men move, efficient, controlled and unmistakably military. And a thought settles in. Maybe, we need to be careful how we show up here. I know we already talked about, reducing weapons if they can, or maybe staying out if this area so they don't scare the people.

By the time the gathering begins to wind down, the sky has shifted. The air feels heavier. Wind threads through the trees, low and restless, and thunder rolls faintly in the distance. The storm is right on top of us now. We say our goodnights, people breaking off in small groups as they start heading back toward the clearing.

Wade stays behind with his team, going over plans for the night. I don't wait, I can't. I am both physically and mentally exhausted from this very long day. I turn and head back toward my tent, letting the sounds of the jungle settle around me. The night is louder than before. Now, that I am away from the hum of the village, the jungle sounds more alive. Somewhere around me, I hear it, the call of a black-headed night monkey, sharp and unmistakable. I slow slightly, listening. Focusing. Wondering if I will see on them in the trees. Because of that, I don't hear him.

"So," Benjamin says from behind me, "you and *Wraith*, huh?" I flinch. Before I can react, his hand closes around my arm, turning me toward him. Too fast. The fear rolls through me instantly. I don't know his intention and we're alone out here.

"I don't know," I say, pulling my arm back just enough to create space. "We're just getting to know each other." I keep my tone even. Neutral.

He lets out a quiet, humorless laugh. "Looks like more than that," he mutters, stepping closer. "He can't keep his hands off you." His lip curls slightly. "*Mouse*?" he adds. "Already giving you pet names? That's not nothing." There's something off in his voice. He's unraveling but trying to keep it contained.

"I think he's just being nice," I say, even though the words don't feel entirely true.

Benjamin's expression hardens. "Nice?" he repeats. "He's a Green Beret, Sarah. They're not *nice*."

I cross my arms slightly, holding my ground. "Do you know a lot of Green Berets?" I ask. He ignores the question. Of course he does, because it's not fitting his narrative.

"That's not the point," he says, his voice tightening. "You're different with him." He takes another step closer, putting him far too close for my liking.

"You were never like that with me." There it is. I feel it settle in my chest, not surprise. Just confirmation. He thinks he has some sort of twisted claim to me.

"I was never interested in you," I say, my voice calm, steady. I'm not trying to be cruel, but I need to be clear. Need him to understand he means nothing to me.

"So you *are* interested in him?" His voice changes again, more intent. He's gearing up to make a point, like he was right all along. I don't answer right away. I don't like the way he's looking at me and I need to get away from him. His smile becomes sinister, something off behind it, like he's enjoying this more than he should.

"He can't offer you anything," Benjamin says quietly. "You know that, right? He's not looking for anything real. Just something easy. A quick fuck."

The words land harder than I want them to. He knew exactly what words to say to hurt. A part of me has already thought that and he knows it. I take a step back.

"I'm not having this conversation," I say, turning slightly.

His hand closes tightly around my arm. He pulls me back roughly toward him, I trip over a branch but catch myself before I collide with him, the camera around my neck swings up, hitting his arm. He looks down at it. Then slowly back at me. His eyes are colder now and my stomach drops. I feel a cold sweat break out over me, I don't know this version of him.

"Let me go," I say, sharper now. "I'm not interested in discussing my personal life, Benjamin."

His grip tightens. "Sarah," he says, low, like he's trying to sound calm. "I know you better than that."

I try to pull free, yanking my arm back. It doesn't work. My heart is pounding, how do I get out of this?

"You heard her." The voice cuts through everything. It's low, controlled. Final. Breaking through the tension and fear.

Benjamin freezes and for a brief second his grip loosens. It's enough for me to try to pull back immediately only again his hands lock on me in a vice. Sparta steps into view, his presence solid and immovable, placing himself just slightly between us. He doesn't look aggressive, but you could see it in his posture, he was dangerous.

His gaze locks on Benjamin. "Let go," he repeats, quieter this time. Benjamin lifts his hands slowly, backing off a step.

Sparta doesn't move. Doesn't blink. "Are you okay, Sarah?" he asks. But his eyes never leave Benjamin.

"I'm fine," I say quickly. "Benjamin was just leaving." Sparta glances at me briefly, just enough to register my expression and then looks back at him. A silent warning.

"She's fine. We were just talking," Benjamin mutters, forcing a smile. "We're friends. Right, Sarah?"

Something in me snaps. "No," I say flatly. "We're not."

I don't look at him again. I turn and start walking. Sparta falls into step beside me without a word. Close enough so I feel safe. Far enough not to crowd. We don't speak until we reach my tent. I drop my bag, unzipping it with hands that are steadier than I feel.

"Are you sure you're okay?" he asks again. I nod. This time, he looks closer at me, assessing me to see if I am telling the truth. I'm not.

"Yes. I'm okay." A small pause. "You're Shawn, right?"

He nods once. "Yeah. But everyone calls me Sparta."

I give a small, grateful smile. "Okay. Thank you… Sparta." And I mean it. I don't know how I feel using their call names like that. It feels weird, like that's just something they call each other and not for outsiders.

"Does he always act like that?"

I hesitate. "Umm… no," I say. "I think he's just used to getting his way. I'm sure he's harmless." The word feels different this time. Sparta's expression doesn't change.

"People like that usually aren't," he says simply. "But now we know." A faint smirk touches his mouth. "And Wraith knows now. He'll handle it."

My head snaps toward him. "Wait, how does Wade know?"

"Sarah?" Wade's voice cuts through the dark. "Are you okay?"

I close my eyes for a second. Of course. I just want to be alone. "Yes," I call back. "I'm fine. Like I told Sparta, he's harmless." Even if I don't fully believe that anymore.

Wade says something low to Sparta, too quiet for me to catch. I don't stay to listen. I just turn and head for my tent. I'm done. The second I'm inside, the exhaustion hits harder. I change quickly, crawling into my sleeping bag as the first low rumble of thunder rolls closer. The storm's almost here.

"Sarah?" His voice again, right outside my tent door. "Can I come in?"

I let out a slow breath. "Why?" I ask, sharper than I mean to.

"I want to know what happened." Of course he does.

I hesitate, then unzip the tent. "Fine."

I shift back to make room, even though there isn't much. He ducks inside, zipping it closed behind him. The space shrinks instantly, this tent was not designed with someone of his size in mind. He sits beside me. Too close to ignore. For a moment, neither of us speaks. The air feels heavier in here, now.

"What happened." he says the quiet demand, brooking no arguments.

"You're blowing this out of proportion," I say, quieter now, but not steady.

"I still want to know." There's no edge to it.

I exhale sharply. "Can we talk about this tomorrow?" I ask. "It's been a long day. You really take this safety stuff seriously?" I hear the attitude as soon as I say it. It may be unfair to him but I'm tired, exhausted really and now I'm a little shaken. I don't want to feel either of those things, I just want to go to sleep.

"I take *your* safety seriously." His voice drops slightly. There is truth that lands between us.

I go quiet, no more retorts coming to the surface. "…He was asking about you," I say finally. "About us." The words are a struggle to get out. This is embarrassing. "And then he said—" I hesitate. "That you're only interested in…" I trail off, heat creeping up my neck. "Something physical."

Silence. Outside, thunder cracks closer. Inside, everything feels like it's crackling with it.

"Okay," Wade says quietly. "We'll come back to that last part. Sparta told me he put his hands on you." His tone doesn't rise. But it sharpens.

"Yes," I say. "He did. But I don't want to make a big deal out of it."

Wade goes still beside me. "If it happens again," he says, each word measured, "you tell me." There's no room for argument in it.

I swallow. "Why do you care so much?" I ask, the question slipping out before I can stop it. Because I need to know. Because I *don't* know what this is. Lightning flashes outside, briefly illuminating his face. His eyes are already on me.

"I care," he says, quieter now, "because I want to get to know you. And I want to see where this goes." My heart squeezes in my chest, before going into overdrive.

"Sparta also told me what he said," Wade adds. "About me." His gaze doesn't waver. "Are you worried about that? That I'm just talking to you because it's easy? Convenient?"

I hesitate. "No," I admit. "I don't believe that, necessarily." I take a deep breath. "But I don't know what to believe either. We just met. I'm not thinking anything." Not true, I've definitely been overanalyzing. I'm just not admitting that.

He nods once. Accepts it. "What do you need from me? I want you to trust me." he asks.

The question catches me off guard. "Trust takes time," I say softly. "You can't expect me to just give it to you."

"I don't. I'll earn it." There's no hesitation in it. "And until then," he continues, "I'll keep an eye on you." A slight shift in his posture. "Not just you. The situation. My team knows to watch him."

That settles some of the lingering fear in me. Even if I don't want it to. I don't know what to expect from Benjamin anymore and he really did scare me.

"Are you okay?" he asks again. His tone is quieter. "When Sparta called it in, I came as fast as I could."

I blink. "You already knew something was wrong," I say. "Before you even got there."

"We're connected," he says. "Earpieces. Always listening. When I saw Benjamin leave right after you, I sent him to keep an eye on the situation." A faint pause. "You didn't answer me." He shifts slightly closer. He's not touching me but close enough that I feel the heat of him. The scent of him. That sun soaked wood, a little rough around the edges now from the day. My breath catches without meaning to. I should move away, especially after what just happened with Benjamin.

"Sarah." My name is quieter this time.

"Hmm?" I murmur.

"Answer my question," he says quietly. "I want the truth. Are you okay?"

I hesitate, just for a second. "Yes," I whisper. "I'm okay now. I was a little scared in the moment. Nothing I couldn't handle."

His gaze lingers on me a beat longer. Like he's deciding whether to believe that. Thunder rolls again, closer this time, deeper, vibrating through the ground beneath us. Rain begins as a soft patter against the tent, light at first. Inside, the air feels heavier.

Wade hasn't moved. Hasn't given any indication that he plans to. The space between us feels smaller than it should, charged with something I don't quite understand. My pulse stutters. Part nerves, part something I'm not ready to name. I shift slightly, drawing in a breath.

"You should probably get going," I say, keeping my tone light.

"Before the rain really starts."

For a moment, he doesn't respond. He just watches me. Lightning flashes, briefly illuminating his face again. Then he exhales, a quiet, almost amused breath. Not dismissive. Like he's choosing something.

"I'll see you in the morning, Mouse." His voice is low. Soft. A promise.

My throat goes dry. I nod, even though I'm not sure he can see it. He shifts, pushing himself up in one smooth motion before ducking out of the tent. The flap falls closed behind him.

And seconds later, the rain comes. Hard. Relentless. I hope he's not out there getting soaked. It drums against the canvas in a steady rhythm, drowning out everything else. I lie back slowly, staring up at the thin fabric above me as the storm presses in. Barely protected by the Kapok tree and the thin canvas.

But inside, all I can feel is the warmth he left behind. And the way my thoughts keep circling around him. Sleep comes easier than it should. After this day, after remembering Carly. After what just happened with Benjamin. My mind should be running through it all but I am pulled under by exhaustion.

Chapter Seven

Wade

I woke to the sound of the rain easing off. Not silence, never silence out here. The jungle didn't do quiet. Water still dripped from the canopy overhead, steady and rhythmic. Insects hummed, birds called. There was movement everywhere, constant, layered noise. This was the normal, baseline noise. Which made it easier to hear when something wasn't. I stayed still for a second, listening. No alarms. No movement out of place. No raised voices. Good. Didn't mean it would stay that way.

I sat up, dragging a hand down my face, jaw tight. I didn't really sleep. My body had rested, but my mind hadn't. My gaze flicked automatically toward the thin wall of fabric separating my tent from hers. Sarah.

The way she'd looked at me before I left last night stuck with me. The hesitation in her voice when she told me to go, like she wasn't sure she meant it. I should have been able to walk away without a second thought. I'd done it before. Worse situations. Harder choices. Instead, I'd spent half the night tracking the storm and every sound that came from her direction. Not ideal. I pushed the thought aside and forced my focus where it belonged.

I shoved the sleeping bag off and stepped out of the tent. The air hit me immediately, thick, damp and already heavy with heat even this early. The ground was soft from the rain. Mud would slow movement today. I stretched out the stiffness in my shoulders, scanning the clearing as I moved. Positions. Sightlines. People.

Reaper was already near our main set up, crouched near the fire pit, stirring a pot of coffee. Casual at a glance, but his eyes tracked everything. Always did. He looked relaxed, but nothing slipped past him. Not movement. Not tension. Not me. Second in command for a reason. I'd trusted him with my back for years. Tactical execution, call adjustments on the fly, if something went sideways, he was already fixing it before anyone else caught on.

He looked up as I approached, a faint smirk pulling at his mouth. "Rough night?"

I rolled my shoulders, ignoring it. Not taking that bait. Reaper just watched me for a second longer, like he was deciding how much to push. He never pushed far. Didn't need to. Guy grew up with nothing, foster homes, rotating through systems that didn't give a damn if he made it or not. Learned early how to read people. How to survive. Now he reads a room the same way he reads a battlefield. I grab a tin mug from the crate and pour coffee, the heat grounding. Familiar. Routine.

"We finalized the rotation," Reaper said, watching me over the rim of his cup. "Two-man shifts. Outer perimeter and inner coverage. We'll rotate with the research teams when they move out. No one goes anywhere alone."

I nodded. "Good. Anything overnight?"

"Quiet," he said. "Storm kept everyone down. Village settled early." He paused slightly. "Only thing worth noting, our favorite scientist stepped out late."

My grip tightened around the mug. "Sarah?"

He nodded once. "Didn't go far. Just stood outside. Watching the rain."

I exhaled slowly, my eyes shifting toward her tent. She was alone in the dark, after everything that happened. I didn't like that, she doesn't know we have someone watching.

"Next time, you wake me," I said.

Reaper raised a brow. "Didn't seem like a threat."

"She doesn't know what is," I replied flatly. That was the problem.

Out here, you didn't get warnings. You got consequences. Probably the same damn thing that kept me up.

I grit my teeth, forcing my expression neutral. "Noted. Anything else?"

Reaper gives me a knowing look but doesn't push. "Nah. Just figured you'd want to know." I exhale through my nose, taking a slow sip of coffee, letting the heat settle me. It's not Reaper getting under my skin. It's her. The thought of Sarah stepping out alone in the middle of the night doesn't sit right. Not after yesterday. Not after him. Benjamin put his hands on her, that didn't go unnoticed. She thinks he's harmless but he's clearly escalating. He's threatened and not thinking clearly. My jaw tightens at the reminder. I haven't decided what to do about him yet. Every instinct I have says to shut it down, make it clear, once and for all, that he doesn't touch her again. But he's a civilian. Which means he's under my protection, too. Doesn't mean I trust him. Doesn't mean I won't be watching.

For now, the mission comes first. It always does. I finish my coffee and set the mug aside, shifting into routine, checking gear, running through positioning, mentally walking the terrain again. Rain changes everything. Slows movement, limits our visibility. Makes people careless and makes mistakes easier. By the time the rest of the team filters in, the camp is already moving. Quiet chatter, gear being adjusted, the low clink of metal and ceramic.

We form up near the edge of the clearing. From here, I've got a clear line of sight to her tent. Intentional, I tell myself it's situational awareness. Coverage. It is, but it's not just that. She'd push back if she knew. I can already hear it, sharp and stubborn voice telling me she doesn't need a babysitter. I almost smirk at the thought.

She doesn't hesitate around me. I thought from our first meeting she would shy and quiet. I'm seeing her differently now, she's outspoken when it matters. When she's fighting for herself or talking about her passion.

Most people are scared of us. Our presence or experience, whatever it is, they usually keep their distance. Not Sarah. She meets me head-on, like backing down was never an option to begin with. It should be a problem. A distraction. Hell, it is a distraction, it's also the first thing in a long time that's pulled my focus in a different direction. She's got fire and for the first time in years, I don't find myself avoiding it.

Once everyone had coffee and gear squared away, I stepped forward, clearing my throat just enough to pull their attention.

"Alright, listen up," I said. "We'll keep it simple." I glance around the group, making sure I've got everyone. "Reaper, Sparta, you're on extended night rotation this week. Sleep during the day, I want full coverage after dark."

They both nod once.

"Magellan, Stitches, you're with the geologists. Stay wide, keep eyes on movement. Don't let them drift. Ghost, I want you to stay on intelligence and comms." Another round of nods.

"Glitch, you're with me. We'll hold the village, coordinate comms, and keep things tight here." I pause. "Questions?"

For a second, no one says anything.

"Yeah." Glitch. I look at him. His posture's off. Tighter than usual. Jaw set. "I've got one," he says, tone clipped. "Why are you staying back? That wasn't the original plan."

The tent goes quiet, not tense yet, but close. I don't react.

"Plans adjust," I say evenly.

Glitch lets out a short breath, shaking his head slightly. "Right. Adjust." His eyes flick toward Sarah's tent, then back to me. "This about the mission," he adds, "or something else?"

There it is. He's trying to be subtle, but he's missing the mark. The air shifts.

I hold his gaze. "Careful," I say, voice low. "You're getting close to stepping out of line."

Silence drops hard after that. Reaper exhales quietly, already reading the room.

"Alright, everyone," he mutters, clapping him once on the shoulder. "Let's give them a minute." The rest of the team follows, no hesitation. They know better. Now it's just us. I don't move closer. Don't raise my voice. Don't need to.

"What's your problem?" I ask.

Glitch holds my gaze for a second, then looks away, running a hand over his face.

"You're not thinking straight," he says. "You're changing the plan for her."

"She's part of the op," I reply. "That makes her my responsibility."

"That's not what I meant."

"I know exactly what you meant."

He exhales sharply, frustration bleeding through now. "You've been locked in for years, Wade. Mission first, always. Now we get here and suddenly you're…" He trails off, searching. "Different."

I let that sit. "She's not a distraction," I say. "And you don't talk about her like that. Ever."

My tone doesn't change. But it lands. Glitch nods once, tension still in his shoulders. "I'm not trying to disrespect her," he says. "I'm looking at you. What happens when this is over?"

There's no edge to it now, just concern. I take a slow breath.

"I don't know how it ends," I admit. That part's true. "But I know what this is." I meet his eyes again. "And I'm not walking away from it before I understand it."

Glitch studies me for a second longer, then nods slowly. "You're serious."

"Yeah."

He huffs a quiet breath, some of the fight leaving him. "Alright."

Then I add, more controlled, "If something's going on with Alex, you bring it here. Not out there." His reaction is immediate, tight jaw, slight flinch. Got it.

He nods once. "Yeah. I know." Another pause. Then, quieter, "I shouldn't have said anything earlier. She was within earshot."

I hold his gaze a second longer, then give a small nod. "Keep it professional."

"Yeah." I step in close enough to get his attention and clap a hand on his shoulder, my grip firm, just enough pressure to remind him where the line is. Not enough to hurt. Just enough to make a point. Glitch flinches slightly. Regret flashes across his face. Good.

He's always been solid in the field. Fast, adaptable, one of the best operators I've got. Comms, breach, direct action, it doesn't matter. He adjusts on the fly and gets it done. But Alex, that's the crack. High school sweetheart. The only thing he's never been able to compartmentalize. Lost his parents a few years back to a car accident. Took leave for the funeral, could've stayed out longer. Didn't. Came straight back to the team, threw himself into the next op like it would fix something. It didn't, it never does. It just delays the inevitable. And from what I've seen, she's never really been okay with this life. With how often he's gone. What it takes out of him. I release him and step back.

"Get your head right," I say quietly. He nods once, then turns and walks off before I can push any further. I let him go. For now. By the time I finish my coffee, Reaper appears at the edge of the tent, arms crossed, expression neutral but curious.

"How'd it go?"

"He's off," I say. "Something's going on, but he's not ready to talk." My gaze shifts past him, toward the village. "Apparently Sarah heard him."

Reaper winces. "Yeah. She didn't look too happy when I checked in earlier. Good luck with that."

I huff a quiet breath, dragging a hand over my face. "Yeah. Appreciate it." He claps my shoulder once and heads off.

I scan the clearing. The group's already moving, filtering toward the shabono and there she is. Camera around her neck, head bent over a small red notebook, jotting something down while Dori and Paya speak with her.

She's focused and locked in, until they step away. This is my window to talk to her. I start toward her, steady, controlled. This shouldn't be hard. I've dealt with militia leaders, negotiations that could turn violent in a second. But this? This has my pulse just a little off.

She doesn't look up when I stop in front of her. I can see the stiffening in her posture, she knows I'm there.

"What do you want, Sergeant Blakely?" Her tone is clipped, too formal, again. She's building a wall up. The title lands harder than it should. I let it go.

"Sarah," I say, keeping my voice even. "You heard what Glitch said." Still nothing.

"Yeah," she replies flatly, still writing. "Hard not to."

I shift slightly, lowering my voice. "I'm not going to defend how he said it."

"But he wasn't speaking for me." That gets her attention. Just enough that her pencil pauses.

"I don't really care what he thinks," she says. "I have work to do." I almost smile. She's trying to shut this down. I won't let that happen.

"I wasn't lying to you," I say, quieter now. "About the mission. We're here to protect you guys, I had a plan and now it's changing because I want to be close to you. Normally, I wouldn't stay close and my men know it. I did think it was a waste at first." I don't sugarcoat it, I want her to know the truth. "But that's changed."

Slowly, she looks up. Her wide blue eyes that reminds me of dawn, before the sun comes up, lock onto mine. Finally.

"And what?" she asks. "That's supposed to make me feel better?"

"No," I reply. "It's just the truth. It changed when I met you and saw what you were doing here. And when I met you."

She paused, her hand hovering over her notebook, but she didn't look at me. "I need to focus on my work," she said, slipping the strap of her camera over her shoulder.

"Can we talk tonight?" I asked.

There was a beat, just enough to think she might say yes. Then she shook her head. "I don't think we need to," she said. "I'm here to do my job. To finish my research. Nothing else."

And just like that, she turned and walked away. Leaving me standing there. The rest of the day, I stayed locked in. On the surface, everything ran smooth, coverage held, rotations stayed tight, no movement where there shouldn't be. But under that, something sat wrong.

A couple hours ago, Magellan checked in, said they were wrapping up and heading back. Right on time. Still didn't like it. When they finally break through the tree line, I'm already watching. Everyone moves like they should. They set all of their gear down and head straight for their tents, needing a quick reset. Magellan and Stitches head for the main canopy without a word. Reaper and Sparta step out not long after. They must've heard them come in. No one says anything. They don't need to. We've been doing this too long. You feel it when something's off.

It's late. Dinner's about to start. I tap my earpiece, calling the rest of the team in. "Wrap it up. Move to central."

Glitch stays on perimeter. I make my way toward the benches, where the group's already starting to gather. Magellan and Stitches are there, talking through the day. On the surface, it sounds routine. But I catch it, the clipped tone, the way their eyes flick between each other. There's more. They're just not saying it here.

I scan the area, instinct kicking in. Looking for her. Usually, I find her without trying. Like my brain already knows where to look. This time, nothing.

Jenna and Willis come in from the tree line. But something doesn't line up. Benjamin isn't with them. That's enough to get me moving. I straighten slightly, shifting my focus toward the edge of the clearing. And then I see her. She's coming in from the opposite side with Paya, the two of them dragging something behind them. It's hard to tell from here, it could be bundled supplies, maybe food or materials. Normal or should be normal. But it's not what has my attention. It's who's with her.

Glitch is walking beside her, talking and she's listening. I feel my chest tighten and I start toward them, pace steady, controlled. No reason to draw attention. Not until I understand what I'm looking at. Sarah nods at something he says, her expression unreadable from here. Then she looks up, her eyes catching on mine and smiles. It's a small, tentative smile but it's real. I'll take what I can get.

He notices me a second later. His expression goes neutral fast. He gives me a short nod, then turns off, heading back toward the perimeter without a word. I slow slightly, watching him go. I don't like it. Not one damn bit. Paya's watching all of it. Her gaze shifts between Sarah and me, the question clear even without words. She says something to Sarah in Portuguese, then bends to grab what they've been dragging.

In the firelight, I finally make it out. A small deer. Sarah steps forward again, putting herself between us. She doesn't look up. That doesn't sit well.

"Everything okay?" I ask, keeping my tone even.

"Yes," she says. "I was helping Paya check traps when Glitch came up to us."

My focus sharpens. "Did he say anything?"

"Yeah. He did." She adjusts the strap of her camera. "Can we talk later? I need to finish up so I can eat and get ready for bed."

Dismissed. I don't like the sound of that.

"Alright," I say. "I'll find you later." She nods once, then turns and heads after Paya without another glance. I watch her go, tension settling low in my gut. Could be nothing. Could be something. Either way, I don't like not knowing.

I head back to the guys and grab food, keeping my position where I've got a clear line of sight on her. I don't say much. Just eat my food and watch. Every now and then, she glances over. Glitch drops down beside us a few minutes later. I look at him. He gives me a brief, neutral smile like nothing's off. I hold his gaze a second longer than necessary.

If he made this worse, we're going to have a different conversation but I let it go, for now. No point making a scene in front of the village or the civilians. That's how things spiral. The guys fall into their usual rhythm, low jokes, easy conversation but they leave me out of it. They know when to.

She thinks I don't take what she does seriously. That part's on me. First impression wasn't great. But that was before I saw her work. Before I saw how she moves here, how the village responds to her.

She's not just along for the ride. She belongs in this environment and I need her to understand that I see it. I don't get many chances to do things right the first time. Not like this.

About an hour later, the geology team calls it and heads back to their tents. Sarah stays where she is, sitting with Paya and Kaori. She's quieter now. Listening more than talking, watching the way they interact. Learning and working. I'm guessing it's hard for her to turn it off and just relax. Every so often, Paya says something to her and Sarah responds, translating, keeping the conversation moving. I stay where I am, tracking all of it without making it obvious. Waiting.

"So," Magellan says, pulling my attention off Sarah. "Trip out was clean. They had a plan, knew what they were looking for. Guide kept them on track." Magellan leans back slightly, casual as ever but there's nothing careless about him. There never is.

He's the one keeping things light most days. Jokes, pranks, running his mouth just enough to keep everyone from getting too deep in their own heads. He grew up in a loud, tight-knit family with Spanish roots, both of his grandparents immigrated from Spain when they were young. Now there's a whole branch of them down in Albuquerque, big, opinionated, and always in each other's business. He's used to chaos. Thrives in it.

But when it's time to switch? He does. Weapons specialist. One of the best I've got, one of the best I have ever seen. Knows every piece we carry like it's an extension of his own body. And right now, he's all business.

He shifts slightly, tone changing. "During a break, Benjamin was talking to Jenna. Trying to flirt."

Stitches huffs under his breath.

Magellan continues, "She asked about Sarah. If they were together."

My jaw tightens. "And?"

"He told her him and Sarah were 'close.'" Magellan glances at me. "Didn't say it outright, but it was implied. More than just friends." That sits wrong.

"He's planting a narrative," Sparta mutters.

"Jenna didn't love it," Magellan adds. "You could see it. She pulled back after that. He didn't take it well."

"Pattern behavior," Stitches says. "Push, test boundaries, get frustrated when it doesn't land."

I nod once, already running through it. "Alright," I say. "We tighten coverage around him. Nothing obvious. I don't want this turning into a scene." They're all watching me now.

"Night rotation, stay closer to the tents," I continue. "Day ops, no one lets him wander off alone with anyone. Keep it quiet. We're observing, not escalating."

Reaper nods. "Understood."

"Let's hope we're reading it wrong," I add.

But I don't believe that. Benjamin's becoming a variable. He's not a threat, yet, but he's trending in that direction. And people like that don't usually correct themselves. Sarah doesn't strike me as someone who'd play into whatever he's implying. If anything, she seemed uncomfortable even talking about him. That tells me enough.

There's more there. She just isn't ready to say it. I look up just in time to see her stand. She glances my way, brief but intentional and then turns toward the trail back to the tents. I take that as my opening.

I push up from the bench. "We'll regroup in the morning," I tell the guys. "Call it if anything changes."

A few nods. No questions. I catch up to her just past the edge of the firelight, falling into step beside her. For a few seconds, neither of us speaks. Just the sound of our boots on damp earth and the jungle settling in for the night.

She missteps on a loose rock. I catch her before she goes down, my hand closing around her arm, steadying her.

"Careful," I murmur.

"Thanks," she says, quiet, a little breathless. I don't drop my hand right away. I let myself hold her steady and she doesn't try to pull away. So I let my hand shift, resting lightly at her side as we keep walking.

When we reach her tent, she unzips it and ducks inside.

"I'll be right back," I tell her quietly.

She pauses just long enough to nod, then disappears into the tent. I stand there for a second, watching the flap fall closed before I turn and head back toward mine. I grab what I need, my sleeping bag, my pillow and hesitate for half a second. This could go either way. She asked for space earlier. But she also agreed to talk. I head back. As I approach, I can hear her moving around inside.

"Sarah," I call quietly. "Can I come in?"

"One second," she says. "I'm changing." I wait, scanning the clearing out of habit. That's when I catch movement. Benjamin. Standing just outside his tent. Watching. I hold his gaze, long enough for him to understand I am watching him. He shifts, then disappears back inside.

"Okay," Sarah says softly. "You can come in."

I unzip the tent and step inside, closing it behind me. She's already curled into her sleeping bag, facing me. The space is tight. Smaller than I expected. She has stuff scattered everywhere. Her camera case and journal sitting out in the corner. Her duffel bag filled with clothes looks like a mini explosion set off inside it.

"Mind if I sit?" I ask.

"No," she says. "That's fine."

I set my things down carefully, keeping my movements quiet. Boots off by the entrance. Sidearm within reach. Routine. Then I settle beside her. There's a stretch of silence. Just the jungle outside. The faint drip of water still falling from the trees.

"I meant what I said earlier," I start. My voice is low, steady. "I was wrong about this mission." No excuses. No deflection. "That was before I met you," I add.

She doesn't respond right away. "I've worked really hard to be here," she says finally, her voice quieter now. "And it just felt like, I was more of a burden. I don't want anything happening with your team because of you guys being here or helping me."

I shift slightly, angling toward her.

"You're not a burden," I say. "I see what you're doing here." I repeat what I said earlier, needing her to hear me. "I didn't before. That's on me."

That gets through to her, just a little. I can tell by the way her shoulders ease just slightly.

"I don't move fast like this, I'm not used to whatever this is." she says, quietly.

"I know."

"And I don't want to lose focus."

"You won't." No hesitation. "I meant that too. I adjusted coverage," I add. "Not to hover but to make sure things stay tight around the village." I don't look away from her. "I take this seriously. Your work included."

That's the truth she needs, not anything else. I don't reach for her. Don't close the space. Even though it's there. Even if I want to build the connection. I wait, because if this is going to happen, it's not going to be because I pushed.

"Okay... I'll try to trust you." Her voice is quiet, but it's there.

"Please do," I say. "This isn't a game for me."

"Okay." She exhales softly.

There's a pause. I don't want to push. But I need to know.

"Can I ask you something?"

She hesitates. "Sure."

"What did Glitch say to you?"

She sighs and then, unexpectedly, lets out a small laugh. It catches me off guard. A light giggle that lightens some of this worry that's been sitting in my chest since this morning.

"I figured you'd ask," she says. "He told me what happened. Said it was his fault. That he's dealing with personal stuff and took it out on you and me."

I nod slightly, even though she can barely see it. "Did he say what it was?"

"No."

"Alright," I say. "That make sense. Can I ask you something else?"

"I guess." She's worried now.

I keep my voice even. "Magellan and Stitches overheard Benjamin talking to Jenna today." That gets her attention. "He implied that you and him…" I choose my words carefully, "…had something going on."

She's silent for only a moment before she erupts. "What?" she snaps, the shock in her voice immediate. "No." There's no hesitation. No uncertainty. Just anger.

"He was flirting with her, or trying to" I add. "She asked about you. That's what he told her."

"Oh my god," she breathes, and now there's frustration layered in. "No. I've never touched him. We were friendly, I guess. Barely that." She shifts slightly, words coming faster now. "Maybe for a short time after everything that happened before. But then he started getting weird. Pushy. I shut that down. I've kept my distance ever since. For five years, I tried to keep my distance. We're not even in the same department," she adds, quieter now. "So it's not hard but somehow I keep running into him."

I let that settle. Then, more gently "So there was never anything between you?" Not an accusation. Just clarity.

"No, I've never been with him." Her voice is firm, steady. There's no hesitation in it and even though I barely know her, I believe her. I should question it. I should keep a layer of distance. But something about Sarah makes that damn near impossible.

"Okay," I say quietly. "I trust you." The words come easier than they should. Maybe it's reckless. Maybe it's too soon but it doesn't feel wrong. The silence that follows isn't awkward. It's heavier than that. I shift slightly, getting more comfortable on the hard ground, aware of how little space there is between us. Aware of her.

"Did I say you could sleep in here with me?" she asks after a minute, her tone dry. A small smile pulls at my mouth.

"No," I admit. "But I was hoping you might." She lets out a soft breath, somewhere between a laugh and disbelief.

"You're unbelievable."

"Yeah," I murmur. "I've been told that."

"Go to your tent, Wade." I don't move right away. Not because I'm ignoring her. Because I'm choosing how to respond. I reach out slowly, giving her time to pull away if she wants to. When she doesn't, I brush my knuckles lightly over the back of her hand. Her breath catches as electricity shoots between us but she doesn't pull away.

"Someday," I say quietly, my voice low but steady, certain, "you're going to let me stay." She swallows, her fingers curling slightly under mine, but she doesn't argue. Doesn't agree either. For now, that's enough. I pull my hand back and push myself up, forcing my body to move when every instinct tells me to stay.

"Get some sleep," I say, softer now.

She points toward the tent flap. "Out."

There's no bite to it. I huff a quiet laugh and duck out into the night. She's definitely not shy and quiet like I thought. The air is cooler now, the jungle settling, the storm long past but still lingering in the damp ground beneath my boots. As I make my way back to my tent, one thought settles in, solid and unshakable. I'm not walking away from this.

Chapter Eight

Sarah

Yesterday went well. With my research. With Wade. At least, on the surface. Hearing Glitch explain himself helped. It settled some of the doubt that had been clawing at me since yesterday morning. But not all of it. There's still something sitting beneath it, this quiet, persistent uncertainty I can't quite shake.

Talking to Glitch yesterday threw me off at first. Then he apologized. Explained just enough to make me feel guilty for assuming the worst. He didn't tell me what was going on in his personal life, but I can guess. It felt heavy. Personal. The kind of thing you don't share easily. It made me realize I needed to at least hear Wade out. It's the adult thing to do, after all.

Also, I'm stuck here for six weeks. Avoiding him isn't exactly an option. If I'm being honest with myself, I don't *want* to avoid him. Was any of that real? Or am I just letting myself believe it is because I want it to be? I've known him for less than a day. No more than twenty-four hours and somehow I'm already trusting him more than I should. That alone should scare me.

Wade is impossible to ignore. Tall, dark and handsome. The kind of man that looks like he walked straight out of a romance novel and into real life just to ruin me. Those golden-brown eyes? They don't just look at me, they *see* me. Like they strip everything back until there's nothing left to hide behind. His jawline alone should be illegal.

The way he carries himself, steady and confident, like nothing in the world could shake him. It's dangerous. Because then there's me. Short. Plain. Covered in a thin layer of jungle sweat and clinging to whatever dignity my deodorant is managing to hold onto at this point. My hair is a mess. My clothes are practical, not pretty. Any effort I made before we got here is long gone, swallowed by humidity and dirt and reality. And yet, he looks at me like none of that matters. Like I matter. No one has ever made me feel like this before. Like my stomach is in constant chaos, butterflies colliding every time he looks at me. Like my face betrays me no matter how hard I try to stay composed. One glance from him is enough to undo every carefully built wall I have.

I stretch slowly, working out the stiffness from another night on a hard ground, reaching for my shirt. As I pull it over my head, a dull ache tugs at my upper arm. A faint but unmistakable bruise is forming, you can just make out the marks where Benjamin's fingers held me tightly. The memory hits instantly, his hand clamping down too tight, fingers digging in just enough to leave a mark. The way he didn't let go right away. Like he didn't want to. The fear coursing through me.

My stomach turns. I press my fingers lightly against the bruise, testing it. It's tender but it's not bad. I just hope the mark will disappear quickly. Even if the feeling doesn't. My jaw clenches, anger simmering just beneath the surface. Not just at him. At myself. I should have shoved him off sooner. Should have made more of a scene, drawn attention, done something. But I'd been caught off guard. Too focused on staying professional. On not making things worse. Not again.

I exhale sharply and finish getting dressed, rolling my shoulders as if I can physically shake the memory loose. He doesn't get to ruin this for me. He doesn't get that kind of power. Stepping outside, the jungle is already awake. Sound surrounds me, birds calling, insects humming, the distant rustle of movement through thick undergrowth. The air is damp, heavy with the scent of rain and earth.

I lift my chin slightly, steadying myself. Today, I focus on why I'm here. But as I move through camp, I feel it. That weight, that awareness. I glance up to see Benjamin across the clearing, watching me. My resolve hardens instantly. The rest of the morning, I stay close to Paya, documenting everything I can, her movements, the way she interacts with others, the rhythm of daily life here.

It settles something in me. Feels right. Like I'm exactly where I'm supposed to be. The moment I get the chance, I ask her where they bathe. I should have asked yesterday. Desperately needed it two days ago.

Dinner tonight is normal. As normal as things can be. I sit with Dr. Willis, Jenna, and Benjamin, making sure to check in about their work, asking if they need help with translating, if anything came up during the day.

"We might want to move locations," Willis says at one point, glancing at Benjamin. "Not far. Just closer to another section of the river. We'll need to explain that." I nod, filing it away.

While they get pulled into a conversation about samples, I lean closer to Jenna. "Paya's going to show me where we can wash up tomorrow morning," I say quietly. "You want to come?"

Her face lights up instantly. "Oh my god—yes."

I laugh softly. "Early, before everything starts."

"Perfect," she says, already grinning.

Both Willis and Benjamin are watching us now. I keep my focus on Jenna.

"What's going on?" Benjamin asks.

"She's taking me to cleaned up in the morning," Jenna says, practically glowing. "Finally."

Something shifts in his expression. Easy to miss if you're not looking for it. But I see it. The slight lift at the corner of his mouth. Gone just as quickly.

"What about us?" he asks, his tone is casual but with a slight edge. "Think we could tag along?"

My stomach turns. A scowl pulls at my face before I can stop it.

"Where are you going?" The voice behind me makes me flinch.

For half a second, I think it's Wade. My heart jumps before my brain catches up. It's not him. I turn and find Ghost standing there, watching me with that same unreadable expression he always has. This is the first time I've really seen him up close since we arrived. He doesn't hang around the rest of the group.

Before I have the chance to answer. Benjamin cuts in, "Sarah's taking us to see where we can wash in the morning, together," looking straight at him. My eyes widen. That's not what I said.

"That might not be appropriate," Dr. Willis says calmly, stepping in before I can. "Sarah, would you mind checking with Paya about separate arrangements?"

Relief washes through me. At least someone caught that.

"Yeah, of course," I say quickly. "I'll go ask her." I'm already moving, needing distance, from Benjamin, from the conversation, from the way everything suddenly feels off.

"You don't have to go right now," Dr. Willis adds gently. "Finish eating first."

"Oh, no, I'm done anyway," I say, maybe a little too fast. I grab my dishes and head off before anyone can say anything else.

Paya is near the edge of the clearing, rinsing dishes. I drop down beside her and start helping without asking, letting the familiar motion steady me.

"Are you okay?" she asks, glancing at me. She knows something is off. I follow her gaze for a second. Ghost is still nearby. Further back, Wade and his team are watching. I can't hear what he's saying, but I can tell by the way he's looking over here, he's paying attention. Benjamin is too. God, this is so awkward.

"Yes," I say, turning back to Paya. "I'm okay." Then I add, "The men, they want to know where they can wash. Or if they take turns."

I slow my words, choosing them carefully. Portuguese isn't easy for either of us. She frowns slightly, thinking it through. For a second, I worry I said it wrong.

I try again, simpler this time. "Men... women... same place? Or different?" Understanding clicks.

Paya tilts her head slightly, thinking. "Same river," she says. "But different places." She gestures vaguely with her hand. "Women go together. Men go... there." She points off in another direction. "Not always. Just... how it happens." It wasn't a rule. Not like ours. Just the way things naturally settled.

She studies me for a moment, curiosity flickering in her eyes. "In your home, you wash separate?" she asks.

I hesitate. "It depends," I say. "Usually, yes. Privacy." I gesture lightly, trying to explain. "Men and women... not together."

She nods slowly, though I can tell it still doesn't fully make sense to her. And why would it? Here, things are simpler. More natural. The jungle doesn't care about modesty or social rules. It just is. It hits me again how different our worlds are. How much we build rules around things that don't exist here. And how far from home I really am. We fall back into washing dishes, the steady rhythm of it calming.

"What did she say?" I jump slightly, turning to find Ghost just behind me. I hadn't even heard him move. He smirks, not in a teasing way, more like he finds my reaction amusing.

"She said it's the same river," I explain, drying my hands. "But people don't all go together. Women usually go together, and men go somewhere else along it. It's not... structured. Just kind of happens that way."

He nods once, like that makes sense to him, then steps back again, giving space without making it obvious. I turn back to Paya, finishing up the dishes while we quietly talk about the morning. One by one, everyone brings their plates over.

When Dr. Willis joins us, I glance up. "We'll just need to go at different times or areas along the river," I tell him. "It's shared, but they kind of... separate naturally."

He nods easily. "That makes sense."

I study him for a second. He's always so calm and respectful, completely unbothered. So different from Benjamin. It makes me wonder if he really doesn't see it. Or if he just chooses not to. We finish up quickly, the last of the light fading as the jungle settles into night. At the edge of the path, I spot Wade. He's standing with his arms crossed, broad shoulders outlined against the dimming sky.

Watching. When our eyes meet, something in his expression shifts, softens and warmth spreads through me before I can stop it. I say my goodnights to Paya and her family, then head toward him. He falls into step beside me.

"There you are," he says, voice low. "How was your day?"

"It was a good day," I say, smiling despite myself.

"Good." He nods once. "I want to hear about it. I'll meet you at your tent. I've got a few things to put away first." I nod and head ahead of him, slipping into my tent. Wondering if I should tell him to stay away. I change quickly, pulling on my pajamas and tossing my clothes into the corner. I'll deal with everything properly in the morning.

Not long after, I hear the zipper.

"Come in," I say softly.

Wade ducks inside, the space immediately feeling smaller with him in it. He moves quietly, pulling off his boots and setting them near the entrance.

"It's cooler tonight," I whisper, shifting slightly in my sleeping bag.

"That's why I brought this," he says, dropping his sleeping bag beside him. Then, like it's the most natural thing in the world, like he expected to stay in here. I don't hate that thought, I just don't know what people will think. This is too fast, too soon.

"So how did your focal survey go?"

I blink. Surprised and, if I'm being honest, I'm impressed. "You remembered that?" I ask, a small smile tugging at my lips.

He glances over at me. "I listen." There's something in the way he says it, so simple and steady.

"It was really good," I say, settling a little more comfortably. "We checked the traps, but there wasn't anything in them today. Honestly, it was just nice. I spent a lot of time with the kids." A small smile tugs at my lips. "Paya helps her mom take care of anyone who's sick or injured too, but there hasn't been any of that lately. So it was mostly just normal."

"That's good," Wade says quietly. "I'm glad to hear that. And I appreciate you letting me know when you were heading further out."

"Of course," I say. "Glitch didn't talk much, but he was fine. He just stayed back and let us work."

Wade hums softly, like he's filing that away. "What about dinner?" he asks.

I hesitate. I knew this was coming.

"Well..." I shift slightly, picking at the edge of my sleeping bag. "I asked Paya about getting cleaned up. She said she could show me in the morning, so I asked Jenna if she wanted to come. She was very excited about it." I let out a small breath. "So we're going to go with her tomorrow."

Silence. "What else?" Wade asks.

I groan softly. "You already know, don't you?"

"Just tell me. Don't keep anything from me." I glance toward him, even though it's too dark to really see his expression.

"Just... don't make a big deal out of it, okay?" He doesn't answer. Of course he doesn't.

I sigh. "Dr. Willis asked if the guys would be able to go too, which is fine. That makes sense." I pause, then force the rest out. "But Benjamin made a comment about wanting to come with us. With me and Jenna." I wrinkle my nose. "While we get washed up." The words feel worse out loud. "That's when Ghost showed up," I add quickly. "It didn't go any further. Dr. Willis shut it down."

Wade doesn't say anything. Just keeps waiting.

"I went to help Paya after that," I continue, my words starting to rush. "And asked her more about how it works. It's not like structured. Just different areas, different groups."

Still nothing. I shift again, nerves creeping in. "Are you going to say something?"

"I'm glad Dr. Willis stepped in," he says, voice low. Controlled. "Benjamin's pushing boundaries," he continues. "And he's not reading the room. That's a problem, I'll be handling," he adds.

That makes my head snap up slightly. "Wade—"

"I'm not going to make a scene," he cuts in, calm but firm. "But I am going to make sure he understands where the line is." His tone isn't angry, just calm and certain.

"And you won't be alone with him," he adds quietly.

"If it makes you feel any better," I say quietly, "I think he's harmless. I think he just... thinks he's flirting." Even as I say it, the words feel thin. Unconvincing. Wade lets out a low, rough sound. Not quite a growl but close enough.

"Harmless?" he repeats, voice tight. "Mouse, he had his hands on you."

My stomach twists. I'm suddenly very aware of the bruises on my arm, hidden but not forgotten. Does Wade know he bruised me?

"That's not harmless," he adds, quieter now. Controlled.

"I know," I say quickly, not wanting this to spiral. "I'm not trying to argue with you. I just...I don't know what to do." I exhale, the words finally spilling out. "We're here for six weeks. I don't want to make things worse. This—" I gesture vaguely around us "—this is my work. My education. I've worked too hard for this."

He reaches out, his hand settling gently against my cheek. The touch steals the rest of my breath. His thumb brushes lightly over my skin, slow, absent, like he's grounding himself as much as me. He studies me for a long moment. Like he's trying to read everything I'm not saying.

I can see the questions in his eyes. Feel them. But he doesn't push.

"Alright," he says finally, voice lower. "Another time, we'll be careful. If it continues to escalate, I will be stepping in." The words settle between us, heavy with everything left unsaid. His hand lingers for a second longer before he pulls away. The loss of his touch is immediate. He exhales slowly, like he's reining himself back in.

"Just promise me something, Mouse," he murmurs.

I tilt my head, searching his face. "What?"

His gaze locks onto mine. "If he crosses a line," he says, "you tell me. Right away. No brushing it off. No waiting. I need to know if you're not safe."

Something in the way he says it, not just concern, not just duty, something deeper that sends a shiver down my spine.

"I promise," I say softly. Even as I say it, my mind drifts back to the bruise. To whether that counts. Or if I'm already breaking that promise.

"Honestly…" I hesitate, then continue, quieter now. "He wasn't always like this. Five years ago, he seemed… normal. Decent. I mean, I was never really a big fan of his. We went through something… bad. After that, I kept my distance. And I've heard he's changed. That he's become more of a… player."

Wade's expression sharpens slightly. "What happened five years ago?" he asks.

My chest tightens instantly. The words are there. But so is everything that comes with them. I shake my head, my voice barely above a whisper.

"Maybe… another time."

Because I already know, if I start that story now, I won't be able to finish it.

"I want to know," he says quietly. "It might help me understand. And I want to get to know you. Give me that chance."

I draw in a slow breath, trying to steady myself. "Okay, but you can't interrupt," I murmur. "If I stop, I might not be able to start again."

He nods once. So I begin.

"We were here," I say softly. "This exact place. It was my first international field school, and my best friend came with me. We were both studying under Dr. Anderson. Dr. Willis and Benjamin were here too, doing their own research."

My voice catches, and I pause, forcing in another breath.

"Her name was Carly. We met our freshman year, random roommate assignment. We just clicked. Same major, same classes. It felt like fate." A faint, sad smile touches my lips. "We weren't opposites exactly. More like we balanced each other. Our other roommate Fallon, was with us and the three of us became inseparable ever since."

I swallow. "She had the prettiest blonde hair and taller than me, I mean most people are. A little shy sometimes, but also kind of boy-crazy," I add, attempting a small laugh that doesn't quite land. Wade's hand moves to my hair, slow and steady, comforting but it almost makes it harder to hold it together.

"When we started grad school, that's when we met Benjamin. He transferred in to work with Dr. Willis. He wasn't like this. Not back then." I shake my head slightly. "Carly liked him. They started flirting. Then dating." Another breath. "We all ended up here together. Same setup. Same kind of research. Just no military team watching over us." I glance at him briefly. "So, you know. Slightly less intimidating."

I try to smile again, but it fades quickly. "I was out in the jungle with Paya that day, checking traps. The village had heard about tension near the border, but no one seemed too worried. So we kept working."

My chest tightens.

"It was our last week." I pause, staring down at my hands. "Dr. Anderson found me out there. Said they'd heard gunfire somewhere in the distance. Nothing close, but enough that they wanted everyone accounted for."

My voice drops. "When we got back, Carly wasn't there."

The words hang heavy between us. "Benjamin came out of the trees not long after. Said he'd just gone off for a minute. Bathroom, I think." I shake my head, like I can still see it happening.

My throat tightens. "So we started looking for her."

I blink, but the tears come anyway. "We searched for days. The whole team. The village helped too. We went through the jungle, the riverbanks, everywhere we could think of.

"We never found her. There was no trace. We had to assume..." I swallow hard. "That she didn't make it." I press my lips together, trying to keep it together, but the tears keep falling anyway. "After that, everything just blurred. Getting home. Finishing the semester. Trying to pretend life went back to normal." I shake my head faintly. "It didn't.

"I remember getting to Belém," I whisper. "My aunt and uncle had flown in to meet me. And then, I went home to meet her parents in Minnesota. To give back her belongings." I choke out the last words, still remembering how her parents looked. I still feel the guilt even after all this time. Like I didn't do enough.

"I'm sorry you went through that," Wade murmurs, his voice low, close. "No one should have to." He pulls me in a little tighter, his hand moving slowly up and down my back. I don't think I've ever had this before. Not like this. Safe. Steady. Like I don't have to hold everything together on my own. For a moment, I let myself sink into it. And then the memories shift.

Carly. Laughing in our tent. Talking late into the night. My chest tightens.

"I remember her talking about Benjamin," I say quietly. "How much she liked him. But she wasn't sure about him. Not long-term." The words start coming faster now. "Toward the end, she said he was getting pushy. About sex. She wasn't ready."

I stiffen as it clicks into place. "The night before she disappeared, she told me they had a fight. She was thinking about ending things." Wade's arm tightens protectively around me. "I don't know," I whisper. "Maybe she said something to him. Maybe that's why he was so upset after."

My voice wavers. "When we got back to school, he wanted to stay friends. Said it would help to talk about her. Remember her." I shake my head faintly. "And then after a few months he just changed. He started flirting with me. I backed off. And after that he just turned into someone else. Like none of it mattered."

The silence that follows is heavy.

"I'm sorry," Wade says again, softer this time. "But from what you're telling me he didn't get better. He got worse."

"I know," I whisper. "I just... I keep thinking maybe he just doesn't handle rejection well."

Even as I say it, it sounds weak. Like I'm trying to make it make sense. Wade doesn't respond. He doesn't have to. A yawn slips out of me, the exhaustion finally catching up. The tears. The memories. The long day. His hand keeps moving along my back, slow, steady.

"I picked this spot because this is where Carly and I stayed," I murmur, my words starting to blur. "I just... wanted to feel close to her again." My eyes drift shut. "Sometimes I'd sit under the kapok tree and write. Or just... draw."

"That makes sense," he says quietly. "You were looking over here when we first got in. You had that same look on your face."

I huff out a soft breath. "I was hoping you didn't notice. I still hope she will come stumbling out of the trees." I whisper my confession, even if it's stupid to hope after five years.

He doesn't respond to that. I don't know what someone could say to that. Just continues to hold me, he's so comforting but he's also confusing.

He shifts slightly. "Get some sleep, beautiful," he murmurs.

I feel him hesitate for a second. Like he doesn't want to leave. And then the warmth disappears as he carefully pulls away. I almost ask him to stay. The sound of the zipper is soft. The jungle hums around me. For the first time in a long time, the memories don't feel quite as heavy.

And as sleep finally pulls me under, one thought lingers at the edge of my mind, not just about Carly. But about Benjamin. And the pieces that don't fit.

Chapter Nine

Sarah

I slowly wake up to Wade running his arm over my stomach. His touch feels like pure electricity and a slow-burning fire that coils low in my stomach. My back is pressed against his front. My breath hitches, my pulse thudding in my ears as his thumb brushes softly against my cheek. His delicious scent envelops me.

"Like what you feel, Mouse?" he murmurs, his voice rough, teasing but there's something else there, something deeper. I should pull away. I should say something sharp, remind him that this isn't happening, that I'm not the kind of girl who just melts at a charming smirk and a whispered promise. But I don't move. I can't. His lips pressing just behind my ear, so close I can feel the warmth of his breath, the maddening anticipation stretching between us like a taut wire.

"Tell me to leave," he whispers, his fingers tightening just slightly, like he already knows I won't.

I swallow hard. My heart is racing, my thoughts tangled, and damn it, I should say the words. But all I can do is stare at his mouth and wonder what it would feel like to close the distance. To give in. To let myself fall. I feel his callused hands slip under my shirt and slide up to my breasts. I lay there holding my breath, not sure if I should let him continue or if I should stop him. He gently grabs my breast and squeezes it before pinching my nipple causing me to inhale sharply.

His other arm that was under me raises and he uses his fingers to gently force my face up to start kissing me. He starts at my neck and starts gently placing kisses across my jawline until he reaches my lips.

His hand roamed with an intimacy that sent sparks through my skin, his touch confident but gentle, as though he was learning every inch of me. I definitely don't want him to stop now. He licks across my lips seeking entrance and I gasp as his hand starts sliding down my belly to the top of my sleep shorts. I can feel his long hard erection pushing against my ass as he kisses me as his hand slips under my pants.

"Wade." I moan quietly.

"You're so soft and responsive, baby. Can I touch you?"

"Mmm, yes, please don't stop."

I jolt awake, hearing my voice broke through my subconscious. My breath catching as the last remnants of the dream cling to me. For a moment, I don't move. Don't think. I just lie there, staring up at the worn fabric of my tent as the jungle slowly comes to life around me. It's early, the morning light just starting to bleed into the sky, but the sun hasn't broken the horizon yet. My heart is still racing. Heat lingers in my body, slow and unfamiliar, like it hasn't quite realized the dream is over.

I exhale slowly. I can't believe I dreamt that. It felt so real, I *wanted* it to be real.

"Sarah?" Wade's voice cuts through the quiet outside my tent.

I jump. "Yeah?" I call back, and I hear it immediately, the slight shakiness in my voice. Great.

"Are you okay?" he asks. "I thought I heard you call my name."

My entire face ignites. Oh. My. God. Did I? Did I actually say his name out loud? Worse, did I sound like I did in the dream? I hope he didn't hear me moaning.

"Yep. Yep, yep, yep." I close my eyes. Wow. Smooth.

"Are you sure?" he asks, sounding unconvinced.

I clear my throat, forcing some semblance of composure back into my voice. "Yes. Did you need something?" There's a brief pause.

"Dori and Paya are heading this way," he says. "Figured you'd want to know."

Right. Reality comes flooding back in and I need to focus. "I'll be out in a minute."

"Okay."

His footsteps fade, and I drop my head back against the ground with a quiet groan. I cannot believe that just happened. I stare up at the ceiling again, dragging in a slow breath. Does he know? There's no way he knows…right? I sit up, running a hand through my hair as I try to shake off the lingering warmth still humming through me. It doesn't fully go away. Not even close. There's still a tightness in my core that needs to be released.

As I get dressed, my thoughts won't settle. Part of me, the part still caught in that dream, feels ready. Like being close to him isn't something to question. Like it just fits and that terrifies me because, the other part of me is screaming the opposite. This is way too fast and way too soon. I barely know him. Fallon's voice drifts through my mind, teasing. *Just have fun, Sarah.*

I huff out a quiet breath. This isn't just fun. Not with him and that's exactly the problem. It feels real. I straighten, grabbing my things and pulling myself together as best I can. I throw on yesterday's clothes, no point in wasting a clean set when I'm about to wash up anyway.

Even standing, I still feel off. Hyper sensitive, like my body hasn't caught up with reality yet. I take one more steadying breath before stepping outside. The morning air hits me, cooler than I expect, damp from the night's rain.

Wade is already walking toward me with two mugs of coffee in his hands. Dori and Paya are already making their way over, and I lift a hand in greeting, smiling as I step forward to meet them. I'm trying very hard to ignore the way my body reacts when Wade gets closer. Or the fact that I can't quite meet his eyes right away. When I glance back at Wade, there's a cocky curve to his mouth. Oh no. He hands me a cup of coffee, his fingers brushing mine just long enough to make my pulse jump.

"Thanks," I murmur, trying to sound normal.

He lifts his own cup, watching me over the rim as he takes a slow sip. His eyes glint with something that immediately makes my stomach flip. Does he know? No. There's no way. But the way he's looking at me—too calm and too amused—has heat creeping up my neck anyway. I take a quick sip of my coffee, mostly to give myself something to do. I glance toward Dori, trying to regain some composure, but the warmth from Wade's proximity lingers, distracting.

Paya steps forward, breaking the moment. "Good morning," she says, smiling.

"Good morning. How are you?" I ask.

"We are well," she replies. Her gaze flicks briefly between Wade and me. "You look well also." My cheeks heat again. Great. They've noticed. I feel like there is a big sign pointed right at me broadcasting what I'm thinking.

"Yes, we're doing well," I say, maybe a little too quickly.

Paya only smiles and nods, completely unfazed. "We came to show you the spring," she says. "We have soap we make, if you need."

"Oh, yes, that would be amazing," I say. "I'll just wait for Jenna, and then we can all go together. I can ask the others if they want any soap too."

I feel Wade's hand settle lightly at my back, and I glance up at him. "You can offer them coffee," he says quietly. "And maybe tell me what's going on."

I nod, turning back to Paya. "They have coffee, if you'd like some," I translate.

She smiles, glancing at Dori. "No, thank you. We had tea."

I relay that back, and Wade nods. Dori is still watching us in that quiet, observant way. Like he's taking in everything without saying a word. I quickly explain the plan to Wade.

"They're going to show us the spring. They have soap if anyone needs it. I'm just waiting for Jenna so we can go."

He leans slightly closer. "Are you feeling dirty?" he murmurs under his breath.

I freeze. Behind him, someone chokes on their coffee, coughing as they try to clear their airway. Then it turns into a laugh. My face goes up in flames. I refuse to turn around. I don't need to know which one of his teammates just heard that. Wade pulls me lightly against his chest, his laughter low and barely contained. I can feel it, warm and steady, through him. Oh my god. He knows. There is absolutely no way he doesn't know. I tilt my head up and fix him with a glare. Do all of his men know? This is humiliating.

"You're enjoying this way too much," I mutter.

His grin only widens. "I'll have my guys hang back," Wade says, his voice low, steady. "Out of sight. But close enough." A slight pause.

"You won't be alone out here." The shift in tone catches me off guard. One second he's teasing me, the next, he's all focus. All control. His hand brushes lightly along my back as he steps away to speak with his team, the touch brief but grounding.

"Everything is good with you, Sarah?" Dori asks, pulling my attention back. His gaze is steady, thoughtful. "You are getting your work done? Seeing what you need?"

"Oh, yes," I say quickly, smiling. "It's going really well. I'm happy to be back." I gesture lightly around us. "Just keep doing your normal routines. That's what helps the most."

He nods, considering that.

"And Wade?" he asks. I feel Wade's attention shift toward us at the sound of his name.

"Yes," I say, trying to keep my voice even. "He's been kind. We're just getting to know each other." Another measured nod.

"If you need anything," Dori says, "you come to me."

"I will," I promise.

"Everything okay?" Wade asks as he steps back toward me.

"Yes," I say. "He was just checking on me." I glance up at him. "Do you need me to pass anything along?"

"Not right now," he says. "Unless Willis wants to shift locations. We'll need to coordinate with his team and their guide if that happens."

I relay that to Dori, who nods again, already processing. Jenna and Dr. Willis approach a moment later, and after a quick explanation, everything falls into place. I duck into my tent long enough to grab my towel and my small bottle of shampoo and soap. Not that it does much. Between the humidity and the jungle, my hair has officially given up.

Camera slung around my neck, I fall into step beside Jenna and Paya. We head out. Wade's team trails behind us, far enough not to intrude, but close enough that I can feel their presence.

Wade.

Ghost.

Reaper.

Sparta.

Watching and protecting us. The walk is quiet, and I don't mind it. It gives me space to listen. The jungle is alive in the early morning, birds calling overhead, insects humming and distant rustling through the trees. Somewhere farther off, I hear the sharp chatter of monkeys waking with the sun.

We move for a while, longer than I expected, before the trees begin to thin slightly. And then we arrive to a small, clear pool sits nestled beneath a low waterfall, the water spilling gently over smooth rock before trickling into a narrow stream. It isn't large. But it's beautiful. The water is a clear blue, almost glowing against the deep green that surrounds it. Thick foliage frames the edges, vines curling down toward the surface, everything damp and vibrant with life.

For a moment, I just stand there. Taking it in. I'm glad I brought my camera. The place steals the breath right out of me. The spring feels unreal, like something pulled from a dream. Clear blue water reflects the deep green canopy above, the surface barely disturbed except where the waterfall spills gently over smooth stone. The sound of it is soft, steady, almost hypnotic.

It feels untouched. Like time doesn't quite reach here. Birds dart between the branches overhead, flashes of red and yellow and blue cutting through the green. I lift my camera instinctively, capturing what I can, knowing it won't fully do it justice but needing to try anyway. I could stay here for hours. Just listening.

A quick glance over my shoulder and I see the guys spreading out, disappearing into the trees like they were never there to begin with. Within seconds, the jungle swallows them whole, no sound, no movement. Only the quiet assurance that they're still there.

Wade had handed me a radio before we left, just in case. The water is cooler than I expect when I step in, but it's perfect, refreshing against the heat that's been clinging to me for days. I don't waste time. We don't. Jenna moves just as quickly beside me, both of us eager for even a few minutes of feeling clean.

I rinse my hair beneath the waterfall, tipping my head back as the water rushes over me, washing away sweat and dirt and something deeper I hadn't realized I was carrying. I just stand there. Eyes closed. Letting it fall over me. Unfortunately, we don't have the luxury of time. Way too soon, we're done and heading back out. Drying off quickly and dressing just as fast.

I lift the radio. "We're good," I say, keeping it simple.

A few minutes later, I see Wade as he steps out of the trees like he belongs there, his gaze finding me immediately. And that slow smile, that is just for me, makes my stomach flip.

"You look beautiful," he says, stopping in front of me. Like it's a simple fact. Heat creeps up my neck again, and I duck my head slightly, smiling despite myself.

"Ghost's walking you back," he adds. "The rest of us will rotate through."

I nod. "Okay."

A fleeting thought danced in my mind, Wade and I alone in the cool water, the waterfall masking our whispered words. His touch, the heat of his body against mine, my cheeks flushed as I shook the thought away. I would love to see him undress, to see what he looked like beneath his uniform. That would be a great image to capture on my camera. I could feel his toned body against my back as he was pressing into me this morning. He could kiss me and feel me as we swam in the water. His golden brown eyes light up and he leans down to me.

"I can only imagine what you're thinking about, beautiful. I would love to get in the water naked with you." He winks at me. "Now, go on. I don't want you seeing any of these guys. I will find you later." He says kissing the top of my head and giving me a tap on my ass nudging me towards Ghost and Jenna.

"I don't know what you're talking about," I mutter, refusing to meet his eyes.

A low chuckle rumbles out of him. "Sure you don't."

Before I can respond, he steps back, giving me space again. "Go on," he says. "I'll find you later." There's promise in his voice.

I nod, turning before I can overthink it and head toward Jenna and Paya. Ghost falls into step nearby, quiet as ever. As I walk between them, I try to focus on the path. On the jungle. On anything that isn't the way my pulse is still racing or the fact that Wade is somewhere behind me. I absolutely will not imagine him taking his clothes off or what he looks like naked.

"So, you and Wade," Jenna says from behind me, her voice light but there's an undercurrent of attitude under it. "Is it serious?"

I keep my eyes forward as we walk. "I don't know about serious," I say evenly. "We're just getting to know each other." It feels like the safest answer. The same one I've been giving everyone. I'm also getting sick of having to explain it, I don't see why it's anyone's business.

"You barely know him, though," she adds. Still soft. But there's something in it now. Something that makes my shoulders tighten as my hackles rise. I don't respond right away. Even without turning around, I can feel her watching me. My earlier excitement, the cool water and the quiet peace of it, starts to fade. This is exactly what I didn't want.

People talking or speculating about it, when it has nothing to do with them. When I don't even know what's going on between Wade and I. I don't know how to feel about it. It feels like it's turning something that's meant to be mine into something else.

"We're still getting to know each other," I repeat, a little sharper this time.

There's a pause, then she asks, "You're sleeping with him, aren't you?"

I stop. The words slam into me, harder than I expect. My heart starts beating like a drum line. Slowly, I turn around. Jenna is watching me, her expression unreadable. Behind her, Ghost is standing still a few paces back. Just watching this whole exchange. My pulse spikes. How much did he hear?

"I don't understand how that's any of your concern," I say, my voice steady despite the heat rising in my chest. "What Wade and I do or don't do, has nothing to do with you." I hold her gaze. "It's not affecting my work. And it's definitely not affecting yours."

Jenna crosses her arms slightly, her expression tightening. "Benjamin told me you two had something going on," she says. "Some kind of friends-with-benefits situation." She takes a breath. "He made it sound like he wanted more."

For a second, I just stare at her. What do I even say to that? How dare he talk about me like that.

"What?" The word comes out sharper than I intend. "That's a lie," I say immediately, my pulse racing now. "Benjamin and I have never been anything like that. Not now. Not before." I shake my head, anger building. "Don't repeat things he says like they're facts."

Jenna hesitates, but I don't stop. "And don't assume you know what's going on with me," I add, my voice firm. "I'm here to do my job. I'm professional and I take this seriously. If this turns into a problem, I will take it to Dr. Willis. I'm not letting rumors or personal nonsense interfere with this work."

Silence stretches for a moment. I don't wait for her response. Turning, I move forward, catching up to Paya without another word. I can still feel the tension behind me. The weight of what was said. Underneath it all is anger. At Benjamin. At the situation. At the fact that somehow, this is already becoming more complicated than it should be. I don't even know if I actually have the authority to report Jenna like that. Or if it would just make everything worse.

But Benjamin? That's different. I *will* be saying something to him.

My hands are shaking. I tuck them close to my sides, trying to hide it, but I can still feel the tremor running through me.

"Is everything okay?" Paya asks softly beside me.

I nod quickly, forcing a smile that I know doesn't reach my eyes. "Yeah. It's fine. She just had some questions."

Paya studies me for a moment. She doesn't push. She doesn't need to. Between the raised voices and the tension, she knows something happened. When we reach the clearing, she pauses.

"I will meet you by my home later," she says gently.

I nod. "Okay."

And then I see him. Benjamin is standing near the larger tent, talking casually with Magellan and Glitch like nothing in the world is wrong. Like he didn't just drag my name through the dirt. Something inside me snaps. I don't think. I don't slow down. I walk straight toward him, each step harder than the last, my pulse roaring in my ears. My hands start shaking again but this time I don't try to hide it. Glitch looks up first, his expression shifting from a friendly greeting to confusion when he sees my face. Magellan follows a second later, his posture straightening slightly.

Benjamin turns. "What—"

"What is your problem?" I snap, my voice louder than I intend. The clearing goes quiet.

For a split second, he just stares at me. Confused. Caught off guard. And that's all it takes. Before I can second-guess it, before I can stop myself. I swing. My fist connects with his jaw with a sharp, sickening crack. Pain explodes through my hand instantly.

Benjamin stumbles back, swearing under his breath as he grabs his face. The world seems to freeze for a second. My hand throbs, but I force it down, clenching my jaw as I try not to react. I don't regret it and at the same time I do. I don't understand why I reacted like that. Too many emotions bubbling up and his stupid face pretending he doesn't know what he did.

Out of the corner of my eye, I catch movement, Magellan and Glitch stepping forward, not aggressive, but alert now. Reading the situation. No one laughs. No one says anything. They're only watching. And I'm still standing there, breathing hard, staring Benjamin down.

"What the fuck?!" Benjamin snaps, stumbling back a step as his hand goes to his face. He presses at his nose, checking for blood. There isn't any. Damn it.

"What Wade and I are doing has nothing to do with you," I say, my voice shaking but I don't back down. "You don't get to make assumptions or talk about me like that. Not anymore."

He doesn't answer right away. Just stares at me. Face going red in anger, embarrassment or both.

He steps toward me. "You bitch," he spits. "You've always wanted me. You're just pretending now that he's here."

My stomach drops. "You're insane," I snap, heat flooding through me. "You dated my best friend. I would *never* want you. You're disgusting, inside and out."

That does it. He lunges. But he doesn't make it far. Glitch and Magellan move at the same time, grabbing him hard and hauling him back before he can reach me. Ghost steps in front of me instantly, solid and unmoving, putting himself between us without a word. It happens so fast I barely process it. Benjamin struggles, trying to pull free, but it's useless.

"Easy," Magellan mutters, not even sounding winded. "Not a good look for you."

"Stand down," Glitch adds, his tone sharp, nothing like the joking edge he usually carries. "You're done."

I'm shaking. Bad. My hands won't stop, and this time I don't even try to hide it. God, I should have reported him before. I should have said something sooner. A small, irrational part of me wishes Wade was here. Another part is relieved he isn't. Because I don't think he would have stopped at one punch.

"What is going on here?" Dr. Willis steps into the clearing, his voice cutting through everything.

Benjamin stills immediately. "Nothing," he says smoothly, like none of this just happened. "We were just talking about where to go next for samples."

I blink. The audacity of it. Dr. Willis's gaze shifts between us. Benjamin. Me. Then back again before falling on the guys still holding him back. Ghost standing in front of me. He doesn't look convinced. My heart is still pounding, but something in me settles.

I'm not letting this slide. "That's not true," I say, my voice steadier than I expect.

Everyone's attention snaps to me. "Benjamin has been making comments about me," I continue. "Inappropriate ones. To me and apparently to others."

I glance briefly at Glitch and Magellan before looking back at Dr. Willis. "He just tried to grab me."

Silence drops over the clearing. Glitch's grip tightens slightly on Benjamin's arm. Magellan doesn't move at all, but I can feel the shift in him, like he's waiting. Ghost stays exactly where he is. Between us.

I was about to speak again when I heard Wade. "What the hell's going on here?" His voice cuts through the clearing, sharp and commanding. Relief flows through me at just the sound of his voice. I turn. He's already moving toward us. Hair still damp, shirt clinging slightly from the humidity, boots barely laced like he didn't take the time to finish getting ready. His weapon sits holstered at his side, and something about the way he carries himself, tight and controlled. It makes him look even more dangerous. More focused.

Everything shifts, they are a practiced machine moving in unison without a single command voiced. Glitch and Magellan release Benjamin and step back, but not far, just enough to give Wade space. Ghost moves with them, his hand closing lightly around my arm as he pulls me a step behind him.

Benjamin straightens, wiping at his face, trying to recover what little pride he has left.

"This doesn't concern you," he snaps.

Wade doesn't even slow down. "Doesn't concern me?" His voice drops, quiet and lethal. "You've got to be kidding." He stops just a few feet away. Close enough to make it very clear, this is not a conversation. "This ends now," he adds.

Benjamin scoffs, trying to puff himself up. "Your job is to keep us safe. Maybe you should focus on that instead of trying to get in her pants." For a split second, everything goes still.

Wade moves. Fast. His fist connects cleanly with Benjamin's nose, a sharp crack echoing through the clearing. Benjamin drops instantly, clutching his face as blood spills between his fingers. Silence.

Wade steps forward, towering over him. He doesn't raise his voice. He doesn't need to. "You don't speak about her again," he says, each word deliberate. "You don't look at her. You don't go near her." A slight tilt of his head. "Or next time, I won't stop there." Benjamin doesn't answer.

"Dr. Willis," he says, without taking his eyes off Benjamin. "You need to know what's been happening. He's been harassing Sarah. Making comments, spreading lies, putting his hands on her." His tone is steady. Professional. But there's something coiled tight underneath it.

"That's not—" Benjamin starts. Dr. Willis's expression hardens, his gaze snapping to Benjamin.

For a moment, no one moves. And I realize something. I expected anger, I expected chaos. Maybe even embarrassment, but instead, warmth spreads through me. The way Wade stands there, controlled and unshaken, like this is just another problem he's handling, like I'm something worth stepping in front of.

No one has ever done that for me. No one has ever made it so clear: *You don't get to touch her.*

I should say something. I should step in. Tell him I can handle myself. But I don't. Because for the first time, I don't want to, I just want it all to stop.

Benjamin mutters something under his breath, pressing his hand to his nose like it might dull the pain. His eyes flick to me. Now, there is no more arrogance or irritation. He looks worried and his eyes flicking to Dr. Willis again.

Wade doesn't look away. He just stands there, watching him, waiting as if he's daring him to try something again. My pulse pounds as I drag my gaze from Benjamin back to Wade. To the rigid line of his shoulders. The tension still locked in his frame. The way his fists are clenched like he hasn't fully come down from it yet. For someone so controlled he looks anything but right now. Before I can think better of it, I reach for him. Just a light brush of my fingers against his arm. A silent thank you.

He exhales sharply. Like he didn't realize he'd been holding it in. When he turns to me, the anger doesn't disappear, but it softens. Just enough. It hits me all at once. I'm in trouble. The kind that doesn't fade. The kind that doesn't make sense. The kind that ruins you in the best and worst ways at the same time.

"Again," Dr. Willis says, stepping forward, his voice tight with control, "what exactly is going on here?"

"I didn't do anything! She just came back from wherever and fucking punched me. You can ask these guys."

"I didn't see anything." Glitch says.

"I didn't see that either, she came in accusing you of telling people you've slept with her." Magellan says cooly. I love these guys just a little bit more, for protecting me. I could get in a lot of trouble for what I just did.

Wade doesn't take his eyes off Benjamin right away. Then finally, he looks at him. "You'll want to handle this," he says evenly. "But understand something, I won't let this happen again. I'll step in if I have to."

It's not a threat. It's a promise. Then he turns back to me. Just like that, the edge is gone. His gaze softens, scanning my face like he's checking for something. Making sure. I don't even know what to do with that. With him. With any of this.

My thoughts are a mess of anger, relief, disbelief, all tangled together. I don't want things to escalate with Benjamin. But I don't think they're going to settle either. Not after this. He wasn't always like this. He used to be…normal-ish. A friend. Someone Carly trusted.

"Come here, beautiful." Wade's voice cuts through everything. Lower now. Steady. He holds his hand out to me. Not demanding. Not forcing. Just there, waiting for me. I don't even bother fighting it. I step into him.

Chapter Ten

Wade

After the fight, I don't say anything. I just take her hand. Her fingers are cold in mine, even in the thick jungle heat. I guide her back to my tent, not giving anyone a chance to stop us. Not Willis. Not the guys. No one. She doesn't argue. Doesn't pull away. That alone tells me everything I need to know. She's letting go and letting me handle it, placing trust in me.

Once inside, I sit down and pull her with me, easing her onto the sleeping bag. Then I lie back, bringing her with me, tucking her against my chest like it's the most natural thing in the world. She's shaking. Full-body tremors from the adrenaline crash. I'm not much better. The anger is still there, sitting just under the surface. Waiting. So I don't talk, I just hold her. One arm tight around her back, the other braced under her head, keeping her close. Letting her feel I'm here. That she's safe.

I'm not happy about what just happened. Not even close. But having her here like this, in my arms, letting me take care of her. It feels like a line we just crossed. One she didn't pull back from.

"This is not very comfortable," she murmurs into my chest, her voice so quiet I almost miss it.

A breath of a laugh leaves me before I can stop it. Of all the things she could say, I tighten my arm around her, pulling her a little closer anyway.

"Yeah?" I murmur. "You'll survive." There's a pause.

"That didn't feel like me." That gets my attention.

I shift slightly, just enough to look down at her. "What didn't?"

"Me, that" she says softly. "Losing control like that. Hitting him." A breath. "I've thought about it before but I've never actually done it. And now…" She swallows. "I feel like I overreacted."

I study her for a second. Really look at her. She's not upset about him. Not really. She's upset about *herself*.

"Sarah," I say, my voice low but steady. "You didn't overreact. You reacted." Her eyes flick up to mine. "He pushed. You pushed back. That's not weakness, that's a boundary."

I brush my thumb lightly along her arm, grounding her. "You don't get to beat yourself up for defending yourself."

She exhales, but I can tell she's not convinced. "My whole future is riding on this," she says quietly. "If this gets back to the school, if they think I'm unstable or unprofessional…" Her voice tightens. "They could pull my research. I could lose everything."

I don't know academia. Don't know how their systems work. But I *do* know people. And I *do* know problems when I see them. Benjamin? He's a problem. I shift slightly, adjusting her against me.

"You're not losing anything," I say, calm, certain because I won't let that happen. I don't say that part out loud. But it's there.

"I'll talk to Willis," I add. "Make sure he understands exactly what happened. If he tries anything again, he won't get the chance to spin it." My jaw tightens slightly. "He's done pushing you around."

I look down at her again, softer this time. "Not while I'm here." And I mean every word of it.

"What's your plan for the rest of the day?" I ask, mostly to pull her out of her head.

"I guess I'll go meet Paya. I just need to change first. I was so excited after getting clean and now he and Jenna kind of ruined that."

"Don't let them take that from you," I tell her, brushing my thumb lightly along her arm. "I, for one, am pretty happy we're both clean." I lean in and press a quick kiss to her lips.

She smiles faintly, her eyes locked on my lips a little dazed. Her cheeks darkening, she was not prepared for the kiss but she's not stopping me or pulling away. "I'll try. Clean clothes and clean hair feel amazing."

"Good. Get changed, and I'll walk you over to Paya and Dori." My tone shifts slightly, more serious now. "Stay with them today. Glitch will have eyes on you, but I want you where we can see you. If you go anywhere, you tell one of us. No exceptions."

She nods, starting to move. I don't let her get far. My hand catches her wrist, pulling her gently back toward me. This time when I kiss her, it's slower. Deeper. It's not rushed or reactive, just deliberate. She inhales softly against my mouth and I feel it straight to my core.

Her hands come up, gripping my shirt like she needs something to steady herself and a possessive heat flares low in my chest. I angle my head, deepening the kiss just enough to feel her respond, to feel her lean into me instead of pulling away. She's not resisting. She's choosing this. Choosing me. I slide my hand to the small of her back, holding her there, keeping her close without forcing it. My mouth moves from hers to her jaw, slower now, testing, giving her space to stop me if she wants to.

She doesn't. Her breath catches and I feel the shiver that runs through her. That sound almost breaks my control. I pause there, my forehead resting briefly against her temple, forcing myself to rein it in before I push too far, too fast.

"Go get changed," I murmur, my voice rougher than I want it to be. "Before I decide I'm not letting you leave this tent at all."

Her fingers tighten once against my shirt, anchoring me to her before she pulls back. I let her go this time. Barely. Her breath hitches, and when I flick my tongue over the sensitive spot just below her ear, she moans a soft, breathy sound that shoots straight to my dick.

When I heard her moan my name this morning I knew she had been dreaming about me. She's wanted this just as much as I have. I *knew* it. I felt it every time she looked at me like she wasn't sure whether to push me away or pull me closer.

Her hips shift, pressing against me and I groan at the friction. My restraint is hanging by a thread, but I won't rush this. I want her worked up, aching, desperate for more.

"You're incredible," I murmured against her skin, pressing a kiss to her temple. "Next time, I can't wait to take my time exploring every inch of you."

Her breath stutters and her body tenses beneath mine—not in fear, but in anticipation. I smirk against her throat, loving the way she shivers for me.

For a moment, I just hold her there, my face pressed into the curve of her neck, breathing her in. I should let her go, give her space, but I don't want to. Not even a little.

"Wow," she whispers, her voice unsteady.

I lift my head, and the sight of that blush spreading across her cheeks pulls a low chuckle from me. I brush my lips over her cheeks, slow, deliberate, like I'm chasing that warmth instead of easing it.

"Yeah," I murmur. "Wow's right."

Her eyes flick up to mine, wide, a little dazed, and something in my chest tightens.

"You're trouble," I add quietly, a faint smirk tugging at my mouth before I press a quick kiss to her lips. "The good kind." If I don't stop now, we're not leaving this tent.

"Come on, Mouse," I say, forcing myself to pull back, grabbing her hand and tugging her up with me. "Let's get dressed before I change my mind."

I grab a clean shirt while she fixes hers, pulling her sweater back on. I don't miss the way her fingers linger for a second longer than necessary.

When we step out of the tent, a few of my guys are hanging around the main setup. I tilt my head toward Sarah. "Go get dressed, I'll meet you over there."

She nods and heads off, and I slide my earpiece back in, scanning the camp automatically. A few people are missing. Willis included. Stitches is crouched near Benjamin, working on his nose. I hear it before I see it, the sharp crack of cartilage being set. He groan loudly in pain. A flicker of satisfaction hits before I shove it down.

Stitches doesn't react. Doesn't flinch. Just resets the bone like he's done it a hundred times before, hands steady, movements precise. That's him, he's always calm and controlled. Doesn't matter if it's a busted nose or something a hell of a lot worse, he handles it the same way. No panic. No hesitation. Best medic I've ever worked with. Guy's got this way of compartmentalizing everything. Locks it down, puts it where it belongs so he can do the job in front of him.

Didn't come easy. Lost his mom when he was a teenager, cancer. Took care of her as long as he could, from what little he's said. After that, he learned real quick how to keep emotions out of the way when it mattered. Now he just fixes people. I watch for another second as he finishes up, already moving on like it's nothing.

"Where's the rest?" I ask, stepping up beside Glitch and Ghost. They're relaxed on the surface, coffee in hand, but their eyes are moving, tracking everything.

"Taking their turn getting clean," Ghost answers.

Makes sense. I catch the look Glitch shoots him, the corner of his mouth twitching. Yeah. There it is.

"Say it," I mutter, already knowing.

Glitch grins. "We were starting to think you went missing, Wraith."

"Funny," I deadpan. "Try that again and I'll put you on perimeter for a week." He just laughs.

I shake my head, already moving on. "I'm walking her over to Dori. Glitch, start a patrol sweep. Keep it tight. Ghost, I want eyes on Willis the second he's back. Before Magellan and Stitches rotate out, I need a word with him."

Both of them nod, the shift from joking to business immediate. Good. That's why I trust them. I take one last look around the clearing, making sure everything's where it should be. Then I head out after her.

"So what happens now?" I ask quietly.

We're off to the side of the clearing, far enough that Benjamin can't hear us, but close enough that I can still keep eyes on him. I don't trust him. Not for a second.

Dr. Willis exhales, rubbing the back of his neck. "I'll be honest, I didn't see most of what led up to that. I walked into Sarah yelling, and then you stepping in and… well." He gestures vaguely. "That."

I nod once. Fair. But that's not the full picture.

"Then let me fill in the gaps," I say, keeping my tone even.

He looks at me, listening now. Good.

"Benjamin's been escalating since day one. Watching her. Tracking her movements. The kind of attention that doesn't sit right." My jaw tightens slightly. "Not casual. Not harmless." I really don't like that she keeps using the word harmless when referring to him, she's trying to convince herself everything is fine when it's anything but.

Willis's expression shifts, just a fraction.

"First night here, one of my guys overheard him cornering her," I continue. "Talking about wanting her. Putting his hands on her, hard enough to leave a mark."

I see the shift in his eyes.

"She's been avoiding him the entire time," I add. "Every time I've asked, she deflects. Which tells me this didn't start here. And then last night—right in front of you—he's making comments about bathing with her and the others."

Silence settles between us. Willis looks away for a second, thinking. Then back at me.

"I didn't connect it before," he admits, his tone quieter now. "But hearing it laid out like that… yeah. That's a problem." Understatement of the year. "We need to get ahead of it," he continues. "Before it gets worse."

I nod. "Already ahead of you. My team's been watching him. That's the only reason he hasn't gotten further with her."

Willis absorbs that, then sighs. "I'll speak with him directly. And Jenna," he adds. "I want to understand what she's been told."

"That might not get you much," I say. "She's already coming at Sarah sideways. Accused her of leading him on."

Willis grimaces. "Noted."

"I'll document everything," he continues. "Formal report. I can log it through the satellite phone so there's a record before we even leave." That's good. That's what I wanted to hear.

"And Sarah?" I ask. That's the part that matters. He meets my eyes.

"As far as I'm concerned, she defended herself verbally. What I saw was you stepping in physically." Fair. "As long as she keeps her distance and I document the full situation," he continues, "this shouldn't impact her academically. I'll make that clear in my report."

A small part of the tension in my chest eases. It's not gone but it's better.

"I'll have her work more directly with me," he adds. "Limit interaction with both Benjamin and Jenna."

"Good," I say. "That's exactly what needs to happen." We stand there for a second longer, both watching the clearing. Benjamin's still sitting off to the side, using a towel to wipe the blood from his face. There's a deep purpling forming under his eyes already, his nose slightly more crooked than it was before.

"Keep your people on him," Willis says quietly.

"They already are." That earns a small nod.

"Alright," he says, extending his hand. I take it, firm.

"We'll handle it from here." I release his hand, but my eyes drift back to Benjamin.

I head back toward the tents, scanning out of habit. Reaper and Sparta are packing away gear, breaking things down with practiced efficiency. Magellan and Stitches are posted up with fresh coffee, looking entirely too relaxed. Glitch's still out on perimeter and Ghost is nowhere in sight, which means he's exactly where he needs to be. Good.

I make a mental note to have him dig into Benjamin when he gets back. There's no way this is the first time he's pulled something like this.

"How was last night?" I ask. "Anything to report?"

"Quiet," Reaper says with a shrug.

"Yeah," Sparta cuts in, smirking. "Right up until your girl came in swinging."

A few of them chuckle and I shake my head, though I can't quite stop the corner of my mouth from lifting.

"Man, you should've seen it," Magellan adds. "Kid didn't even know what hit him."

"And you," Reaper says, pointing his mug at me, "coming out of the trees like you were about to end someone? That was new."

"Didn't think we'd ever see you like that," Stitches mutters. I ignore that part.

"When we first met her, I figured she'd be quiet," Magellan goes on. "All books and notes. Didn't peg her for throwing punches."

"She's got more backbone than you gave her credit for," I say simply.

That earns a few nods. "Yeah," Sparta says. "She fits."

I don't respond to that, but I don't disagree either. "Alright," I shift, bringing it back to business. "Anything from your run with the geologists?"

Magellan shakes his head. "Nothing out of the ordinary. They stuck to their plan. No issues."

"Didn't see much interaction either," Stitches adds. "If anything happened between Jenna and Benjamin, it wasn't out there."

I nod once, filing it away. "My talk with Willis went through, it went as expected," I say. "He's documenting everything. Talking to both of them, logging it with their school."

That gets their attention.

"Good," Reaper mutters.

"As far as Sarah goes," I continue, "she's clear as long as she keeps her distance. That was her main concern."

"She'll be fine," Stitches says. "If it comes down to it, we all back her version. No question."

"I'm not worried about that," I reply. And I'm not. What worries me is everything after. "When we're here, we've got eyes on him," I say.

"He won't get near her without one of us stepping in."

I glance out toward the tree line, where Glitch disappeared earlier. "But when this is over?" I add. "When they go back and we're not there?"

That's the problem. That's the part I don't like. None of them answer right away. They don't need to.

Reaper exhales slowly. "Then we make sure she's not walking into that blind."

I nod once. Yeah. We do. Because one thing's already clear, Benjamin isn't done. And neither am I.

"Well, we all know you'll be there with her, keeping her safe," Reaper says, grinning.

The rest of them pile on immediately.

"Yeah, Wraith's not going anywhere now," Magellan adds.

"Man's already planning the wedding," Stitches mutters. Laughter breaks out.

I shake my head, flipping them off as I turn away. "Yeah, yeah. Laugh it up. Can't wait to see the rest of you fall just as hard." That only makes it worse. "Get to work," I throw over my shoulder, but I'm already moving.

Because yeah, they can say whatever they want. I know exactly where I'm headed.

"Glitch, status?" I murmur into the earpiece as I take the path toward the shabono.

"Perimeter's clear," he answers. "Nothing moving that shouldn't be."

"Keep it that way."

The village is alive when I step through. Kids running, weaving between the adults. Women working with dyed fibers, hands moving fast, practiced. A few men shaping tools, others sorting through goods laid out for trade. Sarah told me about it last night, how they prepare for the rainy season, how everything here has a purpose. Food. Trade. Survival. Everything earned. A few of the kids spot me, then more and just like that, I've got a small group circling me. They start mimicking rifles with their hands, making shooting sounds, darting around like they've done this a hundred times.

I don't need to understand the language. Game's universal. One of the boys points at me, makes a sharp "bang" sound. I clutch my arm like I've been hit, stumbling back with an exaggerated grunt before dropping to the ground. They erupt. Laughter, shouting, running circles around me.

"For a guy who's been in real firefights, your acting's terrible," Glitch's voice cuts through my earpiece, amused. A smirk pulls at my mouth.

"Who says I'm acting?" I mutter.

"You look dead already, Sarge," Magellan adds.

"Somebody get him a medic," Stitches chimes in.

"Fuck off," I mutter, pushing myself up just as Glitch steps out from the tree line and joins the kids, immediately playing along. I watch him for a second. He's looser, lighter. We all are. It didn't take long, didn't take much, just her.

"Down for the count, soldier?" Her voice cuts through everything. I look up. Sarah's standing over me, hands on her hips, that smirk on her face, the one that hits somewhere low and doesn't let go.

"There she is," I say, pushing up onto one elbow. "Thought I was a goner for a second. Turns out I just needed you to come check on me." She rolls her eyes, but there's color in her cheeks. Fire in her eyes. More than there was earlier.

The guys were right. The more comfortable she gets, the more she shows it. And damn if I don't like that.

"Might need mouth-to-mouth, Doc," I murmur, catching her wrist and tugging her down just enough to bring her closer. "Only you can save me." That blush hits instantly, spreading across her cheeks like I flipped a switch. Damn.

"Pretty sure you're breathing just fine," she shoots back, trying for composed, but I can hear the smile in her voice. "I was thinking more along the lines of first aid."

"How would you know?" I lean in closer, lowering my voice. "You're not close enough to check." I pull her just a fraction closer, enough that her breath catches, enough that I feel it.

"Just to be safe," I murmur near her lips. She gives me a quick kiss, fast, almost like she surprised herself and then she's gone, pushing back to her feet.

"Not while we're working," she says, glancing around, cheeks still flushed. "Maybe later."

I push up to my feet, stepping in just long enough to brush a kiss behind her ear. "Yeah," I murmur. "Later."

I give her a light tap at her hip. "Get back to work, beautiful." She walks off, glancing back once, that soft smile hitting me harder than it should.

"I'm surprised she still has clothes on with the way you're looking at her," Glitch says as he steps up beside me. "You know there are kids around, right?"

I don't even look at him. "You're still talking?"

He snorts. "So how's patrol?" I ask, finally shifting my attention to him.

"Quiet," he says. "Been keeping an eye on your girl. Benjamin and Jenna passed through a bit ago. Didn't come near her. Headed back the other way."

I frown slightly. "Didn't see them."

"He's being careful," Glitch mutters. "He's not done."

Yeah. I'm thinking the same thing. "We keep eyes on him," I say. "No gaps."

"Already on it. Heads up," Glitch adds after a second. "Clouds are rolling in. Looks like another storm."

I glance up. He's right. Dark clouds are pushing in fast, wind picking up just enough to shift the air. My gaze drops back down, right to her. Sarah's standing with Dori, trying to talk over the wind, her hair whipping around her face as she pushes it back, laughing at something he says.

Something about that sight, calm in the middle of everything, calm after everything that has happened. She's not going to him stop her, I won't let him get the chance. And just like that, I'm already moving toward her. She drifts away from Dori, already flipping open that little red notebook of hers. Head down, focused, like the rest of the world just fades out when she's working. I slow without meaning to, watching her as she writes something quickly, then flips the notebook over, like she doesn't want anyone seeing what's on the back pages. When she glances up and catches me looking, a blush creeps across her cheeks.

Then she drops her gaze and starts writing again. Interesting. A second later, she lifts her camera, moving through the space like she belongs here, capturing the women sitting in a circle, hands weaving baskets with practiced precision. The kids darting through the clearing, laughter echoing. She doesn't rush it. Takes her time. Waits for the right moments. Then she turns, finds me. Click. I huff out a quiet breath, shaking my head. Sneaky. She lowers the camera, satisfied, then moves to sit with the women, folding herself easily into their circle. They don't hesitate to make space for her.

She smiles easily at them, she belongs here. Since she's settled, I shift my attention back to the job, moving along the inner perimeter. Eyes scanning, tracking movement, patterns, anything out of place. My gaze keeps drifting back to her.

Ghost hasn't surfaced yet, which means he's digging. When Ghost digs, he finds something. Always does. I get up to do a slow perimeter check. I step just inside the tree line, adjusting my path to get a better look at the outer edge of the clearing. Glitch is further out, sweeping wider.

A shift in the air and Ghost is suddenly beside me. No sound. No warning. Just there.

"Timing's impeccable," I mutter. He doesn't react. He never does. "You look into Benjamin?" I ask quietly. He nods once. That's all it takes to set my teeth on edge. "What've you got?"

Ghost's expression tightens, just barely. "It's bad." My focus sharpens instantly. "He's got complaints," Ghost continues, voice low and controlled. "Harassment. Multiple. Some more serious—assault allegations that never made it past initial reports."

My jaw clenches. "Why not?"

Ghost's eyes flick toward the village, then back to me. "His uncle's the dean." Of course he is. "Records buried," Ghost adds. "Reports disappear. Girls back off. Pattern repeats."

A slow burn starts in my chest.

"He's got a type," Ghost continues. I don't like the way he says it.

"What type?"

Ghost doesn't hesitate. "Small. Dark hair. Curvy."

My gaze snaps back to the clearing. To her. Sitting there, smiling, completely unaware.

"Yeah," I mutter, my voice going cold. "That about covers it." For a second, neither of us speaks. The jungle hums around us, it's normal and peaceful calls.

"We're not letting him near her," I say finally. Not a suggestion. Not a plan. A fact. Ghost nods once.

"Already ahead of you." Good. Because if Benjamin so much as looks at her wrong again, I won't be pulling my punch next time.

"Yeah," I mutter, keeping my voice low. "Connections like that don't just make problems disappear, they bury them."

Ghost nods once. "Anything on the dean?" I ask.

"Not yet. I can dig," he replies.

"Do it."

He shifts slightly, continuing. "I checked Jenna. Clean record. Good grades, involved on campus. First field school. Transferred in, no local support system."

I exhale slowly. "So she's isolated."

"Yeah," he says. "Easier to influence."

My jaw tightens. "What else?"

Ghost's gaze flicks toward the clearing before coming back to me. "Benjamin's been messaging her for a while. Pushed this trip hard. Made it sound like a big opportunity."

"Did he ask for anything in return?"

"No. Not directly. Just friendly. Encouraging. Some light flirting."

I don't like that. "Long game," I say. "Build trust first. Get her on his side."

Ghost gives a slight nod. "Could be. When she went after Sarah earlier, she was defending him. Not neutral."

"So she's invested," I mutter. "Whether she realizes it or not."

"Feels like it," he agrees. "If she thinks she's got a shot with him, she's more likely to back him up."

I run a hand over the back of my neck, thinking it through. "Alright," I say finally. "We watch both of them. No assumptions but no blind spots either." Ghost nods once.

"There's something else," I add, lowering my voice. "Sarah told me about the girl who went missing five years ago. They were best friends."

Ghost's attention sharpens instantly.

"They were here. Same field school. Same setup." I pause, jaw tightening. "That girl was dating Benjamin. She told Sarah he'd been getting pushy. She was thinking about ending it." I exhale slowly. "Next day... she's gone."

The silence that follows is heavy. "Sarah hasn't connected it yet," I continue. "But I don't believe in coincidences like that."

Ghost's expression darkens, his gaze flicking toward the camp before returning to me. "Yeah," he says quietly. "Neither do I."

"I want everything you can find," I tell him. "Reports, complaints, anything tied to him back then. I don't care how buried it is."

"I'll dig," he says. "There's always something left behind."

"We loop everyone in tomorrow morning," I add. "No gaps."

Ghost studies me for a second, then says, "We've got trackers. We can slip one on her so no one knows."

I shake my head immediately. "Not like that." His brow lifts slightly. "I talk to her first," I say, firm. "She needs to understand why. I'm not going behind her back, not on this. I want her to start being more aware and taking precautions, too."

"Understood."

"I'll talk to her tonight," I add. "We keep this transparent."

"Got it. I'll update when I have more." I glance back toward the women for half a second, just enough to make sure she's still there. When I turn back, Ghost's gone. Like he was never there to begin with. I huff out a quiet breath, shaking my head. Guy's a damn ghost in every sense of the word.

Wind picks up harder through the trees, leaves snapping and shifting overhead. The air's changing, storm's coming in faster than I thought. Movement in the village shifts too. People are wrapping things up, gathering tools, calling kids in.

"Rain's moving in," Glitch's voice crackles through the earpiece. "Not far out."

"Copy," I respond, scanning the tree line. "Magellan, Stitches—status?"

Silence. I pause, listening harder.

"Magellan, Stitches, check in," I repeat, sharper this time.

Nothing. I look up just in time to see Glitch stepping back into the shabono, his expression already tightening. Yeah. I don't like that at all.

"Yeah, we're about two klicks out," Stitches comes through the earpiece.

"Any issues?" I ask.

"We'll brief when we're back."

My grip tightens slightly on the radio. I don't like that answer. Not one damn bit. But I let it go, if it's sensitive, they won't say it over comms. Not with civilians nearby.

"Copy."

Glitch steps up beside me, eyes on the sky. "We eating early?"

I follow his gaze. The clouds are rolling in fast now, darker, heavier. Wind's picking up, shifting the whole feel of the place.

"Yeah," I say. "Dinner's about ready. We get everyone fed before that storm hits."

He nods once. "Good. Because once they're back, there's something you need to see."

That sets something off in my gut. Right then, Magellan and Stitches break through the tree line, gear slung, moving with purpose. Behind them, I catch sight of the others filtering back in.

"Stitches," I call, not taking my eyes off the returning team. "Keep eyes on Sarah." He nods immediately. No questions.

"Hold up," Magellan mutters, falling in beside me. "I'm coming." We head toward the path where Glitch's waiting. I feel it before I see it, Sarah's eyes on me. I glance back. She's watching, that small crease between her brows. Questioning. I give her a quick wink, letting her know there is nothing to worry about. Not yet. Up ahead, Willis, Benjamin and Jenna are coming through. Willis gives me a neutral nod. Benjamin doesn't even try to hide the glare. Jenna avoids looking at any of us. Noted. We pass them without a word and keep moving.

The wind kicks harder, first drops of rain starting to fall, light, but steady. Glitch doesn't stop until we're far enough down the path. Then he turns.

"After I left you earlier," he says, "I picked up tracks cutting into the brush." My focus sharpens. "We don't go in there," he adds. "Not on standard patrol."

"No," I agree. "We don't."

"Tracks were fresh. This morning, maybe earlier."

"Where'd they lead?"

He looks at me like I should already know. "Back toward camp."

A beat. Then it clicks. "Sarah's tent," I say.

"Bingo."

A cold, steady anger burns through me. "Alright," I say. "I'll talk to Reaper and Sparta, see if anything was off last night."

"That's not all," Magellan cuts in. I look at him.

"When we were out with the geologists, we caught part of a conversation," he says. "Benjamin and Jenna."

My jaw tightens. "Go."

"Benjamin asked her verbatim, 'what the fuck did you say to Sarah?'"

That alone tells me enough. But I stay quiet. "Jenna said she told Sarah it wasn't right to lead Benjamin on while being all over you," Magellan adds.

I exhale slowly through my nose.

"And Benjamin?" I ask.

His expression darkens. "Told her she should've left it alone. Said he has a plan."

That word hits like a trigger. Plan. "Did he say what it was?" I ask.

"No," He says. "But Jenna didn't look confident after that. More like, she realized she stepped into something."

Silence settles between us for a second, the storm building around it.

This isn't random anymore. This is deliberate. Escalating.

"Alright," I say finally, voice low and controlled. "We loop everyone in. No gaps. No assumptions."

They nod. "This is week one," I continue. "We've got five more to go." And suddenly, that timeline feels a hell of a lot longer. "Tomorrow, we regroup early," I add. "New plan. Adjust patrols, tighter rotations. No one moves without coverage."

My gaze drifts back toward camp. Toward her.

"Because whatever he's planning" I say quietly, "he's not done." And I'll be damned if I let him get the chance.

Just as we're finishing eating, the rain starts coming down harder, thunder rolling in behind it. We move fast, cleaning up, securing gear, everyone heading for their tents. This storm is going to be worse than the last one. Sarah ducks into her tent, and I follow without hesitation. She glances back at me as I zip the tent shut behind us, the sound of the storm instantly muffled but still violent overhead.

She's already changing into her pajamas, moving quick, like she's trying not to be obvious about it. Like I haven't been watching her all day. Every glance. Every shift of her body. I felt it. That nervous energy. That anticipation. It's been sitting just under my skin all damn day. More than once, I had to adjust my cargo pants just to keep it from being obvious. Now, in the tight space of the tent, it's worse.

We settle in, the rain hammering against the fabric above us, wind whipping hard enough to make the walls strain with every gust. Lightning cracks, briefly illuminating the inside and I catch the flicker of fear in her eyes as she curls tighter into her sleeping bag.

I shift closer, lying beside her on the ground. "Little Mouse?" I murmur, my voice low.

"Yes?"

"We found some things out about Benjamin today."

She turns toward me, the dim light barely outlining her face. "What? Like what?" The worry is immediate.

I keep my voice steady. Controlled.

"Ghost found reports. Girls complaining about harassment. Things that didn't go anywhere." I pause, choosing my words carefully. "There were also cases, assaults that looked suspicious. He was named several times but it kept getting buried."

She gasps softly, instinctively pulling back. Not happening. My arm tightens around her, pulling her back against me. After a second, she stops resisting, settling against my shoulder with a quiet exhale.

"Buried?" she asks.

"Yeah. Nothing official. Whatever was there got wiped. His uncle's the dean."

"Yeah," she whispers. "Dean Wagner, he's Associate Dean of Research and Field Programs. He tells everyone." There's a pause, then quieter, "What did you say about assaults?"

Before I can answer, thunder cracks overhead that are loud and sharp, breaking the quiet. Lightning flashes through the tent. She flinches hard. I feel it all the way through her body. My hand comes up automatically, steadying her, anchoring her closer.

I say quietly. "I don't have full details. Just enough to know there were complaints and that they didn't go anywhere." Her fingers curl slightly against my shirt.

"That's why I'm telling you," I continue, keeping my voice steady. "Not to scare you—but so you understand why I'm not taking any chances."

Another crack of thunder rolls overhead, closer this time. She flinches again, pressing in tighter without even realizing it. "Hey," I murmur, shifting just enough to bring her closer, my arm settling more securely around her shoulders. "I've got you."

She exhales slowly, but I can still feel the tension in her. "I just... I didn't think it was that serious," she whispers. "I thought he was just being... annoying. Pushy."

"He is," I say. "But he's also been getting away with it for a long time. That's the difference."

Silence settles between us for a moment, filled only with the relentless sound of rain hammering the tent.

"What does this mean?" she asks softly. "For me?"

"It means you don't go anywhere alone," I answer immediately. "You stay with me, or one of my guys. Always. No exceptions." She shifts slightly, tilting her head so she can look up at me when the next flash of lightning cuts through the dark.

"That sounds a little... intense," she says carefully.

"Yeah," I agree. "It is." I don't soften it. Don't dress it up. "Because he's escalating," I add. "And I'm not waiting around to see how far he's willing to take it." She studies me for a second, searching my face, like she's trying to decide if I'm overreacting. Another rumble of thunder shakes the ground beneath us.

"I don't want this to ruin my research," she says finally, her voice quieter now. "I've worked too hard for this."

"It won't," I tell her. "We'll make sure of that. You keep doing your work. I'll handle the rest." Her lips press together, like she's holding back a dozen more questions.

"Willis is filing something," I continue. "Official. So there's a record. And we're tightening everything on our end. Patrols, rotations, coverage."

She nods slowly. "Okay," she whispers.

"Would you consider wearing a tracker?" I ask after a moment. "Just while we're out here. Maybe after, until everything is handled."

She tilts her head back to look at me, even in the dim light I can feel her eyes on me. "Why would I need that? What aren't you saying?"

"I'm saying I don't know what he's planning," I answer honestly. "Maybe it's nothing out here. Maybe it's later. But I don't like the way he's focused on you and I don't like that he's pulling someone else into it." I pause, choosing my words carefully. "I just want to know I can find you. Immediately. No guessing."

She studies me for a second longer, then her shoulders ease just slightly. "Okay," she says softly. "You're right. I'd rather be safe." Relief settles low in my chest.

"Thank you," I murmur, pressing a kiss to her forehead.

I tilt her chin up just enough to brush my lips against hers, slowly, testing her reaction. She kisses me back but there's still hesitation there. Not rejection, just uncertainty. I don't push. I pull back instead. Because the last thing I'm going to do is rush her.

The storm picks up again, wind slamming against the tent hard enough to make the fabric snap. Instinctively, she shifts closer, her hand finding my shirt again. I let her, there's no hesitation, no second thought. We just fit, it feels effortless.

"Try to get some rest," I murmur, brushing my thumb lightly along her arm. "I'm not going anywhere." That earns me a soft breath of a laugh, barely there.

"I should make you leave," she whispers.

"Are you?" I ask, keeping my voice low. If she tells me to go, I will. But I don't want to.

"No." Relief settles deep in my chest.

"Good," I murmur. "I like being here."

"Good," she says softly. "I like you being here." I can hear the shyness in her voice, I don't respond. Letting things settle between us, I know she needs time to adjust to the idea of us.

Outside, the storm rages, wind howling, rain pounding against the tent like it's trying to tear it apart. Inside, she finally starts to relax, her body softening as she settles more fully against me. I stay exactly where I am, between her and anything that might try to get close.

Chapter Eleven

Sarah

The wind howled through the camp, rattling my tent like the storm itself was trying to tear it from the earth. The fabric strained with every violent gust, the stakes creaking in protest as rain hammered down in relentless sheets. Even with Wade beside me, I couldn't fully relax.

If anything, I was more aware. Of him. The steady heat of his body at my back. The solid weight of his arm draped over me. The slow, even rhythm of his breathing against my neck. Every small shift sent sparks of awareness through me, making it impossible to settle.

I curled deeper into my sleeping bag, trying to ignore the way my mind kept drifting back to him, his voice, his smirks, the way his lips had felt against mine earlier.

God. I squeezed my eyes shut, willing sleep to come, it didn't. The storm only grew louder and stronger. The wind roared, snapping the tent hard enough to make me flinch. The ground beneath us seemed to vibrate with each crack of thunder. Then a sharp tearing sound cut through everything.

My eyes flew open just as the side of the tent split. Fabric ripped wide, the seam giving way under the force of the wind. Rain blasted inside instantly, cold, violent and soaking everything in seconds.

I gasped, scrambling upright. "Wade—!"

"I've got you." He was already moving.

One second he was beside me, the next he was braced between me and the opening, one arm out, gripping the torn fabric to keep it from ripping further while his other hand caught my arm, steadying me.

"Are you hurt?" he demanded, eyes scanning me fast, sharp, assessing.

I shook my head, heart racing. "No—just—"

Another gust slammed into the tent, nearly flattening it.

His jaw tightened. "Yeah, we're not staying here." Before I could respond, he was moving again, fast, efficient. "Grab what you can," he ordered, already reaching for my bag and shoving things inside. "Clothes, essentials. Now."

My hands shook as I scrambled to my knees, stuffing whatever I could grab into the bag as rain soaked through everything. "Okay, okay, I'm ready!"

He didn't hesitate. "Stay on me," he said, grabbing my wrist and pulling me toward the opening.

The second we stepped out, the storm hit full force. Rain lashed against my skin, wind nearly knocking me off my feet as we ran. Wade didn't let go, his grip firm, guiding me through the chaos like he'd done it a thousand times before.

It felt like forever but it was only seconds. His tent came into view, already holding stronger against the storm. He yanked the flap open, practically pulling me inside before ducking in after me and sealing it tight. The difference was immediate.

Still loud and his tent is shaking just as bad as mine was but at least it's contained now. Safe. I stood there for a second, drenched, breathless, heart pounding and then I looked at him. Water dripping from his hair, chest rising and falling, eyes locked on me, still scanning, still making sure I was okay.

"I told you," he muttered, breath rough. "That tent wasn't holding."

Despite everything, the storm, the chaos and the adrenaline, I let out a shaky laugh. "You were right," I admitted.

His expression softened just slightly. "Yeah," he said quietly. "I'm just happy I was there."

The air inside his tent was thick with damp heat, the sound of rain hammering against the fabric almost deafening. My breath came in uneven pants as I pushed my soaked hair from my face, shivering from the sudden chill that clung to my skin. Wade dropped to one knee in the dim light, water dripping from his clothes, his jaw tight as he pressed on his earpiece.

"Yeah, we're good," he said low and steady. "Her tent ripped. We're in mine. Anything else?"

I swallowed, watching him as he listened. His shoulders eased just slightly, but when his gaze flicked back to me, it was still sharp, still focused, like he hadn't stopped assessing the situation, even now. The storm raged on outside, but inside the tent, everything felt, closer. His tent is significantly smaller than mine, we're closer together. The warmth in here has nothing to do with being out of the rain and everything to do with being close to him. I was very aware of him. Of how little space there was between us. Of how my heart was pounding for reasons that had nothing to do with the storm anymore.

"Mouse," he murmured, a hint of amusement in his voice. "Didn't know you screamed like that. Think you just proved the nickname fits."

My cheeks burned. "I was surprised," I shot back, trying to sound defensive even though my voice came out softer than I intended. "The tent literally ripped open and then I got hit with freezing rain."

He chuckled under his breath, the sound low and warm. "Fair enough."

Before I could say anything else, he reached for me, guiding me down beside him again like it was the most natural thing in the world.

"You're soaked," he said, his voice lower now, steadier. "You need to get out of those clothes before you get sick."

My stomach flipped. Not because of what he said but because of the way he said it. There was no teasing edge this time, no smirk. No heat laced into his words. Just quiet command and something protective beneath it, that settled around me like a shield.

Warmth crept up my neck, even when he wasn't trying, he affected me. There was a quiet rustle as he shifted, the sound of fabric moving in the dark. My pulse kicked harder, my mind immediately going places I probably shouldn't let it. I couldn't see much, just shadows, movement but I could feel him close to me.

Then something brushed against my arm.

"Here," he said softly. "Put this on." I took it, fingers brushing his for just a second. A dry shirt, that smelled like him. Relief mixed with something else entirely.

"Thank you," I murmured, turning slightly as I pulled off my soaked clothes as quickly as I could, grateful for the darkness shielding me.

His shirt slipped over my head, the fabric falling loose around me, smelling faintly like him, clean and woodsy. I tugged it down, suddenly very aware of how little space there was between us again. How easily that space could disappear. I don't know if I was ready for that. But the fact that I wanted it? That was the dangerous part.

My heart thundered louder than the storm outside. This was uncharted territory, an intimacy I'd dreamed of but never experienced. Was I ready? Would he find my inexperience disappointing? A swirl of excitement and anxiety tightened my chest as I wrestled with the vulnerability of the moment.

Will he find it weird that I am a virgin? Should I act like I know what I am doing? I decided to keep my panties on, everything else is wet and feels weird to just get naked under his shirt.

"Hey," his voice comes softer this time, right near my ear. "You're okay."

I don't move at first, my whole body locked in place from the sudden awareness of just how close we are. The heat of him seeps into me, chasing away the cold but replacing it with something far more dangerous.

"I didn't realize—" I start, then stop, because I don't even know how to finish that sentence.

"That I'd be this close?" he murmurs, a hint of amusement in his voice, but it's gentler now. Careful. I swallow, nodding even though he probably can't see it.

"You can move," he adds quietly. "I'm not going anywhere." There's something about the way he says it. Strong, firm in a way that makes the worry in my chest ease just a fraction. Slowly and oh so cautiously, I shift the rest of the way into the sleeping bag. The space is tight, forcing me to settle against him whether I want to or not. His arm brushes mine, then stills, like he's giving me the choice. My heart pounds. I can feel every point of contact. The warmth of his side against mine, the steady rise and fall of his chest, the faint brush of his breath against my hair.

"Better?" he asks quietly.

"Warmer," I admit, my voice barely above a whisper.

A low hum of approval vibrates through him. "Good."

For a moment, neither of us says anything. The storm rages outside, but inside the tent, everything feels suspended in time. Like the world narrowed down to just this small space, just this moment. His arm shifts, settling lightly around me. Just there. An offer Not a demand. I hesitate then let myself relax into it.

My body betrays me, and as I settle fully into the bag, my ass presses against something—*hard*.

Heat shoots through me like a lightning strike. He lets out a low, barely-there groan, shifting slightly, like he's trying to give me space. But now that I *know* the effect I have on him, something shifts inside me, something reckless, something needy. I move, just slightly. Just enough. My torso slides against his chest. His breath hitches behind me. I hear his hands fist the sleeping bag, the soft scrunch of fabric tightening under his grip. My pulse pounds in my ears, muffling the sound of rain hammering the tent. I don't know what's come over me, but I *need* the friction. A slow, lazy roll of my hips against him and I feel the sharp inhale he takes.

"Sarah," he rasps, his hand coming down on my hip, holding me still. His grip is firm but shaking, like he's fighting something deep and primal. A delicious ache pools low in my belly. "I'm trying to be a gentleman," he murmurs, his breath warm against the shell of my ear. "But if you keep grinding that sweet ass against my cock, I'm going to lose that fight." His lips brush just behind my ear, his teeth grazing the sensitive skin. A shudder rolls through me.

I don't know how long I remain silent, my body warring with my mind. "So do it," I whispered, emboldened by the intensity of his warmth, the storm's chaos around us mirroring the tumult in my chest. When he shifted, his body pressed intimately against mine, and a wave of sensation stole my breath. This was different, raw, all consuming, and utterly undeniable. It feels right.

"If we do this, it means your mine, forever. I won't let you go. There's no hurry, we can wait until you're ready." He tells me quietly. I push up so I can reach his lips. I give him a quick peck.

"Make me yours." I whisper quietly, so quietly I don't know if he heard me. He drags in a deep breath and then suddenly pushes me so my back is on the floor and he is above me.

He starts kissing me, it starts out gentle just little pecks but when his hand glides up my waist and grabs my breast, I gasp into his mouth. Taking the opportunity, he immediately pushes his tongue into my mouth making the kiss deeper. I moan into his mouth when he starts playing with my nipple that was already hard from the cold rain. Now aching as they strain forward eagerly waiting to feel his touch. Sending sparks flowing through my body, making my pussy throb for him. The need to feel him inside me is so strong, I've never felt this way.

He reaches his other hand above my head holding his body up just enough where I can feel every inch of his hard body without the weight. Wade pushes his cock against the wetness gathering on my panties. Right where I need him the most. I moan again and push back against his cock causing him to groan above me as he starts kissing down my jaw. His other hand starts dragging my shirt—his shirt—up my body. I feel the shivers sliding over my body.

"You're so wet, my little Mouse. I can feel the wetness on your panties." He grumbles into my neck as he slowly kisses his way down to my breasts. He starts sucking the hardened peak into his mouth while using his hand to play with the other nipple causing my back to arch.

"Let's get this off you, beautiful." He says softly. I lift up enough for him to pull it over my head. Then he gently lays me back down, I didn't expect this level of gentleness, he's going slow like we have all the time in the world.

Pushing his cock forward to hit my entrance, if it weren't for the barrier of my panties and his boxer he would slide right in. Pulling back just enough so he is hovering above me again and he starts kissing and licking between my breasts as he moves down my body.

When he gets to my belly button he kisses my stomach and slides his tongue around my belly button and down my belly. I gasp again at the phenomenal feeling of tingles erupting all over my body. There's a fire building in my belly and it's spreading.

I never put much thought into how this would feel, but this is the best feeling I have ever had. The wetness is rushing between my thighs again. He chuckles as he keeps kissing down and resting his lips over my pubic bone before he gently bites. His hand sliding down to the edge of my underwear and slips his fingers in them pulling them down my thighs. Gently using a thick calloused finger he slides through my slick folds.

"Mmm, so wet for me. I can't wait to taste you," he murmurs, his breath hot against my skin as he finally reaches the apex of my thighs.

I suck in a sharp breath, part anticipation, part fear. My heart pounds, uncertainty tangling with the need coursing through me. For a fleeting second, I wonder if I should stop him. If I'm ready. His fingers hook into my panties and he peels them away, pulling them down my thighs. His lips brush against me, and the thought disappears. I *don't* want to stop him.

His large warm hands grab my thighs and spread me wide apart. His tongue swipes over the slit and my hips instantly buck up. He grabs my thighs tighter, holding me in place as he gives me what I want and I finally feel his tongue swiping over my clit. I shudder out a gasp. I'm very glad I didn't stop him. He devours me like a man starved, like he's never tasted anything so delicious. Every flick of his tongue, every slow, deliberate stroke sends a pleasure so intense through me that I can barely breathe.

I've never felt like this—never so consuming, never so completely out of my own control. The way he touches me, the way he seems to know exactly what I need before I do, has me unraveling faster than I can stop it. This is different. This is *him*. The way he's worshipping me with his mouth is sending me hurtling toward something bigger, something unstoppable.

His warm callused hand moves from my thigh and his finger slips into my warm, wet, soaking core. I didn't even know I was so wet. His other palms squeezes my other thigh. Carefully he moves his one finger around stretching it out before his hand turns and I feel his finger press on a spot that has me squeezing his finger, nearly coming undone.

All while his tongue doesn't stop its ministrations on my clit and laps up any juices that leaks out of me. I feel the tightness in my core increasing, heightening like the storm swirling around us. Wade moans as a rush of liquid soaks his finger as he curls his finger up in that come hither motion.

"Sarah, you taste so fucking sweet, this is mine," he groaned against me, his voice thick with desire. "You're so perfect, so soft. I can't wait to feel you wrapped around me." He says as he slips a second finger inside me and I fall over the edge.

The orgasm crashes over me and I feel the release as I come so hard all over his hand and mouth. Luckily the storm around us covers my loud moans. He is lapping it up and wringing out every last surge of pleasure from my body. I lay there trying to catch my breath as I came back to myself. He starts crawling up my body and kisses me, I can taste the saltiness from me and my face heats again. I can't believe I did that.

"Oh my goodness." I whisper when he lifts up. He is stroking the side of my face and breathing into my neck.

"That was amazing, Little Mouse. I can't wait to feel you do that with me deep inside you." His words alone are enough to get me ready again.

"Do you want to continue or do you want to wait? I don't mind either way, I promise." Am I ready for this? If I do this there is no turning back. It just feels right, even if this ends between us I can't deny the way he makes me feel now. I know at least if I lose my virginity to him, I will always cherish the memory.

"I want you." I whisper. I don't know if I am ready but I know I want to try. He starts sliding his cock through my folds again. Rubbing it up the slit and against my wet entrance. Just the pressure of him there feels so good, it's so sensitive. I moan out loud and thankfully it's covered by the sound of thunder and the rain. A part of me really wishes it was light enough to see what his face looks like right now. To see how his cock looks. The other part of me is glad we can't see except for small bursts of lightning because I am sure I look as nervous as I feel.

"Beautiful, I don't have any condoms. I promise I am clean. You're protected in all the ways you can be with me." I didn't even think about that. Im clearly so inexperienced at this. Luckily, since I turned 17, mom insisted on birth control. Even though I was not sexually active.

"Umm, I'm on birth control and I am clean, too."

"Okay, baby. I can still pull out if you want?"

"I think it's fine. You—you can inside." I whisper and it's barely audible. This whole thing is so embarrassing, even if I know it's necessary.

My heart thunders in time with the storm raging outside, wrapping around us like we exist in our own world. He doesn't respond, I don't know if he's feeling my discomfort, he just kisses me in response. His body is warm, solid, grounding. I cling to him as he starts to press inside, the thick head of his cock stretching me wider than his fingers ever did. Then he stops just as there is a sharp, unexpected tightness and I freeze. Barely breathing. He must feel it.

His whole body tenses, his grip on my hips tightening, his breath coming in uneven pants against my lips. A low, almost tortured groan escapes him, his restraint vibrating through every muscle as he forces himself to hold still. *He's waiting for me.* I don't know what I expected, maybe pain, maybe something more immediate. But instead, it's just *this*. The weight of him. The slow, almost unbearable pressure of being filled so completely for the first time.

His forehead presses to mine. "Breathe, Mouse," he whispers, his voice raw, reverent. His lips brush over mine, feather-light, coaxing me through it. He presses all the way in, breaking through that thin barrier, the pinch is unbearable for a moment. I inhale shakily, my nails pressing into his shoulders. The discomfort ebbs, giving way to something deeper, something overwhelming and right.

He shudders, pressing his lips to my temple. "Fuck, baby," he groans, his voice rough with emotion. "You. Are. Mine. All mine."

This moment was ours, etched into memory by the rhythm of the storm. Willing any tears not to slip out, thankfully it's dark and he can't see the pain on my face. He slips his hand between us and rubs small circles on my clit helping me focus on something other than being stretched open. Before the next thunder and lightning hit, I am able to force myself to relax further by taking deep breaths.

"Okay, I'm good." I tell him and he starts to slowly move his hard cock in and out and I swear it feels like a smooth steel pipe sliding inside me. He starts a slow rhythm of going in and out until the pain eases and I start to move against him meeting his thrusts. He is groaning in my ear.

"Oh fuck, your so tight. I don't know how I am going to last in this sweet pussy." The sting of him breaking through that barrier is slowly going away and it feels amazing.

I can feel the pressure in my lower belly build again, I didn't think it would feel this good, especially this time. I am trying to stay quiet so no one hears but the moans are slipping out. My fingers glide over his hard back and my fingers dig into his shoulder.

My pussy spasms over his cock and I know I am close again. He is starting to pound into me harder. I am not ready to come yet, I don't want to lose this feeling of ecstasy.

"Let go." He growls above me. I shake my head even though I know he can't see me. His hands slip down and I feel his fingers on my clit, again. My release hits instantly and I barely hold back a scream as I come over his cock as his thrusting grows erratic. My moan is lost in the rain and wind outside the tent. He does one last hard thrust and growls as he empties himself deep inside me.

My heart feels as though it is going to beat right out of my chest. A tear slipped down my cheek, not from the lingering tenderness, but from the depth of emotion coursing through me. This wasn't just about the physical, it was the unspoken promise in Wade's every touch, the certainty that I wasn't facing this alone. For the first time in a long while, I felt cherished, I cling to that feeling like a lifeline in the storm.

"That was amazing. *You* were amazing." His voice is rough, barely above a whisper, but there's something else there—something deeper.

He presses a kiss to my forehead, then my lips, slow and lingering, as if he's memorizing the feel of me.

I swallow hard, my throat tight. I feel like I'm going to cry again, the weight of what just happened settling in my chest. But I don't want to make a fool of myself by getting too emotional. Before I can pull away, he brushes his knuckles down my cheek, tilting my chin up so I have no choice but to meet his gaze.

With the next flash of lightning I keep my eyes on his face. Wanting to remember this moment forever. His eyes are softer than I've ever seen them, filled with something I don't have the courage to name yet.

"Thank you," he murmurs, his thumb sweeping over my bottom lip. "For trusting me. For giving *me* this."

My breath hitches. No one has ever made me feel so… *cherished.*

"It was beautiful," I murmured, my voice trembling with the weight of the moment. "Thank you." His arms tightened around me, his steady heartbeat lulling me as the storm raged on. Somewhere in the chaos, I found a sliver of peace, though a small part of me wondered how long it would last.

He lays down next to me and pulls me close, pulling my front to his back again. His hand reaches around my waist to cradle one of my breasts. My breath evens out, the tension slowly draining from my body as the warmth of him wraps around me, steady and constant. I've never felt so safe and this feeling is going to be both dangerous and addicting. Being held and cared for. I close my eyes, already drifting off as I listen to the storm and feeling his heartbeat under my cheek.

My last thought before sleep takes me is a quiet, stunned realization —I can't believe I just did that.

Chapter Twelve

Sarah

When I wake, the world feels completely different. Sunlight filters through the trees, warm and golden, like the storm never existed. The air is fresh, washed clean, carrying that earthy scent the jungle always has after heavy rain.

For a second, I just lie there, blinking up at the dark olive canvas ceiling of Wade's tent, the material still faintly damp from the storm. Then I stretch, rolling slightly and the space beside me is empty. Cold. The absence hits me before I can stop it. A small, sharp pang in my chest that I immediately try to ignore.

It doesn't mean anything. He probably just got up early. He's military, of course he did. I think they always get up early. Still, I can't help but feel like maybe it didn't mean to him what it meant to me. I push the thought away and sit up, gathering my things. My clothes from yesterday are damp but wearable, I change quickly before unzipping the tent and stepping outside.

The damage is worse in the daylight. My tent is destroyed.

Shredded fabric hangs from branches, tangled in the roots of the kapok tree like some kind of wreckage. Bits of nylon are scattered across the ground, my gear half-soaked and strewn everywhere. I let out a slow breath.

"Okay, yeah," I mutter. "They were right."

As much as I hate to admit it. I move through the mess, collecting what I can, my clothes are scattered everywhere. My bras and panties are strewn about and I look around. Wondering if anyone has seen any of them but I find no one out here. I hope that means they didn't. I start hanging my dripping wet clothes over low branches to dry. Although, I need to find somewhere hidden for my underwear. No way is that hanging for everyone to see. My fingers are still a little shaky, whether from the storm or everything else, I'm not sure.

"Oh no, Sarah, what happened?" I glance up to see Dr. Willis walking toward me, already dressed like he's about to head out on an expedition. Honestly, he looks like he stepped straight out of an Indiana Jones movie.

"Well," I say, gesturing at the disaster around me, "turns out everyone was right. My tent didn't hold up."

He winces slightly, taking in the damage. "That's unfortunate."

"Yeah," I say dryly.

"Are you going to need new accommodations?"

I pause, brushing a piece of wet fabric off my arm. "I think so," I admit. "I'll talk to Dori and Paya today. He offered before when he saw my tent."

And there's Wade's tent, but I don't let myself linger on that thought. I don't know what last night meant to him. Or if it meant anything at all. Better not to assume. Out of the corner of my eye, I see Jenna step out of her tent. Her blonde hair is a mess, quickly twisted into a bun as she looks over at me.

She hesitates, then gives me a small, tentative smile. I return it, polite but measured. I'm not going to be rude. But I'm not forgetting yesterday either.

"Maybe one of the guys has a spare tent," Dr. Willis suggests. "Or you could bunk with Jenna."

I hadn't considered that they might have an extra tent. It might be easier. Less complicated. Before I can respond, movement catches my attention. The guys are coming back from the trees, heading toward their larger tent where they keep their gear and hopefully coffee. Definitely coffee. My gaze shifts automatically and finds him. Wade's walking just behind the group, deep in conversation with Ghost. His expression is focused, serious, like whatever they're talking about matters.

He looks different out here in the daylight. He's sharper but his shoulders look relaxed. My stomach does a strange little flip. Like I'm not sure if I should go to him or wait for him to come to me. As if he could feel my stare, Wade looked up. For a split second, his eyes locked on mine. Then he gave me a small smile—soft, almost private— and went right back to talking with Ghost.

My chest tightened. That wasn't his usual look. No smirk. No heat. No teasing glint in his eyes. Just a smile and then he looked away. I swallowed hard, my thoughts spiraling before I could stop them. He regrets it. Of course he does. Last night was intense, too intense. Maybe he woke up this morning and realized it was a mistake. That I was a distraction. That this, whatever this is, isn't worth it.

That he doesn't want me. The thought lands heavier than I expect. Fine. I straighten my shoulders, forcing my expression neutral as I turn back to my things. Focus on work. That's why I'm here. I don't need distractions. I don't need him. I can keep my distance, keep things professional, throw myself into my research and ignore everything else. Even if a small part of me already knows that's a lie.

"I'm going to get ready for the day," Dr. Willis says beside me, his tone warm. "Let me know if you need anything."

"I will, thanks." I keep my voice steady, even as I continue gathering my things. Thankfully, there isn't much. Most of it I had already packed or grabbed last night when the tent tore apart.

I risk another glance. Wade's still with the guys. Still talking, still not looking at me. Something sharp twists in my chest, and this time I let the anger take over. Easier than feeling whatever this is. Fine. Work it is. I won't let this get to me.

I absolutely will but I'm not admitting that. Turning away, my gaze catches movement, Benjamin is stepping out of his tent. My stomach drops. I immediately look away, refusing to engage. Not today. Not after everything.

"Bom dia, você está bem?" I jump slightly, startled as Paya's voice comes from behind me.

"Sim, estou bem," I reply automatically, forcing a smile that doesn't quite reach my eyes.

Her gaze shifts to my destroyed tent, taking in the damage with quiet understanding. "Do you need to stay with us?" she asks gently.

I hesitate. The image flashes uninvited, Wade's arm around me, the steady rise and fall of his chest beneath my cheek, the warmth that made everything else feel distant for just a little while. Staying in his tent would be, complicated. But staying in the shabono, surrounded by everyone, pretending I'm fine? That might be worse.

"Let me see if they have a spare tent first," I say finally.

Paya nods, but there's a knowing look in her eyes as she turns away. Like she already knows what I'm going to decide. Even if I don't.

A moment later, Wade's hand settles against the small of my back. I jump.

"Easy there, Mouse," he murmurs, his voice low, still rough from sleep. "Why so jumpy?"

My heart stutters at the sound of it, at the feel of him so close again. I straighten, trying to keep my tone even.

"No reason. Just cleaning up my stuff," I say, gesturing toward the sad remains of my tent. "I was going to go get cleaned up. Do I need someone to escort me?"

"Yes." The answer is immediate. No hesitation. "Give me a minute," he adds, already shifting his stance like the decision's made. "I'm going with you."

Then that familiar edge creeps back into his voice, just enough to make my stomach flip. "Wouldn't mind getting you alone again."

I roll my eyes, but it does nothing to stop the heat that curls low in my stomach. *Be strong, be strong.* I chant in my head. He turns to grab his things and then his gaze lands on my packed bag. The shift is instant. The teasing disappears.

"What's this?" His voice drops into something more controlled.

I hate that tone. I shift under his stare. "I wasn't sure where I'd be staying," I say, nodding toward the shredded mess behind me. "Just getting everything together. Drying what I can."

He doesn't respond right away. Just watches me. Jaw tight. Like he's already decided I'm not telling him everything. A slow breath leaves him, like he's forcing himself not to say something.

"Come on," he says finally, holding out his hand. I hesitate. Then shift my bag instead, pretending not to notice. His hand lingers in the air for a second before dropping. He doesn't push but I feel the tension anyway. We start walking. The jungle hums around us, alive with sound, the distant calls of spider monkeys, birds echoing through the canopy, leaves rustling with every movement of wind. Normally, I'd soak it in. Today, it feels distant.

"I talked to Paya this morning," I say after a few minutes, breaking the silence.

"Yeah?" His voice is neutral, but I can hear the edge underneath. "I saw."

So he was watching. Of course he was. "What'd she say?" There it is again. That tightness. He's not angry, but close enough.

"She offered for me to stay with them," I say. "In the shabono." The words hang heavy in the air between us. I don't look at him. Don't want to see his reaction.

The jungle stretches out around us, dense, vibrant, alive with color and movement. Sunlight filters through the thick canopy, catching on bright leaves and flashes of birds darting through the branches. The Spider monkeys are calling to each other while birds sing their morning songs. I can't see any through the thick canopy of trees all around us. It really is a beautiful area, I could see the appeal of living here. Of course I couldn't live without running water and modern amenities but I see the appeal. There are so many vibrant colors in the forest with the flora and also the fauna. This place is so diverse I swear you never see the same thing twice.

It's beautiful. It should feel peaceful. But all I can feel is the tension walking beside me and the question I don't want to ask. Why does it feel like I'm about to lose something I never even had?

"Mouse?" Wade's voice pulls me back, grounding me.

"Oh—what?" I blink, realizing I completely spaced out.

"What did Paya say?"

"Oh." I let out a small breath, trying to gather my thoughts. "She just asked about the storm, what happened to my tent. I told her, and she said they have space if I need somewhere to stay. Like Dori offered before."

I chance a glance up at him. That was a bad idea. His jaw is tight, teeth grinding just slightly. That muscle ticks again, the one that tells me he's holding something back and I don't think it's good. I barely have time to process it before my foot catches on a fallen branch.

"Shit—" I pitch forward but before I get too far he catches me. Wade's arms lock around me instantly, steadying me before I can fall. My hands land against his chest, solid and warm beneath my palms. For a second, neither of us moves.

I look up slowly. He's already looking down at me. That confusion is still there but now it's mixed with something else. Now his eyes look darker, hungrier. His hand slides up my arm, slow and deliberate, until it cups my jaw.

"What did you tell her?" he asks quietly. He leans in just enough that I can feel his breath against my lips.

I forget how to think. "Tell who… what?" I manage, my voice softer than I intend.

His eyes narrow slightly. "Paya," he says, patience thinning. "What did you tell her about where you're staying?"

Oh. Right. That. "I just said I needed to talk to you guys first," I answer, stumbling over my words. "Maybe you have a spare tent or —" His expression hardens. Only this time the anger is brief, before it switches into disbelief and possession. His hand slides from my jaw to the back of my neck, fingers firm as they curl there, anchoring me in place.

"Spare tent?" he repeats, low and then he closes the distance. His lips crash into mine. It's hot, demanding, leaving no room for hesitation. The kiss steals the breath from my lungs. One hand drags down my back, pulling me flush against him, solid and unyielding. The other tightens slightly at my neck, not hurting, just holding me there, like he doesn't want even an inch between us.

It's not soft. Not careful. It's an all consuming, claiming kind of kiss. My body betrays me instantly. I melt into him, fingers gripping his shirt as the world tilts. If he wasn't holding me up, I'd be on the ground already. Time slips. I don't know how long we stay like that. It could be seconds or minutes but it doesn't matter. All I know is him. The heat. The intensity. The way everything else fades. When he finally pulls back, it's slow. Like it takes effort. His lips brush mine once more, softer this time. A contrast that somehow hits even harder. His forehead hovers close to mine, breath still uneven.

"Stop making plans that don't include me," he murmurs, voice rough, edged with possession but quieter now. Not quite a command. Although, close enough to make my heart race all over again. My eyes slowly open, and he's still there.

His face hovers just inches from mine, his gaze locked on mine like he's trying to read every thought I haven't said out loud. The sharp edge from before has softened, that molten gold back in his eyes, there's still a flicker of irritation there. My breath catches. I should say something. Push back. Remind him that he doesn't get to decide things for me but the words don't come.

"Do you really think I'd let you go anywhere else after last night? I told you last night that you're mine. I don't do things half way." he asks, his voice low, rough with something deeper than teasing. His hand lifts, cupping my face, his thumb brushing along my cheek in a way that makes my chest tighten.

"You're mine, Sarah. Not just for a moment, for every moment. Mine to protect, mine to care for." My pulse stumbles. Part of me wants to argue. Part of me wants to believe him. That's the problem, because I don't know him well enough to trust that. Being here in his arms, with the weight of him grounding me, it's too easy to forget that. I shake my head slightly, more to clear my thoughts than answer him.

He exhales, like he expected resistance, but instead of pushing, he just takes my hand again and starts leading me forward. We walk the rest of the way in silence. When the trees finally open up, the sight steals my breath all over again.

The waterfall spills over smooth stone, the clear water catching the light like glass. Mist clings to the air, mixing with the scent of damp earth and something sweet blooming nearby. Birds dart through the canopy, flashes of color against endless green, while distant monkey calls echo through the forest. It feels untouched. Like the world doesn't exist beyond this place. For a moment, I just stand there, really taking it in this time. The quiet. The beauty. The way everything slows.

There's a soft sound behind me. Fabric is shifting and a zipper being pulling down. I slowly turn in fear or anticipation it's hard to tell with my pulse thrumming. Wade's already pulling his shirt off, muscles flexing as he drags it over his head. The light filtering through the trees catches along his shoulders, the lines of his body sharp and defined as he pushes his pants down his thighs without a hint of hesitation. I barely have time to process anything before his cock springs free, bigger than I imagined. My cheeks heat instantly. I never really got the chance to see it last night, not like this. A rush of heat pools between my thighs at the memory of how he *felt* inside me, stretching me, filling me. My breath stutters. Heat floods my face before I can stop it.

"See something you like, Mouse?" His voice is laced with amusement, but there's a hunger behind it too.

My heart does something strange that, I'm not ready to name yet. So instead, I turn toward the water, focusing on the cool mist against my skin and trying very hard not to think about the man standing just a few feet away. I feel his gaze on my back, warming my whole body.

"Relax, Mouse," he murmurs, his arms come around me, turning me to face him. His golden eyes are on me, that familiar smirk ghosting across his lips again. "You've already felt my cock inside you." I swallow hard, forcing my eyes away, failing almost immediately.

"Maybe I just wasn't expecting..." I trail off, because honestly, I don't even know how to finish that sentence.

He chuckles softly, stepping closer to the water like none of this affects him in the slightest. "Get used to it," he adds, voice low, teasing but there's something steadier underneath it now. "You're not getting rid of me that easy." I try to swallow my nervousness, but the way he's watching me, as if he can read every thought in my head—makes it impossible. Still, I refuse to look away. Not this time.

I just stand there like one of the brocket deer we'd seen in the traps —completely frozen—as he slowly walks toward me, that sexy smirk back on his face. I squeeze my thighs together to relieve some of the pressure building. His eyes track the move and he grabs my waist and pulls me forward, my hands landing on his hard abs. I splay my hands over him and feel the hard ridges as he leans down to kiss behind my ear again and I shiver feeling my nipples harden into stiff peaks.

"Get these clothes off." He demands as he starts pulling my shirt off, once that is out of his way his hands instantly go to my bra and quickly pull it off. He kneels down in front of me and I moan so loudly as he puts his mouth onto my nipples which sends tingles straight down to my core.

His hands slide slowly down my waist, I can feel his fingers rough against my soft skin until he reaches my pants. He deftly undoes the button, slides the zipper down and starts sliding them down over my ass. My panties are still on, I can feel them getting wet. Wade leans down and puts his nose against it and inhales.

"I can still smell us," he said, his voice low and rough. "It's intoxicating. I can't wait to feel you again." His tone is hoarse, thick with desire, before he lands a sharp smack on my ass.

Shivers run down my spine from his dirty words, a rush of heat spreading through me. A blush creeps up my cheeks and I bite my lip, unsure how to respond. This is all so new, being wanted like this, hearing words like that meant for me. It should make me shy away, but instead, it only makes me want more.

Coming from him it sounds so hot. I quickly take my boots off and turn towards the water, just as I take a step forward he spanks me again. Suddenly I am airborne and tossed over his shoulder as he wades into the clear water. He smacks my butt hard making me yelp.

"There's that cute little scream again. Now be good or I am spanking you more." He says.

Walking deeper towards the waterfall, it's not very deep, the water reaching to his waist. If he lets me go here it will be up to my chest. He keeps going until we are right next to the waterfall, and sits me on one of the rock outcroppings. The smooth rock, worn from thousands of years of this waterfall flowing over it. Cool against my bare skin, it's a major difference to my overheated body. My feet are in the water, while the rest of me is out. I feel goosebumps rise all over my skin as Wade stands there staring at me, his face perfect level with my soaking wet core. A light breeze flows around us.

At this moment I feel as if it's just us two in the whole world. Something about him made me feel both safe and wild, cherished yet free. I didn't just want him, I wanted this: the way he looked at me, the way he touched me like I was his entire world. It wasn't just lust; it was something deeper, something I wasn't ready to name but couldn't deny. Yet the thought lingers, is this real?

Leaning down he starts sucking on my nipples again and I feel his hands sliding down my thighs, opening them wider for him to step in between them. The cool air hits the most sensitive part of me as he switches to my other breast and I throw my head back on a moan. When he stops, I open my eyes and look down at him. I see the adoration and lust shining through his golden eyes. His body starts dipping lower into the water, my pussy throbs in anticipation. Now I know the immense pleasure that only he can bring me.

"You. Are. Mine," he murmured, his voice softer now, as though he was letting me in on a secret. "I wasn't joking when I said that to you last night. You've woken something in me, Mouse, something I didn't know I was missing." His words seeped into my soul, layering this moment with a gravity that was almost overwhelming.

I don't get a chance to reply because he suddenly leans forward and his mouth latches onto my pussy. A loud moan escapes me. Before I have time to think about it, I quickly put a hand over my mouth not wanting anyone to hear us. I feel his hand slide back up and grab my arm to pull my hand away.

"Don't hold back, Mouse," he said softly, his voice rough and coaxing. "I want to hear every sound you make, just for me." Wade demands with his mouth hovering over soaking wet pussy. I could feel his breath as he talked, making me moan again.

His tongue slid up and down the slit before slowly dragging it through my wet folds. He switches between sticking his tongue into my core and sucking on my clit. I know it won't be long if he keeps it up like this, just as he slips two fingers into me his mouth latches onto my clit and I come loudly all over his hand and face.

Grabbing my waist, he slides me down so my legs are around his waist and turns around so that his back is leaning against the smooth rocks. He slid into me slowly, achingly slow, as though savoring every inch, every sensation. My nails dig into his shoulders, I was not prepared for that stretch.

"Are you sore, beautiful?" He's looking down at me, his eyes scanning my face, at the discomfort I can't hide.

"A little, it felt better after you just, you know." I whispered.

He pulls out slowly and eases back in. "Tell me if it's too much. I will stop."

"I will." He pulls out again, so slowly it's agonizing before pushing back in just as slow. He squeezes his eyes shut and breathes. I know he's struggling to hold back but he keeps going slow until I relax a little more. Until, I can't take it anymore.

"More." I tell him. He pulls out faster and pushes into me harder. My breath hitched at the fullness, the raw intimacy of the moment. His eyes locked on mine, the golden warmth there grounding me even as my body spiraled into ecstasy. He grabs my hair pulling my head back and he continues his punishing rhythm of sliding in and out of me.

His mouth latches onto my collarbone, pressing hot, open-mouthed kisses against my skin. It's a stark contrast to the deep, relentless way he's taking me. My head falls back in pure ecstasy, my fingers digging into his shoulders as pleasure crashes through me. One hand grips my waist, the other sliding around to seize my ass, his hold almost bruising as he drives into me with powerful, consuming thrusts. It still hurts a little and feels so good at the same time.

"Let it happen, Sarah," he growled softly, his lips brushing against my neck. "I've got you."

I shake my head, "I can't."

"You can, let me feel you squeezing my cock again."

He continues pumping into me, lost in using my body for his own pleasure. He looks up suddenly and kisses me and goes even harder. I scream as I start coming again, squeezing his cock inside of me. This one is more intense than the one last night, I didn't think it could ever get more intense. He pulls me closer to him and groans as he emptied himself inside of me. I keep my eyes closed as I catch my breath. He is breathing heavily next to me but is kissing me gently all over my face, hair and neck.

"So fucking beautiful when you come." He whispers next to my ear. I sigh contentedly.

"Oh my god, that was amazing." I slowly come back to my surroundings, I am still clinging to him.

"You're incredible, Sarah," he murmured, his hand trailing down my spine, slower this time. More deliberate. "And if you ever try shutting me out again," His voice dipped, not quite a threat, not quite a promise. "I'll remind you exactly where you belong."

My breath caught, my body still warm from him, from everything that had just passed between us—snap. The sharp crack of a twig shattered the moment. I jerked, my head whipping toward the trees, heart slamming against my ribs. The jungle had gone eerily still, the kind of silence that didn't feel natural. Nothing moved. But the feeling didn't go away. Like eyes were on us. Watching.

Wade's hand tightened on my waist instantly, all trace of teasing gone. His body shifted, subtle but unmistakable, placing himself between me and the tree line.

The air felt different now, heavier. There's another rustle and my eyes shoot in a different direction, towards where come from to get here. There's no more movement, nothing steps into view and there's no more sounds. I swallowed, forcing myself to breathe through the sudden spike of fear. "Probably just an animal," I said, but the words came out thinner than I intended.

"Maybe," Wade replied. But he didn't relax. Not even a little. Every line of his body was taut now, his focus locked on the trees, scanning, calculating. The man who had been teasing me moments ago was gone. The intimacy between us evaporated, replaced with a quiet tension that settled deep in my bones. The jungle shifted around us, shadows moving between thick leaves, the wind whispering through branches. And suddenly, it didn't feel like we were alone anymore.

Chapter Thirteen

Wade

"Tell me why you were upset this morning." My voice comes out low but there's no mistaking the edge in it. She falters beside me. I want her off balance just enough to stop deflecting. She looks up at me with that wide, innocent expression and it hits harder than it should. I can see the worry in her eyes, she doesn't trust this yet, I know that will come with time. I also need her to communicate with me.

We're close to camp now, with too many eyes. I stop walking for a minute and pull her to me. I want to know why she reacted like that so I can ensure she doesn't get too inside her again. I also want to distract her from the thought that someone was watching us. I know it was Benjamin. He was trying to stay hidden in the trees but I saw him.

"Umm… you know, my stuff being thrown around in the storm," she says.

I tighten my grip on her hand. "That may be part of it," I reply evenly, "But that's not all." Her eyes flicker. I step closer, pushing her up against a tree, not giving her space to retreat into her own head.

"You were jumpy. You were pulling away from me again." My voice drops slightly. "I told you last night. I told you again this morning. I'm not going anywhere."

Her chin lifts, that fire sparking back to life. "You can't just claim me."

There it is. I almost smile. Instead, I step in closer, backing her just enough to make her feel the difference between us.

"I can," I say quietly. "And I am."

Her breath catches but she doesn't step away. That's all I need. "This thing between us?" I continue, my tone steady, certain. "It's not random. It's not convenient. And it's sure as hell not temporary." Her eyes flare at those words and I know I hit the nail on the coffin. My thumb brushes lightly over her knuckles, "You mean something to me, Sarah." Her expression shifts from conflict to doubt with a hint of something softer trying to break through.

"I'll give you time," I add, just a touch quieter. "But don't mistake that for me stepping back. I'm not." Silence stretches between us for a beat.

"It's just…" she exhales, words rushing out. "When I woke up, you were gone. And then when I saw you… you didn't look at me the same."

I lean in closer to her, my hand sliding under her jaw, tilting her face up so she has no choice but to look at me. My lips hover just above hers.

"How do I normally look at you?" I ask, voice quieter now.

Her cheeks flush instantly. Pink spreading fast. "You know…" she mutters, barely audible. "Like you're undressing me in your mind."

A slow, satisfied grin pulls at my mouth. "Yeah," I murmur, leaning in just enough for my voice to brush against her ear. "That's because I am."

She shivers before she leans into me without even realizing it. I press a slow kiss just behind her ear, feeling the way her body reacts, how she softens and how she gives in without thinking.

"Listen to me," I say, pulling back just enough to meet her eyes again. "I left this morning to check the perimeter. Not to walk away from you. I meet with my men in the early morning before everyone is up to debrief." Her brows knit slightly, like she's processing that. "And when I looked at you?" I continue, my tone easing just a fraction, "I held back. Because if I didn't, I wouldn't have stopped at looking. I would've rushed over to you and claim you in front of everyone like I really want to."

Her lips part. Her breath catches again. That's the look I'm used to.

The one she was missing. I brush my thumb across her cheek once, slower this time. "Don't overthink this," I add quietly. "You're not something I regret." I let that settle. Then take her hand again, firm but not forcing.

"Now come on," I say, guiding her forward. "Before I forget we're supposed to be heading back at all. Your safety is my top priority," I tell her as we keep walking. "If I have to get up early again—meetings, perimeter checks—I'll wake you first."

She scrunches her nose immediately and I can't help it, I tap the tip of it with my finger, a quiet chuckle slipping out. "Alright," I amend, softer this time. "Maybe I won't wake you." Her lips twitch, I catch her chin lightly, making sure she's actually listening to me.

"But don't shut me out," I add, more serious now. "If something's bothering you, about us, about anything, you come to me. Don't sit in your head and make it bigger than it is. I'll fix what I can. The rest, we figure out together." I release her, stepping back slowly, making sure she has her balance before we start walking again.

She nods, a little slower this time. "Okay. I will. I promise I won't keep jumping to conclusions." There's hesitation in her voice, though, a vulnerability. "It's just, I've never done this before," she admits. "Never had a relationship. And you're way out of my league."

I stop walking. That pulls me up short. It's been obvious she was inexperiences and proven last night when I took her for the first time. I was surprised and so fucking happy when I met resistance. She was mine and only mine, so for her to say out of her league? That doesn't sit right with me. I turn toward her fully, gripping her hand a little tighter, not rough, just enough to make sure she feels me there.

"Don't say that again," I tell her, low and firm.

Her eyes widen slightly. "You're fucking gorgeous," I continue, not giving her a chance to brush it off. "I notice everything. Your body, the way you move, those gray eyes that catch the light, don't think I haven't seen it. Your hair when you pull it back? Yeah, I've thought about that too.

"The way you hold your pencil against your lips when you're thinking. The way you flip to the back of your book and write something when you think no one is watching. The way you jump into every task with the Yanomami. The way you stand up for yourself when you need to and the way you let me handle it when it's too much."

Her cheeks flush deeper, I let my gaze linger just long enough to make the point land. "Smart. Funny. Strong as hell even when you don't think you are," I add, quieter now. "If there's a league here, you're the one out of mine."

She doesn't answer, but I see it, the small smile trying to break through, the color still high on her cheeks. The tears in her eyes. Good, I need her to hear me, to believe every word. I start walking again, pulling her along with me.

"I haven't done the relationship thing either," I admit after a beat. "Not like this. Not where I actually care what happens after." She looks up at me at that. "I know what I want, though," I continue. "And I've said it before, I'm saying it again so you hear it. I want you. I'm not letting you walk away from this because you're scared of it."

Her grip tightens in mine. "I do believe you," she says quietly. "Just be patient with me."

"I will," I answer.

That's enough for now. We fall into a quieter rhythm after that, the jungle sounds filling the space between us instead of tension. When we reach the clearing, I immediately scan.

Magellan and Stitches are gone, already out with the geologists. Reaper and Sparta? Probably crashed after night watch. Glitch's the only one moving around, heading straight for us. Right on time. He hands me the tracker without a word, just a look that says we both know why this matters.

I turn back to Sarah, the weight of it settling in my hand. I don't like this part. Not with her. Not with how she's already looking at me, like she's waiting to see how I handle it.

"It's just precaution, Mouse," I tell her, keeping my voice steady. "I'd rather never need it. But I need to know I can find you if something goes sideways." I step closer, lowering my voice just for her. "This isn't about control," I add quietly. "It's about making sure nothing and no one, gets the chance to put you in a bad position again."

I hold it out to her. Not forcing. But not backing down either. She watches me closely as I explain it. There's worry in her eyes when I tell her she can't mention the tracker to anyone. Not Willis. Not Jenna. Definitely not Benjamin. For a second, I hate it. Hate that I'm putting that weight on her.

But then I see the understanding dawn in her eyes. She nods, even if she doesn't like it. She trusts me enough to go along with it. Doesn't mean I like what it implies. Because this isn't just about militia anymore. This is closer. More personal. More dangerous. I watch her move back to her bag, gathering her things like she's trying to reset the day. When she disappears into the tent to change, I stay where I am, scanning out of habit but my focus keeps drifting back.

When she steps out again, with her camera around her neck. That little red notebook in her hand. Pencil tucked behind her ear like she belongs here, like this is her world. It's a natural, focused kind of beauty. It's not the kind of beauty that demands attention.

It just takes it and holds it. I don't look away. Not until I have to. If I don't, I'm going to drag her right back into that tent and forget we have a job to do. Instead, I shift gears. I give her a nod, subtle, letting her know I'll catch up and then I move. Her tent is a mess. Shredded nylon, damp gear, everything scattered. I don't waste time. I gather what's salvageable, hang what needs drying, and move the rest into my space. Our space. Because there's no version of this where she's sleeping anywhere else. Not after last night. Not after what I know now. What she doesn't know, what I plan on surprising her with later is that our tents can connect. Designed that way for longer ops, when space gets tight or when we need to consolidate. So I set it up. Expand the frame. Link the entry points. Shift gear to one side so there's actual room to stretch out instead of curling up like we're packed in a damn crate.

It's not luxury. But it's better. More importantly, she's not alone. By the time I'm done, sweat's sticking to my back again, humidity already climbing with the day. I take a step back, checking everything over. It's good enough, it has to be because she's going to be here, with me. No question, I will be showing her that I mean every word I tell her.

I don't think about the regulations. The career risk. The lines I've already crossed. Sixteen years of doing everything by the book and I don't hesitate now. That should bother me. It doesn't, because I know my men won't say a damn word. And Benjamin? That problem will handle itself. One way or another. I head toward the shabono, rolling my shoulders as I fall back into routine. Time to relieve Glitch and keep eyes on the perimeter.

As I approach, I spot him immediately, leaning near the edge, watching the flow of people.

"Status?" I ask quietly as I step up beside him.

"All clear," he replies, handing me a quick look. "She's been with Dori most of the time." Good.

"Go run a check on the tracker," I tell him. "Full range. I want to ensure the signal is strong." He nods without question and moves out.

I take his place, eyes automatically scanning the tree line, movement patterns, entry points. Then I find her, my eyes locking on her. Sitting with the women, notebook open, listening, observing and completely absorbed in her work like nothing else exists.

Like she's safe. My jaw tightens slightly. Not because she's doing anything wrong. Because she doesn't realize, she's the center of the problem now and I'm the only one making sure it doesn't reach her. I've got one more day and one more night with her before I rotate to overnight watch. A week. Seven nights of distance. Seven nights of not having her within reach. Yeah, that's going to be a problem.

"When did the other group head out?" I ask Glitch, keeping my voice low.

"About twenty minutes after you and Sarah left," he says. "That's when Sparta and Reaper crashed."

I nod once, but my mind's already moving ahead. "Was there any point you lost eyes on Benjamin?"

Glitch's expression shifts. "Didn't see him at all this morning," he admits. "Not until right before they left. We figured he was still sleeping."

My jaw tightens. Of course.

"He came through the trees looking pissed," Glitch adds, "something set him off."

I drag a hand through my stubble, irritation spiking. "Yeah," I mutter. "He saw us."

Glitch's brows pull together. "At the waterfall," I continue, quieter now. "He must've followed. Had eyes on us the whole time."

That doesn't sit right. Doesn't sit right at all.

"Shit," Glitch exhales. "That's on me. I should've checked."

"No," I shake my head. "I saw him up earlier. Didn't flag it. That's on me."

I don't make mistakes like that. Not when it comes to something I'm responsible for. Not when it comes to her. This just got more complicated. If he's watching, if he's tracking her movements, then he's not backing off. He's escalating. And that lines up way too well with everything Ghost pulled.

"Fuck," Glitch mutters under his breath. "No wonder he looked like that. Like someone pissed in his wheaties."

Before I can respond, I see her. Walking toward us. Her gaze moves between me and Glitch, that sharp little look already forming, curious and suspicious. Smart. Too smart to miss tension like this. I shake my head slightly at Glitch, he knows to drop it. She doesn't need to hear this, not yet.

"Everything okay?" she asks when she reaches us.

I don't hesitate. "Yeah," I answer smoothly. "We're going to test your tracker today. You don't need to do anything, just keep doing your thing."

Her eyes search mine for a second longer than necessary. Like she knows there's more. Then she nods. "Okay."

I lean in, keeping it casual, brushing a quick kiss over her lips. Not for show, enough to remind her and anyone watching, exactly where I stand.

"Go on," I murmur.

She turns back toward Paya, slipping right back into her work like she didn't just tilt my entire focus off balance. Glitch gives me a one-finger salute as he heads off to start the test. I watch her for a few seconds longer. Then force myself back into position. Focus.

Perimeter.

Movement.

Patterns.

Control the situation.

Minutes pass and I feel him before I see him. I don't track it, I don't need to. Ghost drops down beside me like he's always been there. No sound. No warning, he's just there.

I glance over. "Tell me you've got something," I say quietly.

Because with Benjamin watching her—us—like that, we're running out of time before this turns into something worse. "What did you find?" I ask, keeping my voice low.

Ghost doesn't look at me right away. Just watches the tree line for a second longer before answering. "Nothing tying him directly to Willis," he says. "Benjamin's clean on paper. 4.0 GPA. No shared classes, just works under him as a TA. If there's anything there, it's not obvious."

I nod slowly. "Then we don't assume," I reply. "Not yet. Last thing I want is to drag Willis deeper into this if he's not part of it."

Ghost dips his head once. "There's more," he adds. That gets my attention. "I just got word from command. Those militia groups up north? They've crossed the border." My focus sharpens instantly.

"Into Brazil?"

"Yeah. But not near us," he clarifies. "They're pushing through smaller villages, farther north. We're talking thousands of klicks and a river between us and them. This area's still clear."

I don't like it. "Any intel on weapons?" I ask.

"Standard," he replies. "Machetes. AK platforms. Nothing sophisticated but they don't need it. They're taking control of small settlements. Tribes. Anyone without defense."

My jaw tightens. "Alright," I say. "I'll have Sarah pass that along to Dori. They need to know what's happening out there." Even if it's far. Even if it never reaches them. Information keeps people alive.

"I'll also push it to Magellan and Stitches," I add. "They're the only ones getting anywhere near those distances. I don't want them blindsided." Ghost nods. "And we regroup tonight," I continue. "If not, first thing in the morning. Everyone needs to stay in the loop on this."

He starts to stand. "Hey, Jackson."

He pauses. Doesn't move right away. Then slowly turns his head. That look's still there. Same one it's been since that mission. That quiet. haunted look. I don't say his brother's name right away. Don't have to. It's always there between us.

"I appreciate this," I say instead. "All of it. Digging into Benjamin, staying on top of intel, watching her back." His expression doesn't change. But I know he's listening.

"I know it's not standard," I continue. "I know I'm pushing lines I don't usually push." That's putting it lightly. "Sarah matters to me." That part's simple. No way around it. Then, quieter, "I think Jameson would've liked her."

That does it. Just a flicker behind his eyes. Barely there, but I see it. I've seen it before. At the funeral. Back in Asheville, at his mom's place. Their family home is a small green house tucked into the mountains, same one he and Jameson grew up in after their dad died. Old man was military too, both boys followed him in without hesitation.

I remember Ghost standing there, shoulders squared like always, while his mom held onto him like he was all she had left. He looked wrong, not broken exactly, he'd never let himself look broken. But thinner than he should've been. Hollowed out in a way that had nothing to do with weight. His dark hair had been cut short again, uneven in places like it hadn't mattered who did it. Scruff shadowed his jaw, not quite intentional. His nose, already a little crooked, looked like it had been set recently, still faintly bruised along the bridge.

And his eyes those sharp gray eyes with that steel-blue edge were still there but dulled. Like something behind them had gone quiet.

There'd been healing cuts along his knuckles. Faint marks at his wrists. The kind you only get from being restrained too long. Nothing obvious to anyone who didn't know what to look for. But I knew. We all did.

He stood there anyway. Solid. Unmoving. Letting his mom cling to him like he was the only thing keeping her upright. Didn't say a word. Didn't react. Just took it. Like he'd taken everything else. Didn't say a word then either. Hasn't been the same since. Ghost gives a small nod. Doesn't say anything. He never does. Then he's gone again, slipping back into the trees like he was never there.

I watch the space he disappears into for a second longer. Then I shift my focus back to the clearing. Back to the mission. Back to her. No matter what else is going on, she's still the one thing I can't stop tracking.

Chapter Fourteen

Wade

I keep my eyes on Sarah most of the day. Not in an obvious way, at least, not to anyone who doesn't know me. But I track her. She's in her element again, sitting with the women, listening, observing, writing. That little red notebook is constantly in her hands, pages filling fast as she captures everything around her.

Every so often, she flips the notebook over and writes something quickly in the back. The first time I noticed it, I though nothing of it. By the third, I was curious as hell. Now, I'm damn near convinced I know exactly what she's writing. Especially when she looks up, catches me watching, a blush creeps up her neck again. Yeah. That's not research notes. A slow grin tugs at my mouth. Good. If she's not ready to say it out loud yet, I'll take it however she gives it to me.

Glitch checks in about thirty minutes later, tracker's working fine. Clean signal. No interference. We push it further a couple hours later.

"Wade?" I look up as she walks over, that soft energy around her still there, but brighter now.

"I'm going with Dori to check traps," she says. "Do you need to come with me?"

I don't even answer right away. Just reach out and pull her down into my lap. She lets out a small breath of surprise, but she doesn't fight it. Doesn't pull away. I press a kiss to the side of her head, breathing her in for a second longer than necessary. I told her I'd dial it back. That was a lie. Or at least, not one I can keep.

"Yes," I say finally, voice low. "Let's go. I need to stretch anyway." I rub my thigh absently, working out the familiar ache that settles in if I sit too long. Her gaze drops to my hand, lingers there a second before lifting back to my face.

"What happened to your leg?" she asks softly.

I hold her gaze. "Tonight," I tell her. "I'll tell you tonight."

Her expression softens, like that answer is enough for now. "Go on," I add, giving her a light tap as she stands. "Do your thing."

She smiles, a bright, excited smile and turns back toward Dori. I catch his eye for a brief second as she reaches him. I give him a nod and he nods back, an unspoken understanding. Then they're moving down the trail. I fall in behind them, a few paces back. Not close enough to hover, but not far enough to lose sight. Never that far.

My focus shifts automatically, tree line, movement, sound and wind patterns. The jungle's alive, but there's a difference between normal noise and something out of place.

Nothing yet. Still, I don't relax. Not with everything we know. Not with him out here somewhere. Every now and then, my gaze drifts back to her. The way she moves, light on her feet, talking with Dori, completely absorbed in what she's doing. Happy. That's what it is. She's happy out here.

"Glitch," I murmur into the comms, keeping my voice low. "We're pushing deeper into the forest. Track her position, make sure signal holds."

"Copy," he comes back immediately.

I keep moving, staying just behind them, letting them lead while I cover. But my mind drifts. Back to her question. Back to my leg. That mission. The one that changed everything. The one where we lost Jameson. The one where Jackson stopped being Jackson and became Ghost. I exhale slowly, jaw tightening.

Yeah. That's going to be a conversation. One I'm not used to having. But for her, I'll tell it. Just not all of it. Not yet. Ghost went through hell on that mission. More than any of us. He survived it but something in him didn't. Came back quieter. Sharper. Like he peeled away everything unnecessary just to keep moving forward. He still does the job better than anyone I've ever seen, but when it's done he disappears. Keeps to himself. Doesn't go home. Doesn't let anyone in.

A ghost of who he used to be.

And I don't know what happens to a man like that when this is over. I don't know if he'll ever be able to walk away. I don't know if I will either. The thought lingers longer than I like, so I push it aside, focus shifting back to the present as we make our way through the trees.

Dori's ahead of us, carrying a pygmy brocket slung easily over his shoulder. Small. Lean. Deer-like. Sarah's practically bouncing beside him, completely fascinated. She doesn't stop talking, asking questions, pointing things out, completely lit up by the experience. I don't tell her I've seen dozens of them.

Different jungles. Different missions. Different reasons. Some things stay where they belong. In the past. In a world I don't want touching her. Because she sees things differently. She sees beauty where most people see survival. Finds wonder in places I've only ever looked at through a tactical lens. And I want her to keep that. Need her to keep that. Because somewhere along the line, I lost it. And being around her, I catch glimpses of it again.

Sarah's carrying two armadillos and it's everything I can do not to laugh. Her arms are stretched out as far as they'll go, her nose scrunched like she's trying not to breathe too deeply, clearly not thrilled with the situation. But she doesn't complain. Doesn't hand them off. Even when I offer.

"I've got it," I'd told her earlier.

She shook her head immediately. "No, I want to do it." She's stubborn and determined and just a little out of her depth. Dori's noticed it too. Every time he glances back at her, there's a quiet smirk tugging at his mouth. He knows exactly what she's doing and he respects it. Hell, I do too. Before we left the traps, she handed me her camera.

"Take a picture," she said, shifting the armadillos awkwardly. I lined it up, watched her force that bright smile, eyes sparkling despite the obvious discomfort. Clicked the shot. That one's going to be framed in my head for a long time. Because it's her. All of it. The curiosity. The determination. The willingness to throw herself into something unfamiliar just to experience it fully. It's these moments, the small ones. The real ones. That make everything else feel worth it.

Back at the shabono, the tribe moves like a well-oiled machine. There's no wasted motion. No hesitation. Everyone knows their role.

The adults gather around, working efficiently, preparing the meat, separating the skins, setting aside the shells. The armadillo shells are carefully cleaned, set out to dry for later use. Bowls. Ceremonial pieces. Tools. Sarah had lit up when Paya explained that. Of course she did. Now she's right there beside her, sleeves pushed up, completely focused as she helps with dinner prep. Talking, asking questions, absorbing everything like she always does.

And damn if it doesn't hit me again, she fits here. Not just as an outsider studying them but as someone who respects them. Understands them. Watching her laugh softly with Paya while they work. Yeah, that does something to me.

Dinner ends up being armadillo. Not my first time but I hope its the last. It's not exactly something you crave, but it's edible. Reminds me a lot of alligator, something Sparta would swear is a delicacy. I settle in with the guys, waiting until everyone's got food before I say anything.

"So, Mouse," I call casually, glancing over at her, "how was preparing armadillo for dinner?"

The reaction is immediate. The guys freeze. Forks halfway up. Eyes slowly shifting toward her. Sarah blushes under the attention, but there's a spark of pride there too.

"I didn't actually prepare the meat," she says quickly. "I helped with the vegetables."

Reaper stares down at his plate like it personally offended him. Glitch looks like he's reconsidering every life choice that led him here.

Sparta? Sparta just shrugs and keeps eating.

"Armadillo?" Reaper mutters, like he's hoping he heard wrong.

"Yeah," Sarah says, completely unfazed. "It's a staple protein for them. I helped Dori with the traps earlier. Honestly, it's not bad if you don't think about it too much."

Glitch lets out a slow breath. "Not bad? What are we on, Fear Factor now?"

"Armadillo's fine," Sparta cuts in, still chewing. "My grandma used to make armadillo soup back home. Swamp cooking. You'd be surprised what tastes good if you grow up on it."

Reaper groans. "You, Louisiana boys are built different."

"Damn right we are," Sparta shoots back with a grin.

That's Sparta. Grew up in the Louisiana swamps, he has a big family, tight-knit, the kind that teaches you early how to survive off the land and take care of your own. Hunting, fishing, making do with whatever's in front of you. Tough as hell. Doesn't complain. Doesn't quit. And when it comes to the mission? He's the one mapping it out before the rest of us even realize there's a problem. Ops, planning, intel coordination, he sees the angles, the movement, how everything fits together.

This jungle? It's just another version of home to him. Sarah finally catches onto their reactions and loses it. Her laughter spills out, bright and uncontrollable, and before I know it she's shifting right into my lap like it's the most natural thing in the world. Her body bounces and presses against mine as she laughs. That doesn't go unnoticed. At all. I go still for half a second. Then adjust my grip, sliding a hand to her thigh to steady her, pressing her into my now hard cock, before she realizes exactly what she's doing. The moment she stills I feel it, the shift. The awareness. She turns her head just slightly, eyes meeting mine, cheeks flushed.

I smirk. I lean in and brush my lips just behind her ear. "Eat your dinner, Mouse," I murmur low enough that only she hears it.

Her breath catches. She doesn't argue. Just turns back to her plate a little too quickly, suddenly very focused on her food. Across the fire, Stitches narrows his eyes slightly.

"Everything good over there, Sarge?"

I don't even blink. "Just fine," I reply easily. "Eat up. Armadillo's good for you. Builds character."

Reaper snorts. "I've got enough character, thanks."

The rest of the meal settles after that. Mostly quiet. A few jokes. A lot of side-eye from Reaper toward his plate. And Sarah? She's still smiling to herself. When she finally stands to help Paya clean up, there's still a softness in her expression. And I track her the whole way as she goes. Like I always do.

"Anything to report from today?" I ask the group.

"No, nothing of interest," Magellan answers.

"Alright. Meeting at 0500."

They all nod, going back to their food. Except Sparta, he's already nearly done, eating like the jungle might run out of meat tomorrow. Swamp boy through and through. As the night settles in, I move off toward Willis while the others stay near the fires.

"Did you talk to Benjamin or Jenna today?" I ask, keeping my voice low.

Willis exhales, rubbing the back of his neck. "Yeah. Jenna's conversation was... surprising. She admitted Benjamin had been overly friendly, flirty but she thought if she confronted Sarah, it would make him notice her." He shakes his head slightly. "Said she realized afterward how stupid that was. She seemed genuinely sorry."

"And Benjamin?"

"A very different conversation," Willis says, his tone tightening. "He deflected everything. Blamed Sarah. Blamed Jenna. Claimed Sarah had always wanted him, even said they had a 'thing' after the last field school."

My jaw tightens. "Yeah. That tracks."

"I didn't buy it," Willis continues, "but it's concerning."

"Sounds delusional," I mutter.

"I'll keep an eye on him," he says. "And I'm using out satellite phone and calling this into the university tomorrow. It needs to be documented."

"Good." I nod once, firm. "Appreciate it."

We shake hands, and I turn back toward camp just as Sarah finishes up with Paya. I catch movement in the trees, Ghost slipping into the shadows like he was never there and Glitch drifting closer, keeping his distance but still within range.

It's fully dark now. Firelight flickers across the clearing, shadows stretching long between the huts, moonlight barely cutting through the canopy overhead. Then she's walking toward me. And just like that, everything else fades. I reach for her hand the second she's close enough, threading my fingers through hers like it's instinct.

"Ready to head back to our tent?" I ask. I don't miss the way she blushes, her gaze dropping like she's suddenly very interested in the ground.

"Mhm," she murmurs.

I smirk slightly, leaning just a little closer as we start down the trail. "What are you thinking about?"

She glances over her shoulder, checking how close Glitch is, then looks forward again.

"N-nothing," she stutters. Yeah. Not nothing. I don't push. Not yet. But the way her hand tightens in mine? I've got a pretty damn good idea.

"Sure, nothing. Is that what you call what I did to you last night or this morning?" I ask her knowing she is going to be more embarrassed than she already was. I love teasing her. She gasps in surprise and I chuckle.

"Well, don't stop on my account. What did you do to her?" Glitch asks innocently. Her steps falter but I keep her upright as we walk our way through the darkened path with our flashlights. The canopy is thicker here so the moonlight doesn't get through and the fires are too far away.

"We just played a game together right, Little Mouse?" She doesn't say anything, I feel her footsteps quicken and try to pull her hand away from me. No doubt trying to get away from the conversation.

"Was it a naked Twister? I love that game!" he asks.

"Oh my god! Stop! This is embarrassing." She yells and we both chuckle.

"Okay, okay. I don't need to know what kind of games my Sarge is playing with my new sister," Glitch says, completely unfazed as we reach the clearing before peeling off toward his own tent. I watch him go, a small smirk pulling at my lips. He's come a long way in a few days. Whatever's going on with him and Alex, he's not letting it drag him under and more importantly, the team's accepted her.

That matters. She goes still beside me, looking up at me. "Did he mean that?" she asks quietly. "That I'm his sister?"

"Yeah," I answer without hesitation. "Glitch doesn't say things he doesn't mean. He lost his parents a few years ago, no siblings. None of us really have much left outside the team. Only Sparta and Magellan have families left." My thumb brushes over the back of her hand. "So yeah, they're protective of you."

Her expression softens, something deeper settling behind her eyes, but she doesn't say anything as she starts toward our tent beneath the kapok tree. The moonlight filters just enough through the canopy to illuminate it and she stops cold.

"You did this?" she whispers, turning those wide eyes up at me.

I step in behind her, my hands settling low on her hips, grounding her there. "It's not much," I murmur. "But we needed the space. Didn't realize how much gear you hauled around with you."

She smacks my chest lightly, but she's smiling.

"Thank you," she says, softer now. "I love it." She hesitates, then adds, a little shy, "I didn't really want to sleep anywhere else. Well, I just want to use you for your body heat," she adds quickly.

I huff out a quiet laugh, arching a brow. "That so? That all I'm good for?"

"No," she murmurs, already ducking inside. "There's...other things that are useful too."

I follow her in, zipping the tent behind me. The space is dim, lit only by the faint glow of moonlight bleeding through the fabric. I strip down to my boxers, tossing my clothes aside as she shifts around, changing. I don't miss the way she moves. Don't miss anything about her. Didn't plan on it.

She settles into the sleeping bag, and I slide in right after her, pulling her in until there's no space left between us. Her breath catches. I love how vocal she is, how easily she reacts to my touch. I can't wait to get her home and have real privacy with her.

"Hmm," I murmur, my fingers tracing slowly along her side, just enough to make her aware of every inch of contact. "What other things am I good for?"

She hesitates, and I feel it, the tension, the nerves, the curiosity all wrapped together. I don't rush her. Don't push. But I don't let her pull away either. My hand settles more firmly at her waist, anchoring her there as I dip my head closer, my voice lowering.

"Go on, Mouse," I murmur against her ear. "I'm listening."

She hesitates, then whispers, "Keeping me safe, for one. Keeping me warm. And…I guess you're pretty good at kissing too. And some other things."

"You *guess?*" I let a smirk creep into my voice. "I'll have to keep doing it until you're sure."

Her breath hitches just as my lips brush over hers. I reach down, unzipping the sleeping bag a little, giving us more space, before rolling her onto her back. I slide over her, pinning her softly beneath me. Her hips move against my thigh, searching for the friction she's beginning to crave.

I grip her hip with one hand, stilling her. "Uh-uh, Little Mouse," I murmur, my lips trailing down her neck. "I'm in control here. Lay back and enjoy."

She shivers beneath me, her fingers sliding up my arms, clutching at my biceps. I let my hand skim down, teasing the inside of her thigh before running a single, lazy finger over the damp heat between her legs. She whimpers, arching into my touch, but I keep my pace slow, just enough to drive her crazy.

"Wade," she gasps, gripping my shoulders, her nails biting into my skin.

Her reaction sends a sharp bolt of heat straight to my core. I trace slow, deliberate circles against her slick folds, feeling her body open to me. When I finally slide a finger inside her, she lets out a strangled moan.

"Shh," I remind her, pressing my forehead to hers. "Gotta be quiet, beautiful."

Her breathing stutters and I can feel the way her body tightens around me, how close she already is. I keep my rhythm steady, pushing her higher, watching the pleasure wash over her. She bites onto my shoulder as she comes, muffling her cries. Her body is shaking underneath me in pleasure, her tight little pussy is squeezing my finger and I can't wait to feel that around my cock again.

I groan, slowly pulling my hand away, pressing a kiss to her temple. My lips linger there, feeling the warmth of her skin, the way her pulse flutters beneath my mouth. I can still hear her ragged breaths, feel the way she clings to me, her fingers curled into my shoulders like I'm the only thing anchoring her to the moment.

"You're so beautiful," I whisper, my lips brushing over her damp skin. She doesn't answer right away. Instead, she exhales a shaky breath, her body melting into mine, pliant and warm.

"Mmm thank you," she finally manages, her voice breathless and soft.

I grin against her skin, trailing my fingers along her stomach, tracing lazy circles as I pull myself up to settle between her already open thighs, an invitation I don't take lightly. I take my time, letting my palm glide up her smooth stomach, feeling the steady rhythm of her heartbeat beneath my touch. I slowly grab and squeeze her perfect tits. Her hard nipples pressing against my palm. I lean down and lick over one nipple and then the other. Her body, rises searching for more. I don't rush, I don't take, I savor every bit of her.

She shifts slightly, pressing her soaking wet core against my cock. My body tenses, the heat of her nearly undoing me. But this time isn't about rushing. I want her to feel *everything*. I dip my head, pressing a kiss just above her heart, feeling the way it thunders beneath my lips. Slowly, I move upward, brushing my lips against the curve of her collarbone, her jaw, the sensitive spot behind her ear that always makes her shiver.

"Wade," she whispers, her voice barely more than a breath.

I don't hesitate. Grabbing her thighs I bring them up and around my hips. I sink into her, slow and deep, reveling in the way she gasps softly, her fingers threading into my hair, pulling me closer. Her body welcomes me, gripping me with a heat so intense I swear I could lose myself in her forever. I move gently, my thrusts unhurried, my hands cradling her face, my forehead resting against hers. I want her to see me, feel me, know that this is more than just heat. More than just a moment.

This is *us*. Her eyes flutter open, locking onto mine and in that instant, I know. I know I'll never want another woman like I want her. I know she's already inside me, buried deep in a place I didn't think I'd ever let anyone reach.

I start moving a little faster, her legs lock behind me, trying to keep me deep. I pull higher onto my knees, my hands slide against her waist. Just as I pull back, enough to just leave the tip inside her, I grip her harder and slam her against me. The sound she makes is somewhere between a muffled scream and a squeal. I press my hand against her mouth.

"Mouse, I know it feels good but you have to be quiet." I say softly into her ear. "Bite me again if you need to." She nods under my hand so I remove it. I can't wait to explore more with her, but we are limited in this tight cramped tent. I want to hear her scream my name without worrying of others hearing us.

I keep tunneling into her tight little cunt. she starts spasming, around me. Threatening to lock me inside her, I could live like this, forever. My balls are drawing up and that familiar tingle is starting up my spine, I won't be able to hold out any longer.

"Fuck, you feel so good. I want you to come for me. Let me feel you squeeze my cock, Little Mouse." I say quietly into her ear. Her nails dig into my back and she locks her legs tighter against me. I have to fight against her hold to keep pounding against her. She finally lets go, her pussy getting even tighter and I moan at the sensation. I slam into her once, twice and let go. Coming deep inside her, claiming her as mine. Pressing my lips to hers like a vow. A vow that I'm hers and she will be mine.

Before I let myself sleep, I make sure I'm ready. Throwing my pants on, weapon within arm's reach. If something happens, I need to be moving before she even wakes up. I should probably have her put her pajamas on, too. Selfishly, I want to feel her body.

Chapter Fifteen

Sarah

I wake to soft kisses pressed along my cheek and forehead, barely there but enough to stir me from sleep. The tent is still dark, early morning light not yet breaking through the canopy. I roll onto my side, burrowing deeper into the sleeping bag, chasing what's left of the warmth of him. Wade's voice brushes against my ear, low and warm. He has to meet the guys. I grumble something unintelligible, swatting lazily in his direction.

A quiet chuckle. Another kiss against my temple. "I'll be back soon." The soft rustle of fabric follows, boots, gear, movement I'm already used to and it fades into the background as sleep pulls me under again before he even leaves.

When I wake again, the light has changed. The sun is higher in the sky, making everything bright, too bright for the early morning. It's harsh to my eyes that are trying to adjust from sleep. The sun filters through the tent walls, turning everything a muted gold. I stretch slowly, muscles protesting, a dull soreness settling deep in my body.

Heat floods my face as memory catches up. My shirt is on. My panties too. I frown slightly, trying to piece it together. I don't remember getting dressed. Did he…? The thought sends a strange mix of warmth and embarrassment through me and I quickly shove it aside. Focus. I change into clean clothes, grab my camera and notebook, and step outside. The heat hits immediately.

The clearing is too quiet. My eyes scan automatically, tents open, empty. Wade's gone. The others too. Dr. Willis's tent is still standing. Jenna's. Benjamin's. Everything looks normal but something feels wrong. A tightness settles in my chest. I hesitate, just for a second. Then I move. Skipping getting cleaned at the waterfall, I head straight for the trail, quickening my pace, camera and notebook clutched tightly in my hands. The jungle hums around me all of the birds, insects and distant movement are still going strong. Only it feels different now, everything is more intense and amplified.

I don't hear him coming. An arm snakes around my waist, yanking me backward so hard my feet leave the ground. A hand clamps over my mouth, cutting off the scream before it can fully form. My camera and notebook slip from my hands, hitting the forest floor with a dull, final thud. Panic detonates in my chest.

I thrash, twist, claw—anything but the grip on me is iron. Unyielding. My movements feel slow, weak, useless. I can't get free. The world tilts. Then I'm airborne. I hit the ground hard, pain exploding through my spine as I land on my backside. My head snaps back, teeth clacking together, breath ripping out of my lungs in a sharp, broken gasp.

For a second, I can't breathe. Can't think. I scramble, palms slipping in dirt and leaves as I try to push myself up, heart slamming so hard it feels like it's going to break through my ribs. Then I see him. Benjamin. He's standing over me, blocking out the light, his face twisted into something I don't recognize anymore. Not the cocky smirk. Not the annoyance. Something worse. Something wrong. His eyes gleam, completely wide, unhinged and excited?

"You're mine, Sarah," he sneers, voice thick with something that makes my stomach turn. My blood runs cold. His hand moves, slow and deliberate, reaching behind his waistband.

A gun. The world narrows to the black metal in his hand.

"If I can't have you…" he continues, tilting his head slightly, like he's enjoying this. My pulse roars in my ears, drowning everything else out. "…then no one can." The words slam into me. Final. Real. My chest seizes, panic clawing its way up my throat, sharp and suffocating.

I drag in a breath and the scream tears loose.

"Sarah—Sarah—Mouse." I bolt upright, a broken gasp tearing from my chest, the scream still lodged somewhere in my throat.

Wade's hands are on me instantly. Firm and holding me tight. "It's okay," he says, voice steady but urgent as he pulls me into him. "You're safe. Breathe."

Air won't come at first. My chest heaves, lungs burning as I try to drag in a full breath and can't. I'm back in the tent. Back in his arms. It was a dream, it wasn't real. The sleeping bag is wrapped around me, his body warm and solid behind mine, his chin resting against my shoulder as he holds me close.

"It was a nightmare," he murmurs, his hand moving in slow, steady circles along my back. "Just breathe, beautiful."

I focus on that. On him. The rise and fall of his chest. The heat of his body. The familiar scent of sun-warmed wood and fabric and something that is just Wade. Safe. My breathing starts to even out, each inhale coming a little easier than the last. The tears are building in my eyes, they are threatening to spill over. The tent is dim, early morning light just beginning to filter through the canvas, soft shadows shifting along the walls.

Wade's uniform brushes against my bare skin. The material is rough and solid, a quiet reminder that he came back. That he's here. "Are you okay?" he asks softly.

I nod, swallowing hard, still too shaken to trust my voice. His hand moves to my chin, tilting my face toward his. His lips gently brush mine, before he presses a kiss to my forehead.

"Do you want to tell me about it?"

I shake my head quickly. My throat feels tight, raw, the words too tangled to even try. "Later," I manage, voice hoarse. "Not here. Not now."

He studies me for a beat, something sharp flickering behind his eyes, before he nods. "Okay. Later."

He doesn't push. Just holds me tighter. I stay like that for a while, wrapped up in him, letting the last of the panic bleed out of my body. My muscles slowly loosen, my heartbeat finally settling into something normal. But the memory lingers. It felt way too real, too close for my liking.

Eventually, I pull myself together, dressing quickly and gathering my things. When we step outside, the morning has fully broken. The others are already up, gathered near the large tent, mugs in hand. Their eyes flick toward us, toward me, concern written plainly across their faces. Every single one of them. Wade's hand finds mine again, steady and sure, as we walk over. Someone presses a mug into my hands.

"Thanks," I murmur, wrapping my fingers around it, letting the heat seep into my skin, chasing away the last of the chill. Their conversations have gone quiet, mugs paused halfway to their mouths, eyes tracking me in a way that makes my skin prickle, not with fear but with awareness. It feels like I am under a microscope.

Glitch is the first to move. "You good?" he asks, stepping closer, his tone lighter than his eyes.

I nod, even though I'm not entirely sure it's true. "Yeah. Just… a nightmare."

His jaw tightens slightly, but he doesn't push. Reaper shifts behind him, arms crossed, scanning the tree line instead of me. Sparta mutters something under his breath, already moving to check the perimeter like it's second nature. Stitches watches me a second longer than the others, calm but assessing, like he's checking for something deeper.

They're not just looking at me. They're adjusting. Wade's hand tightens around mine.

"I'm taking her to clean up," he says, voice leaving no room for argument. No one questions it.

Glitch just nods once. "We've got it here."

Wade doesn't respond. He just turns, guiding me back towards our tent. He grabs our soaps, I stand there watching him rifling through the bag, my heart is still pounding and the tears are still forming.

"Let's go get cleaned up," he says softly, grabbing my hand again. But when he gestures toward the path, my stomach knots instantly. The thought of being alone, or even going down a path, even for a minute sends a ripple of unease through me.

"I don't want to be alone," I whisper.

His jaw tightens. I see his throat move as he swallows, his eyes dropping to mine, his normally golden-brown gaze now dark, unreadable. Then he nods once. "I'm not leaving you alone. I promise."

Relief floods through me so fast it almost makes me dizzy. I can still feel their eyes on me as we leave. Not intrusive. Protective. The jungle swallows us quickly, the sounds of the camp fading behind us until it's just the hum of insects and distant calls overhead.

Wade doesn't say anything at first. He just keeps walking. His hand never leaves mine. It's warm and steady. Grounding in a way I really needed. My fingers tighten around his without thinking. The path feels different now. Narrower. Darker. Like I'm seeing it for the first time, not as part of my research, but as something unpredictable. Something that could hide things I don't understand.

Wade's thumb brushes once over the back of my hand. A silent reassurance. "I've got you," he murmurs, barely above a whisper. For now, that's enough to keep me moving forward. Something heavier.

I glance around one more time before slowly pulling my clothes off. He does the same, his gaze steady, quiet, watching without saying a word. The air between us shifts, it's more charged, different than before. Not just heat. He grabs the soap and leads me toward the rock outcropping. The same place as yesterday.

When we reach it, he sets everything aside, then turns back to me and lifts me easily, like it's nothing. My legs wrap around his waist automatically, my arms sliding around his shoulders. And just like that, I feel better. In his arms I feel safer. My forehead presses lightly against his as I breathe him in, trying to shake the lingering fear.

"Can you tell me about your nightmare now?" he asks gently.

I nod, trying to steady myself, pulling in a slow breath that doesn't quite fill my lungs. The fear is still there, humming just beneath my skin.

"It started with me waking up alone," I say quietly. "In the tent. You were gone... all of you were gone. Even Dr. Willis, Benjamin, Jenna... it was like I'd slept through everything." His grip tightens slightly around me, not enough to hurt, just enough to anchor me. Reminding me he's right there.

"I was rushing," I continue. "Trying to get to work. I was walking down the path to the shabono and then..." My voice falters. "Someone grabbed me." His arms lock around me instantly.

I swallow hard. "He threw me to the ground. And he said... 'if he couldn't have me, then no one could.'"

My breath stutters. "He had a gun." The words barely make it out before the tears spill over. Wade's hands come up immediately, brushing them away, his lips pressing to my cheek, then my forehead. Soft gently kisses that keep me steady and grounded.

"I know it sounds irrational," I whisper, my voice breaking. "It was just a dream. But it felt so real. I couldn't move... I couldn't fight back.

I felt weak. Like I had no control." The words come faster now, tumbling out between shaky breaths, the tears falling harder the more I try to hold them back.

"If something ever did happen, I want to know how to get out. I don't think I can walk down that path alone right now." I hesitate, my voice softening. "Does that make me crazy?"

His grip tightens slightly at my back. "No," he says firmly. "Not even a little." His gaze holds mine, steady, grounding. "Sometimes your instincts pick up on things before your mind catches up. Doesn't mean you're wrong."

My stomach twists at that. Because I know he's right.

"There was more I needed to tell you yesterday," he continues, voice lower now. "After… everything, I didn't want to ruin the moment. I wanted you to fall asleep peacefully in my arms."

My heart stumbles at his words, but the unease settles right back in. Before I can stop myself, the question slips out. "Could he get a gun?"

His expression hardens instantly. "Benjamin?" I only nod. "No," he says. "Our rifles are locked down when we're not using them. Sidearms stay on us. No exceptions."

I nod, exhaling slowly. That helps. A little. But not enough. "What did you need to tell me?" I ask, quieter now.

"Well, first," he says, his tone shifting slightly, more controlled, "there's been a border breach. Militia groups pushed through." My stomach drops. "But we're far enough south that we should be okay," he adds quickly. "If that changes, you'll know immediately."

I nod, trying to absorb that without spiraling. "Next—Willis talked to Jenna and Benjamin."

My attention snaps back to him. "Jenna admitted she handled things badly. Said she was embarrassed. According to Willis, nothing's happened between her and Benjamin but the way he talks about you made it sound like there was."

I let out a small, disbelieving breath. Of course he did.

"She regrets how she treated you," Wade continues. "Willis wants to extend the same protection to her that we're giving you."

That makes me pause. Jenna regrets it? I don't understand her. The jealousy, the attitude, it doesn't make sense. I never gave Benjamin any reason to think I wanted him. If anything, I've done everything I could to stay away from him.

"I don't know," I say slowly. "I guess, I'd rather be safe than sorry. She did seem different yesterday morning. Nicer." I hesitate. "Does

Willis know about the tracker?"

The question feels heavier now. More real. I hate that. Hate that I'm even thinking like this, like I need protection, like something might actually happen. This trip was supposed to be exciting. Important. The final step toward everything I've worked for. I don't want fear to take that away.

"No," Wade says. "And I want to keep it that way. The fewer people who know, the better." That makes sense, I think. "I'll have the guys keep an eye on her," he continues. "If we think it's necessary, we'll put one on her too. But right now, he's focused on you."

A chill slides down my spine. "Now Benjamin..." Wade's jaw tightens slightly. "That conversation went exactly how you'd expect. He blamed you. Blamed Jenna. Said again that the two of you had something after the last field school."

My heart starts racing. I shake my head immediately. "That's not true. I've never—"

"Hey." His hand presses more firmly against my back. "Calm down, Mouse. I know. I believe you." I try to steady my breathing, but the anger is still there, hot and sharp in my chest.

"Ghost dug deeper," he adds. "Didn't find much more. Nothing tying Willis to him. Grades are clean. No shared classes. On paper, he looks solid." Of course he does.

"Yes," I say quietly. "He is. He's always been smart. Helps the undergrads, tutors, brags about his grades like it's his entire personality." Which somehow makes all of this even more annoying.

"Okay," he says quietly, his tone shifting again. "Now for the harder part."

I let out a small, humorless breath. "Harder? As if this hasn't already been?"

He huffs softly, attempting to run his fingers through my tangled hair. They catch almost immediately, and he gives up with a quiet exhale, his hand sliding down to my lower back instead. His thumb starts tracing slow, steady circles against my skin.

"In your dream," he continues, voice low, measured, "you said you were dragged from the path leading to the shabono." My stomach drops. I don't like where this is heading.

"Glitch found something yesterday. A narrow trail that's hidden. About halfway between the shabono and our clearing." His jaw tightens. "He followed it." I already know what he's going to say.

"It leads straight to our tents." My breath stutters. How—how did I know that?

My chest tightens, panic clawing its way up again. "I can't—" I shake my head, struggling to breathe. "How did I dream that? Wade, how—"

"Hey." His hand presses more firmly against my back. "Breathe. You're safe." I try. God, I try. It's like trying to breathe underwater. His hands rub circles on my back. "In through your nose. Do it now." He commands and I do. "Out through your mouth." I slowly release my breath. "Again, this time hold it for three seconds and release it slowly." I do it again and the breathing comes easier.

"We're aware of it now," he continues, steady and calm. "We've already adjusted. You won't be alone. Not out here. Not for a second."

The words help a little. "I feel safe with you," I admit quietly. "But what about when I go back to school?" My voice wavers. "You won't be there then. What am I supposed to do?"

The fear creeps back in, quieter this time but deeper. "I will be," he says without hesitation.

I blink up at him. "What?"

"I'll be with you. I finish this mission, do my debrief and I'm done." His gaze locks onto mine. "I'm retiring."

That wasn't what I expected. "At my school?" I let out a small, incredulous laugh. "Won't that be a little obvious? A big, intimidating military guy just following me around everywhere?" A memory clicks into place. "Wait—Hazel mentioned something about someone retiring who'd be around..." I shake my head, smiling faintly despite everything. "I was picturing someone old. Like gray hair, slow walk, maybe a cane."

His hand comes down with a light pinch to my hip, making me jump. "I am not old," he mutters. "I'll be thirty-two in September." I bite back a smile. "And I am trained to blend in and I wouldn't be 'military' anymore," he adds, quieter now. "I'd just be your boyfriend." My breath catches slightly. "If not more."

I don't respond. I can't. Because the way he says it—like it's already decided. Like it's inevitable. I look away, focusing on the water, the rocks, anything but him. What does more mean to him?

"A really tall, ridiculously built boyfriend following me around campus," I mumble instead, deflecting. "That won't draw attention at all."

But my mind is already spinning. This is fast. Too fast? And yet, a small, dangerous part of me knows exactly how easily I could fall for him. I just don't know if I should.

Sam would tell me to take my time. This is my first real relationship, there's no rush. Just be open to the feelings, let things happen naturally. She's always been like that. Steady. Protective in a quiet, grounding way. The typical older sister, always watching out for me.

Fallon? Fallon would roll her eyes and tell me men are idiots. Take what he offers, enjoy it while it lasts, then walk away before it gets messy. But she's been through things. Things she doesn't talk about much, but I've seen the aftermath. The walls. The way she shuts down anytime anything gets too close to real. She doesn't trust men. Not anymore. And no one could blame her for that.

Sam's advice is probably the smarter choice. But out here...out here, everything feels different. Stronger. There are no distractions, no noise, no normal life to pull me back. Just the jungle, the work and him. It feels like we're in a very intimate bubble. And I don't know what happens when that bubble bursts.

"Sounds good to me," Wade says, breaking through my thoughts. "I'll just keep the guys back and stare at your ass while I follow you around." I huff a quiet breath, but it doesn't quite turn into a laugh.

"Okay," he continues, his tone shifting. "There's one more thing." My stomach tightens. When is this going to end? I don't think I can take anymore. "That twig snapping yesterday? That wasn't an animal." His gaze hardens slightly. "It was Benjamin. He followed us. Saw us together."

My heart drops. "I didn't want to alarm you," he adds. "Didn't want to ruin the moment. I didn't want you to be worried, those sounds we heard were him. I saw the flicker of movement before he stepped on a twig. But after this morning, we need to be more careful of your surroundings." The words settle heavy.

"Did he see me?" I ask quietly. "Naked, I mean?"

"No." His voice is firm. "I had you covered, my body covered your front and the rocks hid the rest. I would never let him see you like that." That helps. A little. But he heard us, heard me, during something I thought was a private moment.

"Alright," he says, like he's closing the subject. "That's everything for now. I'll fill the team in. And your question about my leg, I didn't forget. You fell asleep on me but I promise I'll tell you tonight."

I nod automatically, but my thoughts are already spiraling. He knew. He knew someone was there. How long did he know someone was there? Was it the whole time and he kept going. Why? The question sits heavy in my chest, twisting tighter the more I think about it. I don't say anything. I can't. Because I don't even know what I'd say. I need to keep thinking about this.

So instead, I force a small smile. "Right. Let's go."

I know he'll be with me all day. And that should make me feel safer. It does in a way. His presence steadies me but that persistent uneasy feeling is still there. How can I trust someone to protect me, when I don't fully understand him? Because Wade does understand me. That's the problem. In such a short time, he's learned how to read me better than most people ever have. He knows when I'm anxious before I say a word. When I need space. When I don't.

And yet, did he know I'd be upset about that? Did he realize, in that moment, that I wouldn't like it? That I'd question why he didn't stop? And if he did…why didn't he? I force the thought down, burying it before it can take hold. But something tells me, I won't be able to ignore it for long.

Chapter Sixteen

Sarah

I'm starting to wish this field school was over. Or that we could just pack up and leave. I know I won't. Not when my PhD is riding on this. Not when I worked so hard to get here. I'm not about to let anyone take that from me. Still, the thought lingers longer than it should. As we walk along the path, something moves high in the trees, and I stop short.

"Wait—" Tilting my head back, I scan the canopy until I spot it. A spider monkey. My breath catches. She's perched along a branch, her long, slender limbs draped with effortless balance. Her body is sleek and black, her face pale with dark rings framing her eyes. Curled tightly against her is a baby, smaller, clinging to her as she shifts.

"Oh my God…" I whisper, barely breathing.

I don't move. I don't want to scare her. My hand instinctively goes to my chest, where my camera should be and I deflate instantly. I forgot it. Of course I did. Wade is beside me, completely still, his presence solid but quiet as he watches with me. He doesn't speak, doesn't move, just lets me have the moment.

The monkey notices us. There's a sharp, echoing *whoop whoop* that cuts through the trees, and in one smooth motion, she gathers her baby and swings away, disappearing into the canopy like she was never there. I finally exhale. Then I turn to Wade, a huge smile breaking across my face.

"I can't believe I just saw that," I breathe. Something softens in his expression, and before I can say anything else, he leans down and kisses me. It's deeper than I expect. For a second, everything else fades, the fear, the tension and the constant awareness of what could go wrong. It's just him. Just us.

He pulls back slowly, his eyes searching mine, and I swear I see it there again. That same intensity, that same certainty. My earlier worry is gone, at least for now. He presses one more quick kiss to my lips, then takes my hand and we start walking again. But it doesn't take long for reality to creep back in. My thoughts drift to this morning. To the scream. Heat rushes to my cheeks.

God... how loud was I? Did anyone hear? The embarrassment settles in my chest as we step into the clearing. Most of the guys are already gone. Glitch is still there, along with Stitches and Magellan, looking like they're getting ready to head out with Dr. Willis.

Dr. Willis stands near the coffee, pouring himself a cup. When he looks up and sees us, there's a kind smile on his face. Not pity or concern. Just a normal smile. Relief loosens something tight in my chest. Okay. Maybe no one heard. Or if they did, maybe they're pretending they didn't. Either way, I'll take it.

"How loud were my screams?" I whisper to Wade.

"Not that loud," he says easily. "We were all by the main tent. I got to you quick, so it didn't last long. I don't think anyone else heard." Relief loosens something in my chest. He walks me back to the tent, and I tuck my soap away before grabbing my notebook, trying to shake off the lingering embarrassment.

"Do you want more coffee?" he asks.

I shake my head. "No, I want to get started. I feel like I'm already behind."

He studies me for a second, then nods. "Alright. I'm going to brief the guys. Glitch will go with you, I'll catch up in a bit."

Before I can respond, he leans in, kissing me quickly before heading off. I watch him for a moment as he talks quietly with Glitch. Whatever he says has Glitch's expression tightening for a second before he nods.

Then his face shifts, he looks lighter, easier as he heads my way.

"Ready, Rocky?" he calls, a grin already forming.

I blink. "Rocky?"

"Yeah," he says, stopping in front of me. "You've got a mean right hook. Figured it fits."

I roll my eyes, but I can't quite stop the small smile. "Clearly wasn't that mean, it did more damage to me than it did him."

"Uh-huh," he hums. "Still badass."

"Seriously, my roommate took me to a boxing gym, she insisted I learn to defend myself. I went one time and never went again. I didn't even like hitting a punching bag." He just laughs, like that's the funniest thing he's ever heard.

I grab my bag, shaking my head. "I'm ready. Let's go."

He steps beside me, then casually offers his arm. Not pushy. Just there. I hesitate for half a second before looping mine through his. It helps. More than I want to admit.

"What's your real name?" I ask as we start down the path. "Calling you Glitch feels weird when we're actually talking."

"Jake," he says. "Glitch just stuck. Tech stuff, comms, all that."

"Makes sense," I say. "You definitely give off 'fixes things people break' energy. Or maybe a breaks people, kind of vibe."

He huffs out a quiet laugh. "Yeah, something like that." We walk in comfortable silence for a few steps, the jungle closing in around us. I glance up at him. His sandy-blond hair is just long enough to look slightly tousled, like he ran a hand through it and gave up. Bright blue eyes, sharp but easy. Lean, strong build and more wiry than Wade, but still solid.

Approachable. Safe. The kind of person who makes things feel normal even when nothing is. For a moment, the heat, the bugs and the tension, it all of it fades into the background. And I can't help the small, fleeting thought that slips in. Fallon would like him. He's exactly her type.

He catches me looking and grins. "You checking me out, Rocky?"

"What? No!"

"Mm-hmm," he hums. "It's okay. I won't tell Wraith. I'd prefer to stay alive."

I laugh despite myself. "No. I was wondering if my roommate would like you."

His grin widens instantly. "Is she hot?"

"She is," I say, swatting his arm, "but that's not the point."

"Feels like it should be the point."

I shake my head, still smiling. "You just seem different. Lighter. Compared to when we first got here."

He exhales, the teasing edge softening just a little. "Yeah. I am." He glances ahead, then back at me. "Once I realized I was screwing things up for Wraith and got my head out of my ass, things started looking better."

There's something honest in his tone now. "There's nothing I can do about my situation anyway," he adds with a small shrug. "And clearly, she wasn't the right girl for me."

I hesitate. "What happened? If you don't mind me asking."

He studies me for a second, then huffs out a quiet breath. "We're basically brothers in this unit," he says. "So that makes you my sister now. You can ask me anything."

Something warm settles in my chest at that. "Okay then, Jake," I say softly. "What happened?"

His expression shifts, not fully serious, but the humor dims around the edges. "High school sweetheart. Alex," he says. "We planned on getting married when I got out. She wanted to wait, finish school, let me finish my deployments. We made it work as best we could." He pauses, jaw tightening slightly. "I'd see her on leave. Not often, but enough. She never said it was too much. Never gave me a reason to think anything was wrong. I mean she wasn't happy I was gone so often, but not enough she was thinking she was done. Then the day we shipped out for this op, I got an email." My stomach sinks.

"She found someone else," he says quietly. "Said she couldn't wait anymore. That she deserved more."

I wince. "Jake... I'm so sorry."

He shrugs, but it's tighter this time.

"Did you tell her you're retiring after this?" I ask gently. "Maybe—"

"No." His answer is immediate. Firm.

"If she found someone else, it means she was already looking." His gaze hardens slightly. "That's not something I forgive." There's no anger in his voice. Just certainty. "It's time to move on," he adds. Then his lips curve again, just a little. "I want what Wraith has with you."

My breath catches. "Someone who looks at me the way you look at him."

Heat floods my cheeks instantly, and I shove his shoulder. "Okay, stop." He laughs softly. "I hope you find her," I say, quieter now. "And... I'm honored to be your sister."

That earns me a real smile. "Careful," he says. "That means I get to be overprotective now."

I snort. "Great. Just what I need."

A thought hits me. "Wait, how old are you?"

"Thirty-two," he says with a small smirk. "Enlisted at eighteen. Been gone most of my life." His gaze shifts forward for a moment. "She was the only thing I ever came back for after my parents died."

My chest tightens. "What happened?"

"A drunk driver," he says quietly. "Hit them both. Few years back."

"I'm so sorry," I whisper. "I can't even imagine."

He nods once, his expression steady but distant. "It was hard. Still is." A faint breath leaves him. "They were good parents. I've got a lot of good memories, though."

Something about the way he says it lingers. "Wade says he's coming to Minnesota with me after this," I say. "You should come too. Fresh start. Maybe you'll meet someone there."

He glances at me sideways, amused. "You think Wraith's going to let me tag along while he's busy trying to keep you all to himself?"

I laugh, the tension finally easing out of my shoulders. "Fair point."

"Did he tell you we saw a monkey?!" I practically blurt, the excitement bubbling out before I can stop it.

Jake chuckles, shaking his head. "Nope."

So I tell him everything. The way she looked, the baby clinging to her, how she moved through the trees. By the time I'm done, he's smirking at me.

"What?" I ask, narrowing my eyes. "What's so funny?"

"You," he says easily. "Getting that excited. I've seen them almost every day since we got here."

I stop walking. "What? That's impossible. They're always hiding."

He shrugs. "They hide when they hear people. Movement, noise, anything like that. But when you're trained to stay still, stay quiet and actually observe?" He glances down at me. "You see a lot more than you think."

I punch his arm lightly. "Show-off."

But the moment fades faster than I want it to. Wade's words echo in my head. *Watch your surroundings.* My smile slips. Without thinking, I start scanning the trees. The ground. The path behind us. Jake notices.

He nudges my shoulder gently, pulling my attention back to him. "Hey," he says quieter now. "Don't worry. We've got you."

I nod, but I don't say anything. Because I don't know what to say. I am grateful. More than I can put into words. But I also hate that I need them this much. We reach the shabono and the conversation naturally fades as the sounds of daily life take over.

Jake gestures with his thumb toward a spot off to the side. "I'll be over there."

I nod, watching him peel off toward the edge of the structure. That reminds me, my research. Yesterday's conversation comes flooding back. The wedding. The excitement comes back, softer this time but just as real. Paya and Kaori are getting married soon. And I get to witness it. Be part of it. Document it. It's everything I came here for. I make my way toward Dori, who's seated with several of the men, speaking as they listen intently.

"Bom dia," he greets me.

"Bom dia," I reply with a smile, asking where Paya is.

"She walks with Kaori," he says, gesturing outward before continuing his explanation to the group. I nod, not wanting to interrupt, and settle nearby. For a moment, I just sit and watch. Life unfolds around me in quiet, steady rhythms.

People cleaning up from breakfast. Others picking at small portions of food. Mothers nursing their babies. Children darting in and out of the open space, laughing, chasing each other. I lift my camera and start taking pictures, capturing moments as they happen. Real, unfiltered and beautiful moments of their daily lives. I move slowly through the space, careful not to disrupt anything, documenting what I can. Near the far side, I spot a group of men working with bundles of cotton they harvested earlier. They're spreading it out, hanging it from the upper structure of the shabono to dry.

I take a few more photos. This—this is why I'm here and for a little while, everything else fades into the background. As I circle the shabono, I spot Jake. He's sitting on one of the benches, back against the wooden support, one arm draped loosely over his knee. From a distance, he looks relaxed. But he's not. His gaze is fixed somewhere beyond the structure, watching the kids as they run and play, but there's something distant in his expression. Quiet. Thoughtful. Sad. I lift my camera without thinking.

Click.

The sound is soft but not soft enough. His head turns instantly, eyes locking onto mine. He shakes his head, a faint smirk tugging at his mouth. So much for being sneaky. I lower the camera, smiling to myself as I keep moving. A few minutes later, Paya returns with Kaori.

They greet me, and I nod in return, stepping aside as they separate. Kaori joining Dori with the men while Paya moves back to the women. I follow along, mostly observing. Taking notes. Snapping pictures and helping where I can.

Today I get to work in the gardens, harvesting vegetables and fruit, documenting everything before joining in. The soil is warm beneath my fingers, the air thick and heavy. Hotter than yesterday, much hotter. By midday, sweat is soaking through my clothes, my shirt clinging uncomfortably to my skin. Every time I wipe my forehead, I just manage to smear more dirt across my face.

I'm a mess. I haven't seen Wade since this morning. But Jake hasn't left my side. Even when he gives me space, I can feel him nearby. Watching. Always aware. And every so often, I catch that same look on his face again. Distant. Like part of him is somewhere else.

When we finish in the garden, I turn to Paya. "I'm going to go clean up before dinner."

She nods easily. "Two hours. Then you come back."

I smile. "Okay."

As I step back, my eyes drift to Jake. He's standing off to the side now, scanning the distance again. Not watching me. Not right now. And for a moment, I hesitate. Because I know what Wade said. What Jake said. *Don't go alone.* But the thought of just being by myself for a little while pulls at me harder. I'm exhausted. Physically. Mentally. Constantly watching. Constantly thinking. Constantly wondering what I should say to Wade, if I should say anything at all. I haven't had a single moment alone since I got here. Not one.

Right now, I need it. Just a few minutes. They probably won't even notice. And if they do, I have the tracker. It'll be fine. I tell myself that again as I turn away, slipping through the edge of the shabono and onto the path that leads back toward the tents. Back toward clean clothes and soap. A quiet moment to breathe. Maybe Wade will be there. Maybe I'll figure out what to say.

When I reach the clearing, it's empty. The others must still be out on their research run. I pause for a second, scanning the area, wondering where Wade is but I don't linger on it. I just want to get clean. I duck into my tent, grab my things, and head back out, moving quickly toward the path that leads to the waterfall. A small voice in the back of my mind tells me I should find Wade. Or at least tell someone. But I ignore it. It's fine. Everyone's gone. If Benjamin was around, they would've told me.

I'm halfway down the path when I hear a twig snap behind me. I spin— "Ghost," I gasp, clutching my chest. "You scared me."

He doesn't move. Arms crossed. Expression unreadable.

"Wraith's on his way," he says calmly. "He's not happy you disappeared."

I huff out a breath, trying to brush it off. "I'm fine. Tell him I'll meet him back at the tent when I'm done."

No response. Just those steady, watchful eyes. "Okay…" I gesture to myself, forcing a small, awkward smile. "I'm just going to go get cleaned up."

Still nothing. I turn away, taking a couple steps down the path, but I can feel his eyes on my back. I glance over my shoulder. He hasn't moved. Not even a little. Like he's rooted there. A strange unease settles in my chest, but I push it down and keep walking.

If Wade's on his way, he'll find me. It's not a big deal. I'm safe. I barely make it ten steps. Strong arms wrap around me from behind, and a scream tears out of me before I can stop it.

"Little Mouse," Wade murmurs against my ear, his voice low, controlled, but edged with something sharp.

My heart is still racing as I sag back against him. "You scared me," I say, trying for irritation.

"You scared me," he returns immediately, turning me to face him. "I'm not happy, you put yourself in danger." His hands stay on me. Not letting me pull away. His golden-brown eyes lock onto mine and there's no mistaking it now, relief, yes, but underneath it? He looks angry.

"I told you," he says quietly, voice dropping, "you're not going anywhere alone. It's not safe."

"I just wanted to clean up," I protest, gesturing down at my dirt-streaked clothes.

"I don't care." The words are immediate. Uncompromising. "I'm coming with you." He takes my hand, his grip firm. Final.

"But my hands are gross—"

"Don't care," he repeats, tightening his hold just slightly. Not enough to hurt. Just enough to make it clear, this isn't up for discussion.

"Where have you been today?" I ask, trying to shift the focus off myself.

He doesn't answer. Not right away. We walk the rest of the path in silence, the heat pressing in around us until the sound of the waterfall finally breaks through. The small spring glints in the light, cool and inviting, and all I can think about is stepping into it.

I drop my things near the rocks and turn. Only to find Wade already pulling his shirt off. Before I can say anything, his hands are on me. He turns me to face him, his grip steady as his fingers slide to the hem of my shirt, tugging it free from my pants. My breath catches as he slowly lifts it, and I raise my arms without thinking, letting him pull it over my head.

He still hasn't answered me. That silence, it says more than words ever could. My hands come up, instinctively settling on his arms as he moves behind me, his touch deliberate. When my fingers press against him, a low sound rumbles in his chest. A warning. My pulse jumps, heat curling low in my stomach in a way I can't ignore.

"I just wanted to make sure no one was around," I whisper, my voice softer now, breathless.

His hands still. "I would never let anyone see what's mine." The words are quiet. But absolute. They send a shiver down my spine. I don't argue. Don't bring up what happened yesterday. Because something tells me now is not the moment. His hands move again, guiding, steady, leaving no room for hesitation. The space between us tightens, the air thick with tension that feels ready to snap.

"Take your boots off," he says, his tone low, controlled. I don't question it. Just bend, hands working quickly, my movements clumsy from the way my pulse is racing. By the time I straighten again, he's already stepping out of the rest of his gear, his focus never leaving me.

For a second, we just stand there. Looking at each other. The world feels smaller. Closer. Like everything outside this moment has disappeared. I take a step forward and before I can even reach him, he moves. Strong arms wrap around me, lifting me effortlessly off my feet. A startled laugh escapes me as I grab onto his shoulders, the sudden shift stealing the breath from my lungs.

"Wade—!" The cold water hits my skin in a rush, sharp and shocking as he carries us straight into the spring. I gasp as we're submerged, the world going quiet for a split second. Then we're back up again, water cascading around us.

His hand comes down as he slaps my ass. The sound is loud, echoing off the water. "Wade!" I yelp.

"I think I need to punish you, Mouse. You're not taking your safety seriously. It's time I teach you a lesson."

"Wh—what?" I whimper. His hand is caressing over my butt as he walks us deeper into the water.

"Mmm, I told you. You. Are. Mine. You put yourself in danger today. You scared me and my team when you put yourself at risk. You need to know, I take your safety and well being very seriously." He growls. My insides turn molten at the sound of his voice.

Then his hand comes down of my ass again, a little sharper than before. The sound is harsher than what it feels but I still jump in his arms. The feeling adds fuel to the fire. My pussy clenches and wetness pools. Why is this is so hot? I should be scared but I want to be his.

I barely have time to catch my breath before he's there. Kissing me. Deep and demanding. Like he's been holding back and finally decided he's done waiting. And just like that, everything else fades away again.

Chapter Seventeen

Wade

I pull back from our kiss, letting her body slide down mine so we're eye level. She slowly opens her eyes and I can see the bright blue shining through over the grey in her eyes. Her pupils are blown wide, she's enjoying this. The water running down her face makes her more ethereal as if she's glowing.

She is so beautiful, I can't help but to slide my fingers through her wet hair pulling it from her face. Wanting nothing more than to wrap it around my hand as I plunge into her. Or better yet, as I guide my cock through her pretty lips. Her lips swollen from my kiss and slightly parted, looks perfect for sliding my cock into. I just keep looking at her as her breathing returns to normal.

The brightness in her eyes was the same as this morning when she saw those monkeys. Pure excitement, unfiltered and radiant. It was a look I wanted to see more of, something that made her seem lighter, untouched by everything weighing us down. When I finished going over reports with the guys, I decided we needed a new call. Something distinct, something *ours*. We practiced making the *whoop whoop* and the answering call, fine-tuning it until it was second nature.

I caught Sarah watching, when she, Glitch and Paya walked through the area. Her lips twitching in amusement as she listened to a bunch of grown men mimicking a damn spider monkey. But I didn't care. If it kept us safe, if it reassured her even a little, then it was worth it.

I set her on the rock outcropping, spreading her thighs wide open so I can fit my shoulders in between them. Her hands are gripping my shoulders, holding herself steady.

"Now, you willingly put yourself in danger. What should we do about that?" I ask her.

"Talk it out?" She says innocently and I smile a wicked smirk.

"Oh, Mouse. My precious girl. I won't hurt you, I'll never hurt you. However, you will feel everything I do to you and when you finally let go. When you finally come, it's going to be overwhelming and I'll be here to catch you. Are you ready?" Her breathing is labored, I can see she is nervous but also excited.

I start with a slow lick over her slit, she's wet with water and her sweet juices. She moans a delicious, sweet moan for me, her eyes closing. I give her one more swipe of my tongue and when she relaxed, I gave her a light tap on her thigh. Her eyes fly open in shock and I smile.

"I told you I was going to punish you, Beautiful. Don't think I'm just going to eat your tasty pussy and let you orgasm. Not right away."

Her mouth forms a perfect O in surprise. She's going to be so much fun. "Just relax, I'll take care of you." She gives me a jerky nod and keeps her eyes on me. I go to lick her again, keeping my eyes on hers but stop, turning my face to bite the inside of her thigh and she yelps. I bite her other thigh and she moans, tangling her fingers into my hair.

I lick over slit, going deeper and pressing against her swollen nub. I spread her thighs wider and start licking further down, dipping my tongue into her tight little hole. She gasps, trying to close her thighs but I hold them open. I lick over her again and she starts to relax again. I slap her thigh again but this time she keeps her eyes closed and just moans. Lost to the sensations, she starts to lay back against the rocks.

I slap her other thigh and enjoy her sweet moans. I go back to eating her out and slip my tongue back into her puckered hole. "Oh, Wade."

"Mm, you're amazing." I slide my finger over her soaking wet core, gently rubbing up and down over her. She's so sweat, her pussy lips are glistening. I slap over her pussy, just as she gasps, I insert two fingers into her tight cunt. She's gushing already, her slick juices sliding out of her body. She spasms just as I reach up and angle towards her G spot. She tries to close her thighs again but I stop her. I bite her clit and she gushes for me again, I think she likes a little bit of pain with her pleasure.

I slide my fingers out of her and she cries in displeasure at the loss but I slide them lower, pressing against her ass. My mouth descends onto her pussy again, I suck on her clit and start licking her. Distracting her from my finger pressing against her puckered hole. Gently pressing in only a fraction. When I finally get past the tight ring of muscle she relaxes and I can slip in all the way. I keep going slow, in and out, not wanting to overwhelm her. I bite at her clit and slip my tongue slides into her pussy. Fuck, she tastes so good.

Her whole body starts tightening and her legs start to shake. I latch back onto her clit, while my finger keeps sliding in and out. As soon as I bite her clit, she comes. Screaming out her orgasm and she squirts all over my face. My dick has never been so fucking hard, but with what little brain cells I have I use my other hand to clamp over her mouth again. Her come is sliding down my chin and I can't help the smile as I clean her up with my tongue.

"Fuck, you're delicious. My new favorite meal." I rub my chin against her thigh and bite it again as I slowly slip my finger out.

"How was that?" I ask her. She's laid back against the rocks just breathing with her eyes closed.

"Mmm. Mhm." Is all she gets out. I pick her up and slide her back down into the water. I start kissing her neck and her face as she comes down. When she finally opens her eyes, I smile.

"We're not done yet. Your punishment isn't over. I need you to take your safety seriously." I whisper. I don't even give her a chance to respond, I turn her around, pressing her upper body up against the rocks. I use my arm under her body to protect her delicate skin from the harsh rocks. I line my cock against her slick pussy

I'm so fucking hard, I'm ready to blow any second. I won't last like this. I slide out slowly and slam back into her. She's using one of her hands to muffle her moans and the other is bracing against the rocks. My other hand is gripping her waist and I keep slamming back into her. My cock is hitting the back of her, I wish my other hand was free to keep spanking her. I settle for a quick fuck, because that's all I can do right now. My balls are already drawing up.

"Damn it. Sarah, I need you to come with me."

"Mhm." She moans behind her hand.

"Now, beautiful. Come with me." I groan out. Her pussy is

tightening over me, threatening to keep me inside her. When she finally lets go she starts moaning and spasming over my cock, my eyes roll back as I let go. Trying to drag in breath as I release everything I have inside her. I rest my head against her back and I regain my breath.

"Fuck, you did so good." She's completely pliant in my arms. I guide her back against the smooth rock, turning her toward me and pulling her in, holding her close. Her body melts into mine, her breathing slow and heavy as she relaxes. Exhausted. It's already been a long day.

My hand moves through her damp hair, smoothing it back gently. "You were amazing," I murmur. "You did so good."

"So good..." she mumbles, barely awake. I press a kiss to her temple, something softer than what came before. "Let's get you cleaned up." I grab the soap and bring her with me into the shallower water, keeping one arm around her as I steady her. She washes her face while I help rinse the rest of her off, my touch slower now, more careful. Giving her comfort. Her body is still sensitive, I can feel it in the way she reacts, the way she leans into me without thinking. I keep my hands gentle, not pushing, just there.

"You're amazing, beautiful," I say quietly, brushing a wet strand of hair from her face. "I'll never get enough of you."

Her fingers trace faint patterns along my back, light and absentminded, there's something real in her eyes when she looks at me. I kiss her again, slow this time, just holding onto the moment. I don't know what this is. Don't know where it's going. But I know one thing, she's mine.

"Come on," I say after a minute. "Let's head back." I guide her out of the water, keeping a steady hand on her as we move toward our clothes. She's slower now, every step deliberate, her body still catching up. The sun is high, heat pressing down on us, making me wish we could stay in that water just a little longer. I help her get dressed, keeping things simple, quick.

"Do you need me to carry you?" I ask.

She considers it, then shakes her head. "I can walk. I'm just... tired."

"It's been a long day," I tell her. "And after everything we just did, it can take a lot out of you. That's normal." My hand brushes her arm. "You can rest before dinner." She nods. I take her hand once we're ready and lead her back toward camp.

"You were so angry," she says quietly when we're almost there. She hasn't looked at me much on the walk back. Too busy watching everything around us. Good, I hope this means she's paying attention more.

"I was," I admit. "But I was more scared." That gets her to glance up at me.

"I never want to hear that you're missing again," I continue, my tone firm but steady. "I'm sorry if I scared you but you need to understand something." I stop walking, making sure she's looking at me. "I'm serious about your safety. I need you to take that seriously too."

She studies me for a second, then nods slightly. "I wasn't scared," she says softly. "I know I barely know you but I know you wouldn't hurt me." The words are quiet. More of the tension in my body, that's been there since I heard Glitch as if anyone has seen her loosens. She trusts me, and I'll be damned before I ever break that.

"You're right," I murmur, my voice lower now. "I will never hurt you." I press a kiss to the side of her head. "Only take care of you." We keep walking, the jungle humming around us, but my mind is somewhere else entirely. Today, after everything that's happened. Everything that could have happened.

"Why did you leave without telling anyone?" It comes out harder than I intend. But I don't take it back. She needs to understand.

Sarah's eyes widen, and I watch her scramble. "I—I thought it was safe," she says quickly. "I just needed a moment to myself." That hits harder than it should, because she doesn't get it. She can't. She hasn't seen what I've seen. Doesn't know what I read this morning.

"It's not safe," I say, my voice firm, leaving no room for argument. "That tracker?" I shake my head slightly. "That's a last resort. If we're using it, something's already gone wrong." I drag a hand through my damp hair, forcing myself to stay controlled. "I can't let that happen to you, Sarah."

Her expression softens instantly, guilt flashing across her face. "I'm sorry," she whispers. "I didn't mean to worry anyone. I just needed a little space. I hate feeling so jumpy all the time. So reliant on other people."

I exhale, some of the tension bleeding out of me. "I get it," I say, quieter now. "I do. But you're not just here for school anymore. Things changed. As for being reliant, I want you to come to me when you need or want anything. You don't need to feel like a burden, I want to take care of you." My hand tightens slightly around hers. "Next time, you tell me. I'll come with you." She nods.

We fall into silence again, but it's heavier now. Not uncomfortable, just full. I can feel her thinking. Her mind is spinning, trying to make sense of everything. Then I hear her small, quiet sigh. It puts me on edge instantly.

"Where were you earlier?" she asks. I glance at her, then forward again, my jaw tightening.

"With the guys," I say. "We were working on contingency plans." Because after what Ghost found? We don't get to take chances anymore.

"Glitch was keeping an eye on you," I add. "He said you weren't going far. Just harvesting nearby." That should've been enough. Should have been safe. I hear it again in my head. Clear as if it just happened. *'Anyone seen Sarah?'* Glitch's voice. Tight. Wrong My stomach drops all over again. The silence that followed was worse than anything. No one answered. Not right away. And in that split second, everything went to hell. Worst-case scenarios hit fast and hard. How long had she been gone? How far could someone have taken her? How the hell did we miss it?

We were moving before anyone even responded. Our training kicking in on instinct. I was already on my feet, heart pounding, adrenaline spiking so hard it felt like my chest might crack open. Ghost was beside me without a word. We didn't need one. We were already moving. I met Glitch halfway down the path, his face tight, eyes scanning like he was ready to tear the jungle apart. Just like me. My fists were clenched, my whole body wired, ready to burn the entire forest down if that's what it took to find her.

Then Ghost's voice cuts through the comms, quiet and steady. "Found her. She's heading to the spring."

Relief hits fast and hard, but it doesn't just wipe out the fear. Not even close. What the fuck is she doing out there alone?

"On my way," I say, already turning, changing direction without breaking stride.

I pass Sparta and Reaper on the way, jerking my chin toward camp. "Get some rest."

They don't argue. Glitch's standing a few yards off, tension written all over him. His jaw's tight, posture rigid. He looks like he wants to say something but he doesn't. He knows he fucked up. What he doesn't know is how bad this could've been. What we just uncovered.

When I reach Ghost, I keep it short. "Fill him in." He nods once, gives a lazy salute, and disappears back into the trees like he was never there.

Then it's just me. The pounding in my ears went quiet. All I can hear is the distant rhythm of her footsteps. I slow down. Just enough. Even though I shouldn't, I'm going to surprise her. I'm going to explain just how much danger she put herself in, how much she scared me. Maybe not everything, I damn sure don't want to lie to her. But the truth? The truth would scare the hell out of her.

"Talking with the guys," I say finally, keeping my voice even. "We had to go over some mission details."

She looks at me. Just for a second. Then her gaze slips away. There it is. That look. Disappointment, again. She doesn't push, doesn't question it, or tell me what's on her mind. Just nods and steps ahead, putting space between us like she needs it. My jaw tightens as I watch her go. Fuck. I don't understand that look. But I know I don't like it. Feels like I just did something wrong.

I don't want to hide things from her, but she doesn't need to know what we found. Not yet. Because it's not just complaints. It's a pattern. Girls who spoke up that got shut down, discredited, buried. Reports that disappeared within days of being filed. Names that kept showing up then suddenly stopped. Ghost didn't just find harassment claims.

He found timelines and overlaps. This wasn't just at their school it was at his previous university and started while he was in high school. Girls who transferred out halfway through the semester. One who withdrew completely. Another who just vanished from records altogether, that disappearance bothers me the most. Especially after what Sarah told me about Carly.

There was never any follow-up. No investigations. Nothing. Like she was never there. And Benjamin? He was always just outside of it. Never named directly. Never caught. But always close enough to make your skin crawl. The dean made sure of that. Cleaned everything up before it could stick. Protected him. Enabled him. And if even half of it is true, this isn't some entitled kid with an ego. This is someone who's been getting away with it for years.

Escalating. Learning. Getting smarter about it every time. I tighten my jaw. No, she doesn't need that in her head. It won't help her. It won't make her safer. All it'll do is make her afraid. Make her start questioning everything with her friend. We'll handle it. We'll keep her safe and when this is over, we'll make sure he pays for it. One way or another.

By the time we hit the clearing, Glitch is already there, pacing near the big tent. He spots us immediately. His expression hardens. "Rocky, what the hell?" he snaps, closing the distance. "I look away for one second and you vanish?"

"Rocky?" I mutter under my breath, glancing at Sarah.

"Yeah," Glitch says, shrugging. "Killer right hook. Fits."

I don't step in. Don't stop him. Because I remember exactly how it felt when he said he couldn't find her. That drop in my gut. That split second where everything went wrong. She needs to hear it, from more than just me. I stay quiet, watching them closely. Tracking every movement. Every reaction. Not because I don't trust Glitch but because I don't trust the situation. Not anymore, not with her in the middle of it. Sarah plants a hand on her hip, staring him down. Fire back in her eyes. Good.

"Now you listen here, *Jake*," she says, dripping sarcasm. Jake. I didn't realize they were on a first-name basis.

"I just wanted some alone time," she continues, hands on her hips. "I already told Wade I was sorry. You don't need to start in too." Too much attitude, way too much for someone who could've gotten hurt. Glitch blinks, clearly thrown by her tone. His eyes flick to me, I lift my hands slightly in surrender. Not my fight. He started it. I already had my moment with her.

"Oh, really?" Glitch says, raising an eyebrow. "Do you know what that would've done to me if something happened to you?" His voice softens at the end, the edge dropping just enough to make it real. That's what gets her. Sarah falters, her gaze flicking back to me for half a second before she looks down.

"Okay," she mutters. "I get it. I'm sorry. I thought I was safe with the tracker."

Glitch exhales, dragging a hand over the back of his neck. "That tracker is a last resort. If we have to use it, it means something's already gone wrong." He jerks his thumb toward me. "And if something had happened to you? Wraith here would've ripped my balls off and served them for dinner."

Sarah's eyes go wide as she looks at me. "He's not wrong," I say with a shrug, keeping my tone casual.

She wrinkles her nose. "Okay, well I said I was sorry. Don't go ripping people's body parts off. That's gross." There it is again. That sass. I have to fight the smirk that tries to surface.

Glitch snorts. "Gross, right?" Then his expression settles again, more serious as he looks back at her. "Just... don't do that again, Rocky. I'd like to keep all my parts where they are."

She huffs, but there's a faint smile this time. "Okay. I promise." It eases something in the air. A little but not all the way. Because I can still feel it, something she's not saying. She's holding onto something that is bothering her and I don't like it.

"It's only three," I say, shifting the focus. "What's the plan before dinner? You heading back to your research? Or do you have time for a little nap?"

"I'm going to head back over to Paya," she says. "I just wanted to clean up. I told Paya I'd meet her again after. I like helping with the food, it'll be really useful for my dissertation."

"How does their food help?" I ask, genuinely curious.

Her whole expression changes. Lights up. Like it does every time she gets a chance to talk about her work. "Food is everything for them," she explains. "They're one of the last nomadic tribes. They rely almost completely on what's around them, what they hunt, what they grow, how they harvest it." She gestures slightly as she talks, slipping into that world like it's second nature. "Even what they throw away matters. Their midden—their waste—it tells a story. What they reuse, what they discard, how they process things. It all ties back to how their ancestors lived."

I glance at her, watching the way she comes alive when she talks about this. "So people have been living here that long?" I ask.

"Yeah," she says, nodding. "That's the current belief. Humans reached North America around thirty thousand years ago and gradually moved south over time."

I shake my head slightly, impressed. "That's... a long time."

She smiles softly. "It is."

"Wow," I mutter. "The more you know, I guess."

She smiles, already warming back up. "Yeah. That's where Dr. Willis's research comes in. It's believed the last ice age ended here around eleven thousand years ago, which means humans were still migrating even when most of the planet was covered in ice." She gestures as she talks, completely in her element. "But Brazil wasn't covered in ice sheets," she continues. "The Amazon would've been smaller, and the temperatures cooler than they are now."

I watch her more than I listen. The way her eyes light up. The way she forgets everything else when she talks about this.

"So you study the people, the food and the land?" I ask. "Feels like you need to know a little bit of everything."

She nods. "You do. Anthropology pulls from a lot of different sciences. You have to understand all of it to build a full picture."

"Is that what you want to do?" I ask. "Teach?"

"Yes… and no," she says with a small laugh. "I want to teach, but I also want to keep researching. That's the goal."

"Applied anywhere yet?"

"Yeah," she says. "A bunch of places before I came out here. But I have to finish my dissertation first before anything moves forward."

"Where?"

"All over," she says. "Montana, Washington, Missouri, Tennessee, Oregon. Anywhere with strong programs for what I want to study."

I nod slowly, already filing it away. Doesn't matter where. I'll go where she goes.

"Hope you get the one you want," I say.

"Me too," she replies.

I wait. Expecting her to say more. To tell me which one she actually wants. But she doesn't. Just gives me a small distant smile, like her head's somewhere else entirely. That same look again, I almost push, almost pull her back into it. But before I can, I realize—Glitch is gone. Slipped off at some point during the conversation without a word. Figures he didn't want to stay for the impromptu history lesson. Sarah turns away, quietly packing her things. I watch her for a second, debating whether to say something.

Ask her what she's thinking. What she's holding back. Instead, I don't. I just fall into step beside her as we head back toward the shabono. Close enough to touch. Far enough that she doesn't have to. The silence between us isn't empty. It's heavy. Full of whatever she's not saying.

Chapter Eighteen

Wade

The rest of the night moves quickly. Magellan and Stitches report nothing new. No movement. No issues. Benjamin stays quiet, I should feel better about that but I don't. Because quiet like this? It doesn't mean safe. It means waiting. And I've got a feeling, he's not done yet. He's planning something, but after everything we've discovered we know to keep a close eye on him and more importantly a close eye on Sarah. We're going to stay ahead of this, keeping this close to the vest is the best thing we can do right now.

We head back toward the tents, the group breaking off one by one. Sarah says her goodnights, polite as always. Even to Jenna. She never looks at Benjamin, not even once.

"You've been quiet tonight," I murmur once we're inside the tent. "What's going on?"

She doesn't answer. I hope she's not upset about earlier. She didn't seem to be, if anything, she leaned into it. Still, it's something we'll need to talk about. I want her comfortable with this. With me taking care of her. Discipline when she needs it. Care when she doesn't. And never—never anything that would hurt her.She starts getting ready for bed. That tight feeling in my chest builds, slow and steady. I follow her lead, going through the motions, but my focus is locked on her. Something's wrong and I don't like not knowing what it is. Information is power.

We crawl into the sleeping bag, her back to me at first. I can feel the tension in the air but I'm holding on to the fact that she's not pushing me away, not trying to sleep anywhere else. I give her space, for only a second. Then I can't take it anymore.

"Talk to me."

She exhales, shaky. "I'm trying to figure out what to say." Her voice is quiet, uncertain. "I'm not good at this. I've never really had to say what's on my mind like this before. I've never been confrontational."

I stay still, letting her work through it. Even though every instinct in me is pushing to fix it now. Even if I don't know what *it* is.

"I told you I wouldn't jump to conclusions," she continues, her voice barely above a whisper. "But all day, I've been thinking." She pauses, taking a deep breath. "I was wondering if I should ask Paya if I could stay in one of their huts." My chest tightens, an ache twisting under my ribs. But I don't interrupt, not this time. She needs to say it, all of it because I still don't know what's bothering her.

"I don't know if I can be with someone…" she swallows, her voice trembling now, "who's okay with other people seeing me like that. During something… intimate." She doesn't say the word, but I feel it anyway. "I'm new to all of this," she adds, softer now. "And I know you're not. But when I imagined being with someone…" Her voice cracks just slightly. "It was just the two of us."

For the first time, I don't have an answer ready. Because she's right, she's completely right and I hate that I'm the reason she's hurting. I shift closer, slow, careful, giving her time to pull away if she wants to. She doesn't. I gently turn her toward me, my hand coming up to cup her cheek. My forehead rests against hers, grounding us both. She sniffles once and I know she's trying to hold back her tears. It guts me, I did this.

"I messed up," I say quietly. No excuses. No deflection. Just the truth. "My focus was on you. On keeping you safe. Watching everything around us." My thumb brushes lightly along her cheek. "I saw him. I knew he was there." Her breath catches. "I made the call to keep going anyway," I admit, my voice lower now. "And I shouldn't have."

That one hurts to say. But it needs to be said. "You didn't deserve that," I continue. "Not from me." I hold her gaze, not letting her look away. "You deserve privacy. Respect. Control over moments like that. I won't put you in that position again."

A heavy silence settles between us. I need to find a way to fix this.

"Beautiful girl, I'm sorry," I murmur, my voice low, steady. "You're right. I should've stopped the second I knew he was there. You didn't deserve that." My thumb brushes along her cheek, slowly.

"I need you to understand something," I continue. "I don't want to share you. I don't want anyone else seeing you like that."

Her eyes don't soften. "Then why would you let him?" she asks, quiet but firm.

The question lands exactly where it should. I swallow, forcing myself not to look away. "Because I wanted him to know you're taken. That he needed to back off." My jaw tightens. "I thought it would send a message." I shake my head slightly. "It didn't. And I knew that before you even said anything." A breath leaves me, heavier this time. "I was wrong." That word doesn't come easy but I don't hesitate.

"I feel like you're purposely hiding things from me." Shit. She's right, I'm not hiding things about that, I am hiding things from her about Benjamin. About him possibly having something to do with Carly's disappearance. Things I don't want her to know, things I don't want her to worry about. I study her face, trying to find the right way to say this without pushing her further away.

"It's not that I'm hiding things," I say carefully. "It's that some of the things we deal with, I can't share. Not fully. There are things that we— my team—will learn and deal with. Some things need to remain top secret until it's handled." She doesn't say anything, so I keep going. "But anything that involves you? This place?" My voice lowers, more certain now. "You deserve to know what I can tell you. I can't promise I can tell you everything, just what I can, I will tell you." It's sort of the truth anyway. She's still not saying anything. "I don't want to protect you by shutting you out," I add quietly. "That's not the kind of man I want to be with you, however, I am going to protect you whenever I can." That seems to reach her.

She exhales slowly. "If it's about me or this field school, I want to know."

I nod. "I hear you," I say. "And I'll tell you what I can. No more leaving you in the dark." Even if I hate it. Even if I'd rather carry it all myself. I pull her closer, letting her settle against my chest, my arms wrapping around her. Not tight. Not controlling. Just there. Holding her, keeping her steady. We stay like that for a while, the tension easing, not gone but quieter. I press a kiss to the top of her head, breathing her in, reassuring myself in the fact that she's still here. Still with me. But I don't miss the truth underneath it all. If I don't handle this right, she could walk away and that's not something I'm willing to let happen.

"There's something else I want to talk about." Her body tenses. "It's not bad. I just know you're still new to all of this and I love that, I really do. I also don't want to scare you off."

"Okay?" She whispers and I smile at her nervousness.

"I want you to feel comfortable with me. Comfortable enough to talk about anything," I say quietly. "I like being in control, yeah. But that doesn't mean I don't listen. It means I need you to trust me." My thumb brushes along her skin. "When you push back, I'll push back too. Like earlier. But I'm not here to hurt you. Ever. It might get intense sometimes. But I'll always take care of you after. You don't go through any of it alone."

My voice softens. "I don't want to control you, I want you to choose this. Choose me."

"I—I really liked what you did earlier at the waterfall," she whispers. I grin wider, knowing she can't see it.

"Good," I say quietly. "Because I plan on doing a lot more. Just… not here. Not with canvas walls and half the team ten feet away." Her hand around my waist squeezes me tighter against her.

"Do you still want to hear about my leg?" I ask after a moment, my voice quieter now. I promised her. Even if it's not a story I like telling. One I don't talk about.

"Yes," she whispers against my chest. "I want to know everything. It's crazy, feeling this close to you when I barely know anything about you. We just met."

A low chuckle slips out of me, not quite amused. "Yeah," I murmur. "I feel it too. Like we've known each other a long time." I pause, my hand brushing along her arm. "It's easy. Effortless."

"Well," I start, my voice quieter now, "my full name's Wade Alexander Blakely. Born and raised in Missouri." I pause for a second, not because I don't know what to say but because I don't usually say any of this.

"You're from Missouri? Me, too!" She exclaims.

I chuckle. "Really, what part?" I already knew that from her report, she lived in Missouri her whole life until she started school in Minnesota.

"Kansas City," she says quickly, "Right near the Kansas line. What about you?"

"St. Joseph," I tell her. "Not too far from you. I grew up with my parents, I was an only child," I continue. "They're still there as far as I know." I let out a small breath. "They weren't really around much. Drinking, partying that kind of thing. They were never interested in having a kid. I pretty much raised myself." Her hand tightens slightly against my chest.

"I had a neighbor," I add. "River. We grew up together. I spent more time at her house than my own. Her family, they were what I thought a real family was supposed to look like." I can feel Sarah listening, really listening. "We kept in touch a little after I enlisted," I say. "Letters at first. Then less. Eventually, nothing."

I shrug slightly. "Haven't talked to my parents since I left."

"Were you more than friends with River?" she asks softly. There's a hint of jealousy in her voice and makes the tension in me ease, she's possessive of me and I like that more than I should.

"No," I say, without hesitation. "Never. She was like a sister to me. That whole family was a family I never had." My jaw tightens slightly. "They were the closest thing I had to one, anyway."

I don't miss the way Sarah processes that, like she's reading between the lines.

"You don't talk to your parents at all?" she asks. "I don't know what I'd do without my family. My parents and my older sister were always very supportive. Always helping me."

I glance down at her. "They never really cared if I was there or not," I say simply. "So it wasn't much of a loss."

Her expression softens. "I'm really close with my family. My sister and I fight sometimes but never anything real, but..." she smiles faintly, "they've always been there. Always supportive." I pull her a little closer without thinking. Good. I'm glad she got that, she deserved that.

Then I nod slightly toward her. "You've got something different. I'm happy you had that."

"I've been in the Army since I was eighteen," I continue. "Made Special Forces four years in. Been a Green Beret for twelve years now."

I let that settle for a second.

"Re-enlisted four times. After our last mission, we decided we were done. Our current enlistment was almost done, we just have to finish out our contracts."

"Wow," she breathes. "That's a long time."

Then she tilts her head slightly. "So… you're thirty-four?"

I huff out a quiet chuckle. "Not quite. Thirty-two. Been doing this long enough to feel older, though."

"Yep," I murmur, a faint smirk tugging at my mouth. "So not an old man." She groans softly, and I press a kiss to the top of her head.

"I didn't forget," I add, my tone shifting. "I'll tell you about the last mission." I take a slow breath, letting it out before I start. "We were in the Democratic Republic of Congo," I say. "Deep jungle. Not too different from here, thick terrain, limited visibility, hard to move without being seen."

Her fingers are still tracing slow circles against my chest. It helps keep me in the moment, not getting lost in the memory.

"We were attached to a joint operation," I continue. "Helping local forces deal with a militant group operating out of the northern region. They'd been hitting villages, taking hostages, using them for leverage, labor, whatever they needed." My jaw tightens slightly. "Our job was twofold. Train their forces in counter-terror tactics and step in when things escalated beyond what they could handle."

I pause briefly, choosing what to say next. "We got intel on a compound. Remote, very well hidden. They were holding multiple hostages there." I glance down at her. "That's where things started to go sideways. Ghost and Jamo were running recon," I continue. "Standard sweep. In and out. Quiet." I shake my head slightly. "Only they never made it back."

I feel her hand still against me. "We lost comms first," I say. "Then visual. At that point, we knew something was wrong." My voice drops a notch. "It took us a few hours to confirm they'd been taken. Ghost is our communications intel, so losing him hurt us more than we would like to admit. We can all do intel to a degree, just not like he can." Her fingers press a little firmer into my chest.

"After that, everything moved fast," I say. "You don't wait. You don't hesitate. You find them. It took us twenty-four hours," I add quietly. "In those moments every second counts, so 24 whole hours was agonizing. It took us way too long to find them. We tracked movement patterns, intercepted communications, worked with local informants. Pieced it together until we had a location."

I stare past the tent wall, seeing it all again. "By then we already knew what we were walking into. Our plan was a rapid assault," I continue. "Hit hard, hit fast. No drawn-out engagement. Get in, secure the hostages, eliminate the threat. Get our men and get out. It should have been simple, on paper anyway. They weren't holding them for trade," I say, my voice tightening. "They were extracting information. Anything they could get."

I take a slow breath, steadying myself. "When we got there... we didn't have time to wait for perfect conditions. We moved. We breached just before dawn," I say. "Low visibility. Minimal external movement. We split into teams, hit multiple entry points at once."

Controlled chaos. Exactly how it's supposed to be. "I was on the lead element," I continue. "We cleared the first structure fast. Resistance was immediate, small arms fire, scattered positions but we pushed through." I can feel her hand tighten again. "We found them in the second building."

I pause. Just for a second. Because this is the part that never sits right. "Jamo..." I swallow, jaw clenching. "He didn't make it. We were too late." The words come out flat, I try to swallow back the lump. "They killed him before we got there," I say. "Ghost was still alive." Barely. "They were together," I add, quieter now. "The whole time."

I don't need to spell it out. She understands. "We secured Ghost, called in extraction and started clearing the rest of the compound," I continue, forcing myself forward.

"That's when it happened. We were moving between structures," I say. "Pushing deeper, making sure there were no remaining threats." I shake my head slightly. "They had rigged part of the compound. Improvised explosives. Hidden in the debris, structural weak points, designed to hit us while we were clearing." They were smarter than we gave them credit credit for. More calculated in their plans.

"I didn't see it," I admit. "None of us did." A breath. "It went off. The blast threw me back and it hit me more than anyone else." I say. "I hit the ground hard." I shift slightly, instinctively. "Shrapnel caught my leg. Knocked the wind out of me, disoriented me for a few seconds." I glance down at her. "Long enough."

My voice stays steady. But I remember it. All of it. "The team pulled me out," I continue. "Stitches had me stabilized within minutes. The team finished the mission, secured the area, got me and Ghost out. Brought Jamo home where he belonged." I let out a slow breath. "That's how I got the pain in my leg. It could have been worse. I woke up stateside in a hospital, they operated on my leg. I had to do physical therapy, eventually it got better. Now it only hurts if I keep it bent for long periods of time."

Silence settles for a moment. Then, quieter, "Ghost… he hasn't been the same since." I grip her waist tighter. "He watched his little brother die," I add. "There's no training for that. No way to come back from it the same." I finally glance down at her. "That's why I said earlier, some things we deal with…" I pause, then finish it simply. "They stay with you."

"When you say little brother, do you mean—?" she trails off. Her voice breaks slightly. I feel the warmth of her tears against my chest.

"Yeah," I say quietly. "His real brother." I tighten my arm around her just a little.

"They were close. Always have been." I pause, choosing my words. "Jamo was different from him. Lighter. Talkative. The kind of guy who could walk into a room and make it feel less heavy. Ghost's always been quieter. Keeps to himself. But after that mission…" I shake my head slightly. "We barely saw him for a while. Even now, when he's around he's not really *with* us. Just does his job."

She shifts closer, like she's trying to hold onto something she can't fix. "They're from North Carolina, his father was military, Marines, he was killed in the line of duty." I continue. "Their mom still lives there. As soon as we were cleared to travel, the whole team went back for the funeral."

"Oh my god…" she whispers. "Their poor mother." There's real grief in her voice. Not just sympathy. Empathy. I pull her closer, pressing a kiss to her hair.

"Yeah," I murmur. "It was hard." That's an understatement. "Our goal now," I add after a moment, my voice firmer, "is to finish this mission and get everyone home. No more losses. Including you."

"How long ago was that?" She asked.

"Almost a year ago now." We lie there in silence for a while. I brush my thumb under her eyes, wiping away the last of her tears. I hate when she cries.

"Did you know what Ghost said to me before you found me today?" Her voice is soft again, but lighter now.

"No. I figured he was just lurking somewhere in the trees." I try for humor. It doesn't land. Never really does, I have my moments but I'm not as funny as Magellan or Glitch.

"At first he just stood there," she says, a small laugh slipping through. "Completely silent. It was honestly kind of creepy." That sounds about right. "Then he goes, 'Wraith is coming,' like that's supposed to mean something to me." She lets out a quiet giggle. "And then he tells me I worried all of you and then nothing. Just silence again."

I huff out a breath, shaking my head.

"Yeah. That tracks." She laughs a little more and I take the opportunity, pinching lightly at her side. She squeals, the sound brighter this time.

"I was scared," I admit, my tone dropping again. "Hearing you were missing, that's not something I ever want to hear again." My hand settles at her waist, steady. "The guys, they've all taken to you. More than you probably realize. They know you're important to me." That's the truth. "They want to protect you."

"I know," she says softly. "And I won't do that again." She shifts closer, her voice quieter now. "I feel safest when I'm with you."

My body settles, hearing her tell me she trusts me and she feels safe with me is important. we're working on building something good, something that's going to last. I pull her in, holding her a little closer than before.

"I've got you," I murmur against her hair. My voice is low. Certain. "I'm not letting anything happen to you."

Chapter Nineteen

Benjamin

Five weeks. Five fucking weeks of watching her. Always just out of reach. Always wrapped up in him. It's infuriating. Every time I see her, it crawls under my skin, this constant, gnawing need to take what's mine. To fix the mistake I made the first time. I let her slip away once. That won't happen again.

When I transferred to that university, I noticed her immediately. Quiet. Focused. Different from the rest. She didn't fawn. Didn't chase attention like the others. Didn't want me. That was new, interesting. I tried, of course. Subtle at first, then less subtle and more persistent. Nothing. Every smile I gave her? Ignored. Every conversation? Cut short. Like I didn't exist. Like I didn't matter.

Carly, though…Carly was easy. Too easy. She was flirty and far too eager, always looking for attention. So I gave it to her. Took her out. Let her think she mattered. All just to get closer to Sarah. To make her notice. To make her react. Only, she didn't. Not the way I wanted. But I saw it sometimes. The tension and the awareness when she saw me. She felt it. She just refused to acknowledge it.

Five years ago, I almost had her. Almost got her alone. Almost got her to stop fighting it. Then everything fell apart. Timing. Always fucking timing. Then Carly got in the way. I dealt with Carly. I'd do it again if I had to. She thought she could leave me. That she could just walk away like I didn't matter. Like there wouldn't be consequences. Like I wouldn't remind her.

My jaw tightens. People always think they have a choice. Until they don't. She was always supposed to disappear during that field school, only I made sure to have my fun before I turned her over. And Sarah? She was supposed to come next. I was careful. Used Carly at first, then used her absence. Tried to build something through shared grief. A connection. A way in but the second I pushed, she shut me down. Every time. Like I was nothing. Like I meant nothing to her.

So I watched. From a distance. Because she's the only one who never came to me, the only one who made me wait. I don't like waiting. Never have. My uncle told me to stay back. Too much attention after Carly. Too many questions. Too many people looking in the wrong direction. So I listened, for a while. But there were nights…when she walked home alone. When no one was around. When it would've been easy. Too easy. I almost did it. More than once.

And now—Wade. Sergeant Blakely, I roll my eyes. That asshole made things complicated the second he showed up. Dr. Willis said we'd have military oversight. Retired. I expected one guy. Maybe two. Someone older, slower, predictable and easy to manipulate. Not this. Not a whole damn team. Not him. The moment he stepped up to our group, I knew.

The way he moved. The way he looked at people. He was the kind of man who doesn't ask, he just takes. She noticed him. Of course she did. I saw it the second he walked up to her. The way she looked at him. The way her body reacted before she could stop it. That soft, nervous energy. That blush. That hesitation. Lust. My jaw tightens. She's supposed to look at me like that.

And now, him. He stepped in like he belonged there. Like she was already his. Like I didn't exist. I've been patient. Watched from a distance. Played it right. Let her think she had control. Let her believe this was her choice. But it's not, it never was. She's mine. She just hasn't accepted it yet. And Wade? He's in the way. That's fine. I've dealt with obstacles before. This time, though…I won't hesitate.

When her tent tore apart in the storm, I thought—*finally*. This is it. She'll come to me. She'll need me. But she didn't. She went to him. I watched her the next morning. The way she looked at him. The way she softened around him. The way she let him close. Let him touch her. And yeah, the slight hitch in her walk telling me she was sore. That was supposed to be me.

I waited for that. For her to look at me like that. For her to *give* me that. I told myself there was still time. That maybe she hadn't crossed that line yet. That maybe, she was still mine to take. That thought kept me steady. Kept me in control. Until the spring.

I followed them and kept my distance. I watched and everything in me snapped. She was his, in a way she was supposed to be mine. She gave him something that belonged to me. She was too close to him, trusting and completely unaware of her surroundings as I watched.

My hands curl into fists. My breathing turns sharp. Uneven. No. This isn't over. I was patient once. I won't make that mistake again. That virgin cunt was promised to me. And yet, there she was, giving it to him freely. Moaning for him. Wrapping her legs around him like a whore. I knew he saw me. That smug bastard had the audacity to lock eyes with me as he buried himself inside her. It was like he was daring me to do something, as if he thought his claim meant anything. Humans aren't wolves. A mark doesn't mean shit. He may have taken her sweet virginity, but she'll be mine soon enough.

I was starting to think she was a nun. No matter what I did, she never wanted anything more than friendship. It didn't make sense. I don't have problems getting girls. They come easy. Always have. But her? No, she had to be different, difficult. The one that didn't fall in line. The one that made me work for it. The one I was supposed to have five years ago.

I tried to play it smart this time. Kept my distance. Let their guard drop. Wait for the right moment. But Wade, he's been watching me. Not just him. All of them. They close ranks around her like she belongs to them. Like she needs protecting. Like I'm the threat. They don't even know how much of a threat I can be.

My jaw tightens. I thought when he switched to overnight rotation, I'd finally have an opening. A chance to get close. To remind her of our special connection. But no. They adjusted, shifted. Kept her covered. Always someone nearby. Always eyes on me.

And her? She won't even look at me anymore. Like I'm nothing. Like I don't exist. Even after I pushed Jenna away. Useless. She got clingy. Possessive. Started acting like she mattered. She was supposed to be a distraction. A tool to use, something to keep Sarah off balance. Instead, she made things worse. She drew attention to me when she wasn't supposed to. She got too emotional and confronted her, when she has no right to. Now she's just a problem. Another loose end. But she doesn't matter, none of them do. Only Sarah matters. And tomorrow, she'll finally understand that.

Dr. Willis has been avoiding me unless we're working. Keeping things strictly professional. Watching his words. That's fine. Everyone thinks they're being careful. That they're in control. They're not. It's all part of the plan.

For now, I wait. I watch and time, everything. Willis finishes eating, mutters something about getting sleep and walks off. One less set of eyes. I scan the clearing. The team's scattered. No one close enough to hear. No one paying attention. Perfect.

I turn toward Jenna. "Hey," I say, my voice easy. Calm, like nothing's wrong. Like everything's normal. She is always giddy over the prospect of pleasing me. Too easy. I do get to fuck her often, again not easy with those assholes watching my every move. The only way I could get off with Jenna was imagining it was Sarah, imagining I was taking her cherry. Jenna clearly liked sex, it's hard to really enjoy her. I didn't break her in. She's too easy, too eager for me. I prefer to give the pain so they only know pleasure from me, before they probably won't feel any pleasure ever again.

"My pet. If they don't follow us tonight, I will fuck you again. Would you like that?"

"Yes, please. It's been so long, playing with myself just doesn't cut it." I inwardly roll my eyes, she is far too easy. Tomorrow night I will finally have my challenge.

When we get up the guys all look our way but they make no indication of moving to follow me. I will have to make quick work of fucking her, for my pleasure. I just need the release as I think about all the things I will do to Sarah.

As we walk towards the darkened path I make sure she's following me. "I will meet you later, at our spot." I say before going into my tent.

Under the cover of darkness, I led Jenna away from the tents. She clung to me, her hands eager and needy. I didn't bother with niceties. In the shadows of the trees, I bend her over, yanking her pants down.

She moaned, but I silenced her with a sharp tug of her hair. I didn't want to call attention to us and it wasn't her voice I wanted to hear. It wasn't her body I wanted to fuck.

In my mind, it was Sarah. In my mind, I am gripping her waist roughly and pounding into from behind her. She's screaming in fear and pain from being taken, but eventually her velvety tight little cunt would relax. Her screams of pain would turn to screams of pleasure.

I would get to feel her pussy spasm as she comes and she still takes it. My hands shift to squeeze her ass tightly, enough to draw pain before I plunge my finger into untouched tight little hole. I don't give it any lube, I just take it. Shoving my fingers into her and listen to her scream in pain again, my favorite sound. When I'm done claiming this cunt I'm going to claim her ass next.

In my fantasy she's not on any kind of birth control and I'm not using any condoms. I'm claiming every bit of her. I moan as I spurt deep inside her. There's no way I'm done. She's gasping trying to regain her breath and her composure but I don't give her a chance. I slip out and shove my dick right into her ass. It's mine. She screams beautifully for me.

She's desperately trying to get away from me but I wrap my hand out of her throat, keeping her body tight to mine. She starts to relax only a little. My eyes roll back in my head, her tight bundle of nerves is squeezing me so good.

I choke her harder and come deep in her. I should have started with her throat so I could claim all of her holes before I got rid of her.

When I come back into myself, Jenna is crouched over panting. I feel sick, I want it to be Sarah. It's always Sarah. Her tight, untouched body, the way she'd scream for me. First in pain, then in submission. She'd learn to love it, just like the others. I'd break her in. Make her mine. As I pull out of her I let her fall to her knees. I got what I needed and I know she got to come.

"Thank you," she whispers softly. "It's always so good."

"I'm going to bed now. I'll see you tomorrow."

I get my pants back on and turn walking back to my tent, leaving Jenna on her knees behind me. A wave of satisfaction washed over me, not from the act itself, but from the anticipation of what was to come. I'll take back what he stole from me and then she'll finally understand who she belongs to.

Chapter Twenty

Sarah

The last five weeks have felt like both a lifetime and a blink. Slow... because I'm exhausted in a way I've never experienced before. Physically. Emotionally. Mentally. Sleeping on the hard ground every night is wearing me down, even if having Wade wrapped around me makes it a little more bearable. Still, I find myself craving the simplest things, my own bed, a long hot shower, soft clothes and a week where I don't have to think about anything at all.

It's gone by in a blink, because everything else has been a blur. The Yanomami have been incredible. Every day with them has given me more than I ever expected, insight, trust and moments I know will shape my research for years. I came here hoping to learn, but I didn't realize how much I'd feel connected. I didn't know how much closure I would find here, not after everything that happened five years ago.

And then there's Wade and his team. What started as intimidation, six men who looked like they belonged on a battlefield instead of in the jungle has turned into something else entirely. Something steady.

Something safe. They've become my family out here. In a way, they've made this place feel less foreign. Less lonely.

Not everything has settled. Benjamin lingers like a shadow I can't quite escape. Always at the edge of my vision. Always watching. There have been too many moments where I've looked up and caught his eyes already on me. There's something in his stare that makes my skin crawl, something that settles deep in my chest and refuses to go away. Thankfully, I'm never alone. Wade or one of the guys are always close. Always watching back.

The nightmares haven't stopped. They're not as bad as the first one, but they're still there. Still vivid enough to leave me shaken when I wake up. I haven't told Wade. I don't want to. He already watches me like I might disappear if he looks away for too long. I can't add more to that.

We only have three days left. Tomorrow is Paya and Kaori's wedding, and despite everything, I can't help the excitement bubbling up inside me. It's going to be beautiful. I feel incredibly lucky to be here for it, to witness something so important, so deeply rooted in their culture.

The day after that, we say goodbye. Pack everything up. Start the long journey back, hours of walking, then the bus, then the flight. Back to reality, back to home. The word feels heavier than it should. Bittersweet, because going home means leaving this place, but it also means stepping into whatever comes next.

Wade and I will be apart for a couple of weeks. He has to finish his discharge, close out sixteen years of his life, figure out what comes after the military. Then he'll come to Minnesota. He's been so sure about it. About us. About everything. He promised, wherever I got accepted for a job he was coming with me. It didn't matter where. Part of me loves that certainty. It steadies me, makes this feel real.

But another part of me…hesitates. Because everything out here feels intensified. Like we're living in a bubble where nothing else exists. No distractions. No real-world complications. Just us. What happens when that bubble bursts?

After the mission, I'll visit my aunt and uncle in São Paulo for a week, white sand beaches, sunshine and a chance to breathe. A chance to just relax. Then it's off to Missouri to see my family before heading back to Minnesota to finish my dissertation.

I spent most of my time with Wade. Mostly at night, when the others weren't keeping us busy. Except for that one week he was on night patrol. I didn't think it would affect me as much as it did, but sleeping without him was harder than I expected. Which is ridiculous considering I had only been sleeping next to him for a few days before that. Still, the absence was noticeable.

And then there was the shift in who stayed with me. Instead of Wade and Jake, first it was Magellan and Stitches. It shouldn't have felt different. But it did. Not worse. Just different.

Magellan—Joel, as I started calling him—was impossible not to like. He grew up in the States, but his family is from Spain, and you could hear it in his voice when he relaxed enough to let it slip. His accent wasn't strong, but it was there, soft, smooth and threaded through his words in a way that made everything sound just a little more interesting.

He was built like the others, broad shoulders and strong arms but there was something more relaxed about him. Less rigid. More approachable. His dark brown eyes always held a hint of mischief, like he was one comment away from saying something he probably shouldn't. He told me after they get out, he's going to go see his family for a while in Albuquerque. Not sure what happens next but he's been away far longer than he's been home and he misses his family.

"They call me Magellan because he was from Spain," he told me one night, leaning back like he had all the time in the world.

I blinked at him. "You do know he was actually from Portugal first, right? Then gained Spanish citizenship before the circumnavigation?" The words came out before I could stop them.

He just stared at me for a second. Then laughed. "I did know that," he said, shaking his head. "Didn't think anyone else would, though."

I shrugged, trying not to feel awkward. "Occupational hazard."

"So," another voice cut in, "I hear you've got a new call sign." I turned to see Stitches, Nick, watching me, one brow slightly raised.

"Rocky, right?"

I groaned softly. "Apparently."

Nick's lips twitched, like he was holding back a smile. He had a quieter presence than the others. Steady. Grounded. The kind of person you didn't notice right away but once you did, you realized he was always watching, always aware. There was something calming about him. Maybe it was his eyes, a cerulean blue and steady. Warm in a way that made you feel like everything was under control even when it wasn't. Or maybe it was just the way he carried himself.

He was controlled and measured like the rest of them, sure, but he was safe. He was solid, muscular like the rest of them, but not overwhelming. Built for endurance rather than intimidation. His black hair was always kept short, his face clean-shaven in a way that made me wonder how he even managed it out here.

"Jake started it," I said, crossing my arms. "Apparently I have a 'mean right hook.'"

Nick huffed quietly. "You did deck him."

"In my defense," I shot back, "he deserved it." That earned me a small smile. A rare one.

"Well, it was entertaining for all of us when you came flying into the clearing and punched that prick."

"I am not ever like that," I mutter, my face burning as they both start laughing.

"Oh, I don't know," Nick says, a hint of a smirk tugging at his lips. "Looked pretty natural to me."

Joel leans back, grinning. "Next time, hit him harder. We should probably teach you how to throw a proper punch."

I groan. "There is not going to be a next time."

"Shame," Nick adds casually. "Can't say I didn't enjoy resetting his nose after Wraith got to him."

I blink at him. "Wait, his nose actually broke? Wade never told me that."

"Oh yeah," Joel says, clearly enjoying this. "He came stumbling out of his tent later. Heard the crack when Nick set it back in place."

Nick shrugs. "Benjamin didn't take it well."

"I think we all enjoyed it," Joel adds with a chuckle.

I shiver. "I'm really glad I didn't hear that." It didn't take long to realize each of them had their own way of watching out for me. Joel kept things light. He's always full of jokes, stories and a constant distraction so I didn't overthink.

Nick was different, he was more quiet and observant. The one who noticed when I was off before I even said anything and even without Wade there that week, I was never alone. Over the weeks, they rotated duties, taking turns going out with Dr. Willis and his team for fieldwork. Simon and Shawn drew the short straw more than once.

"Listen, there is no way I am going out in the field all day with that limp dick, I would end up killing him. I would much rather be here watching your sweet ass walking around." Wade told me.

"Same." Jake said quietly. Wade shot him a look so he quickly added, "Except the ass watching." When it looked like Wade was going to punch him. My face turned bright red when all the guys laughed. They loved to tease me. Constantly. I couldn't say I loved it. But I didn't hate it either.

"No way," Simon—Reaper—said flatly when I told him he needed to stop. "It's too easy."

I narrowed my eyes at him. "You're all impossible."

"That's why you like us," Shawn—Sparta—added with a grin. I rolled my eyes but didn't argue. It would only fan the flames.

I have not seen much of Ghost, unless he was talking to Wade or at dinners. He is the only one that I haven't gotten to know. Based on what happened during their previous mission, I don't blame him. I can't possibly imagine what he went through, or how he is feeling. I certainly wouldn't want to experience the loss of my sister let alone in the gruesome way he must have witnessed. I don't think I'd survive it. He was always there and not there at the same time. Mostly I only saw him when he was speaking quietly with Wade or sitting at dinner, just on the edge of everything. He's always watching and listening. But never really joining in.

The week I spent with Shawn and Simon was different. Somewhere along the way, I stopped thinking of them by their call signs. Not because they weren't important. But because calling them by their real names, Shawn, Simon, felt more personal. Like I wasn't just someone they were protecting anymore. Like I belonged. It also felt like their call signs were meant more for them, a close knit group of men that went through hell together and I wasn't a part of that.

Shawn was louder for sure, and funny. While Simon was focused and structured, certainly more serious like Wade. Still fun but in a completely different way. They were both hilarious. Between the two of them, I learned more about Wade in a week than I had in the five before and not from him.

"He's a tight ass," Simon said one morning, shaking his head. "Used to never smile. Just walked around looking like he was about to ruin someone's life."

Shawn huffed out a quiet laugh. "Still does."

Simon shivered dramatically. "Scary motherfucker. You should've seen him back in the day."

I glanced between them, curious despite myself. "Yeah?" I asked.

Simon leaned forward slightly, lowering his voice like he was about to share something important. "Ask him about the time we were interrogating a terrorist in East Asia."

I froze. Then immediately shook my head. "Nope. I'm good."

That earned a laugh from both of them. I made a mental note right then and there, I did not want to know. Simon had a presence that was hard to ignore.

Even when he was joking, there was something sharp underneath it. He told me his call sign came from the way he operated, deliberate and precise. When he had a target, he didn't miss and I believed it. No reason not to, really. His green eyes were intense, the kind that locked onto you and didn't let go. There was a warning in them, even when he was smiling, like something coiled just beneath the surface. Danger, wrapped in humor. But he was also one of the easiest to talk to. Quick with a joke. Always ready with a story and clearly he was fiercely loyal. The way he talked about Wade made that clear.

Shawn was different from Simon in almost every way. Where Shawn was loud, Simon was steady. Where Shawn joked, Simon observed. He told me his call sign came from his love of history, specifically Spartan warfare. He broke down strategy like it was second nature, referencing tactics, formations, patterns I didn't fully understand but could tell mattered. He was the one who planned. Who structured. Who made sure everything ran the way it was supposed to.

Paired with Simon, they balanced each other perfectly. Energy and control. Chaos and precision. Shawn had a commanding presence that didn't need to be loud. His dark skin seemed to catch the light differently out here, his features sharp and defined under the sun. His posture alone made it clear, he was someone people listened to. Someone people followed. And somehow, I'd gotten to know all of them. His deep brown eyes, that looked almost black, held an intensity that grounded me, but I could tell he was always scanning, always alert, watching for anything that might go wrong. I remembered that first night, when he stepped in without hesitation.

When he pulled me away from Benjamin. A quiet, steady presence in the chaos. I couldn't be more grateful that he had been there or that he'd had the instinct to follow in the first place. Like a Spartan, he carried himself like a warrior, disciplined, deliberate and always ready.

The whole team moved like a well-oiled machine. Years of dangerous missions had shaped them into something seamless, each man knowing exactly where the others would be, what they would do, without needing to say a word. They trusted each other with their lives. And somehow, they trusted me enough to bring me into that circle. The way they treated me? It felt like family. Within five weeks,

I'd somehow gained six overprotective brothers.

I grew up with just my older sister, the kind who was more of a conundrum, we would get into trouble but she always very protective of me. Sometimes borderline smothering but we always had fun. But this was different. They teased me. Protected me and like any real brothers, they refused to let me live down that punch.

Which is how I found myself standing in the middle of the clearing one evening, fists raised, with Simon, circling me like I was an actual opponent.

"Alright, Rocky," he said, a grin pulling at his mouth. "You've got a decent swing when you're panicked. But let's make sure next time it actually does some damage."

I groaned. "Can we not bring up how I failed at punching Benjamin? Again?"

"Failed?" He placed a hand over his chest, mock offended. "Sweetheart, that wasn't a punch. That was a very aggressive attempt at petting his face." Shawn snorted behind him.

I shot him a look. "Wow. So I'm surrounded by comedians now?"

"Only the best," Shawn shot back.

I sighed, dropping my shoulders. "Fine. Teach me, then."

That grin came back instantly. "Gladly."

For the next hour, he walked me through everything. How to plant my feet. How to keep my balance. How to throw a punch without breaking my wrist, which apparently, was very important. How to move. How to react. How to think. It wasn't just about hitting. It was about control.

"Again," Simon said, tapping his hands together. I exhaled, resetting my stance, focusing this time. When I threw the punch, it landed solid against the padding. A sharp *thud* echoed between us.

Simon let out a low laugh. "There you go. That's better."

I straightened, brushing damp hair off my face, a small smile slipping through. "So, does this mean you'll stop teasing me now?"

He tilted his head, pretending to consider it. "Nope." I groaned.

Shawn stepped forward, clapping a firm hand on my shoulder. "Don't worry," he said, a rare hint of amusement in his voice. "We'll make a fighter out of you yet."

And for the first time since being here, I believed him.

"You know I went to a boxing gym once." I told them. They both looked at each other and then back to me.

"Like one time or like once as in it was a while ago?" Shawn asked.

"Literally one time, my roommate dragged me and I hated it. She kept making me follow along with her and I was exhausted. Hitting the heavy bags were the worst. I never went back." Again they both looked at each other and burst out laughing. I just rolled my eyes and started walking away. As I turn around, Wade was standing near our tent, waking up for his night rotation, he had the most incredible sexy smirk. His eyes telling me exactly what he wanted to do to me.

That night, lying in my sleeping bag, I couldn't help but think about how much had changed. Five weeks ago, I came here as a researcher, focused, driven, thinking only about my work. Now? I had a family here. Despite everything that had happened, I wasn't ready to leave them.

I kept my camera with me constantly, documenting everything I could. The tribe. The work. The small, quiet moments. But some of my favorite shots were of the guys. Especially in the mornings, when they dropped the hardened edges and played with the kids. It was such a stark contrast, these men who carried so much, laughing, relaxed and letting themselves just *be* for a little while.

The only one I never managed to capture was Ghost. I tried once. Thought I was being subtle, lifting my camera slowly, angling the lens just right. But the second I looked through it, he was already staring at me. Locked in. Like he'd known exactly what I was doing before I even did. I lowered the camera, caught. For a split second, I *swear* I saw the faintest hint of a smirk. But it was gone so fast I wasn't sure if I imagined it.

There were other moments I captured, too. More discreetly. More carefully. Benjamin. Anytime I caught him watching me, I took a picture. Quietly, without drawing attention. I didn't know if I'd ever need them. But something in me told me to keep them. Just in case.

The past slips away, and I blink back into the present. It had been a long day of checking traps with Dori, helping prepare for tomorrow's feast. The entire village felt different tonight. Anticipation hummed in the air, a quiet excitement building for the ceremony. I couldn't wait to witness it. But exhaustion finally caught up to me.

Wade and I slipped into the tent quietly, I changed into my pajamas quickly and crawled into the sleeping bag.

"Are you okay?" Wade's voice cut softly through the darkness. "You're quiet."

I hesitated for a moment, then nodded, even though he couldn't see it. "Yeah, it's just bittersweet, you know?" I said softly. "I've known her for so long, and after this I might never see her again."

There was a pause before he spoke again. "Would you want to come back?"

I let out a small breath. "Maybe. If I had a research project that brought me back. But even then she'll be moving further inland. There's no guarantee our paths would cross again."

He shifted closer. "Never say never," he murmured. "And even if they don't, you've got the memories."

I smiled faintly, even in the dark. "You're right. This whole trip, it's been mostly good. I'm really grateful I came."

His hand found mine in the sleeping bag, fingers threading gently through mine. "I'm grateful I met you," he said quietly. "I didn't even want this mission at first but I'm glad I was sent here."

He leaned in, pressing a slow soft kiss to my lips. His hand came up to cradle my jaw, grounding me as the kiss deepened just enough to make my heart skip. There was nothing rushed about it. Nothing overwhelming. Just him and I. The familiarity of it settled over me, warm and steady. It reminded me of the first time he kissed me. That same spark. That same pull. Only now, it felt deeper. Like something we were both holding onto, because we both knew time here was running out.

His other hand is sliding to my breast and he uses his thumb and forefinger to pinch my nipple. My back arches off the ground as my hands reach around his neck and slide down his back. When his mouth starts traveling down my jaw to my neck I wrap my legs around his waist pulling him closer to me.

I can feel the wetness pooling between my thighs and I know I am ready for him already. His warm mouth is planting kisses down my neck and he stops to suck on my collarbone before he gets to my other breast and I gasp.

The hand that was playing with my nipple slides slowly down my body. I love the feel of his rough hands gliding over me. When his fingers reach my wet slit I hear him groan.

"So fucking wet for me, every time." He whispers. Wade's whole body starts sliding down mine and he's trailing kisses down it. He stops to lick my belly button, making me mewl and lift my hips.

Working his way down he wastes no time and starts devouring my clit. I know it won't be long, I can feel the pressure building deliciously in my core. Licking from my wet entrance to my clit he groans at the wetness and slips a finger inside me and I come instantly. Lapping up all my juices he doesn't stop, wringing out every last bit of my orgasm.

"Mmm, that was fast, beautiful." He says in wonder. I am laying there panting and Wade is sliding back over me, kissing me. He must have already shed his clothing when I was lost to the onslaught of his tongue. Ever so slowly he slides his cock into me. It feels bigger than I remember, he stops when he is all the way. Or maybe I feel tighter, it's hard to tell but it feels so good.

"Fuck, you're so wet and tight." He growls out. Pulling back until only the tip is left inside me he slams back in and holds it there. I gasp and grip him tighter with my legs and my hands. I bury my mouth onto his shoulder, gently kissing knowing I'm going to have bite down to keep quiet. Like I've been doing every time, he keeps telling me I'm not biting that hard but one time I left marks that lasted more than a day.

Urging him to start moving more. He takes the hint and keeps going. Slowly he makes love to me. This time means so much more. Taking his time he slides in and pushes back in building the orgasm to a crescendo, the now familiar tightening inside me. I know it won't be long before I combust. I never want to lose this feeling.

His thumb slips between us and onto my clit and I can't hold back anymore. I moan as I come undone. Digging my fingers into his shoulders, I moan out his name. He keeps pumping through my orgasm. He moans quietly above me when I start squeezing.

"Fuck, Mouse. I swear you've gotten tighter." He says roughly. He grabs my hips, lifting my higher as backs more onto his knees and starts slamming into me. My eyes roll back as I bite my lips. It's so hard to be quiet when he's going that hard, when he's hitting the right spot inside.

"Wade!" I hiss. I try to be as quiet as I can but I know I'm losing the battle. He starts slamming into me harder and oh, god. He grabs my waist against and hits me deep two more times before he comes, groaning my name.

"I love you," he whispers against my neck, and I freeze.

I've felt it for weeks now, whatever this is between us has been growing and building but I kept the words locked inside. In case it was too soon, I don't want to be pushy or needy. In case it scared him. In case it scared me. In case, we only had these few weeks together and I would never see him again.

He pulls back slightly, bracing himself above me, his hands coming up to cradle my face. His thumbs brush gently beneath my eyes, catching the tears before I even realize they've fallen.

"If you're not ready," he murmurs softly, "that's okay."

My chest tightens. I take a shaky breath, trying to steady myself but the words are already there, already pushing forward. "I love you, too."

"Thank fuck," he breathes, dropping his forehead to mine before pressing quick, warm kisses across my face. My cheeks, my nose, my forehead, anywhere he can reach. A laugh bubbles out of me through the tears.

"I love you," he says again, quieter this time, more grounded. Like he needs me to hear it. Like he needs it to be real.

The tears come faster. "Stop crying, beautiful," he teases gently.

"How did you know?" I sniffle, swiping at my cheeks.

That's when he tickles me. I gasp, squirming as laughter breaks through everything else. "Wade! That's not fair!"

He chuckles, easing off, his hands settling back around me. "Because I know you," he says softly. "I know when you're about to cry. When you're angry. When you get stuck in your head and overthink everything." His thumb brushes lightly over my cheek. "I've been paying attention these last six weeks."

"Oh." It's all I can manage, but my chest feels full, too full for words.

He shifts, sitting up. "Let me get dressed. Then we'll get comfortable." I listen to the quiet rustle of fabric before he slips back into the sleeping bag beside me. He turns us onto our sides, pulling me close and my back pressed to his chest, his arm wrapping securely around me.

"Good?" he murmurs, his lips brushing just beneath my ear.

I let out a soft breath, sinking into him. "Perfect." His arms tighten slightly, like he's anchoring me there. Like he's not letting me go. Everything feels still, right and safe.

Like every night I am in his arms, my mind quiets. I focus on the steady rhythm of his breathing, the warmth of his body wrapped around mine, the way his presence seems to hold everything together. For a moment, just a moment, I let myself believe that this feeling could last. That I could keep this. But somewhere, in the back of my mind, something doesn't settle.

A quiet unease I can't quite name. I push it down. Let myself drift anyway. Because right now, in his arms, I'm safe. And I hold onto that feeling as sleep finally takes me.

Chapter Twenty One

Sarah

I wake to the early morning dawn the sky outside is getting lighter. It must be too early because Wade is still here, his warmth pressing into me. His arm is wrapped around me, his body pressed close. For a moment, I don't move. I just lie there, letting it sink in. Last night, the words we said. The way everything shifted, I still feel worried that it's all a dream. That none of this is real. A smile spreads across my face before I can stop it.

I never expected to find love. Not here. Not like this. It feels like serendipity. Like something that wasn't supposed to happen but did anyway. Carefully, I ease out of his arms just enough to reach for my notebook. Flipping to the back, I quickly jot down a few thoughts before they slip away.

I never planned to use this part of the book but somewhere along the way, it turned into something else. A journal. Mostly filled with thoughts about him. About us. Things I would have like to talk to Fallon about.

"What are you doing?" His voice is rough with sleep, low behind me and I freeze for a second before glancing over my shoulder.

"Just writing," I whisper. He shifts closer, his arm sliding around my waist as he pulls me back against him.

"What are you writing, beautiful?" he murmurs, his breath warm near my ear.

A shiver runs down my spine. "Just my thoughts," I say softly, suddenly very aware of how close he is.

"And those thoughts happen to be about me?" There's a hint of a smile in his voice.

I huff out a quiet laugh. "Of course they are."

He turns me gently, guiding me onto my back so I'm facing him. His golden-brown eyes are softer than I've ever seen them, open and unguarded. Full of something that makes my chest tighten. Tears prick at my eyes before I can stop them.

"Hey," he murmurs, brushing his thumb beneath my eye. "Save that for later, yeah? Paya's ceremony deserves it more."

I let out a small laugh, lightly tapping his cheek. "You're impossible."

He grins. Then leans in, kissing me slowly. I shift, moving closer, settling over him just enough to look down at him, my hair falling around us like a curtain. His hands come to rest at my hips. That smirk I've come to love tugs at his mouth.

"I think my little Mouse finally caught me," he murmurs. "Now what are you going to do with me?" I pause for a second, pretending to think, even though my heart is racing. Even though I already know the answer.

"Hmm," I say softly, leaning down just enough for my lips to brush his. "I haven't decided yet."

His grip tightens slightly, his eyes darkening just a fraction but there's still that warmth there. That steadiness. That *us*. For a moment nothing else exists.

I lean down to kiss him, a quick peck. Wondering if I should tease him or go straight into riding him like I want to. I've never initiated anything with him, even if I have been thinking about it. I've been too embarrassed to try, not knowing what I am doing. I don't want to do the wrong thing and look dumb. I decide to tease him, so I give him another quick kiss and start lifting my leg back over as if I am going to lay next to him. I see the confusion in his eyes before he grabs my thigh and brings me back so I am straddling him.

His hard cock is strained against my ass. "Get up on your knees quick, I need to get pants off." he whispers, there's a gleam in his eye. He's so excited, I can't believe I could get him that excited. I get up on my knees and I help him get his pants unzipped and down his legs. I rest back down and now his smooth hard cock is pressing against my aching core. I know it would be so easy to just lift up slightly and slide right down. My heart is pounding in anticipation at trying this, I can't wait to feel him fill me. I just hope I can do it right.

Reaching his hand behind my neck he brings me back down to kiss him. He takes it deeper right away, licking the seam around my lips and I open for him. His other hand reaches for my breasts and I moan into his mouth. I know I can't wait any longer I need to feel him filling me and stretching me. I lift up slightly and using a hand I reach between us and move his rock hard cock into position and start sliding down onto his length. Keeping my body bent towards him so my head doesn't hit the ceiling.

He hisses as I moan from the pleasure. He whispers "shh" against my lips and I know I must have been too loud.

"Sorry." I mumble.

"Don't be sorry, I can't wait to have some real privacy with you so I can make you scream. To explore more with you. Now start moving. Up and down backwards and forward whatever feels good for you." He grabs my hips and helps me start moving and before long I take over, lost in the pleasure, he's never been so deep inside me. I can barely hold back the moans, this will be the first thing we do when we reunite.

His hands move from my hips to my breasts, gently kneading them and playing with my extremely hard nipples. They feel so heavy and full in his hands, when he starts squeezing them harder I lose it. I start coming, my movements becoming erratic, he throws his head back and comes with me with a quiet growl.

Spent, I lay over his chest, gently playing with the hairs on his chest as he rubs circles on my back. I feel like I could fall asleep again.

"I feel like I could fall sleep just like this." I feel his body shake with his soft chuckle, reminding me that his semi-hard cock is still inside me.

"I'll let you sleep for a little while longer, beautiful. I'll come wake you up, when it's time." he murmurs against my lips.

I don't know how much time has passed but I feel movement over me. Blinking my eyes open Wade is hovering over me, the sunlight filtering through the tent above him.

"Just a few more minutes," I mumble, not ready to give up the warmth, the comfort of him.

"I'd love that," he says, voice low and amused, "but you have to go see Paya, remember? Besides, people are probably already wondering what we're doing in here, if they didn't already notice the tent shaking earlier." My eyes snap open.

Heat floods my face as I shove at his shoulder. "Oh my god." He just grins. We get dressed quickly. I leave my notebook and camera behind for now, I'll come back for them later. Right now, I just want to get cleaned up before the day starts. When we step outside, the camp is already stirring. Most of the guys are up, along with Dr. Willis. The air feels different this morning, lighter but busy. Like everything is building toward tonight.

Jenna's and Benjamin's tents are still closed. For now. We make our way over to the fire, grabbing coffee as the guys talk.

"We have to go out for one more sample," Dr. Willis is saying. "There was one that wasn't cataloged correctly."

"Alright," Joel replies. "Once everyone's up, we'll head out. Do you need the guide, or is it close?"

"I think we'll be fine without him. Just a quick trip, collect the sample, take some photos and head back." He pauses. "Honestly, you probably don't even need to come. Things have been quiet and the militia activity hasn't moved any closer."

"No," Nick says firmly. "We're still going. We're too close to being done to get complacent."

There's a quiet agreement among them. Always cautious. Always thinking ahead. I know a part of it is wanting to keep eyes on Benjamin at all times.

"What about you, Sarah?" Dr. Willis asks, turning to me. "Anything left to cover?"

"I'll be with Paya and Dori today," I say. "There's a lot to prepare for the feast tonight. And tomorrow I'll go through my notes, make sure I didn't miss anything before we leave."

He nods. "Good. I'd say this has been a successful trip, wouldn't you?" We all murmur our agreement, sipping our coffee. For a moment, it almost feels normal.

Then I see movement out of the corner of my eye. Benjamin is stepping out of his tent, stretching like everything is perfectly normal, like he isn't a complete creep. Like he's just another part of this, the second his eyes lift, they find me. That same look. My stomach tightens. The warmth from earlier fades just a little. I take a slow breath, forcing myself to stay calm, to stay normal.

Wade's presence at my side helps. Keeping me calm, reminding me that I am safe. Still. I think I'm ready to go get cleaned up now.

"I'm going to grab my things and get cleaned up," I tell Wade. He nods, already watching me.

When I reach our tent, I move to the far side where we've been keeping our bags. Ever since that first week, we've fallen into a rhythm, our soaps tucked neatly into my carrier, towels folded the same way every time. I grab everything without thinking. Like I've done it a hundred times. If I didn't keep reminding myself this was new, that six weeks together is no time at all, it. It would feel like this has always been us.

When I step back out, Wade is already walking toward me. He takes everything from my hands without a word, just like he always does. He never lets me carry anything. Not once. I can't help the small smile that tugs at my lips. Maybe chivalry isn't dead, at least not with him. Not with any of them. Everything between us is just easy and natural. Sometimes that worries me, it shouldn't feel this easy or natural, surely it should take more time.

His hand finds mine as we start down the path, fingers threading together automatically. Sometimes we talk. Sometimes we don't. Today is one of those days we don't, just a comfortable silence. We haven't had sex at the waterfall since we had that talk, knowing I need my privacy. There was no way I was going to give Benjamin the chance to see me again.

We get undressed quickly and get into the water. He carries the soap to the rock outcropping. We both get cleaned up quickly, he takes his time helping me wash my hair. It never fully feels clean, I can't wait to São Paulo and take a real shower, I'm also ready for the comfort of a real bed, even if I will miss him. I've grown used to sleeping next to him.

After a quick wash and change, we part ways near the clearing. Wade leans in, pressing a soft kiss to my lips. "I'll find you later."

"I'll hold you to that," I say, smiling as I turn away. Jake falls into step beside me without a word.

The path feels different today. The sunlight barely breaks through the canopy, shadows stretching longer than usual, pooling between the trees. The air feels heavier, thicker, like the jungle itself is holding its breath. A quiet unease settles low in my stomach. I don't know why. It's darker, reminding me of that first nightmare. It just feels wrong, I start scanning the trees.

"Are you okay?" Jake asks me.

"Yes, it's just. It feels different today." He doesn't respond but his eyes are scanning, too. He doesn't call me ridiculous or try to tell me it's nothing. He just adjusts for me.

When we reach the shabono, it's already alive with movement. Voices overlap, laughter mixes with conversation, the steady rhythm of preparation filling the space. Villagers move back and forth, gathering food, organizing, preparing for tonight's feast. Everything looks normal. Everything *should* feel normal.

A light punch lands against my shoulder, pulling me out of my thoughts. I glance over to see Jake grinning at me. "Quit crying," he says, but his voice is softer than usual. Like he knows something's off.

"I'm not crying," I mutter, swiping at my face.

He tilts his head, unimpressed. "You're a terrible liar."

I swing at him, using my new found skills that Simon taught me, but he dodges easily, laughing as he steps out of reach. "Jerk," I mumble. But the sound of his laughter loosens the fear in my chest, just a little.

As I make my way toward Dori, that feeling creeps back in.

"Are you ready?" Dori asks, his kind smile steadying me.

"I am," I say. But even as the words leave my mouth, my skin prickles. Like something unseen is watching. Waiting. Just beyond the trees.

Finally. We've been working toward this all day, and now it's here. The sun begins to sink, casting a warm, golden glow through the open roof of the shabono. The light filters down in soft beams, catching on drifting smoke from the fires, turning everything hazy and almost dreamlike. The air feels alive.

Dori steps into the center of the clearing, his presence immediately grounding the space. Conversations begin to quiet, voices lowering as people gather closer, forming a wide circle around him. I've been waiting for this moment all day.

As an anthropologist, this is everything. An opportunity most people only read about. But as Paya's friend, this means so much more. It's a celebration. A farewell. A beginning and an ending all at once.

This last week has been a blur of preparation, gathering food, organizing and preparing for tonight. Paya told me other tribes would bring offerings, and now they are arriving, filtering into the shabono in groups. Families reconnect. Children run between them. Voices rise and fall in bursts of laughter and recognition.

There are so many people. More than I've seen here since we arrived. Tomorrow, Paya will leave. She'll go with Kaori to his tribe, where she'll live from now on. It's tradition. The women join the husband's tribe, weaving new bonds between families, strengthening connections that stretch across the forest.

Tonight is about all of that. The joining of the families, about honoring and remembering. We finished preparing the food not long ago and Paya disappeared with her mother to get ready. I can still picture her excitement from earlier, nervous but her eyes were glowing. When she returns, the entire space shifts.

For a moment everything feels still. Then the sounds begin. A low rhythmic chanting. Layered voices rising together, echoing through the open structure of the shabono. The beat of it settles into my chest, grounding me in the moment.

I step back slightly, lifting my camera almost instinctively. Click. Click. Click. I capture everything I can. The movement. The expressions. The way the firelight dances across their skin. But my vision blurs slightly with my tears. I blink them away quickly, not wanting to miss anything. Not wanting to lose this moment. Not wanting to forget. I move toward the edge of the clearing where Wade stands, watching everything unfold, his posture relaxed but alert, always the soldier. Always aware.

He's even more alert now that there are extra people here. All the guys are spread around the shabono, trying to fit into the group. Trying to look relaxed but it's obvious by the way their eyes scan everything. For a brief second, his eyes meet mine and just like that, I feel steady again.

I lift my camera once more. Because this, this is something I'll carry with me forever. Paya is breathtaking. Red and orange feathers hang from her ears, swaying softly as she moves, catching the glow of the firelight with every step. More feathers are woven through her dark hair, threaded carefully between bright red flowers that burn against the deep shine of it. A garland of blossoms rests around her neck, the petals brushing her skin as she walks, releasing a faint, earthy sweetness that lingers in the humid air.

She looks like she belongs to this moment. Like she was always meant to stand here. Her skin is painted with bold black stripes, each line deliberate, steady, practiced. They trail down her arms, across her shoulders, marking her in patterns that feel both powerful and deeply personal. There's a rhythm to them, a quiet symmetry that speaks of tradition, of meaning passed from one generation to the next. She isn't just a bride. She's stepping into something larger than herself.

Across from her, Kaori waits. His face is marked differently, thick black stripes framed in red, the color vivid and striking against his skin. The red feels alive, pulsing with something deeper than decoration. Strength and power. More lines curve down his chest and arms, intricate and fluid, like the jungle itself has reached out and left its mark on him. And yet, when he looks at her, there's nothing intimidating about him.

The drums begin to rise. Low at first. Then stronger. The sound moves through the ground, up through my feet, into my chest. It settles there, steady and insistent, like a second heartbeat. Voices join in, layering over one another, rising and falling in a rhythm that feels ancient.

The entire village seems to breathe together. To move together. For a moment, I'm not just watching. I'm part of it. I try to take it all in, the colors, the movement and the way the firelight dances across painted skin. I lift my camera, capturing what I can, but it already feels like it's not enough. Like no picture could ever hold this. My gaze drifts back to Paya. To the way she moves forward, steady, certain. To the way Kaori looks at her like she's the only thing that exists.

For just a second, I imagine myself in her place. Marked in paint and flowers. Walking toward someone who looks at me like that. Walking toward Wade. The thought sends a quiet shiver through me. Something warm, something deeper than I'm ready to name. I push it away. Tonight isn't about me or my unknown future.

It's about Paya. About Kaori. About the life they're stepping into together. And I won't miss a second of it. And yet, I can't shake the feeling that I'm witnessing something I may never get to have. I glance over my shoulder, and my breath catches.

Wade is already watching me. His gaze is steady, unreadable at first but there's something there. Something deeper. Something certain. I feel it. His intention. His quiet conviction. He's imagining this future, too. The thought settles heavily in my chest, as a lump forms in my throat. I swipe at the tear slipping down my cheek, trying to steady myself before it turns into something more.

Before I can fully pull myself together, his hand finds my back, warm and solid. His thumb moves in slow circles, a silent reassurance that he's there. That I'm not alone. His attention flickers for a brief second, something subtle passing across his expression, like he's listening to something I can't hear. His focus sharpens, then settles again just as quickly, his hand never leaving me. Always aware. Always working.

The movement draws a few glances. Dr. Willis looks over, his expression neutral, already drifting elsewhere. Jenna's gaze lingers a moment longer, concern softening her features. And Benjamin—his expression darkens. My stomach drops. I look away from and force a small, unsteady smile toward Jenna, hoping it looks more reassuring than it feels.

This isn't some grand, staged ceremony like the ones you see in movies. It's something quieter. More real. Dori's voice rises, steady and rhythmic as he begins speaking in Yanomami. The words flow in a cadence I don't understand, but I can feel the weight of them, the importance. He turns to Kaori. Then to Paya. Then to an older man standing nearby, his presence commanding without needing to speak. The elder. It makes sense. The elders guide these unions, weaving connections between tribes, strengthening bonds that stretch far beyond just two people.

I wish I could understand every word. Every meaning behind what's being said. But Paya promised she would explain everything in the morning, before she leaves.

Leaves. The word gives me a dull ache in my chest. As the ceremony continues, Wade and his team begin to shift outward, spreading along the edges of the shabono. Subtle. Controlled. A quiet perimeter forming without disrupting the moment. Protecting.

I move carefully through the crowd, lifting my camera, capturing what I can. Faces. Movement. Light flickering across painted skin. There are so many people. Bodies moving around me, voices blending together, palm leaves brushing against my arms as I navigate through the space. It's overwhelming.

And through it all, I keep feeling it. That quiet pull at the back of my mind. Like something is just out of place. Like I'm being watched. I can feel Wade's eyes on me the entire time. Not in a way that distracts me but in a way that steadies me. I know it's not his eyes that are making me feel uneasy. Even in the middle of all this movement, all this noise, I know exactly where Wade is.

The shabono is overflowing with people. Bodies packed close

together, voices rising and overlapping, laughter echoing up into the open ceiling. It's far more crowded than I've ever seen it. I get the sense this was meant to be held out in the clearing near our tents, where there's more space but no one seems bothered by the lack of room. They've made it work. They always do.

The feast is in full motion now. Food is passed between hands, shared freely, no hesitation. The smell of cooked meat, roasted roots, and fresh fruit fills the air, thick and rich and impossible to ignore. Smoke curls upward from the fires, mixing with the humid jungle air and the scent of flowers still woven into Paya's hair.

Some of the people from neighboring tribes watch us carefully. Not all of them, some are genuinely curious. But enough. Their eyes linger too long. Expressions harder and less welcoming. Especially when they look at Wade and his men. It makes sense. We don't belong here.

I keep my distance from them, instinctively shifting toward the people I recognize and toward the familiar faces of Paya's tribe. Safer. The noise builds as the night deepens. Louder conversations. Bursts of laughter. Children weaving through the crowd, chasing each other, their energy endless. They dance in loose circles, mimicking the adults, their joy unrestrained. It's impossible not to smile watching them.

This part feels familiar. Almost like home. This is their version of a reception. A celebration that stretches long into the night, fueled by connection, by shared history, by something deeper than just the union of two people. I move through it all carefully, lifting my camera again and again. Capturing everything I can. Faces lit by firelight. Hands reaching, sharing, connecting. Even the people who seemed guarded earlier begin to soften as the night goes on. Not toward us but toward each other. Time slips away. I lose track of it completely.

The sky outside darkens fully, the firelight becoming the only real source of illumination. Shadows flicker along the walls, shifting with every movement, every passing body. I start to feel it then. The exhaustion, heavy in my limbs. Still, I keep moving. Keep documenting. Not wanting to miss anything. A hand slides around my waist.

I jump slightly, instinct kicking in before I can stop it. Then I turn to find Wade. He's smiling down at me, relaxed in a way that almost feels out of place but his posture says otherwise. Alert. Even without their rifles, the team is still armed. Sidearms secured at their hips, barely noticeable unless you know where to look. The second I told them how many people would be here, everything shifted. They started making different plans, adjusting their positions, then planning for contingencies.

Even now, I can see it if I look closely. The way they've spread out. The way they move without drawing attention. The way they're watching everything at once. Protecting and still letting me experience this moment. They didn't bring their rifles. Dori had warned them it would unsettle the other tribes, especially with the growing fear of militia groups moving through the region. Too many weapons would shift the atmosphere from celebration to threat. Which clearly didn't work, some of them clearly don't like outsiders being here.

Wade hadn't liked it. Not even a little. Even now, I can feel it in him, that quiet tension beneath the surface. His body is relaxed against mine, his arm steady around my waist, but there's nothing relaxed about the way his eyes move. Constantly scanning. Tracking movement. Measuring distance. Waiting for something he can't see yet.

The longer the night stretches on, the heavier my body feels. The energy around me hasn't faded in the slightest. If anything, it's grown louder. More animated. The kind of celebration that builds instead of burns out, but I'm fading. My head tilts slightly as I lean into him, the warmth of his chest grounding me. He notices immediately. Of course he does. His hand shifts, tightening just a fraction, pulling me closer as his lips brush against the top of my head. He knows.

Time has blurred into something meaningless. The sky is pitch black beyond the open structure, the only light coming from the fires that flicker and dance around us. It feels late. Really late. My eyes lift, searching the sky out of habit, even though I can't see much through the canopy. It has to be well past midnight.

The celebration shows no signs of slowing. Groups gather and split, laughter rising in bursts. People reconnect, voices overlapping in stories and shared memories. Some sit close to the fires, others move through the crowd, weaving between bodies with practiced ease. This isn't just a wedding. It's a reunion. A farewell. Tomorrow, Paya leaves and everyone here knows what that means.

I shift slightly, stretching out the stiffness in my legs, but the movement only reminds me how tired I am. For a moment, I stop trying to keep up with everything around me. Stop trying to capture every detail. Instead, I just exist in it. The warmth of the fire. The sound of laughter. The steady presence of him behind me. I let my eyes drift closed for just a second, breathing it all in. Trying to hold onto it.

Because something in me knows, this moment won't last and I want to remember it exactly like this.

Chapter Twenty Two

Wade

I'm working with Ghost when the conversation circles back to the same dead end we've been hitting for days. Benjamin. Dean Wagner. Everything we've uncovered. Ghost's been watching the university servers. No report was ever filed by Dr. Willis about what happened here. Nothing about Benjamin's behavior. Either he never made the call or it got buried somewhere along the line. We don't know which.

We've been building the case piece by piece, slow and careful. An attorney outside the university, someone with no ties to the dean. Looping in the right people, laying groundwork to bring it higher if we have to. But it's messy. Too much of what we have comes from places we weren't supposed to be. Journal entries. Private records. Things that won't hold up if they're challenged. And here? Nothing solid. Nothing that sticks. He grabbed her once. Watched her more times than I can count. Hovered just close enough to set every instinct I have on edge. But not enough to put him away.

The attorney is working angles we can't, tracking down the girls who reported harassment, trying to get statements, build something real. Even found a therapist to help approach the ones who reported assault. If we get testimony, if we get one solid thread, everything changes. But right now, we've got nothing that holds.

The frustration sits heavy in my chest. Feels like we're chasing something just out of reach. Ghost throws out the idea again. Setting a trap. Creating the illusion she's alone. Waiting for him to make a move. I shut it down immediately. Not even a discussion. She's not bait. She's not part of the operation. She's mine to protect. I don't say it out loud. But it's there, in every decision I make.

We go back and forth anyway. Different angles. Different approaches. None of them good enough and none of them safe enough. Eventually, we land where we always do—wait it out. Finish the op and handle it once we're stateside where we have more control, more resources. I don't like it. But it's the only option that doesn't put her at risk.

Glitch has been with her all morning. Staying close, keeping an eye on her while they get set up for the ceremony this evening. When she woke up, she was practically glowing. Excited in a way I don't think I've seen before. She's been waiting for this day since we got here. The ceremony. Her friend getting married. Every time she talked about it, her whole face lit up. Like nothing else mattered. Like the world was exactly where it was supposed to be. And then she'd get emotional, tear up without even trying to hide it.

It hit me harder than it should've. Seeing her like that, open and happy. She kept going on about what it meant for her work too. Said this was something most people only get to read about. That being here, seeing it happen in real time, it would change everything for her. I don't pretend to understand that side of it. But I understand what it means to her. That's enough.

The guys gave her shit about it, of course. They've become close to her over the past six weeks, too. Always teasing her, treating her like one of us. Couldn't help themselves. She ignored every bit of it. Didn't even slow down. Just kept smiling. I let myself believe, just for a second, that maybe we'd make it through this without anything going wrong.

"Wraith," Reaper's voice cuts through the earpiece. "Multiple groups inbound. Other tribes are arriving now. Some of them aren't exactly friendly when they spot us."

I'm already moving before he finishes. Ghost shuts his laptop without a word, packing it up fast and clean. We fall into step together, heading back toward the main tent. My mind is already shifting. From investigation, to security. There is going to be too many variables, tonight. Too many bodies and not enough control, for our liking.

"Alright," I say into comms, my tone sharper now. "We're done with intel for the moment. Ceremony's starting soon, and this just turned into a full security op." No hesitation. No pushback. They're already adjusting.

"With this many unknowns, we tighten the perimeter. No one moves alone. No gaps. Eyes on your assigned at all times." I pause, running through the layout in my head. The shabono's structure, its open center and multiple entry points. Exactly zero real barriers.

"Primary objective is the scientists. Secondary is situational awareness. I want constant comms. If something feels off, I hear about it immediately." Ghost mutters something under his breath about priorities. I don't look at him. Don't need to. Assignments come next.

"Stitches, you're on Jenna. Keep her close, don't let her wander. Magellan, you're on Willis. He's going to drift, don't let him. Reaper, you're on Benjamin. I want eyes on him at all times. If he so much as breathes wrong, I hear it. Glitch, you float. You're my secondary. If anything shifts, you move where I need you. Sparta, you take outer perimeter. I want you watching the crowd flow, who's coming in, who's leaving, anyone lingering where they shouldn't."

That leaves one position. Mine. They don't miss it, of course they don't. The comms crackle with barely-contained amusement. Comments I don't bother acknowledging.

"Focus," I snap, cutting it off before it builds. "This isn't a game. We've got unfamiliar terrain, unfamiliar people, and no control over the environment. That means we stay sharp." Silence follows. The right kind.

"Check your gear. Sidearms only. Low profile. No unnecessary escalation." They all know this already, we've been planning. The anxiety in me building, I never get this worried before an operation, but this feels different. We all knew the rifles were a no-go the second Dori mentioned the other tribes. Didn't mean I liked it. Didn't mean I agreed. But we adapt, we always do.

Ghost and I reach the tent, falling into routine without speaking. Weapons checked, mags confirmed and comms tested. Everything methodical. We've done protective details before, even in high-risk environments and in unpredictable crowds. This is different because it's not just a mission. It's her. I don't let that show. Don't let it change how I move, how I think, how I plan. But it's there, driving every decision I make. I've known since the first week. Tried to ignore it. Tried to push it down, but it didn't work. Now, there's no pretending it's anything else.

So I adjust. Not the mission and not the plan. Just the stakes because I'm not losing her. Last night when we made love it felt right. Not just the physical part, everything after. The way she stayed close, the way she looked at me like she was trying to figure out what came next. I knew she's been getting worried about how things will be between us after we're done tomorrow. We talked about it a lot. I hope she is reassured, but she will be when I move to Minnesota to be with her. She won't have to question where I stand.

As I stand in the sweltering heat in my uniform, sweat clings to my back and runs down my spine, but I don't move. The unit is spread evenly around the shabono perimeter, just like we planned, each man positioned with clear sightlines, overlapping coverage, no blind spots. Our rifles are still locked away and we're each carrying our side arms that are hidden.

I watch Sarah flit around with her camera attached to her face, completely in her element. Capturing photos of Paya and Kaori during the ceremony, she's also capturing the guests and moving easily through the crowd like she belongs here. Like she isn't surrounded by potential threats. I notice she is staying away from the ones that look angry about our presence. Good. She's paying attention.

Every once in a while she stops near me and I hand over her notebook and pencil I keep in one of my pockets. She writes something and winks as she hands it back. Like it's nothing. Like this is normal. She has pockets in her cargo pants that she can fit her notebook into. She wanted me to hold it so she had a reason to come by me. I wasn't going to complain.

"How are things going, Little Mouse?"

"Good, it's so beautiful. It's exciting to see the different tribe members. Paya looks so beautiful and people look like they're having fun." Her face is lit up again, flushed from running around in the heat, eyes bright with excitement. She's completely absorbed in this moment. Luckily, the sun is starting to dip lower. I grab her hips and pull her closer to me, grounding her for just a second. Keeping her where I can feel her.

"I'm glad you're enjoying it. Make sure you keep your distance from the angry ones, I don't like the way they are looking at all of us." I whisper to her. She nods, even if I know she doesn't feel the weight of it the way I do. She doesn't need to. That's my job.

"I wonder what Sarah is observing right now?" I hear Glitch say into the earpiece. I look past her head and spot him instantly on the opposite side of the shabono, leaning casually but watching everything, smirking like an idiot. Keeping my hands around her, I flip him off. He starts laughing.

"I don't know what he said, but I can hear his laugh through your ear piece. Tell him he's an idiot." She has no idea. The comms light up immediately, low chuckles, quiet amusement passing between the team. Even Ghost lets out something close to a breath of humor.

And just like that, for a second, it almost feels normal. She giggles as she walks away, disappearing back into the crowd and I let her go. But my eyes never leave her. Not for a second.

"Focus up." I bark into the earpiece. I keep my expression neutral, but I have to fight the edge of a smile. It's funny. It always is with them. But not tonight. Not with this many unknowns, this many moving pieces. Everyone needs to stay sharp.

As the ceremony draws to a close, I catch movement on the far side of the shabono. Benjamin. He stands abruptly, barely sparing a glance at what's still unfolding in front of him before turning and heading toward the direction of our tents. My attention sharpens instantly. A moment later, Willis follows, stepping over to Magellan with that same stiff, controlled expression he always carries when something doesn't interest him.

"We're heading back. Going to finish organizing before dark." They didn't enjoy it. That much is obvious. If anything, they look relieved to be leaving, like the entire ceremony was beneath them. Or like they had somewhere else they'd rather be.

"Okay, Magellan and Reaper, please stay with them. Check the perimeter of the clearing as well. Please continue to report in. Glitch can you run a perimeter check of the Shabono and report back."

Acknowledgments come through one after another. Everyone moves but Jenna stays seated. She watches them go, something uncertain flickering across her face before she looks back toward the celebration. She still seems to be enjoying it, even if there's hesitation there now.

The night stretches on. The celebration doesn't slow. Bonfires burn brighter as the jungle around us sinks into complete darkness. The only light comes from the flames, casting shifting shadows across faces, bodies, the walls of the shabono. Everything feels alive. And still,

I don't relax.

Sarah moves through the crowd, camera still in hand, but I can see the difference now. The pace is slower. Her steps less steady. It's late. When she drifts closer, snapping pictures of the kids running through the open space, I reach out, my hand brushing against her back. She startles, again. I hate that. Hate that she's still on edge. Hate that even with all of us here, she doesn't feel completely safe. That needs to change.

"You're getting tired." I murmur to her. She nods, not even trying to argue. "It's almost 2am when do these things end?" I glance around the shabono, taking in the movement, the energy that hasn't faded in the slightest.

"Hopefully soon, but they have a tendency to go for a while. They don't all get together very often, so it's more of a celebration of being together and seeing old loved ones that they don't get to see much. Like tomorrow with Paya leaving, they won't see her again for a long time." She absorbs that quietly, already weighing the options.

I should send her to bed. Get her out of here. Get her somewhere controlled. However, I know she won't want to miss this and part of me doesn't want to pull her away from something that matters this much to her. The rest of us don't get that luxury anyway.

We'll be up all night. Keeping an eye on everything and rotating positions. Keeping eyes on every movement until this crowd clears out and the risk drops back to something manageable. The researchers will sleep. We'll catch up on it later when we're on the plane, back at base. Right now, we hold the line.

As we continue talking, Jenna comes up behind Sarah. "Hey Sarah?"

Sarah suddenly turns around, startled by someone coming up behind her. Jenna shifts uneasily, her nerves evident in the way she fidgets. A flicker of curiosity sparks in me. What could have her so rattled? I glance over at Stitches, knowing he's been listening through my earpiece. He meets my gaze and simply shrugs, understanding my silent question without me having to say a word.

"Hey, Jenna! Are you having fun?"

"Yes, I am. I was just wondering if you would come with me to go pee? Sorry, I just really don't want to go out there by myself. Normally I would be over by our tents, I feel more familiar with that area."

Sarah and Jenna both look into the trees beyond us and I track their gaze automatically. Total darkness, the firelight doesn't reach far past the edge of the shabono, and beyond that, the jungle swallows everything. I see the worry in Jenna's eyes. She's not faking this she is concerned. Sarah turns to look up at me again, the question clearly written across her face.

"I think it should be safe, but don't go too far." The words leave my mouth before I can stop them. Before I can listen to the part of me that's already rejecting the idea completely. Sarah nods. I don't like this. Not even a little. Every instinct I have is pushing back. Telling me to shut it down. Tell her no. Keep her here. Tell her I will go with her, even if she doesn't want me hearing her.

"Okay, probably a little bit out so you won't hear us," she adds, scrunching her nose in that way that usually gets a reaction out of me. Not this time. Right now, all I can think about is distance.

Glitch's voice comes through the earpiece. "I'm finishing my perimeter walk. Nothing unusual so far. They should be fine up to a hundred yards." I grit my teeth. He's not wrong. Logically, it makes sense. But logic isn't what's keeping me on edge. It's that feeling. That pressure building in the back of my mind. I don't like it. I don't trust it. Privacy be damned. She shouldn't be out there alone.

"No more than a hundred yards," I say, my voice firm. "And you have five minutes. If you're not back, I'm coming in after you." I hold her gaze a second longer than necessary, making sure she understands. This isn't a suggestion. She gives me that small smile anyway. Like she thinks I'm overreacting. And then she turns, walking away with Jenna toward the edge of the firelight.

I watch her go. Every step. Until the shadows swallow her completely. The second she's out of sight, that feeling in my gut gets worse.

I say to Glitch. "Stay close without them noticing. Keep an eye on them."

"Copy. I'll shift towards their side."

Even as I watch her disappear into the darkness, that uneasy feeling lingers. It doesn't fade. It doesn't settle. If anything, it sharpens. Jenna asked her to go, why? Was she really scared to go alone, or did something happen? She's been keeping her distance from all of us, barely even speaking to Benjamin. That alone is suspicious. She has been working more with Willis.

Then there's Benjamin. The fucker has been too quiet these past couple of weeks. Too controlled. Too careful. I haven't forgotten what he did, even if Sarah decided not to tell Jenna about the tracker. Smart move. We don't know who to trust. My eyes flick to my watch. Three minutes. The longer they're gone, the harder it gets to stay put. My fingers flex at my sides, my legs itching to move, every instinct pushing me forward.

Five minutes. Fuck this. I push off the tree and head toward the path. Out of the corner of my eye, Stitches moves to follow me without a word. Ghost is still outside the shabono, watching. Magellan and Reaper should still be in the clearing, keeping an eye on Willis and Benjamin. Sparta is inside the perimeter. Everything should be fine. So why does it feel like it isn't?

"Were they following the path that leads to the traps?" Glitch murmurs in my earpiece. My heart drops, because I already know what he's going to say.

Chapter Twenty Three

Wade

"Yes. They left five minutes ago. Stitches and I are heading that way." Cold sweat erupts along my back.

"I don't see or hear them. I connected with the path a couple minutes ago and headed further away from the shabono." God damn it where is she.

"Fuck. Find them. We're closing in on six minutes, I gave her a limit of five." My breath feels tight, my chest constricting with something I don't let myself name.

"Everyone report in," I grind out, stepping off the path into the trees. Stitches moves just as quietly beside me.

"Magellan and I are still watching the clearing," Reaper says. "No movement. Willis and Benjamin went to bed hours ago. We haven't seen the girls come through here, but we'll do a perimeter check."

"Nothing from inside the shabono," Sparta adds. It's been eight minutes now.

"Sarge." The way Ghost says my name makes my stomach drop.

"Talk." My voice is sharper than I mean it to be, but I don't give a fuck.

"I pulled up her tracker. She's moving north, fast. She's already a couple of kilometers ahead." My vision tunnels. How the hell did she get that far that fast?

"I can't say, but she's moving quickly. Looks like they turned on an adjoining path that goes northeast." I take off. No hesitation. No thought. Just movement. My boots hit the ground in near silence as I push through the jungle, listening for anything—anything—that shouldn't be there.

"Sarge." Reaper this time. I already know I'm not going to like what comes next.

"Copy," I grit out.

"We checked Willis and Benjamin's tents. There's a cut on the back from the middle down to the base. They're gone." I stop dead in my tracks.

The jungle is too quiet. No insects. No movement. Just silence pressing in from every direction. Sarah and Jenna are gone. Willis and Benjamin are gone. And something tells me this was no accident. My grip tightens around my weapon, rage and fear slamming into each other in my chest, sharp and violent. I will find her and God help the bastard who took her.

The jungle is suffocating. The night, usually a source of cover, now stretches endlessly around me, swallowing every sound that isn't the pounding of my boots or the erratic beat of my heart. Sarah is gone. The words slam through me again and again, each time harder than the last.

Anger boils up, mixing with the cold edge of fear threatening to choke me. Did someone take them and we didn't notice? Unlikely. Impossible. And yet, it happened. A distant sound reaches my ears. There. Just barely, I hear the faint, unmistakable hum of an engine. An ATV. My stomach clenches. They're moving her.

I turn sharply, sprinting back the way I came. I need to be better equipped. The jungle is unforgiving, I refuse to be slowed down by unpreparedness. By the time I reach Stitches and Glitch, Ghost has already joined them, appearing from the dark like he was made for it.

"There was an engine," I growl. "Faint, but moving fast. They have the girls." No hesitation. No questions. They all know what that means. Everything changes now. I take off toward the shabono, my team at my back.

Sparta moves the second he sees us coming. He doesn't need to ask what's wrong, he can hear everything through the ear pieces and he can read it on my face. He falls in beside us without a word. We cut through the village, weaving past bodies and worried faces, barely registering Dori and Paya looking on with concern. Voices rise behind us, confusion spreading through the celebration, but I don't stop. I can't stop.

The clearing comes into view. Reaper and Magellan already have the weapon cases open, loading rifles with steady, practiced hands. Metal clicks in the night air. Mags seated. Chambers checked. Slings thrown on. The dim glow from the lanterns flickers over their faces, grim, focused and ready.

Willis and Benjamin's tents are still zipped up. Neat. Undisturbed. But we know better now. The cuts in the back. They never went to bed. They walked out the rear like cowards. I move to the table and set Sarah's camera down, my fingers lingering on it for one brief second. She handed it to me with that teasing smirk, the warmth of her fingers brushing against mine. I should have gone with her. I should have shut it down immediately. I should have sent Glitch sooner. *I should have—no.* I snap myself out of it. Dwelling won't save her.

I force myself to move. To think. To function. Holstering my sidearm. Slinging my rifle over my back. Seating fresh mags into my vest, checking each one by touch before locking them in place. Comms secure. Knife where it belongs. Tourniquet accessible. Every movement is mechanical, rehearsed from years of repetition. My body knows what to do. My mind is screaming.

Ghost is already on the tracker, eyes locked on the signal, feeding coordinates into Glitch's tablet. Glitch has the satellite map up, overlaying terrain, waterways, elevation changes, any route they'd use to move fast without getting bogged down.

Stitches is packing trauma gear with ruthless efficiency, gauze, chest seals, syringes, airway kit, shears, IV starts, fluids. The stuff you bring when you expect blood. I catch him flipping through the casualty cards for each of us, then adding one more blank card to the stack. His jaw tightens. None of us say it, we don't need to. We're all thinking the same thing. This could go bad.

A shadow falls across the tent opening. "Sarah?" I turn. Dori stands there with Paya and Kaori at his shoulders, their eyes moving over the weapons, the gear, the urgency in the air. They already know. No one prepares like this for nothing. I shake my head once. The grief in their faces hardens into something sharper. Resolve.

"Focus up!" I bark, snapping everyone back to task. "She's been gone fifteen minutes. We roll now. Whoever took them has the advantage of transport, we don't. Grab what you need." Mags slammed home. Packs sealed. Bolts checked. Safeties confirmed. No wasted motion.

Dori steps forward. I grip his forearm hard. "I will get her back." He nods once. That's all either of us needs. I move first. Rifle comes forward, muzzle down but ready as I push into the tree line, my team flowing behind me like water finding its course.

Ghost on point. Tracker in one hand, weapon in the other. Glitch just behind him with the tablet, feeding updates, adjusting routes in real time. Stitches center stack. Reaper and Sparta on flank security. Magellan trailing rear watch. A seven-man element that has done this dance in worse places than hell.

"We'll cut northeast, stay close to the river," I say low and steady. "Less dense trees there, better movement. We keep pace without blowing the trail."

Clicks of acknowledgment sound through comms. No chatter. No jokes, now. Just mission mode. We move fast. Disciplined fast. Not a blind sprint. Controlled aggression. Enough speed to gain ground, enough spacing to avoid bunching up, enough silence to hear what matters. The jungle swallows us whole. Darkness presses in like a living thing. Branches rake across sleeves and gear. Mud grabs at boots. Insects whine past our ears. Somewhere overhead, something heavy moves through the canopy.

None of it matters. It's all background noise. All I can think about is her. Every minute passing. Every second she might be scared. Every second she might think I'm not coming. *I'm coming, beautiful.*

An hour in, Ghost's voice cuts through the comms. "They stopped ten minutes ago. Close to the river, still on the south side."

I don't break stride. But every part of me sharpens. Finally. Relief barely registers, she's not moving anymore. That should mean opportunity. A fixed target. A chance to close. But something about it feels wrong.

"How far?" I grit out, jaw clenched so tight it aches.

"Well…" Ghost doesn't usually hesitate. The pause is worse than the answer.

"Well, what?" I snap, anger and fear bleeding through before I can lock it down.

"Well, they were moving at a quick pace through the jungle. They have managed to get 100 kilometers." He says it quietly. Doesn't matter. It lands like a punch to the throat.

One hundred klicks. No one covers that kind of distance on foot in this terrain in that amount of time. Not carrying two women. Not through jungle this dense. They were prepared and used an ATV. They're staying close to the river which means they plan to use a boat, multiple handoffs. This wasn't impulsive, it was planned. I do the math automatically.

At our current movement rate, even pushing hard, it could take the better part of a day to reach that location on foot. Longer if terrain turns against us. Way too fucking long. I send up a prayer to any god still listening that they haven't found the tracker. If they do, we lose our only clean line to her.

"Glitch," I say, forcing my voice level. "Anything on satellite?" No answer right away. Typing. Map layers shifting. Signal processing. I hear the river before I see it. Heavy water. Fast current. Wide enough to matter.

Then Glitch speaks. "There's a structure near her location. Small footprint. Looks like a warehouse or service building. Close to a city with multiple river ports." My blood goes cold. A building. River access for port traffic. Easy movement. Easy concealment. Easy disappearance. My mind connects the dots before I can stop it. Trafficking pipeline. Transit node. Temporary hold site before transfer. I grind my teeth so hard pain shoots through my jaw.

"Keep moving." No one answers. They don't need to. My men feel the anger and the urgency coursing through me. I know they must be angry, too. They care about Sarah but she's my whole world, my future. We increase pace immediately. Ghost pushes point harder, still disciplined enough to track sign and maintain navigation. Glitch keeps feeding route corrections from terrain imagery, trying to shave minutes anywhere he can. Reaper and Sparta widen security intervals, scanning for choke points, ambush terrain, movement. Stitches stays center, conserving energy, protecting the medical loadout.

Magellan checks rear trail every thirty seconds, making sure no one is following and no one is falling behind. A professional movement under pressure. Fast. Controlled. Violent if needed.

The jungle blurs around us. Moonlight flashes through breaks in the canopy. Roots try to break ankles. Vines catch on gear. Branches slap across faces and rifles. None of it matters. Nothing slows me down.

The sounds of the Amazon, howls in the distance, insects screaming in waves, unseen bodies moving through brush. It all just fades into static. She is the only thing in my head.

Ghost calls fresh coordinates. "Still there. Southwest side of the Amazon River where it meets the Tapajós." His voice stays calm.

Mine would not be. So I don't speak. I just move. Adrenaline keeps my legs driving, lungs burning, vision narrowed. But it can't drown out the truth clawing at my insides. Every minute we lose shifts the odds. Every second gives them time to move her again. Every second she spends at their mercy is one too many.

Sarah. Hang on, baby. I'm coming.

The eastern sky starts to bleed orange through the canopy, thin light cutting through layers of mist. Dawn has come on too fast. We've been moving all night. Most of us have been awake more than twenty-four hours. Some longer. Legs heavy. Shoulders burning under load. Feet blistered and wet inside boots. None of it matters. Fatigue is real. So is training. You acknowledge it, compartmentalize it, and keep moving. Giving up was never an option and it isn't now.

My mind keeps running the same questions on repeat. Will this be when they transport her? Are they waiting for daylight movement on the river? Will they sit tight until dark and move under cover again? Which one would I do?

Ghost's voice crackles in my earpiece, sharper now, all business. "Still no movement. But that doesn't mean they haven't spotted the tracker."

The thought hits like a fist to the ribs. He's voicing my concerns. If they found it, they could've ditched it. Fed us bad location data. Moved her hours ago while we burned time chasing a signal. She could already be gone. No, I shut that down immediately. There is no place on this earth I won't go to find her. I may have only known her a few weeks, but she is my future. Every brutal step through this jungle drives that truth deeper into my bones.

Time loses shape. Hours smear together into heat, sweat, and movement. We've been pushing nonstop, rotating point, hydrating on the move, eating when we can force it down. Legs heavy. Shoulders burning under gear weight. Lungs raw from the wet, suffocating air. Still we move. Still no one complains. That's the job.

The sun finally starts to fall again, the worst of the heat easing just enough to matter. Shadows lengthen through the trees. Good. Darkness favors trained men. Darkness favors us.

We tighten spacing and keep pushing, weaving through the

undergrowth in staggered formation. Ghost on point. Reaper and Sparta offset left and right. Magellan rear security. Stitches tucked center with the medical load. Glitch floating where needed, eyes bouncing between terrain and screen. Each step deliberate.

Sweat runs down my spine, soaking into my shirt. I don't feel it. I don't feel anything except urgency. Then I catch the hint of smoke. Faint at first beneath the rot of wet earth and vegetation. Then clearer. Burning wood, a cook fire. Human presence. We're close and if they've laid a hand on her, there will be no mercy.

Ghost raises a fist and the formation slows automatically. Then his voice comes low through comms. "Five klicks out." So fucking close.

"Focus up." My voice stays level even if my pulse doesn't. "We've been moving for hours. The sun's coming up soon, and we'll lose the element of surprise. They'll wait until daylight to move her. We don't have that long."

I drop to a knee behind the cover of a thick trunk and the team follows suit automatically. "Two-minute halt. Final checks." Fresh magazines are seated. Suppressors tightened. Radios checked low and brief.

Ghost rips out a drained battery and slams in a fresh one before doing the same for his GPS unit. Glitch swaps his radio pack, eyes never leaving the tracker feed. Reaper runs a hand over his kit, confirming blades, mags, med pouch. Sparta checks optics and rear security while Magellan scans the tree line toward the shack.

Stitches crouches beside me long enough to press a fresh battery into my palm. I swap it into my radio, key the mic once, then release.

"Comms check." One by one, quiet clicks answer in my ear. Good. I rise, bringing my rifle back up.

"From here on out, no unnecessary chatter. Weapons tight. Positive ID before shots. We hit fast, clear rooms, find Sarah and Jenna, move fast." My jaw clenches as I look through the trees toward where they're holding her. Truth is, it'd be a miracle they waited this long to move her. But miracles happen and they better start now.

Reaper tightens his grip on his rifle. "Let's go get your girl." My girl. Damn right.

We move again, faster but quieter, spreading wider as terrain opens. The jungle begins to thin, dense walls of green giving way to lower brush and broken tree cover near the widening riverbank. More lines of sight. More danger.

Then we hear movement. Ghost drops instantly to a knee, fist raised.

The whole line freezes on instinct. Weapons up. Eyes searching. Breathing slows.

The sky shifts into that pale blue-gray light right before dawn. The same shade as Sarah's eyes. And I swear, I will see them again.

I tighten my grip on the rifle, forcing my breath steady.

"Slow down," I murmur. "Stay spread. Watch for traps."

Because if they planned the abduction, they may have planned our arrival too. The jungle is too quiet. No birds calling. No insect wall of sound. No movement in the canopy. Just the hush that settles when something dangerous has moved in. We're close and I am going to kill anyone who stands between me and Sarah.

"I see a large wooden building," Sparta murmurs through the earpiece.

Instantly, we freeze. Every man drops low without hesitation, rifles covering sectors, eyes scanning tree line, roof line, ground sign.

"How far?" I whisper.

"I'm behind a tree, about fifty yards out. It looks like some kind of dockside shack. No guards outside. No traps that I can see."

A wooden shack. Remote. Weather-beaten. Easy to abandon. Easy to burn. Easy to disappear from. Perfect as a temporary hold site. They're getting ready to move her.

"Sparta, stay put. We're coming to you."

We start moving, slower now, measured footsteps. Silent as men can be carrying rifles and rage. We slip through the undergrowth, using the thick trunks for cover, stepping where the ground is softest, avoiding branches. No one bunches up. No one crosses another man's muzzle. Professional movement under pressure. The structure comes into view through the trees. It's worse than I expected.

Boards bowed outward. Sections patched with mismatched timber. Roofline sagging from years of storms and neglect. One hard kick in the right place and parts of it would fail. But I don't care about the building. Sarah is inside.

"Glitch, get thermal imaging on the building," I order. "Ghost, check the tracker. Any movement?"

"Still there," Ghost confirms. Then voices erupt inside. They're speaking fast and angry in Spanish. I go completely still. The language is rapid and layered over itself, but I catch the cadence immediately. I look to Magellan. He's already listening, head tilted, filtering tone from noise.

"It's hard to hear," he mutters. "They're arguing. Some want to move now, some are saying wait."

Why wait? Waiting means something changed. Waiting means uncertainty. Waiting means opportunity.

"Thermal's up," Glitch whispers. "Seventeen heat signatures inside. Ten clustered in the main room. Seven separated in another room." Seventeen. Too many for reckless. Manageable for us. One of those rooms holds the girls. Maybe both. Maybe one. No assumptions.

"Alright," I murmur. "We stay in the trees. Ghost, Glitch, Stitches you're with me on the left. Reaper, Sparta, Magellan take the right. Stay spread. Check for more exits, then regroup."

Acknowledgments click softly through comms. No wasted words. Glitch is already recording thermal overlays and sending them to the team feed. Ghost starts reading the structure with his eyes the way other men read books. Stitches checks gear one more time, preparing for casualties before bullets fly.

We move. Two elements peeling opposite directions, circling wide through cover. No crossing lines. No noise. No light. When I reach the front angle, I spot double doors opening onto a weathered dock. No guards outside. No immediate transport tied up. But farther out, shapes in the water. Large freighters sitting low and still beyond the morning haze. Anchored. Fuck. That means this isn't random. It's organized. And if we'd been an hour later, she would've vanished into the river traffic.

"At the front," I whisper. "Double doors, no guards."

"We're at the back," Reaper reports. "One exit. No sign of movement."

"I moved further ahead, no other doors," Sparta adds. Good, two exits. That's it. A kill box if we control it right. Anyone trying to run funnels straight into one of our elements. Just as I'm about to signal the approach, a door slides open. I tense instantly, rifle coming tighter into my shoulder, finger indexing along the trigger guard.

Two men step out, AK-47s hanging loose across their chests. Undisciplined carry. Comfortable. They think they're safe here. Behind them, Willis follows. He looks like hell. His usual khaki shirt is wrinkled and damp with sweat, hat gone, hair flattened and sticking up where he keeps dragging a hand through it. Every movement is twitchy, nervous. He should be.

The two gunmen light cigarettes, speaking low while Willis hovers beside them. Smoke drifts into the morning air in lazy spirals. I watch mouths. Hands. Posture. Everything. Numbers. They're talking numbers. Pricing. Timing. Quantity. A fucking deal. I want Magellan closer for clean translation, but moving him now risks compromise. We stay frozen in place, concealed in brush and shadow. No one breaks discipline.

After a few minutes, the men shake hands. Casual. Business concluded. They flick their cigarettes to the dirt and head back inside like none of this matters. Like lives are inventory. My grip tightens on the rifle. They have no idea what's coming for them.

"Ghost, call it in," I say. "We don't know what we're about to walk into."

Ghost slides back a few yards, already pulling the satellite phone, keeping his voice low and clipped as he passes coordinates, personnel estimate, armed presence, trafficking indicators. Contingency on record. Support notified. No expectation of help in time.

I draw one slow breath and force everything back into place. Anger later. Precision now.

"Reaper, Sparta, Magellan get to that back door. Move on my signal." Soft clicks confirm. I picture their routes automatically— angles, sectors, breach points and crossfire avoidance. Ghost finishes the call. I give the signal. We move.

My pulse hammers in my ears as we close the distance, rifles up, muzzles steady. Boards in the walls are warped and split in places. Through the gaps, shapes move inside. If anyone looks hard enough, they'll see us. I raise a fist. Freeze. Everyone locks in place. I listen for a moment, there are boot steps and voices, metal scraping wood. It doesn't sound like they're alarmed, not yet.

"Wraith," Magellan's urgent whisper crackles through the earpiece. I click twice. Send it.

"They're talking about the ship arriving in an hour, there was concerns about the one girl, too much drugs she hasn't woken up when she should have." Magellan breathes. "Said they can do what they want to the girls in the meantime. They're negotiating prices."

My vision tunnels. Everything narrows to a red point. It takes every ounce of discipline I own not to kick the door in right now and kill every man breathing inside. Not yet. I can't afford to be sloppy. Not at the risk of hitting her. I force one breath in. One breath out. The only good news? They're still alive. And now, so are the men inside.

For a few more seconds.

"Get ready," I whisper.

Ten…

Nine…
Eight—
A scream echoes through the trees. I know that voice. "Move."

Chapter Twenty Four

Sarah

Pain detonates behind my eyes, sharp and merciless, each pulse of it crashing in rhythm with the nausea churning through my stomach. My head swims. The room tilts as if I've been dropped into a river, dragged beneath the surface. I blink against a light that is far too bright. It's not wade's tent above me. I need to focus.

Think. I squeeze my eyes shut, forcing my sluggish mind backward. Jenna whispering that she couldn't hold it anymore. Her embarrassed laugh when she asked if we could go just a little farther down the trail so no one would hear her. Me rolling my eyes and using the flashlight to lead us deeper. Knowing we shouldn't go any further because Wade would get worried. The jungle around us had been alive with sound, buzzing insects, distant birds and the heavy rustle of leaves in the dark. The damp earth soft beneath our shoes.

I remember telling her to hurry. Then branches snapping. A hand over my mouth. Another fist in my hair, wrenching my head back so hard stars burst across my vision. I know I needed to scream to get

Wade's attention, but I couldn't.

"Run!" I'd tried to yell, but it came out muffled against a palm that smelled like sweat and cigarettes.

I remember kicking, clawing, my nails scraping skin. A man cursing in a language I didn't know, but I think was Spanish. The beam of the flashlight spinning wildly through the trees before crashing to the ground. Then something pricking my neck. A needle and then darkness. The memory hits like a wrecking ball, stealing the air from my lungs.

I jerk upright on instinct. Agony rips through my wrists, white-hot and brutal. I gasp, yanking again before panic fully registers. My arms won't move. My body thrashes uselessly against the resistance. No. No, no, no. I whip my head to the side, vision blurring from the motion. My stomach lurches. Nylon rope has bitten deep into my skin, binding me to a rusted metal bed frame bolted to the floor.

My pulse jackknifes. My chest caves inward. Breathe. Look. The air shifts, humid and foul, drifting through the slats in the walls. It carries the smell of mildew, old sweat and something rotten. Thin spears of sunlight slip through the cracks in warped wooden walls, slicing across the dirt floor. Dust drifts through the beams. I don't know how long I've been out. I don't know where I am. The air skims over my skin, too much skin. Bare skin. No. My breath stutters and lungs seize, trying to stop the cry threatening to come out.. Slowly, so painfully slowly, I force myself to look down. My shirt is gone. I don't want to look lower, but terror drags my gaze downward anyway. A strangled sound claws up my throat. Only my panties remain. Oh God. Oh God.

A sob swells thick and choking, but I bite it back so hard my jaw aches. Only a whimper comes out. My whole body turns to ice when the door creaks open. I flinch, every muscle locking. Instinct screams at me to run, to fight, to hide. But I can't. I'm trapped.

A small woman enters, her blonde hair stringy and unkempt, hanging in dirty tangles around a face far too young to look this broken. Blonde, unnatural to this part of the world. Out of place, like me. She moves carefully, almost soundlessly, her head bowed as she cradles a small tray with a dented metal cup and a slice of dry bread balanced on top. She's naked. Dark bruises stain her tanned rough skin, blooming across her hips, ribs, and thighs. Fresh cuts criss-cross her arms and torso, some thin and shallow, others deeper, angrier.

My stomach turns. I swallow hard. She doesn't look at me.

"C-Can you help me?" I whisper, my voice hoarse and ragged,

scraped raw from thirst. From the force of trying to keep the lump in my throat at bay. From whatever drug they gave me. The blonde girl flinches so hard the cup rattles against the tray.

Her wide brown eyes flick to mine for only a second. In that brief glance, I catch everything at once. Fear, guilt and a helplessness so deep it feels carved into her bones. I repeat it in Portuguese but there's nothing, just a hollowness in her stare, like she's looking directly at me but not truly seeing me. Like part of her checked out years ago and never came back. Like hope was starved out of her slowly, piece by piece, until nothing remained but instinct and survival.

Something inside her is broken. Not freshly shattered. Worn down, eroded, deadened by time. I can't tell which is worse. Her lips part as if she might speak, but no sound comes. Then her gaze drops to the floor again, shoulders curling inward, she says nothing.

Instead, her gaze darts sharply toward the corner of the room, her whole body tensing. It feels like a silent message, but one I don't understand. I try to turn my head, but pain pulses through my skull, dull and heavy, making everything lag behind my thoughts. The room tilts as I slowly follow her line of sight.

A young girl sits on a thin mattress shoved against the far wall, maybe sixteen, maybe younger. It's hard to tell beneath the fear hollowing out her face. Her skin is dark, her black hair tangled around her cheeks and shoulders. She keeps herself folded inward, small shoulders hunched as if she's trying to disappear into her own body.

She wears a traditional skirt much like Paya's. Nothing else. One wrist is tied to the bedpost with fraying rope, the skin beneath it rubbed raw and angry. Only then do I notice the rest of the room. Two more narrow cots line the opposite wall, stained blankets tossed across them. One is empty. On the other, an older native woman sits rigid and silent, eyes fixed on nothing, her arms wrapped around herself like if she lets go she'll fall apart.

The air changes around me. This wasn't made for one captive. It was made for many. I stop breathing. The realization crashes into me so hard it feels physical. This place. These girls. They're taking women and girls from local tribes. What they're doing here. What they have planned for me. My breath shudders out. My body locks rigid with horror as I stare at her.

Slowly, I drag my gaze back to the blonde girl. Her lips part like she wants to say something, but nothing comes out. I don't know if she understands me. I don't know if she can speak. I don't know how long she's been here. I swallow again, forcing my mind to move. Think. Look for something loose, something sharp, anything.

Before I can try anything, the door flies open. The force of it slams into the wall, rattling the warped wooden boards. I jerk violently on instinct. Fresh pain explodes through my skull as a shadow looms in the doorway And I know, I'm not getting out of this without a fight. If I even get the chance to fight.

A man strides inside, filling the room with his presence before he even speaks. Dark green camo stretches tight across his broad shoulders, sweat-darkened and worn. An AK-47 hangs loose on its strap across his chest, the weapon swaying with each step. His posture is casual. Like this is routine, like girls tied to beds are nothing new.

He grins. He likes the fear. I see it instantly. The gleaming excitement when he looks at my face. His black eyes sweep the room, slow and deliberate, taking inventory of every body, every reaction, every weakness. Then they land on me again and his smile widens. Dread floods my veins so fast it steals my breath. My limbs go cold. My body locks in place even as my mind screams to move.

The blonde girl with the tray retreats immediately, shuffling backward until she reaches the younger girl in the corner. They shrink into themselves like they've seen this too many times. I yank against my restraints, trying to scoot back, trying to make myself smaller. There's nowhere to go. He stops directly in front of me and studies me before he reaches out. Rough hands grab my breasts hard enough to hurt. I scream, at the violation, at the helplessness, at the sheer terror of being touched like this. The sound cuts off when something sharp cracks across my face.

Pain explodes through my cheek. My head snaps sideways. I bite down hard on my lip to stop another scream, copper flooding my mouth. A single tear slips free anyway. It only seems to amuse him. His grip tightens, punishing now, fingers digging deep enough to bruise. I twist and buck uselessly beneath him, every movement trapped by rope and weakness. His laugh is low and pleasant, like we're sharing some private joke.

My stomach churns so violently bile rises into my throat. Then he reaches to his belt. Draws a knife. No. The whimper escapes before I can stop it. When he hears it, his smile turns vicious. The blade presses to my skin, cold enough to make me gasp. It trails slowly across my breasts. Not pressing hard enough to cut my skin, just testing and teasing. Making me fear what's coming.

I squeeze my eyes shut. The knife glides lower across my stomach. Down to the waistband of my panties. I brace for pain. For tearing fabric. For the moment everything becomes something I can never undo. I think of Fallon and try to imagine her strength, force myself to be brave because in this moment I am helpless but they will never break me. I just have to believe Wade is coming, I can fight through this long enough for him to find me.

A shout explodes through the room. The blade stops instantly. "Mio!" I gasp, sucking in a ragged breath as the pressure lifts. The man snarls and spins toward the door. Two figures step inside. Benjamin and Jenna. Oh, God. She's walking in, fully clothed. I stare at them, breath breaking into short, uneven pulls. Trying to make sense of this.

They did this?

Benjamin stands there grinning, blue eyes bright with satisfaction. Jenna lingers beside him, lips curved in a smug little smile that doesn't belong on the face of someone I trusted. My mind refuses to connect what I'm seeing. It doesn't make sense. It can't.

"What's going on?" I choke out, my voice thin and shaking.

Benjamin's grin widens. "What's going on," he repeats mockingly, "is that I finally got you where I want you." His eyes burn with something ugly. Burning with resentment, obsession and ownership. Any semblance of the Benjamin I thought I knew is gone.

"It's about time you woke up. I must've given you too much of the drug." Benjamin clicks his tongue, almost disappointed. "But now there's no more *Wraith* getting in my way."

Wade. A lump rises hard in my throat. How long have I been gone? Does he know? Is he looking for me? Is he coming?

Benjamin tilts his head, studying me like I'm something trapped in a cage. "How did you get here?" he echoes mockingly. "You really don't remember?"

I shake my head once and instantly regret it. The room pitches sideways, nausea crashing through me so hard I squeeze my eyes shut. Benjamin chuckles.

"You're still feeling it, huh?" he says lightly. "Nasty little muscle relaxant." My pulse stutters. Drugs. That's why my arms feel like they weigh a hundred pounds. That's why my thoughts are slow and slippery. That's why I couldn't fight. The needle in my neck.

He leans closer, his breath sour, his eyes glittering with something rotten. "I might've used too much," he admits. "You've been asleep almost twenty-four hours." A whole day. Cold horror spreads through me. What happened in that time? What did they do? What did Wade think?

A slow smile curls across his face. "Don't worry," he says. "You weren't touched." The relief barely has time to register before he keeps talking. "I wanted you awake when I finally took what belongs to me."

My stomach drops so hard it feels like falling. "I was worried I wouldn't get what's mine."

Beside him, Jenna giggles. "It wasn't hard," she says with a smug little shrug. "You're way too trusting." I stare at her, trying to reconcile this girl with the one who shared meals with me, talked with me, asked me for help.

"Jenna... why?" She rolls her eyes like I'm the unreasonable one.

"Because he loves me," she says. "And thanks to you, we had to hide it."

She believes him. She actually believes every lie he's fed her.

"What do you want?" I whisper, voice shaking despite my effort to steady it. "Where are my clothes?"

Benjamin's smirk deepens. "I told you." His hand drags over my stomach and I jerk away as far as the restraints allow. "I'm taking what's mine."

I flinch, and his expression hardens instantly. "You should've been mine from the start," he snarls. "You were promised to me." His eyes flash with fury. "And then you gave yourself to that asshole."

He paces the room, seething, restless energy rolling off him like heat. I stay silent. I don't even know what to say to someone this broken.

"You let him touch you," he spits, turning on me. "You let him have you." His jaw flexes, eyes wild. "But I'll fix that." His voice drops, colder now. "I'll be the last."

No. I force every muscle in my body to loosen, even as terror claws through me. I soften my expression, willing myself to look calm. I look at Jenna briefly to see if she is even hearing any of this, nothing is making sense.

"Benjamin," I whisper, forcing warmth into my voice. "I'm sorry. I never meant to hurt you."

His step falters. For one brief second, uncertainty flickers across his face. Then it's gone.

He shakes his head slowly. "No matter," he murmurs. "I'll take what's mine, and he'll never see you again." A smile creeps across his mouth. "Just like Carly."

Ice floods my veins. "What?" Keep him talking. Keep him

distracted. Right? I think that's what I'm supposed to do.

"Yes," he says almost proudly. "I needed her to get to you. That part was useful." He shrugs like he's discussing something trivial. "Then she disappeared. Everyone looked for days." My stomach twists. "We never found her body," he says, watching my reaction with delight. "Just like before we sold her to the militia group."

The room tilts. I thought she was dead. We all did. He glances toward the blonde woman still standing near the wall, tray trembling in her hands. My eyes follow. And then I see it. Not the filthy hair. Not the bruises. Not the hollow cheeks. The familiar brown eyes.

They widen as they meet mine. The fog lifts briefly from her eyes as she's starting to understand what's happening. Suddenly, not so lost. A girl seeing her friend that lost her, that never found her.

A broken sob tears out of me. "Carly."

The tray slips in her shaking hands, rattling loudly. Benjamin laughs. The sound is sharp and wrong, too loud in the cramped room. I jerk my gaze back to him. He looks insane. He's so proud, so triumphant over everything he's done. Beside him, Jenna's smug expression cracks. She takes two slow steps backward, unease replacing certainty.

"How was I supposed to know they'd keep her for themselves instead of selling her?" Benjamin says with a careless shrug. "Apparently she became valuable."

Carly flinches like each word is a blow. Benjamin smirks, eyes sliding back to me. "Doesn't matter," he says. "Once I'm done with you, none of it will matter."

"That's enough." The voice is calm. I jerk my head up. To find Dr. Willis, standing in the doorway. My mind stumbles over the sight of him strolling into the room as casually as if he's arriving for morning field notes instead of walking into a nightmare.

He adjusts his sleeve, looking mildly annoyed. Like someone interrupted his schedule. A man I've known for years. The professor who praised my work. Who encouraged me. Who mentored me. The one who promised he would keep an eye on Benjamin. My breath shudders out of me. The room swims at the edges, the drugs still dragging at my thoughts. Maybe I'm hallucinating. Maybe this is another trick.

Then he smiles. For one split second, it's the same warm smile I've seen a hundred times in classrooms and offices. He was always so kind and reassuring, then it changes and twists, the rotten underneath finally showing through. A cruel, amused smirk replaces it, and my stomach drops.

"Yes, you stupid girl," he sneers. "Far too trusting." His gaze slides lazily over me. "Though, admittedly, harder to get to than this one."

He gestures toward Carly without even looking at her. I hear Jenna suck in a sharp breath, but I can't tear my eyes away from him.

"I was rather hoping she'd be long gone by now," he continues, glancing at Jenna with naked contempt. "Or dead. No ties. No complications." He sighs dramatically. "But alas. Here she is." Like she's a paperwork problem. Like we are inconveniences. My whole body locks rigid. Heat and ice race over my skin at the same time. He was never helping me. He was never protecting anyone. I was never safe.

"But… why?" My voice shakes, confusion and betrayal knotting together so tightly it hurts. "You helped us. You—" Dr. Willis laughs. Not the familiar chuckle I knew, this sound is more hollow. Cold and detached.

"I had you all fooled," he says, almost pleased with himself. "I was keeping an eye on Benjamin, yes but not in the way you imagined." He clasps his hands behind his back. "He's my assistant, Sarah." His pale blue eyes gleam. "He's the one who's been finding girls for me."

The words hit like a physical blow, air leaves my lungs and my chest seizes. I can't breathe, I can't think and the world is starting to swim again.

Dr. Willis. The man I trusted. The man who signed recommendation letters. Who discussed ethics and research and cultural preservation. Who smiled at me while feeding girls to monsters.

He leans closer, voice light and mocking. "I can see the confusion. Don't worry. It won't matter soon." Bile surges into my throat. I yank hard against the restraints, rope burning into my wrists. I don't care, I have to get out, I have to do something.

"Benjamin," Willis says, dismissing me entirely. "Before you get started, there's been a change of plans." Benjamin stiffens instantly.

"What?"

"I had to renegotiate with the militia," Willis says, bored as if discussing shipping costs. "They're taking both girls now. Same price." He glances between me and Jenna. "And they'll help us get back to camp afterward." Then a pleased little smile. "Making it look as though we simply got lost." My blood turns to ice. Both girls. He meant both of us. I whip my head toward Jenna just as she recoils in panic, the reality finally crashing through whatever lies she'd been fed. Her face drains of color.

"No! Benjamin?"

Dr. Willis only smirks at her reaction. Amused. As if she's just a funny inconvenience and not a real person. Then he turns and walks out. The door swings shut behind him. And then everything happens at once. The same soldier from before moves first, dark eyes bright with anticipation. No. No. No.

He grabs Jenna by the arm and yanks her toward the other bed. She screams instantly, kicking and thrashing so hard the bed frame scrapes across the floor. A second man rushes in behind him. Together they force her down. They tie her wrists. Rip at her clothes. She sobs and fights and begs. Screaming Benjamin's name, but he doesn't even acknowledge her.

I yank wildly at my bindings, rope slicing hotter into my skin. Panic crashes through me in violent waves. Someone has to hear this. Someone has to stop this. I need Wade. The soldier who held the knife to me steps away from Jenna and turns back toward me. He looks to Benjamin. Waiting. Like this is some gift being granted. Benjamin smirks and gives a small nod.

Then Benjamin starts toward me. Not even sparing a glance at Jenna. I barely register his hands on me. The bruising grip. His fingers digging into my flesh. The hot, foul breath against my skin. My eyes catch something else. There's a fast movement from the corner of the room. I snap my gaze toward it. Carly is moving and in her hand is a knife.

The man over Jenna never sees her coming. Carly lunges with everything she has left. The blade drives deep into his neck. A wet gurgle bursts from him. He staggers backward, dropping to his knees, clutching at the wound as blood pumps through his fingers. He makes horrible choking sounds, hands coming away slick and red.

Oh my God. A roar of rage fills the room. The second man whirls, he rips the knife free from the man on the ground currently bleeding out and buries it in her stomach. No. Carly gasps, her whole body jerks. Then, horribly slow, she crumples sideways, striking her head on the floorboards. Blood spills from the wound, spreading beneath her in a widening pool.

The second man doesn't even look down at what he's done. He shoves the dying body aside like trash. Then turns back to Jenna. Blood covering him and excitement stretches across his face as he tears at his pants and climbs on top of her.

A scream rips from my throat. The slap comes so hard my head snaps sideways. Pain detonates across my skull as black spots burst across my vision. The room tilts. Sound warps and echoes. Somewhere far away, I hear laughter. Benjamin.

"Shut up," he hisses, face flushed with rage. Spit gathers at the corner of his mouth as he fumbles with his belt, jerking it loose. He shoves his pants down just enough and my stomach lurches so hard I nearly gag.

His smirk widens. "You look so excited," he sneers. "You must be ready for me."

Breathe.

Focus.

I drag in air through a tight throat, fighting to force my body awake, to make my limbs work, to do anything but lie here helpless. Then something changes. There's a subtle shift in the room, a whisper of movement at the door. A shadow. A wraith. My blurred vision struggles to clear, but I know him before I can fully see him.

Wade. Standing in the doorway. Chest heaving, hands clenched into fists so tight the knuckles look white even through the haze. The familiar golden-brown eyes I love are locked on me. Benjamin doesn't notice. He's too focused on me. Too sure of himself. Too stupid to sense death standing behind him.

"What the fu—" He never finishes.

One second he's over me. The next, he's ripped backward so violently the bed jerks beneath me. I feel myself fading again, as I hear a crash and a loud broken roar. My eyes keep sliding shut. I can't hold them open. Somewhere far away I hear Wade yelling, raw, furious and completely animalistic. Flesh striking flesh. Bodies slamming into walls. Someone screaming.

Maybe Benjamin. I don't care. Warm hands cradle my face. Relief hits so hard it almost hurts. I can't make out all his words, but I know his touch. I'd know it anywhere.

"Sarah," he breathes. Safe. The thought barely lands before everything inside me starts to collapse. The last strands of fear unwind all at once, leaving nothing behind. My muscles shake violently as adrenaline drains away. My vision swims, edges blurring into shadow and light. The humid air, gunfire somewhere distant, voices shouting, it all feels far away now. I try to open my eyes. Try to focus on the steady weight of Wade's arms around me. The warmth of his chest against mine. But I can't. I sag into him, unable to hold myself upright any longer. The last thing I hear is his voice, low and steady, dragging me back from the dark.

"I've got you, Little Mouse." Then softer and broken. "I'm sorry." His breath catches. "I didn't protect you."

His arms tighten around me, fierce and desperate, like he can hold me together by force alone. I want to tell him it's okay. Want to tell him he came. Want to tell him he saved me but my lips barely move. Carly. The name rises through the fog. I force my mouth open.

"Help… Carly." Then darkness takes me.

Chapter Twenty Five

Wade

The world detonates into motion. The doors burst inward under combined force, wood splintering as we flood the room, rifles up, sectors assigned, muzzles already finding targets. Seven armed men. They're too slow, they never get the chance to bring their weapons up. We execute cleanly. Controlled pairs. Failure drills. Center mass. Head if needed.

Gunfire crashes through the shack, deafening in the enclosed space. Muzzle flashes strobe off warped walls and hanging dust. Bodies hit the floor hard. Reaper, Magellan, and Sparta hit from the rear entrance the same second, cutting off escape lanes exactly as planned.

No crossfire. No hesitation. No mercy. Then the silence is deafening. Nine men are down. Blood spreads across warped boards beneath them, AKs scattered uselessly beside twitching hands.

Willis stands in the center of the room untouched. Hands raised. Eyes wide. The remaining five heat signatures are missing. Where is Sarah?

"Oh, thank God!" Willis gasps. "They took us last night, I was so scared! I prayed you were coming for us." It sounds rehearsed. Every instinct I have screams liar. I fight the immediate urge to put a round through his skull. Maybe I should. Maybe I'll regret not doing it.

"Ghost," I order. "Keep your gun on him."

Willis pales instantly. "Why? They kidnapped me! I can help you, I know where they are!" He jerks his head toward a back door.

Glitch is already moving. Zip ties snap tight around Willis's wrists before he can say another word. I don't have time for his games. I move. Weapon high. Stack forms behind me automatically. Door checked. Handle turned. Push.

The room beyond is hell. A tribal women is naked, bruised and completely terrified. A young tribal girl huddles in the far corner, knees to chest, eyes vacant with fear. A blonde woman lies motionless in a pool of blood, hair filthy and slick against her face like she hasn't been clean in weeks. For one awful second I think she's dead, then she moves.

Jenna is tied to a bed, wrists flayed raw and bleeding. And on top of her is a man with his pants down, driving into her while she screams. He never gets to finish. Reaper is past me in a blur. Steel flashes once. The man's throat opens red. He collapses before his body understands he's dead.

I barely register it. Because across the room—is Sarah. My Sarah. Benjamin is on top of her. Pants undone. Hands pinning her down. Her shirt is gone.

Her wide and terrified eyes meet mine. They're far too dilated, mostly black, I don't see any of blue-grey eyes I love. She looks confused, like she can't believe I'm real. A bruise darkens beneath one eye. Angry red marks stain her skin. Something inside me tears loose. There is no more control, no more restraint, no mercy. Before Benjamin can even turn, I'm on him.

I grab him and rip him off her so hard we both hit the ground. "What the fuck!" he shouts, scrambling, hands clawing for balance. Then his eyes find me, focusing and recognition slams into his face. Fear follows right behind it. Good, I don't have time to enjoy it. Before he can move, before he can beg, before he can even think, I'm on him.

My fist crashes into his mouth. Then again and then again. I wasn't joking when I told him I went easy on him before. Every second she was missing. Every mile we ran through that jungle. Every image of what might be happening to her. Every ounce of fear, helplessness, rage, and guilt pours through my fists.

Bone gives beneath my knuckles. Blood sprays hot across my hands.

He moans and cries. With a futile effort he tries to shield face, but I keep hitting him. It doesn't take long for him to go limp and still, I keep hitting him. Justice doesn't feel like enough. Nothing feels like enough.

"Somebody stop him!" The shout sounds far away, like it's coming through water. Hands lock around my shoulders and haul me backward. I fight for half a second before awareness cuts through the red haze.

"That's enough, Wraith!" Reaper barks. I sit back on my heels, chest heaving. Benjamin lies twisted in the dirt, face barely recognizable. Blood covers him. One eye already swollen shut. I watch his chest. There's a very slow rise and slow fall. He's still breathing, barely.

"We'll take care of them," Glitch says, voice hard as steel. "You take care of your girl." My girl. I'm moving before he finishes speaking. I drop to my knees beside the bed, dirt grinding into them, and scoot closer until I'm at her side. Sarah lies motionless on the filthy mattress. She looks too pale and my hands move over her automatically, searching for wounds, checking limbs, ribs, throat, scalp.

Nothing obvious. No gunshot. No stab wound. No massive bleeding. Please God, I press two fingers to her wrist. She has a strong and steady pulse. Relief hits me so hard it almost folds me in half. Then guilt crushes it. She looked terrified when she saw me. Lost. Brokenhearted. She knows, she knows I failed her. She might have been raped. She could have been killed. My one job was to protect her and I failed.

Someone slams into my shoulder, shoving me aside. My hand flies for my Sig before training catches up. Stitches.

"I know it's hard," he says sharply, already climbing over the bed to assess her. "But move."

I blink like I'm waking up. I don't know how long I'd been frozen there with my fingers on her pulse. Seconds, minutes, it could've been hours. Time doesn't exist in this room.

"She whispered Carly's name." My voice sounds wrecked. "The girl who disappeared five years ago. What do you think that means? Is she dying?" I lower my head beside Sarah's shoulder, needing to stay close enough to feel her breathe.

Stitches doesn't look up from Sarah as he checks her over. I don't even register the blood on his hands. "Is that Carly?" he asks, not slowing for a second. "Because if it is, she's alive but barely." I look over to see the unconscious girl now with a bandage around her abdomen. Blood-soaked gauze is piled beside him, his med kit torn open across the floor. He glances toward the rest of the room. "And we've still got multiple women in here, including the young tribal girl in the corner. No clue where any of them belong." My head snaps up Fuck. I glance toward the corner, pulse hammering, and really see them for the first time. Not just one girl. Several women. Two older tribal women huddled near the wall, bodies drawn tight, fear etched into every line of them. Another younger woman crouches beside them, arms wrapped around herself, eyes huge and glassy.

And the girl. Small frame. Terrified eyes darting between us. Far too young to be caught in whatever hell this place was. Judging by the handmade skirt, the woven bracelets, the intricate beaded necklace at her throat, she has to be from one of the local tribes. This is where my girl would come in handy. I grit my teeth. Sarah would know what to say. She'd know the right tone, the right posture, the right words to calm them instead of terrifying them more. She'd know if they spoke Yanomami. She'd know if that necklace marked family or tribe or status. She'd know how to help. But Sarah is limp in my arms, barely stirring.

The thought of her waking in pain, drugged, disoriented and afraid, hits me with a fresh surge of rage. I tighten my hold on her and force myself to think. The woman who could be Carly is down. The women are terrified. The kid is frozen and we are not fucking safe yet. I meet Stitches' gaze.

"We take them all with us. Now," I say, voice low and firm. "We sort it out later." My eyes go back to the young girl. She flinches instantly, pressing deeper into the shadows, dragging one of the women with her. Hell.

"We don't have time for slow and gentle introductions," I mutter, more to myself than anyone else. My hands are full with Sarah, and the last thing I want is to charge at traumatized women carrying rifles and covered in blood.

Stitches crouches slowly, palms visible, movements deliberate and controlled.

"We're not here to hurt you," he says gently. "But we can't leave you here. We need to go." They don't move. Their eyes keep jumping from him, to me, to the dead men on the floor and then to the open door. Searching for danger. Searching for a trap. Searching for any reason to trust us. I swallow down impatience. We don't have time for this and they clearly don't understand us or trust us. Outside could light up any second.

More men could be coming. Sarah would know what to do, but Sarah isn't awake. So I make the call. I nod once at Stitches.

"Get them moving. Carry whoever won't move on their own. We adapt on the fly." If they fight, we handle it. If they scream, we handle it. If they run, we chase. Right now, survival is the mission. Because if anything happens to Sarah before I get her clear of this place, I won't survive it either. Magellan steps into the room first, face hard as stone, and joins Reaper in dragging bodies clear of the doorway. They work fast, efficient, clearing lanes, checking corners, making space for movement.

No one says a word. They don't need to. Glitch comes in next. Knife in hand, he drops to one knee and slices through the rope binding Sarah's wrists first, then moves to Jenna. She jerks away at first, eyes wide with terror, until she realizes what he's doing. He finds the shredded remains of her clothes on the floor and hands them over. Jenna stares at them like she doesn't understand what they are. Then she snatches them and pulls the fabric to her chest. We don't have anything better to give her.

While Stitches continues checking Sarah—pupils, pulse, breathing, responsiveness—I search the room for her clothes. I find them in a filthy corner. My jaw tightens as I gather them. When I check the hidden pocket, my fingers close around the tracker. Thank God. They never found it. That tiny piece of plastic is the only reason I'm holding her now.

Once Stitches gives me the all clear to move her, I dress her as quickly and carefully as I can, every bruise and red mark fueling the fire already burning inside me. Then I lift her into my arms. She folds against my chest, limp and warm and far too still. I move fast through the wreckage, stepping over splintered boards, blood, shell casings, bodies. Part of me is grateful she can't see what we left behind. The dead men. The torn room. The violence. But there's no relief in me, no satisfaction, no justice. Only fear. Cold and vicious, squeezing tighter around my ribs every second she doesn't wake.

I press my cheek to the top of her head, breathing in sweat, dirt and the faint scent that is still somehow her beneath all of it. It does nothing to quiet the panic clawing through me. When I step outside, the sun is already heating up. Blinding sunlight crashes over us, too bright after the darkness inside. The jungle hums with life as if none of this happened. My world has narrowed to one thing.

The weight of her in my arms. The sound of my breathing. The prayer pounding through my skull. *Stay with me, Mouse. Just stay with me.* Then I hear it. A distant rhythmic thunder. Whomp-whomp-whomp, the tell tale sign of fast approaching rotor blades. My grip tightens instantly. Who the fuck is that?

Reaper and Ghost are already looking up, speaking low through comms. Neither one looks alarmed. Not an immediate threat. This is the support Ghost called in earlier. The helicopter drops lower through the canopy break, downdraft tearing through the clearing, blasting dirt and leaves into spirals around us. Brazilian military markings. They must've been nearby to get here this fast.

I still don't loosen my grip, not for anyone. Sarah stirs weakly against my chest. Her fingers twitch. Her lashes flutter but her eyes don't open. *Come on, baby. Give me something.* Reaper steps forward to guide the bird in. Then the sky explodes. A deafening blast rips through the air. One second I'm watching the helicopter descend. The next it's a fireball above us.

Metal shears apart midair, flaming debris spinning outward. The shockwave slams through the clearing like a physical wall, hurling Reaper backward off his feet. Then it hits me. I twist instinctively, trying to shield Sarah with my body as the blast throws us backward. The world flips. Sky. Fire. Trees. Smoke. My back smashes into the ground hard enough to rip the air from my lungs.

Sarah's weight settles against my chest, grounding me through the disorientation. I have her, she's still here and I need to fucking move. My ears ring so hard the world sounds distant and warped. Vision swimming, I shove up onto my elbows, tightening my hold on Sarah as smoke and fire roll overhead.

What's left of the helicopter rains down in burning pieces. Black smoke billows into the sky. Flames claw upward like hell itself just split open above us. Reaper is already on his feet. Rifle shouldered, eyes scanning through the chaos, he pivots toward the river. I follow his line of sight and my stomach drops.

A freighter sits broadside in the channel. Not random or civilian, but it was waiting. Mounted near the bow is a heavy gun traversing toward us.

"Move!" Reaper roars, already sprinting in my direction.

I don't need the order twice. I surge to my feet, Sarah locked tight against my chest, and run for the tree line. Pain protests through my back from the impact. I ignore it. Adrenaline wipes everything clean except one objective: Get her out. Behind me another blast detonates. The shack erupts into flame and splintered wood, shockwave chasing at our backs. Heat lashes across my neck and shoulders.

I don't look back. Benjamin and Willis are still inside. No way to reach them now. No time to care. Automatic gunfire rips across the clearing from the river. Short controlled bursts. Then engines, I glance back once to see men are piling into smaller boats from the freighter, cutting hard toward the dock. They're coming fast. A recovery team or a kill team, it doesn't matter. We are seconds from getting boxed in. Ahead of me, Stitches crashes from the brush carrying the blonde girl in both arms, moving like her weight is nothing. Her head lolls against his shoulder.

Glitch is right behind him, dragging Jenna forward by the wrist while she stumbles and sobs, half dressed and barely coherent. The older tribal woman is clutching the younger girls hand, eyes wild as they push through the brush. Good. They got them out. Rounds snap through branches overhead. Wood explodes off a trunk to my right. They're firing blind into the jungle.

I angle deeper into cover, using the thickest trees, weaving, changing pace, refusing to give them a line on us. I don't stop running. Sarah stirs in my arms again, a weak shift against my chest, but her eyes stay closed.

I lower my mouth to her hair and press a hard kiss there. "Hold on, baby," I rasp. "I've got you. I'm not losing you now."

The jungle closes around us, swallowing smoke, gunfire, and firelight behind a wall of green. Branches whip at my face. Roots try to trip my feet. My pulse hammers in time with every stride. War rages at our backs. My only thought is Sarah and getting her the fuck out of here alive.

Over the headset, Reaper's voice cuts through the chaos—sharp, clipped, controlled. He's already taken charge of the rear element. Assigning sectors. Positioning Magellan, Ghost and Sparta. Building a hasty perimeter between us and the river. Exactly what I'd expect, exactly what we've been trained to do. Then the jungle erupts again, gunfire crashes behind us. The hard, disciplined cracks of our rifles come in measured bursts, controlled pairs, short strings, target discrimination. Between them, the sloppy chatter of AKs answers back. They don't know exactly where we are yet. They're firing at sound. At movement. Their fear is guiding their shots. I should be back there with my team. Instead, I keep moving. I throttle down from a sprint to a fast tactical pace, lungs burning, arms screaming from carrying Sarah over uneven ground. Sweat pours down my spine. Every root underfoot feels like a trap.

Glitch is one side, rifle up, his eyes constantly scanning the brush, canopy, flank lines. Stitches is close on my other side with an unconscious Carly in his arms, eyes scanning everything. No one wastes breath talking. I check over my shoulder every few steps. Nothing moving. No visual pursuit, yet. I raise a fist. We halt. Everyone drops low automatically.

I kneel, lowering Sarah carefully onto a bed of leaves and roots, keeping one hand on her shoulder, the other on my rifle. Stitches does the same with the blonde girl. Glitch guides Jenna down, attempting to keep her quiet when she keeps whimpering, her hands clutching at the clothes that are not really covering her body. No one speaks. The jungle is alive around us.

Distant shouting in Spanish. Boats idling and revving near the river. Rounds snapping through trees farther west. Branches breaking. Men hunting. We stay still and let the foliage hide us. I key my mic twice.

"Reaper, is anyone hit?" Two clicks come back. Negative. Relief punches through me.

"Do you need backup?" Two clicks again. Negative. They can hold.

"Are you almost done?"

A pause.

Then Reaper's voice returns, lower this time.

"More incoming."

Fuck. I glance at Glitch and Stitches. They already know. Enemy reinforcements, likely from the freighter. Maybe additional boats. Maybe militia on foot. There's no time left.

"Copy," I whisper. "Break contact when able. Bound east to rally point. I repeat, get to rally point."

One click. Understood. I look down at Sarah. Her breathing is steady, although shallow. I brush hair from her face and force myself back into command mode.

"Any eyes on Willis or Benjamin?"

Reaper answers immediately. "Willis emerged. No sign of Benjamin." So the professor made it out. Benjamin either dead, buried, or running. I know which one I'm hoping for.

I look to my men, "Any sign of the other women that were in there?"

"No, they all disappeared into the trees when the explosion

happened." Glitch said.

"Alright. We move east. Stay in the trees. Stay off skyline. Keep river orientation but don't crowd the bank. If we need extraction, water's our fastest option."

They nod once. No hesitation. "If we get separated," I continue, voice hard, "split by pairs. Priority is the women. Reach the rally point and hold. Maintain comms discipline."

More nods. This part is familiar. Movement under pressure. Withdrawal under fire. Protect the vulnerable. But this time we aren't hauling packs and weapons. We're hauling broken, terrified civilians and the woman I love.

And failure isn't an option. Not today. Not ever. Stitches and I both readjust our grips as we move, shifting weight before fatigue can become a mistake. Sarah rests against my chest, one arm looped around my neck where I placed it to stabilize her. She feels both familiar and frighteningly fragile in my arms.

Stitches carries the blonde girl in a fireman-style rotation for a few steps, then transitions her lower into a cradle carry to keep her airway clear while we move. Even hauling dead weight through jungle terrain, he stays steady.

Glitch has Jenna. One arm hooked under hers, the other hand gripping the back of her belt to keep her upright. She's walking, barely. Legs dragging over roots and mud, body moving only because he's making it move. Her stare is fixed straight ahead. Empty. Catatonic. I want answers. What happened in that room? How deep was she in this? Was she victim, accomplice, both? One look at her face tells me none of those questions matter right now. She's gone somewhere inside herself.

The gunfire behind us has slowed. But it hasn't stopped. Every distant rifle crack punches through my chest. My men are still back there. Still maneuvering. Still killing anyone trying to reach us. I know what they're capable of. We've trained for chaos. Planned contingencies. Drilled break-contact drills, rally points, casualty movement, lost-comms procedures until they lived in muscle memory. I trust them with my life. But trust doesn't loosen the knot in my gut.

We move fast through the jungle, weaving through thick growth in staggered file. No one steps where the man ahead stepped unless necessary. We vary pace, vary spacing, break pattern. Every footfall matters, very snapped branch carries, every careless movement can turn concealment into contact. Slowly we move apart, needing to maintain distance. Less conspicuous when there are many of us together and easier to hide.

Then Reaper's voice cuts through the static. "We've all successfully exfilled. Willis is in tow. Still no sign of Benjamin." He pauses. "They stopped sending men ashore, but the freighter is moving east. Be on the lookout. We're far from done."

I slow just enough to scan. Left flank. Right flank. Rear trail. Canopy breaks. Listen. Nothing but insects, leaves, and the far hum of water. For now.

"Do we have more backup coming?" I ask quietly.

"Yes," Reaper answers. "Command spun up support. We're to meet the extraction vessel at the rendezvous point. About a day on foot." A day if terrain cooperates. Longer carrying casualties. Longer if pursued. Longer if Sarah crashes medically.

"Keep moving," I order. "Report any issues. Noise and light discipline." Acknowledgments click back. I key off the mic.

Then I feel a slight movement against my chest. Sarah shifts against me. One leg jerks weakly, then a soft moan slips past her lips. Relief hits so hard my knees nearly give out. I drop immediately, lowering with her and easing her onto the ground as carefully as I can. Leaves and soft earth cushion her while I brace her head in my palm. My fingers brush her skin. She's still clammy, but her breathing is slightly stronger now. Less shallow and more present. Her head rolls to the side and then those beautiful eyes blink open. Hazy and unfocused, but alive and that's all I care about. For a second she doesn't know where she is.

I watch confusion turn to alarm. Her breath quickens and her body tightens. She looks around wildly at the trees, the movement, the people, trying to understand.

"Sarah," I whisper, leaning close. My hand finds her cheek, gentle and steady. Trying to get her to focus on me. She flinches. The reaction cuts straight through me, but I don't move away. Then her gaze locks on mine. Recognition floods in. The panic drains from her features little by little and her whole body softens a fraction.

"Hey, Little Mouse," I murmur, brushing my thumb across her cheekbone. "How are you feeling?"

She swallows hard and her lips part but nothing comes out. I don't push. She's here. She's breathing. That's enough for this second. And as long as I'm drawing air, she is never leaving my sight again.

"Water?" she croaks at last. I'm already reaching for my canteen.

I slide an arm behind her shoulders and help lift her just enough to drink. She takes a desperate swallow, then tries for more. I ease it back.

"I'm sorry, beautiful," I say softly. "We have to conserve. I'll give you more before we move again." I run my thumb slowly along her jaw, forcing calm into both of us. "Now tell me how you're feeling."

She closes her eyes for a moment, breathing through it. When they open again, they're clearer. Still bruised by fear. Still exhausted. But clearer.

"You saved me," she whispers. "I knew you would come." The words nearly break me. It's the look in her eyes that does it most. Relief, trust and absolute faith. Even after everything.

"I will always come for you." My voice comes out rougher than I intended, thick with everything lodged in my chest. "Always." I swallow hard. "I'm sorry you were taken in the first place. I should've never let you out of my sight."

Her expression changes. Something sharp flickers behind the exhaustion. "Please don't blame yourself," she whispers. "It's my fault for being so trusting." Her jaw tightens. "I should have never followed Jenna."

The way she says Jenna's name, hard. Bitter, accusing and it sends a warning through me instantly. "What do you mean by that?" My pulse kicks hard, every nerve instantly on edge. I don't realize I've tightened my grip on her until I see her wince and force myself to loosen it.

She closes her eyes for a second and draws in a shaky breath, like she's bracing for impact. I hate that look. Hate the way she's trying to shoulder this alone.

Then she says it. "Jenna was with Benjamin." The words hit like a sledgehammer to the chest. "She was helping him," Sarah continues, voice trembling. "That is until Willis decided to sell her too."

Everything inside me goes cold first. Then white-hot. Jenna, that shaking, crying girl we dragged out. The one who looked terrified. The one I almost pitied. She helped him take Sarah. Helped hand her over to that fucking animal. I'm on my feet before I realize I've moved. Sarah startles, eyes widening, and I curse myself even as rage coils through every muscle in my body. My fingers twitch toward my rifle. Toward action. Toward violence.

But there's nothing to shoot here except ghosts and delayed justice. Not now. Not while we're still exposed. So I pace. Three steps one direction. Turn. Three back. Again, back and fucking forth. Breathe,

Wade. Control it.

I glance over and see tears sliding silently down Sarah's cheeks. No sobbing. No breakdown. Just quiet tears while she tries to hold herself together. Her hands are shaking and her shoulders curled inward. Like she's trying to make herself smaller, trying to disappear. That sight guts me more than anything she's said. I drop back to my knees in front of her. Force the fury down. Swallow every ounce of it, because she doesn't that, she needs me steady.

"Fuck, beautiful," I whisper, voice rough and low. "I'm sorry." The words aren't enough. Nothing will ever be enough. "I'm so sorry this happened to you."

She doesn't answer. Just takes the canteen when I place it in her hands and sips carefully, like even drinking takes effort. I slide beside her and pull her gently against me. Her head settles on my shoulder. I wrap an arm around her waist and hold on, grounding myself in the only truth that matters right now. She's here, I got her back, she's alive. I press my lips to her temple.

"I love you," I murmur.

Her breath catches, then shudders out. "I love you too."

I drag in a deep breath, hold it, let it out slow. Then I force myself back into mission mode. "Glitch, do you copy?"

"Copy," he answers immediately through the comm.

"Sarah's awake. Haven't got the full story yet, but Jenna was in on it. She helped Benjamin take her. Willis turned on Jenna after."

Silence. Then—"God damn it!" Glitch's voice cracks through the earpiece hard enough to make Sarah jump. The channel erupts after that. Reaper swears. Magellan spits out something vicious in Spanish. Sparta mutters a dark, controlled curse. Even Ghost keys in with a low, dangerous, "Figures." Then the line settles.

Glitch comes back first, voice tight with fury. "I didn't touch her. Didn't raise my voice. Just looked at her and she started bawling. Asked if she helped take Sarah." He exhales sharply. "She nodded."

My jaw clenches. "In the confusion," he continues, "the tribal women bolted. All of them. Took the younger girl with them. Slipped into the brush before we could react."

Honestly? Good. If they were going to run from someone, better from us than back to those bastards.

"This whole thing is a clusterfuck," Glitch finishes.

"No argument," I mutter. I glance at Sarah. Her eyes are fixed on me, tired but alert, reading every expression on my face. "There were other women in that room," I explain quietly. "An older tribal woman, the younger girl, they ran during the chaos." Her brows pull together in concern instantly. Even now, even after what she's been through.

"We have to find them," she whispers. Of course that's where her heart goes first. I close my eyes for half a second. Fuck. Before I can answer, Glitch keys in again.

"Tell Sarah, I know exactly what face she's making right now." Despite everything, the corner of my mouth almost twitches. "But those women disappeared fast," he says. "No noise, no trail, no hesitation. They know this terrain better than we ever will. Chasing them blind just slows us down and gets people hurt."

I relay it to her, watching for the argument. Watching for that stubborn chin lift. Instead, she presses her lips together and looks down.

After a long moment, she exhales. "You're right." I blink. My eyes soften, I'm so fucking proud of her. Keeping her compassion even now.

Then she looks back up at me, and the pain in her eyes lands like a blade. "I just hate leaving them," she says softly. "What if they're scared?"

I take her hand and brush my thumb over her knuckles. "Beautiful, they were scared of everyone in that room." I lean closer. "But they chose the jungle." I nod toward the trees around us. "That means this place is safer to them than people. And if they're from nearby tribes, they know exactly where to go." She still doesn't like it, I can see that. But she nods anyway, trying to accept what she hates because she knows it's true. I kiss her forehead.

"Sarah." My voice is low. Firm. Not loud but it leaves no room to look away. She lifts her eyes slowly. Exhaustion sits heavy there, but I don't let up. I need the truth. "I love you," I say, steady. "That doesn't change. Nothing you tell me will change that." My jaw tightens. "But I need to know." The word almost sticks in my throat. "Were you assaulted?"

Her eyes go wide, panic flashing as she processes it. She starts to look away. I don't let her. My hand comes up, firm under her chin, guiding her back to me. Not rough. Not gentle either.

"Look at me." My voice drops. Controlled. Certain. "I'm here. I've got you. But I need to know how to take care of you."

She searches my face like she's looking for something real enough to hold onto. Then she shakes her head. I don't relax. Not yet.

"No," she whispers. "Benjamin said he was waiting for me to wake up… so I was awake for it." Her voice wavers. "You got there before that happened. You got there in time." My chest tightens, but I keep it locked down.

"They only touched my breasts," she continues, quieter now. "Hard. They slapped me. One of them dragged a knife over my skin, but I don't think it cut."

The relief that punches through me is immediate. "Okay," I breathe, dragging a hand down my face. "That's good, baby. That's… so fucking good. You're so brave," I tell her quietly. "Braver than you know."

"I didn't do anything," she whispers. My hand tightens around hers.

"Yeah, you did," I say firmly. "You survived. You kept fighting. You didn't let them break you." I brush my thumb along her skin. "That makes you brave, my beautiful girl." I don't let myself sit in it. Not yet. My focus snaps back into place.

"I know this is a lot," I say, my voice steady again. "I know you're trying to process everything. But we're not out of the woods yet." I hold her gaze, making sure she hears me. "Right now, we get you out. Then I take care of you. All of it. Okay?"

She nods. That's all I need. I slide an arm beneath her knees, lift her into my arms, and turn east, moving fast through the trees.

Chapter Twenty Six

Sarah

We've been trekking through this jungle for what feels like forever. Wade says it's only been six hours. As if that's a short amount of time. The sky above us is fading into bruised purples and heavy gray, what little light remains strangled by the thick canopy overhead. Humidity clings to my skin like a second layer. Every breath tastes of damp earth and leaves.

I'm exhausted. My muscles tremble with every step. The drugs are mostly gone now, leaving behind a pounding soreness in my body, a headache that comes in waves, and a hollow ache in my stomach sharp enough to make me dizzy. I haven't complained once. I won't.

Wade carried me for most of the journey, moving through the jungle with impossible strength, like the weight of me meant nothing. When he finally set me down to rest, I insisted on walking. He didn't like it. I saw that immediately. But after a long look, he gave a single nod and let me try. Now every step feels like punishment. Roots snag at my boots. Mud sucks at my soles. Branches scrape exposed skin. My legs feel unstable, but I keep moving because if Wade can carry the weight of all this, I can carry myself.

I haven't seen the others at all, Wade said they're all moving toward the rendezvous point by separate routes, likely arriving before us. The distance between us and the rest of the team knots uneasily in my chest, but I trust him. Right now, Wade is the only solid thing left in my world. He stops so abruptly I nearly walk into his back. My pulse spikes. His fist rises instantly beside him, fingers curled tight. A silent signal. I don't know military commands, I know enough. Stop. Be quiet and don't move. I freeze where I stand, barely breathing.

Wade shifts slightly in front of me, body changing in an instant. Every trace of softness is gone. He becomes something else out here, still. Lethal. Predatory. His eyes cut through the dense brush ahead. I follow his gaze. At first I don't see anything. Then the shape reveals itself. A small hut, half-hidden through the trees, so weathered it blends into the jungle around it. Gray boards warped by rain and heat. Vines crawling up the sides. A sagging roof bowed with age.

This hut looks like it's one with the forest around it. There is no sign of any kind of life, no smoke, no light and no movement. It looks abandoned, but something in the way Wade tenses makes the hairs rise on the back of my neck.

He turns to me, voice barely above a breath. "Stay here. Behind the tree." I nod immediately.

"I'm going to clear it before dark." His eyes lock on mine, hard and serious. "If you hear shots, grab the pack and run." My throat tightens. "There's a satellite phone inside." Run. Leave him if I hear gunfire. The thought makes panic flash through me, but I force myself to nod again. He sets his pack beside me, checks the magazine on his rifle, then draws and verifies his handgun with quick practiced movements. Everything about him is calm.

Then he slips into the trees. One blink and he's gone. The moment he disappears, the jungle changes. The sounds feel farther away. The shadows feel deeper and a suffocating silence settles over me. I press my back against the rough bark, forcing myself to breathe slowly. In. Out. Again. My heart doesn't listen. It pounds so hard I can feel it in my throat, in my wrists, in the ache behind my eyes. I strain for any sound. A snapped twig, leaves shifting, voices, a gunshot, anything. But there's nothing. Only jungle. The air hangs heavy with the scent of wet soil, rotting wood, crushed leaves. Somewhere far off, insects drone in a steady pulse. A bird lets out a sharp cry, then silence swallows it again.

I try to focus on those sounds. On anything except the truth pressing in on me. Wade walked into something unknown and if something happens to him, I'm alone. My fingers tighten around the strap of his pack beside me. Would I really run? My body is weak. My legs already shake from the hike. My head still throbs. I want to believe I would do what he said. Grab the pack. Use the phone. Move. But if I heard a gunshot, if I heard him go down, would my legs even work? I don't think I could leave him. Minutes drag by like hours. My breathing speeds up without permission, shallow and fast, and I shut my eyes to force it slower. In. Out.

A small quiet sound, a shift in the brush somewhere beyond the hut. My eyes fly open. Pulse hammering, is that Wade or someone else? I don't move, I listen so hard it hurts. Again, the faintest whisper of movement. Too measured to be the wind. Every muscle in my body locks. It's nothing. Just the jungle. Just my imagination. Then something touches my shoulder.

I jerk violently. My body reacts before thought can catch up, stumbling backward so fast the back of my head cracks against the tree trunk. Pain explodes bright and sharp. Stars burst across my vision. A gasp tears from me as I sway, stunned. Then strong warm hands catch my arms. My breath stutters. I blink rapidly, fighting through the haze. Wade. I know him before I fully see him.

His scent reaches me first, sweat, earth, gun oil, something clean beneath it that is only him. Then his face sharpens into view. Eyes fixed on mine.

Concern darkening every line of him. "Hey. Easy." His voice is low, calm, instantly soothing. "It's me." Relief crashes through me so hard my knees nearly give out. I sag forward before I can stop myself. I hadn't realized how hard I was shaking until his hands tighten on my arms, steadying me.

"You okay?" he asks, gaze moving over my face, checking for injury.

I nod automatically, swallowing against the lump lodged in my throat. "Yeah. Just—" My voice breaks. I take a breath and try again. "I didn't hear you."

His mouth tightens. "Didn't want to risk making noise."

I nod once more, still clutching his forearms like they're the only stable thing left in the world. He's back. I'm not alone. And right now, that is enough, it's all I need. I don't know if I could handle being left alone for long. Not after everything. Not with the dark pressing in and every sound feeling like a threat.

He helps me upright, and the second I'm steady enough, I throw my arms around him. The force of it surprises even me. Wade catches me easily, folding me against him without hesitation.

"It's okay," he murmurs near my ear. "You're safe." His fingers slide through my tangled hair, slow and careful, smoothing through knots as if he can soothe the panic right out of me.

We stand there for a while. I don't know how long. Long enough for my breathing to even out. Long enough for the trembling in my hands to settle. Long enough for me to remember what safety feels like. I cling to his warmth, to the solid strength of him, to the simple fact that he came back. Eventually, Wade pulls back just enough to cup my cheeks and tilt my face upward.

"Come on," he says softly. "It's getting dark." His eyes flick toward the hut. "We're staying there tonight. I cleared it. No recent tracks, no signs anyone's used it in a long time. Perimeter looks clean. We'll be safe there."

Safe. The word catches strangely in my chest, but I nod. Even that tiny motion feels draining. Every inch of my body hurts. My muscles feel hollowed out, heavy and weak. Now that the adrenaline is gone, exhaustion crashes over me in punishing waves.

Wade bends, grabs the pack, swings it onto one shoulder, then reaches for my hand. I take it. I try to walk beside him. I really do. But every step feels worse than the last. The jungle floor is uneven and treacherous, roots rising from the earth like traps. My legs shake with effort. My balance slips twice in only a few yards.

Wade notices immediately, of course he does. He stops, turns, and before I can protest, sweeps me into his arms as if I weigh nothing. A soft gasp escapes me. I'm too tired to argue. His hold tightens, secure and careful, drawing me against the broad wall of his chest. His heartbeat thuds a strong, reliable and steady beat beneath my cheek. A rhythm my body seems desperate to trust. For the first time since waking in that nightmare room, I feel something close to peace.

In the fading light, I catch the faintest smile at the corner of his mouth. It's small and tender, then he leans down and kisses me. It isn't frantic or hungry. Gentle enough to make my throat tighten. A promise without words. We survived. I've got you. You're not alone anymore. My fingers curl into his shirt. When he pulls back, I rest my head against his shoulder and let myself believe every unspoken thing in that kiss. For now, that is all I need.

Later, Wade settles us on the hard wooden floor of the hut. His back braces against the wall, rifle within reach, body positioned between me and the door even while resting. I curl beside him, my head in his lap. His warmth seeps into me through every layer of exhaustion. His fingers move slowly through my hair, untangling strands, stroking gently, anchoring me to the present.

Outside, the jungle hums in the dark. Inside, wrapped in him, I finally begin to come down from the terror. Despite the deep ache in my muscles and the cool night air slipping through the cracks in the walls, I feel safer than I have in what feels like forever. Maybe safer than I ever have. The slow rhythm of Wade's fingers moving through my hair pulls me toward sleep, each pass gentler than the last. My body wants to surrender to it.

But the moment I close my eyes, it all comes back. The scrape of rope against my wrists. The rough boards beneath me. The cold drag of metal over my skin. The helplessness. I jerk hard enough to startle myself and my eyes snap open. Wade's hand stills for only a second. Then his fingers begin moving again, calm and steady, like he knew exactly where my mind had gone. The reassurance in that simple touch loosens some of the fear choking me.

His rifle rests propped against the wall beside him, close enough to grab in an instant. Ever watchful. Ever ready, even now. Earlier, he spoke quietly over the radio, checking in with the others, making sure everyone was alive and moving. Some of the team pushed ahead to the rendezvous point to secure our extraction route.

Stitches has Carly. He said he treated the stab wound as best he could and stabilized her before they split routes. But she was still unconscious, the thought lands heavy. Everything feels heavy.

"Don't you need sleep?" I whisper, voice rough and thin. His fingers slide through my hair again.

"No," he murmurs. "I can go days without it." Then after a beat, "I'll rest when I know you're safe." The words should comfort me. They do but guilt slips in beside the warmth. I should be stronger than this. I am stronger than this. I crossed an ocean alone. Built a career. Lived in the jungle for weeks. Survived being taken. But right now, sore and shaken and barely holding myself together, I don't feel strong at all. We fall quiet again. The steady rise and fall of his breathing anchors me better than any meditation ever could. I want to sleep. I need to sleep. Yet every time my eyes drift closed, I'm back there. Back in that room, under Benjamin's hands. Back hearing Jenna scream.

Back watching Carly fall. My pulse races. My throat tightens around screams I barely remember making.

I squeeze my eyes shut and turn my face into Wade's thigh, forcing myself to focus on what is real now. The warmth of him. The rough calluses on the hand stroking my hair. The scent of earth and sweat and safety.

The solid wall of his leg beside my cheek. "You're safe," Wade murmurs, as if he can hear every thought. His hand trails down, fingertips brushing the side of my face. "I've got you, Little Mouse."

A shaky breath leaves me. Then another and slowly, finally, I let my body give in to exhaustion. Because for the first time since I was taken, I believe him. I'm safe. I'm with him. I'm home.

I wake with a violent start, my whole body locking rigid before I'm even fully conscious. The surface beneath me feels wrong. My pulse slams against my ribs as panic crashes over me. Cold air skims across my skin and my mind fills in the rest before reason can catch up. No.

My wrists burn as I yank against restraints that aren't there, phantom pain sharp and immediate. I twist, breath tearing from my lungs in shallow bursts, every nerve screaming danger. How did I get back here? Where is Wade? Was any of it real? Did he never save me?

My eyes fly open, scanning wildly through darkness and shadows. For one disoriented second, I don't know where I am. Then the old wooden walls sharpen into view. The same room I was in. The faint moonlight slipping through cracks in the boards. The warmth wrapped around me. A creak sounds nearby and terror spikes all over again. The door opening. My mind betrays me instantly. Benjamin striding in with that sick smile, his sick eyes crawling over me. That voice, I can hear it clearly. *Did you miss me?*

A scream builds in my throat as I jerk backward, trying to flee something that isn't there. Then a hand covers my mouth. I freeze. Pure terror locking every muscle in place.

"Shh, Little Mouse." Everything stops. Wade's voice, not Benjamin's. The crushing weight in my chest loosens all at once. Reality surges back in jagged pieces. The arm around my waist. The broad chest pressed to my back. The scent of him, earth, sweat and sun-warmed skin, that is steady and clean that my body now knows instantly. His hand eases gently from my mouth the second he feels me recognize him, giving me room, giving me choice.

I don't scream. I spin in his arms and grab fistfuls of his shirt instead, holding on hard enough to wrinkle the fabric. He's here. I'm here. Not there. Benjamin is gone. He's gone.

"You're safe," Wade murmurs again, voice low and rough with sleep and concern. His palm slides over my hair, smoothing it back from my face. The touch is slow. Like he's trying to calm something wild and wounded. I can't answer. I don't know if the word safe means what it used to anymore. At some point after I fell asleep, he must have moved down beside me on the floor, curling around me protectively in the dark.

Now I'm wrapped in his arms, one leg tangled with mine, his body a shield between me and the room. His lips press soft kisses into my hairline. His hand traces slow patterns along my back, grounding me her in this moment. Where I am with him, where he came for me. Where nothing else exists except the sound of his breathing and the way he keeps holding me like he never plans to let go.

"Do you want to talk about it?" he asks, his voice gentle but firm.

I shake my head and burrow deeper into his chest, breathing him in like he's oxygen. The steady rise and fall of his breathing slowly pulls mine back into rhythm. He exhales, fingers spreading across my back, stroking long and slow.

"It would help," he murmurs. "Maybe not now, but eventually. You'll need to let it out. Don't bottle it up."

I don't want to let anything out. I don't want to think about the room. The ropes. The hands that touched me. The fear that coursed me. The absolute helplessness, knowing I couldn't do a damn thing to stop it. How close everything came to being worse. I want only one thing right now. Wade.

My fingers drift lower, tracing the hard lines of his stomach, the tactical vest and gear still strapped to him, all of it frustratingly in the way. My touch is tentative at first, testing. When he doesn't stop me, I grow bolder. My hand slides lower, feeling the solid tension of him through his pants. A rough groan vibrates from deep in his chest, the sound rolling through me where my cheek rests against him. It grounds me. I am here, I am safe. This is my body, my choice and on my terms.

"Make me forget," I whisper, pressing my lips over the pounding beat of his heart. "Make me forget everything but you." His whole body tightens.

I feel the war in him instantly. Need against restraint. Want against protectiveness.

"Beautiful," he rasps, lips brushing my temple. "I don't think now is

the right time. I want you ready for this. You went through something
—"

"I am ready," I cut in, voice trembling with something far deeper
than desire. Right now all I can feel is the desperation mixed with
hope. "I need you, Wade. I need to feel you. I need to be with you."

He leans back enough to look at me fully. Those brown eyes search
mine, filled with concern, hesitation, care so fierce it almost hurts to
witness. He's afraid I'll regret it. Afraid I'm reaching for this for the
wrong reasons. Afraid to fail me. I lift my hand and cup his face,
forcing him to hold my gaze. To see that this isn't about forgetting. It's
about taking something back.

"If this is a dream," I whisper, voice breaking at the edges, "then I
need these memories when I wake up."

Something in his expression softens completely. His thumb brushes
beneath my eye, catching tears I hadn't noticed falling.

"This isn't a dream," he murmurs. Then his mouth finds mine. A
warm, slow kiss that feels like a promise more than passion. When he
pulls back just enough to breathe, his forehead rests against mine. "I'll
prove it to you."

His knee gently nudges my legs apart, his body settling between
them. He takes his time, dragging his hands down my sides, peeling
away the clothes that feel like remnants of another life, another *me*.

"I love you, you're my dream. We have to be quick, I need to stay
connected and alert." he breathes against my skin, pressing reverent
kisses along my jaw.

I shiver. "I love you too."

His lips trail lower, his mouth painting soft promises over my
collarbone. He starts lifting my worn shirt and brings it just above my
breasts. He kisses down to the peaks of my breasts. He pauses just
before taking me into his mouth, his breath warm against my sensitive
skin.

"You are *safe*," he whispers before his tongue flicks out, teasing me.

A gasp catches in my throat as he sucks me deeper, his hands
gripping my waist, holding me still as my body arches beneath him.
His kisses continue lower, slow and deliberate, his voice a steady
reassurance against every part of me. He unbuttons my cargo pants
and pulls them down my legs. He rips both my boots off and takes my
pants the rest of the way off with them before settling back between
my thighs.

"This is *real*." I tremble as his mouth moves down, as his rough hands explore the soft curves of my hips, my thighs. The anticipation coils tight inside me, burning away the last remnants of fear.

"Please," I gasp, my fingers threading through his hair.

His low groan sends a jolt through me. "Fuck, you're perfect."

He licks me once, slow and teasing, before pulling back. His eyes are hooded, dark with restraint as he reaches for his belt, unbuckling it with one swift motion. I watch, enraptured, as he frees himself, his thick length standing hard and ready. Then he's over me, his body caging mine in the best possible way. He kisses me deeply, stealing the breath from my lungs.

"You," he growls, positioning himself at my entrance, "are *mine.*"

And then, he's inside me, pushing into my heat with a slow, steady thrust. A cry escapes me, but Wade is there, swallowing it with his lips, his hand sliding over my mouth with a hushed, amused chuckle.

"We have to be quiet," he whispers against my lips, his voice thick with desire. "I know it feels amazing, but just *lay there* and *feel me*. Only *me.*"

"Fuck, you feel so good, beautiful. I need you to come." He says and his thumb traces over my clit and I moan again. His hips move in a slow, deep rhythm, every stroke a promise, a reminder that I am here, that I am his, that I am safe. And as my body tightens around him, as the pleasure builds and swallows me whole, I finally, *finally* let go. Of the fear. Of the past. Of everything except *us*.

Chapter Twenty Seven

Wade

I keep my movements slow, deliberate, each thrust an unspoken vow, each touch a silent promise. I want her to *feel* it, to know it's not a dream. She is my dream. The only one I've ever had that truly mattered. A soft moan spills from her lips, breathy and sweet against my ear. It takes everything in me to hold on, to keep myself controlled. But when her fingers grip my back, nails biting into my Kevlar vest. She's afraid to let go, something in me tightens, sharp and possessive. I never want her to feel like she has to hold on for dear life. She doesn't have to. I'm *here*. Always.

Her hips start moving with mine, desperate, searching. The rhythm between us becomes something more, more than need, more than pleasure. It's a claiming, a surrender to everything we are together. The way she grips me, her body pulling me deeper, the soft cries breaking from her lips, it undoes me. Her breath hitches, her body trembling beneath mine, her tight, wet heat squeezing me like she's afraid to let me go. And then, with a shuddering gasp, she comes apart.

I groan low in my throat, feeling her pulse around me, drawing me with her. I can't hold back anymore. I bury my face in her neck, whispering her name like a prayer as I shatter, falling with her into the abyss of everything we've just created between us.

Afterward, I don't move. I just hold her. Feel the warmth of her skin against mine. The steady rhythm of her breathing slowly evening out. The fact that she's here, alive, in my arms, still feels too fragile to trust. Her fingers drift across my back in lazy, absent patterns, featherlight touches like she's memorizing every inch of me. Maybe making sure I'm real.

I lower my mouth to her temple and kiss her there, lingering. "Still think this is a dream?" My voice comes out rough, scraped raw by everything we've been through.

She lets out a soft breath, the kind that only comes when someone finally feels safe enough to relax. "No," she whispers. "You feel real." I wrap my arms around her and bury my face in her hair for one selfish second. I'll spend the rest of my life making sure she never has to question what's real again.

Right now, training overrides comfort. I lift my head and listen. The jungle outside has changed. Night insects are fading, morning bird calls are starting. First light isn't far off. Movement becomes easier to spot in daylight. So do tracks. So do bodies and once the sun is fully up, heat becomes another enemy.

"We need to get ready," I murmur, brushing hair back from her face. "We need to keep moving."

She nods, though exhaustion flashes through her eyes. I hate it, I hate asking more from her when she's already given too much. But staying here gets us killed. I sit up and immediately begin shifting back into mission mode.

Sliding my pants on first, I move to my vest, getting that tightened. Check my holster, get my rifle cleared, mag seated and the chamber is confirmed. Knife is secured.

I key my mic low. "Wraith to team. Radio check."

Clicks come back one at a time through the earpiece.

Reaper.

Ghost.

Glitch.

Sparta.

Magellan.

Stitches.

All alive. The tension in my shoulders eases a fraction.

"Status?" I ask.

Ghost answers first. "At rally point. No movement overnight. River traffic increased at dawn."

Reaper keys in next. "Perimeter set. Two observation points. No contact." Good. They're doing exactly what they should be. I glance back at Sarah while I shrug into my pack. She's dressing slowly, soreness obvious in every movement even though she's trying to hide it. Bruises stand out sharper in the early gray light. Rage flickers hot and immediate. I shove it down. Use it later.

I kneel in front of her. "Eat something." I hand her half an energy bar and my canteen. She opens her mouth to protest the rationing. I give her a look, needing to make sure she's taken care of. She takes both, my good girl. While she eats, I inspect her wrists again. Rope burns. Swelling. Skin broken but clean enough for now. I rewrap them with fresh gauze from Stitches' kit.

Then I check her pupils, watch her track my finger. "Any dizziness?"

"A little."

"Nausea?"

"It's less now."

"Can you walk?"

She lifts her chin stubbornly. "Yes." I already know that means maybe.

"We'll move slow. You tell me the second that changes." She gives me the look that means she plans to say nothing and suffer through it. I know this woman too well. I stand and shoulder the pack, then crouch to erase obvious signs we stayed here, shift dirt, scatter impressions and brush back drag marks near the doorway. Not perfect, but enough to slow casual trackers.

I move to the entrance, scan left, right, canopy, trail. There is nothing immediate, just humidity rolls in thick as steam and the jungle is waking.

I turn back and hold out my hand. "Stay close to me. Step where I step when you can. If I say down, you drop. If I say run, you run. No hesitation."

Her small, warm hand slips into mine, completely trusting me. "I'm not leaving you," she says quietly.

I bring her knuckles to my mouth and kiss them once. "You won't have to."

Then I lead her back into the jungle, rifle up, senses sharp, carrying the woman I love through hostile terrain one careful step at a time. As we push forward, the jungle closes around us again. The narrow game trail we'd been following all but disappears beneath tangled roots, hanging vines, and wet undergrowth that fights every step. Broad leaves slap against my shoulders. Thorned runners snag at our pants. Branches claw at skin and gear alike, slowing movement to a grind.

I stay in front, rifle up, one hand clearing the path when I can, the other reaching back for Sarah whenever the terrain gets too steep or slick. She's fading, I hear it in her breathing first. It starts with shorter pulls of air, less controlled. Then I see it in the way her steps lose rhythm. The hesitation before lifting a foot over roots. The tiny sway every time she stops. Her body is hitting the wall. Drug crash. Trauma. Dehydration. Lack of food. Hours of movement through jungle terrain and she's still refusing to complain.

Stubborn woman. "We're close," I murmur over my shoulder. "Just keep following me." She nods, sweat dampening the hair stuck to her temples. I slow our pace half a notch, choosing cleaner footing, scanning constantly for tracks, broken foliage, anything that says we aren't alone.

Then *crunch*, that's not jungle noise. It's weight on leaf litter. I stop so fast Sarah walks straight into my back. My hand shoots behind me, catching her before she falls. I don't look at her. I'm already listening. Another controlled, measured sound that's not from an animal.

I raise a closed fist at shoulder height and freeze. Sarah stills instantly, good. She's staying silent and paying attention. My rifle comes up, muzzle tracking left flank where the sound came from. I shift one step right for a better angle, trying to cut through the foliage without exposing us both.

There. A shape moving between the trees. Low and disciplined, weapon is being carried properly. My pulse hammers once, hard. If it's not one of ours, we're compromised. If it's militia, they may have scouts between us and the river. If they've been tracking—I kill the thought and make the call.

"Whoop whoop." The spider monkey signal rolls soft through the trees. Silence answers.

I tighten my grip, finger finding the wall of the trigger.

Then I hear a "Whoop."

Relief hits like a gut punch. I lower the muzzle slightly and glance back. Sarah's lips part in the smallest smile. We changed the call sign because of her. She laughed the first time the guys used it and now it's bringing friendlies out of the jungle instead of enemies. I squeeze her hand once.

Stitches appears first, ghosting through the foliage like he grew there. Carly is beside him. Fuck, she looks worse than I expected. Too pale beneath dirt-streaked skin, her eyes glassy and half-lidded. A deep cut mars her temple, dried blood tangled through her hair and one side of her shirt is dark with old seepage from the stab wound dressing.

She's upright only because Stitches is practically carrying her. His face tells me everything. She needs evacuation, now. Sarah inhales sharply beside me, pain flashing across her features.

I keep my voice level. "We need to get to the rendezvous point. Now."

Stitches nods once. No wasted motion. He slings his rifle behind him, crouches and lifts Carly into a fireman-assisted carry that keeps pressure off her abdomen while maintaining mobility.

I adjust my pack and look at Sarah. "Can you move?"

"Yes." It's clearly a lie but she's determined. I'll let her walk for now, I need to maintain the use of my weapon, but as soon as I think she can't handle it anymore, we will adjust.

I take her hand again. "We're stepping it up."

Without another word, we move. This time a little faster. No conversation and no wasted energy. Just breathing, foot placement, security checks. I rotate my head every few seconds, front, left, right, rear glance, canopy break, trail sign. Stitches mirrors the pattern behind us. We stagger spacing to avoid bunching up and giving one target cluster if engaged.

The jungle feels different now. Like it knows we're racing something. Humidity hangs thick and hot even in the fading light. Mosquitoes swarm exposed skin. Somewhere distant, monkeys scream warnings through the canopy. Then the trees begin to thin. I smell water before I see it, the telltale scent of river mud, diesel and oil.

We're getting close. Through the foliage ahead, dark movement cuts across the river. A patrol boat, it has a low profile, a fast and it's running dim. Engines are throttled down. My body goes rigid, armed silhouettes shift onboard, scanning the banks. Could be ours or could be militia. Could be both if this day wants to keep testing me.

I raise a fist again and everyone drops low automatically. I bring the rifle up, sights tracking the shoreline. Movement flickers in the brush ahead. Closer this time. Multiple bodies.

I don't wait. "Whoop whoop."

The signal snaps through the trees, there's only one beat. Then the reply.

"Whoop."

My men emerge from concealment in disciplined intervals, weapons out, sectors covered.

Reaper first, Ghost behind him. Sparta wide right. Magellan rear security. Glitch near the bank, already waving us in, they're all alive. Relief slams through me hard enough to stagger. I bury it immediately. We're not safe yet. In the center of the group, Jenna and Willis stumble forward with their wrists zip-tied behind them. Jenna looks hollowed out, shock swallowing whatever bravado she had left. Willis looks furious, offended, even now, like being bound is beneath him.

I don't spare either of them more than a glance. My world narrows to Sarah and Carly. I keep both women on the inside of our movement formation, screened from the prisoners and shielded by rifles. Ghost and Sparta take point. Reaper and Magellan float the flanks. Glitch stays near the prisoners, muzzle never drifting far from Willis. Stitches carrying Carly in front of me.

I stay beside Sarah, always. The dock comes into view through the last wall of brush, weathered planks stretching into the river where a low-profile patrol craft idles in the current. That same dark hull with its suppressed wake. The crew already scanning sectors. Then I recognize the silhouettes. The Full Metal Jackets.

My chest loosens for the first time in two days. At the bow stands a broad-shouldered figure in plate carrier and helmet, beard darker than I remember, rifle tucked like it belongs there, is Nate—Specter, their team lead and one of my closest friends. He sees me and gives one curt nod. No reunion, yet, just business. Not until we're safe.

"We've got wounded!" I bark.

"Copy!" he shouts back. "Load now! Two-minute window!" Perfect. We tighten formation and move. I step onto the dock first, testing the planks for rot as I go, then turn and lift Sarah by the waist onto the boards. Her legs shake the second they take weight. She still squares her shoulders and keeps moving. Unbelievable woman. Carly comes next, Stitches half-carrying her.

The prisoners are shoved behind them. Then the first shot cracks, a supersonic snap. Close enough to feel it pass my ear.

"Contact left tree line!" Ghost roars. Reaper fires before the echo dies, one clean shot. A body drops in the brush. Then the jungle explodes. Muzzle flashes burst from both banks. AK fire rakes the dock, chewing splinters from the planks, rounds punching holes through rail posts and kicking spray off the river.

"Move! Move! Move!" The Full Metal Jackets open up from the boat. Controlled bursts. Disciplined fire. Different than militia panic shooting. Their rounds hammer the tree line with surgical violence. Sparta drags Willis forward by the collar when the bastard freezes. Glitch shoves Jenna hard enough to keep her moving. Magellan and Ghost pivot, firing alternating sectors to keep heads down.

I turn to shove Sarah toward the boarding ramp. "Go!" She stumbles forward. Then pain detonates in my lower back. A hot and violent burn, like getting hit by a sledgehammer wrapped in fire. The impact nearly folds me. My right leg threatens to buckle. Shot. I've been shot. My breath catches but training takes over instantly. No spinal collapse. Legs still working. Bleeding, likely through-and-through or lodged low.

Pain can wait. I stay upright. Sarah is three steps from the ramp. That's all that matters. I grit my teeth and drive forward. Reaper's eyes cut to me mid-reload, he knows and he says nothing. Just shifts closer, becoming my shield without breaking stride.

That's brotherhood. Another burst slams into the dock behind us. Wood explodes at calf height.

"Get him onboard!" Ronan bellows from the craft.

Two SEALs surge down the ramp, rifles slung front, returning fire one-handed while grabbing Carly and Sarah. Stitches passes Carly off to Patch who guides her forward to start checking her over. Stitches immediately turns back to cover. I shove Sarah into waiting hands.

She twists, eyes wide. "Wade—"

"I'm right behind you!" Lie if I need to. Truth if I can make it. I hit the ramp hard, blood running warm under my waistband now. Another round punches sparks off the metal beside my head. Ghost drops the shooter before I can turn. I reach the deck just as my leg finally falters. Hands grab me, Reaper on one side, Sparta on the other, dragging me behind the armored console.

The engines roar, lines are cut and the throttle slams forward. The patrol craft surges into the river as tracers streak over the stern. The Full Metal Jackets keep firing in measured bursts, walking rounds across the bank until the return fire dies. I sag against the bulkhead, rifle still in my grip, blood slicking my hands.

Across the deck, Sarah is alive. Carly is alive. That's enough for now.

The freighter looms behind us, dark and massive against the burning horizon, its mounted guns slewing toward our escape route. We're not clear, not even close and I don't know how much longer I can stay on my feet. The patrol boat surges forward, engines screaming as the hull slaps hard across the river chop. Every impact sends fresh agony through my lower back, pain radiating hot and deep into my hip.

Stay upright. Stay useful. Then I see the muzzle flash.

"Incoming!" someone shouts. Their first round streaks low across the water, missing wide but close enough to throw spray over our stern.

Before they can correct aim, the Full Metal Jackets answer and they answer like professionals.

"Dash, keep us moving!" Specter barks over the engine noise. "Zigzag pattern—don't give them a clean line!" The patrol craft immediately cuts hard across the river, Travis "Dash" Williams throwing the wheel over with practiced aggression. The hull slams through the chop, changing angle before the freighter can walk in another shot.

"Graves, gun up!" Dominic "Graves" Moreau is already on the mounted weapon system, massive frame planted wide as he swings the turret toward the freighter with smooth, controlled precision.

"Signal, feed range!" Owen "Signal" Hayes glances between optics and tablet feed. "Four hundred meters and closing. Portside gun nest exposed."

"Viper, take eyes!"

From the elevated stern platform, Elias "Viper" Cruz drops prone behind a precision rifle, scope already trained downrange.

"Knox, launcher!" Mason "Knox" Keller grins like a maniac as he shoulders a compact rocket tube near the aft rail. "Been waiting all day for you to say that."

"Hold until I say." Rounds snap overhead. Wood splinters off the dock behind us. The freighter's mounted gun begins tracking again. "Now!" The Full Metal Jackets unleash hell.

Graves opens first, heavy rounds hammering across the freighter's deck in brutal, measured bursts. Metal erupts in showers of sparks as the gun emplacement gets shredded. Viper fires once. The enemy spotter on the upper rail disappears backward. Knox launches. The rocket streaks low over the water and slams into the midsection of the ship with a thunderous impact. A blossom of orange fire punches outward, followed by black smoke and screaming men.

"Secondary cook-off!" Signal calls. As if on cue, stored fuel or ammunition detonates deeper inside the vessel. A second explosion rips through the superstructure, blowing windows outward and sending debris raining into the river. Men leap overboard some burning, some wounded. Some already being dragged under by current.

Graves keeps firing in disciplined bursts, walking rounds across the deck to suppress anyone still trying to man weapons. Specter doesn't even look back.

"Enough. Save ammo. Dash, full throttle. Get us clear." The engines roar louder. The patrol craft surges ahead, slicing through the river while the freighter burns behind us like a floating funeral pyre.

I barely register any of it. My vision is narrowing. Not from shock, from blood loss. I need to move before I drop where Sarah can see me. I force my legs forward and pass through the main compartment of the patrol craft.

Inside, red emergency lights glow over metal walls and bolted benches. Weapons cases are stacked under seats. The smell of oil, smoke, blood, and river water mixes in the cramped air.

Sarah is there. Seated at the table beside Carly. She's leaning against Sarah, their hands are clasped tightly together. Carly looks ghost-white, patched dressings wrapped around her abdomen and head. Sarah looks exhausted, bruised, hollow-eyed and still the most beautiful thing I've ever seen. She spots me instantly.

Her expression changes, her brows drawing together. She knows something is wrong, of course she does. I force a smile through clenched teeth. She gives me one back, small and uncertain. She's not fooled.

"Are you okay?" I ask, scanning her again for injuries I missed. She nods, though her body is trembling with delayed shock and fatigue. Strong, so damn strong. No visible bleeding. No new trauma. Good. That's enough to keep me moving another minute.

"I'll be right back," I tell her. "I love you." My voice is steady for most of it. The last words shake. Her lips part immediately. Her eyes drop to my side, then snap back to mine. She knows something is wrong, but I don't let her speak

"Glitch," I bark. "Stay with the girls." He rises from the opposite bench at once.

"You got it."

"Stitches, with me."

From the rear compartment another voice cuts in. "Make that Stitches and Patch." I think it's Reaper but everything is starting to blur.

Lucas "Patch" Bennett steps through the hatch already pulling gloves on, calm as if we're in a clinic instead of a gunfight on the river. Same square jaw and shaved head. Sleeves rolled over tattooed forearms. Combat medic for the Full Metal Jackets and one of the best trauma hands I've ever worked beside. Protocol-driven, steady under pressure, impossible to rattle. Mean bedside manner. Brilliant hands.

He takes one look at me and snorts. "You look like shit, Wraith."

"Good to see you, too."

"No it isn't. Sit down before I sedate you with a frying pan."

Even half-dead, I almost laugh. I move before Sarah can stand, before she can follow, before seeing me bleed becomes another thing burned into her memory. The corridor tilts slightly. Stitches closes in on one side. Patch takes the other without asking. Once we hit the bridge hatch, my knees nearly buckle. Both men catch it, like they knew it was coming.

"Round hit low posterior flank," Stitches says clinically. "He's been compensating for ten minutes."

"Idiot," Patch mutters.

"Badass," I grit out.

They shove me into the bridge, clear a space near the navigation console and force me onto a bench while Dash keeps one hand on the wheel and the other on comms.

He glances back once. "You die on my deck, I'm charging your family cleanup fees."

"Good luck with that." The warm rush of blood down my side tells me exactly how bad it might be. Stitches presses gauze hard into the wound.

White light explodes behind my eyes. "Found the pain," Patch says dryly.

"Make sure Carly is good first," I snap.

"She's already stabilized," Patch says. "Now shut up and let us keep you that way."

The boat races into the dark river while they work and all I can think about is the woman in the next compartment waiting for me to come back.

"Shut the door," I order, my voice rough, breath coming too short. The second the hatch clicks closed, I start stripping off my gear. Plate carrier first. Then belt. Then rifle sling. Every movement is slower than it should be. My fingers feel thick, clumsy, slick with blood. Adrenaline is burning off fast now, leaving pain and weakness in its place.

"Well, well."

Nate "Specter" Smith steps in from the helm, broad shoulders filling the cramped bridge. "Looks like I'm saving your ass after all, Wraith." Same dry tone he's had since the first joint op we ever ran together. Same bastard grin. Team lead of the Full Metal Jackets. One of the few men I trust without question. I try to glare at my friend, but it doesn't have much heat behind it. My vision is tunneling at the edges, black creeping in and out. My pulse thuds heavy and slow in my ears.

Too much blood. Instead of answering, I lift one hand and flip him off before dropping it hard onto the steel table bolted to the deck. My whole back feels like it's on fire. Every breath drags pain through my side. Fuck. I forgot how much getting shot hurts.

Patch is already moving. "Cute reunion," he mutters, snapping gloves on. "Try not to die before I bill you."

Stitches drops to one knee beside me, med pack spread open in seconds, trauma supplies laid out with practiced speed. "Shepherd's hook entry," he says, fingers probing carefully near the wound. "Low posterior flank. Need him prone or side recovery."

"Any exit?" Patch asks.

"Not seeing one."

"Great. Bullet's sightseeing."

Specter's grin vanishes completely. "Shit, Wraith, what happened?"

None of us answer. No time.

"I need him flat," Patch orders. "Now. Specter, you're on pressure. Stitches, cut everything."

Hands grab me under the arms. They haul me onto the navigation table, charts and gear swept aside in one violent motion. My head hits hard metal and I barely feel it. Then Stitches cuts my shirt and undershirt up the spine. Fabric peels away wet and stuck to the wound. When it tears free, white-hot pain detonates behind my ribs. I bite down so hard my jaw pops. I make no sound, no weakness, I just breathe.

"Good bleed," Patch mutters. "He missed kidneys if we're lucky. Maybe soft tissue and muscle track. Maybe not."

"Comforting," Specter says.

"Shut up and push." Specter plants both palms into the dressing over the wound. Pressure crushes the breath out of me. My body jerks despite myself.

"Easy," Stitches says, one forearm pinning my shoulder. "Don't fight us."

Easy. Sure. The room tilts violently. Voices fade in and out beneath engine noise. Metal rattles. River chop slams the hull. Patch starts an IV in my arm without asking permission. Cold fluid hits my vein.

"BP dropping," he says. "He stayed vertical too long." No shit. I close my eyes for one second and Sarah's face appears instantly. Bruised cheek. Shaking hands. The way she looked at me when I told her I loved her. The way she trusted I'd come. The way she smiled in that hut like I was something worth believing in. I can't let her lose me now. I force my eyes open. The words cost everything I have left.

"Keep her safe," I rasp, looking at Stitches. He nods once.

Specter leans closer, not hearing. "Keep who safe?"

Sarah. My Little Mouse. I try to say it. Nothing comes out. The bridge lights smear into white and shadow. Sound stretches far away. Then everything goes black.

Chapter Twenty Eight

Sarah

I look over at Carly. She's still gripping my hand, fingers tense and cold, but her head remains bowed on my shoulder. She hasn't spoken much since we got on the boat. Barely reacted to anything. Just sat there like if she stays still enough, maybe none of this is real. She looks awful. Too pale. Too drained. Like she could faint at any second.

Across from us, Jake leans against the wall, arms folded over his chest, staring at the door Wade and Nick disappeared through. His usual smirk is gone. That alone makes my pulse jump. Something feels off, maybe everyone is exhausted but I don't think that's right. At least, that's not all it is.

The boat moves fast, the steady vibration of the engines humming through the metal floor beneath our boots, but the energy in the room has shifted. Everyone is quieter. I can sill see and feel the tension in the air, they're all still waiting or preparing for more attacks. I really hope this is done, I want to get out of here.

A quiet unease slides through me. "Jake," I whisper. His head snaps toward me immediately, expression softening the second he sees my face.

"Hey, Rocky." His voice is warm, trying for playful. "Glad to see you doing well."

I don't smile. I don't feel like smiling.

"Is everything okay?" He hesitates, only for a second but I see it.

"Yeah," he says easily. Too easily. "They just need to update Nate, notify command. Standard protocol."

It makes sense, kind of. I nod anyway, but the knot in my stomach only tightens.

Jake studies me for a moment, then pivots. "How about you? You need anything?"

I glance down at Carly, then at the untouched canteen on the table. Suddenly I'm aware of the hollow ache in my stomach.

"I'm hungry," I admit quietly. "And I don't think Carly is doing well." Carly still doesn't look up, but her grip on my hand tightens.

Jake exhales through his nose and pushes off the wall, crossing over to sit beside us. "Yeah," he says softly, all humor gone now. "I noticed." Then he brightens his tone on purpose. "I'll get us food. I'm starving too."

A man in tactical gear passes the hatchway, broad-shouldered and moving with the easy confidence of someone who belongs in dangerous places. Jake reaches out and taps him on the arm.

"Hey, Switch, can we get some snacks before these women mutiny?" The man glances over. Sharp eyes and a quick smirk.

"Demanding already. Must be Glitch's people." Without waiting for a reply, he keeps moving down the corridor. I blink at Jake. He spreads his hands dramatically.

"I know. I'm way more charming than you thought." Despite everything, a weak laugh escapes me. It feels strange, but good. A few minutes later, the same guy returns carrying protein bars, crackers, bottled water, and what looks like military ration packs.

He drops them onto the table. "Compliments of the Full Metal Jackets," he says. "Try not to judge the cuisine."

Jake tears into a protein bar immediately. I remember Wade telling me to go slow. Small bites, small sips, I know I need it for strength and energy. So I do. The food tastes dry and bland and somehow wonderful. Carly barely moves until I nudge a water bottle toward her. After a moment, she takes it with shaking fingers.

The more I eat, the heavier exhaustion settles into my bones. The

Adrenaline is gone now, pain and fatigue rush in to replace it. My eyelids keep slipping lower.

Then the engines change pitch and the boat slows suddenly. Every person in the compartment goes alert. I jolt upright, pulse slamming against my ribs.

"Why did we stop?" My voice comes out sharper than I intend, fear leaking through every syllable.

Jake watches me carefully from across the compartment. "We're transferring," he says evenly. "Everything's fine."

I swallow hard, eyes snapping to the door Wade disappeared through. Still closed. Still no sign of him.

"Do you think Wade's okay?" I ask, my voice smaller now. Thinner.

Jake pushes off the wall and kneels in front of me, forearms braced on his thighs. "Rocky," he says, softer this time. Serious. "Don't work yourself up. This is normal for us. We hit the support ship, medics take over, everyone gets checked out."

Support ship. The words should calm me, they don't. I've never been on a naval ship, I've never needed support like this and the one man I need to comfort me is not here. I nod anyway. The knot in my stomach only tightens.

A voice calls Jake's name from outside. He stands as the rest of the team filters in through the aft hatch, mud-streaked and exhausted. Not through Wade's door. My chest constricts. Where is he? Before I can ask again, my eyes land on Willis and Jenna. Their wrists are still bound in zip ties. Jenna's head hangs low, shoulders trembling with silent sobs.

Willis lifts his chin and looks directly at me. The hatred in his stare is so cold and absolute it makes my blood run cold. Jake shifts instantly, blocking my view with his body.

"Eyes elsewhere, Doc," he says flatly.

Willis disappears from sight. The rear hatch opens and hot river air rushes in along with shouted commands, boots on metal, and the clang of secured lines. We're guided up and out. The patrol craft is tied alongside a much larger vessel, gray steel rising several stories above us, floodlights cutting through the early darkness. Sailors move with sharp purpose across the deck while armed personnel secure the perimeter.

A naval ship. The size of it makes me feel suddenly very small. Very far from home. Metal stairs shake beneath my feet as I'm escorted upward. Jake carries Carly up the stairs, her hanging against his shoulder. We're moved through narrow passageways lined with pipes, bulkheads, radios crackling overhead. Everything smells like diesel, salt, antiseptic and machinery. Doors slam. Boots echo.

Voices speak rapid Portuguese and English around us. I feel disoriented and lost all over again. We're ushered into the ship's medical bay. It's brighter than the corridors, with clean white lights, curtained treatment spaces, stainless steel trays, monitors humming softly. Not a hospital exactly, but close enough. Carly flinches the second a nurse approaches.

When they try to guide her to a bed, she panics and grips my hand harder, fingers shaking violently.

"It's okay," I whisper, though I don't know if it is. But there is no way I am letting anything else happen to her. She whimpers when they wrap the blood pressure cuff around her arm. I tighten my hold until some of the tension leaves her shoulders.

I explain where I can, piecing together everything in broken explanations. Kidnapped, held captive for five years, drugged, wounded. The words sound clinical, like they belong to strangers. Glitch never leaves our side. He stands near the curtain entrance, posture rigid, eyes scanning every movement in the room.

But something is off, his jaw is too tight. His gaze keeps flicking away whenever I look at him. He knows something and he isn't telling me. My stomach twists. Where is Wade? They separate us into adjoining curtained bays but keep us close enough to still touch hands between the gap.

IV lines. Vitals. More questions I have to answer about myself. About what happened in that room before I was rescued. They give us fresh gowns for which I am grateful, these clothes are disgusting, crunchy with dirt and sweat. We get warm blankets, the whole time Carly doesn't speak. Just huddles into the blanket.

When they finally bring us food, rice, bread and broth, I force myself to eat. They all insist my body needs something. Every bite feels like sandpaper scraping down my throat. Jake stands by the door like a guard carved from stone. He hasn't sat once, hasn't joked once. Barely spoken, he's hiding something and I don't like it. Every minute Wade doesn't walk through that door makes it harder to breathe. My now full stomach makes me drowsy, but I fight the pull of exhaustion.

I need answers. I need to see him. "Jake." My voice is hoarse enough that it barely sounds like mine. He looks up immediately, dark circles carved beneath his eyes.

"Where is he?" I ask, heart pounding so hard it hurts. A beat of silence stretches between us.

"Try to get some sleep." His voice is too careful, too neutral. "I'm sure he'll be here when you wake up."

That's not an answer. My pulse stutters, panic threatening to claw its way up my throat, but my body betrays me. The exhaustion wins and everything goes dark.

White. Too much white. Too bright. This isn't the olive green color of Wade's tent above me. I blink against the harsh fluorescent lights overhead, my body heavy and sluggish, every limb weighted down. Something tugs at my arm. I look down to find an IV line snakes into my wrist.

A monitor nearby gives off a steady constant electronic pulse. The medical bay, I'm still on the ship. The realization moves slowly, through layers of fog. I try to turn my head and immediately regret it. My muscles ache. My skull throbs dully behind my eyes.

Then I hear it. A soft snore. I shift my gaze. Nick is slumped in a chair beside the bulkhead, arms crossed over his chest, head tipped back at an angle that looks painful. His mouth is slightly open. Even asleep, he still looks alert somehow. Carly is in the bed beside mine, curled on her side beneath a thin navy blanket, breathing evenly. She made it. We made it. But I don't see Wade, where is he?

The hatch door opens with a metallic click. My heart leaps into my throat. For one wild second I think it's him. I expect broad shoulders. Golden brown eyes. The solid feeling of safety walking into the room. Instead, a medic steps inside carrying a tablet and a tray. The disappointment hits harder than it should. Why isn't he here? I don't remember much of the next stretch of time.

Questions. Vitals. Someone checking my pupils. A woman in navy medical scrubs speaking calm, clear English. I answer some things. Miss others. Everything blurs in and out.

Later, a doctor comes in. She looks to be in her thirties, blonde hair secured tightly back, kind but efficient eyes. She offers me a reassuring smile and holds out her hand.

"Dr. Souza," she says in lightly accented English. "I'm overseeing your care." I take her hand weakly. "How are you feeling?"

"Tired," I admit. "Is that normal? I feel like I should be better."

"Yes," she says gently. "Your body is still metabolizing the muscle relaxants they gave you. From what we were told, it was an excessive dose. That's why you lost consciousness for so long."

A chill runs through me. Twenty-four hours. Gone. Stolen. I swallow hard and stare at the blanket over my legs.

Dr. Souza's voice softens. "You are safe now."

Drugged. I knew that already, but hearing it spoken aloud drags me right back into that room. Benjamin's smile, the course rope holding me in place. The utter feeling of helplessness. A chill races through me and my fingers tighten around the sheets.

Dr. Souza studies me for a moment, then glances toward Nick still half-asleep in the chair by the wall.

"Davies," she says politely, switching to English. "Could you give us a few minutes, please?"

Nick straightens immediately, eyes narrowing just slightly. "Everything okay?"

"Yes," she says smoothly. "Private medical information."

His gaze flicks to me. I nod, though I'm not sure why. He rises, stretching stiffly, then points a finger at me.

"No escaping while I'm gone, Rocky."

Normally I might smile. I don't. The hatch shuts behind him with a metallic click. I look over at Carly, she is still asleep, her monitor beeping steadily.

Dr. Souza waits until it seals before turning back to me. "There is something else," she says gently. "When we ran your bloodwork, we found elevated hCG levels." I stare at her blankly. The letters mean nothing right now.

She hesitates, then says, "You are pregnant." I blink. The room goes strangely silent except the blood rushing in my ears and the sound of my heart monitor speeding up.

"Pregnant?" I repeat, voice rough and thin.

She nods once. "Yes. Pregnant."

Pregnant. The world tilts so sharply I grip the mattress to steady myself. Like, I might fly right off of it. I can't breathe. Pregnant. How? I mean, I know how. But I was careful. I was on birth control. Wasn't I? I try doing the math, I know I got the shot not long before I came here, it hasn't been three months.

Wade. The thought of him crashes through everything else, I need to see him. I need to tell him. He must still be here. He wouldn't leave me. Right?

"Are you okay?" Dr. Souza asks softly. I nod automatically. It's a lie, I am not okay. Not even close.

She continues in a calm, practiced tone. "It appears early. When you get home you will want to confirm with additional testing and ultrasound when you are stable, but the bloodwork is clear. I understand it was just yesterday you were taken and in your notes you said you were never assaulted?"

"No, no." Is all I can think to say, I don't even know if that made sense.

"Okay, do you know who the father is?" I nod.

Dr. Souza places a gentle hand over the blanket near my knee and her eyes soften. "This is a shock. You do not need to decide anything today. Okay, I'll leave you be for now. Let us know if you have any questions and when you get home, make an appointment with your doctor." I don't respond again, my mind is spinning. Early. Wade's baby. The realization hits so hard tears sting my eyes. Where is Wade? Why isn't he here? Why am I hearing this alone?

Dr. Souza gives me one last compassionate look, then quietly leaves. The room suddenly feels enormous. Too white. Too bright and too empty, despite Carly still out beside me. Panic tightens around my ribs. The hatch opens again. I jerk so hard my IV tugs painfully.

Nick steps back inside, ducking through the doorway. He takes one look at my face and all humor disappears. He shuts the door behind him.

"What happened?" he asks carefully.

I swallow against the lump in my throat. "Where is Wade?"

His expression softens, but there's something guarded beneath it. "Good to see you awake," he says, trying for lightness. "Back to your fiery self."

I glare at him. He's stalling. The attempt dies instantly.

Nick drags a hand over his face and steps closer. "No need to punch me," he mutters. "And I need you to stay calm, okay?" Every nerve in my body goes cold. "Now, before you freak out—"

A sinking feeling opens beneath me. "You and Carly are being discharged today," he says carefully. "Ghost contacted both of your emergency contacts."

I barely hear the rest. My voice comes out low and deadly steady. "Where. Is. Wade?"

He exhales slowly, jaw tightening. "When Wraith was getting everyone onto the ship, he was hit."

The world tilts. My stomach drops so hard it feels like I'm falling. I shove back the covers and swing my legs over the side of the bed before Nick raises both hands.

"He's okay," he says quickly. "Easy. He's okay."

I freeze, chest heaving. "The round went through clean," he continues. "Lower back, missed the spine, missed anything major. We got bleeding under control, Patch helped stabilize him and they moved him straight into surgery."

Surgery. The word slices through me.

"He lost a lot of blood," Nick says carefully. "He went unconscious for a bit, but they got him squared away. Last update I had? He should be waking up soon."

My hand flies to my chest, trembling so hard I can barely press it there. I can't get enough air.

"So when I kept asking Jake what was going on, when I begged for answers, he knew? You all knew?" My voice rises with every word. The monitor beside me starts chirping faster. "When I was sitting here terrified, all of you knew he could've been dying and no one told me?"

Nick's gaze drops. For the first time since I met him, he looks uncomfortable. "We were trying to protect you," he says quietly. "You'd just been drugged, assaulted, dragged through the jungle. You were exhausted. We didn't want to dump that on you unless it became necessary."

A sharp, humorless laugh tears out of me. "Not necessary?"

My hands curl into fists. "He's my—" The words catch hard in my throat. Mine. Everything. Future. I can't say any of it. "I want to see him." The demand comes out shaking. Nick nods once, expression gentling.

"Of course." Then he lifts a finger.

"But let me finish first."

I cross my arms, furious and impatient, but I stay where I am. "Our mission here is almost wrapped," he says. "You and Carly are being transferred ashore once medical clears it. Secure escort the whole way."

My eyes flick to Carly.

She's still asleep in the neighboring bed, face pale against the pillow but less ghostly than before. Some color has finally returned to her cheeks.

"Your aunt and uncle are en route," he continues. "They'll meet you at the naval terminal once we dock. Carly's family has been contacted too." Relief and anxiety twist together in my chest. "Willis and Jenna are detained," Nick says. "Separate holding. Full statements pending."

I nod stiffly. "But until we get more intel," he adds, voice tightening, "we still can't confirm whether Benjamin is alive or dead."

All the air leaves my lungs. The room turns cold. My skin prickles. That name alone is enough to drag me straight back into the dark.

Nick notices immediately. His tone softens. "Hey. Look at me." I force my eyes up. "You're safe," he says firmly. "You hear me? Safe. Wraith made damn sure of that."

I swallow hard and manage a nod. "We still have to return to command, debrief, file reports, clean up this mess." He gives me a tired half-smile. "Then we're officially off the clock."

A thought cuts through the panic. "How did you know to call my aunt and uncle?"

Nick shrugs one shoulder. "When we got tasked with the op, we received files on everyone in the expedition. Background checks, passport data, emergency contacts, medical notes if available. Standard protective package."

My pulse stutters. "So you knew who I was?" My voice drops to a whisper. "He knew who I was before I bumped into him?"

Nick goes still for half a beat, realizing exactly where my mind went. Then he nods once. "Yeah." The room shifts around me. That first meeting. The collision. His stare, the way he always seemed to know me. None of it was chance. Nick starts talking again, probably explaining, probably trying to soften it, but the words blur into noise.

Only one thing matters now. "Take me to Wade."

Nick studies me for a long moment, then exhales. "Yeah," he says quietly. "I figured that was coming." He helps me to my feet when my legs wobble, steadying me with a hand beneath my elbow before guiding me into the corridor.

"He's down there," he says quietly. I follow his gaze. At the far end of the passageway, outside a closed medical room, a man stands with a nurse. Dark green clothes. Thick, structured fabric that doesn't look like anything people normally wear. Boots. A gun strapped at his side. Broad shoulders. Completely still. Watching everything. Guarding the door.

My heart starts pounding. My body moves before my mind can catch up. As I approach, both of them look up. The nurse steps back. The soldier turns fully toward me.

"I'm here to see Wade." I mean for it to sound firm. Instead it comes out thin and fragile.

The man's expression doesn't change. "Ma'am, he's restricted at the moment."

I blink. "What?"

"He's post-op," he says evenly. "Still under observation. No visitors authorized yet."

My throat tightens. "Is he awake?" I ask quickly. "Tell him it's Sarah."

Something flickers in the soldier's eyes, recognition maybe but his posture never shifts. "He gave standing instructions before surgery," he says. "No one comes in until medical clears it."

The words hit me like a physical blow. No one. No visitors. No one comes in. My mind doesn't hear policy. It hears rejection. I stare at the closed door. He knows I'm here. My limbs move. My thoughts don't.

By the time I make it back to my room, I feel hollowed out. Inside, Nick is seated beside Carly's bed, leaning close, speaking softly enough that I can't make out the words. His hand is wrapped around hers. She's listening, present in a way she hasn't been before.

The second I enter, he straightens and steps back, eyes scanning my face. "How's Wraith?" he asks automatically, not realizing I am breaking inside.

I lift my gaze to his and glare. Confusion flashes across his features.

"Tell me something," I say, my voice eerily calm. "Was it all a lie?"

His brows draw together. "What?"

"Did my report tell you I was naive and stupid?" My voice cracks on the last word, humiliation burning hot beneath my skin. "Was I just some girl you all studied? Manipulated?"

"Sarah—"

"I can't believe this." I shake my head, tears threatening now. "You know what? Thank you for saving me. Tell everyone thank you for saving us." I swallow hard. "I will forever be grateful." My eyes lock onto his. "But please go get whoever I need to get off this ship."

"Sarah, what happened?"

"Just go." The room goes still. Nick stares at me, jaw tightening. I can see the questions in his eyes. I can see he wants to argue. Wants to fix it. Wants to know what happened in the hallway but one look at my face must tell him none of that is happening right now. I'm done asking. Done begging for scraps of truth.

I turn to Carly instead, softening instantly. "Are you ready to go home?" I ask quietly. She looks between us, then gives a small nod. When I glance back, Nick is still standing there for one last second. Then he leaves without another word. I don't look at the door after it closes. I won't break in front of him. I won't break in front of anyone.

Chapter Twenty Nine

Sarah

Carly and I are headed home. The thought still doesn't feel real, even as the naval transport hums beneath us and the shoreline comes into view through the small window. The base rises from the coast in layers of concrete, steel fencing, floodlights and guarded entry points. Uniformed personnel move with clipped efficiency across the tarmac and docks below. Helicopters sit farther down the runway, rotors still. Trucks roll between buildings painted in weathered military gray.

Order and security. The opposite of everything I just came from. My pulse pounds harder as we disembark. Then I see them. My uncle Tony is already moving before the escort even clears us forward. Tall, broad, salt-and-pepper hair windblown, eyes locked on me with relief.

"Sarah." My name breaks out of him like prayer. I barely make it two steps before he reaches me, pulling me into his arms so tightly it knocks the breath from my lungs. And I let him. For one suspended second, I let myself be held like a child again. Safe. I know it's not the same kind of safe I felt in Wade's arms, knowing he would do anything to protect me.

His chest shakes once before he steadies it. "You're okay," he murmurs hoarsely. "Jesus Christ, kid. You're okay."

Then my aunt Luciana is there. One hand pressed to her mouth, eyes shining with tears she's trying not to let fall. She cups my face gently, taking in every bruise, every shadow beneath my eyes, every piece of damage I tried to hide.

"Oh, querida," she whispers. Then she folds me into her arms too, softer than Tony, but somehow just as strong. Behind me, Carly stands frozen until Luciana turns and opens one arm toward her without hesitation. Carly breaks instantly. She steps forward and lets herself be gathered in.

No words. Just trembling. Tony clears his throat and gets practical fast, because that's who he is. "Bags are handled. Car is waiting. We'll get you girls fed, showered, rested, then to the airport."

I nod, but another urgency claws through me. "My phone."

Tony's face shifts. "Already handled." He reaches into his pocket and hands me a brand-new phone still in its protective case. "Picked it up on the drive in. Your parents called your provider. Same number."

My throat tightens. Of course he did. I take it with shaking hands. Within minutes I'm connected to the base Wi-Fi, fingers fumbling as I dial home. My mother answers on the first ring. The sound she makes when she hears my voice will stay with me forever.

I cry before I can stop myself. "I'm safe," I choke out. "Mom, I'm okay." Then for a few minutes I try to calm her and my dad down.

Then I call Fallon. When she answers, I can barely speak. "Sarah?" she says sharply. "Sarah, is that you?"

"Yes." A sob escapes me.

"I'm safe. Carly is too." There's silence. Then Fallon's voice turns fierce and shaking all at once. "I'm going to kill everyone who touched you."

Despite everything, a weak laugh breaks through my tears. Tony squeezes my shoulder while Luciana guides Carly toward a bench and kneels in front of her, speaking softly in Portuguese and English. Carly doesn't understand Portuguese unless that's changed now but she's met my aunt and uncle a couple of times. I asked Carly if she wanted to use my phone to call her parents but she just shook her head no, she hasn't spoken a word since we found her.

Tony takes care of everything without asking to. Hours later, after paperwork, escorts, and security clearances, they walk us all the way to the terminal attached to the base airfield.

Tony hugs me again, longer this time. "You call if you need anything," he says. "Anything."

Luciana kisses both my cheeks and smooths my hair back like she's done it a hundred times. "Come back when you're ready," she says gently. "Not before."

They make sure we board safely, waiting at the gate until the last possible second and when I look back one final time, they're still standing there. Promising to visit soon.

The flight back to Missouri was long. Carly slept through most of it, or maybe she only pretended to.

I tried to sleep too, but every time I closed my eyes my body jolted awake before I could drift under. Every change in engine pitch made my pulse spike. Every footstep in the aisle made me look up too fast. Every male voice nearby sent a cold flash through my stomach before my brain caught up.

Benjamin. What if he was alive? What if they were wrong? What if he escaped? What if this wasn't over? I kept scanning exits without meaning to. Counting rows, watching where hands were going. Tracking who moved where. I hated that I couldn't stop. When I did manage to close my eyes, my mind circled somewhere else entirely. Wade.

The fact that he knew who I was beforehand. The first time we met. The way he always seemed one step ahead. The way he looked at me like none of it was strategy. Was any of it real? Then the harder thought. He knew I was there, he knew I was asking for him and he didn't want visitors. My throat tightened. He doesn't even know I'm pregnant. I pressed a hand low against my stomach beneath the airline blanket, a private reflex no one noticed.

Fear twisted with grief so tightly I couldn't separate them anymore. Fear of Benjamin. Fear of what happened. Fear of what comes next and grief for something I wasn't even sure I'd really had. Next to me, Carly never opened her eyes.

By the time we finally make it through the airport, both of us are moving slowly, exhaustion dragging at every step. I keep my arm looped through Carly's as I guide us toward the waiting area. Then I see them, both my parents are standing there with my sister, Sam. Beside them are Carly's parents.

Carly's mother sees her first. Her hand flies to her mouth as a broken gasp escapes her, then she starts crying. Her father folds forward like someone physically struck him, one hand braced on his knee before he forces himself upright again. I stop walking. I watch as they rush toward her. Five years. Five years of believing their daughter was gone. Five years of grief, unanswered questions, birthdays spent mourning someone they never got to bury and now she's here. Alive, breathing even if she is not the same girl she used to be.

I let go of her arm as they reach her and wrap themselves around her. She flinches at first. Her body locking on instinct. It takes her a moment for her to relax, she lets them hold her. My chest tightens so sharply it almost hurts. Her mother clutches her like if she loosens her grip for even a second, Carly might disappear again. A fresh wave of emotion crashes over me. Not just for Carly. For all of us.

Then my mom, reaches me and throws her arms around me so fast I barely have time to breathe before I'm buried in the scent of vanilla, laundry soap and home. She's crying openly. One hand cradles the back of my head while the other grips my shoulder like she needs proof I'm solid.

"I'm so glad you're safe," she says through tears.

My throat burns. "Me too," I whisper.

My father steps in next, he doesn't say anything at first. He just pulls me into a hug so tight it steals the air from my lungs. My quiet, stoic father. When he steps back, his deep blue eyes rake over every bruise and shadow on my face. "I can't believe that asshole," he mutters, voice low and dangerous.

"I know," is all I can manage.

Because I don't know where to begin. Sam reaches me last. A couple inches taller than me, darker chestnut hair falling over one shoulder, warm brown eyes already glossy.

She grabs my face in both hands. "You scared the hell out of me."

Then she hugs me hard enough to make me laugh and cry at the same time. My family surrounds me, touches my arms, my shoulders my hair. Like they all need proof too but even standing there in the middle of them, part of me is somewhere else.

Still on that ship. Still outside Wade's door. Is he okay? Was it all a lie? Was I just convenient? Accessible. Available. An easy target. Eventually I pull away and walk back to Carly. Her parents step aside enough for me to reach her. She looks dazed. Small. Like the airport noise is happening a thousand miles away.

I hug her carefully. "Your parents have my number," I tell her softly. "Call anytime. Day or night. I mean it."

She gives me the smallest nod. It's enough. I say goodbye, then watch as her parents guide her toward another terminal for their connecting flight home.

Then I turn back to my family. "Please just take me home," I say. "I want a shower and my bed."

No one argues. I hold it together through the entire walk through the airport. Through the parking garage. Through loading the car. Until the doors shut. Then I break. The first sob tears out of me so violently it surprises even me and then I can't stop. I cry the entire hour drive home.

Ugly, shaking sobs that leave me breathless. My mother keeps turning in her seat to talk softly. My father reaches back once and squeezes my hand. Sam curses Benjamin at least six times. I hear none of it. All I can hear is the echo of two words. No visitors.

By the time we pulled into my parents' neighborhood in Kansas City, the sky had gone black. Their subdivision was exactly the same as I remembered. Wide streets and trimmed lawns. Porch lights glowing warm against brick facades. Two-story homes lined with maple trees just beginning to leaf out. Everything I used to take for granted. So different then the world I just escaped out of.

My dad parked in the driveway of the house I grew up in, a large brick home at the end of a quiet cul-de-sac with white shutters, flower beds my mother obsessively maintained, a wrap around porch and the porch swing where she drinks coffee every morning. Home. The word still felt unreal.

The second I stepped inside, warmth wrapped around me. Soft yellow lighting. The faint scent of cinnamon and laundry detergent. Family photos lining the entry wall. Holiday cards tucked into mirror frames. Proof of a life untouched by jungle darkness.

My mother had already got my room ready with fresh sheets because she knew I would need the safety of my room. I moved through the house like a ghost. Past the formal dining room where no one ever sat unless it was Christmas. Past the kitchen island where Sam and I had done homework. Past the living room with the same oversized sectional and the throw blanket my mom never let anyone actually use.

Upstairs, down the hall my bedroom was the last one on the left. She'd kept it mostly the same. The walls were still a soft pale blue. My old white bookshelf still held half-read novels, framed pictures, a ceramic horse I painted badly in middle school. The quilt on the bed had been freshly washed. A lamp glowed beside it. Clean pajamas folded neatly on the comforter. I nearly lost it again right there.

My mother hovered all evening. Bringing tea. Soup I couldn't eat. Fresh towels. Asking if I needed Advil, water, silence, company.

Eventually my dad came to get my mom, "Claire, let the girl be. She's safe, we'll see her in the morning." He started steering her out of the room as she was sniffling back tears, both of them saying goodnight.

"You're not sleeping alone tonight," she said matter-of-factly. She came in carrying a blanket and two bottles of water. My dad came to the bedroom door to check on me one more time.

I was too tired to argue. So hours later, we lay side by side in my childhood bed, shoulders touching. We hadn't shared a bed like this since thunderstorms scared me when I was ten and she'd sneak into my room with snacks and a flashlight. Now the comfort of her beside me felt like something sacred. The room was dark except for moonlight filtering through the blinds.

"I'm sorry this happened," Sam said quietly.

I nodded into the pillow, my head pounding from crying all day. But there was more. So much more and it was eating through me from the inside.

"That's not all."

She turned immediately, propping herself on one elbow.

Her brows furrowed. "What else happened?"

My stomach rolled. Right now, I feel so stupid and naive. "I met someone," I whispered. She stayed still, waiting.

"He was one of the Special Forces guys." My throat tightened around the words.

"I didn't mean for it to happen. I didn't even like him at first. I tried not to anyway, he was the one I texted you about in the beginning." A humorless laugh escaped me. That got the faintest smile from her.

"But then…" I stared at the ceiling. "It was just so easy, being around him. Talking to him. Like I'd known him forever. It just felt so natural, the way he took care of me. Protected me from Benjamin even from the very beginning." I swallowed hard. "I fell for him."

Sam's expression softened. "And then?"

I closed my eyes. "He didn't want to see me when we were at the hospital."

Her jaw tightened instantly. "Excuse me?"

"And I'm pregnant." That got a reaction. Her eyes widened so fast I almost would've laughed under different circumstances.

"You're… pregnant?" I nodded once. "You're sure?"

"The doctor told me. Bloodwork." My voice shook. "I need to make an appointment. Figure out how far along. Everything."

Sam lay back for a second, staring at the ceiling beside me. Then she blew out a long breath. "Okay. We'll circle back to the pregnancy." She turned her head toward me. "Tell me about him."

So I did. I told her about Wade. His golden-brown eyes that always seemed to see too much. The way he looked at me like I was the only person that mattered. The way he smiled when he teased me. How safe I felt in his arms. How terrifying it was to need someone that fast. How he came for me. How he carried me through hell. How he made me believe something real could exist in the middle of chaos.

When I finished, the room was quiet. "Wow," Sam breathed finally. "I genuinely don't know what to think."

I laughed bitterly into the dark. "Yeah. Me neither."

"Maybe there's an explanation," she said carefully. "Maybe he'll come through."

I didn't answer. Because I didn't know if I wanted him to. Because even now, loving him hurt. Because if I ever saw him again, I had no idea whether I'd kiss him or slap him first.

"When are you going to make an appointment?"

"I was thinking when I got back to Minnesota. I have three weeks before school starts. I want to get back and get situated. Meet with Dr. Anderson and prepare for all the things with school."

"Do you think you'll be back here to have the baby? I would hate for you to move far away without any support."

"I don't know. Probably. Maybe. I haven't thought that far ahead yet."

"Yeah, that makes sense. You know I am here for you right?"

"I know. Thank you."

"When are you going to tell mom and dad?"

"I'm thinking tomorrow, I wasn't trying to hide it from you guys, I just… I have been a mess. I feel better after telling someone though."

"Yes, don't hold anything in. Maybe you should think about seeing a therapist too, you know. It was something traumatic you went through." I nod my head, not knowing what I think about that. I do think I will need some help though. I fell asleep replaying all the moments between Wade and I. Wondering if any of it was real. I tried to keep my mind distracted but if it was him it was Benjamin's cruel smile hovering over me.

At breakfast, we are all sitting down at the table when my phone rings. It's an unknown number and I really don'y want to answer. Too scared at what was on the other end. So my dad grabbed it.

"Hello?" His voice gruff, ready to fight whoever was on the other line. Then he looks at me, "Sarah, it's an Agent Ramsey with the FBI." He said.

To say that I wasn't terrified would be a lie, my stomach dropped so hard it felt like I was going to throw up. I knew I hadn't done anything wrong. I knew I was a victim. I knew, logically, they were calling to help build the case. None of that mattered. Wrapped in one of Sam's sweatshirts, hair damp from the longest shower of my life. My bruises had darkened overnight. My eyes were swollen from crying. I looked like someone I barely recognized. I just stared at the phone as they all stared at me.

My father immediately stood. "We're taking putting this on speaker. Sarah we're here for you, okay?" Morning light spilled through the large windows over the sink, catching the granite countertops and polished wood floors. The coffee pot hissed. My mother hovered near the island but didn't interrupt. Sam sat across from me in leggings and a messy bun, arms folded tight.

Dad pulled out the chair beside mine and sat close enough that our shoulders touched. Grounding me without saying it. He hit speakerphone.

"Miss Maddox?" the voice said. His voice was very deep and controlled, it reminded me of Wade.

I straightened instinctively. "Yes." It came out mostly a whisper.

"This is Special Agent Ramsey. We spoke briefly in Brazil. First, I want to say I'm glad you're home safely."

His voice was calm, steady, professional in a way that made breathing easier. "We're recording this statement with your consent," he continued. "You may stop at any time, take breaks at any time and decline any question you don't want to answer today. Understood?"

"Yes."

"And Sarah?" Something softened in his tone. "You're not in trouble."

My eyes burned unexpectedly. "Okay."

For the next two hours, I told him everything. Every detail I could remember. The wedding. Jenna asking me to go with her. The walk into the jungle. The hands over my mouth. The needle in my neck.

Waking in the shack. The women. The younger tribal girl tied to the bedpost.

Benjamin's smile. Dr. Willis stepping into that room like he belonged there. The way he spoke about selling us. The negotiations. The men. Jenna and what they did to her. Carly. My voice broke more than once. Each time Ramsey waited, he never rushed me. Never filled silence just to fill it.

When I described what Benjamin said, how I was "his," how he talked about Carly, how proud he sounded, my father's hands curled into fists on the table. When I described Willis casually discussing prices, my mother covered her mouth and cried silently.

When I repeated the words *both girls now, same price,* Sam muttered, "I hope they rot."

Ramsey's voice stayed even. "Did Benjamin admit involvement in Carly's disappearance?"

"Yes."

"Did Dr. Willis acknowledge prior knowledge of trafficking activity?"

"Yes."

"Did either man reference names, locations, militia groups, buyers, routes?"

I answered everything I could. Sometimes clear memories. Sometimes fragments. Sometimes just tone, smell, fear. By the end my throat felt scraped raw. My whole body trembled. Ramsey must have heard it.

"We can pause."

"No," I said quietly. "I want it done."

There was a brief silence. "You're doing exceptionally well."

No one had said that to me yet. That was something Wade would say to me. I stared at the kitchen table and blinked hard. Eventually the questions shifted to identification. Photos would come later. Statements. Medical releases. Follow-up interviews. Possible grand jury testimony. My chest tightened again. Dad noticed immediately and put a hand over mine.

Ramsey's voice cut through the panic. "One step at a time. Right now, you're safe at home." Home. The call ended with him promising someone local would coordinate anything further. Then, after a pause: "And Sarah?"

"Yes?"

"You helped save multiple victims by surviving long enough to talk to us."

The line clicked dead before I could respond. The kitchen stayed silent. The kind of silence that comes after something heavy settles over a room. Then I turned to my family. There was no putting it off anymore.

"I didn't tell him everything."

Three faces lifted. "What else is there?" my mom asked carefully. I looked down at my hands, twisting my fingers together in my lap. Then looked at Sam, needing a little support and strength.

Then I told them the truth. Not just about what happened in that jungle, not just the rescue. I told them about Wade. About how we met, how he got under my skin almost immediately. How he made me feel safe in a place that should have terrified me. How fiercely he protected me. How he came for me.

"I fell in love with him," I whispered, trying to hold back tears already burning in my throat. "And I'm...I'm pregnant."

I must have said it badly or wrong. Because my mother gasped so sharply she burst into tears all over again. My father went rigid beside me. It took me three horrified seconds to realize what they thought.

"No!" I blurted, shaking my head so hard it made me dizzy. "No, no —it wasn't like that."

All three stared at me. "I'm not pregnant because of them," I said quickly, cheeks burning. "I—I fell so hard for him and maybe it was stupid, I don't know. I'm on birth control. I've always been consistent with it."

The room went dead silent. My mother slowly lowered her hands from her face, still crying but quieter now. My father's brows drew together. His jaw hardened and I've never seen him look so furious. I realize he's not mad at me, but mad at Wade, angry about the whole damn situation. Join the club.

"I don't know what to say," my mom whispered.

"I know." My voice cracked. "I don't know what to say either. It was an accident."

"Where is this man now?" my dad asked, each word clipped and controlled.

"He was shot during the rescue," I said softly. "He was still in the hospital recovering when Carly and I left." My mother inhaled sharply again.

Dad's expression darkened. "Does he know?"

I shook my head. "No. I was told he didn't want any visitors. Didn't want anyone in his room." That landed like gasoline on fire.

My father pushed back in his chair slightly, eyes flashing. "So he led you on," he said, voice low and dangerous, "got you pregnant, then abandoned you?"

"Thomas," my mother warned softly. But he didn't look away from me. I stared down at my hands again, throat tight. I shrugged one shoulder because I honestly didn't know. Maybe. Maybe not. I didn't know what to believe anymore, even if that was exactly how it looked. That's how it feels.

Chapter Thirty

Sarah

A week after I got home, my parents brought me to the airport so I could get back to school. They wanted me to stay longer. My mother especially, she cried the second we pulled up to the terminal, then tried to pretend she hadn't. It only made me cry too. She clung to me like she could physically hold me together. Like if she kept her arms around me long enough, the cracks inside me wouldn't spread any farther.

"I can stay," I whispered more than once. But that wasn't true, I needed movement. A routine to stick to. Something that felt like my life before everything shattered. So I promised her I was okay. I promised I'd call every day. Promised I'd come home for Thanksgiving, a normal family holiday. Normal food. Normal conversations. Normal me.

I promised to keep her updated about the baby, though even saying the word still felt surreal. Baby. Mine. Ours. I desperately wanted to finish my degree before the world shifted again. I was so close. One more push and I'd have something solid to stand on. My dad hugged me next. Shorter than Mom's and he squeezed me into a bear hug.

"Call if you need anything," he said. Which, in Dad language, meant: *I will drive across three states in the middle of the night if you ask.*

Sam squeezed me last and slipped a packet of crackers into my tote bag. "For nausea," she murmured.

I laughed through tears. Then I walked inside before any of us could change our minds. The whole time, I waited. For Wade. For a call. A text. Anything. We never exchanged numbers, but I knew Ghost and Glitch could probably find my blood type if they wanted to. So if Wade wanted my number, he could get it. I told myself if I had his, I would have called. Maybe screamed first. Maybe cried. Maybe both. If he even answered my call, but I didn't have his number and he never reached out. Not once.

So I started forcing myself to accept what I didn't want to believe. This was over. He saved me and for that, I would always be grateful. But saving someone and staying were two different things. By the time I reached the gate, I decided the waiting was done. Done grieving what almost was. Done hoping. Done aching for a man who should have been there but wasn't. I tried not to think about him. I really did, it was impossible. Especially every morning when I threw up. It was like once my body realized it was safe—or maybe once I knew I was pregnant—it all caught up to me. I never felt any symptoms before this, I was also terrified it was because of the drugs. I'd kneel on cold tile, one hand gripping the sink, the other pressed over my stomach, wondering if this was all some cosmic joke. Then I'd sit there afterward, rubbing my belly, trying to feel something other than confusion.

As I sat in that airport by myself, I decided I was done waiting. I needed to move forward.

Then my phone buzzed.

Unknown Number: Hi, Little Mouse. How are you?

My heart stopped. Wade, I thought instantly. He was the only one who ever called me that. *Little Mouse.* Then another memory slammed into me just as fast. Benjamin on that first night in the forest. Mocking the nickname with that cruel smile. My blood ran cold. What if it wasn't Wade? What if they never found Benjamin because he was still out there? Watching. Waiting. Finding ways back into my life. My thumb hovered over the screen, suddenly numb.

It could be Wade. But fear had already sunk its claws in. His name—

real or imagined—felt like a ghost in my chest, rattling something loose and painful. This was what I'd wanted, wasn't it? Proof he cared. Proof I mattered. Proof I hadn't imagined all of it. But relief never came. Anger did, fast and hot.

I stared at the screen, breathing too hard. Where was he when I couldn't sleep through the nightmares? Where was he when I woke choking on panic? Where was he when I was sick every morning, alone in my bathroom, clutching the sink like it could hold me together? Where was he when the fear would creep in and for a moment worried he wasn't contacting me because he died. Then to reassure myself he was fine, Stitches confirmed he was okay. He wasn't here. And now a text? Like nothing happened?

My fingers shook as I typed. *Who is this?*

I stared at the words. If it was Wade, he'd answer. If it was Benjamin, my stomach twisted violently. I deleted it. Typed again. Deleted that too. There was too much to say. Too much hurt. Too much pride. Too much fear. I saved the number, for later or maybe never. Then I changed the contact name. **Jerk.** A tiny, bitter satisfaction. Then I blocked him.

My thumb hovered afterward. Uncertainty crept in. Was that fair? Was I overreacting? Then I saw again the closed door, with the guard blocking it. *He isn't taking visitors.* I locked the screen. No, I was done waiting. I tucked my phone away and boarded my flight. Because I had bigger things to focus on. Like my research. Like finishing school. Like the future. Like the baby growing inside me. His baby. For now, that future did not include Wade Blakely.

Minneapolis-Saint Paul International Airport was loud, bright, and far too normal for the way my world felt. People rushed past with rolling suitcases, kids whining, phones ringing, flight announcements echoing overhead. Meanwhile, I stood near baggage claim feeling like I'd been dropped onto the wrong planet. Then I saw Fallon.

She stood near the carousel scanning every face that came through the crowd. Even from a distance she was impossible to miss. Five-ten and built like strength wrapped in curves, she carried herself with the kind of confidence that made people move around her without realizing it. Her fiery red hair spilled in thick waves over the shoulders of a fitted black jacket, vivid as flame beneath the airport lights. Emerald-green eyes sharp and searching.

She looked adorably comfortable in leggings and an oversized university sweatshirt. Controlled, like she always did when she was trying hardest not to fall apart.

The second those eyes landed on me, everything in her face cracked. "Sarah." My name broke out of her like a prayer. I barely got two steps before she was there.

She hit me hard enough to make me stumble, arms wrapping around me with desperate force. The scent of citrus and soft floral shampoo filled my lungs as I buried my face against her shoulder.

And then we were both crying. Not graceful tears. Ugly, shaking, breathless sobs. She kept pulling back just enough to cup my face, looking me over like she needed proof I was real.

"Oh my God," she whispered thickly. "Oh my God."

"I'm okay," I tried to say. It came out broken.

"You are not okay," she said immediately, voice fierce through tears. "But you're here." Then she hugged me again, even tighter and I clung back just as hard. People stared. I didn't care. Neither did she. It was relief and heartbreak tangled together. Joy that I was alive. Grief for everything that had happened in between.

When she finally pulled back, she wiped under her eyes and tried for her usual sharp composure.

"You look terrible," she said shakily. I laughed through tears. "You're crying too hard to insult me properly."

"Shut up."

She grabbed my bag with one hand and my hand with the other. "Come on," she said, squeezing my fingers. "I'm taking you home."

It's a hot, sticky August day. The kind where the air hangs heavy even before noon, pressing against the windows and making everything feel slower. Tomorrow, I start school again. I've been back in Minnesota for a couple weeks now, trying to piece myself back together in quiet, uneven ways. Sleeping when I can. Throwing up more than I'd like. Avoiding mirrors on bad days. Pretending I'm fine on the good ones. It's been a whole month since I've seen Wade and I'm not doing any better at convincing myself I'm fine without him.

This morning, I woke to a knock at the door. A delivery man showed up with with a box, then another one and another one. Three plain cardboard boxes stacked inside my kitchen. No return address. No note on the outside. No warning. Just brown tape and my name written in black marker. Something in my chest tightened before I even brought them inside. I carried them to my bedroom and sat cross-legged on the floor.

For a full minute, I only stared. Afraid of what could possibly be inside. Then I cut the first box open and broke. I sank to my knees so fast the box tipped sideways. Sobs tore out of me before I could stop them. Because inside was everything I thought I'd lost forever. My journals. My field notebooks. My camera wrapped carefully in clean cloth. Sample files. Printed maps. My worn research binder and nestled inside a small pouch is the necklace Paya gave me.

My fingers shook as I lifted it free. Everything I left behind with the Yanomami. Everything I needed for my research. Everything tied to the version of me that existed before I was taken. The scent of the jungle still clung to the fabric of my field bag. Earth. Rain. Smoke. Green things growing wild. It smelled like memory and grief. Like home and heartbreak at once.

Whoever packed it had done it carefully. Deliberately. As if they knew every item mattered. As if *I* mattered. On top of the second box sat a folded sheet of paper. My breath caught instantly and my fingers trembled as I opened it.

> **Little Mouse,**
> **My beautiful girl.**
> *I'm sorry for the way things ended.*
> *I promise I would never refuse you anything.*
> *I am coming to you once I am finished here.*
> *I am coming home.*
> *With all my love,*
> **Wade**

My vision blurred so badly I could barely finish reading. I pressed the letter to my chest and curled over it on the floor. As if that could bring him closer. As if it could erase the weeks of silence. As if it could undo the ache I'd been carrying alone. *I am coming home.* I didn't even know what that meant. To his childhood home in Missouri? To me? To us? Hands shaking, I opened one of my journals. I flipped through pages of field notes, interviews, sketches, plant records until a second folded page slipped free. I froze. Then opened that one too.

> **Beautiful,**
> *I read all your notes about me. I loved every one.*
> *I wasn't trying to invade your privacy. I just miss you so much. I needed a*
> *piece of you with me.*
> *Everything you wrote was beautiful, I feel the same about you.*

I can't wait to write you more letters for the rest of our lives.
I love you,
Wade

A broken sound left me. Half laugh. Half sob. I was crying so hard I barely heard the bedroom door open.

"What's wrong?!" Fallon rushed in, panic already in her voice. "Is it the baby?" I shook my head and held up the letters. She took one look at my face, then at the handwriting, then at the boxes spread around me.

"Oh no," she whispered. Then, to both our surprise, her eyes filled too. She sat beside me on the floor and wrapped an arm around my shoulders.

"That idiot," she murmured, sniffling. "I had a feeling there had to be more to it." I laughed wetly through tears.

Today was the day of my first doctor's appointment. Maybe it was coincidence, maybe a sign or maybe life just liked dramatic entrances. But for the first time in weeks, the tight knot in my chest loosened.

I'd spent every day fighting with myself. Whether to call him, let him back in or keep trying hate him and protect myself. Now I didn't know what I felt except overwhelmed. I was lucky enough to find a doctor who could get me in quickly and Fallon insisted on coming.

She'd thrown herself into this pregnancy with enough enthusiasm for both of us. Talking color themes, should she start buying or yellow or wait until we know the sex. She was looking up the best prenatal vitamins, books and found an app to start tracking the size of the baby. After my appointment today we could input the official due date. I'm so glad I wasn't in this alone, but I wouldn't let her derail her own future for mine.

She'd been applying for research opportunities, fellowships, field placements. Big ones. Life-changing ones. She's been talking about an upcoming research opportunity happening in Chile, helping identify red dwarf stars that might help find life on other planets. I refused to become the reason she stood still.

Still, as she helped me gather paperwork and tissues off the floor, she pointed at me sternly.

"We are discussing names after the appointment." I stared at her. "I'm nine minutes into accepting this is real."

"Great," she said brightly. "Plenty of time."

"Sarah." I jerk at the sound of my name. The waiting room suddenly feels too bright, too warm, too full of people pretending not to listen to everyone else's business.

Beside me, Fallon squeezes my hand. "You've got this," she murmurs. I give her a look that says *I absolutely do not*, but I stand anyway and she gets up with me.

The nurse smiles kindly. "Come with me, dear."

I follow her through a maze of beige hallways and framed pictures of smiling babies. Cruel décor choice. She points to the scale first, I step on, then height, blood pressure, pulse and temperature. Routine things that somehow make this feel more real. Inside the exam room, she asks questions while typing. Date of last period. Medical history. Allergies. Birth control. Symptoms.

Nausea? Constant.

Fatigue? Crushing.

Mood changes? I glance at Fallon. She just snorts. The nurse smiles without looking up.

Before leaving, she hands me a paper drape and gestures toward the table. "Undress from the waist down. Doctor will be in shortly." The door clicks shut. I stare at the exam table like it insulted me personally.

Fallon rises from the chair immediately. "You okay?"

"No," I admit. She helps me unfold the paper drape, then sits back down once I'm settled.

My hands won't stop fidgeting. Everything is about to change. It already has changed. I'm sad, angry, terrified and somewhere beneath all of that, excited. I look down at my phone in my lap. Still blocked. Still no Wade. Still too many feelings. My thumb hovers over his contact. Two quick knocks sound before I can decide anything. The door opens.

A young tall male doctor steps inside. Dark hair and a disarming smile and, annoyingly close enough to Wade's age and build to make me instantly tense.

"Hi, Sarah. I'm Dr. Henderson. Congratulations, you're pregnant." He says it cheerfully like he's announcing raffle winnings.

"Thanks," I mumble.

He glances at Fallon. "You're welcome to stay if Sarah would like."

"She would," Fallon answers for me. I nod quickly. "Hi, Dr. Hunky, I'm Fallon, best friend to this one."

He gives her a once over with an amused smile before he goes back to reviewing the chart. And she blushes, actually blushes. She never does that. I just roll my eyes at her, ever the flirt.

"It looks like your last period was in May, and your last contraceptive injection was in April. Do you know approximately when you were last sexually active?"

I want the floor to swallow me whole. "Third week of July," I say quietly. He nods, matter-of-fact. No judgment, no reaction. Bless him for that.

"We'll do a transvaginal ultrasound today. Since it's early, that'll give us the most accurate dating." I nod again.

Then the fear that's been clawing at me all morning surges forward. "There's something I need to ask first."

His expression shifts, attentive. "I was taken a few weeks ago." My throat tightens. "In Brazil."

Fallon's hand finds mine instantly. "I was drugged. Sedated. I don't know exactly what they gave me. A doctor on a naval ship said muscle relaxants and other things." My voice shakes now. "Could that have hurt the baby?"

The room goes very still. Dr. Henderson sets the chart down. "I'm really sorry that happened to you."

Something in his tone that seems gentle, direct, human and makes my eyes burn. "We don't know enough yet to assume harm," he continues carefully. "Many medications and stressful events do *not* automatically mean injury to a pregnancy. Right now, the best first step is to evaluate growth, heartbeat, and development. Today's ultrasound will tell us a lot."

"So the baby might be okay?" I whisper.

"It very well may be," he says. "And if we need extra monitoring, we'll do that."

I nod, swallowing hard. "Thank you."

He steps back toward the machine. "Whenever you're ready, lie back and place your feet in the stirrups." I do. Fallon moves beside my shoulder like a bodyguard with mascara.

"This your first pregnancy?" he asks gently.

"Yes."

"You're doing fine." I don't feel fine, right now I feel split open. Cold gel. Machine hum. The screen flickers to life in shades of gray. Shapes I don't understand but then a fast rhythmic sound fills the room.

I freeze. "What is that?" I whisper.

Dr. Henderson smiles. "That's the heartbeat."

My hand flies to my mouth. Beside me, Fallon gasps so loudly she startles herself. Tears spill before I can stop them. On the screen is something tiny and miraculous. Small and curved, like a little bean. My baby.

"Oh my God," Fallon whispers. "Oh my God." I'm crying too hard to speak.

Dr. Henderson takes measurements quietly for a moment. Then he turns the monitor slightly toward me.

"You're measuring at approximately ten weeks," he says. "Still first trimester." Ten weeks. My mind instantly counts backward. June… Wade. So basically the first time we made love. My chest tightens.

"The heartbeat looks strong," he adds. "Growth appears appropriate for gestational age."

Relief crashes through me so hard I nearly sob again. "The baby looks okay?" I ask.

"Everything I'm seeing today is reassuring."

Fallon starts crying now too. "This is ridiculous," she sniffles. "I didn't even know I was emotional."

Dr. Henderson prints images and hands me tissues. "We'll let you get dressed, then we'll talk next steps, labs, prenatal vitamins, follow-up appointments, and any trauma-informed support services you'd like." He says the last part gently. Not pushing. Just offering. When he leaves, I stare at the black-and-white image in my hands.

Ten weeks. Alive. Strong heartbeat and suddenly nothing feels simple anymore.

When we get home, I call my mom. She's crying but excited to be a grandma, she's downloading the same app so she can keep up with everything. After I get her to calm down, I say my goodbyes. I decide to make dinner just to give my hands something to do. Something normal. Something I can control. Chopping vegetables feels safer than thinking. Following a recipe feels easier than sorting through everything happening inside me. I'm ten weeks along, inching toward the second trimester, and somehow that fact still doesn't feel real.

Across the apartment, Fallon is sprawled across the couch with her laptop open, six tabs too many, highlighter in hand like pregnancy has become a competitive sport. Every few minutes she shouts a new discovery toward the kitchen.

"Did you know aversions can hit out of nowhere?" I hum in response. Thirty seconds later, "Oh my God, your boobs are going to get huge!"

I nearly drop the wooden spoon. "Please stop researching me like I'm a science project."

"You literally are a science project right now," she calls back.

I shake my head and keep stirring. Despite everything, a smile threatens. She has been my rock through all of this uncertainty. Steady when I'm spiraling. Gentle when I'm angry. Funny when I feel like I might drown. There are moments, small ones, when I catch a shadow pass over her face after she says something comforting, like she knows too well how fear can hollow a person out. She learned survival the hard way. She never talks much about a certain time of her life. Never about the man whose name she once almost said in her sleep. Never about why loud male voices in parking lots make her shoulders lock. I don't ask. Whatever cracked something in Fallon, she carries it quietly. She still shows up whole for me.

Just as dinner finishes cooking, a sharp knock hits the front door. The spoon slips from my hand and clatters into the pan. My whole body jerks. Heart racing. Breath caught high in my throat. I turn so fast my shoulder nearly hits the counter. For one sick second, all I can picture is Benjamin standing on the other side. Smiling that sick disturbing smile, waiting and watching, ready to take me again.

Fallon is off the couch instantly, laptop forgotten. Her face changes in a flash, soft friend gone, something sharper underneath. "Sarah," she says quietly. "Breathe."

Another knock. I can't move. I keep staring at the door, pulse pounding, every nerve in my body screaming that danger found me again.

"Expecting someone?" she asks. I shake my head. My apartment is tiny, so it only takes five steps to reach the door, but each one feels heavier than it should. Loud knocks still make my nerves spark. I peer through the peephole. My breath catches. Jake is standing there. I yank the door open so fast I nearly hit myself with it.

"What are you doing here?"

"Rocky." He grins like the world is a game built for his amusement and steps forward like he's already been invited in. "I told you. I'm moving in with you and Wraith." The name hits me like a jab to the ribs. I flinch. Jake sees it immediately.

I hate the flicker of pity that crosses his face before he smooths it away. I still haven't unblocked Wade. I was going to tonight, maybe or I just needed more time. One more pocket of silence where I didn't have to decide anything.

"Well," I say, forcing brightness I don't feel, "there is no Wade and I."

Jake snorts. "Oh, please. No one believes that." He drops a duffel bag beside the door like he means to stay a week. "I haven't seen him in a couple days," he continues, eyeing me carefully, "but I know that man. He's already figuring out how to fix whatever stupid thing happened."

My chest tightens. Before I can answer, he opens his arms. "Now come here. I want to know how you are." I let him pull me into a hug. Warm and familiar enough to break something loose in me. Then chaos detonates.

A blur streaks past my shoulder. Suddenly Fallon is in front of me, both fists pounding into Jake's chest with shocking force.

"You son of a bitch!" she yells. "I will kill you! She does *not* need you here pretending to care!"

Jake stumbles backward, hands raised. "What the—"

She hits him again. "I know places to hide a body, you piece of—"

"Fallon!" I lunge forward and grab her around the waist, dragging her back while my face burns bright red.

"This isn't *him!* This is Jake!"

She freezes mid-swing. "Oh." Her eyes dart from me to Jake. Then back. Jake straightens slowly, rubbing his chest. Then he grins. He looks Fallon up and down with open interest.

"Well," he drawls. "Who's the firecracker?" To my absolute disbelief, Fallon blushes. Full pink cheeks. Eyes wide. What the hell is happening? Twice in one day?

"This is Fallon," I say, pointing between them like I'm introducing feral animals. "My roommate."

Jake places a hand over his heart dramatically. "Fallon. Love the welcome."

She crosses her arms. "You came in cocky."

"I'm always cocky."

"I noticed."

I stare at both of them. "This is Jake," I say flatly.

They keep looking at each other. Long enough to be annoying. Long enough that I clear my throat. Nothing. I clear it louder. Still nothing. Jesus Christ.

"Dinner's ready," I say sharply. "Should we eat, or are you two going to eye fuck each other all night?"

They both blink like they've returned from another dimension. Fallon coughs and looks away.

Jake laughs. "Yeah," he says, still rubbing where she hit him. "I'm starving."

I roll my eyes and head for the kitchen. Thankfully, I cooked enough food for an army. Which is good because apparently one just walked in. We ate on the couch with plates balanced on our laps and some random reality show playing too loudly in the background. No one was actually watching it. It was just noise. Something to fill the spaces between thoughts.

He fit into our apartment far too easily, stretched across one end of the couch like he'd lived there for years instead of twenty minutes. He talked while he ate, filling me in on what happened after he got home.

"So I got another email telling me what storage unit and code to get in," he said, gesturing with a fork, "Alex had packed every single thing I owned into boxes and shoved it all into storage."

"What a bitch," I muttered automatically.

Jake grinned. "Thank you. Nice to feel supported."

"I'm serious."

He shrugged, unbothered in that way only Jake could manage. "Probably for the best. Saved me from seeing her face."

I frowned. "Where's all your stuff now?"

"Still in storage," he admitted. "Haven't found a place yet." Across the room, Fallon and I exchanged a glance. He had absolutely no intention of finding one tonight. He was staying at least for now.

Honestly, I didn't mind as much as I should have. Most nights I was still half convinced Benjamin would appear outside my door. Every creak in the hallway. Every engine outside. Every unfamiliar footstep. Sleep had become something thin and unreliable.

Having Jake here felt safer. Even if he came with emotional collateral damage. After dinner, Fallon and I carried plates into the kitchen while Jake stayed on the couch, texting someone and pretending to care about whatever dating disaster was happening on TV. Fallon loaded the dishwasher while I rinsed glasses. She kept glancing at me.

Finally, she lowered her voice. "Are you okay?"

I paused, drying my hands on a towel. "No," I said honestly. Then sighed. "I mean... kind of." She waited. "It's just..." My voice wobbled. "I was doing better. Not thinking about Wade every second. Then the boxes came. Then the appointment. Now Jake is here and he's..." I swallowed. "A reminder."

Her expression softened. "But he's also my friend," I added quickly. "He became like a brother to me. He saved our lives." I rub my belly, something I've already started doing a lot. Emotion rose too fast, burning hot behind my eyes. Damn hormones. Damn trauma. Damn all of it.

Fallon crossed the kitchen and wrapped me in a hug. "You do not have to be strong all the time," she whispered. I nodded against her shoulder, blinking hard.

When we pulled apart, she leaned closer. "Are you going to tell Jake you're pregnant?"

Before I could answer, that I absolutely was not going to tell him we hear, "You're pregnant?" My entire body went cold. I turned slowly. Jake stood in the kitchen doorway, one shoulder against the frame, phone forgotten in his hand. His expression shifted too fast to track. Shock. Confusion. Sadness.

Then something heavier. "Shit," Fallon whispered, stepping back.

Jake took one step toward me. "Rocky?" His voice had lost all humor.

I swallowed hard. "Um... yeah."

His eyes dropped briefly to my stomach, then snapped back to my face. "Does Wraith know?"

I shook my head. "No."

His jaw flexed. "When did you find out?"

"The day I woke up on the naval ship." My throat tightened. "I wanted to tell him then, but..." I forced myself to meet his eyes. "It was pretty clear he didn't want to see me."

Jake flinched like I'd hit him. His shoulders dropped. For once, he looked every bit as tired as he probably was. Then he crossed the room and pulled me into a hug before I could react.

"I'm sorry," he murmured into my hair. "That's not what happened." I stiffened. He tightened his hold just slightly. "I promised him I'd let him explain," he said quietly. "So I'm not gonna betray that. But Rocky, don't give up on him yet."

I pulled back enough to glare at him. "Easy for you to say."

His eyes held mine. "He's hurting too."

I snorted and stepped away. "Yeah, well. I'll tell him eventually." The words tasted defensive. "But I'm not setting myself up to be hurt again."

Jake exhaled through his nose. Like he wanted to argue, he knew I was only half-convincing myself. But for once, he let it go.

I cleared my throat and forced my voice steady. "Do you have a place to stay tonight, or are you crashing on our couch?"

"Duh, little sister." He said sliding an easy smirk back on his face.

"Told you I was staying with you."

I rolled my eyes and went to the linen closet for extra blankets. Behind me, Jake and Fallon had already started talking in low voices like they'd known each other longer than an hour. Traitors. When I came back, Jake was watching me.

"How far along are you?" My grip tightened on the blankets. I looked at Fallon, silently asking how much I should say. She gave me the world's least helpful shrug.

Jake leaned forward, elbows on knees. "Are you going to tell him?" When I didn't answer right away, the room seemed to narrow.

I inhaled slowly. "No."

His brows drew together. "No?"

"I don't know," I snapped. "Eventually. Maybe."

Jake's jaw ticked. "I think you should."

"Why?" I challenged. "It won't change anything. He doesn't owe me anything."

Jake stared at me like I'd said something offensive. "You really believe that?"

"I believe what I heard."

He shook his head hard. "You don't get it. He's broken without you. He—"

"I blocked him," I cut in. "So it doesn't matter."

Jake swore under his breath. Then he pulled out his phone and held it toward me. The contact name on the screen hit me like a punch.

Wraith

My fingers trembled. "Call him," Jake said quietly. I didn't move. "Rocky, I was there when you two met. I watched you fall in love." My throat tightened. "And I watched what it did to him when he woke up and realized you were gone."

I looked away. "He thinks he failed you," Jake continued. "He thinks he lost you. But he's coming back for you." His voice softened. "You two are not over. A love like that doesn't just disappear."

My chest hurt. I squeezed my eyes shut. Then before I could stop myself, I grabbed the phone. Hit call. Put it on speaker. The room went silent. One ring. Two.

"Hello?" A woman's voice. I froze. Everything inside me dropped.

"Hello?" she said again, cheerful and distracted. Jake looked as shocked as I felt. I couldn't speak.

Jake cleared his throat. "Uh… I'm calling for Wade."

"Oh!" she said brightly. "He's in the shower. He should be out in a minute." I ended the call. Then threw the phone across the room. It smacked the wall with a crack and hit the floor. I was already moving. Straight to the bathroom. The second my knees hit tile, I started violently throwing up. My whole body shook with it. I knew I shouldn't have called. Knew it. What did I expect? That he'd answer alone? That he'd been pining dramatically in some empty room? Idiot.

I rinsed my mouth, tears burning my eyes. From the living room, Jake started yelling. I moved closer to the cracked bathroom door, heart pounding.

"Are you out of your goddamn mind?!" he shouted.

A muffled response I couldn't make out. "I was over here pleading your fucking case and *that's* what answers your phone?"

More muffled words. "Fuck, man. You have any idea how that sounded?" Silence. "It wasn't me calling, you asshole. It was Sarah." My stomach twisted. Another pause. Then Jake again, angrier now. "I don't know how you fix this one. I gotta go."

The apartment fell quiet. Then a knock at the bathroom door. I jumped backward.

"Rocky?" Jake's voice was softer now. "You okay?" I didn't answer. I didn't want comfort. Didn't want excuses. Didn't want to hear another reason why Wade hadn't really hurt me while I bled anyway. I needed to move on because he clearly already had.

At the thought, I slapped a hand over my mouth. Too late, the sob broke free. The door opened an inch. Jake's head appeared carefully through the gap.

His expression changed the second he saw my face. "I don't want to talk," I told him. He ignored that completely and lowered himself onto the bathroom floor beside me. The tile was cold. The silence colder.

After a beat, he glanced at the toilet and said, "I'm just glad you weren't peeing. This would've been awkward."

I turned my head slowly and glared. He lifted both hands.

"Too soon?" I said nothing. We sat there in silence for several minutes. The kind that isn't comfortable but isn't hostile either. Just full. Heavy with the unspoken works I could feel him wanting to say. Trying to decide if he should.

For once, I was grateful he didn't because I'd been stupid enough to hope. Even while telling myself not to. I had been ready to unblock Wade. Ready to open that door again, even though it terrified me. I was going to tell him. About the baby. About how hurt I was, how I still loved him anyway. And now, some woman answered his phone.

If he was moving on, then so was I. "Tell him I love him," I whispered finally.

Jake's head turned sharply. "You tell him yourself."

I shook my head. "He's coming back to you," Jake said. "Probably already on his way."

I gave a humorless laugh. "Sure."

"And by the way," he continued, nudging my shoulder, "when you two get back together, I'm calling dibs on matron of honor."

Despite everything, I blinked. "What?"

"I need that officially noted. Because I have a feeling I'll have to physically fight the spitfire out there for the role."

A watery laugh escaped me before I could stop it. I saw the sadness in his eyes, though. The way he tried to bury it under jokes. I remembered that look from when he talked about his ex.

"Maid of honor, you have to be married to be matron. Best man," I corrected. "Fallon gets matron of honor."

He considered that. "Counteroffer. I get ordained and marry you both myself."

"Fine," I said. "As long as you don't say anything dirty."

"No promises." I almost smiled.

"Great," he said. "I'll tell Wraith when he gets here."

I rolled my eyes. "Thank you for trying to cheer me up," I said quietly. "But I never said he was welcome here and I definitely never said I'd marry him."

Jake opened his mouth. "He left me," I continued, voice breaking. "And if that wasn't enough, he moved on." The words hurt even as I said them. "It's time I do, too."

Another sob pushed up my throat. "I have a whole new life to figure out," I whispered, pressing a hand to my stomach. "And it won't involve him."

Jake's expression tightened. "Rocky, I love you like a sister, but don't be stupid. I promise he wasn't wi—"

"Time to go, Rambo." We both looked up. Fallon stood in the bathroom doorway, arms crossed, her green eyes sharp enough to cut glass. Jake ignored her and looked back at me. Pleading. I shook my head.

"I'm tired," I said. "I need to sleep." He held my gaze another second. Then sighed and stood. Fallon stepped aside just enough to let him pass, then immediately herded him toward the front door like a hostile cattle handler. When he glanced back in disbelief, she shut the door in his face. The shocked expression he wore almost made me laugh. It was enough to dull the heartbreak for half a second.

"Come on," Fallon said softly. She helped me to bed.

I curled onto my side, clutching the sonogram picture in one hand. My baby. My future. Mine. I cried quietly into the pillow until exhaustion dragged me under and before sleep took me, I made myself one promise. I would start forgetting him. As far as I was concerned, I tried. I reached out. That was enough. Tomorrow I would focus on school. I'd teach lab to undergrads. Assist Dr. Anderson, work on my dissertation. My life went on, whether Wade was in it or not.

Chapter Thirty One

Wade

Beep. Beep. Beep. The steady rhythm drags me up from the dark one jagged inch at a time. Each pulse is too sharp, like someone driving nails into my skull. I try to move. Pain tears through my right side so violently my vision whites out.

"Fuck—" The word comes out raw and broken. My body feels like it's been stitched together with rusted wire. Every breath pulls at something deep in my ribs. My shoulder burns. My mouth is dry enough to choke on. I force my eyes open to white overhead lights. Metal bulkheads and a low ceiling. The faint vibration beneath the bed.

Not a hospital, a naval med bay, I've woken up in worse places. The smell confirms it, antiseptic, machine oil, recycled air and salt threaded underneath. Then memory hits in fragments. The patrol boat. The freighter. Sarah in my arms. Gunfire. Getting her onboard. The impact. Then nothing. My chest seizes. Sarah. I jerk my head to the side hard enough nausea rolls through me. No Sarah. No blue-gray eyes. No soft voice asking if I'm okay.

Just Stitches slumped in a chair beside the bed, boots kicked out, arms crossed, chin to chest. Even asleep he looks ready to stab somebody. I brace a hand on the mattress and shove upward.

A brutal spear of pain rips through my ribs and side. "Jesus Christ." His eyes snap open instantly. Hand already moving toward the sidearm clipped to his belt before he registers where he is. Then me.

Relief flashes across his face. Gone a second later. "Welcome back to the land of the living," he says. Classic Stitches line. Not classic Stitches tone, he's being careful about something.

My throat feels like broken glass when I force out one word. "Sarah?"

His jaw tightens. That silence hits harder than the bullet did. He stands and moves to the bed controls. "Easy."

The mattress rises slowly, bringing me upright. I grit my teeth until my jaw aches. Sweat beads across my forehead. He fills a plastic cup from the dispenser and presses it into my hand. I drink too fast as the pain detonates under my ribs. Black creeps in at the edges of my vision.

When it clears, the cup is half-crushed in my fist. "Where is she?"

He looks away for half a second. That half second tells me everything.

"Home," he says quietly. "Back in Missouri." Everything inside me goes still. The cup collapses fully. Water spills across my hand and blanket. I don't feel it.

"Why?" The word comes out low. Dangerous.

Stitches drags a hand over his face. "You were unconscious almost two days," he says. "Needed surgery. Lost more blood than I liked. We didn't know when you'd wake up."

I stare at him. "That's not an answer."

"No," he says. "It's context."

Then he steps closer, forearms braced on the bed rail, voice calmer than mine could ever be right now. "She asked for you the second she was coherent." My pulse stutters. "She was weak as hell, pissed at all of us, and stubborn enough to try getting out of bed on legs that barely worked."

That sounds like my girl, a flash of pride hits so fast it hurts. Then dread follows.

"She insisted on seeing you. I helped her out of bed and made sure she knew where to find you, your room wasn't far from hers. I stayed back with Carly after."

The room narrows. "She saw me?"

"No." My chest caves inward. Stitches holds my gaze, giving it to me straight.

"You were still out cold. Specter was outside your door keeping the hall clear." Something in his expression changes. Annoyance. Guilt by association. "He followed protocol," Stitches says. "No visitors in medical until cleared."

I hear the hesitation. "How did he phrase it?"

He mutters a curse. "Told her no one was allowed in. Then apparently clarified it like an idiot."

My blood runs cold. "How."

Stitches meets my eyes. "'He isn't taking visitors.'"

The pain in my side has nothing on what tears through my chest. She came to me. She fought through fear, drugs, exhaustion, humiliation and thought I turned her away.

I close my eyes. A sharp breath saws through my ribs. "Fuck."

"She came back furious," Stitches says quietly. "Wouldn't look at me. Wouldn't look at Glitch either." Each word lands like another round. "Then she demanded transport off the ship. Wanted to get home."

"She left thinking I rejected her."

"Yes." No softness now. Just truth. I grip the rails until my hands shake. This feeling is old and familiar, the same black-edged guilt from years ago when Jamo went down and Ghost got dragged into that tunnel because I was one step late making the call.

One second too slow. One wrong read. Men bled for it. I've carried that weight ever since. And now Sarah. Taken under my watch. Drugged. Almost broken. Then handed one more wound because I wasn't conscious enough to stop it. Maybe this is what I do. Protect badly. Love dangerously. Ruin what gets close.

Stitches watches something ugly cross my face. "Don't start that shit."

I open my eyes. "What shit?"

"The martyr garbage." He straightens. "She was taken because traffickers betrayed an expedition and had inside help. Not because you blinked."

"I let her out of my sight."

"You're not God."

"I was responsible."

"And you brought her home." His voice sharpens for the first time. "You crossed a jungle, bled out and put her on that boat. Don't rewrite the story because you're hurting." I look away. Because hurting is exactly what this is.

He softens again. "Listen to me, brother. She's alive. She's home. She's angry. She's good. Angry means breathing."

Despite myself, a rough laugh escapes me. It hurts like hell.

"There he is," Stitches mutters.

Then his medic face returns. "You're not going anywhere today."

"I'm getting to Missouri."

"You're getting cleared first."

"Command can kiss my ass."

"Command already wants you upright for debrief." That tracks. Paperwork before pulse.

"What about Benjamin?"

His eyes harden. "No body."

Of course. The room goes cold.

"What about Willis?"

"Detained. Talking through lawyers." Coward.

Stitches folds his arms. "I'll get you her number. Her address. Whatever I can legally hand over." I look at him sharply. "But," he adds, "you're going to heal enough to stand before you go chasing her across continents bleeding through a bandage."

"I don't need sleep."

"You need blood volume, stitches, and common sense."

"I've never needed that."

He snorts. "Fair point." Then he grips the rail once, hard. "You want any shot with her?"

Every part of me stills. "Yes."

"Then don't show up half-dead and self-loathing. Handle command. Heal up. Then go tell her the truth." The truth. That I never stopped wanting her. That I woke up asking for her. That I would've crawled to that hallway if I'd been conscious. That losing her scares me more than the bullet did. I lean back against the pillow, exhausted all over again.

Outside the compartment, boots hammer past in the corridor. The ship keeps moving. So does time.

And somewhere in Missouri, Sarah thinks I sent her away.

"Command wants us back in debrief the second you're cleared conscious and coherent. It's all a goddamn mess with those Brazilian forces being killed. They want freighter intel. Willis. Trafficking routes. Brazilian liaison statements. Missing suspect. You disappearing right now isn't happening."

"I don't give a fuck what command wants."

"I know." His voice sharpens. "But if you tear yourself open trying to play hero, you won't be helping anyone. Including her."

I look away because I hate that he's right. He softens a notch. "I'll get Ghost working her contact info. Home number, cell, whatever he can legally pull."

My jaw clenches. "Today."

"Today," he confirms. "But first you rest, let Patch check the wound, then you sit through debrief without passing out."

I say nothing. Because every second I'm stuck here, she's home believing I rejected her.

They keep me on the ship another twelve hours. Twelve slow, useless, miserable hours. Patch checks the wound twice, changes the dressing once, and threatens to chemically restrain me if I try to "play action hero with fresh stitches." He says it with a calm smile that somehow feels more threatening than yelling.

Patches signs off on transport only after I can walk the corridor unassisted and keep food down. I almost fall during the walk. I lie about the dizziness. He knows I'm lying and lets it go anyway. By the time we transfer to the airstrip, dawn is bleeding across the water in streaks of gold and blood-orange. Engines whine in the distance.

Crewmen move pallets and evidence crates toward a waiting transport. Somewhere behind me, Ghost jogs up holding a boxed replacement phone. He tosses it to me. "Don't break this one with your feelings."

I catch it one-handed. "Did you get it?"

He knows what I mean. He nods once. "Everything I could. Cell number, home address, emergency contacts, university records, travel manifest, recovered property inventory," he says quietly. "Anything we legally had."

I tuck it under my arm without opening it. If I look now, I'll want to walk off this runway and steal a plane.

My pulse kicks hard for the first time since waking. I tuck the phone into my pocket like it's something fragile. Like it matters more than the rifle slung over my shoulder. Because right now, it does.

Dr. Willis and Jenna are being loaded separately under guard. Wrists restrained and heads down. No sign of Benjamin. Still missing. Still breathing, if I'm unlucky.

Ghost falls into step beside me, tablet in hand, eyes hollowed out by too little sleep and too much work. "Command moved debrief to

Comalapa International Airport," he says. "FBI and Brazilian federal police dialing in remote."

"Of course they are."

He glances sideways at me. "You look worse than yesterday."

"Thanks."

"You're welcome. Don't do anything stupid before debrief," Ghost adds.

"No promises."

"That's what I was afraid of."

Inside the aircraft, the cabin vibrates with engine thunder and cold recycled air. Bench seats line both sides. Cargo straps web the center aisle. Weapons cases are locked down beside pallets of recovered gear. I move slower than I want to. Every step pulls at the stitches in my side.

Reaper jerks his chin toward an open seat and drops beside me the second I sit. He studies my face for half a beat. "You look like shit."

"Feel like it too."

"Good." I glance at him. "Means you're alive." That's Reaper's version of concern.

Across from us, Glitch is already arguing with Signal from the SEAL team over comm logs and chain-of-custody timestamps. Sparta sits silent, eyes closed, conserving energy. Stitches pretends not to watch me from three seats down. Near the front, Specter boards last with Ridge, speaking low to a loadmaster before strapping in.

The ramp closes and the engines surge a the bird starts to lift. Once we level out, Reaper leans back and gets to business.

"While you were napping the last couple days, we went back to the tribe." My head turns. "We brought a translator," he continues. "Told Dori Sarah was safe. Unharmed as far as we know. Told him Carly was recovered and both were home."

My jaw tightens at the careful wording. "As far as we know."

"Exactly." He doesn't sugarcoat things. "Explained Willis and Benjamin were behind it." The names alone sour the air. "To say Dori was pissed would be putting it mildly," Reaper says. "Apparently he always thought something was off with those two." That makes two of us. I was too slow to the game though and they got her.

"He said he hopes he sees Sarah again someday. Wishes her peace." I stare at the cargo netting across from me. The old man grew on me. More than I expected.

"I should've known," I mutter.

Reaper hears it anyway. "Known what?"

"Benjamin. Willis. Any of it."

He snorts once. "You knew Benjamin was a snake. You didn't know the doctor was trafficking women out of the jungle."

"I should've protected her."

Reaper turns fully toward me now. "That's ego talking." I look at him sharply but he doesn't flinch. "You got ambushed by a coordinated betrayal involving insiders, militia support, hidden transport and drugs," he says flatly. "Then you crossed hell to get her back."

"She was still taken."

"And she still came home." I look away first. He keeps going. "You carrying guilt over Jamo and Ghost is one thing. We all carry ghosts."

At Ghost's name, our tech glances up without missing a beat in his argument with Signal. "Still here," Ghost says dryly.

Reaper ignores him. "But don't start rewriting this into some curse where every bad thing that happens near you is your fault."

My jaw flexes. "You don't know what's in my head."

"No," he says. "I know what's on your face." He nods to the box holding my new phone in my hand.

"You want to punish yourself, fine. Do it later." His gaze hardens. "But when this plane lands, you need to be useful."

The engines drone around us. The wound in my side throbs with every breath. The phone feels heavier than ammunition. Right now I need to focus on debrief. So I can get to Missouri, get to Sarah. If she'll even hear me. He continues before I can argue.

"We packed the camp. Recovered all electronics, field notes, hard drives, sample logs, passports, sat devices, ledgers, anything that could matter. FBI wants every scrap tied to Willis, Benjamin and Jenna." Of course they do. There's probably enough dirt in those boxes to bury half a university. "Sarah's stuff?"

Reaper nods. "Boxed separately. Camera too. Clothing, passport, notebook, personal effects. We tagged everything clean. It'll be shipped once legal clears release."

A knot I didn't know I was carrying loosens slightly. She'll need all of her research, everything she worked so hard for, "Thank you." He gives one curt nod like gratitude makes him uncomfortable.

My mind drifts back to Sarah and for the first time in a long time, I'm not sure charging forward fixes a damn thing.

Reaper reads enough of that on my face to speak again. "If you call her just to ease your guilt, don't." My head lifts. "If you call her," he says, voice low and steady over the engine roar, "call because she deserves all of you."

That lands harder than it should because guilt is loud. Truth is harder. The plane jolts through turbulence. Cargo straps rattle. Somewhere near the front Ghost swears at his tablet. I tighten my grip on the phone. Missouri feels a thousand miles away and somehow not far enough.

We've been back at command for a week. Seven days of fluorescent lights, locked briefing rooms, bad coffee and answering the same questions twelve different ways.

Every helmet-cam clip, drone feed, sat-phone transcript, recovered hard drive, handwritten note and evidence bag from that jungle was seized, cataloged, and handed over. Legal teams descended like vultures. Intelligence officers wanted names, routes, militia affiliations, shipping manifests, offshore accounts. The FBI wanted timelines, statements, chain of custody, victim contact points and anything tying Dr. Willis and Benjamin to prior disappearances. They got all of it.

And then they asked for it again. Command was pissed. Not publicly, of course. Publicly they called it a successful rescue with evolving complications. Privately? We killed a pile of militia fighters in a foreign jungle, a helicopter filled with Brazilian forces was shot down, detonated a freighter, detained two civilians we were originally tasked to protect and failed to recover one primary suspect.

Benjamin never turned up. No confirmed body. No blood match. No remains. Which means one thing. He could still be breathing and if he's breathing, then Sarah is still in danger. That thought has lived under my skin every waking second.

I need out of here. Need wheels up. Need to get to Missouri and put eyes on her myself. Instead, I get another conference room. Another analyst. Another colonel asking whether my use of force was proportionate when armed traffickers were raping hostages.

No one says anything directly about Sarah and me. But I catch looks. From my men. From Specter. From Stitches. The kind of glances that asks if I'm going to reveal my relationship. I ignore every one of them. They've all tried talking to me. Reaper with blunt logic. Stitches with threats disguised as concern. Even Ghost, which means hell is freezing somewhere. I shut them all down. Because rage is easier than anything else right now. Rage at Benjamin. Rage at command. Rage at Specter's mistake. Rage at myself.

My knuckles are split from the cinderblock wall behind the barracks. Twice this week. Maybe three times. I stopped counting. The team knows the signs. When I get this close to losing control, they usually give me space. Usually. I'm in the team room staring at a mission map I'm not seeing when Ghost finally breaks the silence.

"You need to get your shit together, Wraith."

I turn so fast the chair nearly tips. "The fuck did you just say?"

He doesn't flinch. Doesn't step back. Ghost never does.

"I said get your shit together," he repeats evenly. "Because if you don't, you're gonna lose her for good."

The words hit center mass. I bury it under anger. "You don't think I know that?" Every head in the room lifts. Reaper stops cleaning his rifle. Stitches slowly lowers the med kit he was inventorying. Sparta looks up from the corner.

Ghost keeps coming. "Pacing holes into the floor and punching walls isn't helping." I'm half a second from crossing the room and proving I still hit hard with one good side.

Instead I force my hands open. "Don't you think I know that?" I ask, voice like gravel.

He sighs, rubbing his temple. "Yeah. I do. I got you a new phone."

"I know." I grit my teeth. I've been staring at it for days. Wondering what to say.

"Sarah left angry, hurt, convinced you rejected her. She made her choice?" he adds. "No. She made the only choice she thought she had."

My jaw flexes. "The fuck she did." I drag a hand down my face, exhaustion clawing through the fury. I hate this place. I hate these meetings. I hate being stuck while she's out there thinking the worst of me.

Ghost studies me for a long moment. "And if you text her right now?" he asks quietly. "You really think that fixes anything?" I open my mouth. Nothing comes out. Because no. A text doesn't fix this. Which is why I haven't texted her. That and the thought that she deserves someone better.

Hey, sorry command and a miscommunication made it look like I abandoned you after you were kidnapped. That isn't a message. That's gasoline.

"She has every right to be pissed," Ghost says.

"I know." It comes out lower than I intended. Honest. For the first time all week.

He nods once. "Good. Then stop acting like the victim."

That one nearly gets him killed. Reaper stands between us before I move. "Enough," he says.

Stitches folds his arms. "Actually, no. He needs to hear it." I glare at all of them. Traitors.

Ghost steps closer, voice still calm. "You want her back?" My pulse kicks once. "Then start earning it."

No one speaks after that. Because we all know one thing. Sooner or later, command is going to release me and when they do, I'm going to Missouri. When I get back to the barracks, the guys are scattered around the room pretending to relax.

Reaper is stretched across his bunk cleaning a knife that doesn't need cleaning. Ghost has three screens open on his laptop, because apparently one source of misery isn't enough. Stitches is half-asleep with earbuds in. Sparta is reading. Glitch is gaming on his phone and muttering profanity at strangers. No one says a word when I walk in. Good. I drop onto my bunk, reach into my pocket and pull out the phone Ghost finally gave me.

My thumb hovers over her contact. Sarah. Just her name is enough to make me worry again but I can't keep going like this. She might deserve better than me but I will make damn sure I become someone she deserves. I've been thinking about it all day and I have no idea what the hell to say. How do you start this?

Sorry you thought I rejected you?

Sorry I let you get taken?

Sorry I'm in love with you and somehow keep making everything worse?

I type the first thing that feels real.

Me: Hi Little Mouse, how are you?

I stare at the screen. Delivered. Then, after what feels like an hour but is probably three minutes—Read. My pulse kicks hard. The typing dots appear. Disappear. Appear again. Disappear. No message comes. I exhale slowly through my nose. Maybe that was too soft, that wasn't right. That's not enough to make up for what I did.

Me: Please give me a chance to explain. I am coming home to you.

I hit send. Nothing. Then the message flips red. Failed to send. I stare at it and try again. Failed. Again, failed. She blocked my number. The room narrows instantly. She thinks I didn't want her. She thinks I let her come to me and turned her away. Stitches told me what she thought, that it was all planned. That I just used her. I thought it was did a good job convincing her she was always more to me.

"Who are you talking to?" Reaper's voice cuts through it.

Every head in the room lifts. I lock the screen and toss the phone onto the mattress harder than necessary.

"Just trying to talk to her." I look at none of them. "She's not interested." The warning in my tone is clear enough. No one pushes. One by one they go back to whatever they were doing. But I can feel them watching anyway.

Once we finally get temporary release from command, we're sent straight to D.C. Not fully released yet, not home and definitely not freedom. Another cage with better hotels. It has been a month since I've seen Sarah. A fucking month. She's back at school now, I've had Ghost tracking her.

Longer than I thought possible. Long enough for bruises to fade. Long enough for anger to harden. Long enough for her to move on. The bureaucrats in D.C. keep us waiting another week before formal testimony starts. Government rate hotel, per diem. Daily reminders not to leave the metro area. I don't care if they're paying. I'd rather sleep in the dirt if it meant getting to Minnesota faster.

Most of the guys make the best of it. Glitch and Sparta go find bars. Stitches disappears and returns with expensive whiskey and zero explanation. Reaper goes running every morning like a psychopath. Magellan somehow finds someone selling a nice ford truck, a 1995 F-250 supercar. Apparently the hard sell came from the fact that the engine will outlive us all.

Some of them head to Arlington National Cemetery one afternoon. I stay in my room staring at the ceiling while my blood boils. I check my messages anyway. Blocked. Still blocked. I call once from the hotel line. Straight to voicemail. I don't leave one. What would I even say?

When they finally drag us into the federal building, Special Agent Ramsey is waiting with two DOJ attorneys, three analysts and enough paperwork to bury a body. He looks annoyingly calm. Like he sleeps eight hours a night and enjoys this.

Ghost and I present first. Recovered drives. Encrypted copies. Journal backups. Benjamin's files. Search histories. All of his photos, logs and fantasy notes. Surveillance notes on Sarah and her schedules. All thing I tried to protect her from. Everything that proves obsession. Everything that proves escalation. Everything that proves he was planning this long before the jungle.

We also confirm what Ghost uncovered afterward. The university dean was Benjamin's uncle. Dean Wagner, he's the school's Associate Dean of Research and Field Programs and the one who pushed to hire Dr. Willis and pushed for budget cuts for this expedition which meant Willis was the one to lead.

Ramsey's pen actually stops moving at that. Let him feel shocked for once. Then we show the worst part. Documented entries detailing what Benjamin had already done to other women and what he fantasized about doing to Sarah. Our communication with a lawyer who was trying to contact the girls.

The room goes dead quiet. Even the attorneys stop pretending to be detached.

Ramsey closes the file slowly. "Jesus Christ." For the first time since meeting him, he sounds human. I lean back in my chair, jaw clenched so hard it aches. All I can think is one thing.

If Benjamin is still alive—I'm going to find him first. Those were the worst files to walk through. The journals. The surveillance notes. The fantasies. Every twisted line Benjamin wrote about Sarah like she was something to possess instead of a person. Even reading summaries of it made my hands itch for violence. Of course, the asshole across the table had to open his mouth.

One of the DOJ attorneys adjusted his glasses and said, "Defense will argue the digital materials were obtained through unlawful seizure in a foreign jurisdiction."

Ghost actually laughed. A short, humorless sound. We already knew this.

"What helps," Ramsey said before I could speak, "is that every operator present independently documented suspicious behavior from Benjamin and Jenna over six weeks."

That part mattered. Their secrecy. Jenna's manipulation. Benjamin's escalating obsession. The tracker. The lies. The fact that none of this came out of nowhere. What really pisses all of us off is Dr. Willis. He fooled everyone. He played the academic mentor well. Pretended to want to protect Sarah and Jenna, meanwhile he was coordinating trafficking routes and feeding victims into the machine. He'll be harder to prosecute. He worked smarter, cleaner.

Then there's Wagner. We all know he stinks. But suspicion isn't evidence.

Ramsey tapped a file and said, "We're actively digging into the dean's role."

Good. I hope they burn the whole structure down. Then Ramsey leaned back in his chair and pinned me with those sharp green eyes.

"It's incredibly inconvenient," he said dryly, "that you killed all the armed men before we could question them."

The room went still. I smiled without humor. "Yeah, well, we did our job." His brow lifted. "We neutralized an active threat holding hostages," I continued. "Per regulation." Then I let the snark land. "I suppose your training happened behind a desk, so I understand why real-time lethal threats might be confusing."

Reaper coughed into his fist to hide a laugh. Ghost stared at the ceiling. Stitches openly grinned. Ramsey looked like he wanted to hit me.

Instead, he folded his hands. "You're difficult."

"You're slow." That one cost me a kick under the table from Reaper. Worth it. I'm tired of being treated like we're mindless drones who stumbled through chaos. We saved lives. We ended monsters. Yes—we were all hell-bent on protecting Sarah. Though he doesn't need to know what she means to me. If detainee interviews start revealing personal dynamics, so be it. He never asked. We never told. After another hour of circular questioning, I stood.

"If we're done," I said flatly, "any further questions can go through command."

Ramsey studied me for a long second, then nodded. "We're done for today."

Good. Because if I had to sit there another ten minutes, someone was leaving in handcuffs. But when we stepped out into the hot D.C. air, none of that was what stayed with me. Not Willis. Not Wagner. Not Ramsey. Not Benjamin. What keeps my pulse razor-tight is simple: We don't know if he's alive or dead.

And my gut? My gut says this isn't over. Men like him don't vanish. They hide. They obsess. They wait and if he's still breathing, then somewhere out there he's watching. Waiting for the perfect moment to strike again. The thought sends a fresh surge of fury through me. I should have made damn sure he was dead because if he ever comes near Sarah again, I won't just kill him. I'll erase him.

Chapter Thirty Two

Wade

I decided I should stop and see my parents first. At the very least, I could see how they were doing. At best, maybe close the last chapter of a life I'd outgrown years ago. At worst, nothing would be different. They'd still be the same people who loved liquor more than responsibility. The same people who treated parenting like an inconvenience. The same people who never once, in twelve years of deployments, rotations, injuries, and silence, sent a single letter.

No emails. No birthday messages. No *are you alive?* Nothing. Still, some stupid part of me wanted to know. So before I headed to Minnesota to fix what mattered, I drove home. The neighborhood looked smaller than I remembered. Lawns tighter, the driveways looks shorter and the trees were older. Memory always makes places bigger than they are.

I parked in the driveway and stared at the house I grew up in. Same peeling grey shutters. Same cracked walkway. Same gutter hanging crooked over the garage. Only it looked like everything was falling apart. That should've warned me. I stood on the front walk longer than I needed to, duffel bag slung over one shoulder, keys in my hand.

Not sure I wanted to do this after all, maybe it wasn't too late to just turn around and leave. A car pulled into the driveway next door. A woman stepped out. Long blonde hair with athletic build. She glanced my way while grabbing grocery bags from the backseat. There was something familiar in the shape of her face, but distance and time blurred it.

Maybe the neighbors moved. Maybe everyone had. Wouldn't be the first place I came back to that forgot me. I turned and knocked. Shuffling footsteps answered. Then the door swung open. My mother stood there and for a second, I barely recognized her. She was only sixty-two but she looked closer to eighty. Hair thin and unwashed. Skin dull and papery. Eyes bloodshot and floating slightly out of sync. A stale wave of cigarettes, liquor, and old carpet rolled out behind her.

"Wade?" she slurred. I said nothing. Surprised she even recognizes me. Her face cracked into something that might've been a smile. "I missed you."

I didn't acknowledge that either. "Where's Dad?"

I stepped inside automatically, scanning the room. Same stained brown recliner that they found at the end of someone's driveway when they were throwing it out. Same overflowing ashtray. Same glass bottles of Skol vodka on the counter. No sign of him.

She blinked slowly, like the question took effort. "Oh." She waved vaguely toward the living room. "He got in a fight at a bar. About a year ago, I think." I went still. "The guy had a gun," she continued casually. "Shot him dead. It was awful." She pointed toward the mantle. A cheap brass urn sat between dusty framed photos and a ceramic duck. "I've got his ashes right there."

My brain lagged behind the words. "He's dead?" I heard my own voice but barely recognized it.

She nodded once and wandered toward the kitchen. "Terrible business."

I stared at the urn. At the man who spent my childhood calling me weak, lazy, ungrateful. At the man who taught me what rage sounded like through walls. At the man I still somehow thought I might get one final conversation with. Gone. And no one told me.

I turned slowly. "Why didn't anyone contact me?"

She frowned like I was being difficult. "Oh, psh." A dismissive flick of her hand. "We knew you were busy."

Busy. Twelve years and not one phone call to tell me my father was dead. Not one message. Not one attempt.

"I didn't want to bother you," she added. That did it. Any tiny, pathetic hope I'd carried in here died right then. No reconciliation. No hidden regret. No sudden realization that they'd failed me. Just the same selfishness wearing older skin. I was their only child and they couldn't be bothered to tell me my father was in an urn on the mantle.

I laughed once. A short and empty, disbelieving laugh. My mother blinked at the sound.

"What's funny?" I looked around the room one last time. At the house that raised me badly. At the woman who never noticed. At the ghosts I didn't need anymore.

"Nothing," I said. Then I picked up my bag. Because I had wasted enough time on people who never cared. And there was someone in Minnesota I prayed still might. As she keeps talking, I watch her sway slightly in the kitchen chair. Head dipping, her eyes were glass and speech was slowing. Judging by the bottle in front of her she's halfway to passing out already, and it's barely six in the evening.

Some things never change. I hadn't even bothered bringing my bags in from the rental car. Two duffels. That was it. Everything I owned from the last sixteen years of service, deployments, temporary housing, safe houses, barracks rooms, and rented apartments fit into two military bags sitting in a trunk. That should probably feel sad. Instead, it feels clean. Light. Because if I'm honest, most of those years weren't living. They were surviving. Mission to mission. Objective to objective. Stay sharp. Stay breathing. Don't get attached. Don't look too far ahead.

My real life starts now. If she'll let it.

"Would you like me to cook you something?" my mother asks, words slightly blurred together.

"No. I'm fine." I glance at the clock. "I'll eat on the road." I absolutely won't be staying here. Every second in this house feels wasted.

"You're not staying?" She frowns vaguely. "I was hoping you were home now. I could use some help around here." The vodka on her breath reaches me from across the table. Home. I almost laugh again.

"No," I say evenly. "I've got an opportunity waiting for me. I just came to check on you."

There is no chance in hell I'm telling her about Sarah. About the future I want badly enough it scares me. Some instincts don't need explanation. I know better than to drag this mess anywhere near something good.

"I'm gonna look upstairs," I tell her. "Mind if I shower?"

"Oh sure." She waves lazily toward the hallway. "I'm gonna watch TV. *The Price Is Right* is on, you know."

I don't point out it's six p.m. I just nod and head outside. The evening air feels better than the house. I grab soap I bought at a gas station, a clean shirt, and my charger from the rental. Then I head upstairs. My old room smells like dust and stale heat. The same warped dresser still leans against the wall. Same cheap blinds. Same dent in the drywall from where my father once threw something that missed me by inches. Some of my old things are still here.

High school trophies shoved in a box. A cracked baseball glove. A stack of books with water damage. But most of it is gone. Sold or most likely pawned to thrown out. Whatever fed their habits at the time. I kneel and dig through drawers anyway. Nothing worth keeping. Nothing I need. I should just leave. Say goodbye. Get in the car. Start driving to Sarah. I know I've got a mountain to climb when I get there. I know sorry won't be enough. I know I'll probably have to beg. On my knees if that's what it takes. I checked every day to see if she'd unblocked me.

No surprise. She hadn't. I found her social media too, completely silent. No new posts since before the mission. That worried me more than anger would have. Glitch texted yesterday saying he was on his way to Minnesota. The idiot thinks he's running advance recon for my love life. Claims he'll "soften the target." I hope to God he's right. Because there is no universe where I'm getting off easy. I stand and head across the hall toward the bathroom for a quick shower.

Then I hear my mother yell from downstairs. "Wade! Someone's here to see you!"

I stop mid-step and rub a hand down my face. Who the fuck would be here? I don't have time for visitors. I need to be on the road to my future, but the second I stepped into the living room, I froze. The blonde woman from next door stood near the doorway, smiling like she'd just been invited in. It took me a second. Then the years peeled back. River. She'd changed since the last time I saw her. We'd been teenagers then. Now she looked polished in the way people get after learning exactly how to present themselves. Long blonde hair, perfectly tanned skin, fitted jeans, all of it screams money. Paired with a carefully casual smile. Still pretty. Still dangerous in the ways I remembered.

"Wade?" she said, stepping closer.

"Hey, River." I gave her a short nod. "Been a long time."

She tucked a strand of hair behind her ear. Nervous habit or performance. Maybe both. It's hard not to analyze, because my instincts are telling me she's got a plan.

"Oh, I know." Her gaze swept over me openly. "You look… different."

I said nothing. "Bigger," she added with a light laugh, eyes dropping to my arms. I ignored that too.

"You moved back?" I asked her, although to be fair I know nothing of her life after I joined the army.

"Yeah." She sighed dramatically. "After my divorce. Didn't have many options."

"Sorry to hear that." Flat enough to freeze water. She either didn't notice or didn't care.

"I saw you outside and figured I'd come say hi." She tilted her head. "Are you home for good?"

"No." I didn't soften it. "Just stopped by to check in before I head out again."

Her mouth turned down in a practiced pout. "Oh. When are you leaving?"

"Soon." That should've ended it.

Instead, she stepped closer. Close enough to smell perfume under the summer heat. One finger curled around a strand of blonde hair. Flirting, it did absolutely nothing for me. There was only one woman I wanted to see and she wasn't the one standing in my mother's living room.

"You sure you don't want to stay the night?" River asked sweetly. "It's kind of late to drive."

Not a chance in hell. "I've got someone waiting for me."

I adjusted the duffel on my shoulder. River blinked in surprise.

"Oh. Like… a girl?" My jaw tightened. Too personal. Too familiar.

"Yes." I was already turning toward the stairs. "Nice seeing you, River."

I didn't wait for a reply. I took the steps two at a time, grabbed my bags, then checked my phone. Nothing. No new messages. No missed calls. No miracle. Sarah's number still blocked me. Just like every other time I'd checked. Which was embarrassingly often. I dragged a hand through my damp hair and grabbed clean clothes. I just wanted a quick shower before I hit the road.

Followed by groveling. that was the plan. Until I heard River's voice as I was getting out of the shower. Inside my room. I went still. Then moved fast. I yanked my shirt and sweats on as I crossed the hall, barely toweling off, and stepped into my bedroom. River sat on my bed. Holding my phone.

For one full second I just stared. Because surely no one was that stupid.

"Oh," she said brightly. "You're done already?" She set the phone down like she hadn't been touching it. "You got a call from... Glitch?" she said. "I tried to answer."

Rage went cold and immediate. "You what?"

I crossed the room in three strides, snatched the phone off the bed, and checked the screen. No active call. No voicemail. No new messages. I looked up slowly.

"What did he say?"

She shrugged. "Just asked for you. When I told him you were in the shower, he hung up."

A sick feeling dropped through my chest. Why would Jake call instead of text? Unless it was Sarah. Maybe she'd borrowed his phone. Maybe she'd changed her mind. Maybe she'd finally reached back and River answered. I scrubbed a hand over my face. Jesus Christ.

I looked at her again. "Get out."

Her smile faltered. "Wade, I was just—"

"Out."

This time there was enough steel in it that she stood immediately. Good, because one more second and I was liable to throw both her and the mattress outside. I scribbled my number onto a scrap of paper from the junk drawer and held it out to her.

"Not for you," I said before she could smile. "If something happens to my mom, have your parents call me." Her expression flickered, disappointment slipping through before she masked it. She took the paper anyway, fingers brushing mine like it was intentional.

"I was really hoping we could catch up," she said softly.

I gave her the tightest version of a smile I could manage. "Take care, River." Then I was gone. I jogged down the stairs, tossed a quick goodbye toward the living room. I got no response beyond the blare of television.

My mother was half-asleep in her chair, glass tilted in one hand. Didn't even look up. I stepped outside, slammed my bags into the rental and dropped behind the wheel.

The second the door shut, I called Glitch. He answered on the first ring. "Are you out of your goddamn mind?!"

I jerked the phone away from my ear. "What?"

"You think you can just—" He cut himself off with an audible inhale. "I was over here pleading your fucking case and that's what answers your phone?"

My stomach dropped. So it had been Sarah. "Nothing happened," I growled. "My old neighbor showed up uninvited. She was acting weird as hell. I don't know why she answered my phone, but I never touched her."

Jake scoffed. "You have any idea how that sounded?"

Ice spread through my chest. "What did Sarah say?"

He exhaled hard enough to crack concrete. "It wasn't me calling, dumbass. It was *her*."

I gripped the steering wheel until my knuckles blanched. Jake kept going, each word clipped and sharp. "She finally worked up the courage to call you and some random chick answered your phone." I closed my eyes. "Do you have any idea how that fucking sounded to her?"

I slammed my fist into the steering wheel. Then again. Pain barely registered.

"I don't know how you fix this one. I gotta go," Jake snapped. The line went dead. I sat there breathing hard, pulse hammering in my neck. I'd done it again. Somehow. Some fucking how.

Through the windshield, I saw River step onto her porch and glance my way. I threw the car into reverse so hard gravel sprayed the curb. Then I was gone.

Eight hours of driving on the dark highway. Gas station coffee keeping me fueled that and the fact that every mile field by panic and adrenaline. I drove straight through the night. I only stopped once and only long enough to use the bathroom and fill up my gas tank. Didn't think about anything except getting to her.

By the time I pulled into the apartment lot, it was a little after two in the morning. We're in a dingy looking lot in Minneapolis, not far from her campus. Lights out in most windows. Humidity hanging thick over everything. I called Glitch as I grabbed my bag and took the stairs two at a time. Jake opened the door before I knocked. He looked me over once. Said nothing. Then stepped aside.

"Which one?" I asked quietly, eyes on the small apartment, there were two doors that sat on either side of the living room. The tv was on and I can see a makeshift bed on the couch. He pointed left.

"She's gonna kill you," he muttered. Then he dropped back onto the couch like he wanted no part of what came next.

I took one slow breath and opened the bedroom door. It was dark in there besides the little bit of moonlight cutting pale lines through blinds. There was a soft fan noise coming from the corner, an open doorway on one side of the bed. I stepped inside and shut the door quietly behind me.

Her scent hit me first. That lavender vanilla scent I remember from when I first bumped into her. Something warm and unmistakably Sarah. It hit harder than any bullet ever had. My duffel slipped from my shoulder to the floor. I stripped off my shirt, suddenly needing skin, her, something real. Then I moved to the bed. She was curled on her side beneath the blanket, hair spilled across the pillow. Even sleeping, she looked exhausted. I wonder if she's been sleeping okay or if she's been having nightmares like me. Most nights I wake up in a sweat, in my worst fucking nightmares instead of finding her in time I usually find her dead. Instead of what was happening to Jenna, it was Benjamin doing that to Sarah, or instead of finding her, we lose her forever. When we get to the hut her clothes and tracker are there but she's gone.

There was a paper on the mattress beside her. I lifted it carefully and set it on the nightstand without looking. Then I pulled back the blanket and slid in behind her. My body curved around hers instinctively. Like it had always known where to go. For the first time in a month, I breathed. I pulled her gently against me and buried my face in her hair. She stirred, a soft sleepy sound leaving her lips.

Then she rolls toward me without waking. One small movement. Instinctive. Unthinking. She presses her face against my bare chest and exhales like she's finally found somewhere safe to land. Trusting me in sleep before she's ready to forgive me awake. The emotion hits so hard I have to close my eyes.

My throat tightens. A slow, shaky breath leaves me as I wrap my arm around her more carefully, holding her like something precious I almost lost. Everything before her falls away. The years of missions. The empty houses. The bullshit with my mother. The wasted anger. The loneliness I'd convinced myself was normal.

None of it matters in this moment. Only this woman curled against me. Only the warmth of her breath on my skin. Only the chance I almost missed. I lower my mouth to the top of her head and stay there. Breathing her in. Grounding myself in the simple fact that she is here.

Alive. With me. Maybe I don't deserve another chance. Maybe I deserve every ounce of anger she's carrying. But with her tucked against me like this, with dawn still hours away and silence wrapped around us, one thought settles deep in my chest. Maybe, just maybe. There's hope for me yet.

Chapter Thirty Three

Sarah

My alarm blares at six-thirty. I jolt awake and slap at my phone until the sound dies. Tuesdays and Thursdays I have to be on campus by nine to teach lab sections. For a minute I just lie there, staring at the ceiling, willing my heart to slow down. I was dreaming about Wade, the best night of sleep I've had since before I was taken. About the jungle. About those nights in the tent when everything outside felt dangerous, but inside that tiny space somehow felt safer than anywhere else. The sun warming the canvas. His voice low in the dark. His arms around me while we whispered about nothing and everything.

For one soft, dangerous moment after waking, it still feels real. Like I'm back there. Like warmth is wrapped around me. My body goes rigid because warmth is wrapped around me. An arm is draped over my waist. A large hand rests low across my stomach. For one fractured second, I can't breathe. Every nerve in my body lights up at once. My pulse slams hard against my ribs as panic claws straight up my throat.

No. Not again.

I jerk instinctively, muscles locking, breath trapping in my chest. My mind is suddenly nowhere near my bedroom. It's in darkness. In ropes. In hands I didn't ask for. In helplessness. The weight on me feels too heavy. I bite back a cry and force myself still, swallowing air in sharp, silent pulls.

Think. Think. This bed. My room. In my tiny apartment in Minneapolis. Fallon should be across the living room in her own room. I stare at the hand on my stomach, trying to ground myself in what's real instead of what memory wants to make real. The grip isn't tight. Not restraining. Just resting there, protectively.

Definitely not Fallon. My heart is still racing when another thought cuts through the panic. If Jake climbed into bed with me, I will kill him before breakfast. Very slowly, trembling despite myself, I turn my head and stop breathing for a completely different reason. Wade. He's asleep behind me. One arm heavy across my middle. Face buried in my hair. Dark lashes against tanned skin. Bare chest warm against my back. For a second I can only stare. Because my body is still in panic while my heart is doing something else entirely. He's here. Actually here. Not a dream. Not memory. Not wishful thinking.

My pulse pounds wildly, but now from shock, relief, anger, longing, too many things at once. I force myself to stay still so he won't feel me shaking Then horror hits. The sonogram picture. It was with me when I fell asleep. Oh my God. Moving inch by inch, I carefully lift his arm and slide out from under him. He shifts in his sleep, reaching automatically. I panic, grab my pillow, and wedge it into his arms. He tightens around it instantly. I nearly laugh.

Then I see it. The sonogram picture on the nightstand beside him. My stomach flips. Did he see it? Does he know? I snatch it up and shove it into the top drawer of my nightstand like it's contraband. Then I gather clothes and hurry into the bathroom. The second the door shuts, I brace both hands on the sink. What the hell? When did he get here? How did he get in? Did Jake let him in? Did Fallon know? Did he see the picture? Did he know before he climbed into my bed and wrapped himself around me like he belonged there?

I strip and step into the shower. Hot water pours over me, but it does nothing to calm the riot in my head. I shampoo twice. Condition. Shave. Then, in a moment of complete insanity, I blow-dry my hair and curl it. I never curl it. I'm trying to kill time, keeping away from him. Half the time I barely brush it before throwing it into a ponytail. But today is the first day of my final semester. That's all this is. School, professionalism. This is just for teaching. Definitely not trying to look good because Wade is asleep ten feet away.

I meet my own eyes in the mirror. Liar. Still, I keep going. Mascara. Light makeup. Lip gloss. I chose my favorite black dress pants, the pair that makes my ass look phenomenal. Petty? Maybe. Healing? Also maybe. Time will tell. I add black ankle boots and my favorite blue blouse, the one that makes my eyes look brighter and hangs loose enough to skim over my stomach.

Practical now and will certainly be necessary later. My hand drifts there automatically. Ten weeks. A tiny secret growing beneath soft fabric. Our baby. The thought steals my breath every time. I rub my belly once, gently. Then straighten my shoulders. Not because I care what Wade thinks. Not because I want him stunned speechless when he sees me. Not because part of me hopes he regrets every second we lost. I'm doing this for me. Mostly.

"Well, baby," I whisper, resting a hand over my stomach. "Let's get started." I draw in one deep breath, square my shoulders and step out of the bathroom. Then stop dead. Wade is sitting upright in my bed, sheets pooled around his waist, wearing nothing but black boxers.

His hair is messy from sleep, like he'd been dragging his hands through it all night. Dark strands falling across his forehead, it's grown even more in the last month. His chest is bare, all hard muscle and warm tanned skin, but my eyes snag lower. A pale strip of medical tape crossed one side of his ribs, just above an angry pink scar that disappeared beneath the waistband of his sweats where the bullet had torn through him. Proof he'd really been hurt. Proof he'd bled while I was in the next room begging to see him.

Even healing, exhausted, rumpled from sleep and half-dressed, he still looked offensively good. Like a problem I never should have touched. Like a temptation I definitely shouldn't touch again. If I wasn't so furious, I might've jumped him. Instead, I just stand there staring, wondering how far I'd get if I punched him and sprinted for the door.

His eyes lift fully to me. Golden-brown and warm and entirely too soft. "Hi, beautiful." The words hit me like a body blow.

I clap a hand over my mouth to trap the sob trying to escape. Hearing his voice. Hearing *that* voice. Calling me beautiful like nothing happened. It is too much. I can't do this.

"You look like shit," I manage, trying for confidence and landing somewhere near wounded aggression.

The corner of his mouth lifts. "You look fucking radiant."

His voice is still rough with sleep, deeper than usual, thick enough to curl straight through me. Absolutely dangerous. No. Do not get sucked in. We stare at each other for a long beat. He takes me in slowly. His eyes scanning over my hair, my clothes and then back to my face. Like he's memorizing me again and I'm trying not to break apart under the weight of it.

"Is that what you were telling that other woman?" I ask, once I trust myself enough to speak.

Pain flickers across his face instantly. "Sarah—"

"Nope. Answer the question."

"No." His voice is firm. "I wasn't with another woman. I have never been with another woman since you." My pulse stutters. "There is no one but you." I hate how badly I want to believe him. "I'm sorry for how things ended," he says quietly. "Please give me a chance to explain everything."

He looks wrecked, that almost makes it worse. Because I want to forgive him. I want to crawl back into that bed and let him hold me until none of this hurts anymore.

Instead, I grab onto anger with both hands. "I need to go," I say sharply. "I have school."

I turn before he can answer and storm out of the room. The apartment goes dead silent the second I step into the kitchen. Jake and Fallon stop talking mid-sentence. I don't look at either of them. I march straight to the coffee maker.

If the world is ending, I'm ending it caffeinated. I pour a mug and add an aggressive amount of French vanilla creamer. The smell alone almost makes me emotional. I missed stupid things in the jungle. Hot coffee. Privacy. Creamer. Doors with locks. Then my brain catches up. Wait, am I allowed to drink coffee pregnant? I stare into the mug. Great. I don't think I am, I do remember that much. I dump it down the drain, instead of offering it to Fallon. My body is beginning to shake with all the frustration and probably lack of food. At least I didn't throw up today. Yet.

It's eight-thirty. Campus is a ten-minute walk, but I need to leave early if I want time to compose myself before teaching students while my ex-lover/current problem lounges shirtless in my bed.

"Hey, Rocky," Jake says carefully, like I'm a wild animal that may bite. "How'd you sleep?"

I shoot him a look over the rim of my mug.

"Why do you keep calling her Rocky?" Fallon asks, glancing between us.

Jake smirks immediately. "She didn't tell you?" I close my eyes. Of course he's enjoying this.

"Good morning," I say brightly, with enough fake cheer to poison the room. "I slept great. How did *you* sleep? Probably not that well. That couch is ancient." I take a slow sip of coffee. "Or maybe it was because you were up late letting Wade in."

He doesn't even flinch. "It's still better than sleeping on the ground," he says casually. "Or those busted cots at base." Completely ignoring the accusation.

Just then, Wade walks out of my bedroom and every coherent thought leaves my body. He's wearing gray sweats that hang low on his hips, the word ARMY printed down one leg. Nothing else. No shirt. No shoes. Bare feet against the hardwood. His chest is on full display—broad, muscled, scarred, the medical tape still visible along one side. I have never seen him dressed like this. Or undressed like this. My mouth drops open. I snap it shut instantly. Too late. I catch the smug, wicked smirk that curves his mouth. He saw.

"Holy fuck," Fallon whispers beside me. I don't even look at her. I'm too busy being furious. Did she know he was coming too?

"Hey," Jake says lazily, leaning one shoulder against the wall. "Eyes over here, Sunset." Both Fallon and I jerk our heads toward him. I stare.

"Sunset?" Fallon repeats. Judging by her startled expression, that nickname was just born. Jake starts chuckling into his coffee.

"I'm getting ready to leave," I announce stiffly. "I have to be there by nine." I turn to Fallon. "When do you leave?"

"A little after you. My first class isn't until ten."

"Okay. Lunch?" We always try to eat together when schedules line up. But first day of semester lunches are tradition. Started years ago. Back when it was me, Fallon, and Carly. The thought pinches unexpectedly. I need to check in with Carly's parents soon.

"Of course," Fallon says quickly. "Student lounge?"

"Perfect." I grab my bag and keys.

Then glance at Jake. "Do you need my number? In case you leave and need to get back in?"

He shakes his head. "No. Already have it."

I freeze and slowly turn. "You already have it?"

Jake stops mid-sip, realizing too late what he said. "Uh…" His eyes dart toward Wade. Coward. "Ghost programmed it into all our phones," he says finally. The words land harder than they should. So they all had my number. All this time. Every one of them could have reached out. Checked on me. Said *anything* and none of them did. The hurt surprises me with its sharpness. Maybe because part of me believed at least Jake would have. Maybe because it feels too much like the rest of it. All of it was planned, they always knew my information from the start. How much of it was a lie? How much of the narrative did they control from the start? I don't even know what I'm angry about anymore.

Them. Wade. Myself. All of it. I want to ask more. Demand more. But if I start now, I'll never leave. So I shoulder my bag and head for the door. I don't look at Wade. Don't look at anyone.

Right before it shuts behind me, I hear a low, frustrated, "Fuck." Good. Let him be frustrated.

Outside, the morning air is cool enough to wake me up. I curse under my breath when I realize I forgot a jacket in my rush to escape. Too late now. I shove in my headphones, hit play and start walking. Ten minutes to campus. Ten minutes to become Graduate Student Sarah again. Ten minutes to pretend my life isn't imploding in a tiny apartment behind me.

Once I step into the building, I notice people glancing my way. At first, I think nothing of it. First day of the semester. Hallways are crowded, people always look around. But then it keeps happening. A girl near the vending machines does a double take. Two guys talking by the stairwell go quiet when I pass. Someone farther down the corridor whispers my name. My stomach tightens.

I glance down at myself, checking for some obvious disaster. Shirt buttoned. Pants zipped. No mascara streaks. No toilet paper stuck to my shoe. Everything appears normal. So why does it feel like I'm walking under a spotlight?

I turn toward the anthropology wing and head straight for Dr. Anderson's office. Her door is cracked open.

I knock softly. "Come in." I step inside.

She looks up from her desk and gasps. Then she's on her feet before I can blink. "Oh my God, Sarah."

The next second I'm wrapped in a hug that smells like linen spray, old books, and peppermint tea. I stiffen automatically. Then force myself to breathe and hug her back. She pulls away only to grip my shoulders and look me over like she's making sure all of me is still here.

"I didn't know if I should contact you," she says, eyes shining. "I heard bits and pieces. Campus police called. Then federal agents asked questions. Then no one would tell me anything. Just that two people were in custody, one was missing and two girls were safely on their way home."

My throat tightens. "I'm okay." It sounds weak even to me.

Her expression says she knows it. She says gently. "It looks like you're functioning."

That lands too close to the truth. She softens immediately. "I'm sorry. That was unfair."

"It's okay. It's all a long story. I can tell you some things but it's an ongoing investigation, but maybe when I'm done for the day?"

She studies me another second. "You don't have to teach today if you're not ready." The offer nearly undoes me. Because part of me wants to crawl into one of her office chairs and cry until noon.

But I shake my head. "I need normal," I say quietly. "I need something to still be mine."

Her eyes warm. "That sounds exactly like you. I would love it if you came back after, I want to know how you are."

"I will." Is all I can manage around the lump in my throat. Imagining retelling the story again sounds harder than I intended.

She gathers a stack of folders, lab keys, safety sheets, and attendance rosters from her desk. "I updated the syllabus. Added a new section on field ethics and informed consent."

I huff out a laugh. "Subtle."

"Trauma makes radicals of us all." She hands me the materials, then hesitates. "If anyone gives you trouble, asks invasive questions, bothers you in class, you send them to me."

I blink. "Seriously?"

"Sarah," she says dryly, "I've been waiting twenty years to weaponize tenure."

Despite myself, I laugh for real. She smiles, satisfied. "There you are."

Emotion rises so fast I have to look away. "Thank you."

She squeezes my arm once. "Go teach your class. Scare undergrads with bones and colonialism."

"That's the plan." As I leave her office, the hallway feels a little steadier.

Until I notice people staring again. More openly now. Someone quickly looks down when I catch them. Another whispers to a friend. My nerves return full force. I grip the folders tighter and keep walking. By the time I reach the lab room, voices are spilling through the open door. Students already seated. Laughing and talking, completely normal. Until, I step inside. The room goes dead silent.

Heat rushes to my face instantly. Great. Perfect. Exactly what I needed. I set my materials down and start organizing them with shaking hands. I've taught this lab for years. Dozens of sections. Hundreds of students. Today it feels like my first time standing in front of people.

I clear my throat. "Good morning." My voice sounds steadier than I feel.

We begin the way I always begin. Names. Majors. Why they took Anthropology 101. As they go around introducing themselves, I write each name down and explain the structure of the course. Professors handle lecture Mondays and Wednesdays. I run Tuesday and Thursday labs, hands-on material, discussion, artifact work, cultural application.

Today is syllabus day. Easy. Safe. No one can ruin syllabus day. I finish outlining expectations and ask if there are any questions.

A guy in the back raises his hand. "Yes?" I say. "Sorry, what was your name again?"

"Jason." He smiles nervously. "And I was wondering if you could tell us about your field school you were just at."

I freeze. My pulse spikes. "Yes," I say carefully. "I can absolutely discuss my research and the Yanomami community when we cover ethnographic methods."

He shifts. "No, I meant… what happened. With that student and professor."

The room goes still again. Every eye on me. I straighten slowly. Professional voice. Calm face. Hands no longer shaking.

"No," I say evenly. "I cannot discuss an active federal investigation." Silence. Then I add: "But I *can* discuss why asking invasive personal questions in an academic setting is a terrible anthropological method."

A few students snort. Jason turns bright red. And somewhere deep inside me, a tiny piece of myself returns.

"We heard you were sleeping with a hunky Army dude," a girl near the middle calls out. "I would *love* that kind of field school."

My heart stutters so hard it hurts. The room erupts in nervous laughter. I grip the edge of the desk until my knuckles ache. Professional. Stay professional. How could they possibly know what happened in that jungle?

"Yes," I say evenly, though my voice sounds far away to my own ears. "Well, if you have specific questions regarding research methods, cultural immersion, or the Yanomami people, I'd be happy to discuss those." I let my gaze sweep the room. "Anything else is not relevant to this course."

The laughter dies quickly. "If that's all, you're dismissed." I start gathering papers. "Bring your binders Thursday. Complete the online reading and quiz before class."

No one says another word. Chairs scrape. Backpacks zip. Students file out in awkward silence. The second the last one leaves, I collapse into the chair behind the desk. My hands are shaking and I feel sick. How do they know about Wade? No. Not *how*. Campus gossip spreads faster than viruses. The real problem is that soon it won't matter what they know. In a few months, everyone will know something happened.

I rest a hand over my stomach and close my eyes. I still have one more lab. Then I can escape to lunch with Fallon. Then maybe I can survive the rest of the day.

I eat half a granola bar, force down water, then sprint to the bathroom to dry heave dramatically over a toilet. Pregnancy is beautiful. Lies.

The second lab goes smoother. No direct questions. No jokes. But I can feel the curiosity in every glance. Like I'm a person and rumor all at once. When it ends, I pack my things, lock the lab, and head toward the student lounge. Twice I glance over my shoulder. That strange sensation again. Like someone is watching me. Every time I turn, there's no one there.

By the time I reach the lounge, I'm tense enough to snap. "Look at you, positively glowing!" Fallon practically shouts it across the room.

I whip around in alarm. "Jesus Christ!"

She bursts out laughing. "No one's here. It's just us." She lowers her voice. "I wouldn't tell anyone, I promise." Then adds thoughtfully, "Besides blurting it to Jake, but that doesn't count."

I drop into the chair across from her. "It absolutely counts."

"Technicality."

I rub my temples. "Sorry. It's been a long morning."

Her smile fades. "Does he know?"

I hesitate. Then tell her everything. Waking up with Wade in my bed. The students. The weird feeling of being watched. The sonogram picture on the nightstand.

"I never said anything," Fallon says immediately. "And I left right after you."

"I know."

"Did he say something to you?"

"No. But I fell asleep with the sonogram beside me." I lower my voice instinctively. "I don't know if he saw it. He didn't mention it."

She leans back, thinking. "He didn't say anything in front of me either."

Then her eyes narrow.

"Who do you think is watching you?"

"I don't know."

"Do you think maybe Wade followed you here?" I blink, considering it. I know it's not his eyes that are on me though, I don't know how I know, I just do. "To keep an eye on you?"

"No," I say quickly. "How would he even get in? You need badge access for half these buildings."

Fallon gives me a look so pointed it should have its own weapon classification. "Sarah."

"What?"

"They're Special Forces."

I sigh. "So?"

"According to you, Ghost can hack satellites, encrypted phones, probably even NASA if he got bored."

I stare at her. She raises a brow. "And you think a campus badge reader would stop them?" I hate that she has a point. I slump lower in my chair.

"I don't know. Maybe I'm just on edge. Even if he was here watching, I just know it's not his eyes that are on me, if that makes sense."

"It does and you *are* on edge," she says gently now. "Anyone would be." She reaches across the table and squeezes my hand. "First day back. Trauma. Pregnancy. Shirtless ex-boyfriend in your apartment."

I snort despite myself. "When you say it like that, it sounds like a lot."

"It is a lot." She studies me. "But if Wade *is* skulking around campus like some wounded jungle boyfriend, I need warning so I can enjoy it. Have you found a therapist yet?" She asks it gently, casually enough that it doesn't feel like pity.

"I really love the woman I see. She's helped me a lot." Her voice softens. "I mean… you know."

I do know. There are things Fallon carries that she rarely names out loud. Things that changed her. Things she survived and because of that, when she says something helps, I listen.

"Yeah," I say after a moment. "Maybe that would help." It feels strange admitting it. Like weakness. Like failure. Like something my old self would've insisted she didn't need. But my old self didn't wake up screaming. My old self didn't scan exits in every room. My old self didn't flinch at footsteps behind her.

"Give me her number," I say quietly. "I'll see about an appointment."

Fallon smiles immediately. "I'll text it to you."

Then she reaches across the table and squeezes my hand. "I'm here for you. You know that, right?"

Emotion rises unexpectedly. "I know." I squeeze back. "And I appreciate how amazing and supportive you've been."

She straightens dramatically. "That's right." One hand lands on her chest. "I am now Auntie Fallon."

I laugh despite myself. "You promoted yourself fast."

"I'm a self-starter." She stands and grabs her bag. "Now let's get lunch. I'm starving, and I'm sure the baby is too."

I shake my head, smiling as I follow her. She is already fully committed. Already making plans. Already loving someone she hasn't even met. And I'm still trying not to panic every ten minutes.

We head to the cafeteria. The smell of fries and coffee hits first. Then the realization that there are way too many people. Too much noise. Too much fluorescent lighting. I choose soup and a salad because it feels like something responsible adults eat when they're pregnant and emotionally unstable

Fallon gets pasta, garlic bread, and a brownie the size of my face. "For balance," she says.

We eat and talk about classes, schedules, and whether my students deserve grades after today. By the time we finish, I almost feel normal. After lunch, I head across campus to the photography studio. Cooler air. Dimmer lighting. Chemical scent. It's quiet here, my sanctuary. I unpack my materials and begin setting up to develop the photos recovered from my trip.

My trip. Like it was a vacation. I pull out my camera carefully. The same one I thought was lost forever. The same one Wade somehow made sure found its way back to me. My chest tightens instantly. He noticed what mattered to me. He always seemed to know what I needed before I said it. No. I close my eyes briefly and inhale. Do not think about him. Do not think about the way he looked in my bed this morning. Do not think about his hand over my stomach. Do not think about how badly part of me wanted to crawl back under the covers.

Work. Focus on work. I switch on the enlarger and begin.

Chapter Thirty Four

Sarah

There is something deeply calming about the darkroom. The red safelight. The cool hush of the space. The measured steps of the process.

Developer.

Stop bath.

Fixer.

Rinse.

Repeat.

In a world where everything feels jagged and loud, photography still obeys rules. Images appear slowly. Patiently. Honestly, I could do most of this digitally. I have to anyway. But I like printing by hand first, partly for the art of it, partly because if I screw something up, I still have the negatives. Lately, I've had enough loss.

The first prints are easy. Children laughing near the riverbank. Women weaving baskets beneath filtered sunlight. Smoke rising through the open roof of the shabono. Hands painting natural dyes

385

across skin. A close shot of Paya smiling at me, chin lifted proudly, the necklace she later gifted me resting against her collarbone.

I set that one aside carefully. Then more. Elders in discussion. Men returning from a hunt. Feet pressed into mud after rain. The kind of images I dreamed of capturing when I chose this field.

Then I slide the next print into the tray and go still. Benjamin. He hadn't known I was photographing the group. Everyone else had been moving toward the shabono. He'd stopped behind them. Turned his head slightly and stared straight at me. Even in black and white, there is something wrong in his face. Too intent with a smile barely there. The kind that never reaches the eyes. My stomach turns. How did I not see it then?

I force myself to keep going. The next image hits harder. Wade on our first night there. Everyone else was walking ahead. He'd paused. Looked directly at me the exact second I clicked the shutter. The image steals the air from my lungs. His expression is unreadable to anyone else. Stoic. Watchful. But I know that face, the slight pull at one corner of his mouth. The softened eyes. The focus that always felt like being chosen. My pulse kicks up hard enough I can hear it.

I pack everything up, leaving the pictures to set overnight. Except for one, the picture of Wade I take with me. Suddenly unable to stay there another second. I walk home with headphones in, though I barely hear the music.

Halfway there, my phone rings. Unknown number, my heart starts pounding so I don't answer it. It stops ringing then I immediately get a text.

Unknown: It's Jake, Rocky. Answer your phone.

It rings again and this time I answer it.

"Hey, Rocky."

"What?"

"We've got an appointment."

"With who?"

"You'll see." That means absolutely nothing. "We don't know when we'll be back. Need a way in."

I sigh. "There's a spare key in the drawer by the fridge."

"See? Trust. Family. Beautiful."

"You're exhausting."

"Love you too." He hangs up before I can insult him properly. I change his contact to, Jerk Number 2. It's probably not that funny, but it amuses me. By the time I get home, the apartment is empty. I'm relieved and weirdly disappointed. Wade's bag is still in my room, though. So I know he's coming back. That knowledge sits strangely in my chest. I spot his worn t-shirt by his bag and for some masochistic reason I put it on and change into leggings. I dump my backpack onto the bed. Folders. Notebook. Camera supplies. Then the picture of Wade, I pick it up, even frozen on paper, he looks solid. Dangerous. Those gold flecks in his eyes catch the light.

There's the faintest smirk there too. I used to think I could see love in the way he looked at me. Now I don't know what I saw. Or what I invented because I wanted it so badly. The lock clicks. I jump. Then panic-shove my pillow over the picture and hurry into the living room. Jake and Wade walk in carrying grocery bags. A ridiculous number of grocery bags.

"Looks like you bought the whole store," I say to Jake as he dumps six bags on the counter and starts unloading them.

I do not look at Wade. I know it's childish. I know I'm pretending. I do it anyway.

Jake grins. "Your fridge was a hate crime."

"It was fine."

"It contained mustard, half a lime, expired yogurt and vibes."

"That is called being busy."

"That is called malnutrition." He gives me a pointed look and I know he's referring to the baby before he starts pulling things out. Fresh produce. Pasta. Eggs. Chicken. Bread. Coffee. More creamer, my traitorous heart notices the French vanilla first. Even though I can't have coffee. After a few quiet minutes, Wade says nothing at all. Just picks up his bag and disappears into my bedroom.

The door closes softly behind him and suddenly I can't stop wondering what he's doing in there. He's going to find my picture, I should have hidden it better.

"I didn't know what you liked," Jake says, unloading groceries like he's hosting a cooking show. "So I bought options. How do you feel about tacos?"

"That sounds amazing, actually." It does. Mostly because I suddenly realize I'm starving.

"Good." He points a spatula at me. "I make the best tacos ever."

I roll my eyes. "That level of confidence usually means disappointment."

"It usually means excellence."

He starts organizing ingredients with unnecessary flair. Then his tone shifts.

"Rocky?" I look over.

He rubs the back of his neck, suddenly less sure of himself.

"I'm sorry. I should've messaged you." I don't say anything and he keeps going. "But at the same time, we were buried under command reviews, debriefs, evidence turnover, then the FBI." He grimaces. "Mostly, we were trying to survive Wraith." Despite myself, my brows lift. "He was a fucking bear without you," Jake says. "None of us knew peace. We were living in fear."

He's trying to make me laugh. Normally, it would work. Today, I can't quite get there. My eyes drift to my bedroom door. Still partly closed.

Still hiding the man who detonates my nervous system just by breathing nearby. "Does he know?" I whisper.

Jake glances toward the room too. "I haven't said anything," he says quietly. "And he hasn't mentioned anything."

Relief slides through me before I can stop it. Good, I don't know when I want Wade to know. But I know I want it on my terms. My control. Something in this mess should belong to me.

Jake turns back to me. "You never answered my question yesterday."

"What question?"

"How far along are you?"

I hesitate. "Ten weeks." His eyes widen. "Still first trimester."

"Wow." He stares at me like I've announced I'm hatching a dragon. "So you got pregnant like… immediately."

Heat crawls up my neck. "Yeah. I guess." I glare at him before he can think of any other joke to say.

"Wow," he says again, because apparently vocabulary has abandoned him. I snort softly. Then glance at him.

"Can I ask *you* something?"

"Of course."

"What's your plan?" I gesture around the apartment. "Are you staying here for a while? Getting your own place? What about your parents?" I lift a hand quickly. "I'm not trying to get rid of you. I'm genuinely asking."

He just smiles. "Oh, I don't know," he says casually. "Might stay close to that redheaded spitfire."

My eyes narrow. He grins wider. "To answer your question, my parents passed eight years ago. No siblings. No real family left."

Some of the humor drains from the room. "I'm sorry."

He shrugs lightly, but his eyes soften. "Appreciate it." Then the mischief returns. "As much as I'd love to freeload off you lovely ladies forever, I think *we* are looking to find a place to lease."

My stomach flips. "We?"

He gives me a pointed look. "Yes. We."

Absolutely not. I open my mouth. Nothing comes out. He smirks and returns to the stove.

"Are you hungry? I can start dinner." He knows exactly what he did.

"Yes," I mutter. "I can help."

"Good."

He nods toward the cabinets. "Grab me a skillet."

I do, because apparently I'm participating now. He browns the meat while I dice tomatoes and onions. There's something weirdly normal about it. Domestic. Comfortable. Dangerous in an entirely different way, a way that fills me with hope for a better future.

The scent of seasoning fills the apartment. I'm shredding lettuce when the front door opens. Fallon walks in, drops her bag, sniffs once, then freezes.

"Why does it smell like a handsome man cooks here now?" Jake nearly drops the spatula laughing.

"I'll cook for you anytime, Sunset. It's done, let's start eating." He announces.

"Thank God, I'm starving," Fallon announces the second she walks over and starts loading tacos like she's competing professionally. Without waiting for permission, she slides into the seat beside Jake, or maybe it's by design. A second later, Wade comes out of my room. Taking the empty seat beside me, my pulse trips over itself. I get my first good look at him since they got back. He changed into jeans. Dark green knit sweater pushed over broad shoulders. The fabric fits too well. The jeans should be illegal. I hate how fucking good he looks.

We eat in silence. The kind of silence so thick it has personality. Forks scrape. Shells crack. Ice clinks in glasses. Every few seconds I swear someone looks at me. Whenever I glance up, they're suddenly very interested in their food. Cowards.

"This is delicious!" Fallon blurts, making me jump.

Jake points at himself proudly. "You see? I told you I make good tacos."

Fallon and I roll our eyes in perfect sync. He looks offended. She keeps talking through dinner. Animatedly. Wild hand gestures. Stories about class, trying to explain to them about astrophysics and what she does. A professor who wears sandals year-round. A girl in her seminar who cried over MLA formatting. Whenever she isn't talking, she's shoving taco bites into her mouth at record speed. She is absolutely over-performing.

Either trying to impress Jake or distract from the awkwardness. Possibly both. Jake matches her energy easily. They bounce from topic to topic while I stay quiet. Wade barely speaks either. But I feel him. Every glance, every shift in posture. Every second of his attention pressed against my skin.

Then Fallon casually detonates the table. "Did you tell them what happened today?"

Wade's eyes lift straight to me. "What happened today?"

"Oh, nothing," Fallon says too brightly. "Just some students asking questions."

His jaw tightens. "What kind of questions?"

I sigh. "Just details."

"What details?"

"The mission. Me. You."

His stare sharpens. "And what did you tell them?"

I finally look right at him. "I didn't tell them anything." My voice comes out colder than I expect. "It's an ongoing investigation." I hold his gaze. "And I thought you knew I don't like sharing my personal life."

The words land harder than I mean them to or maybe exactly as hard as I mean them to. Before he can answer, I stand, take my plate to the sink, and walk straight to my room. I shut the door behind me. My hands are shaking. I don't know what I'm feeling but mostly it's anger, followed closely by embarrassment. Hurt, all of it mixed together. I'm barely two breaths into being alone when footsteps approach.

Heavy. Certain. The door opens. His combat boots step inside. My eyes drop instantly to them, scuffed leather and laces tight. I trace upward before I can stop myself. Jeans hugging powerful thighs. Sweater stretched across a chest I know too well. Strong throat. Stubble-shadowed jaw. Then those eyes, golden brown and locked on mine. My breath catches.

"Hey, beautiful." His voice is low enough to slide over skin. "I didn't mean it like that." He steps farther inside, closing the door behind him. "I know you'd never share anything personal."

I say nothing. Because silence feels safer. "Can we please talk?" Another step forward. "I know you hate me." His expression shifts. "But please?"

Damn him. Damn the way one look from him can crack every defense I build. This is what happened before. He wore me down patiently. Smiled through every wall. Told me he'd break them one by one and then he did. He walks closer until he's standing next to my bed, too close now. He's so handsome, I hate that I've never seen him dressed like this before. No uniform. No tactical gear. Just a devastatingly attractive man in jeans and a green sweater making the color of his eyes look brighter. I fold my arms tightly across my chest. Mostly to hold myself together.

He looks sad, not quite broken, just devastated. Contrite enough that it makes me want to punch him. Honestly, knowing how well punching went last time, I should probably kick instead. More force. Better reach. I don't know when I became so violence-forward, but Jake calls it character growth.

"I don't hate you," I whisper. The words feel dangerous. Because hate would be easier.

His eyes soften immediately. "You look beautiful." My jaw tightens. "I've thought about you every second we've been apart."

I grit my teeth so hard it hurts. "Even when you were with other girls?"

The question slips out before I can stop it. I hadn't meant to ask. Not yet. Maybe not ever. But there it is now, ugly and exposed between us.

His expression changes instantly, into fierce determination. "Like I said this morning, there is only you." He steps closer, voice low and steady. "Only you since the day we met." Something in my chest twists. "I know how that call sounded," he continues. "But I swear to you, she just showed up." I say nothing. "She was the childhood friend I told you about. The neighbor."

I remember him telling me vaguely. Old history. Still annoying.

"She saw me arrive at my parents' house and came over." His mouth hardens. "Said she wanted to check on me. Offer condolences."

My brows knit. "Condolences?"

He exhales slowly. "Well..." His gaze drops for the first time since entering the room. "I thought maybe before I fixed things with you—" He gestures vaguely between us. I lift one eyebrow, bold of him to assume. "—I should at least close that chapter of my life."

I remain silent. He scrubs a hand over his jaw. "I hadn't checked in on my parents in twelve years." My chest tightens slightly. He told me enough before for that to make sense. "They never contacted me either. Drinking, partying… themselves first. Always." His voice has gone flatter now. Detached. Like facts he learned not to bleed over. "Well, apparently my dad died last year. Bar fight. Guy had a gun."

My hand flies to my mouth. "Oh my God."

He gives one humorless shrug. "They never told me." The horror on my face must show because his eyes flick up. "My mom said she didn't see the point."

My stomach turns. Who says that to their child? Who does that?

I whisper before I can stop myself. "They never told you?"

"No." The word is simple. Heavy. "She was drunk by six p.m. Didn't seem to understand why it mattered."

Something inside me softens despite myself. Damn him. Damn this.

"I'm sorry," I say quietly.

He watches me carefully. "Thank you." Then continues. "The neighbor showed up while I was there. Told me she was divorced. Started hovering." I can picture it. He's so handsome, strong, warm, who wouldn't want him? "She made me uncomfortable," he says bluntly. "I wanted to leave. Fast. I wanted to get on the road and get to you."

My pulse jumps traitorously. "I didn't know you were the one calling." His voice roughens. "I didn't know she went upstairs while I was showering." I search his face. There's no arrogance or manipulation, just frustration mixed with regret. Something raw enough to hurt looking at. I believe he's telling the truth. That's the problem. Because I believed him before too and look where that got me.

I'm doing everything in my power not to rub my stomach. Apparently that's becoming a thing now. My new nervous tell. Hands drift there when I'm anxious. When I'm scared. When I'm thinking too hard. Right now I am all three. Part of me wonders if I should tell him. The other part reminds me to stay strong. To remember how quickly he breaks through every defense I build. How dangerous that is.

"I'm so sorry," I say quietly. "I know you weren't close to your dad, but that still couldn't have been easy to hear."

"It wasn't." His gaze stays locked on mine. "But I'll be okay." Then his voice lowers. "I know I'll be a better dad to our children."

My head snaps up. Our children? Does he know? My pulse stumbles hard but I force my face blank. Jake said he didn't tell him.

Fallon said she didn't tell him. So why would he say that? Plural, no less. I school every feature I can.

Inside, I'm chaos. "You sound very sure of a future with us," I say after a beat, my voice tighter than I want. "For someone who didn't want me anymore."

Pain flashes across his face so fast it almost looks like anger. We stare at each other for several long seconds. Then he clears his throat, steps forward and drops to his knees in front of me. The movement shocks me enough I freeze. He reaches for my hand. I pull it back before he can touch me.

His jaw flexes once. Then he nods like he expected that. "I will never stop wanting you." His voice is rough now. Quiet. Honest enough to hurt. "I can't begin to tell you how sorry I am." He looks up at me from where he kneels. "If you let me, I'd like to explain everything."

I say nothing. "I know it won't undo how it ended. And I know I blamed myself for what happened to you." My throat tightens. "But I'm too selfish to stay away from you."

I swallow hard, then nod once. Telling him to go on. That's why he's here. So he tells me, everything. Waking up on the ship. Learning I'd gone home. How long he'd been unconscious. How the man outside his room was one of his closest friends following lockdown protocol. How no one meant to hurt me. How they mishandled everything anyway. He needed to get out of his own head, he thought for a minute I deserved better because he failed me. That park nearly broke me, I'm safe because of him. His child is safe because of him. It started wearing on him, what happened with Jamo and Ghost and comparing it to me. The guys were all yelling at him. How he tried to contact me. How I blocked him. How he drove straight here once he was free.

I start crying halfway through and hate myself for it. Because I'm tired of crying over this man. Over all of it. He reaches for my hand again. This time, I let him. His fingers close around mine carefully. Like I'm something fragile.

"I'm sorry," he says again.

I shake my head. "No." My voice breaks. "I'm sorry how it went down too." I wipe at my face with my free hand.

"But you all lied to me." His grip tightens slightly. "You were in the next room basically dying from a gunshot wound and no one said anything."

He closes his eyes briefly. "Then Nick tells me the next day like it's information I can calmly process." I'm crying harder now. "You could have died." My chest heaves. "And no one would tell me."

He bows his head. I keep going because once it starts, I can't stop. "Despite all of that, I still needed to see you." My voice drops to a whisper. "I needed to feel you. To know you were alive. To know I mattered and I was turned away." I pull my hand from his.

Fresh hurt rises, hot and immediate.

"Like I was nothing to you. Then on top of that to learn you had a full background check before you even met me, thinking everything between us was staged. I was just something easy and available to you when I thought you truly loved me."

"Mouse, please don't ever apologize." His voice is wrecked. "This is on me." He looks up at me from where he's kneeling, regret written into every line of his face. "I didn't want you worrying about me. I told Stitches to protect you. I knew I wasn't dying," he says quietly. "But even if I had been you're right. I wouldn't have wanted you to see me like that. As for everything else, we do get reports on civilians, but, Beautiful? Bumping into you in that airport like that, it was a chance meeting. Meant to be, I didn't stage it. Everything between us was real, from the moment you bumped into me. Every moment was real, my love for you is real."

I stare at him. Honest. Infuriating. Still trying to shield me even now.

"I don't know," I whisper. My chest aches with the truth of it. "I don't know what to do. I'm scared to trust you." The words hang heavy between us. "It was horrible, what happened to me." My voice shakes harder now. "But through all of it, I thought *we* were okay."

Tears spill faster. "I thought whatever else was broken, *that* wasn't." His eyes close briefly. "Then I was sent away like I meant nothing to you." I swipe at my face angrily. "Like I meant nothing to any of you."

He flinches. "Like those six weeks never happened." I suck in a ragged breath. "I've spent the last month trying to convince myself I was just stupid." My voice cracks. "That I was just some convenient fuck."

The sob that tears out of me is loud and ugly and impossible to stop. He surges upward instinctively, then checks himself like touching me without permission would break something sacred.

"Little Mouse." His voice is shattered. "I am so sorry I made you feel that way."

He rises slowly to his feet in front of me now, close enough to touch, careful enough not to. "You are everything to me." My heart hurts so badly it feels physical. "If you let me, I'll prove it." He swallows hard.

"I swear to God, I would not be standing here if I didn't believe my whole future was right in front of me." He has no idea how true that sentence really is. No idea what future is already growing inside me. I try to calm my breathing. He reaches forward slowly, giving me time to stop him, and takes my hands again. Warm and steady. Every few seconds his thumbs brush my knuckles.

"Fuck," he mutters roughly. "It's killing me not to hold you." My resolve fractures further. Because it's killing me too. I pull my hands free and stand. Pacing two steps away because if I stay close, I might cave completely.

"I don't know what to do." I repeat. He turns with me immediately. "How do I let go of all the hurt from the last month?" My arms wrap around myself. "I don't know if I should keep you away to protect myself…" I meet his eyes. "Or give you another chance."

"Please give me one." No hesitation. "I promise I won't leave your side." Emotion crosses his face so openly it almost undoes me.

"I don't know if I can," I whisper. "I don't know if I can really trust you."

His expression crumples. Then, slowly, carefully, he steps forward. Giving me every chance to move away. When I don't, he wraps his arms around my waist and sinks to his knees again, pressing his face against my stomach. The contact steals the breath from my lungs. His arms tighten. Like he's holding onto the only thing keeping him upright.

"I will prove it," he says against me. His voice muffled. I stare up at the man standing before me, holding me like I'm precious. I don't know if I believe him but I know a very large part of me desperately wants to.

Chapter Thirty Five

Wade

I wake to sunlight spilling through Sarah's curtains and blinds in warm gold bands across the bed. She's curled against me. One arm wrapped over my ribs. One leg tangled with mine. Her face tucked into my chest like sometime during the night her body decided I was safe again, even if her mind hasn't caught up. The bed is too small. My feet hang half off the edge.

My shoulder is jammed against the wall and I've never been more comfortable in my life. We're used to worse. Weeks in a cramped tent with jungle heat, bad sleep and barely enough room to breathe. I'd take this over any luxury bed on earth. I don't know what time she usually wakes up. I know she set an alarm last night, but I didn't look at it. I was too busy listening to her voice in the dark.

We talked for hours. Really talked. Painful things. Necessary things. If not for hearing how badly I hurt her, it would've been perfect. Just lying there with her in my arms again. She told me about Carly. How quiet she still is. How much her roommate Fallon has apparently turned into the most supportive person. She's been helping through everything. How they helped reunite her with her family. Sarah passed along her number to Carly's parents but she hasn't heard from them yet. Understandable. Healing doesn't happen on a schedule. I lie there thinking through a hundred ways to earn Sarah's trust back. What kind of gifts to buy her, flowers is a no brainer but I want something more personal. I know I need to have patience and persistence. Two things I know well through my time in the Special Forces. I will start with dinners and keep proving I will never leave her side again.

Then I hear a whimper. Soft at first. Then another. Her body tightens in sleep. The sound breaks into a cry that turns quickly into a scream. I'm moving before I'm fully aware of what's happening. I roll her gently onto her back and crawl over her, thinking maybe the shift will pull her out of it.

Instead she screams louder. Pure terror.

"Sarah." Nothing.

"Sarah, wake up." Her hands thrash once against the sheets.

"Sarah!" Her eyes snap open. Wild. Unfocused. Breathing hard. That look hits me like a blade straight through the chest. I run my fingers through her hair, pushing it back from her face.

"It's me. You're okay." I kiss her forehead. Then again. I remember how that used to calm her. Her palms come up against my bare chest. Grounding herself. Checking I'm real.

She stares up at me, still breathing too fast. "Are you okay?" I ask softly. She nods. But tears are already gathering at the corners of her eyes.

I wipe one away with my thumb. "What was it about?"

She swallows. "That day. Mostly." My jaw tightens. "Sometimes it's Benjamin trying to get further than he did." Rage flashes hot and immediate. "But you always stop it."

I lower my head and kiss her forehead again. "Sometimes," she whispers, "I see what happened to Carly instead." Her voice cracks. "And I can't stop it."

Jesus Christ. I roll back to my side and pull her into me carefully, keeping pressure off my healing ribs. She comes willingly. Like instinct still remembers us.

"I will always protect you, I will always come for you." I murmur into her hair. The promise feels carved into bone. "Have they been happening a lot?"

"Yes." A small pause. "Most nights." I close my eyes. "I thought it was getting better," she says quietly. "Maybe you being here brought it back to the surface."

Guilt moves through me sharp and clean. "I've been having them too."

She tilts her head slightly against me. "Yeah?"

"Mostly seeing your body on that bed." The words taste like acid. "Not moving." I tighten my hold unconsciously. "Sometimes Jamo. Sometimes Ghost." Old ghosts. Old failures. The ones that never fully leave. She goes still for a second.

Then softer than breath, "I'm sorry."

I frown. "For what?"

"I wish you weren't hurting." That nearly undoes me. Even wrecked. Even healing. Even after everything. She still trying to comfort other people.

"Don't be sorry." I tighten my arms around her, fitting her closer against me. "Being with you helps." It's the simplest truth I know. "The therapy will help too." I brush my mouth over her temple. "Have you thought about seeing someone?"

"Yes," she says softly. "I've been looking."

"Good." I mean it. She deserves every tool that helps her heal. Every ounce of peace she can claw back. I settle deeper into the mattress with her tucked against me. She feels softer than she did in the jungle. A little fuller through her hips, her stomach, her thighs. Healthy. Safe. It looks fucking beautiful on her. More than that, it eases something ugly that's lived in my chest since I lost her.

She's taking care of herself or at least trying to. She won't have to anymore, I will be taking care of her now. Getting her anything she wants or needs. We stay like that for a long time. Morning light creeping higher. The apartment is quiet.

I press slow kisses along the side of her neck. Behind her ear. Across her shoulder. Nothing demanding. Just learning her again. Eventually the tension leaves her body piece by piece. Her breathing evens out. She falls back asleep in my arms. I stay another minute, watching her, before I carefully slide out of bed. I pull on sweats, grab my shirt, before step into the kitchen.

Glitch is at the counter making coffee. Only wearing boxers.

I stop dead. "You better not have been walking around like that in front of my girl."

He doesn't even turn around. "Why? Worried she'll take one look at me and dump your sorry ass?"

He stirs sugar into his mug like a menace. I glare. "No. I'm worried she'll throw up."

He finally looks at me. Offended for half a second. Then the smirk comes back. "Rude."

He takes a sip. Not black. Creamer and sugar. I stare harder. "What happened to you?"

"What?"

"You drink coffee like a chick now."

He shrugs. "I've evolved."

I grunt and pour my own cup black. The way civilized people do it.

He leans against the counter. "Maybe I'm not trying to impress Sarah."

I glance at him sideways. "No?"

"Nope." That smug look says everything. "There's another girl here I wouldn't mind noticing me."

I smirk despite myself. "Fallon?"

He grins wider. "She hits hard."

"You earned it."

"Worth everything I've been through."

I shake my head and take a drink. Then I remember. "Yeah, how did it go with Alex? You meet with her?"

The grin fades some. "No." He looks down into his mug. "I just went to the storage unit she rented." Damn. "Found some of my stuff. Some things from my parents too."

His voice is lighter than it should be. Detached. The way guys talk when something still hurts. "Once we get settled into the house, I'll make another trip and pack the rest."

I nod slowly. "Did you get your ring back?"

His jaw flexes. "No. Guess I'll have to ask what she did with it." He looks irritated now. "I've been avoiding talking to her."

"Yeah," I say quietly. "I'm sorry, man."

He shrugs once. "Could be worse."

But we both know it cut deep. "Maybe when I go back," he says, "we all make a road trip out of it."

I snort. "You trying to trick us into helping you move?"

"Absolutely."

Then his expression turns more serious. "I don't want to see her alone." That honesty lands heavier than he probably meant it to. "I'm ready to move on."

He glances toward Fallon's closed door. "Start over."

I follow his look and smirk. "Fast worker."

He points at me with his mug. "Don't judge me. You moved Sarah into your tent in just two days."

"Fair." He lifts his mug in salute. We drink in silence for a second. Then I look back toward Sarah's room. Toward the woman sleeping in her bed. Toward the life I almost lost.

"I'm trying to start over too," I say.

Glitch nods once. "Then don't screw it up this time."

"Yeah, that's the plan," I say, leaning back against the counter. Changing the subject because I already know I need to do everything I can not to fuck it up. "Driving to Kansas and back wouldn't be bad."

Glitch nods, sipping his coffee. "Did you talk to that realtor about the loft?"

"Yeah." He brightens instantly. "If it all works out, we can move in a couple weeks."

We. This asshole really did decide he lives here now.

"I talked to the guys too," he continues. "They're all slowly making their way here. Once everyone lands, we can start working on our plans." That part matters. The next chapter. Starting over as civilians, something built by choice instead of command, deployments, blood and orders. No handlers. No chain of command. No waiting for the next mission to decide where we sleep or whether we live. Just men trying to figure out who the hell they are when the war finally stops following them. Something real. Something ours.

Reaper and Stitches already decided they're coming out first. Neither one said it with any emotion, just the usual version of loyalty they pass off as annoyance. Reaper claimed somebody had to keep us from making stupid decisions. Stitches said someone needed to keep us alive once we no longer had military doctors and regulations babysitting us.

Which, translated, means they're in. Ghost is taking a detour to see his mother first. He hasn't spent much time with her since Jamo's funeral. Hasn't spent much time with anyone, if we're being honest. He still shuts down anytime his little brother's name comes up, jaw going tight, eyes going empty. I don't know how long he'll stay there, or if he'll even talk once he does. But maybe being home will do something the rest of us never could.

The last two coming are Sparta and Magellan. They have real families waiting on them. Parents who answer calls, siblings actually excited to see them again. Homes where people ask when they're arriving and mean it and from what I understand, enough nieces and nephews between them to form their own small platoon. No one gives them shit for taking time first. They've spent years bleeding beside us. If they need a little while to remember who they are outside the job, they've earned that too. Still, once they get here, once we're all in one place, maybe for the first time in our lives, we get to build something that isn't temporary.

Then he grins. "Now I just need to convince Fallon to move in with me."

I bark out a laugh. "Yeah. Good luck with that."

He shrugs like he enjoys impossible missions. "I've definitely got my work cut out for me."

Then his expression shifts serious. After a beat, he nods toward the hallway. "Was she having a nightmare?"

"Yeah." I glance toward her closed door.

"Did she have one the night before?"

"Not that I heard."

I finish my coffee just as Sarah's alarm starts chirping from the bedroom. I grab two fresh mugs.

"Put some fucking clothes on, man," I call over my shoulder. "No one wants to see your junk first thing in the morning."

Glitch starts laughing. "Speak for yourself!" Fallon yells through her closed bedroom door.

I freeze. Then hear Glitch choking on his coffee. Noted. Thin walls. I step back into Sarah's room and shut the door behind me. She's sitting upright in bed, blanket around her waist, phone in her hand. The dark circles under her eyes are worse after the nightmare. But that's not what stops me. It's the look on her face.

Sadness, hurt and underneath both—anger. I cross to her slowly and hand her the coffee. She takes it without a word. Then hands me the phone. Mine. I frown and glance down. A text notification fills the screen.

Unknown Number: Wade thanks for the great time and giving me your number...

The rest is cut off. My blood goes cold. River. Jesus Christ. I look up fast. Sarah is already standing. Before I can speak, she storms past me and slams herself into the bathroom.

The lock clicks. "Little Mouse—"

Nothing. "It's not what it looks like." My voice sounds pathetic even to me. "I know how stupid that sounds, but I swear to you, I never touched her. I was trying to get away from her."

I press a hand to the door. "Please believe me. I would never do that

401

to you."

Then I hear it. Soft crying from the other side. It guts me cleaner than any blade ever has. I stand there helpless. Five minutes. Ten. Maybe more. Eventually the lock clicks.

The door opens. She steps out with wet cheeks and red-rimmed eyes, like she tried to wash the hurt off her face and failed. She doesn't look at me. Doesn't speak. Just brushes past me and starts yanking clothes from drawers.

My chest tightens. "Sarah—"

Nothing. She grabs an armful and disappears back into the bathroom. The lock clicks again. I stare at the door. Then lower myself to the floor beside it, back against the wall, shoulders slumped. Wondering if kicking the damn thing in would somehow be easier than this. She doesn't come out for thirty minutes. Thirty of the longest minutes of my life.

I stay on the floor outside the bathroom door the whole time, listening to water run, drawers open, cabinet doors shut. No crying now. No sound at all, really. That's somehow worse. When the lock finally clicks, I'm on my feet before I realize I moved. I feel the hitch in my side, pulling at my still healing wound from moving too fast.

She steps out fully dressed. Black slacks. Blue blouse. Boots. Hair curled in soft waves around her shoulders. Makeup brushed carefully over skin that was tear-streaked half an hour ago. She looks beautiful. Untouchable. Like she built armor while I sat outside the door. Her eyes are brighter from the makeup.

Redder from crying. She grabs her backpack and starts moving around the room, shoving notebooks, folders, pens, chargers, whatever she can reach into it. Purposeful. Efficient. Avoiding me like I'm poison.

"Sarah, please—" She lifts one hand. I stop instantly.

"Just don't." Her voice is thin from crying and somehow still sharp enough to cut. "I'm going to school." She zips the bag hard. "I have things to do for my dissertation."

Then finally looks at me. "I think it might be best if you left." The words hit center mass. "And take Jake with you." My jaw clenches. "I don't know how to feel about you. I don't know if I can trust you."

Jesus Christ. "Beautiful, you *can* trust me." I step closer carefully. "I promise you, that's not what it looked like." She says nothing. "I didn't do anything with her." Another step. "I never touched her."

Her eyes shine silver-grey with tears she refuses to let fall.

"The only reason she has my number is because I told her to give it to her parents." I hear how insane that sounds and hate myself. "In case something happens to my mom, they can reach me."

Silence stretches. She studies my face for several long seconds. Searching my face, weighing my words, wondering if they are true. Looking for cracks.

"I need to go," she says finally. Every word sounds like effort. I nod once because if I speak, I might beg. She shoulders the backpack. Then stops at the door. "I want you gone by the time I get back."

The finality in it hollows me out. She shoves on her shoes, grabs her keys, before walks into the living room. Glitch starts to say something. Fallon does too. Sarah ignores both of them. The front door slams hard enough to shake the frame. Silence follows. Then both of them turn to me. I walk to the kitchen table, sit in the same chair I was in yesterday, dropping my face into my hands.

No one speaks for a second. "What happened?" Fallon asks first. She already sounds pissed. Protective as hell. Fair. I'm glad Sarah has that, even if her anger is directed at me right now.

"What happened," I say into my palms, "is I'm an idiot."

"I already knew that," Glitch says. "What'd you do *this* time?" I drag my hands down my face and look up.

"That woman from my mom's house."

"The blonde one?" he asks.

"Yes."

"I gave her my number to pass to her parents." Both of them stare. "In case my mom dies and they need to reach me."

Glitch blinks once. Then twice. "That sucks."

I deadpan at him. "Thanks for stating the fucking obvious."

He shrugs. "I'm trying to support you. I also told you not to fuck up anymore."

Fallon crosses her arms. "Did something happen with her?"

"No." My answer is immediate. "Nothing happened." I look toward the door Sarah just walked through. "I only want Sarah. I gave the number because apparently my dad died while I was deployed and no one told me."

Both of them go still. "So," I continue, voice flat, "if my mom drinks herself into the grave, I figured someone should let me know this time."

Fallon's anger fades into something more complicated. Glitch just watches me and for the first time in a long time, I have no idea how the hell to fix anything.

"Shit, man." Glitch leans back against the counter, coffee in hand. "No one told you he died?" I shake my head once.

"That must've been a shock."

"Yeah." I stare at nothing for a second. "It was." Then I shrug. "And not really, either." Because when two people spend their lives drinking themselves stupid and chasing the next party, you always know how the story probably ends. You just don't expect to find out a year late. Fallon studies me more carefully now. She's hard to read when she wants to be.

Tall for a woman, nearly eye level with Glitch, with the kind of athletic build that says strength wasn't handed to her, it was earned. Thick red hair falls in wild waves around her shoulders, impossible to ignore, and those sharp green eyes miss damn near nothing. She carries herself like someone used to handling her own problems. Maybe everyone else's too.

Even in leggings and an oversized sweatshirt, there's something deliberate about her, practical, capable, no wasted movement. The apartment smells faintly like coffee, dish soap, and that eucalyptus scent that seems to follow her everywhere. But what stands out most isn't how she looks. It's the way she keeps positioning herself between me and Sarah without even thinking about it. Protective. Alert. Ready to go to war for her friend at a second's notice. I respect that. Hell, I'm grateful for it. Sarah needed someone in the last month when I wasn't here. Looks like she had Fallon.

"Does Sarah know about your parents?" Fallon asks quietly.

"Yeah." I nod. "Told her some of it when we were deployed." My jaw tightens. "Told her about my dad last night."

Fallon exhales and leans her hip against the counter. "I think it's hard for her to know if she can trust you." No accusation. Just fact. "You really broke her heart."

The words land harder than getting shot. "You tossed her into a future of complete unknowns," she continues. "Before she left, her life was mapped out. School. Research. Graduation. Everything."

I say nothing. Because she's right. "Then you came in and made her feel…" Fallon searches for the word. "Chosen." My chest tightens. "You made her feel loved. Desired."

She folds her arms. "And that matters, because trust me, I've watched men flirt with her for years."

Jake snorts. "She never noticed?"

"Not once," Fallon says dryly. "It all went straight over her head."

I almost smile. That sounds exactly like Sarah.

"You were the first man who ever got through to her." Fallon's gaze hardens. "Then she got sent away alone." My stomach drops. "In her mind, everything was a lie." I close my eyes briefly. Every version of this keeps coming back to the same truth. I failed her.

Jake points at Fallon. "How come *you're* helping him?" She raises a brow. "When I showed up, I got punched."

"You startled me."

"You committed assault."

"You survived." He grins. I drag a hand down my face.

"How do I fix this with her?" Both of them go quiet. I hate how desperate I sound. Fallon must take pity on me.

Finally she sighs. "I'll show you where to find her today."

I straighten immediately. "She doesn't have classes. She's working on dissertation stuff."

Hope flickers sharp and dangerous. "While I get ready," she says, pointing at me, "you need to go buy flowers, chocolate, or something thoughtful."

Jake mutters, "God help us."

Then Fallon steps closer to me. "Make no mistake." Her voice turns terrifyingly calm. "If you hurt her again, I will rip your balls off and feed them to him."

She points at Jake. Both of us stare at her. Jake slowly lowers his coffee. "Why am *I* involved?"

"Accessory, liability." She shrugs.

I nod quickly. "Understood."

Chapter Thirty Six

Wade

An hour later, I'm walking across campus beside Fallon. Jake came too. Claimed he didn't want to be alone. Reality was he wants front-row seats to my suffering. I changed fast after Fallon left, then ran to the Target down the road like I was assaulting an objective. Spent twenty damn minutes standing in the card aisle like a confused hostage.

Eventually I bought, a bouquet of roses, a box of chocolates and a small stuffed bear. It's not ideal, I wish it was more personalized, something that actually means something to her, I just don't have time. Tonight I will look into more, I plan on spoiling her as much as I can. Now I feel ridiculous. I'm six-four, built like a threat. Walking beside Jake, who's only a couple inches shorter and somehow smugger than anyone alive.

On my other side is Fallon, tiny and redheaded and striding like she commands a battalion. We absolutely look insane. Students openly stare as we pass. Some glance at the flowers and the bear in my hand. Some are staring openly at me, probably trying to determine if this is romantic or criminal. Given my track record lately, fair question.

I shift the bouquet in one hand.

Jake grins. "Nervous?"

"No."

"You're crushing those roses."

I look down. Bent stems. "Shit."

Fallon sighs dramatically. "This is going to be harder than I thought."

We enter the building and move down a long hallway that opens into a larger office space. Next to one door is a plaque that reads Grad Student Lounge. There's a keypad mounted beside it. At least they take security seriously here.

Fallon punches in the code without slowing down and pushes the door open. Inside, a couple students glance up from laptops and coffee cups before going back to whatever they were doing. I scan the room automatically. All the corners, exits and faces. Sarah isn't here.

"Wait here," Fallon says. She crosses the room and talks quietly with two people near the back. Glitch drifts beside me, hands in his pockets, pretending to be relaxed. I know better. He's scanning too. Training doesn't switch off just because you change clothes.

Fallon returns a minute later. "She was here earlier," she says. "Left not long ago."

My chest tightens. "Where?"

"She might be downstairs in the photography lab." We're moving again before she finishes the sentence. We follow this five-foot-nothing redheaded menace through another set of halls, down a stairwell, and into the basement. The air changes down there. It's cooler and a lot quieter. My skin prickles. That old instinct crawls awake between my shoulder blades.

Watched. I sweep the corridor casually. I don't see anything obvious, there's no one down here, no movement. No sound except our footsteps. Beside me, Glitch alternates between checking sightlines and blatantly watching Fallon when she isn't looking. I cut him a glance. He grins without shame. I file that away for later. He just got out of a long-term mess. If he's looking for a rebound, he's not doing it in Sarah's apartment. I already brought enough chaos into her life.

The basement hallway stretches long and narrow with a series of closed doors. Just concrete walls, doors and no windows. The fluorescent hum overhead. I hate the idea of Sarah being down here alone. There's a part of me that still believes danger is one corner away. That she still isn't safe. Maybe she never will be, not in my head.

Fallon stops outside a room and looks back at us. "I don't know how familiar you two are with darkrooms," she says dryly.

"We're not," Glitch answers.

"If she's developing photographs, we wait. If we open the door, we can ruin everything."

I nod once. Understood. She punches another code into the outer photography lab and lets us inside. The room opens wide, tables, computer stations, cutting mats, printers and supply shelves. At the far side is another door. A red light glows above it. That must be the darkroom.

Fallon walks over and knocks lightly. "Sarah! It's Fallon. Can you come out?"

A muffled voice answers from inside. "Yes! One minute!"

My pulse jumps at the sound of her voice, relief just hearing her, knowing she's close, alive, safe. Right there. I move to one of the tables and sit before I pace holes into the floor. I set the flowers and gift bag in front of me. Suddenly feeling like an idiot carrying roses into a basement lab like some oversized teenager begging for prom.

Glitch leans against a counter, smirking. "You've adjusted those flowers three times again."

I look down. "Shut up." Then all I can do is stare at that red-lit door and wait for her to come back to me. On the opposite side of the room from the hallway entrance sits the second door. I've never developed a picture in my life. Never had time for hobbies that required patience, precision or standing still in the dark. Unless it's for an op with a rifle in my hands. So I have no idea what she's doing in there. Only that it matters to her. Which means it matters to me.

Glitch drops into the chair across from me and leans it back onto two legs, angled so he can watch both me and the main entrance. Relaxed on the outside. Working security on the inside. I debate asking them both to leave when she comes out. Part of me wants to talk to her alone. Part of me knows if I corner her right now, she might bolt.

"Did you get that feeling of being watched when we came down here?" Glitch asks quietly.

So it wasn't just me. "Yeah." I keep my eyes on the door. "I felt it." Then lower, "I've got this feeling none of this is over."

He studies me. "With her?"

"With Benjamin. The whole thing." My jaw tightens. "Feels like something else is coming."

He nods once. "Do we know how the investigation's going with the

FBI?"

A humorless laugh leaves me. "No. You know that asshole won't tell us shit." Special Agent Ramsey liked to talk like he was running the world. Liked even more talking to us like we were blunt instruments he tolerated.

"I don't think it'd hurt to call him," Glitch says. I hear the amusement in his voice. He knows exactly how much I disliked Ramsey.

"And say what?" I glance at him. "Hey, I'm stalking Sarah on campus, mind giving me a case update?"

He grins. "No. Ask about the investigation." Then shrugs. "If he gets vague, ask specifically whether the people involved are still detained."

"Yeah. Fine." I rub my jaw. "I'll call him tonight. Or I'll have Ghost hack something open."

Glitch snorts. "Subtle."

"Who are you calling?" Every muscle in my body locks at the sound of her voice. "And what are you hacking?"

I'm on my feet before I realize I moved, Sarah stands just outside the darkroom door, one hand braced on her hip. Her beautiful chestnut hair is pulled into a ponytail, exposing the graceful line of her neck I know too damn well. Something about that look, practical, irritated and all business, hits me harder than it should. She looks tired. The exhaustion is there around her eyes and annoyance. Definitely annoyance. But she's here. Looking at me.

"Hey, Little Mouse." My voice softens automatically. "You look beautiful." I reach for the bouquet and the small gift bag. "I got you these."

In the corner of my vision, Fallon casually drifts away and ends up beside Glitch. Giving us space. Smart woman. I focus on Sarah again. Her eyes hold more blue than grey right now. Less storm, more wounded sky. I've learned to read those eyes better than maps or terrain. They're softer than this morning. Not soft enough but softer. Maybe I'm not dead in the water yet. Maybe that psychopath from Missouri didn't finish sinking me.

"Thank you," she whispers. Quiet enough I almost miss it. Her fingers close around the flowers, then the little gift bag. She glances behind me and back again so fast most people wouldn't catch it. I do. Her cheeks flush pink. That soft rosy color I've always loved. Embarrassed.

I turn to see Glitch and Fallon openly watching us like this is premium entertainment.

"Guys," I say flatly. "A little privacy."

Glitch grins wider. Fallon rolls her eyes. "Rambo, come on," she says to Jake. "You can walk me to class." Then she looks at Sarah. "Sarah, I have my phone on me. Let me know if you need anything. I can bring you food if you're hungry. You didn't eat this morning." She says it pointedly.

Like there's a second meaning I'm not getting. "I can take care of her," I cut in. "I'll get anything she needs."

Fallon gives me a look that tells me she thinks I'm an idiot. Glitch laughs. What the hell am I missing? Is she sick, has she not been taking care of herself? They head for the door. Once it shuts behind them, the room goes quiet.

I turn back to Sarah and she looks worried. That alone puts me on alert.

"What's going on?" I step closer. "Are you sick?" Her eyes lift to mine, thoughtful, uncertain. Like she's deciding what truth to hand me.

After a long breath, she shakes her head. "No. I'm not sick."

The wording catches somewhere in my brain.

Before I can grab it, she continues. "I'm at a good stopping point for the day." She shifts the flowers in her hands. "I know we need to talk." My stomach drops. "Should we walk back to my place?"

I was uneasy before. Now I'm on edge. No phrase in the English language has ever ended well after *we need to talk*.

"Sure, beautiful." I keep my voice steady. "Let's gather your things. I'll walk you back."

"I just need to grab stuff from the darkroom. Then my bag upstairs."

She steps backward, holding the inner door open. A small invitation but I'll take anything she gives me. I follow her inside. She shuts the door behind us and flips on the light. The room glows red. Low, strange, almost unreal.

Chemical scent hangs in the air. Metal trays filled with liquid sit on a center table. Clips and wire lines stretch overhead. Photographs hang drying in rows. I move closer. The first one stops me cold. Me. Sitting on a bench in the shabono talking to Ghost, unaware she'd taken it. Another shows Yanomami women weaving baskets, hands blurred mid-motion. Another jewelry laid in sunlight. Then I reach the last one. Benjamin, he's staring directly at the camera. Mouth tight, eyes ugly with contempt. Like he knew he was being watched and hated it.

A clean surge of rage tears through me. Hot. Instant. My hands fist so hard my knuckles ache. It takes everything I have not to rip the photograph down and shred it. She shouldn't have to look at him. Shouldn't have to develop his face with her own hands. Shouldn't have to carry one more image of the bastard after what he did. After what he almost did to her.

I keep my voice level through sheer force. "Why keep this one?"

Her soft hands slide up my arm

Then both of them wrap around my bicep. Small fingers trying to circle muscle they can't quite reach around. The contact is gentle. She's trying to comfort me, it nearly wrecks me. I look down slowly, fighting to keep every raw emotion off my face.

"He's gone," she says softly. "He can't hurt me anymore." Her grip tightens. "He can't hurt us anymore."

The word hits me hard enough to hollow out my chest. Us. She still says *us*. I swallow against the knot in my throat. She doesn't know. Doesn't know I'm not convinced he's gone. Doesn't know I've spent every day waiting for the next move.

"I just hate what happened," I say roughly. "I hate myself for ever letting you out of my sight." The truth tastes like blood. "If anything happened to you…" My voice breaks. "I don't think I'd survive it."

She closes her eyes and leans her forehead against my chest. Instinct takes over. I wrap my other arm around her and pull her in close. Mine to hold.

For one selfish second, I do nothing but breathe her in and thank God I found her before something worse happened.

"I did survive," she murmurs against me. "And it's not your fault." I almost laugh at that. It absolutely is. "I should never have trusted Jenna," she continues quietly. "I could have had you come with me." I tighten my hold. "You know what got me through it?"

"No." My throat works hard around the word. We still haven't talked about the worst of it. I read her FBI statement. Every line of it. I'd rather be shot again than read it twice. She steps back enough to look up at me.

"When I started understanding what was happening, I knew I needed to delay Benjamin. Keep him talking." My jaw clenches. "Once I realized my clothes were gone and he hadn't said anything about finding the tracker…"

She places a hand over my heart. "I knew." My pulse pounds under her palm. "I knew you were coming for me." Jesus. "I trusted you wouldn't be far behind." A tear burns hot behind my eyes. "I knew you'd never let me out of your sight the whole time we were there."

Her mouth trembles faintly. "And I knew you were serious about that five-minute warning." Despite everything, a broken laugh leaves her. "You probably didn't even wait the five minutes."

"I didn't." My answer is immediate. Would've burned the jungle down to find her if I had to.

"I had complete faith you were coming," she whispers. "It wasn't until I knew for sure you were there that I could finally relax." She searches my face. "Do you know why?"

I shake my head, though I already do. "Because I felt safe. You were my home." My chest caves inward as I watch a couple of tears slip free and roll down her cheeks. "My comfort. My safety."

"Are."

She blinks. "What?"

I slide two fingers beneath her chin. Lift gently until she's looking directly at me. I need her to see every word.

"You keep saying *were*." My voice is low and steady. "Past tense." I brush away the tear on her cheek. "It's *are*. Present tense." Her breath catches.

"I fucked up." No point pretending otherwise. "But I promise you, Little Mouse..." I lean my forehead to hers. "I am your home." My thumb strokes her jaw. "Your family." My hand settles at her waist. "Your comfort." I press a kiss to the corner of her mouth. "Your safety." Then lower, rough with truth, "I am yours."

Another tear slips down her cheek. "And you are mine."

She closes her eyes and breaks quietly in front of me. I pull her closer and rest my chin on top of her head. She fits there too easily, she was made for every place against me. I don't know if I already broke this beyond repair. Don't know if the damage I caused can be undone. But I know one thing with absolute certainty. I'm not giving up and I'm not going anywhere.

"You're right," I murmur into her hair. "I didn't wait the full five minutes." That earns the smallest breath of laughter against my chest. I'll take it. She stays quiet after that. Then the silence is interrupted by the unmistakable growl of her stomach.

I look down. She flushes instantly. "Come on," I say, smiling despite everything. "Gather your things."

I brush my thumb across her cheek. "I'm taking you to lunch."

We walk hand in hand back to the grad lounge. I carry her bag, careful with the photographs inside. She carries the roses. Every few steps she lowers her face to them and smiles softly. A shy, private smile. The kind I haven't seen since she first collided with me in the airport and tried pretending she wasn't flustered. It hits me harder than it should.

At the lounge she grabs the rest of her things but I notice she keeps glancing over her shoulder. Checking behind us. I wonder if she's been feeling watched too. If I'm not the only one whose instincts are screaming. I say nothing for now. Just take the extra bags and lead us out. We walk back to her apartment still holding hands. She never once tries to pull away. That alone feels like mercy.

At the apartment, she disappears into the bathroom for a few minutes. When she comes back out, her hair is down again, chestnut waves falling around her shoulders.

I stare shamelessly. "You look beautiful." I step close and run my fingers lightly through the strands.

"I love your hair like this." Then quieter, "I also love it up."

Her eyes shift from guarded to softer. I see it happen in real time. Maybe I'm getting through the steel walls she rebuilt around herself again.

"Thank you," she says, trying for casual and almost succeeding. Then points toward the door. "Now feed us." One brow arches. There's that word again, us. She's still giving me a chance.

"I know a great place that's never very busy." There's amusement in her voice now. Another miracle. We head out again.

She takes me to a small diner tucked just off campus. Nothing flashy but it is warm and inviting. Mostly empty. I like it immediately. We slide into a booth near the back, away from everyone else. Private. There's still too much left unsaid.

A waitress drops menus and coffee. The second we're alone, Sarah narrows her eyes at me.

"What are you hacking into?" I blink once. Then remember.

"The FBI," I murmur. Keeping my voice low. Her eyes widen. I can't help laughing.

"Why?" she hisses. "Won't you get in a lot of trouble for that?"

I shrug. "If they catch us." Then wink.

She gives me a look that says *you cannot be serious*. I laugh again. God, I missed making her look at me like that.

"Why do you need to?" she asks.

My smile fades. "I want to know how the investigation's going." My thumb brushes across the back of her hand on the table. "Did they call you?"

"Yeah," she says softly. "A nice agent called me." My brows lift. "It was hard reliving it, but my family was with me, that helped." Her fingers tighten slightly in mine. "The guy mostly listened. He was understanding."

"Do you know the agent's name?"

She thinks for a second. "I think it was Ramsey?" What the hell? Ramsey was *nice*? I'd have believed in mermaids first.

"What?" she asks, eyes narrowing. "Why do you look surprised?"

"I met him." I lean back in the booth. "In person."

"And?"

"And he kept us waiting for weeks while we repeated the same story twelve different ways." Her lips twitch. "I'm pretty sure he got off on thinking he was in charge."

That earns a bright, warm laugh. God, I missed that sound.

"Were you being impatient?" she asks. I squint at her. "When you get impatient, you get grouchy."

I reach across the table and take both her hands. The victory of making her laugh nearly has me beating my chest like a damn gorilla.

"Of course I was impatient." I squeeze gently. "I needed to get to my girl." Then flatly, "He was also an ass."

She giggles again. The waitress appears before I can enjoy it longer.

"Ready to order?"

We both glance at untouched menus. Apparently not. Coffee gets topped off. We order quickly, two burgers and fries. Simple.

Once she leaves, Sarah's smile fades. Her eyes grow serious. "I want you to tell me the truth." I go still. "I want to know what happened with the girl."

Fair. Completely fair. So I tell her everything. How River showed up uninvited. How I felt wrong the second she stepped into that house. How the place didn't feel like home, if it ever did. How obvious it was what she wanted. How I kept my distance. How I showered to leave faster. How I came out to find her in my room with my phone. How she answered a call that should have been mine.

"The only reason I gave her my number," I say quietly, "was for her parents." My thumb strokes the back of Sarah's hand. "I told her to give it to her parents in case something happens to my mom." I exhale slowly. "She's not taking care of herself." I stare down at the table for a second. "It's only a matter of time before that life catches up to her."

My throat tightens despite trying to lock down those emotions, I shouldn't even give a shit. They clearly didn't extend the same courtesy to me. "I didn't get to know when my dad died." I meet Sarah's eyes again. "I'd like to know when my mom does."

Her breath catches. She sniffles softly. I see tears gather, then vanish when she blinks them back. The waitress returns balancing plates, saving us both. We let go of each other's hands as she sets everything down. Neither of us speaks at first.

We start eating in silence. Normal things in a conversation that feels anything but normal. I let the quiet settle. Give her room. If she has more questions, she'll ask them and I'll answer every single one.

When she takes a bite of her burger, a soft sound slips out of her throat. Pleasure. Unthinking. Barely audible to anyone else. It hits me like a live round.

My gaze locks on her face. Her eyes flutter closed as she savors the first bite, lips parting slightly. Jesus Christ. I can't tell if she's doing it on purpose. Knowing Sarah, probably not. She has no idea how fucking sexy she is, how much she effects me.

I drag in a slow breath and look down at my fries like they personally offended me. Because all I can think about is getting her home. Back to her apartment. Back somewhere private where I can touch her properly. Use an actual bed for once instead of dirt floors, cramped tents, or stolen moments. Not that I believe she'll let me anywhere near that yet.

She looks up and catches me staring. Pauses mid-chew. "Why are you looking at me like that?"

"Like what?" My voice comes out rougher than intended. I clear my throat, though it doesn't help.

"Like you want to eat me." The second she realizes what she said, color explodes across her skin

Pink rising from the top of her blouse all the way to her ears. I missed that blush so much it almost hurts.

"Because," I say slowly, leaning forward just enough, "I do." Her breath catches.

A savage, possessive satisfaction moves through me knowing I can still affect her. Still get under that beautiful skin. I glance at her untouched fries.

"Finish your food so we can get home." The command slips out naturally. Her eyes widen, then narrow. But she obeys anyway, taking faster bites of burger and fries. I'm grinning before I can stop it. When she's done, I toss cash on the table and stand. Then hold out my hand. For half a second I'm not sure she'll take it. Then her fingers slide into mine. We move fast after that.

The drive back is torture. Every red light feels personal. Every stop sign a direct attack. When we finally pull up outside her building, I'm out of the car and around to her side before she gets the door fully open. I help her out and pull her straight into me.

My hand slides beneath her chin, tilting her face up. I lower slowly, giving her every chance to pull away. She doesn't. Instead she rises onto her toes and kisses me first. A low sound tears from my chest. I deepen it instantly, tasting her, holding the back of her neck, a month of missing her pouring into one kiss. I've missed everything. Her mouth. Her warmth. The way she softens for one breath before fighting me the next.

I break away only because I need air. Then grab her hand and hurry us inside. The moment the main door shuts behind us, I pull her back against me again. Another kiss. Hungrier this time. My hand slides down to cup the curve of her ass. She gasps into my mouth as I lift her clean off the floor. She laughs breathlessly, arms going around my neck. I carry her toward the stairs like a man who finally found his way home.

Grabbing the keys from her I unlock her door and rush in. Throwing the keys onto the table I push her up against the wall and take the kiss deeper. Pushing my achingly hard cock against her pussy, that's straining against the zipper of my jeans, eager to sink into her wet heat. I thrust against her again and she moans beautifully.

"Ahem, you should know before clothes come off that I am here." I look over and see Glitch sitting on the couch. I pull her away from the wall and walk to her room.

"Get the fuck out, Glitch. We need privacy." I say shutting her door behind us and depositing her on the bed.

Chapter Thirty Seven

Sarah

I lay there panting. The need coursing through me. After he put me down on the bed he came down on me. We hear the door to the apartment slam close and Wade instantly starts kissing me again. It's a frenzy of kissing and him taking my clothes off. My shirt gets peeled off and he starts kissing down my jaw, to my ear. I moan so loudly, the intense feeling radiating through me. I feel so hot and the need to be touched burning through me.

"Fuck, baby. I want to hear you. I can't wait to be inside you." His voice is rough with need. I know he's been desperate for me. I wonder how much he's been thinking about me but I get distracted when he gets my bra off, and he starts kissing and sucking my breasts. I have lost all control and pushed them into his face while using my hands to force him down. I feel like I could come from this alone.

"I think your gorgeous tits are even bigger, fuck I am a lucky bastard." My heart drops thinking he's going to guess that I am pregnant. But quickly lose track of that thought when he starts sucking a nipple again and using his fingers to play with the other. It takes like point-two seconds of that and a wave of pleasure courses through me and I start coming with a scream.

I am vaguely aware of him pulling back from me, when I come back from that I slowly look at him, he has a mixture of awe and shock on his face.

"You've never orgasmed like that. Never that fast." He muses with wonder in his eyes. I don't want him questioning it.

"Don't stop. I need you." I whisper. He gives me that sexy grin that makes me putty in his hands. Not that I would ever tell him that.

"You have me. I missed you. I want to hear you, we don't need to be quiet anymore." He says and then he is diving back in, kissing down the length of my stomach as he is unbuttoning my jeans. As he kisses my stomach my breath hitches knowing he's kissing our baby. He doesn't notice or he just assume it's from pleasure. He stands abruptly and starts ripping my pants down my legs. Immediately after he starts rushing to take his own clothes off, if I wasn't desperate for him to hurry I would be laughing.

He's standing there breathing heavily staring down at me, I'm left in my panties. Suddenly happy that I wore my light blue thong. Something I never wore for him before. When I packed for the field study it was all about being comfortable and practical.

"Fuck beautiful, I love you in that thong. I hope you have more." Before I have a chance to say anything he flips me over and pulls my hips back so my ass is in his face. He groans out loud and it gives me a heady feeling, knowing that I make him feel that way.

"I can't wait to start exploring more with you. All the things I want to do to you and with you." He says. I don't respond, I can't, to distracted by his touch.

I hear the sharp slap before I feel it. I squeak when he spanks the other side. He does it again and it feels amazing when he hits right in the center. I gasp as he starts sliding his rough calloused hands down pulling the thong out of the way, to dip his fingers into my soaking wet pussy.

"Mmm, so ready for me." I don't even get a chance to respond when he starts ripping the panties down and spreads my thighs. His cock is nudging my entrance and he slowly starts slipping in.

It feels tighter than before, I don't know if it's from this new position we never tried before or just because it's been so long. Once he gets all the way in we both sigh and relish in the feeling of coming together. I don't know if this really changes things between us or if I can fully forgive him but for now I just focus on the feeling.

The feeling I know that he will only bring me. He slowly slides out and slides back in, stretching me out. As he starts sliding in easier he grabs my hips roughly and starts pounding into me. I try to hold back my moan but he spanks me. "I want to hear you." He growls out.

He feels much deeper than ever before and more pleasure than I remember ever feeling before. He continues thrusting in and out, switching from gripping my hips, he thrusts in harder with a deep groan. I'm so lost, I didn't feel him lift his hand only the sharp slap before the sting on my ass. I can't help the scream that erupts out of me. I feel so close again, my thighs are shaking.

Wade suddenly reaches up to my breasts and pulls me up so my back is against his hard sweaty chest. His hand is wrapping through my hair and pulls my head back so he has access to start kissing my neck. Pressing one hand firmly against my stomach, pulling me harder against him and that's when I lose it. I erupt on a loud moan and I can feel him start fucking me harder through my orgasm. This is one long orgasm, I feel the spasms all over me, my legs shaking.

He keeps going hard, gripping me tighter as growls. "God damn, I love when your pussy tries to keep me inside you." He thrusts one last time and he groans as he empties himself into me.

When his grip on me finally loosens, I collapse back against the bed, panting and boneless. Wade drops beside me a second later and immediately drags me into his side like he can't help himself. His breathing is still rough as he presses slow, lazy kisses behind my ear. The tenderness of it undoes me more than everything that came before.

I melt against him, right now everything outside this room doesn't matter. I'm perfectly safe and warm. Sleep pulls at me fast.

"I love you," he whispers against my skin. A smile finds me before darkness does.

I wake tangled in warm sheets and stronger arms. Wade is still wrapped around me, one heavy arm across my waist, his face half-buried in my hair. He's asleep and he looks so peaceful, it's strange seeing him like this. No guarded eyes. No tension in his jaw. No constant readiness. Just a man sleeping deeply beside the woman he loves. My chest aches at the sight.

Very carefully, I begin slipping free. I need a shower, a moment alone. I need space to think before those golden-brown eyes open and scramble everything inside me again. As quietly as I can, I wiggle out of his hold.

He shifts once, brow furrowing, but doesn't wake. I tiptoe into the bathroom and close the door softly behind me. The shower sputters to life. Steam begins to curl through the room. I brace both hands on the sink and stare at myself in the mirror. Flushed cheeks. Messy hair. A woman hopelessly tangled up in a man who can ruin her with a look.

My mind goes to him. To the man sleeping in the next room. I know I believe him about River. I do. I want him to be there for his mother if that's what he needs, even after everything she's put him through. I don't know whether he wants a relationship with her or just closure. But I hate that no one told him when his father died. I can't imagine carrying that kind of abandonment.

Then the harder part rises. The gunshot. The lies. Being kept in the dark while he bled in the next room. Begging to see him only to be turned away. That hurt lives deeper than I want to admit. He promised me over and over he would be with me and still, I left believing I meant nothing. I love him, that much is undeniable. I think I always will. Which makes everything harder.

And then there's the other truth. I'm carrying his child. I haven't told him. Guilt presses heavier every day. Especially after tonight. I was dropping hints and hoping he'd somehow figure it out on his own, which is ridiculous. I know it's time. I was just hoping for certainty first. Closure. Some sign of whether trusting him again would destroy me. Can I let go of the last month? Can I hand him my heart a second time and believe he won't break it? Can I trust him with *ours* now?

Because the truth is, for all Wade's faults, he's always known exactly what to say. What I still don't know…is whether I can trust what he means.

"I am not going anywhere."

I jump so hard I nearly slip. My heart launches into my throat. Spinning around, I find Wade standing in the doorway of my bathroom. Naked. Broad shoulders filling the frame, completely unapologetic and offensively gorgeous. Water from the sink still beads on his skin, tracing over hard muscle and the deep lines of his stomach before disappearing lower.

But it isn't that which steals my breath. It's the scar. Pink and fresh along the side of his lower torso. The place where a bullet nearly took him from me. My eyes lock there. A sharp ache moves through my chest so suddenly I have to grip the bathroom counter.

He notices immediately, his expression softens. "Oh my god, you scared me," I breathe, dragging my gaze back to his face. "How do you know what I was thinking?"

He steps closer, boundaries apparently mean nothing to this man.

"Because I know you," he says quietly. "I know you're trying to decide if you can forgive me." Another step. "I know you're hurt. I'm just asking for a chance."

His fingers brush my waist. "You won't regret it." A slow, devastating smile curves his mouth. "I'll make sure of that."

I groan. "He's always good with his words," I mutter.

He laughs under his breath and wraps both arms around me. The second he does, some tight place inside me loosens. This is still where I feel safest.

"You're right," I admit against his chest. "I was thinking that." I draw in a shaky breath. "I'm scared." My fingers trace once near the scar before falling away. "You promised me again and again. and then bam—I was sent away." My throat tightens. "Getting crazy news and learning the man I loved was shot and almost died."

His hands tighten on me. "Love," he corrects softly. "Not loved." My eyes sting. "I am so sorry it happened like that." He kisses my forehead. "I will spend the rest of my life making it up to you."

The sincerity in his voice terrifies me more than lies ever could. "What if it happens again?" I whisper. "What if I get taken again?" The memory of yesterday prickles over my skin. That watched feeling. That crawling sense something was wrong.

"What if something happens?" I force the words out. "Am I going to be kept in the dark?"

He goes very quiet. Then he cups my face. "No." Simple. Absolute. "Never again."

I want to believe him so badly it hurts. Instead of answering, I turn and step into the shower. He follows immediately. The stall is small enough for one normal person. Wade is not a normal person. He tries to squeeze in behind me and instantly knocks an elbow into the wall. I snort. He glares at the shower like it insulted him. Then ducks because the shower head hits him square in the forehead. I laugh harder. He bends his knees, attempting to fit under the spray with some dignity left. It does not work. At all. Water splashes mostly off his shoulder while I stand directly in the warm stream trying not to laugh myself to death.

"You enjoying this?" he asks dryly.

"Immensely." He crowds forward anyway, trapping me between tile and six-foot-four stubbornness. Then lowers his mouth to my shoulder.

"You're lucky I love you." I smile before I can stop myself, I feel safe.

"What makes you think it will happen again?" he asks, fingers threading gently through my now-wet hair. I don't want to answer. I don't want fear in this room again. I just want one soft moment before reality crashes back in.

Instead of pressing me, he reaches for my shampoo bottle. He pops the cap, smells it, and smiles faintly.

"Vanilla." Then he pours some into his palm and starts working it through my hair. His fingers massage my scalp in slow circles, strong and careful. A sound almost slips out of me. I lean back against his chest without thinking. He rinses his hands, adds more soap, then quickly scrubs through his own hair before ducking his head under the spray.

I laugh when he has to crouch again. "This shower was not built for giants," I inform him.

"It was built wrong," he mutters.

I grin. When he straightens, his hands return to me. One glides down my shoulder, over my arms, along my waist. Soapy palms moving slowly over my skin with maddening patience. I focus on rinsing out my hair while he washes me like he has all the time in the world. When I start on conditioner, his hands drift higher. He cups my breasts absentmindedly, warm and possessive, like he can't help touching me whenever I'm near.

I shake my head, laughing under my breath. "You are impossible."

"You love me anyway."

I don't answer, he knows. When I finish, I step aside so he can rinse off properly. Which means more crouching. More glaring at the shower head. More of me trying not to laugh. He catches me smiling and gives me that crooked grin I love far too much. We dry off in comfortable silence. I dart out first, grab him a towel, then dress quickly in leggings and an oversized shirt. He pulls on jeans. Leaves his feet bare. Leaves his shirt off. My eyes keep drifting to his chest like they've forgotten how to behave.

"You never answered me," he says. That pulls me from my very distracting thoughts. "Did something happen to make you think it'll happen again?"

I sigh and sit on the bed. He stays standing in front of me, still damp, still shirtless, still unfair. "It's just… yesterday and today at school." I twist my hands together. "It felt like I was being watched." His expression changes instantly. All softness gone. He's back to his tense alert self, his jaw tightening and eyes sharpening.

"Every time I looked around, no one was there," I continue. "So I don't know if I'm still shaken from what happened or if I'm just being paranoid."

His stare hardens. "I felt it too." My head snaps up. "So did Glitch when we came to find you."

My stomach drops. "That's what you were talking about outside the darkroom?"

He nods once. "You are not crazy." Relief and terror hit at the same time.

"That's why you wanted to hack the FBI?" I ask quietly. "You think someone got away?" My pulse starts racing.

"I don't know," he says. "That's what I want to find out." There's something darker under his calm now. Something lethal. He steps closer until he's between my knees. Then lowers himself enough to look me directly in the eyes.

"But I promise you, Mouse..." He brushes damp hair back from my face. "I will be your shadow. I'm not leaving your side." His thumb strokes my cheek. "Nothing is going to happen to you this time."

A chill skates down my spine. Not from fear. From the weight of his words. From the certainty in his voice.

Still, something doesn't sit right. I search his face. "What aren't you telling me?"

His jaw flexes. For a second, I think he's going to dodge it. Then his expression turns grim. "When some of the guys went back..." he says slowly, "they never found Benjamin's body. No remains. No sign of him." My stomach drops. The room suddenly feels too small. His hand tightens at my waist. "And until I have proof otherwise, I'm not letting my guard down."

A tremor moves through me. That watched feeling. The unease on campus. The sensation of eyes I couldn't find. Maybe I'm not imagining any of it. Maybe this really isn't over. My arms wrap instinctively around my stomach. I wish none of this had happened. I wish I didn't have to wonder what danger might still be out there. I wish fear didn't live in my body now.

"Hey." His voice softens immediately. "You're safe." He sits beside me and pulls me into his arms. Only then do I realize I'm shaking. His warmth steadies some of it, I rest my cheek against his bare chest and I listen to his strong, steady heartbeat. Things could have been so much worse for me. I know that. I'll always know that and yet I will never forget the terror. The helplessness. And what happened to Carly was so much worse than anything I endured. The guilt of that never leaves. This is it. I have to tell him now. I've never been so scared to speak in my life.

"I know," I whisper. "I know I'm safe." My throat burns. "I just still remember the fear." I stare at nothing. "I don't know if it will ever fully go away and I don't even know if I have the right to feel this way when nothing truly horrible happened to me."

He tenses. "Sarah—"

"I can't imagine what Carly went through." My voice cracks. "How do I fall apart when she had it worse?"

He turns me toward him immediately. Both hands on my face. "You have every right to feel what you feel." His eyes lock on mine. "It does not diminish what happened to Carly." His thumbs brush away tears. "You were taken. Drugged." Pain flashes across his face. "And it could have been worse." His forehead rests against mine. "I still fear what happened too. I fear what almost happened every damn day." Emotion swells so hard in my chest I can barely breathe.

"I can't lose you," he says. "And I won't. I will make sure nothing happens to you. You are my future. My whole world."

I take one long, shaking breath. Then stand. He looks up at me from the edge of the bed, concern flashing instantly. I turn to face him fully. My hands tremble as they lower to my stomach. There is no easy way to say this. So I choose the truth.

"You already are protecting your future." I see him watching me with open curiosity and worry. I know he doesn't know where I am going with this.

"I need to tell you something." My voice shakes. "I don't want you to go all crazy protective like a papa bear."

Another hint. He looks almost amused. "No promises." He shifts closer. "Just tell me."

I draw in a deep breath, then blurt it out before I can lose my nerve. "I'm pregnant." The words rush out of me fast and breathless.

For a second, Wade just stares. Then his eyes widen slightly, real surprise breaking through that controlled expression he always wears. His gaze flicks down my body, to my stomach, then back to my face again like he's trying to process what I just said.

"You're serious?" he asks quietly.

A nervous laugh slips out of me. "Very serious."

"How far along?"

"Ten weeks." He goes still for half a heartbeat. Then I actually watch the realization hit him. The jungle. The timeline. Us. Relief crashes over his face so fast it almost steals the air from the room. He lets out a rough laugh, dragging both hands over his face before looking back at me again.

"Ten weeks," he repeats, sounding a little wrecked. Then he smiles. Not one of his teasing smirks or controlled half-grins. A real one. Bright. Almost disbelieving. "That baby is mine."

Warmth floods through me. "Yes." He closes the distance between us in seconds, both hands sliding carefully to my waist like he can't stop touching me now that he knows.

"Fuck," he breathes, laughing again under his breath. "We made a baby." I laugh too, tears burning behind my eyes. His forehead presses gently against mine before he drops to his knees in front of me, hands spreading over my stomach like he already treasures what's there.

"Hi, baby," he murmurs softly, and that almost breaks me. Then he looks up at me, eyes shining openly now. "You have any idea how happy you just made me? You're carrying our baby? H-how?" I blink down at him. There goes my relief. Is that a serious question? Confused and slightly offended, I just stare at him.

His eyes widen, then he groans. "No—don't answer that." A crooked smile pulls at his mouth. "I remember exactly how."

Despite myself, I snort. "That's all you have to say?"

He stands and takes the seat beside me again, tugging me gently onto his lap. His hands settle around my waist, bringing us nearly eye level.

"Sorry, beautiful." His thumbs brush lightly over my sides. "I'm shocked." His gaze drops to my stomach, his palm spreading there possessively before lifting back to my face. "I wasn't expecting that." A softer smile appears. "But I guess it makes sense."

My brows knit together. "How?"

"Your body's changed."

I look down instantly, offended. "I have not changed."

That earns his full grin. The dangerous one. "Oh, you have." His gaze drifts over me shamelessly. "Your body looks incredible."

I narrow my eyes. "Wade."

"Your breasts are fuller." His grip tightens slightly at my hips. "Your stomach is perfect." His voice lowers. "And your ass?" He shakes his head slowly. "Don't get me started." Heat floods my face. He leans forward and presses a teasing kiss through my shirt just above my chest. I smack his shoulder.

"What I intended to ask," he says, clearly amused, "is when."

"When what?" I stiffen. "When did I get pregnant or when did I find out?" I point between us. "Because those are two very different conversations."

His expression shifts immediately, teasing fading. His hands slide from my hips back to my stomach. Gentle now. Protective.

"Judging by that look, I'm suddenly nervous," he mutters. Then he exhales. "Both."

I swallow. "I found out the morning I woke up on that naval ship." His eyes shut instantly, pain flashing across his face. I keep talking before I lose my nerve. "The doctor said they ran bloodwork and I was pregnant."

He bows his head once, a quiet curse slipping under his breath.

"As for how far along I am…" I continue softly. "I saw an OB a couple days ago. I told them what happened—about being drugged and everything else. They did an ultrasound, and so far the baby looks healthy." A small smile tugs at my lips. "Oh. I got a picture."

I slide off his lap and reach for the nightstand, pulling the ultrasound photo from the drawer before handing it to him.

His eyes scan the tiny image. "It's so small," he murmurs.

I smile softly. "The app says the baby's about the size of a strawberry." He sets the picture down carefully and looks up at me. Then both of his hands spread across my stomach, warm and steady.

"I'm gonna need that app," he says. Then he leans down and presses a kiss against my stomach through my shirt. Slowly. Reverently. After that he rests his cheek against me like he's listening for something impossible. My heart does an embarrassing little flip. There he goes again. Making me weak.

"I'm sorry I wasn't there," he says against me. "I'm sorry you found out alone." He looks up, eyes wet again. "And now I'm kicking myself even harder for almost losing my whole future." One hand strokes over my stomach. "My whole world in one tiny package."

Then, because he is impossible, "Ten weeks? Damn." He smirks. "I must have super sperm if I got you pregnant on the first try."

I scoff so hard I nearly choke. "You're insufferable." He looks proud of himself. "I was on birth control," I say quickly. "Apparently it wore off early. I didn't know until I talked to the doctor."

The words tumble out faster than I intend. I don't know why I suddenly need him to understand. Need him to know I didn't plan anything. His expression changes immediately.

Both hands framing my face. "Sarah. I do not care how it happened." His forehead presses to mine. "I don't think you tricked me." A kiss to my nose. "I think I'm the luckiest bastard alive."

A sharp sting lands on my hip and I yelp, instinctively pushing into him. "Stop worrying," he says.

I glare up at him. "Do that again and you'll lose a hand."

His grin only widens. "Seriously, beautiful. I'm incredibly happy." The teasing fades from his face, replaced by something rawer. "When I first met you, I knew."

"Knew what?"

His thumb brushes my cheek. "I knew I was going to marry you."

"Oh my god, stop." Emotion rises so fast it startles me. "You're going to make me cry." I smack his shoulder.

He catches my hand and kisses my palm. "I am absolutely going to be a crazy overprotective Papa Bear, just like you said." I laugh through the tears threatening me.

"I have this instinct something's wrong," he continues, expression sharpening again. "So you better talk to whoever you need to at school." His hand settles over my stomach. "Because I'm going to be glued to your side."

I groan. "That's going to be awkward."

He arches a brow. "How?"

"Because I'm going to start showing soon." I gesture vaguely at myself. "Apparently people already know I was with one of the soldiers." His eyes darken. "And then what? I'm supposed to walk around campus with this giant man shadowing me who clearly doesn't belong there?"

"First of all," he says, offended, "I belong wherever you are." I roll my eyes. "Second, I cannot wait until you're showing." His grin turns wicked. "I'm going to make sure everybody knows. As for how they already know..." His smile vanishes. "That part bothers me. The people who knew are either arrested or my men." The room goes quiet for a beat. Then my stomach growls loudly enough to break the tension.

He looks down at me, instantly amused. "Well." He leans close to my belly. "Daddy's going to feed you." I burst out laughing just as he scoops me up.

"Wade!" He carries me into the kitchen like I weigh nothing.

I glance around, we're still alone. He sets me on the counter and steps between my knees.

"What does Mommy want to eat?" he murmurs against my lips.

I snort. "Can you even cook?" He looks offended. "Besides MREs," I add.

That earns a glare. "If it comes from a box," he says proudly, "I can read directions."

I laugh harder. "How about I cook and you relax?"

He shakes his head once and kisses me. His hand slides to the back of my head while the other slips beneath my shirt, warm against my spine. I'm halfway to forgetting my own name when the apartment door swings open.

"Did you not get enough of her earlier?" Jake strolls in and drops into a chair. "I was hoping it was safe to come back."

Wade doesn't even look at him. "I will never get enough."

Then finally glances over his shoulder. "We're starting dinner. You hungry?" He looks unbearably smug. Like a man trying not to explode with news.

I cup Wade's face and pull his attention back to me. "He already knows," I say quietly.

His brows shoot up. "What?" Then hurt flickers there. "How did he know before me?"

Guilt stabs through me. "I didn't tell him." I rush on. "He overheard Fallon and me whispering."

Jake lifts a hand proudly. "Elite hearing."

"That's when he convinced me to call you," I add pointedly. The memory of that woman answering still stings. Wade's face falls. Then he exhales slowly and nods.

"Who else knows?"

"Besides Fallon?" He nods. "My parents and my sister."

Another nod. Jake leans back in the chair, grinning. "Well, I'm glad he knows. I hated keeping that secret." He points at Wade. "Luckily I knew my man here would make it right."

We both glare at him. "What?" he says innocently. "I'm usually right." Then to Wade, "I also already called officiating your wedding."

Wade blinks. "What the hell are you talking about?"

I start laughing again. Before I can hop off the counter, Wade catches my waist and lowers me gently to the floor like I'm made of glass. Overprotective already.

"Rocky here already said I get to marry you two," Jake says proudly. Wade just looks at me, smugly.

I roll my eyes so hard it hurts. "Go sit down," I tell Wade, pushing him toward the table.

"I'm making dinner." He resists for half a second. "It'll help me think."

That gets him moving. He sits down by Jake but keeps his eyes on me. Mostly my stomach and keeps smiling. Still looking like a man who just got handed the whole world.

Chapter Thirty Eight

Sarah

The next day, I walk into the Anthropology department trying to act like this is normal. It is not normal. Wade has stayed beside me the entire walk from the apartment, one hand wrapped around mine like letting go isn't an option. His thumb brushes over my knuckles every few steps and every so often he gives my hand a reassuring squeeze. His other attention is everywhere else. His eyes watching every door, looking through every window. The students that pass by too close. The blind corners, anyone lingering too long or anyone looking twice.

"Breathe, Mouse. Everything will be fine."

I glance over and realize I'm crushing his hand. "Sorry."

"Don't be." I love the hand-holding. I really do. What I don't love is the feeling crawling over my skin. That prickling sensation between my shoulder blades. The certainty that someone is watching. The closer we get to the building, the worse it becomes. Students openly stare as we approach. Though if I'm honest, I don't think they're looking at me.

They're looking at the giant man beside me who looks like he belongs in combat boots on some dangerous mountain, not on a university campus. He does not fit in here at all and that only makes him more noticeable. I scan my badge to let us into the building and lead him down the halls toward the anthropology wing. The whole way, Wade's eyes move constantly. Again his eyes miss nothing, every person and every intersecting corridor. Like a one-man security detail in jeans and boots. People step out of his path without even realizing they're doing it.

It should make me feel safer. Instead, it makes everything feel more real. It feels more dangerous, maybe it isn't Wade making me nervous. Maybe something really is off.

By the time I reach Dr. Anderson's office, I'm fighting the urge to laugh or cry. I'm not sure which one will come out. It doesn't help that I'm about to ask for permission to bring a personal bodyguard to campus like I'm someone important enough to need one. The thought sounds ridiculous even in my own head.

I stop in front of her door. Staring at the name plate beside her door that reads Dr. Hazel Anderson, Professor.

"Are you okay?" Wade asks quietly.

I look up at him. "Yeah. Just nervous." We talked about this last night and again this morning. His stance never changed. Awkward doesn't matter. Attention doesn't matter. People talking doesn't matter. Keeping me and the baby safe is all that matters. And he still has that same gut feeling. That this isn't over.

"It'll be okay," he says softly. "I promise." He steps closer, lowering his voice. "We'll make it work. We'll do our best not to make it too obvious what we're doing." I snort, yeah right, there's no way people won't suspect. He leans down and kisses the side of my head. The gesture is gentle and comforting.

With his hand in mine and his mouth brushing my temple, I feel steadier. I lift my hand and knock.

Taking a deep breath, I knock lightly. "Come in," she calls.

I open the door and step inside. "Good morning, Dr. Anderson." Then glance back. "This is Wade. Is it okay if he joins us?"

Maybe I should've said boyfriend. Or partner. Or giant overprotective caveman. Hazel looks up and freezes. Her eyes widen so noticeably I almost choke trying not to laugh. Because yes, Wade is filling most of the doorway.

"Sure," she says quickly. "Yes. Of course. Come in."

She starts shuffling papers into neater piles that were perfectly fine two seconds ago. Then smooths her hair. Then her blouse. I absolutely do not look back at Wade. Because if I do, I'll lose it. We sit in the two worn chairs across from her desk.

I clear my throat. "So, this is Sergeant Wade Blakely." Hazel's brows rise. "He was in charge of the unit assigned to protect us in the jungle. He's also the one who saved me." Her gaze moves between us. Taking in the tension. The closeness. The fact his knee is touching mine. The way his hand is resting on the chair behind me like he owns the space around me.

"Hi, Dr. Anderson," Wade says smoothly. "It's nice to meet you." Then with a faint smile, "Sarah talked about you all the time."

Hazel visibly brightens. "Oh please, call me Hazel." Then glances at me. "All good things, I hope?"

"Yes." Wade doesn't miss a beat. "My girl only says nice things." I close my eyes. Oh my god.

Hazel smiles slowly. "My girl?" she repeats. Looking between us with open delight now.

"Yes," Wade says easily. "When she bumped into me at the airport that first day, I was done for."

My face goes hot. Hazel laughs. "Well." She folds her hands. "I had heard the rumors. I didn't know they were true." Her eyes sparkle. "Or that you were bringing home more than just research."

Wade leans back casually. "Yeah." His hand settles on the back of my chair. "I'm pretty excited to be out and finally start my life with her."

Why does every sweet thing he says hit me directly in the chest?

"Rumors?" I ask sharply. I mean I knew the students were talking, but I don't understand how anyone would know anything that happened in that jungle. Especially something so personal. My embarrassment evaporates. Hazel's smile fades into something more cautious.

"Yes." She hesitates. "Apparently several professors were nearby when Dean Wagner was escorted out by the FBI." My stomach tightens. "He was screaming." Wade goes still beside me.

Hazel clears her throat. "Saying you were a liar." My jaw clenches. "And that of course you would side with the military..." She winces. "Since you were sleeping with one of them."

Heat floods my entire body. My face burns so badly I drop it straight into my hands. Oh my god. Oh my god. So now the entire department, the entire school, thinks—I want the floor to open and swallow me. A warm hand begins rubbing slowly up and down my back. Keeping me steady. I can feel him coiled tight but dangerously calm. I peek through my fingers.

Wade's expression has gone flat. Cold.

"Where," he asks quietly, "is Dean Wagner now?" I look back at Wade and glare. He's sitting there so still it's somehow more threatening than if he were pacing.

Hazel answers before he can. "I'm not sure where he is yet, but we were notified he's returning today." Her mouth tightens. "We received an email from the university president this morning. He was released by the FBI. They said he hadn't done anything wrong and they couldn't hold him any longer."

The temperature in the room seems to drop ten degrees. I don't even need to look at Wade. His anger fills the small office like smoke, it's heavy, silent and dangerous. Hazel's eyes flick between us, concern deepening. I try to offer her a reassuring smile. It probably looks more like a grimace. My mind spins. Could the feeling of being watched have been him? Had he been back already? Lurking around campus, watching me. I don't know how involved he really was. I only know what Wade and the team were uncovering in the field. Enough to make my stomach turn now.

Hazel folds her hands together. "Can you tell me what's going on?"

I glance at Wade once, then back to her. "It's still part of an ongoing federal investigation." My voice sounds thin to my own ears. "But I can say he was implicated in what happened in the jungle."

Her eyes widen instantly. Color drains from her face. "I can't believe it," she whispers. "Why? Why would he do something like that?" Her gaze drops to her desk. "Why would any of them?" There's grief there too. The betrayal of realizing someone you worked beside might be monstrous.

When she looks back at me, her eyes shine. "I'm so grateful you and Carly were brought back to us." Emotion catches me off guard.

I swallow hard. "Thank you."

Beside me, Wade finally speaks. Low and lethal calm. "If Dean Wagner comes anywhere near her..." Hazel and I both turn toward him. His eyes are fixed on the wall. Jaw tight. "He won't get a second chance."

"Good," she says softly. There's steel under the word I don't hear often from Hazel. Then her expression gentles again.

"I'm so sorry this is happening, Sarah." She folds her hands on the desk. "This has to be a lot. And I'm sure it doesn't exactly help with finishing your dissertation."

I let out a weak laugh. "No, not really."

"I know the gossip probably makes it worse," she continues. "Some of the professors here have a terrible habit of treating rumors like research." That gets a real laugh out of me.

"It's fine," I say with a shrug. "I guess that explains why some of the undergrads already knew on the first day of class."

Hazel grimaces. "I'm sorry. Hopefully it dies down soon enough." She leans forward slightly. "And if you need help, you come to me. For anything." My throat tightens. "Even if you need a few days to yourself, okay?"

"Okay," I say quietly. I glance at the clock on her wall. "I need to get to class soon." Then I straighten, forcing us back to why I came. "I was wondering about the possibility of having Wade with me on campus as protection." I keep my voice even. I do not mention feeling watched. I do not mention the dread crawling under my skin.

But judging by the way Hazel studies me, I don't think I'm fooling her. "Is everything okay?" she asks carefully.

How do I answer that? Nothing feels okay. Everything is still under investigation. I have no idea what I'm supposed to say and what I'm not.

Before I can stumble through it, Wade speaks. "We have reason to believe Sarah may still be in danger." His voice is calm. "We can't discuss the details." His hand settles behind my chair again. "But I intend to make sure she's protected."

Hazel listens without interrupting. "Myself or one of my men will be with her while she finishes her dissertation," he continues. "Once we understand the campus layout, I'll personally make sure we stay out of the way." I almost smile at *one of my men*. Like this campus is about to become a deployment zone.

Hazel exhales slowly. "I think that sounds reasonable." Her gaze moves between us. "I don't know what the two of you aren't telling me. But I suppose the truth tends to come out eventually. I don't know if there is paperwork you need to fill out or if we can find another alternative to explain his presence. I'll look into it." A beat passes. "The only thing is our campus, like most schools, is gun free."

"That won't be a problem, ma'am," Wade says immediately.

Hazel blinks. Then giggles. "Oh, call me Hazel."

I glance back at Wade. He gives her a polite nod. "Hazel." And judging by the pleased look on his face, he absolutely knows the effect he has on people.

"Okay, my lab starts in five minutes. We should head over."

After saying goodbye to Hazel, Wade and I walk quickly across the hall to the lab room. Most of the students are already gathered outside, backpacks slung over shoulders, chatting until they notice us approaching Or rather, notice him. I unlock the door and step aside, letting everyone file in. More than a few heads turn.

Several girls openly stare at Wade as they pass, their eyes lingering far too long for my liking. The irrational flare of jealousy catches me off guard. I look back at him sharply. He's watching me with that slow, knowing smile. He absolutely notices and enjoys it. He leans closer like he wants to kiss me right there in the hallway. I glare. He chuckles under his breath and gives one obedient nod.

"Before you start," he says quietly, "I'm checking the room." My stomach does an odd little flip at how serious he sounds. "Then I'll be right outside making some calls."

I nod and step in. He holds the door for me, then enters after the last student. The room goes nearly silent. Wade moves through the lab quickly but thoroughly, checking corners, storage closets, the prep room, even glancing beneath the counters. There's nowhere for anyone to hide, but that clearly doesn't matter to him. He doesn't rush. He doesn't care that twenty students are staring.

When he reaches me again, he pauses close enough that only I hear him. "You're good." Then he winks.

My pulse betrays me instantly. He steps back out and closes the door behind him. The second he's gone, every student in the room suddenly remembers how to breathe. I turn toward the front bench and begin gathering my materials, pretending not to notice the looks being exchanged.

Each movement is deliberate, measured. A way to steady myself before the inevitable questions start. I inhale deeply and face the class. Thankfully, no one asks anything personal. At least not yet. The same girl that asked if I was sleeping with the army guy was openly staring. She looked surprised and maybe even a little apologetic.

Between classes, we had a fifteen-minute break. Wade took full advantage of every second. The moment the last student cleared the room, he shut the door behind them and crossed to me like he'd been counting down the seconds. His hands bracketed my waist, then he kissed me hard enough to steal my breath. The kiss was hungry and possessive, like he needed to reassure himself I was still here. I melted into him before I could stop myself. When he finally pulled back, I was breathing as hard as he was.

"You can't keep doing that between labs," I whispered.

"Yes I can," he murmured against my mouth, then kissed me again anyway. I laughed softly into the kiss, but the sound died when he pulled me fully into his chest and wrapped both arms around me. Holding me close and holding me still. My cheek rested over his heartbeat. It was pounding harder than it should have been. Whatever call he took before coming in had rattled him. I could feel it in the tension locked through his shoulders. In the way his jaw stayed tight. In the controlled anger humming beneath his skin. He hadn't said a word about it. He just kept me closer. My hands slid beneath his jacket, over the hard planes of his back.

"What happened?" I asked quietly.

"Nothing you need to worry about."

"That answer never means nothing."

His exhale stirred my hair. "I'll handle it. We'll talk about it tonight." There was steel in the words. Danger in the promise. Right now, we don't have time for me to keep questioning him, it will have to wait. Then his hand moved instinctively to my stomach, spreading wide there like it belonged. The touch changed something in the room. His expression softened. My throat tightened.

"We're really doing this," he said quietly.

I tipped my head back to look at him. "Doing what?"

"This." His thumb brushed lightly over my belly. "Us. Our baby. A real life."

Emotion hit so suddenly I had to blink it back. "You're ridiculous," I whispered.

"And you love me."

Unfortunately, before I could answer, footsteps sounded in the hall. Voices. Students returning. We sprang apart like guilty teenagers. I smoothed my shirt. He looked entirely unapologetic. The next two labs went by quickly. Each time a new group entered, Wade checked the room first, then stationed himself right outside the door. No one questioned the six-foot-four wall of muscle silently looming in an Anthropology lab. But more than one student whispered. More than one girl stared. More than one guy suddenly sat up straighter. The rumor mill would be in flames by lunch.

This semester was supposed to be easy. Just a few labs that I had to teach. Finalize my dissertation, then defending it before I can finally graduate. Now I had a protective ex-soldier shadowing me and enough gossip to fuel campus for months. Which reminds me I really need to call my parents and explain what's going on. I just know they are going to insist on coming up here. As the last class wrapped up, I gathered my notes while students filtered out.

When the room emptied, Wade stepped back inside. One look at him told me everything. He was still angry. Or maybe this was new one, he was wound tight. And trying very hard to hide it from me, he was not doing a good job.

Walking down the hall toward the main exit, I'm already reworking my schedule in my head. We still haven't fully discussed it, but if I don't absolutely need to be on campus, I won't be. Most of my dissertation prep can be done remotely. My notes are at the apartment. My research files are there. And if I'm being honest, I feel safer there.

"I need to use the bathroom." Wade nods immediately. No argument. No teasing. Just reaches for my things and takes them from me without a word. The tension in him is impossible to miss now. His jaw is tight enough to crack teeth. His eyes are darker as they scan all over, harder than he was earlier. His shoulders are rigid beneath his shirt. His fingers flex once around the strap of my bag like he's resisting the urge to break something. Whatever happened on those phone calls has him on edge. I feel all of the tension bleeding into me and I hate not knowing why.

"I'll be right outside," he says quietly.

I nod and slip into the women's restroom. The fluorescent lights buzz overhead, it's too bright and sterile for the mess of feelings going on inside me. I move to the sink and brace both palms against the cool porcelain, staring at my reflection. My eyes are shadowed, clearly broadcasting how exhausted I am. From stress and lack of sleep, I look like a very pale woman trying very hard to pretend everything is normal when nothing feels normal anymore.

I let out a slow breath. My nerves are shredded. My stomach twists uneasily. I want to ask Wade what's wrong. Force him to tell me. Make him stop carrying everything alone. But this isn't the place. Right now there are too many ears and too many unknowns. Too many things still happening around us that no one will explain.

I try to take another deep breath, I need to actually use the bathroom before Wade comes barging in for taking too long in here. I'm sure he's outside pacing, watching the time to come bursting in. I close my eyes. Try to steady myself. Try to breathe past the dread clinging to me like smoke. How long do we live like this? Always waiting or bracing for the next thing that might try to hurt me, always checking over our shoulders. How long until I stop jumping at footsteps? How long until Wade unclenches? How long until this is over?

I finish quickly and find out I don't have long to wonder. Because when I step out of the stall and look up a man stands in the doorway of the other stall. Gun raised. Pointed directly at me.

Chapter Thirty Nine

Wade

"What the fuck do you mean it's not my problem, Ramsey?" I keep my voice low, but just barely. My grip on the phone is so tight my knuckles crack. Sarah is in the next room, teaching her lab to a bunch of undergrads students. The rumor mill apparently is already flying, I don't need anyone hearing things they shouldn't. I will not let her hear this.

On the other end, Agent Ramsey scoffs like I'm inconveniencing him.

"Just like I said, Blakely. We have your report." Paper shuffles. "As far as we're concerned, your mission is over. You're out. Move on."

I stare at the wall hard enough to burn through it.

"Unless," he adds lazily, "you have something new to report?"

I see red. "No," I bite out. "What you should've reported was the investigation into Wagner."

Silence. Then a bored sigh.

"Now I find out he's not being held?" I continue. "That he's coming back to the same fucking school Sarah goes to?" My voice drops lower. "The same place you know damn well puts her at risk?"

Ramsey exhales like I'm stupid. "I didn't have enough to hold him on." He sounds amused. Like he enjoys saying it. "How do you even know that?"

"That's not the point," I snap. "Did you even consider Sarah's safety?"

"Oh, don't worry." His tone turns slick. "I'm keeping an eye on the situation." My jaw locks, not like his tone at all. "On her." Every muscle in my body goes tight. "She's actually really cute. I thought so when I heard her voice over the phone. Maybe once all this is over, I'll take my shot."

For one violent second, I consider finding this man by GPS signal alone. "Fuck you," I growl. "She's taken. Try being a professional for once, asshole."

He chuckles. "Interesting you say that." I hate this prick. "Imagine my surprise this morning when I saw her walking into school holding hands with a certain sergeant." My pulse kicks hard. So he was there. Watching. "Looking like a pair of star-crossed lovers."

I blink once. Then scowl. "Star-crossed lovers? What kind of pussy shit is that?"

"Fuck off, Blakely." His voice sharpens. "My point is you're obviously protecting her. And I'm willing to bet there's information you conveniently left out of your report."

Ice slides down my spine. "Things came out after the fact," he says. "So cut the shit. I already knew." Then, almost annoyingly casual, "And I don't care. What I *do* care about," he continues, "is getting concrete evidence on Wagner. We need to know who he's working with. Unfortunately," he says dryly, "your little cowboy rescue operation gathered intel illegally."

My teeth grind. "So it's useless in court."

He isn't wrong. That only pisses me off more. Ramsey sighs dramatically. "I don't know how you got my personal number." I smile grimly. Ghost. "But don't call me again unless you have something real."

The line goes dead. I stare at the phone in my hand. One second. Two. Then lower it very carefully before I put it through the nearest wall. I stare at the phone for a second, forcing air back into my lungs.

Then I dial Glitch. He answers on the first ring. "Yo. What's up?"

I pace two steps, then back again. "They let Wagner go."

"Fuck."

"He's coming back to campus," I continue. "Ramsey says it's not my concern."

Jake mutters something vicious under his breath. I fill him in fast, every word pushing my pulse higher. By the time I finish, my body is humming with adrenaline and rage.

"Do you want me to call Ghost?" Jake asks immediately. "He's been working Wagner's digital footprint."

"No." I'm already pulling up the next number. "I'll call him now." I hang up and dial Ghost.

He picks up on the second ring. "Yeah."

"They fucking let Wagner go." I don't bother with hello. "He's coming back. The FBI says it's not my concern."

Ghost grunts once. "Want me to break into their system?" Typical Ghost. "See what they have on him."

I drag a hand through my hair. "No." The last thing I need is him catching charges because Ramsey's an asshole. "I'm not getting you arrested for hacking the FBI." A keyboard starts clicking anyway. "We need another way in."

Ghost is quiet for a beat. "We could track Wagner's phone." More keys. "But I guarantee the Bureau already tried that. And Wagner doesn't strike me stupid."

I curse under my breath. "Yeah." He's right. I hate when he's right.

"What's your plan?" Ghost asks.

I stop pacing. Look toward the door where Sarah is teaching. I can hear voice speaking through the door, its low and muffled but unmistakably her. And answer with the only truth that matters.

"I need to keep them safe." Silence.

"Them?"

I exhale slowly. "Sarah." My hand tightens around the phone. "And our baby."

This silence lasts longer. "Holy shit. When did that happen?"

Despite everything, a grin pulls at my mouth. "Found out last night. She's ten weeks." Saying it out loud again hits me square in the chest. Mine. Our baby. My family. Ghost actually chuckles.

A rare enough sound it nearly distracts me. "Damn. You don't waste time."

I smirk. "Guess not."

His tone hardens again. "Alright. Listen carefully. I'll dig. But we need to be smart. We're civilians now." Every word is pointed. "That means most of what we do from here on out is technically illegal."

"Fuck legal," I growl. "We do what we have to."

Ghost sighs the sigh of a man used to dealing with idiots. "I'll start small. I can install trackers on both their phones. It's a start."

I nod automatically. "Do it."

"Then we order more field trackers," he continues. "Keys, bags, jacket lining. Make sure she always has one on her."

"Yeah." My eyes cut again to the classroom door. "Do that." Another thought hits me. "Get one ready for Fallon too."

Ghost doesn't question it. "Done."

"Thanks, brother."

"Don't thank me yet," he says. "Keep your head on straight, Wraith."

The line clicks dead. I slide the phone into my pocket. Roll my shoulders once and turn just as the door opens. When Sarah's lab lets out, I fall into step beside her immediately. Close enough to touch. Close enough to shield. My eyes never stop moving. I keep getting that same feeling. The one that starts at the base of your skull and slides down your spine. Being watched but every time I turn toward it, there's nothing obvious there. No visible threat. No clear target.

Just the unease settling deeper into my gut. Sarah walks beside me unaware of the war raging inside my head. I tighten my grip on her hand. Her fingers curl trustingly through mine. A small, warm gesture that means everything. She's mine. She's carrying my baby. I failed her once. I will die before I fail her again.

When we reach the restroom near the exit, she stops. "I'll be quick," she says softly, handing me her bag.

I take it automatically. "I'll be right here."

She gives me a small smile and disappears inside. The door swings shut behind her. I plant myself outside it, listening for any sounds that shouldn't be here. Force slow breaths in through my nose. Out through my mouth. I need control. If I let the anger take over, I stop thinking. If I stop thinking, people get hurt.

My phone buzzes in my pocket. I glance down.

Ghost: Trackers are installed. Pinging close together. Within a few feet. Glitch is on his way.

My blood turns to ice. A few feet. No. No. I slowly lift my head. Eyes locking on the restroom door. Everything inside me goes still. Then violent. I drop Sarah's bag where I stand and surge forward. The door slams open under my hand. My pistol is out before I fully cross the threshold.

There he is. Dean Wagner standing inside the restroom. Gun aimed at Sarah. Her wide terrified eyes meet mine. And the world narrows to a single target. Wagner turns slightly at the sound of the door crashing open. He's still standing between me and her.

Irritation flashes across his face. "Well," he says, almost amused. "That was fast."

I take two slow steps forward. Measured. Controlled. My Sig Sauer locked steady in both hands.

"Drop the gun." Sarah stands frozen near the sinks, chest heaving, eyes darting between us. Wagner laughs under his breath. A thin, desperate kind of laugh, he's breathless and unhinged. It's never good when someone get's this desperate.

"You ruined everything," he sneers. "The plan was supposed to go smoothly."

My finger tightens against the frame, not the trigger, yet. But ready for whatever his plan might be.

"Sarah was the only one going with Ben."

The room goes dead silent. Even Sarah stops breathing.

"He wanted her." Wagner's smile turns vile. "I gave him permission to have her first before we sold her."

A roaring starts in my ears. The edges of my vision darken. Every instinct in me screams to kill him where he stands.

"But then you showed up," he spits. "Fucked the whole thing up."

I don't blink, I just take another two steps forward. Don't give him one inch of the rage clawing up my throat. Because rage gets people killed and Sarah is still in the line of fire.

"You have one chance," I say quietly, deadly calm. "To walk out of here alive."

Wagner glances at Sarah. Then back at me and smiles, a wicked cruel smile that sets my blood on fire. "I think I'll keep my leverage." His hand trembles. His eyes flick between us. Calculating what his chances are. He's looking for a way out of this that doesn't exist. He's panicked now and the last thing I need when Sarah is still in his line of shot.

I see the decision the second he makes it. The smallest tightening of his finger on the trigger. I fire first and the tiny restroom erupts in gunfire. My first round hits his hand just as his weapon discharges. His shot goes wild, deafening in the tight space.

Wagner screams. His gun flies from his shattered grip, skidding across tile as blood spatters the wall behind him. I don't hesitate. I fire again, aiming lower this time. The round punches into his thigh and drops him hard to the floor in a twisting heap. Walking forward I kick the gun further away, then I hear it. A broken sound behind me. A moan.

I whip around and my heart stops. Blood is spreading beneath Sarah's leg.

"No." The word rips out of me. I'm on my knees in front of her instantly. My hands search frantically over her body, checking for more wounds, scanning every inch. Please no. Please no.

"Sarah." My voice breaks. "Baby, stay with me."

Her breathing is wild, way too fast. Sharp, ragged pulls of air that never seem to fill her lungs. Her eyes are huge, the pupils fully dilated. Wild, terrified before pain carves across her face. I find the wound high along the outside of her thigh.

It's just a graze, it's bleeding hard but not center mass. Not her stomach. Thank God. I rip off my jacket and clamp it hard against the wound. She cries out and grabs my forearm. Her whole body shaking.

"Little Mouse, look at me." She can't seem to focus. Her chest heaves faster. She's spiraling.

"Sarah." I cup her jaw with my free hand. "Look at me." I command firmer now.

Her eyes finally lock on mine. "That's it." I force my voice steady even though I'm falling apart. "You're hit in the leg. That's all." She tries to suck in another frantic breath. I shake my head. "No. With me now."

I exaggerate one slow inhale. "In." Then exhale. "Out."

She stutters through it. Again.

"In." I keep pressure on the wound. "Out." "For the baby, Mouse. For our baby. Come on."

She's tries again, taking another breath, it's still shaky, although slightly slower.

"That's my girl." She looks at me through pain-clouded eyes.

"I love you," she whispers. Everything inside me cracks open.

"Don't do that." My voice comes out wrecked. "You're going to be fine." I brush her tears away with my thumb. "You hear me?" My hands are shaking so hard I can barely keep pressure.

"I am not losing you." Her lashes flutter. Her body goes slack for a second. Then her eyes close.

"Sarah!" The scream rips out of me. The restroom door slams open. Ramsey comes rushing in, weapon drawn, takes one look, then holsters. I barely register him. All I can do is hold her tighter. Pray to anything listening.

"Relax, Romeo." I look up murderously. Ramsey crouches, checks her airway, pulse. "Her breathing's normal." He glances at me. "It's probably a pain response."

If my sig were still in my hand, I might have shot him. Footsteps pound in the hallway. Glitch appears first, with Fallon right behind him. Fallon sees the blood and starts crying immediately. Jake catches her around the shoulders. EMTs flood in seconds later. They take over fast. Efficient. Hands replacing mine. Bandages. Vitals.

Questions I don't answer. I help lift Sarah onto the stretcher because I refuse to let strangers handle her alone. When they wheel her out, I stay glued to her side.

"I'm riding with her," I snap at anyone thinking otherwise. No one argues. At the ambulance doors, Jake grips Fallon and looks at me.

"We'll meet you there." Fallon is crying openly now. I nod once. My eyes never leave Sarah. The doors slam shut and sirens erupt. The ten-minute drive to the hospital becomes the longest ten minutes of my life. We hit the ER bay doors, the world turns into motion and noise. Doctors and nurses running up to take over the stretcher. A hospital bed already rolling toward us. Hands reaching for Sarah. Voices barking orders.

I stay beside the stretcher until they physically force space between us. Her face is too pale. There's blood on the sheets. Blood on my hands. Blood on my jeans. I didn't protect her. Again. Didn't protect either of them.

"She's pregnant," I bark at the first nurse close enough to hear me. "Ten weeks." This time there's no pride in saying it. Only fear. The nurse nods sharply and relays it down the line. They rush her through double doors. I follow until another nurse intercepts me with a clipboard.

"Sir, can you tell us what happened?" Her voice is calm. Professional. Completely detached. My whole world is bleeding out behind those doors and she sounds like she's asking for a mailing address.

I grit my teeth so hard my jaw aches. "Gunshot incident."

Words come clipped and hard. "Female, twenty-six, bullet graze right outer thigh." I point toward the doors. "Ten weeks pregnant." I swallow rage. "Assailant neutralized. Police on scene."

She scribbles notes. "We'll take care of her. We'll update you as soon as we can."

Then the sentence that nearly gets her killed. "Please have a seat in the waiting room."

I stare at her. "I'm going with her."

"Sir, she's in excellent hands. I understand this is stressful, but—"

"She's my fiancée." The lie leaves my mouth like truth but they come out hard and absolute. The nurse pauses and studies me. Looks at the blood on my hands. At the way I'm barely holding together. Something softens in her expression. But not enough.

"As soon as she's stabilized and settled, we'll let you see her." I want to punch through the nearest wall.

Instead, I step back. Barely, every bit of me what's to burst through those doors anyway. Then turn and stalk into the waiting room before I explode in front of civilians. They don't need to be worried about me out here, I need them focused in there. On my whole world.

I can't sit. Can't breathe right. Can't stop moving. So I pace. Back and forth. Every second feels like punishment. This hallway. This helplessness. The not knowing. It drags me straight back to the jungle. To searching for her. To wondering if I'd find her alive. And now we're here again. Because I let my guard down. Because I didn't act fast enough. Because I failed.

The doors slide open. Ramsey strides in like he owns the building. His usual smugness is dimmed, but not gone. I stop pacing slowly. Turn toward him.

"Well," he drawls. "Wagner had to be brought here too." My hands curl into fists. "He's unconscious." Ramsey shrugs. "But don't worry. He's handcuffed to the bed."

I take one step toward him. "You think that makes me feel better?"

My voice is quiet enough to terrify. Ramsey's eyes narrow slightly. "As soon as he's patched up, he'll be transported to D.C."

I say nothing. All the violence in me simmers just below the surface. I don't want that bastard in the same building as Sarah. I don't want him breathing the same air. Ramsey sighs like I'm exhausting him and drops into a chair. Looking comfortable and relaxed, like he's got all the time in the world. I keep staring at him. Trying to decide which one of us I hate more right now. I glare at him.

"You don't have anywhere else to be?"

He arches one brow. "You look like you're about two seconds from putting your fist through the wall." He leans back in the chair. "Figured I'd stay and make sure you don't."

Fucker. I don't answer. I turn and resume pacing. The waiting is torture. Sarah is bleeding and hurt. Pregnant with my child. I don't want her to wake up without me being there. And I'm out here while some nurse who doesn't know shit tells me to *have a seat*. My hands shake with the need to do something. Anything.

The ER doors burst open again. This time Glitch and Fallon rush in.

"What's happening?" Jake demands.

"I don't know yet." My voice sounds shredded.

Fallon looks up at me, breathless and crying. "Is she going to be okay?" Her voice cracks. "Do they know she's pregnant?"

"She will be." I say it like fact. Like law. "And yes. They know."

Because the alternative doesn't exist. Fallon nods shakily. Then finally notices Ramsey.

Her eyes widen. "Oh." She fans herself dramatically. "Wow."

Jake looks offended. "Hey."

Ramsey ignores both of them. Of course he does. Instead he smirks at me. "Pregnant, huh?"

He folds his arms. "When did that happen?"

My patience snaps clean in half. "Fuck off, Ramsey."

He chuckles. "Just making conversation." Then glances at my fists. "So touchy."

"Well don't."

His smile sharpens into a fake smile. "It's funny, actually." He tilts his head. "I've been investigating this case for a month." His eyes lock on mine. "And I keep learning so many new things."

I step slowly toward him. Tension dangerously coiled tight. "My personal life has nothing to do with this investigation."

"Oh, I beg to differ." He says it mockingly.

"Maybe if you'd given me all the information, I could decide that for myself."

My jaw ticks. I am one sentence away from rearranging his face. Jake must see it because he steps between us.

"Alright." He puts both hands out. "Everybody sit down before we need another hospital room." I step back. Barely. Breathe in. Breathe out. Clench fists. Unclench.

The doors open again. An older doctor with greying hair in blue scrubs walks in. "Sarah?" I spin so fast my vision blurs. Fallon moves to my side instantly.

"I'm her fiancé," I say before he can ask. The lie comes easier this time. The doctor nods, faintly amused.

"I'm Dr. Keys" He checks a chart. "The bullet only grazed her leg."

My lungs unlock a fraction. "Took a section of skin, but no major structural damage. We cleaned it, stitched it and she's awake."

Relief hits so hard my knees nearly give. "She's asking for you."

I swallow against the burn in my throat. "And the baby?"

Dr. Keys smiles slightly. "The baby is fine." A shaking breath tears out of me.

"We're moving her to a monitored observation room," he continues. "Mostly as a precaution because of the pregnancy, the blood loss, and everything her body has been through today. I want to keep an eye on her overnight, but I fully expect she'll be discharged in the morning."

Fallon exhales loudly beside me. "When can we see her?"

"We're getting her settled now."

Then he looks at me. "Come on. I'll take you." I don't hesitate. I follow immediately. The halls feel too long, he's moving too slowly. Fluorescent lights hum overhead. My pulse pounds in my ears.

What if she blames me? What if she doesn't want me there? What if I broke us again? We turn into the observation unit. The automatic doors hiss open to a colder, quieter world. Fluorescent lights glare off polished floors. Monitors beep in uneven rhythms behind half-closed doors. The sharp smell of antiseptic hangs in the air, mixed with burnt coffee and stale vending machine snacks.

Families line the hallway in plastic chairs. A woman clutches a rosary so tight her knuckles are white. An older man stares blankly at a muted television bolted in the corner. A kid sleeps curled across two chairs while his mother whispers into clasped hands. Everyone here is waiting for news that could break them.

"Room four," Dr. Keys says, gesturing down the corridor.

I nod once and move fast, stepping inside. Then stop dead, the room is empty. Fresh sheets folded tight across the bed, rumpled slightly like someone had sat down but not for long. Heart monitor dark. No nurse, getting everything ready like I thought. There's no movement, no sound.

No Sarah. My stomach drops through the floor. I check the bathroom. Empty. The shower curtain hangs open, the sink is dry, unused towels. My hands start shaking. I storm back into the hall and find Keys speaking with a nurse at the station, chart lights glowing blue across their faces.

"Doctor." My voice barely sounds human. "There's a mistake." He turns. "There's no one in that room."

His brow furrows. "What?"

The blonde nurse beside him twirls a strand of hair around one finger. "Oh!" She brightens like she solved a puzzle.

"Someone from radiology took her for more tests."

Keys goes still. "I didn't order any tests."

Her smile falters. "Oh." She blinks twice. "Um... he said the doctor wanted them."

The hallway narrows around me. "What did he look like?"

She swallows. "A young man in scrubs." Then, absurdly, "Cute." My jaw clenches so hard pain shoots into my temple. "Only he had some scar on his face, like maybe he'd been burned? I don't know I didn't want to be rude and stare too long. He must be new."

Every word out of her mouth is worse than the last. I step forward. Slowly. Every syllable carved from violence.

"Where. The fuck. Is she?" She blanches and lunges for the desk phone.

Dials radiology. Waits. Listens. All color drains from her face.

"They... they don't have her."

Something feral tears out of my chest. A sound so raw I don't recognize it as mine. Sarah is gone, again. This time, I'm going to tear this entire hospital apart.

I'm already pulling out my phone. Behind me, Dr. Keys is shouting at the nurses' station.

"Get security on the line now!" Phones start ringing. Voices rise. Someone says lockdown. Someone else says call the police. I don't listen to any of it. None of that is fast enough.

I dial Glitch. He answers on the first ring. "Glitch." Not his usual humor, no smart ass tone. He already knows something's wrong.

"Get back here now." My voice is ice. "She's gone. Someone took her."

I hang up before he answers. Dial again

He picks up immediately. "Ghost."

"Track her phone." My chest heaves. "She's been taken again."

Keys start clacking violently in the background.

"On it." I hear movement too. A door slamming, fast footsteps. I turn toward the ICU entrance. Glitch is barreling through the doors first, shoving past two nurses trying to stop him. Fallon is sprinting behind him, red hair flying. Ramsey comes after them flashing his badge and barking at staff to move.

"Sitrep?" Jake snaps the second he reaches me.

"Ghost is tracking her phone now." I scan every exit. Every hallway.

Every face. They couldn't have gotten far. None of them are hers.

Glitch's jaw hardens. "How the fuck did they get her out?"

I point toward the pale blonde nurse now crying at the desk. "She let some guy in scrubs take her. Said he was from Radiology," I sneer. "Pretending to be staff."

Ramsey mutters a curse and grabs the nearest hospital landline. "Pull camera feeds. Every exit. Now."

"He—he had light blue eyes and long messy brown hair. Tall… um… thin." The blonde nurse is stammering to a hospital security guard, mascara smudged under her eyes. My body locks, every sound around me dulls.

I turn slowly. "What did you say?"

She startles and points shakily toward the elevators. "Light blue eyes. Brown hair. Kind of shaggy? He had on scrubs and a mask at first but—"

I don't hear the rest. I look at Glitch and I see it in his face. He already knows. The same cold recognition tearing through me. Benjamin. He's alive, he's here and he just took her. My pulse pounds so hard it blurs the edges of my vision. Rage crashes through me so violently I nearly black out.

"He's supposed to be dead," Fallon whispers somewhere behind us.

"No," I say, voice flat and lethal. "He was supposed to stay gone."

My phone is still pressed to my ear.

Ghost's voice cuts in. "Wraith?" I drag air into my lungs.

"It's Benjamin."

"Son of a bitch." He curses.

"We need a car." I start moving before anyone answers. "If she doesn't have her phone, we've got nothing."

Ghost comes back immediately. "She has it. Signal still live." Thank God. "She's moving north. Fast."

I bare my teeth. "Then let's go get her."

"I have my car, let's go." Ramsey says. We're all storming down the hallway. Boots pounding over polished tile. Nurses flatten themselves against walls. Visitors jump out of the way.

Glitch is at my shoulder, jaw locked and eyes sharp. Fallon is keeping pace behind us, face pale but determined. Ramsey is on his phone, barking orders fast enough I can barely make them out.

"State patrol. Interstate cameras. Patch me through now."

My phone is still pressed to my ear. Ghost's voice feeds me updates between bursts of keyboard clicks. "Still northbound. Speed increasing.

Just merged onto Interstate 35W."

Sarah is in that car. Scared and hurt, she was only stitched up less than twenty minutes ago. Carrying my baby and that sick bastard has his hands on her again. Something savage claws up my throat. I shove through the exit doors so hard they slam against the wall.

The parking lot stretches wide under harsh lights, ambulances idling, tires hissing over wet pavement.

"Car's this way!" Jake barks. I'm already running. My blood is thunder in my ears. My mind is a single violent promise. I lost her once. I lost her twice. There will not be a third time.

Chapter Forty

Sarah

Pain dragged me awake in sharp, burning waves. I jerked, sucking in a breath, and immediately regretted it when fire ripped through my leg.

"Easy, Sarah. Easy." A woman's voice. It's both calm and professional. I blinked against the bright overhead lights and found myself back in a curtained ER room. White ceiling tiles. Monitors beeping steadily beside me. The sharp smell of antiseptic filling the air. A nurse stood beside my bed while a doctor worked near my thigh.

"What—" My throat felt raw.

"You were grazed by a bullet," the nurse said gently. "The doctor is finishing a few stitches now. You're okay."

Memory slammed back all at once. Being in that university bathroom, stepping out of the stall to see Dr. Wagner standing there holding a gun. Wade shouting, thank goodness he wouldn't wait outside for long. The gun shots were deafening and at first I didn't feel the pain, my eyes just watching Wagner go down before the pain even registered.

My hands flew to my stomach. The nurse caught them quickly.

"The baby is okay," she said before I could speak. "We checked. Try to breathe."

A sob broke out of me before I could stop it. relief coursing through me, shock and fear come next. I can't believe that even happened, a distinguished doctor, dean of the school. The desperation in his eyes, everything tangles together.

"Wade? My boyfriend?" I whispered.

"He's here," she said. "He's waiting outside." Of course he was. Probably terrifying half the hospital. That almost made me smile, I just want him with me.

The doctor tied off the final stitch. "All done," he said. "You're lucky. Painful, but superficial. No muscle damage."

Lucky. That word felt strange after everything. They wrapped my thigh in a thick dressing, then helped slide me onto a fresh bed. The movement sent another flash of pain through me.

"I know," the nurse murmured. "We're moving you to an observation room. Just overnight monitoring because of the pregnancy and blood loss."

I nodded weakly. My body felt heavy. Boneless, exhausted in a way not even sleep could fix. They wheeled me through bright hallways that blurred together overhead, the elevator. Voices that were not the voice I wanted to hear. Shoes squeaking on polished floors.

Eventually they rolled me into a quieter room with softer monitor lights. A single bed is in the center, with freshly folded blankets and sheets. A large window that shoes a roof top. A small chair in the far corner. Much calmer than the ER chaos.

"This is better," I whispered.

The nurse smiled while adjusting the bed rails. "We'll get you settled and then bring your fiancé back." Fiancé. Heat touched my cheeks. Before I could correct her, she says, "Give me one moment, we need to get this bed made for you." She leaves for a moment and grabs another nurse, she's blonde and younger. She apologizes quickly and makes the bed.

The other nurse tells me she is leaving me in good hands. I don't feel like I am in good hands because as soon as she leaves, the new one says, "I just need to grab one more thing from the station," she said. "I forgot your admission paperwork and another pillow." She fussed with the blanket once more. "I'll be right back."

Then she hurried out, leaving the door cracked open behind her. She didn't even set up my monitor and I really want to hear the baby's heartbeat again. The room fell quiet. I stared at the ceiling, listening to the distant hum of hospital sounds. Voices far away. Rolling carts being pushed. Muted announcements overhead. I should have felt safe.

Instead, a cold unease crawled slowly down my spine. The nurse comes back and after fussing with my blankets and nearly tripping over the cords again, the nurse gave me an embarrassed smile.

"I swear, I'm making a mess of this." She glanced at the monitor beside me. "I still need to hook up your leads and grab another IV bag. Don't go anywhere." The attempt at humor barely landed.

My leg throbbed beneath the bandage. My body felt shaky and drained. "I'll be right back, okay?" She hurried out, leaving the monitor dark except for a standby light, the IV line hanging loose beside the bed, not yet connected.

The door stayed cracked open. Right outside, I heard a soft giggle. Her voice. Then the low murmur of a man speaking too quietly to make out.

"Yes, go ahead," she said lightly. "Be quick though. I think the doctor will be bringing one of her visitors back to see her." Be quick?

A chill slid through me. "Knock, knock." The voice was casual, warm, even. Completely unassuming but the second the door opened wider, every muscle in my body locked. A tall man in blue scrubs stepped inside, head bent over a clipboard. Fluorescent light glinted off dark hair. Mask pushed up over his mouth but it's not covering his nose. Something about the way he moved, the set of his shoulders, the lazy confidence in every step was wrong. My heart slammed against my ribs.

No, that's impossible. He lifted his head slowly. Deliberately and smiled. The same sick, amused grin that still lived in my nightmares. Benjamin. A strangled sound caught in my throat. He may have been trying to hide beneath the mask but there was no mistaking him. There was no monitor to betray me yet, no machine screaming my panic for me. Only the thunder of my pulse in my ears.

His grin widened. "Well," he said softly. "There's my favorite girl."

I couldn't breathe. Wade's voice slammed through my head. *Little Mouse, breathe. Don't let them see fear. Think.*

But I couldn't think. The room shrank around me. The walls were closing in. The air was getting too thick and hard to breathe. Sweat was forming at the base of my neck. My hands shook against the sheets.

How is he here? They said the place exploded, how did he get out and get through a jungle on his own. I thought he died there. I hoped he died there.

Benjamin took one slow step closer. My stomach lurched. The right side of his face was ravaged with burns, shiny uneven skin dragged tight from temple to jaw. One ear curled slightly inward. His forearm was worse. Scar tissue twisted up from his wrist and disappeared beneath his sleeve. The jungle hadn't killed him. It had only marked him. He'd crawled his way back and now he was here. With me. Alone.

My fingers clench the thin hospital blanket. My breath comes shallow. My pulse is a wild, desperate drum against my ribs.

"You look like you've seen a ghost," Benjamin muses. His voice is smooth. I wish he *was* a ghost. "I was hoping to prolong this," he says, shutting the door quietly behind him. "But obviously, you know it's me."

He tilts his head, smile sharpening. "My girl knows me so well." Revulsion crawls up my throat. My mouth is dry. My tongue feels too thick.

"How?" I croak, forcing the word out.

His grin stretches wider. lazy and cruel, as if he ha no concern besides whatever he has planned for me. My fingers dig deeper into the blanket.

"You know Wade is here," I say, grabbing for the only weapon I have. "There's nothing you can do." His expression changes instantly. Amusement curdles into something darker.

"That's where you're wrong, my love." My stomach flips violently. *My love.* I want to vomit.

Memory crashes over me. His hands pinning my wrists. The smell of sweat and dirt. His breath hot against my ear. The laugh he made when I fought him. The exact moment I understood I was trapped. The ropes cutting into my skin as I fought as hard as I could.

And Wade came for me. Wade found me. Wade saved me. But Wade isn't here now.

"You need to leave," I whisper. I try to make it steady but the tremor ruins it.

Benjamin smiles again, pleased by my fear. "Oh, my love." He steps closer. "I'm afraid you don't have a choice."

My whole body shudders. "You're going to get up and come with me." He gestures toward the hall. "I have a wheelchair outside the door." Then he smiles like he's offering flowers. "And we're finally going to be together."

No. No no no. "I'm not going anywhere with you."

He exhales dramatically and shakes his head like I'm being unreasonable. "You will." His voice goes flat. Cold. "Or I'm going to cut you open and remove that baby that belongs to him." Ice floods every vein in my body. My hand flies instinctively to my stomach. How does he know? I hadn't even told Wade until last night.

A scream surges up my throat. He moves fast. Benjamin lunges forward and clamps his burned hand over my mouth. The skin is shiny and rough against my lips. The smell of antiseptic mixed with sweat turns my stomach.

"No screaming," he says quietly. His blue eyes go flat. "I have a knife in my pocket, and I'll use it now if I need to."

Terror spikes so hard my vision blurs. Then something colder settles beneath it. I stop fighting. Not because I'm giving up, because I need to think. I stare at him and begin wondering how to kill him first.

"That's right," He says smugly when he slowly removes his hand. "You don't have a choice." He steps back toward the bed. "Now sit up, and I'll start removing all these cords."

Think, Sarah. Don't panic. Think. I squeeze my eyes shut for one second. Wade's warm brown eyes flash through my mind. *You're strong, Little Mouse. Stronger than you know.*

My eyes open. Benjamin starts tugging at the lines attached to me, pulse clip, blood pressure cuff, the loose IV tubing not yet connected. I force my body to cooperate. Slowly. Carefully. I sit up and pain slices through my thigh. The room tilts. My legs tremble the second they touch the floor. I bite the inside of my cheek hard enough to taste blood. Not just for me. For the baby. I scan the room without moving my head.

Door. Sink. Metal tray. Call button too far away. Then I see my phone, sitting on the counter just behind him. If I can get it, if I can text Wade, he'll find me. He always finds me. But my balance is shot. My leg is weak.

If I make the wrong move, he'll know. I don't have another option. I take one shaky step. Then another. Then I let my knees buckle. My body pitches sideways with a cry. Benjamin curses and lunges, grabbing my arm to keep me from crashing to the floor. I let myself fall toward the counter. My fingers slap blindly across the surface, then close around my phone. Got it.

He jerks me upright before I can do anything else. "What the hell is wrong with you?" he snaps.

I whimper and sag against him, playing weak. Everything in me hates touching him.

"Leg hurts," I whisper.

His irritation softens into smug satisfaction. "Poor thing." He shoves me down into the wheelchair waiting outside the room. Pain shoots through my thigh. I gasp but my phone is hidden beneath the blanket draped over my lap. I can take the pain for as long as I need to make sure I keep my phone and get safe. My fingers lock around it. Benjamin turns the chair and starts pushing me down the hallway. He keeps his head down, pace even, like he belongs here. No one stops us. No one looks twice. I keep my breathing shallow. Keep my face frightened. Keep my phone hidden underneath me.

Wade's voice echoes in my head. *I will always come for you.* I cling to it like oxygen, because this time, I need him to find me before it's too late. Before he hurts our baby.

He gets us out a side door without anyone batting an eye. No one questions the man in scrubs wheeling a pale woman wrapped in hospital blankets through the corridor. The automatic doors slide open and cold air hits my face. Outside, an older beat-up sedan waits at the curb, engine idling. Rust along the wheel well. Cracked rear taillight, mud crusted along the lower panels. Nothing memorable, exactly the kind of car no one notices.

Benjamin glances once across the parking lot, then grabs my arm and hauls me upright. Pain tears through my thigh. I bite back a cry.

"Move," he mutters. He shoves me into the passenger seat.

I slump sideways like I'm weaker than I am, using the motion to tuck my phone deeper beneath me. Hidden between my hip and the seat. Please let it stay there. Please let Wade track it. Benjamin rounds the hood, slides behind the wheel, and peels away from the hospital. My heart pounds so hard it makes me nauseous.

Streetlights streak past, traffic blurs around us. He navigates through the city with disturbing ease, cutting through turns like he's planned every second of this. Within minutes we're climbing the ramp onto Interstate 35W heading north. Away. I keep checking the side mirror.

Again.

Again.

Again.

Every pair of headlights makes hope flare in my chest. Then die. No Wade. No rescue. Does he even know I'm missing yet?

Benjamin notices. "Looking for your soldier?" His voice is amused. I say nothing. My hand presses subtly against the hidden phone. Come on. Come on. Find me. He chuckles and accelerates harder. The city begins to fall behind us. I briefly consider throwing myself from the car. The thought flickers, wild and desperate, but I force it down. *Not smart, Sarah. Think.* If I jump now, I could break something or hurt the baby. If I don't, I might never get the chance again.

The car hums steadily beneath me as we head farther north. Tires singing over pavement. Wind pressing against the windows. The rhythmic thump of seams in the highway. I glance at the dashboard clock. 3:00 p.m. The afternoon sun still hangs in the sky, pale and cold, but time is slipping through my fingers. A few more hours and it'll be dark. No one will see me. No one will hear me scream. Wade always said he worked better under the cloak of darkness, easier to keep hidden.

My phone vibrates once beneath my thigh, a faint buzz against my skin. I don't dare look down. But relief flashes hot through me. It still has power. I curl my fingers tighter around it, hidden under the blanket and my body. Wade's voice echoes through my head. *Hold on, Little Mouse. I will always find you.*

Benjamin hasn't said much. That scares me more than his usual rambling. Silence means thinking. Planning. Every few minutes he glances at me. I keep my face blank, eyes forward. Let him think I'm broken. Let him think I've given up.

"Where are we going?" I ask finally. My voice sounds steadier than I feel.

His mouth curves into that awful smile. "My family has a cabin." He taps the steering wheel casually. "About an hour north of here."

My blood turns cold. "No one will be able to find us there." An hour. Too far. If we make it there, I may not get another chance. He keeps talking like we're discussing weekend plans.

"From there, I can get you clothes. Food. Anything you need before we make our next move." My stomach twists so hard I nearly double over.

"I can see you're excited," he says with a soft chuckle. Like we're sharing a joke. "It's going to be great." His eyes flick to me again.

"Just you and me." My nails bite into my palms. "Then once we get rid of that thing growing inside you—" He says it casually, cruelly. "—I can put my own baby in there."

Bile surges into my throat. For one dangerous second, I almost launch across the console and rip his face apart. Instead, I lock my hands on my thighs and breathe through my nose. Wade's voice again. *Breathe, baby. Don't let fear control you.* I stare straight ahead. He thinks I'm helpless. He thinks I'm trapped. He thinks I'm his. Let him believe it.

"I'm sorry my uncle shot you," he says quietly. "I wanted this to be different. I never wanted to sell you." His eyes flick constantly between the road and me. "You were always mine to keep." A cold wave of disgust crawls down my spine. I don't respond. What does he expect me to say? *It's okay?*

Forty minutes pass in agonizing silence before he finally takes an exit off the freeway. Then another twenty minutes of winding county roads. Trees crowd both sides of the pavement. Patches of open field. Farmhouses set far back from the road. The farther we go, the emptier everything becomes. My pulse climbs with every mile.

Then a sign appears ahead. Scandia. The name means nothing to me. Just another place between me and safety. We roll into town, and it's nothing like I expected. Historic brick buildings line the main street, sturdy and beautiful, the kind that have clearly stood there for generations. Old storefront windows gleam in the afternoon light. Fresh paint trims doorframes. Flower planters sit beneath benches. Flags hang from a few lampposts.

Everything looks cared for. Proud. Quiet in that small-town way where people know each other and notice when something is off. For one wild second, hope surges through me. There are people here. Witnesses. Help. Safety. But Benjamin doesn't slow. He doesn't stop near the shops or the gas station or anywhere someone might see me too clearly. He keeps driving straight through town. Past the places where I might have had a chance. Past every person who could have helped.

And toward the empty roads beyond it. We come up to some buildings in the middle of nowhere. A gas station, a hardware store, a church with peeling white paint. And a small rundown bar sitting near the edge of town, The Rusty Nail. Its weathered wooden siding has faded to a dull gray. A neon sign in the window buzzes weakly, the red letters flickering in and out like they're struggling to stay alive. The parking lot is a patchwork of cracked asphalt and gravel, crowded with pickup trucks, motorcycles and one rusted sedan missing a hubcap.

Above the door, a dented old beer sign hangs crooked in the wind. The whole place looks tired. Forgotten. Exactly the kind of place where no one asks questions.

Benjamin pulls into a gas station just outside town, tires crunching over gravel before stopping beside a pump. I glance out the window. The convenience store is attached to the station, sharing the same lot with a small diner-style counter inside. Pickup trucks sit near the entrance. A woman is pumping gas two lanes over. Two teenagers lean against a truck laughing.

An older man carries coffee cups toward the door. People. Witnesses. Hope punches through my chest so suddenly it hurts.

"I need gas," He says, shutting off the engine. He looks over at me like we're on a road trip together. "You just stay in the car. I'm sure your leg is hurting." It is. A deep throbbing burn radiates through my thigh with every heartbeat.

"I can get you some medicine and water." He's leaving me alone. My pulse races so fast I feel dizzy. This is my chance. "Do you want anything else?" His tone is almost affectionate. I nearly recoil, I force myself still. Pain screams through my leg, but I shove it aside. I can hurt later. I can panic later. Right now I survive.

"No." I shake my head quickly. "I don't need anything. Water and something for pain would be great." His smile softens, like he's relieved I'm finally cooperating. Good. Let him believe it.

"Okay, my love. I'll be right back." Revulsion crawls up my throat. I give him nothing. He steps out and closes the door, then walks toward the store. His reflection flickers across the tinted windows. For a second I lose sight of him. I grip my phone so tightly my knuckles ache. Do I call Wade? Text him? No, no time. If Benjamin looks back and sees me lit up by a screen, it's over. I scan the lot. Trying to figure out the best course. Store entrance that would bring me right to Benjamin or the bar entrance that's not much further.

The Rusty Nail, it is. If I can make it inside, I might be safe. Someone there might help me. Someone might call the police. Someone might lock the door behind me. Every instinct in me screams to run. But my leg pulses like fire. Each heartbeat sends pain slicing through the wound, a brutal reminder of the bullet that nearly tore through more than skin.

My fingers fumble for the handle. Please don't be child-locked. Please don't be stuck. Please let this work. I glance once toward the gas station doors. No sign of Benjamin. *Move, Sarah. Move now.*

Chapter Forty One

Sarah

I shove the car door open and push off the seat. Pain explodes through my thigh. A sharp, blinding burn that nearly drops me back onto the gravel. I catch myself on the doorframe, sucking in a breath through clenched teeth. Then I run or the closest thing my body can manage. An awkward, limping sprint across cracked pavement and loose gravel.

Every step sends fire up my leg. My hospital bandage pulls tight beneath my borrowed blanket. My vision blurs and black spots dance at the edges, but I don't stop.

I reach the door of The Rusty Nail and yank it open with shaking hands. Warmth and noise hit me first. Dim yellow lighting. The smell of spilled beer, fried food, cigarette smoke long soaked into wood, and something smoky from a back kitchen fryer. Old wooden floors scuffed raw and sticky in places under my shoes. A long L-shaped bar stretches across the back wall, dark with age and stained by decades of elbows and spilled drinks.

Two battered pool tables sit off to one side, torn green felt under hanging lamps. A dartboard with a bent wire hangs crooked near a faded chalk scoreboard. An old jukebox hums in the corner, halfway through a classic rock song that skips once before continuing.

Hand-painted signs behind the bar read:

Cash Only

No Fighting Inside

Everything stops when I stumble in. Pool balls go still. Conversation dies. Six sets of eyes snap toward me. An older man behind the bar polishing a glass. A middle-aged couple squeezed into a booth near the wall. Three men by the pool table, cues in hand. All staring. I know what they see.

Barefoot. Pale. Hair tangled. Hospital gown with a matching bracelet. Blood seeping through the bandage on my thigh. Fear written all over my face. I grab the doorframe to stay upright.

"Please," I gasp. My voice cracks. "Help me."

The bartender frowns deeply. "Miss, are you okay?"

I shake my head so hard it makes the room tilt. "No." I clutch the back of my hospital gown closed with one hand, the other braced on the bar to stay upright. "I've been kidnapped."

The words crack out of me. "He's in the gas station. He brought me here. I don't have much time." My breath stutters. "He's going to come looking for me."

The entire bar goes still. Even the jukebox seems quieter. The three men by the pool table straighten. The couple in the booth stare openly. The bartender is the first to move. He sets the glass down slowly and steps out from behind the bar. Up close, he's broad and stocky, mid-fifties maybe, graying hair, faded flannel stretched over thick shoulders. Kind eyes and hard expression. No nonsense.

"Come on, sweetheart, My name is Jason, I own this place," he says, voice low and steady. "You can hide in my office."

He jerks his head toward the back. "Door locks from the inside." Relief nearly buckles my knees. He catches my elbow before I fall.

"Easy now." Then he turns to the room.

"Earl, watch the front." One of the pool players nods.

"Denny, call 911. " Another man is already pulling out his phone.

Jason guides me quickly toward a narrow hallway beside the bar. The smell changes back here. Old mop water. Beer soaked into wood. A hint of bleach trying and failing to cover everything else. Two bathroom doors sit crooked on either side. At the end, a door marked

OFFICE. Jason shoves it open. The hinges groan. Inside is a cramped little room. Old wooden desk, with one folding metal chair. Onto is a stack of receipts and a security monitor that looks ancient, showing a fuzzy black and white camera feed. A metal filing cabinet sits in the other corner.

"Sit tight and lock it after me." His voice is firm but kind. "We'll handle the rest." I nod, shaking uncontrollably.

He steps back out. I slam the door shut behind him and turn the lock. The click sounds pathetically small. I stagger to the chair and collapse into it, gasping for air. My phone vibrates again in my hand. I look down for the first time. Missed calls. Texts. So many texts.

Jerk: Sarah, I'm coming.

Jerk: I love you. Stay strong.

Then the newest one.

Jerk: I will always find you and our baby.

A half sob half laugh tears out of me. I unblocked him but I never changed his contact name. My fingers tremble as I start typing back. A violent bang slams from somewhere outside the office door. I freeze and grip my phone tighter. Benjamin is here. Even though I shouldn't yet, I click Wade's name and hit call.

He answers on the first ring. "Mouse?" His voice is rough, urgent. "Are you okay?"

The sound of him shatters whatever control I had left. A sob rips out of me. Then another. Suddenly I can't stop crying. My whole body shakes so hard the chair rattles beneath me. I try to breathe. Try to speak. Try to tell him where I am. But panic has my throat locked tight.

Then I hear another voice. Too close. I go dead still.

"She must be in here somewhere." Benjamin says from outside the door, his tone smooth and casual. Like this is nothing.

"This is the closest place. I'm just worried, my girlfriend isn't well." I slap a hand over my mouth. Squeeze my eyes shut. The office door handle rattles hard.

I nearly scream. "That's my office." Jason's voice cuts through the room. It's deep, firm and completely unmoving. "No one goes in there but me. Now if you're not buying anything, you need to leave."

Silence. Then slow retreating footsteps or pretending to, it's hard to tell. I don't move or breathe, I don't trust it.

"Sarah, baby." Wade's voice comes softer now. Steady. Coaxing. "Can you talk yet?"

I lower my shaking hand. "I'm not sure," I whisper. "I don't know if he's still out there."

A whimper slips loose. I bite it back too late. My whole body feels like it's splintering apart.

"Okay." His tone shifts instantly. Calm. "We're on our way." I hear road noise on his end, an engine revving. Voices in the background.

"We're not far." A shaky breath leaves me. "I'm so damn proud of you for grabbing your phone." My eyes burn. "Ghost has been tracking you since we realized you were gone."

Relief crashes through me so hard I nearly slide out of the chair. If I weren't already sitting, I'd have collapsed.

"How much longer?" My voice sounds small. Childlike. "I'm scared." The confession breaks me open again. "I just want to go home."

"Five minutes, baby." No hesitation. Absolute certainty. "Just five more minutes."

I nod even though he can't see me. Five minutes. I just have to survive five more minutes.

"Are you in a safe location?" He asks, his tone sharpening into pure command. "Benjamin can't get to you, right?" Just hearing that name sends panic clawing back up my throat. Fresh tears spill harder.

"Yes." My voice breaks. "This nice bar owner brought me to his office and had me lock the door." I glance at the thin knob like it's the only thing holding the world back. "He said he was calling the police, but I don't know what's happening out there." My fingers twist in the hem of my hospital gown. "W-Wade..." I choke on the next words. "He threatened the baby." There's a sharp inhale, the kind that tells me he's barely holding himself together.

His voice drops low. Thick with fury held on a leash. "Shh. It's okay." Every syllable controlled. "You kept yourself and the baby safe. That's all that matters." I press my hand over my stomach. "You stay right there until I come get you."

His teeth grind audibly through the phone. "Let's hope, for his sake, the police already have him in cuffs."

A shaky breath leaves me. "Okay."

"We're pulling in now." Urgency floods his voice. "I'm going to hang up." I can hear the sound of tires screeching on his end. "Do not leave that office until I come for you."

"O-okay." My throat tightens. "I love you." Barely louder than a whisper.

"I love you too." No hesitation. "See you soon."

The line goes dead. I stare at the door, my pulse hammering. Any second now. Any second—a violent crash explodes outside. Wood scraping. A chair skidding hard across the floor. Someone screams. Then Wade. A roar of rage so primal it freezes me in place. The sound of fists hitting flesh. Heavy. Brutal.

Again.

Again.

A sickening crack. A weak moan of pain. My hands clench into fists so hard my nails bite skin. My whole body shakes.

"Blakely! That's enough!" Another male voice that's sharp and authoritative but one I don't recognize. The pounding stops. Muffled shouting fills the bar. Bootsteps. Someone groaning. More voices layering over each other. I want to throw open the door. I want to run to him. I want to see with my own eyes that it's over. But I don't move. I stay exactly where he told me. I don't know how long I can keep waiting, my heart slamming, knees trembling. Listening for the sound of him coming for me.

A knock sounds against the office door. Gentle this time. Then his voice. "Little Mouse, it's me."

My breath leaves in a broken sob. Relief hits so hard I almost fall off the chair. I shove up from the chair on shaking legs. Pain rips through my thigh instantly. My knee nearly buckles. I catch myself on the desk, gasping. When I glance down, blood is trailing along my calf, soaking through the side of the hospital gown. Fresh red. I must have torn the stitches when I ran. I limp to the door as fast as I can, hands fumbling at the lock. It feels like forever before it clicks. I yank it open. Wade stands there filling the doorway.

Chest heaving, his hair is disheveled. Knuckles split and reddened, his eyes are wild, I see it all at once. The relief, terror, rage barely contained. His whole body goes rigid as he takes me in. Then he reaches for me. I collapse into his arms. Everything inside me gives way. I clutch at his shirt, sobbing against him as the last hour crashes through me all at once. He wraps me tighter. Buries his face in my hair.

"Jesus, Sarah." His voice is wrecked. I try to stop crying. I can't. He pulls back just enough to look at me, hands framing my face while his eyes sweep over every inch of me. Checking. Then his gaze drops to my leg. His jaw locks.

Fresh fury flashes in his eyes. "Are you okay?" The questions come rapid, rough. "Did he touch you? Are you in pain?"

"I'm okay," I whisper. My voice trembles. "No, he never touched me." I swallow. "Yes, I'm in pain." Another sob catches. "But I just want to go home." His face changes instantly. Softens. The violence drains out of him. Only tenderness remains.

"Okay," he murmurs. He presses a kiss to my forehead. "We're going to get you to a hospital and then I will take you home." Then he bends and lifts me effortlessly into his arms. Careful of my leg. Careful of everything. I wrap myself around him and hide my face in his shoulder as he carries me out of the hallway and for the first time since waking up in that hospital room, I feel safe again. The bar is eerily silent.

No jukebox. No pool balls cracking. No low murmur of conversation. Just my uneven breaths breaking into hiccups as I try to stop crying and the heavy sound of Wade's boots crossing the floor. Every eye in the bar is on us. I lift my head just enough to look.

Near the exit stands a man in a black suit, posture straight and deliberate. Tall. Almost as tall as Wade. Broad shoulders under a perfectly tailored jacket. Dark brown hair neatly styled. A sharp jaw set tight and striking blue eyes that miss nothing as they track me in Wade's arms.

My stomach tightens. Who is that? Then my gaze catches on the floor. Benjamin lies facedown in handcuffs, blood smeared at the corner of his mouth. Coughing. Groaning. A uniformed sheriff stands over him with one hand near his holster. I swallow hard. This is real. He's caught. He's actually going to jail.

I look up at Wade and whisper, "Who is that?"

He glances down at me, then follows my gaze. His jaw hardens instantly.

"Your eyes stay on me, Mouse," he mutters darkly.

A smooth voice cuts in. "I don't mind if she looks."

I jump against Wade. The suited man has moved closer. Too quiet for someone his size. Too confident. Wade's grip on me tightens.

"Fuck off, Ramsey. I'm taking her to a hospital."

Ramsey's mouth twitches like he's amused. So this is the FBI agent. I barely have time to process it before Wade strides past him, not slowing for anyone.

"I need to ask some questions," Ramsey calls after us. His tone is maddeningly casual.

Wade doesn't break stride. "You can stop by tomorrow." He shoulders open the front door. "Right now she's going back to the hospital, then home." His voice drops into something lethal. "Where I can keep her safe. Because the FBI apparently can't do shit."

Cold evening air hits my face as we step outside. In the lot, Glitch is standing there and he already has the back door open.

"Always with the dramatics, Rocky," he says, shaking his head. Normally I might laugh. Right now I have nothing left. I just curl tighter into Wade as he lowers me carefully into the back seat, keeping my injured leg supported. Then he climbs in beside me immediately, pulling me against his chest.

Ramsey appears outside the car window. "I'm serious," he says. "I need a statement. This whole investigation is a damn mess."

"You'll get one," Wade says flatly. Then he slams the door in his face. Glitch doesn't hesitate. The engine revs. We pull out fast, tires spitting gravel as we head back toward the highway. I exhale slowly. Every inch of me aches. My thigh. My chest. My soul, but for the first time in hours, I feel safe. I melt against Wade. His arms tighten around me. His lips press to the top of my head. The exhaustion is pressing in and I don't fight it, I just let it take me knowing I'm safe.

I wake in a hospital room I don't recognize. This one is different. Bigger, quieter and a little nicer. Soft lighting glows from the wall instead of the harsh fluorescent lights from before. A wide window lets in the first hint of morning, pale gold stretching across the floor. There's a recliner in the corner, a couch against one wall, and actual framed pictures instead of blank beige emptiness.

Panic flares before I hear the, beep. Beep. Beep. The steady rhythm beside me and another sound layered with it. Faster. Rapid. Beautiful. I turn my head. A smaller monitor sits beside the main one, numbers flickering across the screen. I follow the cord down to my belly. My breath catches. The baby's heartbeat, it's strong and quick. The same sound I heard the first time. The sound I will never forget. Tears sting my eyes instantly.

I lift the blanket enough to see I'm in a clean hospital gown. Fresh bandages wrap my thigh, white and neat where blood and panic used to be. Then I look left.

Wade is slumped in a chair beside the bed, far too large for it, head resting near my uninjured leg. One hand is draped over mine like even in sleep he had to make sure I was still here. On the ugly little couch, Fallon is curled on her side, dead asleep beneath a thin blanket. And in another chair, legs stretched out and head tipped back, Jake is snoring softly. My chest aches with love so sudden and fierce it steals my breath.

I don't feel much pain right now. For that, I am deeply grateful. Because I remember all of the pain from trying to run. I turn my hand beneath Wade's and lace my fingers through his. He wakes instantly, eyes opening, alert in half a second.

Then softening when he sees me awake. "Hey, beautiful," he rasps. His voice is rough with sleep. Emotion lodges in my throat.

"I love you," I choke out. There are a thousand things I should say. A thousand questions. Fears I should be voicing. The palpable relief flowing through me, but that is all that comes. His eyes warm.

He lifts my hand and kisses my knuckles. "I love you too." Another kiss. "I'm so damn glad you and the baby are okay."

"They checked on the baby?" I ask quickly.

He nods. "Checked everything." His thumb strokes over my hand. "Baby's perfect. Exactly how they should be." His mouth twitches. "They said they didn't need to keep the fetal monitor on all night..." I glance at the machine. "...but I liked hearing it, so."

A laugh escapes me before I can stop it. So he bullied an entire hospital staff into leaving it.

"Your leg is okay too," he continues. "You tore some stitches, but they fixed it." Then his expression turns serious. "We get discharged tomorrow." His hand tightens around mine. "And I'm taking you home and never letting you out of my sight."

I swallow hard. "I don't think I ever want to be alone again."

He stands, leans carefully over me, and presses his forehead to mine. "You won't be."

My eyes burn again. "What about Benjamin?"

His jaw ticks. "Federal custody."

"And Wagner?"

"Also locked up." He glances at me. "Ramsey swears neither of them are seeing daylight for a very long time."

The room goes silent except for the monitors. I search his face. "It's over?" The tears spill before I can stop them. He kisses my forehead. Slow. Certain.

"It's over, Sarah." His voice is steady enough for both of us. "Now we get to move on." I close my eyes and let myself believe him. For the first time in months, I finally can.

Epilogue

Wade

It's been two weeks since Benjamin took her for a second time, it's carved into me deeper than any scar I carry. I still see the hospital room every time I close my eyes. The neatly made bed, the empty sheets. No Sarah. No sound. No sign she had ever been there. Then that nurse's bright, careless voice telling me someone had taken her for more tests. Like it was routine. Like my whole world hadn't just vanished again. I remember the exact second it clicked. Radiology never called for her, no doctor ordered anything. She was gone. Again.

The rage that hit me in that moment was unlike anything I've ever known. Worse than combat, worse than getting shot. Worse than burying brothers. Because this was her, my Little Mouse. The woman I love, the mother of my child and she was in the hands of a monster because I let myself believe she was safe in that hospital. I still hear the sound that came out of me when the nurse admitted they didn't have her.

Not a yell, not a word. Something animal. Something broken. The world tilted all over again, one minute I was ready to bring her home and the next I was back in hell. Knowing I had failed to protect her a third time. Even now, I wake in the early morning, the sun isn't up yet but I keep reaching for her. Checking that she's still beside me. That no one has taken her, ensuring this bed is full. That she's real.

I slide my hand over her stomach and hold it there until my breathing settles. She isn't due for another five months, but there's already the faintest curve there. A small swell that wrecks me every damn time I see it. I was right about her body changing, too. Her breasts are fuller and her skin glows when she laughs. Every sign of what we made together feels like a miracle.

Her leg is healing, she walks with only a slight limp now when she's tired. The first week was rough, pain meds and bandage changes. Watching the incision for infection after tearing the stitches open and needing them redone. I hated every wince, every flinch and I hated it more when she tried to hide the pain from me.

After everything happened, Ramsey and I had one last conversation. One that cemented my hatred for the man.

"You're off the case, Blakely," Ramsey had said, arms crossed as he leaned against a desk at the FBI field office. "You got your girl, your revenge and your happy ending. Let us handle the cleanup." I'd clenched my fists so hard my knuckles popped.

"You think I'm stepping aside? After you let Wagner walk? After she got shot because of it? After Benjamin somehow made it back into the country without anyone flagging him?"

Ramsey had only smirked, his blue eyes cold and filled with calculation. "That's exactly what you're going to do," he said. "Because you've got a woman to take care of, a kid on the way and you're not military anymore." He straightened his cuffs. "You're a civilian now. And civilians don't get involved in federal investigations."

That was the moment I knew I was done waiting for other men to protect what was mine. Done trusting the systems. Done asking permission. That was the day ShadowLink stopped being an idea and became a plan.

The university had no issue giving her time off. Normally missing those teaching labs would've hurt her dissertation standing. Now they're terrified of what she could do to them and they should be. She was assaulted by a student. Kidnapped and trafficked by a professor and that same student. Shot by a dean.

If that sounds impossible, it's because it should be. Instead, it became national news. A scandal so big every network wanted a piece of it. Reporters called nonstop. Camped outside her apartment. Shoved cameras in our faces, asked for statements, asked for tears. Asked if we were "the couple from the jungle case." I wanted to break every lens I saw.

Instead, I took her home and now I'm focused on the only thing that matters. Keeping her safe, keeping our baby safe and building the life we almost lost before it even began.

We packed everything we could in a single day and disappeared. Or as close to disappearing as possible when half the country suddenly knows your names. I found us an Airbnb for a couple of weeks while the media circus died down and the apartment stopped being a campsite for reporters.

Four-bedroom house that had a private driveway and a full tree line in the back. A small gym in the basement with a bench, free weights. There's a treadmill that sounds like it might die any second, so I don't use that. Perfect enough, just her and me. Sarah packed every notebook, hard drive, article and research binder she needed so she could keep working remotely. I offered to carry all of it, she turned me down instantly and I still somehow got yelled at for touching the "organized piles."

She was more than happy to leave. After everything that's happened she wanted privacy, no cameras, no gawking students or professors and no strangers whispering her name. She needed to feel safe, just us. I picked a place not far from where I found her. In Scandia, a small quiet, kind of town people pass through without noticing. Now it means something entirely different to me.

Last week, I ordered enough takeout to set up a proper dinner in the Airbnb. I'm still learning what foods she likes and unfortunately this far out we don't have a lot of options. I bought candles and a large bouquet of flowers. I even used actual plates instead of containers. Sarah laughed the second she walked in and saw it. Said it looked like a mercenary's version of romance. She wasn't wrong, she knows I can't cook very well.

Earlier that afternoon, I'd left her with Glitch and gone ring shopping, he claimed he was honored to be trusted with her safety. Sarah said he spent most of the time eating our snacks and giving terrible relationship advice, believable. By the time dinner was over, my nerves were worse than they'd ever been before a mission. She was smiling, relaxed, happy and I wanted to give her something untouched by fear.

I pushed back my chair and got down on one knee. Her eyes went wide instantly.

"Sarah," I said, voice rougher than I wanted. "My beautiful girl. My Little Mouse." She covered her mouth with both hands.

"From the moment you bumped into me, I felt something click into place. Like the world shifted and I finally found where I was supposed to be." My throat tightened, but I kept going. "Before you, I didn't know what my future looked like. I had no plan beyond the next mission, the next deployment, the next fight. But because of you, I have one now." I glanced down at her stomach, then back up. "You changed me in ways the Army never could."

A tear slid down her cheek. "I have a home now. A purpose. A family." I opened the ring box. A simple, elegant diamond ring that was perfect for her.

"You're the love of my life. I want forever with you, with our baby and with however many more babies you decide not to murder me over later."

She laughed through tears. "You'll be my partner in everything. My equal. My better half. Will you marry me?"

She was already crying openly now, smiling so wide it nearly broke me. She gave me a tiny shaky nod.

"Yes," she whispered. Then louder. "Yes. I would love to marry you."

Relief hit me like a freight train. I slid the ring onto her finger, it's just a little loose and stood just in time to catch her when she launched herself at me. I pulled her into my arms and held her there, breathing her in like oxygen. Then I carried her upstairs. Careful of her healing leg. Careful of the life growing inside her and I spent the rest of the night loving the woman who chose me back.

Later today, when the bar opens, I promised Sarah I'd take her to The Rusty Nail so we can thank Jason properly. I owe that man more than I can repay. He hid and protected her. Bought us the few minutes we needed, I never really got to thank him that day. I was too busy reaching her, too busy making sure she was okay. Too busy beating Benjamin bloody on Jason's floor. I remember Jason watching the whole thing from behind the bar like he'd seen worse.

Sarah's finally walking without grimacing every time she puts weight on her leg, so today feels right. Reaper, Stitches and Ghost are flying in this afternoon. Glitch is picking them up from the airport. After we finished getting interrogated by the FBI in D.C., Reaper took a train to New York City and apparently decided trauma recovery meant sightseeing and bad decisions. Ghost has been with his mom, I'm assuming he's mostly been been buried in laptops and burner phones.

Magellan and Sparta are still with their families. They were all pissed they missed the action but happy Sarah's safe and made it out relatively unharmed. They've promised to celebrate properly once we're all under one roof. Right now, space is tight. But that won't last long. Because this temporary hideout is only the beginning. We've been looking at different properties. The loft Glitch and I originally wanted in the city is dead now. Too public, too many windows and right now too many neighbors with cameras, questions and nothing better to do. What we need now is privacy.

Land, room to build something no one knows exists. A place peaceful enough for Sarah and secure enough for what ShadowLink is going to become. She'll be done with her dissertation soon. According to her, it's basically finished. She just has to prepare for her defense. She was more than happy to walk away from the teaching portion after everything that happened. I don't blame her. She's been worried about what comes next, what she's supposed to do now. Where we're supposed to live. I told her the truth—I have enough money that she never has to work another day if she doesn't want to. If she wants to teach somewhere out here, I'll support it. If she wants to move to another state and start over, we'll do that too. If she wants to stay home with the baby, I'll make sure she can.

The problem is, she doesn't know yet and I'm learning that after trauma, uncertainty can feel heavier than fear. The baby threw a wrench into every plan she had but every time I catch her touching her stomach when she thinks no one notices, I know she's happy too.

"Stop worrying," Sarah whispers beside me. It still amazes me how easily she reads me when most people never could.

"Just thinking," I tell her, palm spread over the gentle curve of her belly.

"About what?"

"About you." I kiss her shoulder. "How much I love you and our baby."

She groans dramatically into the pillow. "Well, think about that at a more reasonable hour." I grin into the dark. I'm learning she is absolutely not a morning person. She managed it in the jungle because she had no choice. Now that she has one, she treats sunrise like a personal insult. She also blames the baby for making her tired, which might be true. Hearing her mutter it half asleep is adorable.

"Sorry, beautiful," I whisper. "Go back to sleep. I'm going to get a workout in before the guys get here."

She mumbles something unintelligible, rolls away from me, and burrows deeper under the blankets. The sun isn't even up yet. But the tension inside me is, it coils in my chest almost every morning now. The fear of losing her, of waking up and finding an empty bed again. I don't know if that ever fully goes away.

So I go downstairs to the gym in the basement, it's small but enough. I use the bench and the free weights, I don't trust the treadmill, it sounds like it's coughing up bolts. I don't trust it will handle my weight or how fast I really need to go. Instead, I load the bar and lift until my muscles shake and my head finally quiets. Just as I rack the weight, my phone chimes.

Glitch: Got the assets, on our way.

I roll my eyes and send back a thumbs up. Assets. Apparently that's what my team calls themselves now. After a shower, I head upstairs and start breakfast. It's nearly ten, I've let Sarah sleep long enough. Cooking breakfast has become my thing. Dinner is still a gamble but I've mastered eggs and bacon. She gets some morning sickness, though thankfully not too bad and by some miracle, the two things I know how to make don't bother her.

So I cook, because feeding her feels good because taking care of her matters. Because every ordinary moment we get now feels like something sacred. When breakfast is finished, I take the stairs two at a time to wake her. The bed is empty, every ounce of calm I built in the gym evaporates instantly. My heart stutters for a moment before it goes into overdrive. That same panic crashes through me so fast it makes me dizzy.

"Sarah?!" I shout, scanning the room. Blankets tossed aside, lazily but there is no sign of her. I cross the room in three strides and throw open the bathroom door. Steam rolls out. She peeks around the shower curtain, water dripping from her hair. Wide-eyed for half a second, before turning amused.

"Were you coming to creep on me?" she asks cheekily.

I brace a hand on the sink and force myself to breathe. "Mouse," I say darkly, stepping closer. "I'll look at your beautiful body anytime I want."

She laughs softly. The sound fixes something in me. I lean in and kiss her quickly.

"Breakfast is ready. The guys will be here soon."

"Yay." She brightens immediately. "I can't wait to see them again." Then she wrinkles her nose. "I'll be out in a minute. I just wanted to freshen up. I'm certain I smelled like sex."

I grin. "I love when you smell like sex."

She rolls her eyes and pulls the curtain closed again. Not before I catch the smile she's trying to hide. By the time I get downstairs, a truck is pulling into the driveway. Glitch's new truck, he parks like he owns the place and all the doors open. They all pile out. I open the front door before they even knock.

Reaper comes in first, gives me a quick one-armed hug, then smacks my back hard enough to bruise. Stitches does the same, minus the hard slap to my back. Ghost stands there awkwardly like he forgot humans hug now. I drag him in anyway. Glitch struts in last like he's arriving at a red carpet event. He's been visiting often, mostly because of Fallon, she's been insisting on seeing Sarah as much as she can.

"Where's mommy?" he asks. I punch him in the gut. Not full force, just enough to fold him. He doubles over, wheezing.

"Don't call her mommy, you asshole."

"I was kidding," he coughs. "Jesus." Then straightens slowly. "Where is she anyway?"

"She'll be down soon."

Right on cue, Sarah comes down the stairs. Comfy sweats, one of my t-shirts hanging off one shoulder. Her wet hair is in a messy bun, no makeup. The most beautiful thing I've ever seen.

She pauses on the bottom step. "Why is Jake clutching his stomach in pain?" She looks between us like she already knows.

"He's an idiot," Reaper answers dryly. Then he walks over and pulls her into a hug.

"Simon," she says, smiling into his chest. "It's so good to see you. How are you?"

"I'm good." He leans back, studying her carefully. "I should be asking you that." His gaze drops briefly to her leg. "Kidnapped again, shot in the leg, you're definitely one of us now."

She laughs. "Yeah, official member. That's not exactly comforting," she mutters, making him grin.

Stitches steps forward next, quieter than the others. "It's good to see you up and walking again, Sarah."

She smiles softly and reaches for him too, pulling him into a quick hug. "It's good to see you too."

"Try not to get shot again," he says casually.

She snorts. "I'll do my best." Then she turns to Ghost. They were never as close as the others, but that's never stopped her. She steps forward and hugs him briefly.

"How are you?" she asks, searching his face like she's checking for hidden damage.

"I'm doing good," he says quietly. "How are you?"

"I'm great." She smiles wider. "Almost done with school, living with an overbearing man and carrying his child." She pats her stomach.

Glitch has already wandered into the kitchen and is stealing bacon straight from the pan. "He's always been overbearing," he calls out. "He's just your problem now."

She laughs. The house fills with noise. With people. With life and standing there watching her smile in the middle of all of it, I realize something I haven't felt in a long time. This feels like home.

"Damn it, Glitch. I made that for Sarah." He lifts another strip of bacon straight from the pan and shrugs. "Then you should've guarded it better."

I point at him. "Get out of the kitchen before I bury you in the woods."

He grins and saunters over to the kitchen table like he owns the place. I tell the others to go claim a room. They all start dragging bags upstairs and arguing over who gets what room. Reaper wants the one with the better view. Ghost wants the quietest one. Glitch insisted he's happing staying in Sarah's room at their apartment she shares with Fallon. Idiots.

I pull out a chair for Sarah and guide her carefully to the table. She gives me a look that says I'm hovering too much. She's right and I don't care. I build her plate myself, filling it with eggs, toast and what's left of the bacon. Fruit I cut too big because apparently that matters.

The guys are grinning like wolves from the hallway, no doubt preparing material to roast me later. I ignore them. Right now it's just me, Sarah and Glitch at the table while the rest get settled. She starts eating immediately. That alone makes me feel accomplished.

"My mom called," she says between bites. I glance up. I haven't met her parents yet, but I've talked to them on the phone. More than once. The first conversation included concern, suspicion and several pointed questions about why their daughter had been kidnapped twice and shot while in my orbit. Fair questions. They want to visit soon. Sarah promised we'd come to them for Thanksgiving. I fully intend to make a good impression. Preferably one that doesn't involve federal crimes or gunfire.

"Yeah?" I ask. "How's Claire doing?"

"She's good." Sarah smiles softly. "Just checking in. Making sure everything's still okay." She rubs her stomach absently. "We talked about the baby. I told her we're going to see Jason today." Her expression shifts. Subtle enough most people wouldn't catch it. I do.

"They're still worried," she says quietly. About her. About me. About the fact I wasn't there when I should've been. That she was taken again. Shot, traumatized, pregnant and somehow still standing. Yeah. That wasn't a fun phone call. I reach across the table and lace my fingers through hers.

"They have every right to worry," I tell her honestly. "But they'll know one thing when they meet me."

She looks up. "What's that?"

"That I'd burn the world down before I let anything happen to you again."

Glitch gags dramatically. "Jesus Christ, Wraith. Save the romance novel lines for after breakfast."

Without looking away from her, I flip him off. Sarah laughs and hearing that sound in a kitchen full of friends, sunlight and ordinary life, I know we're going to be okay.

We spent the next couple of hours looking at properties that Ghost has already been sending us. He knew we needed acreage, foreclosures, forgotten farm, old hunting parcels no one wanted. Most were wrong the second we pulled in, too close to neighbors. Too exposed from the road and too many places someone could watch from.

Ghost knew exactly what we needed, land and privacy with multiple access points and room to build something hidden. There was one listing he kept pushing harder than the others. The interior phots were not worth a damn and a very minimal description. The thing that had me the most interested was the cash buyer preferred, as-is, perfect to keep everything private.

So we drove out to see it. The entrance was easy to miss, just a narrow break in the trees off a county road, half swallowed by brush and low hanging branches. The gravel driveway had nearly disappeared beneath weeds and moss. Grass grew through the center and tree limbs scraped the truck as we eased forward. It looked abandoned and unwanted. We drove nearly half a mile before the trees opened enough for the property to reveal itself.

Even Sarah went quiet. An enormous old bank barn rose out of the hillside like it had grown there naturally. Built into the slope so part of the lower level vanished into earth and stone. The front facade was old brick, weather-darkened and cracked in places, ivy creeping up one corner. The upper structure above it was faded red wood gone soft with age, sections silvered by years of Minnesota winters.

Some windows were boarded and broken, the roof sagged slightly on one side but still held strong. It didn't look dead but rather it looked like it was waiting for something. Behind it sat a massive steel-sided pole barn, dented and rust-streaked, one sliding door hanging crooked on its track.

Beyond that was woods and more woods, thick stands of pine and oak wrapped three sides of the property like a wall. No neighbors in sight. No traffic noise. No one to hear anything they shouldn't. I stepped out first and listened. Wind through the trees, birds and loose metal tapping somewhere on the garage. That was it. Sarah climbed out slower, one hand on the truck door, still favoring her healing leg. She stared at the barn for a long moment.

"It looks haunted," she said finally.

Glitch snorted from beside me. "Good. Keeps people away."

I ignored him and kept studying the structure. The lower hill-built section would stay cool year-round, it had a strong foundation and looked easy to reinforce. The upper loft space had enough square footage for multiple apartments if gutted and rebuilt. The main level could become open common space. The pole barn would handle vehicles, fabrication, storage. The woods made surveillance and security easy, disappearing easiest of all.

I looked at Ghost. "You already ran maps?"

He nodded once. "Two back approaches through timber. Creek line east side. No direct sight from road. Nearest neighbor over half a mile." Of course he had.

Sarah moved closer to me, slipping her hand into mine. "You're doing the thing," she said.

"What thing?"

"The one where you pretend you're calm while mentally building an empire."

Glitch barked out a laugh. "She knows you way too well."

I looked back at the barn. My eyes roaming over all of the weeds, the broken bones but most all the hidden strength underneath all of it. Then down at the woman holding my hand.

"No," I said quietly. "She knows me exactly enough."

Sarah squeezed my fingers. "You like it."

I let myself smile. Like it? No. I could already see what it would become. A home. A fortress. A business no one would ever understand until it was too late.

"Yeah, Mouse," I said, eyes still on the barn. "I think we found it."

We pull up outside The Rusty Nail. The farther we drove from town and the closer we got to this place, the more Sarah talked. Her side of what happened, how Benjamin got her out. What he said in the car. How scared she was. Every word lit my nerves on fire. I'd heard her statement to Ramsey already, but hearing it from her mouth, quiet and matter-of-fact beside me, was different. More personal and more brutal. I didn't want her reliving it and I definitely didn't want to imagine it.

The bar looks exactly the same, weathered gray siding and cracked gravel lot. A weak neon sign buzzing in the window. The kind of place most people drive past without noticing. We walk in just after opening.

The smell of stale beer and fryer grease. Wood smoke soaked into old boards. No customers yet, just Jason behind the bar, wiping down the counter with a rag that probably needed retiring years ago. He looks up, surprised for half a second. Then recognition lands.

"Well," he says, eyes moving to Sarah. "You look a hell of a lot better, sweetheart."

She smiles softly. "I am doing a lot better." She reaches for my hand. "I made them bring me back so I could thank you."

Jason waves that off immediately. "No need to thank me. I just did what anyone should."

"No," Sarah says firmly. "You didn't have to help me. But you did." Something gentler moves through his face at that.

I step forward and offer my hand. "Wade."

He takes it in a solid grip. "Jason." His mouth twitches. "I definitely remember the guy who stormed in here and beat that kid into hamburger before the FBI dragged him out." Sarah snorts beside me.

"Yeah, he definitely had it coming. He's lucky I couldn't do worse," I mutter.

"Looked pretty justified from where I was standing," Jason says.

I nod once. Then meet his eyes. "This is my fiancée." I feel Sarah squeeze my hand again. "She was taken a second time by that asshole. You hiding her bought me the few extra minutes I needed to get here." My voice roughens. "You helped save her. And my child." Jason glances down at Sarah's stomach, then back up at me. Real understanding settles in.

"Well," he says quietly, "guess that changes the math a little." He clears his throat and shrugs like none of it matters. "She came in terrified. Bleeding. Barefoot in a hospital gown." His jaw tightens. "There wasn't a chance in hell I was handing her back to anybody."

I reach into my jacket and set an envelope thick with cash on the bar. "For the trouble. For damages. For anything we cost you." He stares at it like I insulted him. Then pushes it back across the wood.

"No."

"Jason—"

"No." His tone sharpens. "If I took money for doing the right thing, then it wouldn't be the right thing anymore."

Sarah's eyes immediately fill. Mine burn a little too.

He notices and points a finger at both of us. "Now knock that emotional shit off before I regret helping either of you." Sarah laughs through tears. I grin despite myself. Then Jason jerks his thumb toward a high top table.

"Sit down. I'm making you two lunch."

"We can pay—"

"You can shut up," he says. Then he glances at Sarah. "You still look too skinny." She beams.

"What, do I get a free lunch too?" Glitch asks from behind me.

Jason doesn't even look at him. "No."

We all laugh. Even Glitch, though he looks deeply offended. We head toward the high top table together, the sound of boots on worn wood floors and Sarah's laughter filling the quiet bar. For the first time since all of this started, the place where she was almost lost becomes something else entirely.

Not a place of fear. Not a place of trauma. But a place where good men stood their ground and where, somehow, life moved forward anyway.

Acknowledgments

Writing this book has been an incredible journey, and I couldn't have done it without the support of some amazing people.

To my husband, thank you for always believing in me, listening to my endless brainstorming sessions, and supporting me every step of the way. Your patience, encouragement, and love mean more than I could ever put into words.

To my friend Liz, thank you for reading and proofreading this book multiple times, offering feedback, and constantly cheering me on. Your time, enthusiasm, and support have been absolutely invaluable.

To my sister, thank you for reading my work and supporting me through this process. Knowing you were invested in this story made writing it even more special.

And finally, to my aunt and uncle in Brazil, thank you for sharing your stories, experiences, and love for such a beautiful place with me. Visiting Brazil and experiencing parts of that world firsthand deeply inspired the setting and atmosphere of this book. Your influence is woven throughout these pages in more ways than you probably realize.

This story would not exist in the same way without all of you. Thank you for helping bring it to life.

About the Author

Hi! I'm Ali Wren, an independent author with a passion for blending adventure, suspense, and romance. With a background in biological anthropology, I love weaving real-world science into my stories, pairing brilliant scientists with elite operatives in high-stakes and emotionally charged adventures.

When I'm not writing, I'm a mom, a science enthusiast and an advocate for alopecia awareness.

My *Whiskey Tango Foxtrot* series takes readers across the world, following dangerous missions, fierce love stories and the kind of heroes who never back down.

Looking for bonus content, sneak peeks, and exclusive first chapters? Visit my website here:

https://aliwrenauthor.com

I'd love to connect! You can find me on TikTok, Instagram, and Facebook: **@AliWrenAuthor** for updates, behind-the-scenes content, and more.

Want to know what happens between Glitch and Fallon? Jake "Glitch" Thompson never thought he'd get another chance at love, not after his past with Alex left scars deeper than he'd admit. But Fallon isn't like anyone he's ever met–sharp-tongued, fearless and impossible to ignore.

When her research project in Chile takes a dangerous turn, Jake and the team will have to race against time to save her. But with trust broken and lies between them, will she even want to be saved?

Keep reading for an exclusive sneak peek at Book 2 in the *Whiskey Tango Foxtrot* series.

Whiskey & Lies

9 Years Ago
Fallon

Tonight is the night.

I've been waiting for months—for the perfect moment to make my escape—I feel it thrumming in my bones like a second heartbeat. I lie in the dark, the air stale and thick with the scent of sweat, bleach, and old metal. I've been in this hellhole for over a year. At least I think it's been a year, all of it has been a blur. I'm only relying on bits of conversations I hear from the guards when they talk loudly from outside my door.

Sometimes, I still can't believe how fast it all happened.

One moment I was standing at my mom's funeral, staring at her coffin like it had swallowed my whole world whole. I was sixteen, wearing a borrowed black dress and scuffed shoes from my mom's closet, trying to understand how the strongest woman I'd ever known could just... stop existing.

Breast cancer. Gone at 40.

She used to fill every room she walked into. Copper hair that burned in the sunlight, freckles across her nose like scattered constellations. Loud laughter. Fierce hugs. She wore red lipstick even to the grocery store and danced in the kitchen while dinner burned. People always said I had her fire.

After she died, the house went quiet. Too quiet.

My father stopped shaving. Stopped going to work. Stopped looking at me. Sometimes, I'd catch him staring like he was trying to place me, like I was something almost familiar but not quite. Like he was looking at a ghost instead of his daughter.

I told myself grief does strange things to people. That's what everyone said. At school, I avoided everyone. Their pity scraped at my skin worse than silence. I used to be the girl everyone knew. Friends filling every corner of my life, cheer practices after school, games under bright lights. Now I walked the halls like a ghost. Guidance counselors with soft voices and practiced concern told me they were "there for me" when I was ready.

So I went. I told them I didn't feel safe at home. I told them things were wrong, that I couldn't go to my father with this. She nodded. Took notes. Smiled in that careful way adults do when they think you're fragile. I tried explaining that when his half brother was coming over to 'help out during our time of need' he was really there to take advantage of the fact that I had no one. That my dad was too far gone in his grief to even care. They called my father anyway.

I was right, when I told my father what he had done, he said I was struggling. Acting out. Imagining things. Exactly what Mrs. Craig told him. Of course she did and a few days later, I was walking home, eyes fixed on my shoes scraping against the sidewalk. I didn't notice the dented white van parked outside my house. Didn't hear the footsteps behind me until it was too late.

Rough hands.

A sharp sting in my neck

The world tilting sideways.

Then—darkness. Too quick. Too clean. I didn't even get a chance to fight. Like someone had been waiting for the right moment.

Tonight plays out like the others. The door opens, the creak of the rusting hinges and he enters. J.

I don't know how often he comes, I keep losing sense of time but I do know he comes here more often than anyone else. None of the other men bother with names. They come in faceless and leave the same way. But this one, this one wanted to be known. Like that makes him different. Like that makes him human. It doesn't.

The first few months are fog. They kept me sedated so heavily I barely remember learning how to breathe in this place. But I remember him. I remember brown eyes hovering over me while the world swam in and out of focus.

"My name's J," he'd whispered once, like it was a gift.

The room is dim, lit only by the dull red glow bleeding in from the hallway bulb. It paints everything the color of dried blood. The air smells of mildew, old hay, bleach that doesn't quite mask what it's meant to cover.

The walls are wood—rough, splintering panels warped with age. Not drywall. Not concrete. Wood. There are thin gaps between the boards where night air slips through in icy threads. Sometimes I hear wind pushing against the structure. Once, I heard something that sounded like animals.

I think it's a barn. Or it used to be. The window across the room is small and set too high to reach, but through it I can see a slice of sky. Vast. Unreachable. It feels crueler than a solid wall would.

Beyond it, the stars stretch wide and infinite. I imagine myself out there instead, lying in grass that doesn't stink of rot and rust. I trace constellations in my mind the way I used to as a girl, back when the world felt bigger than my pain. I cling to them like lifelines. If I focus hard enough, maybe I'll catch a shooting star. Maybe it'll carry me somewhere else. Somewhere I belong.

The bed beneath me groans when I shift. Old iron frame. Rusted in patches but not enough to break. They made sure of that. My wrists are bound to the posts with reinforced cuffs, newer than the bed, newer than anything else in this room. I've tested them and they don't give.

Now, he

J's gaze drops to my wrists, and something flickers behind his eyes. Not hunger. Ownership. They're a pale, cold blue, sharp and unblinking, like nothing ever really touches him.

"Well, hello, Ginger," he murmurs, slipping off his suit jacket like he's stepping into his own office. Expensive fabric. Polished shoes. Dark hair, neatly styled, just starting to gray at the temples. The kind of man who probably shakes hands and signs contracts during the day.

"I only get an hour tonight," he says conversationally. "Someone paid well for the rest."

I let my head loll slightly to the side. Slow blink. Empty stare. They stopped drugging me weeks ago. They think I'm docile now. Broken. I feel broken but I'm not ready to give up. I've just gotten better at pretending.

I'm always restrained unless the guards come in to "clean" me. That's what they call it. By cleaning, I mean they drag me to a boarded room that smells like livestock and chemicals. Spray lukewarm water over my skin. Run a bar of soap across me like they're washing equipment, not a person. Once a week someone comes in to wash our hair. Quick. Efficient.

That's it. Maintenance. Like we're animals they're preparing for auction. They don't care about us. They care about the product. Until recently, they kept me too drugged up to notice.

Too numb to feel the tearing. Now? Now I feel everything. And tonight I have to endure it stone-cold sober. I brace myself, nails carving crescents into my palms, as he folds his clothes neatly over the back of the chair like this is some kind of luxury suite.

His eyes drag over me slowly.

I leave my body. Count cracks in the ceiling. Fourteen long ones. Three short. A water stain shaped like a continent I'll never visit. The bed creaks.

I focus on breathing. In. Out. In. Out.

He crawls between my legs. No lube. Just spit. The first thrust makes me flinch. The rest, I endure in silence. Tears slip past my lashes. I don't bother wiping them away. He talks while he moves, low and pleased with himself, like this is intimacy instead of an invasion. He tells me to look at him. Calls me Ginger again, like it's a pet name instead of a cage.

"Open your eyes, Ginger," he commands, breath ragged. "I want to see those sharp green eyes while I breed you." I force them open. Not because he wants me to. But because I refuse to disappear. He moans louder.

When he finishes, he groans into my skin, leaving the weight of his sick promise behind.

He unties one wrist and flips me roughly onto my stomach. More spit. Another violation. I bite the inside of my cheek until I taste blood.

When it's finally over, he presses his mouth to my shoulder and whispers promises that sound more like threats.

"I might just buy you," he says softly. "Keep you all to myself." Like I'm an investment. Like I'm livestock. When he leaves, the door shuts with a final creak that should be in horror movie. Except this is my horror movie.

Silence floods back into the room, before the door opens again. My new guard. He's younger than the others. Late twenties, maybe. A scar cutting through one eyebrow. He doesn't look at me the way the buyers do. Doesn't smile. Doesn't leer. But he still unlocks the chains. Still does his job.

I keep my eyes closed. Pretend I'm still passed out. Weak.

He swears under his breath when he sees the bruises blooming across my skin. Just before he steps fully inside, I hear voices in the hallway. "Victor is coming," one of the men says. "Just got word we have an important client arriving. We're told to make sure all the girls are clean and presentable."

A pause.

"Fuck. Alright," my guard mutters as he pushes farther into the room and shuts the door behind him.

"Damn it," he mutters under his breath. "He didn't have to go that hard." Like that's the line. Like *there* is a line. He crouches and lifts me, careful—almost awkward—like he isn't sure where to put his hands. I let my head fall against his shoulder. Let my body go slack. Dead weight.

The hallway smells like rust and wet wood. Like something rotting slowly behind the walls. He carries me into the bathroom. If you can call it that.

It looks like someone tried to build it in a hurry and gave up halfway through. The walls are mismatched plywood sheets nailed unevenly over what used to be open beams. Insulation peeks out in places. The floor slopes slightly toward a drain that doesn't quite work.

The tub is old cast iron, chipped enamel stained permanently orange from years of mineral-heavy water. The claw feet are missing; it sits directly on uneven concrete blocks.

A single copper pipe juts up from the wall, bent slightly to one side, fitted with a cracked plastic shower head that leaks even when it's off. No curtain. No door that fully closes. Just a warped slab of wood that doesn't latch.

Privacy was never part of the design. He sets me in the tub. The porcelain is cold enough to steal my breath but I don't react. He turns the knob. The pipes scream before coughing out water that smells faintly metallic. It hits me in uneven spurts before settling into a steady, punishing stream. The cold water is enough to wake me up more, to give me the push I need.

When he grabs the same gray bar of soap they always use. An industrial kind of bar soap that was scratchy, impersonal, with no distinguishing scent. He focuses on adjusting the temperature, tapping the pipe with his knuckles when it rattles.

That's when I move.

Slowly.

Carefully.

Silently.

My fingers slide toward his hip. The weight there. Cold metal. For a second, my pulse is so loud I'm sure he can hear it over the water. I've never held a gun before. Don't know if it's ready. Don't know if it'll even fire.

All I know is this: it's heavier than I expected. And for the first time in over a year... I'm the one holding something dangerous. I raise the gun. My hands are shaking so hard the barrel trembles.

I squeeze my eyes shut. And pull the trigger. The blast is deafening in the small room. It punches the air out of my lungs. My ears ring instantly.

When I open my eyes, he's on the floor. There's blood. I don't look long enough to see where. I scramble out of the tub and I run. The hallway outside is empty, but the cries behind the closed doors aren't. Muffled sobs. A voice begging. A thud against wood.

I don't stop. I can't.

My bare feet slap against warped wooden planks layered in dirt and old straw. The building stretches longer than I realized from inside my room. A wide corridor framed by rough beams, overhead lights strung haphazardly along exposed rafters. Some flicker. Some are burnt out completely.

The air smells like damp hay and rust. This was a barn once. I see it now. The high ceiling. The crossbeams. The large sliding doors at the far end. Stalls have been boarded up into rooms. Padlocks on every one. Cages dressed up as walls

The double doors loom ahead, massive, reinforced with metal brackets bolted into old wood. Please. Please. I shove and they swing open.

Cold night air slams into me like a wave. It steals my breath. It smells like dirt and wet grass and open space.

Freedom. Not safety. But freedom.

Behind me, a shout. "Hey!" A groan. "STOP HER!" He's alive. I don't look back.

Just before I clear the trees, I see movement near the road. A black SUV sits idling at the edge of the property. Engine low. Windows tinted.

A man stands beside it. Tailored suit. Immaculate. A deep caramel colored skin and black hair. Completely out of place against the dirt and decay behind him.

He's not shouting. Not chasing. Just watching. Dark eyes follow me with calm calculation. Like he's measuring the odds. A faint grimace touches his mouth. Not surprise or panic. Annoyance. I don't slow down. If he's with them, he'll chase. If he's not, he'll call someone.

Either way—I run. Past him. Past the gravel shoulder. Across the narrow strip of road.

On the other side, another thin stretch of trees, they're smaller and patchy. Not enough to hide a secret like that barn, but enough to conceal it from casual drivers. I sprint across packed dirt, past a rusted tractor half-swallowed by weeds. A sagging fence line. Floodlights mounted on poles that haven't been turned on yet or maybe never are.

The barn sits alone in a clearing carved out of trees. No neighboring farms. No distant porch lights. Just darkness swallowing everything beyond the property line. Gravel bites into my feet. Then grass. Then underbrush tearing at my legs.

The tree line is closer than I thought. The woods are thin, more of a barrier than a forest but they're enough. Branches whip against my skin as I crash through. Twigs snap. Leaves scrape. I've only been running for a little while. But it feels like miles. My lungs burn like I've swallowed fire. My legs shake so badly I nearly trip twice. I'm weaker than I realized. A year of confinement has hollowed me out.

Adrenaline is the only thing keeping me upright. It only takes a few more minutes before houses appear. Old ones. Sagging porches. Peeling paint. Overgrown lawns. The kind of street people forget about. The barn wasn't in the middle of nowhere. It was hidden in plain sight.

My legs finally give out as I stumble onto the sidewalk. I grip a mailbox to stay upright. My whole body is shaking now—not from cold, but from the crash after adrenaline.

Minutes. It couldn't have been more than five. It felt like escaping a continent. I stagger to the first house with lights on and slam my fists against the door. My knuckles split against rough wood.

"Please," I rasp, though I don't know if any sound comes out.

This is a gamble. For all I know, they're connected. For all I know, that man by the SUV is already turning around. But standing still means going back. And I would rather die on this porch than ever step foot in that barn again.

"Please!" I sob. "Please, help me!" The porch light flicks on before the door even opens.

It creaks inward slowly. A woman in her fifties stands there, gray threaded through soft brown curls, reading glasses slipping down her nose. Her eyes—wide, warm, startled—take me in.

"Oh my God..." I must look feral—bruised, filthy, completely naked. Blood dries in streaks along my arms, dirt clings to my legs, and my feet are torn open from gravel and brush.

"I've been held captive," I choke out. "For over a year. Please."

She doesn't ask for proof. Doesn't hesitate. She reaches for me like I'm something precious instead of something broken.

"Come inside, sweetheart." The word almost breaks me. The door shuts behind us with a solid, final click. That sound it feels like safety. I sway, the room tilting slightly, but I force myself upright. The gun slips from my fingers and clatters to the floor.

She freezes for half a second at the sight of it. Then she looks back at me. Not at the weapon. At me.

"George!" she calls, voice steady despite the tremor in it. "George, honey, come here."

A man appears from down the hall, tall, broad-shouldered, wearing a flannel shirt and house slippers. His expression shifts from confusion to horror in seconds.

"Jesus..."

"She needs help," the woman says firmly. "Now."

He nods immediately. No questions. No suspicion. Just action. She grabs the scratchy old blanket on the couch, that looks like she made it herself. From crochet maybe I'm not sure but it feels nice when it's wrapped around my body, shielding me. This is the most privacy I've had in so long, the sob breaks out of me.

She guides me down a narrow hallway lined with framed photos, school portraits, beach vacations, Christmas mornings. A life lived in ordinary, beautiful moments, a life I used to have.

The bathroom light flicks on. Lavender. Lemon cleaner. Warmth. The scent hits me like something from another lifetime.

"You can shower," she says gently. "I'll grab some clothes. My daughter's old things. They should fit you." Daughter. The word lodges somewhere deep in my chest.

The door closes softly behind her. I lock it. Then I collapse into the tub. The water takes a second to warm, and when it does, steam curls around me. It doesn't smell metallic. It doesn't sputter out in angry bursts.

It just flows. My sobs rip out of me before I can stop them, loud and ugly and completely uncontrollable. The water runs red, then pink, then brown with dirt and mud before finally turning clear. I scrub at my skin like I can erase the past year. Like I can scrape away fingerprints and voices and the sound of metal doors.

I don't even remember bleeding. The realization hits harder than anything. It's not my blood all over me. I stay until my breathing evens out, until my hands stop shaking quite so violently.

A knock sounds. "Dear?" the woman's voice is soft through the door. "I've got some clothes. May I come in?"

"Yes," I whisper. I pull the shower curtain tight around me, like thin vinyl could protect me from the world.

She slips inside, careful not to look at me directly. She sets folded clothes on the counter, soft cotton. Faded jeans. A sweatshirt that looks well-loved.

"I'm Fallon," she says gently. "That's George. You're safe here." Safe.

The word feels fragile. I know I should give my name. I haven't spoken name in over a year, it starts to feel foreign like a life that is over.

"We'll call the police," she continues. "They'll help—"

"No." The sharpness in my voice startles both of us.

"If you call them, they'll come back," I say, forcing the words out. "They'll hurt you. They'll hurt anyone who helps me." I don't know if that's true but I don't want to find out. I'm not naive enough to think they're not coming after me, but I just want to get away. Her eyes search mine. Not disbelief.

Concern fills her eyes and then she nods. "Okay," she says simply. "We'll wait."

George appears in the doorway behind her, arms crossed, not defensive, protective.

"Do you have family we can call?" he asks gently.

"No," I say. "Not anymore." Something unspoken passes between them. Grief recognizing grief.

"All right," Fallon says quietly. "Supper's nearly ready. Come out when you feel up to it. There's no rush."

No rush. The door closes. I finish washing and dress slowly. The sweatshirt swallows me whole, and for the first time in over a year, fabric feels like comfort instead of restraint. The first time in a year, I even get to cover my body.

Later, I sit at their kitchen table. The room smells like roasted chicken and fresh bread. A small light glows over the sink. A clock ticks steadily on the wall. Ordinary sounds. George sets a plate in front of me like he's feeding a daughter home late from school. I take a bite. I can't taste it. They ask gentle questions, careful ones.

I don't have answers. Only fragments. Only nightmares.

But for the first time in a long time—I'm not alone while I carry them. I won't share the horrors—they don't need to know. I just need to get through this, find a way out of here safely. For now, I tell myself I'm safe.

Just as the last dish is set in the drying rack, a knock hits the door. Not polite. Not neighborly. Sharp and demanding. I freeze. They found me or perhaps they knew where I was the whole time.

George doesn't. He moves fast, faster than a man in house slippers should. "Come with me," he whispers. Fallon's hand finds mine, squeezes once, firm and steady.

The pantry door opens. He shoves aside a crate of potatoes, revealing a square wooden hatch cut into the floor.

"I put this in years ago," he murmurs. "Storm cellar. Nobody knows it's here." He lifts it. Cold, stale air rises from the darkness below.

"Go," he says. I don't argue. I climb down into blackness that smells like damp wood and earth. Old metal shelves line the walls. Canned goods long expired. A single pull string for a lightbulb that doesn't work. Before he lowers the hatch, he presses something into my palm.

"If anything happens," he says quietly, "call this number. It's our daughter. Ellie. She'll know what to do, she can help you."

The hatch closes. The scrape of the potato bin slides back into place.

Footsteps hit the porch. The door flies open.

"We saw her come in here!" a man shouts.

I know that voice. My guard. I must not have hurt him as bad as I thought, for him to take a bullet and get back up again. Fallon's voice floats back—calm, almost offended. "You can't just barge into someone's home."

"Don't play games with me." Heavy boots thud across the floorboards overhead. Drawers yanked open. Furniture shoved aside.

"It's just us," George says firmly. "My wife and I. Our daughter moved out years ago."

A brief pause before two gunshots. Close together. The sound is different inside the cellar. Muffled. Thicker. Final. I clap my hand over my mouth to swallow the scream clawing up my throat. My whole body shakes so violently my teeth chatter.

Boots move again. Cupboards slam. The pantry door creaks open above me. Dust trickles down through the seams of the hatch, sprinkling over me. I stop breathing.

A long silence before I hear, "Fuck. She's not here."

"She had to come somewhere."

"Boss is going to lose it."

"Yeah, well, that's on you."

"Shut up. We'll sit on the road. She's not getting far." The pantry door slams.

The house goes still. I don't move. Not when something skitters across my ankle. Not when my legs go numb. I count my breaths the way I did in that barn.

In. Out. In. Out. Minutes pass. Maybe more. Eventually, the silence becomes heavier than the fear.

I push the hatch open. The kitchen light is still on. The clock still ticks. Everything looks exactly the same. Except—George lies on his back near the sink, one hand stretched toward the hallway like he tried to stand.

Fallon is beside the table. They aren't moving. Blood spreads slowly across the hardwood, dark and shining in the lamplight. The house still smells like roasted chicken. I fall to my knees.

"No," I whisper. "No, no, no…"

My chest caves in on itself. The sobs rip out of me, loud and broken. I press my forehead to the floor like if I don't look at them, this won't be real.

I should have kept running. I should have gone to the next house. I should have—I killed them. The scrap of paper is still crumpled in my fist.

Ellie. My hands shake so badly I almost drop the cordless phone twice before I manage to punch in the number.

It rings once. Twice. A young woman answers, distracted and warm. "Hey, Mom?"

The word shatters something inside me. She sounded so light, happy but confused why her mom would call her this late. "I'm sorry," I whisper. "Is this Ellie?" I can barely squeeze the words out of my throat.

A pause. "Yeah. Who is this?"

"My name is—" I stop.

Harley. The name slips out automatically. The name my parents gave me, from a different life, I don't feel like Harley anymore.

"My name is Harley," I say, voice barely holding together. "Your dad told me to call if something happened."

Silence stretches thin. "What do you mean?" she asks slowly.

I stare at George's outstretched hand. At Fallon's glasses lying crooked on the floor.

Squeezing my eyes closed. "They helped me," I choke. "I didn't have anywhere else to go. And men came looking for me and—"

I can't say the word. Dead.

"They're gone," I whisper. There's a sound on the other end. Not quite a sob. Not quite a breath.

"No," Ellie says softly. "What do you mean?"

"I'm so sorry," I say again. Over and over. "I'm so sorry." I don't know how many times I repeat it. It's all my fault.

And somewhere in the wreckage of that kitchen, surrounded by blood and lemon cleaner and shattered kindness—a connection is born. Not from safety. Not from joy. But from shared loss.

www.ingramcontent.com/pod-product-compliance
Lightning Source LLC
Chambersburg PA
CBHW060811120726
47909CB00006B/1870